MW01095103

THE
ASSIGNMENT

JILL M. SLAWSON

Copyright © 2022 Jill M. Slawson
All rights reserved
First Edition

PAGE PUBLISHING
Conneaut Lake, PA

First originally published by Page Publishing 2022

This is a work of fiction. *Unless otherwise indicated,* all the names, characters, locales, and/or incidents either are the product of the author's imagination or are used fictitiously, and any resemblance to actual persons living or dead is truly coincidental. Miles City and Fort Keogh are real, and both are in Montana. The pony express was also real. Along with the aforementioned, any errors, in writing, subject, or time, are purely that of the author's imagination, choice, or mischievousness.

ISBN 978-1-6624-5602-2 (pbk)
ISBN 978-1-6624-5600-8 (hc)
ISBN 978-1-6624-5604-6 (digital)

Printed in the United States of America

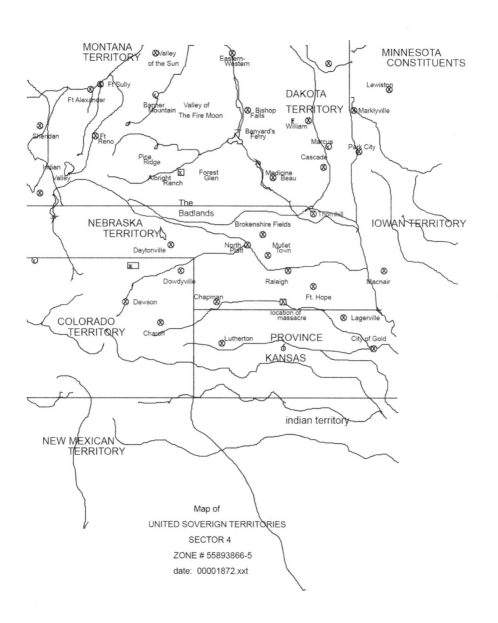

MONTANA TERRITORY

⊗ Valley of the Sun

⊗ Eastern-Western

MINNESOTA CONSTITUENTS

⊗ Ft Sully

⊗ Lewiston

DAKOTA TERRITORY

Ft Alexander

⊗ Banner Mountain

Valley of The Fire Moon

⊗ Bishop Falls

⊗ Marklyville

F ⊗ William

⊗ Sheridan

⊗ Ft Reno

Banyard's Ferry

⊗ Marcus

⊗ Park City

Cascade

Indian Valley

Pipe Ridge

⊗

⊗ Albright Ranch

Forest Glen

Medicine Beau ⊗

The Badlands

⊗ Thornhill

NEBRASKA TERRITORY

Brokenshire Fields

IOWAN TERRITORY

⊗ Daytonville

North Platt ⊗

⊗ Mullet Town

⊗

⊗ Dowdyville

⊗ Raleigh

⊗ Ft. Hope

⊗ Macnair

⊗ Dawson

Chapman

location of massacre

⊗ Lagerville

COLORADO TERRITORY

⊗ Charon

Lutherton

PROVINCE

City of Gold ⊗

KANSAS

indian territory

NEW MEXICAN TERRITORY

Map of

UNITED SOVERIGN TERRITORIES

SECTOR 4

ZONE # 55893866-5

date: 00001872.xxt

To my mom.
Our very own walking encyclopedia—
whose wish it was
to see her children learn and enjoy reading
at least one-tenth as much as she did.
Jeanne E. Barthelmess
December 10, 1923–April 2, 1988

And

To Connie Nadine Svani.

Whether she had pink, blue or gray hair; whether she walked

her dachshunds up and down the roads of Woodhill Estates

twice daily or not, she was my BFF for over 30 years.
I will miss her dearly.
December 22, 1932–June 26, 2021

And finally,

To my beloved husband, Randy.
I am so sorry, Love, but the brain tumors took over
long before we knew what was happening.
Sadly, there are no words that can truly describe our joyous
forty-five plus years of marriage together.
May your kind, humorous and wonderful self
rest in peace for the rest of eternity. Visit me often, will you?
November 22, 1951 – October 20, 2021

Contents

Book 1

Book 2

Book 3

Book 4

BOOK 1

I

you've been volunteered

She was tall. She was defiant, and she was deadly. She was mischievous, inventive, and mysterious. She was full of life, independent, ornery, dedicated, and kind. She was all these things and much more, but no one dare look, because of who they were.

They were the lifeblood of the Academy. The Academy where dregs were molded and taught for centuries. Taught and transformed into the very best of the best. The elite. The proud. The capable.

She was the captivating young woman with skin the color of ivory, long brown-black hair, whose eyes were the strangest shade of gunmetal gray that anyone had ever seen. She was the one who had been summoned while in the midst of survival training and who'd disembarked from the interregional shuttle shortly thereafter and consequently was found silently and patiently standing at attention in the outer office of the chancellor's private chambers.

Chancellor F. Lunette was the man who not only headed their sector, but whose untimely and unwonted request she questioned. She questioned it because it was the second in as much as two weeks. The first was during the last new moon, when they'd discussed the many different aspects of her training, the contents of her personnel jacket, her value to the organization, and her special and unexplainable talent of identifying unusual circumstances. *That day* she sat erect and proud while attentively listening as he told of the recent incident involving the renegade Jesse Loame and the rumored strategies of the Network. It was of a very confidential nature she was informed and was sworn to secrecy.

This day would prove to be different.

The long hallway and its silence grew on her, and in doing so she unknowingly began to relive her past and her untimely enroll-ment into the Academy at the early age of 2,587 days. She could remember it vividly. She was but a young thing scampering around her parents' home while they watched. It had been her birthday, and as birthdays are usually happy and joyous, this one seemed solemn and gloomy. Something was wrong, or amiss, but whatever it was, she had no clue.

Later that night after cake was served, a stranger stopped by. Both parents acted as though he was a long-lost friend, but some-thing told her otherwise. She sensed he was there for another rea-son, but for what, she did not know. As the evening came to a close, her need for sleep became insistent; afraid to leave her parents' side because of the stranger's presence, she fell asleep with her head rest-ing on her mother's lap. By morning it was over; upon waking she found herself in a strange bed within a strange room with a locked door.

The life she knew was gone.

Her years at the Academy hadn't been too bad; in fact, the staff treated her as one of their own. As to special wants and desires there was no time. Every minute of every hour of every day was focused on every aspect of weapons, strength, agility, and endurance training, hand-to-hand combat, sharp shooting, and reconnaissance, (to men-tion just a few). There were also historical facts pertinent to various time periods, mathematics, communication skills, military strategies, etiquette, poise, weapons, and intelligence. All intended to ensure a sixth sense of self-preservation into each and every trainee and team.

She wasn't disrespectful to her instructors, but her ornery side and her love of life did intercede now and again, and that infuriated and frustrated them. Never before had they had so much trouble weeding out such personality flaws as hers. Having such attitudes were not considered desired characteristics of such commissioned products as the elite of Cyclops, which she was soon to become.

Being a loner since her early days encouraged self-preservation, which also eliminated her dependence upon others. This independent side had its drawbacks. She had no friends, and no one wanted her on their team *(as if they were given such a choice)*. She'd tried finding a solid friend, someone she could like and who would like her, but like so many other times she had learned the hard way: trust no one—no one other than the Gray Wolf, *(her secret childhood playmate)*.

Returning to the present she found the receptionist standing before her.

"You may go in now, 5686. Chancellor Lunette awaits."

Just what she always hated, being addressed by her corporate number instead of Grant. Brina Louise Grant was her name, her real name, and it had been given to her by her real parents. That was something no one could take from her. That and so many little phrases she'd burned into her memory, like the not-so-common phrases her mother so eloquently made mention of when the moment was right. Those and so much more were a part of herself that even The Organization couldn't extract, no matter how they tried.

Upon receiving the summons, she was in the midst of survival training. She was just returning from a twelve-day drop into "the void" when an unknown met her on the beach with an envelope. Once the time and date were noted, it was understood that there was no time to change and still be at the office of the chancellor, so she saluted the unknown and left the site.

Once inside the complex, she was escorted under armed guard to the central section where he left her standing alone after notifying the proper authorities. There she stood at attention in her standard-issue black pants, shirt, boots, hat, gloves, and optional filth while waiting for admittance. Once in his office, she stood at attention directly in front of his crescent-shaped desk while he intently and silently watched her from his chair.

It was so quiet that for her not to take advantage of the opportunity would be pointless, so she tuned in her seventh sense and listened while waiting to be addressed. At first, all she could sense was the calm and steady sounds of their breathing and heartbeats. Then came a whispered sound from the other side of the door behind her. A sound similar to that of someone trying to tiptoe across a floor.

Whoever they were, they stopped just short of their door. Their manner of approaching suggested an unauthorized intruder; whether or not the chancellor picked up on the sound up as well, he gave no indication. Then as if on cue, she heard a whisper-soft sound of someone barely knocking on the door. It was then she knew something was up. According to the Systems Operating Manuals, all office personnel were required at all times to use the intercom systems for announcing visitors. This particular circumstance very much warranted it, yet it wasn't coming.

She watched the chancellor while maintaining her mind's eye on the door. Slowly he reclined in his chair, placing his hands behind his head, legs stretched out, his feet atop the desk. His eyes were on her. He was watching for something. Waiting for something. Such an action, plus the inappropriate behavior of the outer office personnel, led her to suspect that something was rotten in upper Locanny.

Before she had time to think further, it happened. The door burst open, and in charged two men dressed in camouflage garb. Brina wasted no time in taking flight out of their line of trajectory and into the center of the office where she had more room to maneuver. With more maneuvering room as opposed to cramped quarters, she could easily use her physical ability, all her training, personal knife, and the power of her mind.

The power of her mind was hers alone. It was a resource she'd kept secret from her instructors as well as her parents. Wolf had told her when she was very young not to divulge that to anyone. Not even to family members, because once they knew, they'd use it against her. Now, unfortunately, she had no choice.

In one fluent motion she launched herself with such speed and agility that the two attackers were caught totally off guard. Before they knew what'd happened, she was in their face. The taller of the two she left in a semiconscious state on the floor after a sideways punch to the head. With him now temporarily immobilized, she turned on the second. Extracting her knife, she drew a beeline on him and charged.

The second of the two intruders watched as the woman incapacitated his partner, then watched in amazement as she whirled towards him, with knife in the ready. Within seconds she was on him. Brina drove her pearl-handled beauty hilt-deep upwards into his chest then gave it a quick twist of her wrist. When the lifeless body began to slowly drop towards the floor, she withdrew it then pivoted around to again face her first opponent.

When the first assailant's head and vision cleared, he turned towards the commotion. There he witnessed the deadly attack on his friend unfold. Silently he cursed her and those involved while returning to an upright position. While doing so, he pulled out from under his jacket a Dragunov carbine. Without further ado, he fired a single shot into the ceiling.

Brina froze. There stood her opponent not more than 6 feet 5.243 inches away from the executive chair pointing a Dragunov carbine directly at Chancellor Francesco Lunette, Chief Secretary of Cyclops.

Seeing the intent in his eyes and the ugly sneer upon his face, Brina knew he thought the situation was now under his control. Unfortunately, he wasn't paying as close attention to her as he should have. Instead, he was yelling worthless demands of anyone who would listen. The beauty of it all gave her enough time to bring together the eerie power held within her mind. This power for her was child's play. So, of course, when their eyes met, she hurtled it his way.

He froze in his tracks, staring at her with eyes as blank as his mind. No movement, no voice. Everything had just come to an immediate stand still. Brina now had him right where she wanted him, and while in this state she stepped up to him undetected. Prying the carbine from his hands she returned to her previous spot, released him, and waited for his reaction.

At first, he blinked. Then noticed the lack of weight in his hands and looked down to see that his weapon had vanished. Using sight alone he frantically searched the room.

Brina, on the other hand, had taken the Dragunov, moved it and herself to the far side of the room—allowing extra room for safety's sake—and had taken aim.

When he spotted her, he faced her, directly. There it was, in her arms. His carbine. In her arms, and she? She was in firing position, and he in her line of fire. He searched those gunmetal gray eyes for intent and knew she'd shoot. No questions asked, no remorse. A quick glance at the chancellor then at her was all that time allowed as the sound of a woman's voice interrupted his brief moment of thought.

"Don't. One move, one slight move from you 'till the sentries arrive and your part in this will be over. Your life will be over," Brina said with deadly assurance.

He shook his head and stared at her. "You're bluffing. You wouldn't kill an unarmed man."

"Don't think it and don't do anything stupid! Put the commas where you like."

Angry, he made his move.

She fired. He crumpled. It was all so stupidly simple.

She stared at the two bodies on the floor. It had all happened in less than eight seconds. She figured the three of them had been setup from the beginning. They were dead, really dead, and only because her training and self-preservation had subconsciously kicked in. She was sure the whole episode was staged because of some stupid decision made from some upper-authority flunky (trying to justify his job).

She had been played like a pawn in a chess game. They maneuvered her into position then waited for her to counteract. What was their belief, to determine whether or not she was qualified to play the game? She was sure that if she'd failed there was a long list of applicants being considered for the next same stupid and moronic game. For the first time in a long time, she was utterly furious. Usually such an emotion as anger is squelched during the early days of training as it can get in the way of positive thinking and planning, but apparently, they hadn't done such an efficient job as they'd thought. Brina slowly swung the carbine, taking aim at the chancellor.

The chancellor had expected a reaction, but not this one. A moment ago, it was surprise and awe as to what she'd done, but now fear gripped his very soul. Fear, she would again pull the trigger without remorse, without hesitation.

She saw what she wanted in his eyes. Lowering her weapon, she searched deeper for what had forced his hand.

"Now that I have your undivided attention, Chancellor, I have a few questions." In his eyes she could see surprise and something else. Something she couldn't make out. Brina held fast to the rifle's butt but allowed the barrel tip to slowly slip towards the floor. She pulled up a chair, but strategically situated it should she need to watch the door, and for maneuvering room.

Even though her body was tense, she tried to relax. She knew caution and common sense were imperative at times like these but felt her cockiness infiltrate and side with her anger during this moment of tension. "Ya know I don't do windows, I don't do carpets, and I certainly don't like being manipulated by fools. Was this little game your idea or someone else's?"

Chancellor Lunette pushed back, slowly swung his chair around, stood up, then walked around to the front of his desk, sat on its edge, and tried not to see her as a woman but as the capable killing machine she just proved herself to be. And as much as he wanted to answer all her questions, he knew he couldn't. Not that he wouldn't, but he couldn't. What he wanted, instead, was to take a moment to consider the "other" spectacle he'd just been privileged to witness.

"Listen, Chancellor, if you recall, only one assailant had a gun, and if this hadn't been a setup, one or both of us would be dead now. What happened? Were they not given all the facts either?"

His mind was churning with thoughts of her. Then of course he had known she wouldn't have appreciated his little exercise, but unfortunately, he had no choice, his orders were clear.

"5686—"

"Don't address me so," she demanded.

After a moment's consideration, "Okay. Grant. That is correct, isn't it?" At her slight nod, he continued. "That power you wield is quite impressive. Have you always had it?"

Brina knew deep down inside he wouldn't answer any of her questions unless it was under his terms. "Yeah...and as you well know, there's no known observation or written documentation on it. And if you report this, plausible denial will be my defense," she stated defiantly.

They sat in total silence for quite some time, while thoughts churned in both their minds. After a bit, the chancellor spoke.

"Grant, let me take this time to explain to you a few things. Those two men were given a rare opportunity to earn a pardon for their crimes and with it their freedom by assassinating the two of us. It was someone's undeniable faith in you that prompted this little exercise, and yes, it was a test of your abilities." He hated lying. "It all stems from the episode last week."

"What happened last week? Sir," she asked, remembering again her place.

He ignored her question. "I've watched you for a long time, Grant. You've proved beyond a shadow of a doubt to be one of the best in your field." At least her file was accurate. "Not so long ago, I was informed of an incident that occurred on your 7,884th day. A day in which during a training maneuver you managed to overtake and disable Dr. Jarlath, Master Trainer of Field Research and Control. I was notified immediately of his injuries upon his admittance to level 32 at the Centre here. Do you realize overtaking him is not an easy task, let alone disable him as well?" He didn't get a response, just an unwavering glare. "Once again, you've exceeded the expectations of your trainers, teachers, several in higher positions, and as a result, they've unanimously agreed and authorized your acceptance into Cyclops. Well, now Cyclops has a special assignment just for you."

An assignment just for her? That's what that stupid game was for? To see if she was capable enough to be sent out into the field? If that wasn't a load of crap, she didn't know what was. Why were they going through all this trouble? It drove her crazy, but she kept quiet. Besides, why question their decision? Their methods really sucked—especially for those dead on the floor—but if this was at all an avenue for her to get out, and she'd just proved herself to the man in charge of the northern sector, then by the All Mother herself, she'd take the assignment and get the hell out of Dodge.

For Brina, the Academy was occasionally fun, but mostly she considered it a contact sport. A constant, never-ending, grueling, mind-boggling training exercise. Oftentimes it got boring (except for her visits to the void), but to actually prove oneself in the field? That was another thing altogether!

The chancellor watched her from behind his desk. Watched the wheels turning behind those lovely eyes. He knew all the information, training, skills, and knowledge contained in that lovely form was just lying in wait. Waiting for its chance to emerge and take its place among the greats of time.

"Grant, you are about to be briefed, but first, I need to know if you are willing to accept this assignment without question, without all the details, and know you will be going at it alone. Without the assistance of a team."

He was giving her a choice? He had to be kidding. Brina knew if she didn't take him up on it, she could be stuck in the Academy forever. She'd already been offered an instructor's position, but why beat your head against the wall for such a job as that would entail? Without further thought, she said, "Where do I sign?"

"Good. You remember the briefing on Jesse Loame?" At her nod he continued. "We have learned, through our informants, he has also managed to obtain the original copy of Chapter XXI titled 'Channeling of Power, from the Text of Operation Manual for the Neptune Sphere.' We've also found a dead technician near the entrance to the Franciscan Lifter. The calibrations were set for the year of 00001872.xxt. The dial set at 55893866-5. We are assuming that he has returned to the past in search of Maximillian Rider."

Her eyes became saucer size.

"Yes, the same Rider who originally stole the sphere six months ago. As I am to understand it, the sphere is useless without the operating instructions. Last week Jesse Loame escaped, and it is believed he has the missing pages. The *lifter* has been disabled, trapping him within those calibrations. Under such circumstances, the only means of transportation and time continuum travel available to us now is the Zodiac Field.

"I am volunteering you to those of higher authority on the condition of acceptance."

Before he could continue, she interrupted. "Sir?" When Brina had his attention, she continued. "A question."

He responded with a nod.

"Why was I chosen for this test, sir?" The rest really didn't make a hill of beans difference to her, it all boiled down to a means of escaping this place, but she was a little curious as to the whys involved.

She had accepted the assignment sight unseen, and because of that he couldn't see why it was so necessary to keep so much classified material from her. "Grant, your identity number is 5686-44-2222-E. Do you know what the E stands for?" he questioned.

"No, sir. Never."

"Expendable."

Everything from past to present slowly came into focus.

"Everyone, and I mean everyone who is affiliated with The World Protection Organization such as Cyclops or the Academy has a letter at the end of their identification number depicting their status within the organization." He gave her a moment to think about that before continuing. "Let's get back to your assignment—to search out and destroy Jesse Loame. Any accomplices of his you happen to run into, fall into the same category and are to be dealt with accordingly.

"Now, since you will be returning to the ancient times of the Wild, Wild West, you'll be needing period clothing and equipment. That, my dear, is in the process of being assembled by Dr. Jarlath, and yes, he is recovering quite nicely. You will be properly equipped and will leave approximately one week from today. Is there anything special you would like to add, or are there any more questions?"

She had accepted Chancellor Lunette's explanation of the letter located at the end of her and everyone else's identity number and its meaning as just another stupid idea held over from the last hierarchy of the organization. Once she left for the Wild, Wild West, not only would she leave the Academy, but her number would remain here as well. Other than that, she couldn't believe her luck! Here was her chance to finally do something good for the organization, herself, and more important, the people of their world.

He'd asked if there was anything special she wanted to add; he meant comments, of course. She had no more comments; there were no more questions to be asked. Not now, not ever. At least until she thought about her options. The Zodiac Field was a one-way-only trip. She knew that, yet it didn't upset her; she had no one here. Her family of late was the Academy, and now they were sending her away. There was only one friend she had left in this world, and to leave him would mean an end to the beginning. She had to ask.

"Chancellor Lunette, sir, I do have a special request. I understand what you're asking. I also understand about the Zodiac Field. I can and will accept this assignment if you would allow me this one small request. I would like very much to take a little extra...security with me, just in case I need it."

"Is there anyone in particular you have in mind?" She was no fool this gray-eyed vixen, and if the rumors were correct...

"Yes, sir, I would like to take along with me the Gray Wolf. Sir.

"You must understand, Grant, he must meet certain requirements before I'll authorize his transfer."

"Name them, sir." Brina knew the Gray Wolf had the capability of fulfilling any requirement.

"Fine. The first and foremost concern—you must be looked upon as going alone. If he is able to fulfill this requirement, the others are of little concern to us." He had heard rumors of this Gray Wolf, but there was no substantial evidence to prove them true and factual. But if there was an official way to "lose" him, it would be well worth it. He wondered if she knew of the rumors.

It was all decided; everything was prepared. Assignments, transfers, and all paperwork processed. Travel vouchers were authorized with Chancellor Lunette's official seal. Even their wardrobe was assembled and made ready. Once Brina completed her study on what little information she could find on the Neptune Sphere, along with its supposed properties, she received her final briefings on the mission before entering The Chamber. There they boarded the platform of the Zodiac Field and waited for their departure time for the 14:47.5062 a.

II

another time, another place

Our story begins in a little town nestled near and about the northwest corner of the Dakota Territories. Its name, Eastern-Western. It was named thus because of the location of the two rivers near it, one being on the east, the other being on its west. One was the Missouri; the other had no name at all.

On a miserable, cold, windy, freezing January day, we find Marshal Dillon Frasier sitting at the only desk in his office, staring out one of the windows in the room, while watching the weather from a warm and toasty spot on his favorite wooden chair. In his hand, a warmed cup of black hot liquid. Close by, his cozy, warm woodstove with an old brown coffee pot resting on its rim.

It was almost noon, yet our hero Marshal Dillon Frasier was not ready to eat; instead, he was muddling over a few things.

Yesterday's thoughtful muddle was of a few of the more colorful characters in town. With a smile, he thought of them: Mrs. Fitzwilly and her collection of cats—sometimes it seemed she had them all. The local whores: Bertie, Louise, Deirdre, and Cassandra—who were always willing to lend a hand. N. Marlow, who called himself a doctor, but a doctor of what—they never could find out. Cornelius Thatcher, down at the livery who said he came from across the "great waters" just to take up blacksmithing, and to shoe horses by himself without an assistant. Annabelle Drearylane, who had a mind of her own, yet was courting Thatcher—enjoying his attentions but not his ideas of childbearing (he boasted his love for children and wanted twelve or so).

Thinking of that phrase stopped him for a moment. Thatcher's often-overused phrase "great waters" reminded Dillon of his deputy. "Johnny Soars Like an Eagle" is an English version of a name which was given to this capable and intriguing man by his Cherokee grandmother during his thirteenth summer. All the marshal knew about him was that he was half-Cherokee, and unfortunately, Dillon also knew, when one is half-Indian, one has a difficult road to travel, so, in order to get the townsfolk to better accept him and for what he could do for them, Dillon changed his name from Johnny Soars Like an Eagle. To Johnny S. Hartley.

The question here might be, why during those times deputize a half-Cherokee Indian? In this case, Johnny had stepped up to the plate during a time when the ball was heading directly towards the marshal. That particular incident, that most definitely got the marshal's attention happened in the general store. That morning, just like all others before it, after chores are finished, some folk often-times head to the general store for either gossip or shopping. This day the marshal was doing a bit of both. While chatting with the owner and a few others, all inside the store were shocked when outta the blue some feller charged in with both guns drawn. The marshal was totally caught off guard and a bit surprised too, because within seconds he watched a second man rush the first from behind, knocking the first to the ground. They later figured that the first man must've mistaken the store for the bank, and the second man, of course, was Johnny. Johnny, who had been watching this "out of place" kinda fella from across the alley. Suspicious of this character, Johnny followed him around the corner and down the street to the general store. When Johnny saw him draw his guns before entering, then fumble with the door handle finally getting it open, decided to act, and he without a gun, charged this jerk like a northern gale. The gunman went down, was cuffed, placed in a cell, and both the day and the marshal were saved.

That very day when Marshal Dillon Frasier laid eyes on Johnny Soars Like an Eagle, or rather Johnny "Wanbli Kinyan" (which was his given Cherokee name, pronounced wahn-blee keen-yahn, which for propriety's sake, translates as "Soaring Eagle"), and what he had done changed his mind about a lot of things. Consequently, since then, the marshal had given Johnny, and those like him, more respect. For within Johnny, Dillon saw something not often found. From the first moment and throughout their friendship, this exceptional young man exhibited an unbreakable sense of pride, honor, and an inner strength most cannot even begin to understand or penetrate. And as far as the marshal was concerned, as long as Johnny took and carried out orders, brought him back to the jail when the marshal was too drunk to stand, continued to be his friend, watched his back, and stood by his side when warranted, the rest would fall into place nicely.

By the next day, the marshal was beginning to feel a bit worn 'cause the night before had been quite busy. Mrs. Fitzwilly had been in complaining about her one of her many cats. As it was explained, Whiskers did not want to come out from under the nice, warm stove to go outside for nightly duties. For that matter, neither would he, and so *why come to the marshal's office about a cat?*

There was that drifter, a townsfolk found, who after spending an entire night playing poker and drinking, froze to death after passing out on the outhouse seat. Jonathan Bunker, sometime during the night, had had enough of his wife's constant complaining to provoke him into outright shooting her. Needless to say, he found himself unceremoniously thrown into one of the jail cells. There he sat, awaiting the end of winter and the arrival of the circuit judge.

As that week progressed, so did the weather. The winds and temps went from mild, to quite windy and chilly, finally to a ghastly and freezing gale. It brought with it an eerie sound not unlike that of harrowing atrocities, pain, and suffering. It was as though the spirit of some long-lost soul was trying to reach out to the marshal (*or anyone else who would listen*) from beyond the grave. That dreaded howling sound and banging after a time began its work on the frail edges of his sanity as he sat behind his desk staring at endless paperwork. He'd been trying to catch up on his work but was having a hard time of it, so instead he paused a moment to stare out the window. Good thing too. So lost in thought, he failed to recognize the banging he'd been hearing was that one of his office shutters had broken loose, as it slapped back and forth against the jailhouse wall with a fever to match that of a Sioux uprising. At least that was until now. *Crap*, he thought. Out of his chair he rose, back on went the winter gear, out the door he charged, fighting the winds and fixed the damned thing. Looking around, realized he didn't want to be outside anymore, went back inside, fixed himself a hot cup, stripped down layers to where he felt comfy, sat back in his chair, and continued to stare at the endless paperwork. Now, he thought, it was quiet, and he could concentrate. Unfortunately, boredom again overtook the paperwork issue, and off he faded back into a day dreamy-like state.

At first light the next morning, believing the weather would get worse as time passed, he hit the general store up for supplies: additional coffee, flour, jerky, sugar, and salt. Heading back to his office, he stopped short when he spied a coal-black horse with a left hind sock that ran up to his rump standing tied to a hitching rail. He stared at it for longer than a moment. He knew that horse. Knew him from somewhere, or one of similar markings. Thinking about it, he finally remembered. With a smile on his face, a vigorous pace to his step, he returned to his office while recalling the face of another. A face of a dear friend. A long-ago-kinda friend. A feller named Cordell Chevalier. With that thought on his mind, after getting comfy again, he let it take hold. Sitting in his chair, he mentally relived those long-ago days when and how he and Cordell met.

Back on *that* freezing winter day, around high noon, cabin fever settled in. In attempts at shaking it, the marshal bundled up, cold or no cold, and took a short walk around town. Passing the livery, gunfire was heard up the street. Whirling around on that ice-covered walkway, he slipped and went down.

It was a bank robbery. Four riders were struggling with their mounts as both they and the horses slipped across that treacherous film of ice. As the marshal watched, one horse lost his footing, and when it did, his rider lost his seat and went flying. The other three managed to gain fairly good ground and control of their mounts, fleeing the scene. As that snow-covered ex-rider attempted to also escape, he again slipped a good one and bulldozed his head right into a snowbank. By then, the marshal was on him. Searching for something solid to grab and hold, seized his arm, then tried dragging him up as he himself clamored to his feet. Once up, the little stinker kicked the marshal in the shin trying once again to escape. *How soon they forget.* Not expecting it, the poor little fool then slipped on that ice and fell back down into the fluffy snow. All who were watching just stood there and laughed. When the kid finally realized he was going nowhere, he began to whimper. The marshal watched him for a moment; then remembering some of his own past escapades, he stopped laughing and held out a hand for support. This time the snow-covered culprit took it. On his feet, he stood, instead of trying to flee. The marshal had to crouch down a tad to get his attention, look into his face, and in doing so, got a good look at his bank robber.

This was just a boy. Actually, to get right down to it, so was the marshal, in a way. Watching him, the marshal was reminded of his own circumstances and what brought him to where he was today. In his eyes, Dillon Frasier saw himself. And if he and his brother hadn't been taken in by Mr. Hamilton all those years ago, that young man standing before him could very well have been himself. Looking into his soft-brown eyes Dillon gently tugged on his sleeve.

"Come, boy." At first, the youngster wouldn't budge, but finally gave in to persistent tugging. Urged to come, he was asked if he realized what kind of trouble he was in. He never said a word, just walked in front of the marshal with his head lowered as though he was heading towards the gallows.

When they reached the door of the jail, the boy made another break for it and again had forgotten the ice. Young boys can be so stupid. This time he was not so lucky. He landed so solidly against the plank walkway that it knocked him cold. Dillon threw him over his shoulder, then carried him to a jail cell. This was no easy task mind you. He was heavier than he looked. After carefully laying him down upon the cot, the cell door was shut then locked as he was left in an unconscious state, covered with a blanket.

While the marshal was out—both with supply gathering and culprit collections—the cooler winter air had filtered into the office through the tiny cracks in the wooden walls. And since there was no one at home to chase it away, the office was now chilly. With the chill came the goose bumps. Not wanting either, Dillon brought in more wood to add to the coal box and his depleted supply sitting nearby, before sitting down, settling in, making himself feel once more at home. With both shutters now securely nailed shut and the fire finally going full blast, the large room was once again transformed from an ice cave in the Antarctic back to a warm and toasty place of business. Once the shivers finally stopped, he could focus on the problem at hand—going through the stacks and stacks of wanted posters, searching for a face that might possibly match the one on the cot.

It wasn't too long before movement was heard from the cell. Slowly Dillon turned while leaning back in the swivel chair to assess his newly found prisoner. The kid stood with his hands resting between the bars, like he had already been sentenced.

"Mmmm, Mr. Sheriff…sir?" The young man paused.

In the next flash of a second, the marshal saw many things. That first tear forming in the boy's left eye brought it all back in a flood. You see, Dillon Frasier had seen plenty of ruffians and hard-core criminals in his time, and here in his jail cell was another young man with his life before him. Another young man afraid, unsure, and alone. Another young man facing an unknown future.

"What's your name, boy?" he asked. He might as well see what he could find out. After all, the marshal had nothing better to do at the time, other than check on Mrs. Fitzwilly and her stupid cat.

"Cordell, sir. Cordell Chevalier," was all he had to offer.

"Well, Cordell Chevalier, how does your head feel?" Dillon felt bad for him. He'd hit that walkway pretty hard. "Do you feel steady enough for some chow?" It was past lunchtime.

"That's mighty nice of you, Mr. Sheriff, sir. Why, I'd be pleased to share my last meal with you."

What a well-mannered kid. Sounded like maybe he had had a decent family life at one time. Not many youngsters addressed their elders with respect nowadays. Kinda made Dillon wonder what brought him here.

"Cordell?"

"Yes, sir, Mr. Sheriff, sir?"

"I'm not the sheriff. I'm the federal marshal for this sector."

If being in jail and the thought that this might be his last night on this earth had him spooked, Dillon figured learning his own status had done him in.

"MARSHAL? YA KNOW I DIDN'T WANT TO ROB THAT BANK! Them guys I was with, they talked me into it, said we could be rich, and I wouldn't have to slop manure anymore. They found me in an old livery stable cleaning horse stuff. That was after I had left St. Louise in search of my fortune." *Sniffle, sniffle.* "Ya see, my parents live there, I got tired of all that schooling, and got restless. One of my teachers suggested that I go West and find adventure." *Sniffle, sniffle.* "Them guys made it sound so easy are you going to hang me for helping those guys steal that money?" *Sniffle, sniffle.*

Not laughing was very hard. The poor kid never stopped for a breath of air, or so it seemed. All Dillon could do was stand there and look the bad guy.

The boy just stood there all humble and innocent with a lower lip quivering like a leaf in a breeze. It was like watching someone standing in the corner waiting fer a whippin' from their dad. Dillon got the impression he'd been stripped of a precious and safe existence, then just as suddenly thrown unceremoniously into another, and that wasn't fair. Right then and there he decided to step in and help this young man—*because there was something about him, he liked.*

"No, Cordell. I'll not let them harm or put ya away. The circuit judge is due come spring, how 'bout I wire him about your situation. Perhaps, instead of sending you to prison, maybe they'll let you work off your time helping me, *without pay of course.* Don't worry, though, I'll see to it that you'll have a place to sleep, are taken care of, and receive three square meals a day."

Cordell's face brightened like a moon's reflection in still waters.

It was done. Cordell worked faithfully under Dillon's direction for three years then alongside him for three more. They became as brothers. Dillon's real brother, Kane, and he hadn't seen each other for ten years. Cordell had now filled that hole.

For those three years he apprenticed under the marshal with the intention of learning the law and its benefits. Later, he decided that marshalcy wasn't challenging enough for him and decided to move on in search of adventure. Dillon's wishes went with him, so did a coal-black bald-faced horse with a *right* hind sock that ran up to his rump. That horse was his parting gift to him as a constant reminder of their friendship.

Similar to the one spotted just this morning.

III

the $64 question

Marshal Dillon Frasier sat in his office chair with feet on the desk staring at the piles of papers awaiting attention. The night was giving way to the dawn as the morning sun and warmth filtered its way between the curtains of his office windows. He was lost in thought. He missed Cordell. It seemed like forever since he had left only four years prior, yet whether he be here or gone in search of his own niche in life, the coming of the new day was inevitable, bringing the old familiars along with it. If one was observant, and aware, the early morning sounds could be soothing. The greetings from the birds who make their homes in the few trees of the town and against the walls and crevices of its buildings were what were normally heard first. Those like the *coo-oooh coo, coo-coo* of the morning dove, the flute-like tones of the meadowlark, and all the other unknowns that sing, chirp, warble, and dumped their loads wherever they choose, in and around their own little corner of the world. Even the hustle and bustle of morning activities by store owners and early risers gently put his mind at ease. And since Dillon didn't quite feel up to working quite yet, he allowed himself a moment to reflect back upon childhood memories of home, family, and his younger brother Kane.

Kane and he were a pair. Of course, they had to be. Brothers raised together with no other children to play or fight with for miles around tend to be that way. They played hide-and-seek, oftentimes with Dillon cheating, heading for the house, followed by Kane giving up the hunt hours later. When Kane finally did go inside, many times he would find Dillon eating cookies and enjoying a glass of milk or two with Mom. Angry that he be fooled, Kane rushed in pushing

Dillon off his chair. Dillon, in turn, would pick himself up amid the spilled milk and all and then punch him, and the fight would ensue.

He remembered other cherished times when their dad was in the fields mowing hay with the team of blondes, and Mom would be playing tag with them in the front yard, enjoying the hell out of her two sons. Dillon could even go back as far as to remember when Dad had put up a rope swing behind the house. Both kids took turns swinging on it. High into the air they'd sail, then let go at the last second before dropping into the creek with a big splash. Those times were always the most fun. Simpler times, happier times.

During those wonderful years, he remembered how his mom always made sure there was enough time for even the simplest things. Picnics, games, warm fireplaces, school, and of course there was the year of the cow. One year, Dad surprised Mom with a milk cow for the holidays. She didn't mind the early-morning and evening milkings, just as long as they had more than enough fresh milk every day. Mom was a wise one. Since there was more than the family could use, she sold the excess to the neighbors and anyone else who wanted it. That extra money came in handy. So handy, in fact, that once she managed to save enough to surprise Dad with a beautiful bay mare she bought from that Mr. Hamilton down the road. Their dad was thrilled, as were the kids. No longer would they have to hear all those stories about how, without a horse to ride, he had to walk all those miles, uphill, in ten feet of snow, to town, 'cause now the horse could fight the snow and the uphill climb.

And like always, the bad memories barged in when least expected. Before Dillon could redirect his thoughts, visions of that horrible day came. Kane and he had just ridden home from school on their own newly gifted brown gelding and found their house and barn burned to the ground. That nice Mr. Hamilton was there with the federal marshal who said it was a band of outlaws and marauders who had attacked their farm, killed their parents, and stole all the stock including Dad's bay mare. They said the Territorial Riders had been after them renegades for some time because they'd burned other families' homes down after looting them in other places within the territory. That nice Mr. Hamilton, well, he looked down upon those boys' sodden faces, knowing good and well what would be in store for them if he didn't do something, so he stepped in, took, and raised those two brothers as his own.

The morning stage broke Dillon's concentration. It never failed. Every time he would hear the arrival of that morning stage, he'd pull out his pocket watch. The time was twelve noon, and they still called it the morning stage. At least it had broken his concentration on his daydreaming, and in its place was anticipation. He had been hoping for another letter from his brother for months now. The last one received was vague and mysterious. Something about the "Ivory Tower" and how the First Citizen had enlisted him for a secret mission.

Knowing the "morning" stage had arrived, he thought about meeting it, but remembered had there been anything of importance, Johnny would bring it directly to the office. Well, within minutes that very thing happened. In burst Johnny with a letter addressed to "Federal Marshal Dillon Frasier, Dakota Territories."

"For you, Marshal. It looks important," Johnny excitedly stated.

Marshal Frasier held out his hand for the delivery. He looked at it closely, spotting the official seal signifying importance. Slowly it was opened, and the contents read. The symbols on the page, as he read, began as words, but as each meaning of each word became clear, he found himself slowly lowering back into his chair and seeing only letters upon a page.

It most definitely was from the Ivory Tower. It was a large mail pouch containing Kane's death certificate along with a letter of explanation, dated and signed by the "Ivory Tower's" First Citizen.

"Shit," the marshal stated.

"Bad news?"

"Yeah. Give me some time alone if you would."

As Johnny left the marshal, Dillon's thoughts turned to Kane and *their* reason for his death. According to the letter, his brother had been killed while on assignment. The letter further explained that the regiment in which he was assigned to and traveling with, in crossing the southernmost part of the Sioux Nation, was attacked and slaughtered. As he read, tears began to form in his eyes.

Kane was a planner and wanted to become all that he could. That was why he continued on with his education. Dillon, on the other hand, left Mr. Hamilton's embrace and took up with the federal marshal who originally found their farm in ruins. Through him, Dillon had learned the hard way what kinds of people were out there in the world. There were those like Mr. Hamilton and the marshal who were strong, yet kind and understanding of folks, and then, on the other hand, there were the kind like those who raped, pillaged, plundered, and took advantage of innocents—innocent folks like his parents. Both Kane and Dillon, in a way, had now been stripped of a precious life and consequently were in a situation that neither one liked and believed to be totally unjust, unfair, and unforgiving. Dillon was not suggesting that life with Mr. Hamilton wasn't good; it just wasn't home. Everything they had known and cherished had been destroyed in one fell swoop by evildoers, and because of that, both had to grow up much sooner than later.

During the first few years under the wing of Mr. Hamilton and his teachings, he used to say to both boys, "The only way to make things right is to be honest, trustworthy, and law abiding. If you feel cheated because of what happened to you and Kane, don't grow up hating life. Do something noble instead. Become an instrument of the All Mother and help protect those less fortunate than you. Serve those out there who might otherwise be wronged because of individuals like those who put you and your brother in my embrace. You, son, are the stronger, your brother is different than you, he will follow a different star."

Mr. Hamilton felt Dillon had the perfect persona to be become a lawman. And after many months of serious consideration, he followed his advice and did just that.

Dillon continued to stare at that letter, long after the tears stopped falling. His anger rose. Who had slaughtered that regiment and his brother? For what reason would someone slaughter, as the letter stated, a regiment of twenty Territorial Riders and one civilian? Indians? Surely not, he knew in his heart that something definitely was not quite right here. Kane had mentioned in his last letter that it had been a secret mission that he had been assigned to. Was that true? Perhaps, he hadn't been kidding after all.

Dillon had only to say good-bye to a few more friends, when Johnny Hartley again barged into the office shouting about another official-looking letter. This one apparently had been missed in all the excitement of the discovery of the first. As Hartley handed Dillon the envelope, he noticed the handwriting. This hand was very familiar. It was Kane's writing. He had sent the promised letter. As Dillon tore into it and began to read, many of the questions he had collected over the last week or so were answered.

It read,

> *Dearest brother,*
>
> *I take pen in hand and write to you in loving memory of our beloved parents, who unfortunately, were unable to tell us what we so desperately needed to know, if any unforeseeable tragedy should strike. I want you to know that I love you dearly and will never forget all those pranks you pulled on me when Mom wasn't looking.*
>
> *I am under direct authority of the First Citizen as one of his special confederates. I have recently received orders to report to Fort William in the Dakota Territories, which is under the command of a Major James Northrup of the Territorial Riders for that area. When I arrive, I'm to be assigned my own regiment to guard me, along with the secret document that I carry, on a very dangerous trek across country to Fort Hope. There I'm to meet a Mr. Jon J. Nobody, hand over the sealed document, then my orders are to continue. The document will state where we go from there.*
>
> *Dillon, I don't know what is going on here. Bizarre happenings have surrounded this assignment. I'm concerned for my life, dear brother, and even though this is*

38

hush-hush, there are those outside the Ivory Tower who know of this. I'm afraid this may be my last letter.

As I mentioned before, this assignment is supposed to be secret, and no mention of this is supposed to get out. However, since you are all that I have left in the world, I felt you should know. After all, if anything should happen to me, under these circumstances, remember this: those connected with the Ivory Tower will tell you nothing, and if by chance they do, it's probably a lie. Remember, I'm supposed to be on a mission of utmost secrecy. I guess you could say now that I've broken that confidence.

My dear brother, since I have gone this far, there is something else you must know. There is a man out there by the name of Maximillian Rider. Beware of him. I cannot tell you more.

Someone is coming.

Your beloved brother,
Kane

Kane. What in the *mother's* name had he fallen into? At least Dillon now had something to go on. The official document didn't say much but did give him a direction. Dillon decided the best avenue to take was to utilize his authority as a federal marshal to discover all that was possible. Once all was gathered, whether it be information or supplies, he would inform Deputy Hartley that he carried the badge until the marshal's return. By the time the marshal's bags were packed and his trusty steed, Cody, was newly shod, they were ready to head out.

Dillon left town heading easterly. His first road would have led to the Ivory Tower, but that was before Kane's letter. If they denied Kane's existence, what was the point? So instead of plan A, he decided on plan B: to follow his nose. Unfortunately, when he couldn't find Fort Hope, regardless of how many Territorial Riders headquarters he inquired at, he was at wit's end. No one seemed to ever have ever heard of it. It was as if it didn't exist.

Sitting upon his trusty steed overlooking the Platt, Dillon pulled out Kane's last letter. When he read that one sentence again, *"Dillon, I don't know what is going on here. Bizarre happenings have surrounded this assignment"*—the hair on the back of Dillon's neck stood on end; goose bumps ran down his arms. *Bizarre* was a definite way to describe the nonexistent Fort Hope. Thinking further, he decided to head towards the River James and Fort William. Since there really was a Fort William, perhaps he would learn something there.

IV

just around the bend

$\mathbf{A}$s the leaves of the trees began their annual descent to the base of their beginnings, so did Dillon ride into Bishop Falls. It was a quiet little town on the north bank of the Oahe and definitely what some would consider a one-horse town.

Riding in from the south side, he found the livery stable conveniently located across from the hotel. *Hotel.* What a wonderful word. He was desperately in need of a bath and a decent night sleep. Sleeping under the stars night after night after night is a treasured experience, but after a while the ground gets awful uncomfortable; the insects crawl into your blanket finding their way into your drawers, your ears, your nose hairs, etcetera. The owls talk all night, the trails are not well marked, and you have to cook for yourself—if you can get a fire started with wet matches. So, after all those many months spent out on the trail, a needed break from the investigation was a blessing in disguise.

What had he learned so far? Zip.

Dillon checked Cody into the livery stable, making sure he had a decent and dry place with plenty of care for the duration of their stay, not knowing how long that'd be, then headed back across the street and stepped up to the Shallenberger Hotel.

Once his signature was in their register, he checked out the room, depositing things not needed for a few hours, stepped back outside, and surveyed the rest of the town from the top step. He stood there, looking up and down both sides of the street till a drinking and dining establishment caught his eye, The Dew Drop Inn and

Saloon. With his mind quickly made up, Dillon headed over to the saloon for a drink, (*'cause he hadn't had a glass of whiskey in a coon's age*).

After sauntering through the swinging doors of the saloon, almost crashing directly into a drunk as he stumbled out through the same opening, he surveyed the room. Had he been sitting down, he would have fallen off his chair, 'cause there in the far corner, sitting at a table playing poker, was an old friend. Marshal Glen Harper. Cursed be the day for he spotted the marshal before Dillon could run. Not wanting to be recognized by anyone or to explain his being out of his area to anyone, he found himself trapped.

"Dillon! Is that you, my old friend?" Harper hollered as he began to lift himself from the chair, excusing himself from the game.

Even though Dillon hadn't seen Glen for some years, he still looked the same. Very tall, well-muscled with light-sandy hair atop his head, and the strangest green eyes. No one, in all the years they'd known each other, had ever tried to cross him. He was a very capable lawman, very strong and extremely fast with a gun. Perfect for the job.

"Glen," Dillon answered, then boldly stepped up to him and firmly shook his hand. "How've you been?"

"Fine. Thanks, Dillon. And you, what have ya been up to?"

They stood toe to toe, eye to eye, and just by his stance, Dillon knew something was up. Glen was here for a reason.

"Just doing a little traveling." Dillon didn't want to tell him any more than need be; unfortunately, he believed it was too late. Rumors in the West spread like wildfire.

"Let's step outside, shall we?" Gently yet firmly Glen guided Dillon out of the saloon and into the street. Glimpsing around making sure there was no one within earshot he cautiously said, "Dillon, the Magistrate's office has been receiving continual rumors of your unauthorized investigation into Kane's death. Do you realize what that could mean?"

"It means that I am determined to find my brother's killers. Glen, you know Kane was the only family I had left. He deserves more than just a hole in the ground, don't you think?"

He looked the marshal straight in the eye. It was then all was revealed. The rumors of his apparent obsession with Kane's death had not gone unheard. The magistrate's office had sent this man out to find and warn Dillon, hoping then his actions would cease. How many others were out there looking for him?

"Well, now what? You know me better than any of the others out there in the wild blue. What do you suggest I do?"

With a look of unquestionable authority and something else that he couldn't quite grasp, Dillon was arrested and escorted to jail.

What a fine mess.

Not having anything pressing to do at the moment, Dillon got himself comfortable in the newly offered accommodations, thinking of those long hours spent in the saddle with nothing to show for it. Then there was Glen. He'd provided Dillon with hot food and all the comforts of home during his two-week stay here in the local jail and brought his other belongings from the inn without delay. What was going to become of our hero? That was the main concern now.

Dillon was awakened by the sound of footsteps in the outer office. Whoever they were, from the sound of it, they were approaching the prisoners' cells which he occupied. He remained reclined in the bunk till he heard the jingling of keys along with the sound of his cell door being unlocked. He watched the door. There stepping through it was Glen Harper and behind Glen was another gentleman whom Dillon did not know. It was Glen who began.

"Dillon, I want to introduce you to a friend of mine. This is Carl J. Stewart. Carl is a special representative of the chief magistrate's office. He has come because I telegraphed him. You see, when I received word of what you'd been up to and of my orders, I sent back to them my reply. 'Cause if it had been *my* brother and the circumstances were similar, I'd be doing the same things as you. Then when I found you, instead of one of them others out there, I sent word to Carl asking him to come here. When he arrived two days ago, we discussed the possible advantage of using you in *their* investigation. Dillon, your future relies on what the two of you can work out. Now, gents, if you'll excuse me, I'm heading for the saloon. If you need me, you'll know where I'll be."

"So, you're Dillon Frasier, the marshal of the Dakota Territory. I've been hearing a lot about you lately. What do you think you can accomplish by sticking your nose in places where it doesn't belong?"

Well, that certainly was a good question. The marshal was beginning to wonder that himself. He should have realized his obsession with this investigation would not go unnoticed. Wondering how serious this breach was, he needed to know what this man was all about. So, while scrutinizing the man before him, Dillon stared at the other side of the room, looking as though deep in thought.

Carl J. Stewart of the magistrate's office was approximately a head shorter than himself, with hair and eyes the color of coal. Dillon could tell from the way he held himself that this was a man not to be taken lightly. So, to avoid any undesirable consequences, he got down to grass roots.

"May I call you Carl?" he began.

"No. You may not. You'll address me as Mr. Stewart," he interrupted, then continued. "What you're attempting, Marshal Frasier, is a serious breach in security. I don't know if you realize what kind of consequences you may be facing, but until we have reached some kind of agreement, we must keep this entirely formal. After all, if we, my office, decides to prosecute, I'd rather be considered an opponent rather than an associate. Do I make myself clear?"

What had he gotten himself into? Conducting an investigation wasn't classified as this type of security breach, as he put it, and besides, this was a family matter. Something else was going on here. Something deeper. What had Kane really been up to? It had to have something to do with that assignment he was on, and until he could learn more he decided to play along. "Yes, 'Mr.' Stewart, I understand. *Perfectly.*"

At that he raised his right his eyebrow at Dillon and continued. "All right, Marshal, take a seat. We need to talk and git down to brass tacks."

Sitting at opposite sides of the desk, "Carl" pulled up and placed on the desk the satchel he apparently had brought with him, just for this occasion. After thumbing through its contents, he found what he wanted, studied it, laid it on the desk, then sat back in his chair and scrutinized Dillon to the point of making the marshal increasingly nervous.

"Marshal Frasier, I have been authorized to make you an offer. An offer you can't possibly refuse. First, how determined are you to find your brother's killers?"

Dillon knew had the circumstances been reversed, and it was he who had been slaughtered, Kane would not stop until someone stopped him. After all, they were the only family each other had.

"Determined enough to attempt escape and continue as a wanted man," he said, hopefully with the sound of conviction in his voice as well as on his face.

"Very well then. One thing you should know: due to your obsession with your brother's death, my original orders were to remove you from the office of Territorial Marshal, have you labeled a renegade and outlaw, and hung from the nearest tree—if/when caught." He looked at the man in front of him with the conviction of the devil himself, and he knew it. "Unless, of course, you are willing to make a deal.

"You have an outstanding record, marshal, and so my office has formulated a plan. If you agree, you may keep your badge, yet would still be considered a renegade, but you'll be free to pursue the investigation of your brother's death and that of the regiment he was assigned; however, nothing you do can or will be linked in any way to the marshal's office. If you refuse this offer and continue on your present course, you will be prosecuted immediately! Consider what you're taking on and your options. I will return in the morning for your answer." At that, he led Dillon back to the cell, watched him enter, closed, and locked the door behind him. They were taking no chances.

For a long time, Dillon paced his cell thinking of this guy's "generous" offer. He was right about one thing: it definitely was an offer Dillon couldn't refuse, unless he could come up with a way to escape, avoid recapture, and manage to live through their punishment if caught—ha-ha. He didn't want to even think about a necktie party. But here they were giving him an opportunity to fulfill his determination in getting to the bottom of Kane's death. That was really all Dillon cared about. Of course, he did care about his position as marshal back home in Eastern-Western. He wasn't born yesterday, ya know. He knew after finding Kane's killers, he still had a future to think of. A paycheck to bring in. Shelter, food, his horse's welfare, ya know, important stuff like that—maybe even a wife?

By the time morning arrived, his decision had been made. All Dillon had to do was inform Mr. Carl J. Stewart, special representative to the chief magistrate.

Back to the same seating arrangement as the night before. And with cups of coffee in hand, they began.

"Well? Did you come to a decision?" asked the devil.

He knew Dillon's answer before a word was uttered. After all, it was do it their way or die—gee, that was a hard one. No one in their right mind would want to suffer any more than absolutely necessary. So, at Dillon's nod, he continued.

"Very well. You've chosen wisely. I will notify the magistrate and all those concerned of your decision. Your badge will be in my possession until this matter is settled, and until that time arrives, you are acting on your own behalf. Your decisions on this matter are of your own choosing. However, we will not recognize your actions or inquiries pertaining to this matter. That of all things must be understood. If, for some reason, you get in trouble or are in need of our assistance, *we will not be there*. Do you understand and accept these conditions?"

The answer Dillon gave was as though he was giving an oath, his word, his first-born (had he had any)—all with his right hand raised.

"Yes, sir, I do." Hearing himself say those words made Dillon think how nice it would be if these words were being spoken to a beautiful woman holding his hand with a preacher in the room, instead of this jerk in front of him.

"Good. Now, to fill you in on the information you'll need to proceed: Your brother, Kane William Frasier, son of Sean A. and Megan C. Frasier, was enlisted by a special branch under the direct orders of the First Citizen. His orders were to deliver a sealed document to an agent of this office. This document contained a location where a weapon of great power lay hidden. This particular device or object was confiscated when we raided a stronghold belonging to a Maximillian Rider. This happened two years ago come March. Are you with me, Marshal?"

"I have a couple of questions about this." It was all so very confusing.

"Not now, Dillon. May I call you Dillon?"

Dillon mentally rolled his eyes upward, all the while thinking how much of a jerk this guy really was.

At Dillon's slight nod, Carl continued. "As I speak, your questions should be answered. I'll go slow, in order to make it easier for you to absorb. This object has been hidden in a safe, yet secret location known only to myself and a few others. Kane's orders were to deliver this document to a representative of our office. Our representative would then follow the orders in the document, continue on under the protection of said regiment with Kane in the lead.

"This is only a guess, you understand, but we're believing there was an unknown traitor afoot. This traitor or traitors somehow learned of the mission, got word of it to an outlaw by the name of Jesse Loame and with a gang of outlaws, intercepted, attacked, and slaughtered the regiment. Now, he's on the run. What he was to do with the information contained within the document was unknown to us. We know he has it because it was missing. As a precautionary measure, we have decided to have him tracked down for trial and imprisonment. You are the man to do just that. If you have any questions, now is the time to ask." He sat there patiently waiting.

"I have several. First, what is this object of such great importance?"

"I'm sorry, that's on a need-to-know basis. You really don't need to know."

"Okay, can you tell me what it looks like, just in case I run across it?"

"Again, I'm sorry. That's on a need-to-know basis, and you really don't need to know. Although, I can tell you this: if you do find it, you'll know what it is, because it's not like *anything* you've ever seen before, or so I'm told."

"You've never seen it?"

"No. But I've certainly been told about it."

"How do you know those you're talking to are trustworthy?" Why was Dillon getting the feeling they weren't telling him everything? This object they keep referring to must be of great importance for them to go to all this trouble. If it wasn't just for Kane, his curiosity had been sparked enough that he himself would have gone just for the sake of it.

"Marshal, to answer some of your unvoiced questions, may I suggest you masquerade as a bounty hunter or some such menial profession. If you did that, then you'd have the presumed authority to track down and bring in Jesse, or any other lowlifes you run over with that horse of yours. And since he is already a wanted criminal, any Territorial Marshal's office will take him. In regards to your badge, when Jesse is brought to trial and imprisoned, they will process his paperwork, and by that time, we will have heard of it, then we will get in contact with you. Although I wouldn't take him to a local sheriff's office, they usually don't have the extra security needed to contain such wanted criminals. You also need to realize he still has a gang with him; that is as far as we know. Who knows since the slaughter. Anything else?"

"As a bounty hunter I am entitled to bounty on all prisoners brought to an office of lawful authority. Will that also be true of Jesse?" Stewart's explanation of the situation was as clear as mud, but the bounty hunter thing he could relate to.

"As a bounty hunter, yes, that is correct. Since he is a wanted man anyway, yes, you are entitled. Is that it?"

"What does this Jesse look like?" He had to know; otherwise, how would he know he had the right man?

"He's about six four, has sandy-blonde hair, and green eyes. One other thing, Marshal, he is a very capable opponent. He is as skilled with his left hand as he is with his right, and when it comes to using firearms, he's a master. Is there anything else?"

If anyone had done his homework, this man had. Unfortunately for Dillon, he had missed that one particular class.

"Who is Jon J. Nobody?" Dillon had a feeling something wasn't right, and the astonished look on this man's face reaffirmed his suspicions. Kane's second letter was unknown to them. Like previously thought, this man was someone not to be taken lightly. Dillon watched his face for further signs of anything. It was not in his face, but in his eyes.

"How did you learn of Nobody? Never mind, Kane must have written you. When did you receive his letter?"

"Kane's letter came just after the notification of his death. It must have been mailed a month or so before the slaughter."

"Dillon, I'm sorry about your brother. He was a very special person." Then he paused. "If there's nothing else, I must be going. You have received all the information I'm authorized to tell you, then some."

"You haven't explained about Jon J. Nobody," Dillon stated

"That's right, I haven't. Sorry, Dillon, but that's on a need-to-know basis, and you really don't need to know."

This was going nowhere fast.

"What about this Jesse feller. Where was the last known whereabouts him? If I know that, I have somewhere to begin." Somewhere to begin.

"In the Dakota Territories, not far from Eastern-Western," he answered with a smile and a sparkle in his eyes. "You'll be fine, Dillon. Oh, one word of caution. Beware of Maximillian Rider; he is not what he seems. And by the way, as far as money is concerned, I'll have an account at the bank set up for you. You may draw upon it when needed. Other than good luck, I can't tell you anymore." At that he raised himself from the chair, picked up his satchel, shook Dillon's hand, and left him sitting there to digest all that was said, and *not said*.

V

on the road again

Dillon finished up his missed week of restful relaxation by gathering many of the supplies needed for an extended trip to Fort William. If he could only retrace the route in which the Territorial Riders had gone, there might have been a possibility of coming up with something tangible.

He arrived at Fort William two weeks later. It was a medium-sized fort as forts go, with typical territory buildings and corrals. Riding up to what appeared to be the main headquarters, he dismounted Cody, then began his way up the stairs arriving at the office of the commanding officer. Just before turning the knob to the outer office door, everything came at him in a whirl.

This was where Kane was dispatched with a unit of men who unknowingly were to meet their deaths. Letting go of the knob, Dillon turned to face the grounds then leaned back against a pillar for unexpected yet needed support. Once that moment passed, he surveyed the grounds seeing a normal fort. A place where officers and enlisted men alike worked, drilled, brushed horses, cleaned up whatever needed attention; played and/or directed music; and on occasion took photographs of local tribe members. Nothing seemed out of the ordinary, but of course, it wasn't expected to be.

Turning back to the door, he grabbed the knob entering the office. He was greeted by a Corporal Weston, the company clerk. After speaking to Weston for a few minutes, Dillon discovered, the corporal was apparently one of the very few of his rank able to read, write, and do his numbers, and was very proud of it too. After Dillon introduced himself, stating his business and interest, Weston escorted him into the office of Major James D. Northrup, Territorial Riders. Entering the office, they found the major standing at the window staring out towards the center compound of the fort. Dillon couldn't see his face, for his back was to him, but the manner of which he stood suggested an easygoing-kinda fella.

At the sound of silence (and the door closing), he turned away from the window, facing Dillon. Now Dillon could see him. His eyes were kind, expelling a sort of pleasantness that is not often found in territorial command posts. Then when he smiled, Dillon knew it to be true. Immediately Dillon held out his hand and introduced himself. "Major Northrup, Dillon Frasier."

"Nice to meet you, Mr. Frasier…Frasier? Any relation to Kane Frasier?" He was also very sharp.

"Yes, sir. He was my brother." Dillon wondered just how much information he could get, especially after what Kane had written.

"Was. Then you've heard. I am very sorry. Ya know, I lost a total of twenty officers and enlisted men in that engagement. It hit us all pretty hard, and I can imagine how you feel. Please sit down, is there anything I can do for you?"

Now was his chance. "Major Northrup, thank you for your condolences. And yes, maybe there is something. Perhaps you could enlighten me a tad. Where did it happen, the massacre? If I knew that, at least I'd have someplace to start." But before he could say anything, there was a knock at the office door.

It was Corporal Weston. "Sir, I hate to bother you, but there's a gentleman outside who is inquiring about enlistment into the Riders. Should I ask him to wait, sir?"

"By all means, Corporal Weston, ask him to wait. I'll be with him soon enough." He then dismissed the corporal and returned his attention to Dillon. "Now, Mr. Frasier, you say you need the location of the massacre. Is there a special reason you ask?"

"I'm investigating my brother's death, and I'm hoping once I discover the location, I might be able to discover something from the remains. I've had no other leads at this time, and you are my last best chance. Please, Major." Dillon had plenty of answers, just no solid evidence.

"Very well. The map here on the wall depicts my territory and jurisdiction. I can show you here." At that, Major Northrup rose up from his chair, turned, and preceded to tell Dillon what he knew.

Meanwhile, in the outer office, the young man waited patiently.

"Thank you, Major Northrup, I appreciate all you've done for me." At that they shook hands, then Dillon turned to leave. As Dillon was escorted out the door and into the outer office, his thoughts were suddenly interrupted.

"Dillon? Dillon Frasier!" Dillon instantly raised his head in the direction of the voice. There standing by the corporal's desk was his brother. *His other brother.*

"Cordell!" Before they knew it, the gap that separated them closed instantly while finding each other amid a brotherly hug that stretched the time they'd been apart. During this greeting, all was totally forgotten, where they were and who was in the room with them. Their joy at finding each other once again after all these years was short-lived when both realized there were other entities in the room. Turning simultaneously, they took note of the forgotten Corporal Weston and his commanding officer, Major James Northrup of the Territorial Riders, both curiously watching them. The look on their faces brought gentle laughter from both Dillon and Cordell.

"Excuse me, gentlemen. I don't wish to break up this, a… reunion, but," Major Northrup addressed Cordell, "did you wish to see me?"

"Oh yes. I mean no, no, thank you, Major Northrup, sir. If you'll excuse the interruption, I believe I'll be going. Thank you for your time, Major, maybe some later time." Cordell stepped on over to the major, shook his hand, turned, and then joined Dillon going out the door.

The information needed and a companion for the duration is what was found at the fort. As they rode out the main gates together, Cordell filled the marshal in on everything he'd been doing since their last meeting, including a yarn about him picking up some fancy knife he inherited, one that had been kept in a safe place for him back east. Dillon wanted to see it, but Cordell was unwilling to share, so they let the subject drop. Instead, Dillon supplied him with all that had transpired since their last parting. Taking a few minutes to digest both tales left Dillon wondering. On the other hand, Cordell needing no direction at all decided to ride along with his friend.

Once they arrived at the approximate location provided by Major Northrup, their search began. What were they looking for? Just about anything would do at this point. The first day there they had expected to find something of value to the investigation, but the more they looked, the more disappointed they became. That forced them to re-engineer their previous plan. Perhaps if they set up camp somewhere within the perimeter of the original incident, they'd find something tangible.

When morning arrived the following day, they started anew, thus beginning again from a different point of view. Since the vicinity of the incident that'd been mapped out by the major had been in a region surrounded by rolling foothills with a river running through its center, the new strategy was to look at the surrounding terrain in hopes of figuring out from which direction the troop approached and where the best vantage point would have been for the attackers to commence their onslaught. Fort William lay to the north of the massacre sight by many miles. This led them to believe the riders were traveling southward. That of course made sense. The River Republican, on the other hand, was directly across from where Dillon and Cordell stood, which meant Jesse must have placed his gang in various locations using the river as a wall not easily crossed. Looking towards the west side of the investigation site was a rock outcropping, and the more Dillon looked at that, the more it appeared to be strategically placed, as if planned for this occasion. Dillon asked Cordell to start over there by the outcropping. Perhaps if they had used the rocks for cover, he'd find something hidden within.

While Cordell searched the rocks and crevices of the outcropping, Dillon moved towards the river and the easterly side of the massacre site. Mounted, he found nothing but open country. On foot was easier.

While in the midst of searching the tall grass, Dillon heard the old signal. Cordell had fired a single shot into the air.

Arriving at his location, Dillon found Cordell just emerging from the rocks. There within his upheld palm, undiscovered by the cleanup crew, was their evidence.

"Whatcha find?" The marshal was excited.

"I know what they look like, but I've never seen ones like these in my life."

There in his hand were what appeared to be some sort of empty cartridge cases. That was when he took a whiff and mentioned a vague odor of gun oil instead of the sulfur used in gunpowder. Even after all this time, the odor was still present.

There were thirteen of them in two distinct sizes. All of them were of a bluish-green color that neither of them had seen before. And when turned over so their butts were upright, there were letters and numbers imprinted onto what he was sure were their head stamps. What was there read as "TC Co. 32-40" on the one; then on the other was "WRA Co. 44 S&W"—which normally on an up-to-date cartridge case meant "Territorial Cartridge Company 32 caliber, 40 grains powder" and the other one "Winchester Repeating Arms Company, 44 caliber, Smith and Wesson." If this was correct, these were definitely empty cartridge cases of some kind from somewhere. Dillon believed they couldn't have been anything else, but where in the world did they come from? Never in his entire life had he run across any weapon or piece of machinery constructed of such a substance.

"Did you find any others, or are those it?" He was hoping there was something else out there other than these funny-looking cases.

"These are it. I'm sure there are more out here, but I think we have the evidence you've been looking for. We've searched for two days, Dillon, and if these are the only evidence we have come up with, and if this Jesse Loame is the instigator in this massacre, maybe we ought to begin our search for him."

"I was thinking along those very same lines. But let's keep them casings. You never know, they just might come in handy."

They never did find Jesse. Although, along his escape route they did find something. A trail of dead and decomposing bodies. As it appeared, they were executed gang members. Again, if this was the Jesse they sought, he wasn't accepting any partners, welcoming any company, taking any chances in the sharing of his find. Each body had been found in a secluded location with a bullet hole right between his eyes. Nearby was an ejected and empty cartridge case just like those in Cordell's saddlebags. At least they knew now they were on the right trail.

VI

what in the name of momma pearlbody…?

Would you believe Dillon if he told you that Jesse and whatever gang he still had with him still eluded them at every turn? It got downright silly. Both he and his partner, Cordell, searched the sector from one end to the other. They haphazardly searched up and around, hither and yon, back and forth, north and south, over and under every rock, braved cliffs and crevices, traveled over hills and dales, everywhere searched the northernmost portion of Sector 4 for two bloody years. This guy just wasn't there. If he was, he was as elusive as a bathtub on the prairie. Although Dillon did have to admit, during their travels they heard and found *some* clues. There were rumors of disemboweled bodies, and on occasion they did find more of those strange-colored cartridge cases. But unfortunately, the rest of what was really needed—like the indispensable information, witnesses, a solid trail to follow, or other solid clues necessary to prolong such a search—just weren't to be found. No one was alive who did recognize, would recognize, or was willing to accept bribes to recognize the sketch of the man on the wanted poster Dillon carried on his person at all times.

This rotten, stinking, exhausting, and seemingly never-ending assignment was driving Dillon batty. The constant hunting, searching, chasing after, had become more frustrating and difficult as days dragged on, more so than any other bloody assignment he'd been on. There were no solid leads, there was no definite trail to follow (as much as Cordell tried), no one had heard of Jesse's whereabouts, no one had remembered seeing him, nor had they heard as much as a peep in regards to the mysterious "item" he searched for—whatever in the hell that was. After a while, not only did it get downright frustrating, but Dillon also began to wonder if any of it was true. So much so that he found himself dwelling on all spoken and unspoken avenues almost continually. This assignment drove him crazy. The only one saving grace? They both saw some beautiful country.

Until one totally bizarre day.

It was in March. He knew this because March, in Zone #78275532a, plans of the All Mother were always in full swing. Everything within view—animals, trees, and wildflowers—were at their utmost in count, color, and greenery. The offspring of the various species of animals were in abundance. The purples, pinks, blues, and reds of the surrounding flowers were as vivid as the leaves and stems at their base. The tall trees reaching towards the sun and her life-giving rays were just as green and bright as their leaves and spindly branches that hung down towards the milk of the land. It was as it should always be. Because here, as usual, whether or not Jesse was real, life continues on, and the life the All Mother gives is never ending.

It had been a long day of riding, late in the afternoon. They'd been giving the horses a nice, easy ride after finding a large meadow earlier in the day, where the horses could graze on tall grasses, while they munched on jerky, old biscuits, and washed it down with water from their canteens. With hunger satisfied, they laid back for a spell then finally moved on down the trail to the next encounter—whatever that may be.

Abruptly, Cordell shouted, "GO!"

He'd caught Dillon totally off guard and before Dillon realized what had happened found himself in a cloud of dust. Cordell must've again noticed Dillon's lack of direction and decided to wake him from his stupor. Dillon shook his head in bewilderment at Cordell's never-ending sense of adventure.

Everyone, and especially Dillon's horse, knew that Cordell's mount, Baldy, was no match for him. Cody could and would catch up, pass, and again win this, as he did all their races. Sometimes Dillon thought that it was the challenge, the excitement, and the thrill of the moment that enhanced Cordell's need for such a show. But who knew? And for that matter, who cared? Whatever his reasons, they generally worked, and Dillon enjoyed them all.

Dillon sunk spur. Cody leapt forward with such force that he almost unseated his rider. Dillon embraced the moment and all the sensations that followed. Sitting on an animal with raw unleashed powers such as a horse at a flat-out run continues to amaze. As the animal gains speed, the excitement of the chase grips one's soul like the call of a good woman. It's the strangest feeling. Everything within view—the trees, the rocks and the terrain—seem as though they've been transformed into a single blur as the excitement of the competition and the power of the animal under one storms forward. As each hoof strikes the ground in its turn of the unleashed three-beat gait of the gallop that is now quite fast, one can feel the muscles and the sheer power of the beast surge forward towards the eventual end of this and all, or anyone's, competitions. Faster and faster Cody charged on, until up ahead through the dust, he could just make out a dim outline of a horse and rider.

Cody sensed his adversary was close at hand, because within those last few yards he managed to find the last burst of energy needed to catch up with, pass, and leave in the dust the surprised pair. By the time Cordell and Baldy caught up with Cody and his rider, Dillon had him down to a walk.

"Thanks. I needed that," Dillon chuckled.

"Damn you, you of all people know that one of these days I'm gonna beat you! And not because your horse is faster. It's just that that he's taller, his legs are longer, his strides cover more ground. He doesn't have to work quite as hard to get as far." Cordell knew that Cody was the better of the two horses, but usually refused to admit it.

While the horses enjoyed their breather, they rode side by side enjoying the scenery and the beautiful colors of spring.

It was around the next bend where it was discovered the most beautiful array of color that either had seen in a long time—and the strangest thing of all, it was out in the middle of nowhere. It looked like a lake of floating flower petals. The place was filled with greens, blues, yellows, oranges, purples, reds, whites, plus shades leaning towards and away from all the aforementioned primary colors, all looking like small five-dollar gold pieces. It was a treasure chest of color to behold. There were also tall grasses and/or weeds that were intermingled between some of the little treasures, but those needed pulling to make everything perfect. It was strange; the groups of colors belonging to these little treasures looked like a rainbow had been placed on the ground, a rainbow of flowers in need of a gardener. Many of these little treasured rainbows looked as though they'd been arranged by some creative sort, just for their pleasure. Curious, the two veered in for a better look.

Before they got too close, there came a sound from beyond the tallest of the many grassy clumps. At first Dillon thought it was the scream of an eagle but changed his mind as nothing from the sky was flying. He also didn't see any shadows cross their path from high above. As a matter of fact, he didn't see anything flying—no doves, no black birds, no hawks, no birds, no butterflies, no nothing. Everything was still.

Suddenly as if out of nowhere, across their path from way high above, came a shadow larger than anything anyone had ever seen before. Neither Dillon or Cordell could describe it to anyone, 'cause it was there one moment and gone the next. He really didn't even get a chance to think about it. He just knew it was there. Cordell saw it too. Dillon could tell by the look on his face when he turned towards his friend, but before a comment could be uttered, both horses' heads shot up with ears perked straight forward. Something was here. Something besides them, but what?

All four of them looked straight ahead. Both steeds' attentions were glued to the far side of the flowers, as were the men's, but as far as Dillon could tell and/or see, there was nothing to be seen. There was nothing there.

"Whatcha think?" Dillon asked Cordell. He knew there was something out there, something here, something close by. Whatever it was, it truly sparked both his curiosity and his caution. And because curiosity was led first in the sentence, that was his strongest ally.

"Could be anything. Could be an eagle, some sort of bird, who knows?" Cordell said matter-of-factly.

"What you want to do about it?"

"You're the marshal. You want to ride closer, have a look-see?"

"Ya know, this could be considered another adventure. Ya want to make a go?" Dillon asked.

"I've already had my adventure for the day, thank you very much," Cordell said as he was still trying to brush off the dust from their earlier escapade.

"That was not my doing."

"Yeah, I know, I know."

"Let's go see. We haven't got anything better to do unless you want to race again."

"Naw, I think not. One humiliation a day is enough for me."

Before they had a chance to urge their animals forward, Cody began his own line of investigation, by softly nickering, as though there was something out there that might want to nicker back.

There were no animals, no birds, no nothing as far as the eye could see. At least nothing that Dillon could see. Nothing except someone's strange creative talent for arranging colorful flowers in the midst of nothing. Cody, however, bewildered everyone as far as him seeking out a counterpart in this strange place. As to the rest, Dillon was beginning to believe it was just the sun playing tricks, the wind or breeze doing the same. Only there weren't no breeze, and it was March, so the heat wasn't an issue. Befuddlement overtook curiosity and as the two looked at each other, they heard a return whinny.

Bemusement now overran their curiosity. Surprise and shock overrode all. For there on the far side of the rainbow treasures stood another treasure.

It was a horse.

"Is that our noise maker?" Dillon pointed towards the animal.

"I see him. Ya know, Dillon. He weren't there a moment ago."

"Ya know, he might've been. Could've been lying down in the grass sleeping." Anything was possible.

"Better go see what's afoot." It doesn't matter who said this; they both thought it.

As they grew closer to the horse, something was found rather surprising. Not only was the animal fully rigged, bridled, and standing alone, but he was also huge. Much taller than either of their mounts. And his color was the strangest shade of gray ever seen on a horse. Dillon thought that perhaps a light gunmetal gray was what fit. This animal was of good flesh, well groomed, and basically gorgeous. As they grew closer still, they also found him to be very vicious. The damned thing charged them when they grew closer. Pinned his ears, bared his teeth, and charged.

Of course, they didn't stick around for long. Seeing what was being offered, decided they didn't want any, and as fast as possible, high-tailed it outta there away from those threatening molars, sharp hooves, nasty attitude.

Hearing only their retreat, both pulled up, stopped, and turned to look back. They were alone. The gray had not pursued them.

Dillon's insatiable need to know overrode shock, it overrode the fear of being trampled, eaten by the devil, and/or pounded into the ground by a huge gray horse. Curiosity or stupidity, Dillon wasn't sure which, and not knowing any better or not knowing anything about hindsight, the two of them headed back towards the gray. It kept eating at Dillon: here was an animal in the condition that he was, wired for sound, tacked up, groomed, and in fantastic condition, but no rider in sight.

So once more they tried to approach the gray. And the closer they got, the closer he watched. About the time they got within a measurable distance, Dillon yelled, "LOOK OUT!"

The gray had again pinned his ears and charged with teeth bared. And once more they left the scene in a hurry. After several minutes Dillon again chanced a look behind them. This time, the gray hadn't given chase.

"I'll be damned," Dillon mused. This was the strangest encounter with a horse he'd ever had.

"What do you think his problem is?" he asked Cordell while the two of them calmly watched from a seemingly safe distance.

"Hell if I know!!"

By this time, the animal had returned to almost the exact same spot as before.

This was getting old. Why would a saddled horse be out here alone to begin with? Perhaps he'd bucked someone off? Maybe he'd wandered off? Perchance he'd broke his lead and run off. There were a dozen reasons why, but no answers were forthcoming unless they could get close enough to catch him.

Both men must have been of the same mind, 'cause simultaneously they looked at each other, nodded their heads, reined both horses towards the beast, and gently urged them forward. In a split second, the animal pinned his ears, bared his teeth, but this time didn't charge. He stood his ground looking as though the devil himself was one within. Dillon kinda got the impression it was a warning, or threat, not to approach. So, as Cordell sat there deciding what to do, Dillon took a form of action and slowly dismounted.

"What the hell are you doing?" asked Cordell.

"What does it look like? I'm gonna walk over and catch 'im."

"What makes you think he's gonna let you?"

"I don't know. I just have to try. Besides, there might be a clue on his rigging to whom he belongs."

Cordell just eyed his friend with skepticism.

"You got any better ideas?" Dillon retorted.

"It's your skin. But I'll tell you what, I'll be here to pick up the pieces and take 'em back to Glen with an explanation. He'll enjoy a good laugh."

"Gee, thanks." What a friend, what a friend indeed.

Hoping and praying that maybe a foot approach would be more readily accepted, Dillon took hold of Cody's reins and gingerly walked towards the standing horse. As he approached, the gray appeared weary, but seemed calmer. Once he got within a stone's throw from the animal, he glanced around. Dillon considered maybe an injured rider? That would explain a lot of it. It wouldn't explain everything, but at least it'd give them something. If this was the case, then search he must and at the same time watch the beast very carefully.

As he approached, he noticed something near to the horse's feet that caught his eye. To his surprise, there on the dusty ground not too far from the gray lay a hat. Just as Dillon went to retrieve it, Cordell screamed, "Dillon! Watch out!"

The animal had whirled towards him, teeth bared. Dillon scrambled for safety by unceremoniously yanking Cody around using him as a shield between himself and the gray.

A mystical exploration all its own was being conducted simultaneously.

With Cody between them, the animal mysteriously stopped. Removing his hand, he wiped his sweat-lined brow with his sleeve, silently thanking the All Mother for saving his worthless hide.

"Dillon!" Cordell yelled. "You still in one piece over there?"

"Yeah. I'm fine. What's he doing now?" Dillon tried to say in a more controlled tone.

"Just standing there peacefully. Whatcha gonna do now?"

Dillon wasn't too sure what he was going to do.

"You want me to shoot 'im?" Cordell was just kidding. He'd never shoot a horse.

"Naw, I don't think so." Dillon wasn't quite ready to do that. Not yet anyway. If they chose to, they could just leave and not worry about any of it. But he wanted to see what the horse was so upset about. It had to have been something.

Dillon peeked around Cody just for a minute to see where the animal was and in what frame of mind, he appeared to be in. He needed to know if it was safe enough to lower his living shield.

Just then came a slight shift in the grass followed by a muffled sound. The horse instantly moved towards it, then lowered his head as if checking on something hidden within the tall fescue.

"What the hell?" he asked of no one in particular. It was as though the animal could read Dillon's mind, for at that very same moment he raised his head, stared directly at the marshal with ears forward, alert, and softly nickered. If curiosity wasn't sparked before, it definitely was now. Turning back towards Cordell, Dillon asked, "What do you think?"

"About what?"

"The horse."

"Don't rightly know." Cordell paused to consider. He had begun his own approach, while scratching his chin through the mass of thick, black, and curly hair. "Give 'er a shot, I guess. If'n he charges again, I'll fire a shot in the air to scare him off. If that don't work, brother, you're on your own." Cordell stopped, pulled out his hogleg, cocked it, and held it ready just in case.

"Thanks, 'brother,'" Dillon sarcastically responded.

Silently he prayed while stepping closer towards the animal and the recently discovered disturbance in the grass. "Easy, boy. Easy. No one's gonna hurt ya. I just want to see." Dillon tried to convey his message using the most reassuring voice he could utter. If there was something, or someone, in the grass who needed help, then by golly, they'd get it. And the horse, why, he'd receive the same, at least until they decided what to do with 'im. Gingerly he approached the gray beast.

"Be careful, he's watching ya awful close," Cordell warned his friend of the horse's odd behavior but as of yet had no indication whatsoever if the animal would strike or not, and therefore didn't shoot.

"I know. I can see him out of the corner of my eye. Spooky, ain't it?"

"*Spooky* ain't the word I'd use."

This time, what surprised Dillon most was the nicker heard as the gap was closed between the two. Upon reaching the gray, Dillon gingerly held his hand towards his nose so that the horse could smell his scent. Then when he didn't bite or pin his ears, Dillon stepped to his left shoulder and laid his hand against his soft, velvety coat. The gray turned his head back towards the tall grass, lowered it halfway to the ground, and nickered softer still.

"Anything there?" Cordell asked.

About six inches below the horse's gray velvety nose lay a body. "Here he is," Dillon called out.

"Is he alive?"

Before investigating further, he felt warm air being blown into his right ear causing him to immediately tense up. Squeezing his eyes tightly shut, he waited for the inevitable.

"Dillon?"

He was afraid to answer. Afraid that any sound or disturbance would break the spell of the moment. Instead, he slowly raised his hand and waved it a tad in a gesture of "easy." When nothing happened, except for the intermittent bombardment of the horse's warm breath upon the side of his face and in his ear, Dillon slowly opened his eyes to chance a peek the gray's way. Surprisingly how the head can remain stationery, yet at the same time find that the eyes can turn remarkably well. When still nothing came except the air flow, Dillon gingerly took two steps to the side, away from the animal. This he did cautiously, again avoiding any sudden moves on anyone's part. With no attack forthcoming, he took another chance by turning towards the animal. What he saw in his eyes surprised him. Innocence, pure and simple.

"Dillon?" Cordell hesitantly asked.

"Yeah?"

"What are you doing?"

What was he doing indeed? Having a staring contest with a horse, of course. That sure sounded silly, and especially so when the animal blinked directly at him, as though he was nuts.

"Dillon, what about what's in the grass?" Cordell pressed. What in the name of the All Mother herself was Dillon doing with that damned horse anyway?

"The grass? Oh yeah, the grass," Dillon softly mentioned aloud. Patting the horse's muzzle, he turned towards the disturbed grass. There on the ground, facedown and apparently out like a light, was the thrown rider. Was he alive? Dillon couldn't tell for sure and wouldn't be until he rolled him over, straightened him out, and checked to see if he was breathing. With the toe of his boot, he slipped it under the rider's torso and gently but firmly rolled 'im over.

"Well, I'll be damned. Cordell!"

"Yeah?"

"Come on over quick, but not too quick!" Not only couldn't he take the chance of the horse going nutzoid on them again, but he also honestly couldn't believe what he'd found. Slowly, but most assuredly, Dillon knelt down to take a closer look. It seemed like forever before he heard the thundering hooves of Cordell's horse.

In a cloud of dust, Cordell had halted, then jumped down off'n his horse. All of this happened without the gray pulling anything funny.

In an excited voice that showed a telltale sign of panic, Cordell pressed, "What, what is it?"

"Looky what we have here."

Cordell knelt down opposite his friend and took a look. "What in the name of momma Pearlbody...?

They stared at each other in total disbelief. The assumed man was no man. He was a she! And a pretty she at that. Whoever she was, her clothing was very different for the times. Cordell confirmed it when, as if the material was on fire, he reached down and took hold of a piece of her vest between his fingers.

"It's not of anything I've ever felt before."

Dillon reached for a feel of the fabric. "Me neither. And what about those colors? When you were in Saint Louise did you ever seen anything like those?" The colors of her attire were gray and black. They looked her up and down. She even wore a yellow ribbon in her hair. And her boots were blue!

"Blue?"

The young woman's conscious self was just beginning to emerge from its protective shield when she was alerted to an unfamiliar presence nearby. That and the excruciating pain that emanated from her head advised her to remain still. So instead of opening her eyes and allowing whomever they were to begin their interrogation of her, or her of them, she decided to play out her role as an unconscious and injured rider.

"What the...I thought you said it was a man?" Cordell questioned.

"I assumed that it was. Who on the All Mother's world would've guessed it'd be a woman?"

They gently shook her to see if she would awaken; she did not.

"Look. Blood," stated Cordell.

Sure enough, he had spotted blood on the side of her head just above the ear. Deciding she was indeed in need of attention Dillon gently tilted her head enough to get a better view of her newly discovered injury. From what they could tell, it was only a flesh wound, and by the look of the wound, it could've only been made by a bullet, and not too long ago. She was damned lucky. If whomever had been slightly a bit more on the mark, she'd be dead. But why hadn't the assailant finished the job, and stolen the horse? He alone would be worth a kings' ransom, unless of course he wasn't able to get any closer than they had. That brought forth a chuckle.

"What's so funny?" asked Cordell.

"Nothing. Just thinking." Just the thought of a gunman being chased off by a horse would be a comical sight. He must be a treasured animal to be aggressive enough to have done that, to have protected her like he did. Then the thought of what they'd just been though came back to remind him, and it weren't quite so funny anymore.

VII

friends are known in time of need

It was still kind of strange how everything was working out, but it mattered little; she was with them now. And all the time they had been tending to her immediate needs, the gray, as Dillon was referring to him, hadn't tried anything else—yet. Feeling she was relatively safe now that both Dillon and Cordell were by her side, they decided to get her to safer ground. Unfortunately, because the area they were now in was too open and vulnerable for ambush, that meant taking her with them.

The next task was to get her onto one of the two horses for the trip across the territorial boundary and to safety. Due to the complexity of the impending situation, their attention was again momentarily forced off the gray and onto the girl; unfortunately, it didn't take long for them to realize that had been a big mistake.

"Look out!" They whirled around finding the gray had decided to charge again. For a split second, Dillon would have bet his bottom dollar he was acting like a bull buffalo in the midst of breeding season, the way he was trying to scare them off, but hell and damnation, that was a different species altogether.

As much as Dillon had had enough and wanted to hightail it outta there, Cordell wouldn't. Instead, without a second's thought, he grabbed the gray's reins.

"Whoa. Easy, big fella, we're not going to hurt her," he kept saying. Cordell had always had a special and unusual way with horses and was having little trouble calming this one.

Even though they sounded friendly enough, she should be cautious as was Wolf. Let them maneuver her into whatever position they chose. Once she willed herself to remain relaxed and limp, they would believe her to be unconscious. If she was in any danger at all, she'd know, and before they could act, on surprise alone, she'd make good their escape.

As much as Dillon didn't want to spend the next several days caring to an injured rider's needs, let alone a woman's, he figured taking her with them and dealing with the inconvenience was better than shooting himself in the foot.

The moment his hands took hold of the reins and his butt hit the saddle's seat, Cody and he were ready to take on the unconscious bundle Cordell was soon to lift his way. With the command of "whoa" reinforced, Cody stood perfectly still as though someone was handing him a lost calf to be returned to its mother or to the main ranch house.

Cordell lifted her with ease high into the air, and Dillon managed to take most of her from him. With awkward handling from both their ends, as she was definitely larger and more shapely than any calf ever handled, Dillon almost lost her when making contact with certain parts of her anatomy.

"Haven't you got hold of her yet?" asked an irritated Cordell.

"Damn it, no! You still got a hold of 'er?" Dillon returned.

"If I didn't, she'd be on the ground by now! You knucklehead, what in the devil are you doing up there, knitting a sweater?" Cordell asked amid strained laughter. "Get hold of her!" Cordell added.

"But what about her...?"

"Never mind about those, she's unconscious, remember? It ain't gonna bother her none, so just grab 'er and set 'er in front of ya. As long as you don't bruise her, she ain't gonna know nothing!" Cordell couldn't believe this.

While Cordell held the young woman in his arms waiting for Dillon to make ready, he had time to notice that she was no bigger than a kitten, and just as precious. With her head nestled in the crook of his arm, he got a real good look-see at this beauty. He thought about her face. Her hair looked to be the color of burnt wood, with a face the color of the stars, but it was hard to tell beneath all that dirt. She did look as though she shoulda still been in school, but the way she filled out her clothes suggested a slightly more mature girl.

Dillon, on the other hand, was finally ready for her the moment Cordell held her upright to him for the second time. It was then that he too saw a beauty. Her age, neither could guess at, but the contours of her figure suggested another story. Once they finally got her situated, Dillon realized that it was going to be an interesting ride for the remainder of the day, for him especially. While holding her in position while Cordell mounted his own horse then grabbing the reins of the gray, Dillon felt as though he was holding a baby in his lap. He was a trifle concerned, however; what if she woke while still in his lap? That would be a might difficult to explain. All they could hope for was that she remained out like a light, until a decent campsite could be found.

She was still unconscious, yet looking as though in peaceful sleep, when Dillon finally stepped away from the young woman they bedded down next to the warm fire. They had arrived shortly after sunset at a protected glen that had a moderate-sized stream running through its center. This way it was assured of having fresh water and shelter should the need arise. Dillon held the young woman in his arms, while Cody patiently waited for Cordell to start a fire and set up his bedroll for their charge. With one of the extra blankets carried for cooler nights, Cordell set up her bed as though they were in a hotel.

Dillon watched in fascination as Cordell gathered armfuls of grasses, leaves, and pine needles to be covered by the extra blanket he had left hanging on a branch so it'd stay cleaner than what he would lay on the ground for himself. Then when all was prepared, he covered his mattress with the one blanket then went to Dillon for her. Careful of where he put his hands, Dillon gently lifted, swung free of the saddle horn, then lowered his charge into Cordell's strong and awaiting arms. While dismounting, Dillon's eyes remained fixed on Cordell as he handled the young woman as though she were a newborn calf. It always amazed Dillon the way Cordell dealt with life. He always treated it as though it was so very precious.

That evening there was an odd feeling that floated around the campsite as she slept. Neither man slept very well. That damned stallion of hers—yes, it was a stallion—kept stamping his feet in apparent irritation when they tried tying him with their own horses. Dillon didn't know what his problem was, but when Cordell went to investigate, Dillon was surprised shortly thereafter when he returned leading the gray.

"What are you doing?"

"I really don't know, but I don't know what else to do." Cordell had decided to tie the gray horse next to his owner.

"Are you addlepated or something?"

"Well, think about what happened today. Remember how he acted when we approached and then afterward when you tried to reach her? Maybe she raised him from a foal, and the two of them have never been separated. Did you ever think of something crazy like that?"

"No. I hadn't. Ya know, now that you bring that up, it does make a bit of sense. Go ahead—give 'er a try. Anything is worth some sleep. Even if it's only a couple hours."

The gray settled down immediately.

They both stared at him for a moment in total fascination. Had it been true after all? Was Cordell right in his assumption? That's when Dillon really noticed the eyes of the gray. They had a strange quality to them. And the more he stared, the sooner he realized that the horse was watching them, watching everything. As the evening progressed, the gray's eyes seemed to follow their every move. Almost as though he was watching out for her. Dillon took it as his imagination and tried to ignore it as he took the first watch.

The young woman's inner clock brought her to a state of awareness long before her rescuers awoke the following morning. After listening to them discuss their concern for her well-being till the wee hours of the previous night, instead of discussing her demise and the selling of the horse, she decided that the coast was clear, and they were decent and considerate men at heart. She would play the rest by ear.

With Dillon's second cup of steaming hot morning coffee still in hand, he quietly stepped towards the woman who still lay asleep next to the fire. For some reason, the fact that she was still asleep worried him a tad. Had she been injured worse than they thought? Should they again try to wake her? He had no idea how to tend to an injured person. And until she came around on her own accord, there was little they could do about it, other than make sure she was warm, comfortable, and protected.

When she finally did begin to stir, Cordell stepped slightly away. He did this in an attempt to avoid startling her. Waking up in unfamiliar surroundings was one thing, waking up amid strangers, especially one of formidable size, was another. With Cordell out of sight for the moment, Dillon knelt closer to her bed, then on her same level spoke to her softly using the same hushed tones that Cordell had used on the gray the day before. This was in hopes that they would have the same effect on her, as they had him. If she didn't recognize the words, perhaps she'd understand their meaning by the gentle tone used.

Her eye lids fluttered, then finally opened. For a split second she looked frightened; then within the blink of an eye, it was gone. Gone as though it was never there to begin with. Slowly, she tried to sit and with Dillon's assistance got there without mishap.

"Thank you," the young woman said, while repositioning herself after the hazel-eyed one helped her up.

"You're welcome," he answered.

The gray horse nickered.

The young woman immediately turned towards the sound. "Oh, Wolf, good. How…oooohhhh." Apparently, it wasn't just sleep that she needed to catch up with. With the sudden onslaught of pain came an overwhelming desire to choke the living shit outta the person responsible, but since that looked to be impossible at the moment, she closed her eyes and placed her head in her hands, trying to abate the dizziness that was trying to overtake her.

The moment the young woman showed distress, both men were at her side immediately.

"You'd better lay back down, missy," Cordell began, "that's a mighty nasty-lookin' head wound there. You don't want to be aggravating it none."

"Head injury?" the young woman said to no one between clenched teeth.

"Yeah," Dillon reaffirmed.

The young woman could barely focus on what they were saying, the pain was so intense. "How did you find me?" she inquired.

"We were riding across the territory and heard your horse," Dillon said.

"No. I said, how," the young woman again asked. Even though her head hurt, her brain was as sharp as a tack.

"How?"

The young woman couldn't believe that they couldn't understand the question. She'd learned the night before that she was in the company of descent menfolk who sounded intelligent and decently schooled but was surprised to discover that the form of the question and its meaning eluded them. It had to have something to do with the time frame. She decided to rephrase it. "In what condition was I in when you found me?"

"Oh yeah, well, yesterday afternoon…" Dillon went on and explained their story, at least all but the close calls with the horse.

The young woman considered the words. "Well, I guess that means that I owe you my thanks. What can I do to repay you?"

"Actually, if you have nothing better to do, and if'n you don't mind, you can visit with us a few days." It would give them their break, and in return they could make sure she was all right before parting ways.

The young woman considered the offer. It would be nice to be able to get one's bearings before heading off into the sunset after who knew what. He sounded sincere, and if he wasn't, either she would've picked up on it or Wolf would've informed her. Besides, her head was still spinning a tad; maybe it'd be a good idea after all. "I accept your generous offer."

"Great." Cordell was thrilled.

With a wince, the young woman got to her feet. Cordell being the closer was there for her when she reached out for support.

"Guess I'm a bit shakier than I thought." Immediately she removed her hand from his arm. She was not used to help and was having a hard time dealing with the need.

"That's okay, missy. I'm here if'n you need me."

The young woman glanced around the area for the nearest tree. "If you'll excuse me for a moment, gentlemen."

"Uh, there's a stream over that way too, if you care to partake."

"Thanks." Just thinking about it gave her goose bumps. "I'll do that." The young woman stepped over to the gray stallion and begun rummaging through her saddlebags for the items she'd need, then left for the water.

Now that she was gone, Dillon asked his friend, "Whatcha think?"

"Sure is pretty," Cordell stated absentmindedly.

"Is that all you think about?" Dillon asked.

"No, but you have to admit she *is* pretty."

Pretty wasn't the word he would have used to describe her; that was for sure. Dillon tried remembering how she looked the day before, covered with all that dirt and filth. She was downright pretty then. And when Cordell lifted her up to his lap, she was pretty then too, even though she was out cold. Then when she opened her eyes this morning, Dillon felt his heart skip a beat. He saw them then. Her eyes. He couldn't pull his own from hers. It was as though it was a dream. At the time, he thought they were gray, but there's no such thing as gray eyes.

"Dillon? Dillon—are you in there?"

"Huh?"

"Did you hear me?" Cordell asked.

"Hear? Hear what? No, I missed it. What?"

"Thought so." The dark man snickered, then mumbled, "Daydreaming again."

Just then the young woman stepped out from behind a bush. "There. Much better. I feel so refreshed now. The water was wonderful."

"The water? It should've been freezing!" Dillon exclaimed. "How are you gonna get better, if you go swimming in freezing water?"

"Freezing? The water wasn't that cold. Cool maybe, but definitely not freezing." Her skin was glowing from the bath. She knew it and didn't care. Her hair was dripping wet, as was her shirt. She hadn't removed her shirt, modesty wouldn't allow it, neither would training.

She had found the stream so easily and had found its beauty to be more than anything she'd ever dreamed. Once on its bank, she stood and took in its all-encompassing view. Knowing her time was limited, she hurried her pace. Down the stream bank she carefully stepped while glancing off into the water searching for a deep-enough hole to bathe in. "There you are, you little devil you." She had sat down on the bank next to the deep hole with its swirling patterns and listened for any dangerous entity afoot.

She could sense malice, but it was eons off. Knowing she was safe, she removed her boots, her ribbon, her belt, her jeans, her undergarments, and her vest, yet did not take the plunge, not yet. From where she sat it was possible to lean forward and peer into the murky depths of the mountain stream. There was a stranger staring at her from below. It was the face of a woman, yet it was so filthy that it did not resemble anyone she knew. The face was mud smudged, and the hair looked unwashed and stringy.

"You look like Horace the Horrible from the Sixty-Ninth Scavenger unit back home. Do you know that?" she said to the face. Not wanting to think about home and what she'd left, she plunged into the icy depths of the mountain stream.

VIII

the life and times of no one in particular

She *was* beautiful. It was as though this woman who'd appeared out from behind the bushes was a different person altogether. She stood erect, confident, and did fill out her clothes quite nicely. Dillon guessed again at her age, believing somewhere between twenty-two to twenty-six years old. She looked strong and able, not like most young women he'd known. Her height, maybe five to six inches shorter than himself. Her hair, now that it was cleaner, was the color of burnt wood, and her skin was very much like vanilla ice cream. The contrast between the two was stunning.

He snuck a peek at her eyes. Their color was as he had previously imagined, gray. A dark gunmetal gray would be closer. Suddenly instead of just admiring them as well as the rest of her, Dillon found her staring directly into his very own eyes. He tried saying something, doing something, but found he could not. Couldn't even move. It was as though he'd sprouted roots and had taken to the ground. Couldn't even take his eyes off her. He tried looking towards Cordell to see if he was suffering too, but that wouldn't work either. What had gone wrong, and why was Dillon suddenly frozen in time? He had no idea, nor could he consider one until whatever had him in its grasp let go.

At first Cordell had no idea what had happened, nor would he after it was over. But he did know something was wrong. "Dillon." No answer. "Dillon?" Still no answer. "Dillon!"

Recognizing the fear and strength in the other man's voice, the young woman immediately released the hazel-eyed man.

"What happened?" Dillon directed his question to the woman.

"What happened what?" she replied.

"Just now."

"I'm sorry. I don't know. I don't know what you're talking about," she lied.

"With your eyes."

"I was just staring off into space thinking about nothing in particular. Did I miss something?"

"You were just staring off some place? I thought…?" He was confused.

"You had said that I'd been shot. Right?" *Get his mind off it.*

"Right. But what does…"

"I was thinking about the incident. And sometimes when I think, I stare off into space. I know, some people mistakenly assume that I am staring at them when in reality I am staring past them. It's a flaw of mine. Please forgive me if I caused you alarm."

He was still confused, but maybe it was just her beauty that had him by its magical spell. Sounded like a silly explanation, but what else could it have been?

Realizing she didn't know their names, nor them hers, she began to extend her hand in what she'd hoped was the tradition of the times to initiate introductions.

"Brina Louise Grant at your service," said the young woman.

"Nice to meet you, Brina Louise Grant. I'm Dillon Frasier, and this is my cohort in crime, Cordell Chevalier." Dillon knew they all were way overdue for introductions, but she wasn't up to anything last night, except rest.

"Dillon Frasier…?" Her hand was still out yet not grasped in return when she suddenly froze in midstream. Hearing, digesting, and finally recognizing his name had suddenly caught her off guard. She paused to think about it.

Dillon watched as she started to offer her hand in friendship but stopped before reaching its full extension. Not knowing what else to do, since shaking hands with a woman was not a common occurrence for him, he slowly reached for it then gave it a gentle squeeze.

The squeeze brought her back to the present, or better yet the past. "I'm sorry." Realizing the error of her ways, Brina again offered her hand to Dillon Frasier.

She wanted to shake hands, again? Not wanting to offend her, he did as she asked. This time, she took his firmly in hers and shook it with an iron grip that was so strong that it totally caught him off guard.

If he was who and what the name implied, Brina was in luck. Back home, luck and she didn't share the same tent. Here and now, however, was different, and she thanked the All Mother for her bloody-good fortune. It was just like that ancient story from her childhood told to her by her mother, before the organization took her; this one was about a house that fell out of the sky and landed on the bad guy. Then, she didn't truly believe in such luck, but now it'd happened, and to her. And with a wily grin on her face, she digested the newly discovered information while formulating a fly-by-the-seat-of-her-pants kinda plan.

The sudden and peculiar look upon her face, Dillon mistook for discomfort, and his concern arose anew.

"Do you feel dizzy? Do you need to sit down?"

She silently smirked at his question. Something wrong? Now there was an understatement if she ever heard one. Dillon Frasier, Dillon Frasier, now where had she heard that name before? Suddenly she had it. It had all come back in a whirl. All those years of history were unfolding before her eyes. It was truly kismet.

"No. Nothing's wrong at all. Actually, everything is falling quite surprisingly into place, much sooner than expected." She meant it to be silent, but it hadn't. Now she had to do something about it.

"What do you mean by that?"

An off-the-wall question to an off-the-wall occurrence. "Do you believe in fate, Dillon Frasier?"

"No. Why do you ask?"

Great. Just what the doctor ordered, a nonbeliever. Brina knew it was going to be fun trying to convince these guys of what was to come, and because of that, she knew before she even got started, she wanted a drink. "Anyone got any whiskey?"

"Whiskey? Now?" It was at this moment that Cordell realized that he'd never learn to understand the rational of women.

"Yeah, I think it's going to be a long day." Brina sighed.

Shortly after lunch, Brina reclined against the nearest tree. "Cordell Chevalier, you said your name was."

"Yep. Why?"

"Just wanted to make sure I heard you right." She'd heard of him, but not from her studies. Somewhere else in her past teachings his name had been mentioned, but from where and in what context? She knew it'd come to her sooner or later.

Now that she was cleaned up and the introductions had been made, Dillon was curious as to how and why she had been in that clearing in such a condition as she had been.

"Brina?"

"Yes?"

"Earlier, you said you were thinking about the incident. Did you mean how it was that you got shot and who it was that shot you? Ya know, I am a Territorial Marshal in this sector. I can help you."

He was offering his services to her? In what context, and what was to be payment? She'd read about these rough and rowdy times. She'd heard of what rowdies did to unsuspecting and defenseless women, of which she was neither. Wolf hadn't indicated a thing. Perhaps she had fallen in with two exceptions to the rule.

How *had* she gotten shot? She still hadn't quite figured that one out. Of course, she had an idea, but what it was she sure as hell couldn't tell them. "I'm not really sure, but at this time I'm not concerned."

"You're not concerned?"

"Not at this time."

"May I ask why?"

"Not at this time."

She was full of answers. Dillon wondered for a moment if she was also running from the law. "Are you in any trouble yourself? I mean with the authorities."

"No."

"Then why would you not want justice?"

"I do want justice. Don't ever think that I don't. It's just that I have more pressing problems."

What could be more pressing than catching, trying, and eventually hanging a gunman? Especially one who had tried to kill you? He didn't understand.

But before they had a chance to question her further, she began, "Frasier, Frasier. Hmmmmm. Tell me, what nationality is that?"

"What does that have to do with anything?" He was puzzled at the inquiry.

"In my case, it might carry a lot of weight," Brina stated.

"In my case, it's really none of your business."

"That may be true. But if you are who I think you are, this may turn into a marvelous adventure for the three of us." She knew it'd be dangerous traveling with strangers not of her own accomplishments and abilities, but she needed someone now. Someone of this time, on her side, who knew the terrain, the locations of the towns, the whys and wheres of townsfolk and their customs, as well as assistance at this particular moment in time. Once she learned all she could from these two, she would break away, initiate her own search-and-destroy methods for Jesse Loame and all who rode with him. Maybe she'd even be lucky enough to find that Neptune Sphere thing.

That was all Dillon needed: another marvelous adventure. If he didn't already have his hands full of marvelous adventures, he just might take her up on a couple of his own. Unfortunately, something in the back of his mind told him this young woman was going to be trouble. Especially after whatever it was that had happened between the two of them earlier. She may have brushed it off as nothing, or as a mistaken assumption, but he knew something had happened. He could hear Cordell call out, but could not respond. Yes, there was something disturbing about her. Yet she was beautiful, and her grip most assuredly hinted on an inner strength and integrity not seen often anymore. That compelled Dillon to trust her. He didn't know why, but after all, it was better than shooting himself in the foot.

But before he'd sit down and tell her his *life story*, he decided to fix another pot of coffee. Maybe even finding a little something within his saddlebags they could eat would help the moment. While he began another pot, Cordell headed over towards the horses and their supplies. Apparently, he had felt the same way. And as he passed the gray, the horse's head followed his movements as though to watch. As Dillon returned his attentions back to the coffee and their new guest, he realized that she, too, had been watching him. Again, something in the back of his mind said both of them were both being watched. What in the name of momma Pearlbody was going on here?

"Well?" Brina inquired.

"Well, what?" Dillon returned.

"Are you going to tell me what I need to know, or are you going to keep me in suspense?" Brina didn't know how hard to push for the information. If these two were the correct two, she would need their willing cooperation, not their resistance. Too much resistance would require threats of all sizes, shapes, and realms, but she didn't want their hatred; she needed their friendship and help. At least that was what her briefings suggested.

Giving in, Dillon asked, "Okay. What was it you wanted again?"

"Actually, your parentage and where your families originated," she said this matter-of-factly.

"Why?" Cordell asked.

"Because I need help. Local help. I would prefer yours."

"Why do you need help, if not to track the person who shot you? And why do you want our particular help?" Cordell again asked.

"I want to tell you, really I do. But you need to understand that I cannot divulge any more explicit details, until I know exactly who the two of you are. And to do this, I need to know from where your families originated. Believe me, the nationality of your last name, your family's heritage, and that of your dark friend here are the only links I have."

"The only links to what?" asked Cordell.

"The only links that will meld in some assemblage of order, certain chain of events. The chain of events that will bind the two of you to me, in this.

"In this what?" Dillon cautiously asked.

"Why, in this adventure. Of course," Brina said with a grand smile upon her face.

"Adventure?"

"Are ya game?" she said with a twinkle in her eye.

Dillon glanced at Cordell and Cordell at Dillon. They really didn't need this just now, or did they? They were bored from the present assignment and had been wondering if any of it was real. Dillon guessed it all came down to what kind of help, how long it might take, and what did her adventure entail. But he knew they wouldn't get any information from her unless she got what she asked. Perhaps then they could decide which direction to take, whether it be by her side, which wouldn't be too bad, or to flee as far from her and that gray horse as they could get.

His silence suggested either thought or resistance. She couldn't tell which. Far be it from her to win trust with threats, so she searched his face, finally settling on his eyes. Then, although not quite as intensely, Brina held him, reaching into his essence in search of his true feelings. Satisfied with what she found, Brina turned him loose. "I'm sorry, gentlemen, let me explain. I'm searching for two men I've never met." Before continuing she focused on Dillon. "One carries your name, Dillon, and travels with a Frenchman. If you are them... then again, due to my occupation, of which you are unaware of at this time, I must always be extremely cautious. I'm hoping all is correct, and you are the pair I'm looking for, but I must know for sure."

Cordell and Dillon had just turned back towards each other, again, both wearing a look on their faces suggesting a possibility of being in the company of a complete lunatic, *with a grip of iron.*

Brina got the impression they were unwilling to answer her. Nevertheless, she was bound and determined to get the information come hell or high water. If resistance was their game, she would show them how serious she was and how dangerous she could be if provoked. Turning towards the horses, she nonchalantly walked over to her saddlebags where she kept the matched pair of pearl-handled Colt Army revolvers Dr. Jarlath, Master Trainer, had given her.

Pulling them out, she turned back towards the two men with them drawn and ready.

"Not to alarm the two of you too awfully much, but gentlemen, there is one thing you should know. I can be a very patient person. But let me warn you now, it will be safer for the two of you if you're totally honest with me and agree to answer my questions *now*." She was losing her patience and valuable time. It wasn't much time, but as it had been established in her time, minutes, sometimes even seconds, could save a life or change history. "Another warning to you, if any of the information you give me is incorrect because you believe you're protecting yourselves, someone else, or if you are truly not who I seek, I will know. And because you've seen me and the Gray Wolf, I would have to modify your situation."

"What do you mean *modify our situation?*" Dillon asked, a bit perturbed.

"There will be no sunrise tomorrow for you two to enjoy, for both of you will be shot dead. Is that plain enough?"

They stood, totally shocked as she cocked both pieces. Dillon looked into those steel-gray eyes seeing the intensity as they stared back. She knew exactly what she was doing. She would follow through with no questions asked and not care of the outcome. There was no point in attempting to beat her draw. It was like looking into the eyes of hell itself. This woman with the unusual-colored boots, horse, and the mystery that surrounded her suddenly frightened Dillon, quite considerably. It was an unfamiliar feeling, and he didn't like it one bit.

So, there they stood. The three of them. Waiting. Waiting for what seemed to be an eternity. Dillon felt totally helpless. What was he to do? There they were, out in the middle of nowhere in the company of a very enchanting woman who held the most magnificently crafted pistols he'd *ever seen* their way. He stood there silently watching his life pass before him. He really didn't want to give her the information she wanted, due to his stubborn streak, but then again, what did it matter? His parents were now long gone, yet he still held them close. Such information as she was asking was privileged, but then, so was watching the sunrise, sunset, and everything in-between.

"Don't get all huffy. I'll tell you. I'll tell you."

"I'm sorry, but I have to have it. There's no other way at this time for me to convince you how serious I am and how important this is."

"Okay. I was born near here in the Valley of the Sun on the easternmost side of this zone. There I grew up with my…parents, Megan C. O'Flannery and Sean A. Frasier." He was about to say something about Kane but decided she needn't know.

Brina held up her hand as though to halt any further explanation of heredity. She was satisfied with the information received. And according to her briefings, he was the one for whom she searched, but what about the black man who rode with him?

She stood as still as the Rock of Gibraltar with that one pistol trained on Dillon. When it appeared that she had what was needed, she shifted her attention and her second pistol towards Cordell. What would he tell her?

After Dillon told what he felt was necessary, Cordell felt miserable. His father's story was so very special to him. Retelling it in front of even Dillon was going to take courage. But when Dillon nodded in response to his questioning gaze, Cordell turned to the gray-eyed woman, stood proudly, and began.

"My father's name was Jacques. He was a captain of a trade ship that sailed under the French flag. While crossing the Sargasso Sea, they were attacked by another ship that was carrying slaves from the south seas to our eastern shores. With the threat of attack always in the minds of the French, they were prepared and equipped for battle on all voyages. After the battle, they managed to sink the slavery ship, but not before they managed to confiscate and take aboard all contraband. Slaves were brought on board, with chains still attached to their legs.

"My father oversaw it all. As the contraband stood on the deck waiting for whatever fate awaited them, my father spotted a beautifully darkened young slave woman who seemed to stand out from the rest. She was like a rose among the thorns, which he felt should not be destined for the slave markets. He knew when and if their eyes met, it would be love at first sight, and it was." He stopped.

Brina's reaction was instantaneous. The look on her face told them she had found what she was hoping to hear. Gently she eased the hammers down and dropped her hands, even though the pistols were still tightly gripped. As Dillon watched her eyes close, he spotted a tear so slowly roll down her cheek. He wondered what it was in Cordell's story that caused such a reaction. Could it have been the intensity in which it was told, or possibly did the story touch a tender spot in her heart? He couldn't tell which.

When she realized her feelings were probably written all over her face, she quickly wiped the tear away and again took on the composed and controlled look they saw only moments before.

"I deeply apologize to you both for threatening your lives with my Colts. I really had no right to do that; unfortunately, due to a lot of things, I felt it necessary. I hoped you would be not only truthful, but also be the two that I seek. It will save me a lot of heartache. Please, do not allow my appearance to deceive you in any way or at any time. When I tell you that I am capable of doing great harm to anyone, I am, I can, and I will." She gave that a moment to sink in then continued. "If you have questions now, I will do my damnedest to answer what I can." She returned to her saddlebags and put the pistols back. Then visibly relaxed.

After that little show, Dillon didn't think there was a relaxed second in her life. He even began to wonder how she managed to sleep, then remembered the stallion.

"Now that you've put away your threats, how do you know we aren't lying?" Dillon asked.

"Trust me when I say I know what you tell me is the truth. You, Dillon, could be lying, but we know you aren't. Cordell's story, on the other hand, it's too elaborate to be made-up."

"All right then, where are you from?" asked Cordell, turning the tables on her.

"Frisco," she answered simply enough.

"What's your nationality?" She had asked theirs; why couldn't they ask hers?

"I have no idea."

"What about your parents?"

85

"I haven't seen them in a long, long time."

"Where did you get those Colts?" They were beautiful. If Dillon could only get a pair like those.

"A friend."

"What's his name?"

"You'd never be able to find him, believe me."

They were getting nowhere fast. "Perhaps it'd be better if you told us what you can."

"Fine by me. I've got to ask you something first." Brina knew, if they hadn't been informed of Jesse, then all her questions would sound like gobbledygook.

Another question, swell. Dillon was beginning to really wonder if rescuing her had been wise. Cordell, on the other hand, seemed totally enamored with her and couldn't tear his eyes away. Regardless of the unsaid issues, Dillon nodded as she began.

"Great. Now, do you know, or know of, an outlaw by the name of Jesse Loame?" She tossed their way.

Jesse Loame! Shit! Where in the name of the All Mother had she picked up that name? Dillon didn't know what to say. He had been informed that this assignment from the beginning was hush-hush. And as far as he knew, no one save Cordell, Glen, and Carl J. Stewart, and he knew for certain the story behind Jesse and the *item*. He knew for fact that Cordell, without question, would tell no one, so who spilled the beans?

"Before we answer, Cordell and I must speak alone." They needed to get their heads together and decide what and how much to tell her.

"That's fine, gentlemen, take all the time you want. Wolf and I will go for a walk." Brina stood then headed towards the horses.

Just short of her reaching the reins, Dillon hollered, "Wait! Who's Wolf?"

She turned to them smiling, holding the reins up, expecting them to understand. It took only a moment to understand the bewildered looks on their faces. Giggling, she added, "I'm sorry. I forgot to complete the introductions made earlier. May I present to you,

Wolf." She stepped aside, allowing the horse to be the focal point as though he was someone to be noticed.

Considering this, Dillon believed her to be one card short of a full deck.

"His name for the most part is the Gray Wolf, but I just call him Wolf. And if you haven't realized by now, he is a *very special* animal."

Dillon didn't doubt that for a moment.

"Gentlemen, once you answer my question, and hopefully give me what I need, I will make an attempt to explain my side of this story. I'll return to hear your answers after a bit." At that, she swung onto the back of the horse with the agility of someone who was born there and rode off.

After she left, Cordell was beside himself.

"Dillon, what in the name of my great-grandmother was that all about? She treats that animal like it was someone worth paying attention to. Not saying that what she says about him being exceptional isn't obvious, but come on now—"

"Cordell, forget the horse. Didn't you hear? Jesse Loame. She wants to know about Jesse Loame. Damn it, man, don't you get it? No one save a few others besides us knows of his existence. What are we supposed to do now? Tell her what we know? Or should we just play it by ear?"

As they discussed the problem at hand, Dillon was beginning to realize just how long Brina had been gone and was just beginning to worry about her out there by herself. They already had an opportunity to see how she handled those pistols, but that was no indication whether or not she could hit what she aimed at or if she could at all handle herself under unknown circumstances. Her accident, whatever had caused that one, was proof of that. And no matter what she said of her abilities, she could just be very good at bluffing. Even though she was of no real concern of theirs, she was a woman and a lone one at that. Dillon guessed it was just a paternal instinct surfacing from somewhere deep in himself. After all, just a short while ago he was regretting running into her at all.

"Well, I guess the best-laid plans of mice and men are usually shot all to hell. What do ya say? It's probably best to tell her the truth. Especially since that's the nature of the beast in both of us. As we also found out earlier, it's also the safest."

"The question, Dillon, is how to do it. How much do we tell her? If we told her everything we knew, she'd think we were the ones not playing with a full deck."

With their cards shuffled and ready to play, Dillon pulled out his pocket watch and noticed the time. An hour had passed already, and there still was no sign of the woman or horse. Dillon was now getting worried, but before he could say anything about it, there came a not-too-faraway yet out-of-place sound from the direction where Brina rode.

"Listen," he quietly said to Cordell.

They stopped talking and listened. It came again. It almost sounded like someone carrying on a conversation. It always amazed Dillon how any sound or noise traveled so well and so far at night. Sometimes you could even hear a coyote in an adjoining valley. Yet here, it was not a coyote. What or who could it be? He motioned to Cordell to be very quiet and to follow closely. This they had to investigate.

They headed off towards the sound, hoping not to sound too much like a bear crashing through the brush, and stopped about four hundred yards or so from a small clearing from where the voice could clearly be heard. There in the shadows, beyond the cut bank, they spotted them.

"It's Brina and that horse." Dillon's concern for her vanished once he could see she was all right.

"Dillon?" Cordell, on the other hand, was inclined sometimes to notice what others didn't.

When Dillon turned to him, the look on his face indicated that he had just told him pigs could fly. "What is it?"

"Why is the breeze blowing over there and not here?"

He was right. Dillon could see and feel it for himself. He could see there was a definite breeze blowing where she and the horse stood. He could see the grasses, the ends of her hair, and the last foot or so of his mane and tail, all were leaning to the left with the wind. And where he and Cordell stood, it was calm.

"Can't answer that. Don't know."

Dillon was so caught up in what he was seeing, he almost ruined everything by standing up to get a better look-see. Even though he saw it with his own two eyes as did Cordell, his mind wouldn't believe it. It almost looked as though the breeze was circling the girl and the horse only, leaving all else on the outside of it still. Out of fascination, they moved in for a better look. Finding a believed to be a better spot, they sat. Just as they got comfortable, Dillon looked up and saw Brina's eyes pop open. Not having the slightest idea how, but the second she came to attention, the breeze and the leaves it carried suddenly stopped.

Within a fraction of a second, Wolf's ears perked up, turning his head their way. Before Dillon realized what had happened, that horse's eyes were instantly locked onto his. How did they know? They were over four hundred yards away.

Dillon had a terrible time trying to break the connection between Wolf and himself. He couldn't remember if he broke it, or if the horse broke it, but before he knew what had happened, Brina was there not six feet away staring down at them from atop Wolf.

"Gentlemen, I'm sorry to barge in on your discovery, but is there anything I can do for you?" She was going to let the other pass. Perhaps with their minds occupied elsewhere—like on Jesse—they'd forget all about the swirling leaves. "Is there a possibility you've made your decision on how much you were willing to divulge? Yes, gentlemen, I knew right away that you both knew about Jesse the moment you decided to speak privately. Sorry, guys, it's a dead give-away." They had tried to deceive her, and it failed. They were lucky she was in such a good mood and that she desperately needed their help.

Both boys just stood there dumbfounded. Had it been so obvious? What about what they had just witnessed just a couple of minutes ago? That, if anything was in need of an explanation more so than what she wanted to tell. "While we were out looking for you because of our concern for your safety, we heard a strange sound out this a-way. Would you mind explaining what we just happened to see just now?"

"Why, nothing, of course. I was just relaxing with my horse. Since you don't know me from Adam, you have no idea what idiosyncrasies I carry within. No, boys, there was nothing unusual going on as far as I'm concerned. Sorry."

Dillon still wasn't convinced. "Listen, we know what we saw." As he took a moment to recall all that had transpired, he remembered Jesse Loame and the mysteries therein. Suddenly he realized that many of the answers to many of their questions perhaps lay within this mysterious woman and the mystery that surrounded the horse as well. They had to know the truth. So there Dillon stood with arms crossed over his chest waiting for an explanation.

"Well, since you were concerned for my welfare, I guess that means you were looking for me. Does that mean the two of you have decided to bring me into your confidence? If that is the case, maybe it'd be best if we talked about it back in the comforts of camp rather than risking the possibility of discovery from outsiders. The choice, gentlemen, is yours."

Did she mean they would finally get to the bottom of all this? She was right, of course. If this was to be a long night, they all should be comfortable.

Back at camp, they sat by the fire that by this time had died down enough to require refueling. Dillon took a moment to gather a few sticks of wood for the fire and while doing so glanced over at Cordell. Again, he was watching her. There was something unexplainable going on between the two of them. He didn't know what it could be, didn't even think Cordell was aware of it.

Once they were all settled, Dillon took a moment to step back and look at the setting. It had the appearance of an Indian powwow, with each of them waiting to hear about the other's visions.

"I have a better idea," Brina began. "This has been a very long day, especially for me. Gentlemen, instead of beginning our tales now, let's begin first thing tomorrow morning. Now would be a nice time to just kick back and enjoy the rest of the evening without any pressure. I'd like to just have something to eat, maybe even enjoy an after-dinner drink, and to just sit around and watch the fire until I fall asleep."

Brina chatted away in mindless wonder. Looking up towards the heavens she was able to avert their attentions towards where her finger was pointing. "Look, guys, it's a full moon tonight. The sky is free of clouds and the stars are so bright. Look there!" Brina pointed straight up. "Do you see them? The constellations? I'm sorry, I mean the stars in the sky?" She wouldn't give them enough time to comment on that last comment and continued. "I mean, if you use your imagination, you can create animals and things by just connecting the dots." She hadn't had much experience in star watching but did know how to find the north star if need be. At their confused expressions, Brina turned her attentions back towards hers and hopefully their stomachs.

"Who wants to get dinner?" Cordell was always hungry. "Or do we just want to chew jerky?"

Brina was the first to speak up. "Well, gentlemen, now that you mention it, I would really appreciate it if one of you would do the honors. After all, isn't it the man who is supposed to take care of the womenfolk? I, myself would really like to sit this one out and allow Wolf a little time for a good rest before taking watch tonight."

Dillon and Cordell must have misunderstood her.

"Are you saying that you'd take the first watch? How do we know you won't just ride off into the sunset?"

"Guys, guys, guys. I didn't say that I'd take the first watch. I said Wolf would take the first watch. You needn't worry about me, I'm going to sit up for a while, then crash."

Crash? What was she going to crash into? They looked at each other knowing good and well that this was not going or sounding the way it should. Besides, who had ever heard of giving a horse this kind of needed rest before taking watch? What did she take him for anyway? *He was just a horse.*

Since Dillon sorta wanted to sit and watch, he turned to Cordell and asked if he would like to stay or if he'd do the hunting for this evening's supper. Dillon had hoped that his friend would have wanted the honors, but as he figured, under the circumstances, asked if a-hunting Dillon would go. Very well. Hoping should anything happen, between him and her, it would be while Dillon was gone and be taken care of before it even got started.

Leaving the camp, mounted on Cody, Dillon glanced back. There sitting by the fire was a peaceful setting. The fire was the center of focus for Brina as she stared into and possibly beyond its depths. Next to her stood Wolf, and for the first time, his eyes were closed. Then, there sat Cordell directly across from Brina, with his eyes locked on target.

When Dillon returned, Cordell met him at the picket line. "Dillon, I'm glad you've returned safe and unharmed."

"Cordell, I expected to see you at the fire with Brina. Why are you here instead? Did something happen while I was gone?" He acted in a way that immediately made Dillon think that he had been caught with his hand in the cookie jar.

"It's kinda hard to say," he replied, then continued. "I sat there for a long time trying to decide whether or not to approach her."

Dillon could see the turmoil in his face.

"She just sat there staring into the fire for what seemed such a long time. Then she sighed, leaned her head way back, closed her eyes, and acted as though she was asleep. She never said a word to me. It was something else, like…"

Dillon could see that something really had happened in that hour or so he was gone. Whatever it was, he was visibly shaken. Somehow, he finally managed to get the rest out.

"Then, it came to me," he stated.

"What came to you?" Dillon asked.

"The voice. Inside my head."

Dillon could see his friend was upset. "Cordell, what voice? Tell me what happened! She didn't hurt you, did she?"

"No. Not at all. The voice I heard in my head wasn't hers. I don't know whose it was. All I can remember was what it said."

Dillon waited, patiently.

"It said, 'Let sleeping dogs lie.' It was then that I glanced up and thought I saw that damned horse looking right at me. I rubbed my eyes and took another look and found his closed. Maybe it never happened! Dillon, am I starting to lose my mind?"

Cordell was really shaken. Dillon could see it in his eyes and was beginning to wonder if maybe Brina was right after all, and that it had been too long a day for all of them.

"Cordell, we're all very tired. Maybe it was just your imagination. How 'bout we take this up in the morning."

He accepted Dillon's suggestion with a nod. After supper they did just that. But just before Dillon felt himself fading off to sleep, he glanced over at Brina. There standing near her bed was the Gray Wolf, her protector, as she called him, keeping a watchful eye out for anything or anyone that would be a threat to her. It was freakish. And as Dillon faded off to sleep, he wondered what kind of a place she had come from. As far as he knew, nothing of which she spoke of or anything that had happened since their first encounter of her and the gray stallion suggested they'd come from anywhere familiar.

IX

getting down to grass roots

The next morning Brina's inner clock woke her just before the coming of dawn. Sensing no one else around other than those still in their bedrolls, she, as quietly as a mouse, gathered herself up out of bed, slipped on her outer clothing and boots, then slowly and cautiously began to pick up and pack away her gear. Once everything belonging to her was safely tucked away, she began her morning ritual by cleaning her Colts.

These were the same Colts Dr. Jarlath had presented to her a week before her departure. As proud as any parent could be, and as a token of all they had been through, for her and her alone, he broke up his historical 150th Anniversary Colt's Manufacturing Company collection. The one ring he always wore on his right index finger—a silver, gold, and black titanium treasure, depicting the Colt emblem of a single silver rearing horse with gold inlaid on each of its two sides and on its face, a fancy gold-and-black titanium circle containing two silver pistols, muzzles crossed, with the "Colt" name above. There was also made mention of a second ring, one with the "Colt" name engraved in gold on both of its silver-titanium sides, and on its top was a rearing horse scrimshawed into its true ivory face—but that ring had mysteriously vanished from the collection years ago. Some said it was stolen by a student; others thought it was the devil. Anyway they looked at it, it was gone. There were only two guns in the collection. Both were ornately engraved with fancy scrolling. Each of their cylinders held a white horse rearing within a circle with the words "Colt 150" next to the animal. Just short of the cylinder, on both weapons, was a man's silhouette. Directly below the circle with the white horse in its center were engraved numbers, and those read "1836-1986." The fancy antique bowie-type knife, which hung on his office wall on a display plaque, also depicted the same fancy scrolling as the guns. In two distinct places, it also had the "Colt" emblem engraved; the silver-and-black titanium was engraved into the top portion of the blade; the gold was encased in the creamy-white ivory portion of the teak handle. It was quite a collection.

He tried explaining to her how the set had come to him but couldn't really remember any of his family knowing. They did know the set was short that one piece in order to make it complete and extremely valuable, but how that one ring was lost, again, no one had an inkling. Ancestral records stated the five items had been in his family for centuries. And since he himself had totally dedicated his life to the Academy, he had no family of his own. No one to pass on his knowledge or his possessions. No one was left for him other than his students and his life at the Academy. His parents, dead. There were no siblings, no spouse, no offspring. And not having any family over time developed a love for Brina as though she was his. It was sort of sweet and ironic at the same time, her becoming the son he never had. Therefore, he broke up what was left of the collection, passing the pistols on to her in loving memory of all the trials and tribulations they had encountered in her years under his instruction—hoping, if at some time in her newfound future she needed his help, in a rather unusual way he'd always be there for her. The last two pieces of the collection stayed home.

Brina treated those cherished guns as though they were a part of her, and in fact, they actually were. Strapping the gunbelt around her hips buckling them securely into place, she stood there for several moments practicing drawing, then reholstering hers and Dr. Jarlath's Colts over and over, and over again. This she did just for the fun of it. Not to mention the fact that practice always made perfect, and perfection was just what the Academy ordered.

On completion of that task, Brina once again surveyed the campsite for any stirrings of the *other campers*. Not only was she able to tell just by watching, but if there was any slight movement that needed her immediate attention, she'd find out through Wolf or through her second sight. But since he was silent, she knew they were still very much asleep. Knowing this, she began to wonder whether or not to start the coffee and would its aroma enhance their awakening. Once she decided, the fire was started, and the coffee began its brewing.

Brina left Wolf where he stood, just in case the other campers just happened to awaken while she was gone (this way they'd known she hadn't gone far). Then off she headed, off into the woods in search of something edible for her morning meal. Maybe while she was at it, she'd find something for them as well. She arrived at a small clearing, one she felt was far enough away from camp, hopefully avoiding any unwanted company, then located a tree of desired size and shape to hide alongside. There she stood silent as the morning dew, with her eyes, ears, and senses at their peak of awareness for the picking up of any and all sounds within her range of perception.

Her ears were the first to pick up the sound of rustling grasses. Once the location of the sound was pinpointed, like a predator she shifted her eyes towards that direction and sound. There one hundred yards away gingerly approaching the clearing was a young doe and her fawn. How beautiful they were, she thought. The fawn still had its spots. The doe appeared with nose held high, nostrils flared, sniffing the air for unsuspecting dangers lurking anywhere ahead. Brina was one with the tree as she watched in fascination at an animal she'd only read about and looked at in the *Manual of the Sciences* textbook. But before she allowed her mind to travel back to memories she no longer wanted to think about, she refocused her concentration on the challenge at hand, breakfast. Once the deer's approximate location was calculated as near as she could figure, Brina stored that information away just in case other animals arrived; that way she wouldn't get them confused.

It wasn't too much longer when she again picked up another sound. This one was very similar to the last, only on a much smaller scale. When the location was pinpointed, she again shifted her eyes. Just emerging from a hole in the ground was a rather large-looking rabbit. She again recognized the animal from the photos in the manual. And again, was fascinated, so fascinated that she was unable to tear her eyes away. The longer she watched, the more surprised she became, because when that rabbit got farther out of the hole, Brina noticed another smaller one just beginning to emerge behind the first. A *tiny rabbit.* And as she watched in total absorption several more, tiny rabbits emerged from behind the first, then it finally dawned on her. *This must be a litter of rabbits. Of course, Brina, you silly twit, it's springtime. Springtime is the time for parturition with hopes of survival.*

Brina suddenly realized she could no more kill one of the procreators of these youngsters than the youngsters themselves. They looked so precious and innocent. And innocence had a special meaning to her. And with that thought in mind, she turned and headed back to camp, reached her saddlebags, pulled out a small amount of flour and spices she'd carried all the way through the *field* and began to conjure up her idea of homemade biscuits for breakfast.

Her second plan would be to wait out the spring. Either that, or she'd have to find their next meal when it wasn't with its family. Even though she had in the past and most definitely would kill offspring and anything else she deemed necessary, here at this time and place it wasn't as engraved.

By the looks of things, her original plan had begun its work. The aroma of biscuits and coffee looked as though it had wafted its way across the far reaches of their camp to swirl its way downwards into unsuspecting nostrils. From there it continued towards the center of the brain, whereas its meaning was fully digested by the two, who were just beginning to reach the outer reaches of awareness. As she finished up the coffee and opened the cast-iron Dutch oven that contained the golden-brown biscuits, she began to pick up slight sounds of certain someone's attempting to awaken from a restful night's sleep.

Cordell, she saw, was just beginning to come around as he had just thrown back his covers. When she turned her attention towards the marshal and his bedroll; she was mildly surprised to find herself staring straight into a pair of hazel eyes that peeked at her from above the edge of a blanket.

"Good morning, Marshal. Did you sleep well?"

Did he sleep well? That was an understatement. "Yes, I did, thanks for asking." He broke off eye contact with her just in time to notice how light it was and how far up into the sky the sun had gotten. "Sweet Bridget! I must have been dead last night. Hey, you over there, you up?" Dillon inquired towards Cordell as he scrambled out of his bed roll.

"Sorta," Cordell replied. He also just noticed the time of day. "What did we do, sleep the day away?"

"Calm down, guys," Brina began. "There's nothing cooking today, other than what you smell and more of what went on yesterday and last night. Obviously the two of you needed the sleep, and with Wolf standing guard, you must have felt secure enough for extra Zs." There was no need to be so concerned, but then again, they didn't know too much about her and Wolf, and that was cause enough for concern. "You're fine, really. Not much happened while you were sleeping, except that I managed to fix us something for breakfast. Is anyone game?"

Cordell ignored the remark and instead recognized the aroma in the air as food. And whatever it was, it sure smelled good.

Sensing her error, she quickly corrected it. "Coffee's on, and the biscuits are ready." Brina turned, took the few short steps back over towards the fire and her cooking, lifted the lid off the oven, found the couple cups left over from last night's meal, the ones she cleaned up as best she could the night before, and filled them with the dark-brown liquid. After each was filled, in their turn, she carried them over to Cordell, offering him one. After accepting his, she then headed over towards the marshal and offered him the other.

"Now, if you wish to try the biscuits, you'll have to come over to the fire. I'm not a waitress." When she noticed the confused looks on both their faces, she added, "There are no plates to serve you food." Then she quietly began chuckling more to herself than for their benefit. They didn't know how good they had it. She'd been in a lot of strange places, eaten a lot of bizarre things in all manners of condition, fully appreciating and taking pleasure in this simple meal.

"Brina, these biscuits are wonderful, and this coffee…how do you manage to get the full flavor without that added yucky taste?" Her coffee was worth killing for. Dillon had never ever experienced such flavorful coffee, even on a trip he took once to St. Louise.

"Sorry, boys. It's a secret recipe that belonged to my great-great-grandmother. When I die, it will die with me, unless miracles do happen, and I ever have a daughter to pass the recipe down to." It had always been a sore spot in her past, not being able to reproduce. The doctors had told her mother that she'd been born with an unknown organ in her body cavity. And in the process of exploratory surgery, in order to examine the organ, its removal inadvertently caused her sterilization.

But before she'd allow that to get her down, she'd taken hold of life and ran rampant. This mission was proof of that. How many others would have been willing to take this assignment sight unseen? Enough of that kind of thinking, she must return to the present, which was now her life.

"So, you see. The only way you can enjoy a decent cup of coffee, as you have discovered, is to allow me to fix it for ya." She said that with a genuine smile.

"Are there any more surprises you're keeping from us?" asked Cordell.

"Why, of course. Everybody has a secret or two hidden away in some dark closet that they wish to remain hidden," she calmly answered.

"Will you share some with us?" asked Dillon, curious now.

"Well, to be honest with you, I have enough secrets to keep the two of you guessing for many years to come. But, before we begin extracting information from one another, there's something I need to get off my chest."

That could prove entertaining was a thought that briefly crossed Dillon's mind.

"Don't be concerned, gentlemen, about certain information regarding Jesse, 'cause believe me, when I tell you, nothing you've seen, heard, or wondered about I'd question. No matter how strange to you it may seem."

99

Suddenly the air crackled with electricity, almost as though a lightning storm was just overhead. But when both men looked up, neither saw anything but the morning light.

Brina never took her eyes off them. "Trust me, gentlemen, *I will believe.*"

Dillon's mind returned to earlier encounters with her at their center: those guns, that horse, the unknown shooter, her eyes, and their effect. That was when he realized something really strange was about to intrude into their lives. He was eager to participate in the future that was yet to unfold with this woman, yet at the same time dreaded what chain of events may result from their meeting. His gut feeling told him to keep silent, but she already had asked about Jesse herself. Did she not know everything, or was she testing their secrecy? He had a feeling that she was being honest, but everything seemed so strange. What was he to do?

Dillon decided to shoot himself in the foot.

"It might help you to better understand what we know of Jesse if we told you a bit about ourselves and how we came to be here. I'm also going to take that earlier gun episode as though it never happened." Turning sharply to Cordell, he added, "Fair?"

Cordell nodded in agreement. He was a curious as a kitten to learn as much as he could about her. And if turnabout was considered fair play, so be it.

Brina sat near to the edge of the fire to enjoy the heat and what was to come.

"Let's see…back 'bout five years ago, I was a federal marshal in the Dakota Territories. My brother…" Dillon told of Kane, his position as a marshal, his assignment, and the letters. "I was notified of his death." Taking a deep breath as it is always difficult to relive the past, he continued. "I was deeply stricken with remorse. I felt destined to find his killers. My decision was perceived as a direct security violation from the higher authority over which I report, but they decided not to prosecute due to my record and achievements. Instead, I was granted a chance to keep my badge if I agreed to *certain terms.*"

She sat totally absorbed yet looked totally at ease.

"Any action that I took in tracking down the assailants would not be connected in any way to the Federal Marshal's office. Other than that, I had my freedom to do as I wished as long as they were brought to trial."

This didn't surprise her. The circumstances surrounding the upper authorities and their denial of certain actions on the grunt's part reminded her of time spent in the *void*.

"You see, Brina, I am determined to find my brother's killers. They just gave me the avenue in which I could carry out my plans." That took a lot of energy to rehash that terrible period. It's funny, Dillon had not realized it, but not only did he find himself afoot pacing back and forth while reliving his past but was also surprised to find that the light of day had faded. It had slipped away without notice. He couldn't remember anything other than explaining to this gray-eyed beauty his story. She must have seen something in his eyes, because before he continued, she stopped him.

"Marshal, I think that's enough for now. It's been a very long day for all of us, you especially, it seems. It's very late, and I know we're all very tired. Your story was very interesting, and I can understand how tensed up you must be feeling right about now. I, of all people, know reliving painful memories can be extremely stressful. Let's turn in and start fresh tomorrow."

"Thanks." Now Dillon's only problem was to get to sleep after reliving those experiences all over again. She was right. He was so tensed up that he could hardly sit down. Leaning up against a tree didn't work. Closing his eyes wouldn't erase the past either; instead, it brought it back more vividly than telling it. That damned letter. Dillon could almost see each and every word written on that page as though it was in his hand instead of in his saddlebags.

Dillon couldn't remember how long he stood there, when suddenly felt he was not alone. He slowly opened his eyes to find Brina standing there directly in front of him, with a cup of something in her lovely hands.

"Here, take a sip of this. It will help you relax."

She handed him the cup that was filled with a liquid that had a smell he didn't recognize. As exhausted as he was, he did as requested, then glanced around to find Cordell already asleep. He almost looked as though dead. Fear gripped his soul.

Brina saw the terrified look in his eyes as her actions had been misinterpreted. In order to halt any further fears, she decided to use the same soothing, relaxing voice they used on her the other day. It worked then; it ought to work now.

"Marshal, he's fine, really. Come. Come over here and sit with me by the fire. If I had wanted you dead, I would have taken care of that long before now. Let me assure you, the tea I had you sip is made with leaves from a plant called sweet balm. It's a plant that grows in open meadow-like fields between here and our eastern shores. It has several medicinal qualities, one of which is a sedative. It should help relieve your tension, and if you don't mind, I'll help it along."

Brina could still remember the strong and powerful hands of her masseuse and the benefits thereof. Perhaps a good, relaxing rub-down would be just what the doctor ordered.

What she said should have made him aware, but after a while, he could feel the tea work its magic, as she put it, because he could feel himself unwinding. Then she motioned him to stay put as she stepped quietly behind. He heard her kneel, and again he tensed up not knowing what was to come.

"Take it easy, Marshal, I'm not going to hurt you. I can help. Let me help you."

On his shoulders she set her hands, using the strength within them to gently work the tension from his mind. It was heavenly. Dillon closed his eyes allowing his mind to focus on the strength and gentleness in this woman's touch. He could see in his mind's eye her fingers as they worked their way around and into the muscles of his shoulders and neck. Then just when he felt as though slipping off into a dream, she stopped.

"Now," she began.

As he continued to sit, she got up, then gently put her hand on his shoulder as though she wanted him to stay put, then stepped away. As the sound her footsteps returned, Dillon gingerly opened his eyes to find that she had laid out his bedroll. What was she going to do? Closing his eyes once again, he waited.

Brina knew, if she was to do a complete and adequate job on this man's back, she needed him on his stomach. "All right, Marshal. What I want you to do is to take off your outer coat, shirt, all the way down to your skin. I want you to lie down on your bedroll facedown on your stomach. I know it sounds crazy, but if you want my help, you must trust me."

Dillon was too tired to argue. His body had already betrayed his mind. It craved the miracle of her hands on his skin. Not being of sound mind at the moment, he decided to trust her. But like she said earlier, if she wanted them dead, she could have carried that out quite nicely beforehand. Per her request, he removed his coat, shirt, then finally made an attempt to unbutton the upper portion of his union suit. By the time everything was removed in accordance with what she asked, he felt naked and vulnerable under the scrutiny of this woman, the elements, and the stars above.

Brina wondered whether or not the marshal was having any problems dealing with her seemingly unusual requests. Once he found his bedroll and laid facedown upon it as she'd requested, it became obvious to her that he was more than in trouble. Both shoulder muscles had begun to twitch and jerk, which indicated to her they were in the midst of light spasms, which also meant he was hurting more than she'd realized. Immediately she knelt beside him, starting with the top of his neck, then worked her hands gently downward towards his waist, via the spine, all the while working outward towards his sides and along those long back muscles.

Dillon felt as though he was a thousand miles away—so wonderful it was. And as his mind drifted, he heard angelic singing. Singing that seemed to drift across the heavens, only to find its eventual resting place there with him during these treasured moments of eternal contentment and relaxation. It had to have been a dream.

When his eyes opened, the sun was peaking at him from between the branches of the trees. That could've only meant that he slept the night away unknowingly. How long had he been asleep? By the looks of things, it had been all night and most of the morning. He must have been truly exhausted last night. A whiff of coffee brewing brought him around (that same wonderful coffee from yesterday). He sat up and glanced over towards Cordell and saw that he too was looking half-asleep with eyes at half-mast. He, too, must have had his own long but restful night. Then Dillon looked for Brina and found her tending the coffee fully dressed, with gun belt strapped on, Colts holstered.

He arose, put away his bedroll, realizing the soreness that was in his back and shoulders the night before had vanished. By golly, if they could only bottle what she did last night, they would be rich beyond the world. Oh well, so much for dreaming.

After putting up his bedroll, Dillon glanced towards the fire to see what was going on. Brina was tending to something, and Cordell, well, he was watching *her*.

Before Dillon could say anything, he again heard an angel's song. It hadn't been a dream after all. His angel *had* returned. There by the fire cooking breakfast was Brina, singing so very softly. Dillon stopped in midstream to listen then found himself being lulled slowly back into that same peaceful state of last night.

Brina had long ago found herself to be one with nature, song, and the pleasures they brought. So, whenever the occasions presented themselves, she'd absently utter her own musical expressions by humming a happy tune from years gone by.

"Good morning," she interrupted her tune to greet her breakfast guests. "Did you have a good night?" she queried, then turned back to the fire, and absently continued her song.

"Yes," Dillon replied, then continued, "are you singing?"

"Oh, I'm sorry. Is it bothering you?"

"No. Not in the least." She didn't need the truth about it.

"Actually, I hadn't thought about it much. As a matter of fact, I'm not singing. I'm humming. Let's see, what was it?" Lost in thought, Brina tried to remember which tune she'd been so absorbed in. "I can't recall its name, but it's a happy tune, a happy tune my grandmother taught me when I was just a small child. You guys hungry? I've got rabbit cooking. If you'd like to join me, you're more than welcome."

She'd gotten lucky this time and found a single rabbit out in the open, away from the protection of the underbrush. If *she* hadn't gotten him, another large predator would have.

For the first time, Dillon thought she looked totally at ease with what she was doing. At the same time, he wondered how she managed to get the rabbit.

"Brina?" Dillon began.

"Yes?" Brina responded.

Before Dillon asked, he picked up his own bedroll and headed over towards Cody and the rest of his gear. "How did you…acquire the rabbit?"

Yesterday, she'd pulled her guns on them, but that didn't mean she knew how to use them. Dillon was about to step back towards the fire and breakfast when his question was answered in less than a heartbeat. With a speed he never knew existed, left-handed even, she drew and fired her pistol so fast he never saw it coming. With it still pointing in his direction, she approached. He stood rock stock-still. Now what? This little show of hers put her in a totally different category than all the other women he had known in his life. Cordell, on the other hand, was off in the bushes doing something when the shot was fired and had missed the show.

When she reached Dillon's side, they stood eye to eye and toe to toe. She reholstered the weapon. She bore into his eyes, showing him for just a second, the eyes of a hardened killer. For a split second it was there; in the next it was gone. Her eyes shifted to the ground. She slowly knelt, and as his eyes followed her descending hand, he spotted the dead rattlesnake inches from his leg. As she stood up holding up the snake by its head, she looked at Dillon with those steel grays of hers, then turned, and nonchalantly walked back to the fire, leaving him standing there with the same look on his face most of her male classmates had after she pulled one of her many unbelievable feats.

He was so dumfounded that it took a minute or two for his mind to register all that had just happened. This woman was not like anyone he had ever known before. Dillon turned back to camp, sat back down quietly on a rock, and relished the rest of his coffee, in total silence.

Cordell finally returned and asked about the shot he heard. Brina explained that she had rabbit for breakfast and snake for lunch, if that would be all right with him. He didn't even think about it, just sat down, picked up his cup, and downed his remaining coffee.

With breakfast behind them they decided it might be better if they broke camp. Dillon hated like the dickens to be caught out there unawares by robbers, who may have been watching them for hours or even days. Besides, moving on might be the break he needed, especially since that episode with the snake.

They were about an hour from camp when their previous conversation resumed.

"Marshal, do you feel up to continuing your story of last night?" Brina asked. She felt he'd had enough time to regroup his thoughts on the past and deal with them on his own accord.

"Why do you keep referring to me as marshal? I do have a name."

"I'm not accustomed to informalities. I'm not used to calling others by their first names, nor am I used to others calling me by my first. In my line of work, they're not used."

"Why, what is your line of work?" Cordell asked.

"I'd rather not say at this time. I'd rather talk about the two of you and of Jesse. Perhaps later we'll get to me. Fair enough?"

"Fair enough," Dillon reluctantly agreed.

"Continue, please."

"After I left the position of marshal, I headed for Fort William. There I met with Major James Northrup. He was kind enough to show me on his map the location of the massacre. As to Jesse, I have no idea. Someone had gotten to his gang before us. One by one they were found dead. Apparently, Jesse, or another very clever assassin, didn't want to share what he had learned with anyone. So, to ensure secrecy, they added murder to their list of activities."

Dillon turned to Cordell expecting him to fill in some of the blanks, but instead of doing so, Cordell asked, "I'm hungry, when do we eat?"

Blessed be the All Mother, Dillon thought. Was that all he ever thought about, food? No. Now he thinks of her, too.

"That rabbit earlier was just an appetizer, not enough to keep a coyote happy. Brina, do you still have that snake, if so, let's stop. I always talk better on a full stomach," Cordell added.

That took care of their afternoon.

Just in case they failed to get going again, which Dillon felt would probably be the case, he found an ideal location and set up camp.

While Brina was again tending the fire and preparing the snake, Dillon's mind shifted back to the episode that brought that snake to their fire. He realized she just may have saved his life by killing that rattler. He was the largest one he had seen. Over six feet in length and as big around as his arm. If she hadn't shot it, he probably would have stepped on it when returning from the picket line, making things worse. Dillon took a moment to think about all the times he had been faced by gunslingers, bank robbers, and others bent on doing him harm, yet never had he considered the unknown dangers the All Mother had safely hidden away waiting for their turn at fun. Before he knew it he needed to sit down. He ought to be paying more attention on where he was putting his feet.

With Dillon sidetracked, Cordell came over with some of the cooked snake. It was cut up in little pieces and fried to perfection. Dillon took a whiff and knew that it didn't smell like any snake he had ever prepared. Sampling the meat, he found it to be delicious. This woman could cook; that was for sure.

With his stomach full, Cordell set his plate down and began his side of the story. "After my father found his fortune in trading with various countries for France, he left the high seas with his new bride and settled near St. Louise, hub of the Mississippi and beyond. There, they found happiness. As I grew older, I found my only excitement was in the form of endless studying. Some of those stories were pretty good, but it was only after I finally finished my schooling that I was compelled to break away. I decided to follow the line 'Go west, young man, go west, east, north or south, go anywhere, but just go.' That was told to me by one of my teachers, who realized that I had the same type of attitude as my father and needed unbridled challenges to satisfy my hunger for life. Shortly thereafter, I left my home and followed his advice.

"There comes a time when all adventurous children try their hand at taking out unapproved loans from various sources, especially when people make it so darn easy. Unfortunately, they also discover the authorities hot on their little tails. I found myself in one of those predicaments yet was fortunate enough to be caught by a territorial marshal with sympathy and understanding of my circumstances.

"He offered me another chance. And after hearing my side of the story, he figured that I had just gotten in over my head with a bad bunch. I took the chance he offered and served my time working for him. Eventually I found myself working with him. And as the years went by, we both grew very close. Close enough to consider each other brothers." He paused long enough to pass on to Dillon a look of brotherly love. "We traveled extensively throughout the northern territories within this sector, and I assisted whenever possible. I left him after a difficult decision to move on and find my own niche in life. I traveled for several months, crossing back into the Dakota Territories, eventually stopping in at Fort William. You see, I'd been thinking about enlisting with the Territorial Riders and was discussing that idea with the sergeant when suddenly the inner door opened and out stepped the major and Dillon.

"Seeing him brought back everything. It was then that I decided the Territorial Riders was not really what I wanted. I wanted to ride with *him*. We exchanged greetings, then I made my excuses to the major, and out the door we headed. Once outside, he explained everything."

Dillon knew about Cordell's story, so he didn't really have to listen too hard. Dillon was more interested in watching the look on Brina's face while Cordell was speaking. She listened with utmost concentration and fascination. Dillon could see the wheels turning once again behind those lovely eyes. What was she thinking? He knew from experience that there was more going on in that pretty little head of hers than she let on. She just sat there staring straight ahead looking far off into the distance. He again wondered what the reason was for her determination in finding Jesse.

Brina now had most of the information she needed. "Okay, guys, let's move on to more important things. I need to know if there were any unusual circumstances found during the initial investigation. Anything. No matter how trivial they appeared to be."

So, there she stood, waiting. For what? The only thing Dillon could think of doing was to give her everything: lock, stock, and both barrels.

"Okay. Since then, we've been tracking down the members of Jesse's gang. As I told you earlier, we found them one by one, already dead. It wasn't just the bodies, but we also found unusually colored empty cartridge cases near each of the bodies. These were of unknown origin and identical to the ones Cordell found at the original sight of the massacre. Plus, each bullet hole in each body was located in the exact same location. Right between the eyes."

"Do you have them with you, and may I see them?" she asked. "Cordell?"

"I'll get them," he answered.

As Cordell headed off towards his horse and saddlebags, Dillon wondered what this woman was going to do or say when she saw the empty cartridge cases.

Cordell returned from his horse with palm open holding one of the empty cases. "Here's one." He handed it over to her.

Brina gingerly picked it up with her fingers, then brought it up to where she could see it more clearly. Turning it over so it was possible to read the head stamp, she scrutinized it till she was sure of her assessment. Then returned it to Cordell. "You may put this back."

Brina quickly stood up from her sitting position on the log and began pacing around the camp in an excited manner. "This is good! This is very good. I was wondering when you were going to get down to the nitty-gritty. Now. Are *you* ready?" It was a statement, not a question.

This time, she looked serious. Dillon knew without a doubt that the truth was coming. Was he ready to hear it? It made no difference; it was going to come, anyway.

"Please sit down."

They did. Dillon watched her head towards her saddlebags and pull something out. It looked like *a flask of whiskey...?* She must have been reading his mind. Dillon had a feeling before this was over, they would all need a drink.

She returned to the fire with Wolf walking right behind her. She was not leading him. He was following on his own accord. This was weird. She sat down with Wolf standing by her side, then handed over the flask.

"Here, you're going to need some of this."

Was she kidding?

"Before I start, you must understand something. All the things I'm about to tell you are true. Unfortunately, there are some things I cannot tell you. At least not now, and maybe not ever—we'll have to see. Because if told, or showed, you'd probably lock me up somewhere and throw away the key. To make it simple, I know from where that casing came, I know of the *item* you seek, and I know who *Maximillian Rider really is.*"

Brina knew right away she'd hit the mother lode by the shocked expressions on both faces.

"Hold your horses, boys. The time hath come to explain a few things. Some things about me and why I'm here." Before beginning, she asked for the flask, took a healthy swig, then sat down with her newfound associates to begin her unbelievable but true story for being here, with them, in the 1800s.

"I am from the future. How I got here and whether or not you believe that is of little concern to me. What is important is that I have been sent by an organization called Cyclops. My orders are of extreme importance: to track down Jesse Loame before he meets with Maximillian Rider. *Your Ivory Tower* wants Jesse for trial and imprisonment. 'We' want him *dead.* Any questions?"

Who was she kidding? From the future? Yeah right, sure, she was. Dillon did have to admit she had some amazing skills for one of her age and beauty. But if what she was telling them was the truth, what would one ask of someone from the future that would verify such malarkey?

"I have several. Are you willing to answer all of them truthfully?"

"As best I can. Let me first warn you, some of what you hear might sound pretty crazy." She sat, patiently waiting. This was going to be interesting. What would they ask?

"What did Jesse do for you to be sent here to find him?" Dillon had an endless list of questions to ask. If she was willing to answer them, he'd best get on with the important ones. That is if she answered any of them at all. Ya know, like what was Wolf, really?

"To put it simply, Jesse Loame is a criminal. He assassinated someone of great importance. He escaped through a device we call the Franciscan Lifter. It is a device we use to travel across the Barriers." At the confused looks on their faces she added, "Don't worry too much about what you don't understand. Just focus on what you can. Remember, there is another criminal out there some-where—Maximillian Rider. Rider is an associate of Jesse's. He had been incarcerated but managed to escape with a device called the Neptune Sphere to this part of the United Sovereign Territories." Just to be sure, she slipped the name of the sphere in just to see their reaction. When there was none, that reaffirmed her beliefs that they knew only enough to be of great help.

"We're not sure, but we believe Jesse managed to get informa-tion on how to channel the sphere's power. This he got from a previ-ous position he infiltrated. Once he had what he wanted, he decided to come here to locate Rider.

"The specific department was contacted, where our fears were confirmed. Dr. Horacio Dimwit, the head of Time Travel Research, explained that once the Neptune Sphere's power is properly chan-neled, anyone can cross the Neptune Barrier to permanently escape our pursuit. Once across the Neptune, where only the sphere can take them, they can continue to create mayhem in whatever form they choose. My mission is a search-and-destroy mission. Wolf is with me for additional security, protection, and companionship."

Dillon needed a drink and bad. She was right on two counts. The whiskey was definitely needed; and locking her up did sound like a fine idea. The thought of even shooting her to end the misery she must be suffering sounded like a good idea too.

"You said Wolf is with you for added security. Would you mind explaining that, in detail? Like who or what is he?"

"Wolf is my horse. Don't you know what a horse is? You have one of your own." It broke some of the tension. They all laughed, but Dillon's was strained and slipping towards hysteria.

All that she'd just said was a bit too far-fetched. It was obvious she was making light of the conversation, and perhaps she truly felt that way, but she was a little too spooky for Dillon to take into his full confidence any further, until something returned to normalcy.

Brina didn't see the sudden seriousness on the marshal's face. She was focusing on Cordell.

"You two were getting too serious. I had to break the tension. *Wolf* is difficult to explain. As you can see, he is most definitely a horse. However, he is also, let me think a second here. He also has a mind of his own and uses it quite extensively." She paused momentarily to gather her thoughts.

In the meantime, Dillon was beginning to think maybe he didn't want to hear any more. Unfortunately, it was now too late for that.

"I'm not sure how much I can tell you about him. We can communicate with each other, but that process works differently from yours and mine. I verbally speak to him, yet his voice comes to me in my head. He is my companion and watches out for me."

Sounded like a devoted dog to Dillon. He used to have one he talked to all the time and did answer—in his own way, but not in his head. Dillon tried to listen to her with an open mind. She was right: a lot of what she was saying was unbelievable. Then he remembered the other night when the horse stood over her while she slept. "You said he watches out for you. You mean like when you sleep?"

"You're getting the idea," she replied.

Dillon was still confused, but not so much that he didn't know the time. "Let's continue this tomorrow, shall we?" He had had enough for one day. Way more than enough.

At her nod, they ended the day quietly. When evening came all was quiet. Everyone was lost in their own thoughts. When it was time to turn in, just as she had explained earlier, Wolf took his watch next to her as they all said their good nights.

X

back to basics

Cordell had fallen asleep with only one thought on his mind, and by the time the sun arose along with himself, he was ready to ask it.

"Brina. I'm confused, if what you say is true, why you? Why did they send a woman?"

Brina wasn't too surprised at his question. It always amazed men how someone could expect a woman to complete such an important task. This period in time was no different than all the others. This time in history, it was considered a man's world, and women raised the children and took care of their man. Sexual equality wasn't expected to begin to surface till later in the century, nor was its foothold to really kick in until sometime during the following century—if her memory served her right.

"Cordell, there are things far beyond your comprehension. Where I come from men and women are trained for the same things. The same jobs you would expect only men capable of accomplishing women can do—within reason. Where I trained, women do have a few disadvantages compared to the men, like strength, power, and others I'd just as soon not discuss. The women, however, are taught in other ways to overcome such handicaps. I'm very good at what I do. My fellow trainees, instructors, and the board of directors all recommended me for this assignment. Not only are my roots here in this time, but when it also comes to special circumstances and other unusual talents, I'm one of the best in my field. And I've been training for a mission such as this since I was a small child. Where I come from, it's not whether you are male or female; it's the training, knowledge, how well you handle yourself, and how well you accept your duty that it all falls back on.

"It's very hard to describe, this sense of duty that I am bound to, body and soul. It's like taking the bullet that was meant for someone else. Sacrificing your life so that others may live. Kind of like how your and Dillon's friendship is or will be. Between the two of you, you have protected each other by standing for what you both believe in: *the good and the right*. You stand by each other just by your word. You're both honest, trustworthy, and dependable. You've been to hell and back, and as long as the two of you are together, you know you have a chance. For you stand together—do you understand what I'm trying to say?

"Wolf and I stand together, and we are bound by forces you can't begin to understand. And it's our duty to carry out this assignment."

Dillon was still in his bedroll, awake and listening intently. Regardless of the strangeness of her story, it held too many hidden truths to be false. Especially after listening to her describe honor and duty as though she knew exactly what they were and had experienced both firsthand. The truth that she claimed to hold dear was obvious, as it was written all over her face as she spoke.

Dillon chimed in, "Brina, I understand the meaning of *duty* as well as the next man." Although it was an unusual moment in one's life when confronted by a woman who also understood it, that left just one question.

Brina knew what the next question was before he asked. She could see it in his eyes. If the tables were turned and she was in his position, her next question would come as no surprise to him, either. Without even knowing what she'd done, she turned from them as though afraid her eyes would reveal the feelings she so desperately tried to hide, even from herself. For as much as she tried to accept the impossibility of returning homeward, the knowledge in itself was still a hard fact to swallow.

"Brina. Look at me, please."

The moment she turned to face Dillon he knew. Without a shadow of doubt, he knew what she was about to say even before she said it. At the same time, he thought how terrible it must have been to take on such a mission knowing there was not a chance of ever returning to those you knew and loved.

"No, Marshal. I cannot return. Not ever," Brina said that proudly with her head held high before him. Knowing it wasn't just because of the machine that brought her here only provided one-sided travel, but it was also the knowledge of her not wanting to live under the rules and regulations of Cyclops for the rest of her life either, that, if anything, forced her to come.

Dillon tried putting himself in her shoes as he considered all that they'd been told. Would he have done the same thing if the situation was similar? What would it have been like to know you were never to have the chance to see, love, or communicate with your family and those you loved ever again? Seeing what he thought to be sadness and other unidentifiable emotions in her eyes, he began to turn his feelings towards her, her story, and away from some of the suspicions held for her earlier, *truth be told*.

Brina knew there were still more questions to be asked and answered and yet understood most of what they wanted to hear would only confuse them more. The need to know was written all over their faces. To attempt to wipe them clean, she decided to jump in with both feet until the need to stop or at least to slow down was obvious.

"Let me try to explain a few things, boys. As you would travel across country on horseback, by stagecoach, or train, where I come from, we have three methods of transportation for different planes of travel. I will explain. One is called the Franciscan Lifter. That is a device that was created in the twenty-sixth century. It allows each component of the Protection League to skip across time, usually the Barriers, and to cross from one sector of the planet to another with or without detection, depending on the circumstances, in the blink of an eye. That's how Jesse made his escape. Through the *lifter*. When Cyclops realized what had happened, the upper echelon of the organization removed a critical part from the lifter, making it inoperable.

"Once they realize, through the historical references, that Jesse didn't resurface elsewhere, they will be assured the mission they sent me on was successful. You have to realize, where I'm from, Jesse had assassinated someone of great importance, then left.

"The rest of my tale and the explanation gets pretty wiggy from here, and if you don't want to hear it, I'll understand."

Wiggy? What in the hell was *wiggy*? It made little difference. Dillon got the picture.

"No, please continue." She was, however, driving Dillon crazy. One minute he was inclined to believe her story, yet the more she explained, he began to believe she had escaped from some mental hospital in the east. Glancing Cordell's way, Dillon found him totally fascinated with her once again, which didn't help one iota.

"For what I am going to say now, you *will* need to sit down." She waited until they were seated and comfortable.

"I will now continue. From the assassination comes the down-fall of Cyclops and eventually our world leadership. From there everything turns to crap, followed by the eventual destruction of everything on the planet. If Jesse continues to survive, the dastardly deed cannot be rectified. If he is killed, hopefully by the two of us, then what had originally brought me here never happens, and the world stays intact. Only because of his one fatal error can we fix this. You see, instead of escaping to the future where the assassination could not be rectified, he escaped into the past, where events can be changed in order to alter future events. That's where I fit in. If I can correct the error, Jesse and the assassination of this emissary will never have happened, and all will be as it should be. Unless of course someone else tries something just as stupid."

"Then what about you?" Dillon asked.

"We'll still be here, Wolf and I. We were sent through the Zodiac Field. That device is still in operation, but since it was an earlier model of the *lifter*, travelers could only depart on one-way tickets. Once the door is opened, someone steps through, and the door closes. I knew that when I was volunteered. And since the circumstances surrounding this period were unknown to all of us, I asked specifically for the Gray Wolf to accompany me.

"Another reason they sent me is because my ancestors came from this period. My roots are here. I am, in reality, returning home.

Remember what I said. We were given a one-way ticket to complete a mission that was sure to be difficult. If I'm killed before Jesse, then this trip was wasted, and all will be lost."

She had to be pulling their legs now. "I'm sorry. You'll have to do better than that. I don't for one second believe one word you've just said. You had me convinced for a while with that bit about honor and duty, but this other junk is bunk."

"You don't believe me, Dillon? You mean after all I've put you through and all the things I've done in front of your eyes, you still don't believe me? What about the color of my boots? Have you ever in your day seen blue boots?"

"Nope. You've got me there, but those crazy people in the east are always thinking up something new and different," he said.

"How about the way Wolf watches over us?"

"You raised him from a foal. That I'm sure of. It's like having a devoted dog. That's all." Dillon couldn't, nor wouldn't believe such a cockamamy story as that one.

"What about my story, do you think I made all that up too?"

"As a matter of fact, yeah."

"How many other question-and-answer periods do we have to go over before you'll begin to believe anything that has happened within the past two weeks?" He was driving her nuts. Yet she knew what would do the trick. "If that's the case, how do you explain this?" All the while she was throwing her questions, she had eye contact with him. But until now, she'd been just looking at him. Now she used his undivided attention against himself, by reaching towards his inner core with her eerie power to hold him once again against his will.

Cordell had sat closely watching the whole episode take place before his eyes; they sounded like spouses bickering over dinner plans. Then when he realized Dillon had halted all movement and voice, as it appeared Brina had him under some sort of control, he got to his feet, quietly pulling his pistol from its holster and tippy-toed his way towards her.

Brina immediately picked up the sound of Cordell's movements. Without breaking eye contact with the marshal, she raised her arm, level with her shoulder, held her palm out to him, and stated, "Stop where you are, Cordell. He's not being hurt. I'm just making a point. If you'll just sit back down, you'll see what I have in store for him."

Apparently her sudden and unexpected attention on him caught Cordell totally off guard. He stopped dead in his tracks. As she held the marshal, she listened for any further motion behind her. When nothing came, she continued with her plan by doing basically the same maneuver to the marshal what she'd done to that assassin in the chancellor's office, which seemed so very long ago.

Brina walked up to the marshal, with him still locked in place with her mind. Standing directly in front of him not only gave her a chance to look deeply into those beautiful hazel eyes, but also gave her a moment to decide which items on his person he'd notice the most if found missing or moved. His gun belt, hat, or maybe even his pants perchance? It had to be something that could be easily removed. She hadn't all the time in the world to play with these guys. Once her decision had been made, she followed through with her arrangements, then stepped back for a better look. Glancing towards Cordell for a note of approval, she was quite surprised to find a whimsical smile upon his face, followed by the nod she had hoped for. He was a strange one, this Cordell Chevalier; he had accepted her story and all that went with her, at face value. At least there was one she didn't have to try and convince.

On acceptance of her task, from the only one who believed her cockamamy story, the marshal was released.

Brina slowly came back into focus with Cordell standing next to her with a rather-large smile on his face. "What are you two smiling at?" Dillon asked.

That's when he felt something in his hands. He looked down in astonishment to find that his left hand was holding several little pebbles. The other held up a small bunch of wildflowers. How in the name of his great-aunt Fanny had she done that? His attention turned from the flowers towards the gray-eyed beauty not fifteen feet away, who innocently stood next to his friend. They were both smiling. Brina had made her point, but what about Cordell's shit-eating grin?

When their eyes met once again, Dillon was able to discern within them a laughing quality, which switched from silence to sound in the blink of their eyes.

Once the belief could be read on the marshal's face, Brina began to giggle uncontrollably.

"How in the hell did you do that?" He stopped for a moment while recalling something of a similar nature happening at an earlier time in her company. Now, there was no question. Something was going on here that was totally unexplainable from anything he had ever read, learned, witnessed, or known. She had done it. The things she'd accomplished during the time in their embrace was most definitely not of this time or place. She was not from around here, and even though she had proved her point, and Dillon did somehow believe her, it was still so unbelievable that believing her was difficult.

"I can't explain it," she began. "It's just a special talent I've had since I was a small child. And according to those of my time, I'm the only one they've ever encountered who has the ability to carry out what you've just experienced. Do you now believe and understand some of my story?"

Thinking about it, yes. He now understood the importance of her being here, and with those special talents of hers experienced, he hoped they could do this together. And the more he thought about it, the more he realized, from that moment on, they would join forces with this totally unusual, mysterious, and beautiful young woman. She had become an asset worth the cost. Not just because of what had just transpired, not for the reasons why she needed their help, not for the fact that she searched for them—*wait just a minute.*

"Brina, you said the other day that you were searching for someone you'd never met. Your previous information tells us why. Would you like to explain how you knew of us?" Dillon felt it wasn't an unreasonable question.

"At the Academy where I was initially raised and instructed, one of the many fields in which I was taught was of our/your Western period. Probably because like I mentioned before, my roots are here. I believe, for each student who is under instruction there at the Academy, there is a period or three of history, in which he/she is more than familiar with. Their reasoning? Well, I always figured it had something to do with the ancestral connection.

"Then after the discovery of Jesse and the assassination, my trainers instilled in me more detailed information pertaining to the two of you and a few others. With such information, I felt my approaching you wouldn't be too awfully difficult. Instead, you stumbled upon us in the clearing. The clearing, gentlemen, was my point of arrival. So, as you can see, it was just dumb luck you found me. You have to remember, Marshal, I had your name, a basic description, and knew you traveled with a Frenchman. It was just a matter of pulling the background information out of you to verify it."

Brina stopped short, with a strange look on her cream-colored face.

XI

visitation rights

There she stood, rock-solid still. Dillon turned towards his friend and found him in fairly the same state. What the hell was going on? But before he could open his mouth to ask, she had abruptly raised her hand up, palm towards him as though to hush.

Cordell had fallen head over heels in love with this woman from the very moment he laid eyes on her just like Captain Jacques had from years gone by. And because of that, he wanted so desperately to believe her stories. He understood how Dillon felt in regard to her strange tales, but Cordell wasn't as hard to convince. The mysteriousness of both the woman and the horse surprised and amazed him, yet they were no more strange, and wondrous than the many things he'd seen during his travels across the territories. And to him it hadn't been the big shock that Dillon seemed to believe it to be.

Since their meeting with this unusual and beautiful woman, Cordell hadn't missed a single beat. He watched her constantly, not only for her continual surprises, but her beauty, charm, and her facial expressions as well. Everything she did intensified his feelings towards her. In doing so, it gave him the advantage of interpreting various movements of hers as signals vital to certain situations they'd encountered. Years ago, he had discovered that in order to acquire anything of value, one must stop, look, and listen to what's going on around you. Which was exactly how he had picked up instantly on her awareness, of her sensing something somewhere off in the distance. The moment before she had raised her hand towards Dillon to stop, Cordell had already froze.

The moment she raised her hand, Dillon looked towards Wolf. He didn't know why he did that, but there the great beast was, standing alert and at attention, with his head up and ears directed northward. Brina was also searching the northward horizon. Dillon immediately hushed, halting all further questions, and directed his line of sight with that of theirs. What was he waiting for? He didn't know. He did know, however, that all night noises had stopped. Even the crickets were silent. All that could be heard was the sound of the fire crackling and the beating of his heart. Turning back towards Brina, he watched as she turned silently towards Cordell.

"Quietly. As silently as you possibly can, get up and find a place to hide over there, by those trees would be preferable. Once you're there, don't speak, don't breathe, and most importantly don't move. No matter what you see or hear, anywhere, right here especially, do not utter a sound. Do you understand me?" she whispered this with deadly assurance.

He turned to Dillon with a questioning look on his face, and in turn, Dillon nodded in agreement. Whatever was to happen, it was obvious—she wanted him hidden and out of sight. With what they had recently learned of her, Dillon wasn't going to ignore anymore warnings from either of them.

Brina knew something was up when she heard a branch snap far off in the distance. She knew it was an animal, but not one indigenous to the region and the All Mother's plan. Someone or some ones were out there. Wolf reaffirmed her suspicions with a mental connection.

"Cordell, there's no time to waste. Go. Go now!" It was an urgent whisper. And just as she'd hoped, he got up, and as silent as a mouse, hurried over to the stand of trees finding his hiding place among them.

It was then she turned back to Dillon, and again, he felt her assault his mind. Only this time, instead of being blind and immobile, he felt a pressure deep within his skull, then came the voice inside his head.

"Wolf says three riders approach. Danger rides
with them, and to hide Cordell."

Shit! She blew it now, although it was now way tooooo late to fix the error. And by the look on the marshal's face, he was just as shocked as she. Regaining her composure instantly, she smiled at him with her gray eyes as she whispered aloud, "I told you I wasn't from around here."

Dillon jumped suddenly, the sound of her voice startling him. This was really turning into some experience.

"Dillon." This was the very first time she used his given name. She needed his undivided attention, and the personal touch usually worked on nonmilitary personnel. "Please, pass the whiskey. I need a drink."

She needed a drink? *He* needed the drink! But just as he began to unscrew the lid of the flask for her and a goodly sized one for himself, he heard the sound of horses approaching, followed by voices.

"Hey! Is anyone there? Anyone at the camp? If you are, please don't shoot. We're just passing by when we smelled your coffee," one of them said.

Dillon was so absorbed with the voice and the thought of a stranger entering their camp, he missed seeing Brina head towards Wolf. What he did eventually see was her pulling out from her scabbard, which hung from her saddle, her rifle, then return. He watched her sit by the fire with it across her lap. She was ready for whatever was to happen.

"Come ahead!" Dillon hollered. Just before they reached their camp, he watched her stand and position herself cautiously and skillfully between the unknowns and where Cordell lay hidden.

"Sorry to bother you, folks, but we'd been riding all day. Your coffee sure smells mighty good. Would you mind terribly if we joined you?" The question was asked by the first one entering the light of their campfire.

There were two coming in, instead of three Wolf warned about. Then Dillon saw the third slowly sneak in behind them. He stayed mainly in the shadows, probably to avoid recognition. Three of them there were, nonetheless. Whoever they were, it would have been unwise to act suspiciously in order to avoid suspicion. Cheerfully, yet with great wariness, Brina invited them in.

"By all means, gentlemen, have a seat and warm yourselves by the fire. I'll fetch you each a cup." Giving Dillon a warning glance as she set her rifle down near the fire after finding a couple of cups and began pouring the coffee, she inquired, "How many of you are there? I need to know so that I can prepare enough for all to eat." She felt this type of approach might be wiser than just shooting them outright.

While she chatted away, Dillon watched them. The one who was doing all the talking was tall and real mean looking with a long stringy black mane and a full face of hair. His frame was lanky and appeared to be about six feet tall. The second of the two was similar in description but shorter with dark-brown hair. The third was kinda hard to see, as he remained hidden in the shadows, but from what Dillon could make out, he was maybe tall like the first but without all the hair on his face. All of them wore sidearms. Dillon could tell, even though Brina appeared to be ignoring them, she was alert and ready for anything. What did these motley-looking *gentlemen* have on their minds?

"Sorry, ma'am, I think we'll pass this time round. I gotta question for ya though, if ya don't mind me asking."

Brina just stood her ground saying nothing.

"Have ya seen a tall, dark-skinned bugger with long curly hair around these here parts?" asked the one.

Wolf was right. They were searching for Cordell, or at least someone who matched his general description. Falsely pondering, Brina took a moment then looked directly into the one man's eyes and responded with sincere honesty (*haha*), "No, I'm sorry, I haven't. Are you sure you won't join us?" Brina lied; she wanted them out of her face and now.

"Nope, sorry. We've other things that need doing. Thanks for the coffee though; it was very good," said that same one, then picked up his reins, mounted, and rode off without another word.

A short time later, after the coast seemed clear, Brina asked Dillon to fetch Cordell from the trees. By the time they returned to camp, Cordell had an explanation for both of them.

"Well, from what I could gather, them boys were the ones that rode with me that fateful day all them years ago when Dillon caught me in the snow. And by the way, it shore was a good thing that you sent me a hiding in them trees. I want to thank you for that. They must have gotten out of jail and figured me an expendable liability. I could have been in big trouble if you hadn't done somethin'." Cordell was all over himself with gratitude and had forgotten all about how Brina had possibly known.

"Hey, that's what friends are for. Isn't it? Remember the duty and honor stuff we talked about the other day? This is part of it. Friends, comrades in arms, and the likes—that's what we are, or if not now, we will be." She was remembering the void and those who didn't make it home, as well as those who did, and why.

With the little things they had already been through and the information they had exchanged, there could be no other explanation. Friends they were to the bitter end. They all sensed it, felt it, within their hearts and souls. It was a strange feeling, strange yet comforting. Neither Cordell nor Dillon had ever had a woman as just a friend, or comrade before, and both were beginning to cherish her company. Actually, *strange* wasn't the word for it, but because of what they had learned, what she'd done to Dillon earlier, and what she had now done for Cordell, it could be no other way.

"I think some extra security measures oughta be considered tonight, what with our little uninvited company this evening. Whatcha think, boys?" asked Brina.

"You might have something there. Them fellers were real friendly and the likes, but it was a bit too coincidental if you ask me."

With that said, they drew straws for the first watch. Brina got the shortest one of the three, which meant she was to take the first watch—and later, after all that had happened, Dillon kinda wondered whether or not she'd planned it that way.

At first Brina thought about strapping on her Colts, but thought better of it; instead, she left them on her pillow. Finding the Henry under her bedroll where she placed it after those creeps left, she picked it back up, checked the magazine making sure it was fully loaded, then headed over to Wolf, and slipped into her saddlebags an extra box of cartridges. Mounting her trusty steed, she waved to the men in her charge, then left to begin her rounds.

Dillon opened his eyes come morning and realized that Brina hadn't awakened him for the midnight watch. He knew then that something was wrong, terribly wrong. Neither she nor the horse were anywhere in sight. Since Cordell was a better tracker than himself, he sent him out to look.

He was gone longer than Dillon felt necessary, and he began to wonder if Cordell had traveled all the way back to Frisco to find her, or if something had happened. Dillon was getting worried. It was a silly idea—really, but he did finally return 'bout two hours later with no news. They say no news is good news, but in this case, Dillon didn't think that fit. What the hell could've happened? Why were there no tracks? Why no trace? Who had intervened? He had to take deep breaths to calm his anxiety.

"Did you go out far enough?"

"Don't you think I'm trying? I'm just as worried about them as you are." Cordell was beside himself. The only love in his life, gone.

"You may have missed something. Did you think of that?" They had just gotten used to her, and now they'd lost her. Dillon didn't like that one bit.

"I went out far enough, damn it! There was no sign of her or that blasted horse." He had gone out as far as he thought he should. "Let's pack it all up and take another good long look all around the area. There has to be some sort of trail to follow."

They did. As a matter of fact, they searched all morning till they finally found three sets of tracks they assumed were left by their visitors the night before. But there were only three, and Dillon had expected four sets. Had they been mistaken in their assumptions? Could those men truly have been searching for a man of Cordell's description, and in not hearing any word of him, moved on? Somehow, he didn't think so, especially when Cordell had recognized them from years gone by. That left only one question unanswered: where was Brina?

They searched another two hours, both in different directions. Suddenly there was a single rifle shot. That was a signal from

Cordell. He had found something. Dillon hightailed it to his side. As he approached, Cordell was frantically waving him to a spot on the trail that appeared to disappear into nowhere.

"Dillon, come quickly! I've found the extra set of tracks." He had followed the tracks left by the three riders to an area where they'd split up. Two had double-backed, and the third rode northward.

Dillon spurred Cody till he was in a full gallop then pulled him to a sliding stop just short of Cordell. Jumping down from the saddle, he quickly stepped over to where Cordell was kneeling, examining his find. "What is it? Have you found her?"

"Yep, I think so. Looky here." Cordell pointed to the ground. "While you were off thatta way searching for a single set of tracks, I followed our guests' tracks till I located a place where they'd split up. Then I followed two of them back towards camp. About halfway out, they stopped for a smoke, I even found the rolled cigarette butts, then turned west till they again stopped behind a large rock that'd be a perfect place to hide. There, they picked up a third rider. I followed those tracks to here, where they met up with the fourth. It's her all right, I'm sure. Looky here, the tracks lead off down this trail and into that little valley there, see? The one with the river running through it. Either that, or it's four other riders out on a moonlight ride." Cordell knowingly glanced first at the valley below, then at Dillon. The mirrored look he received confirmed his beliefs.

Moonlight ride? The hell it was. Dillon had been right. Something had happened last night. Brina was right, too. They had been checking out their campsite hoping to find something of value. They found it, her. Thoughts of things unheard of came crashing into his thoughts. Dillon had heard of horrible things that outlaws and lowlifes did to unsuspecting women—and they were not pretty. Brina had special talents, but against three men? He was getting frantic. They both knew finding her intact and sane was slim, but finding her was of utmost importance, regardless.

Back at camp, they spied her bedroll. There on her pillow lay her Colts—damn. And as Dillon picked them up, preparing to tuck them safely away with the rest of her belongings, he noticed some sort of engraving on one of the grips. It read, *Brina, if you need me, I'm here for you always. MJ.*

MJ? Who was MJ? Dillon figured should she come out of this alive, maybe he'd ask her.

Once they had all their belongings with them, it took only a kick in the ribs to get Cody to follow Cordell and his horse down the treacherous downhill grade. With each careful step Cody took, Dillon felt and heard the shifting and rolling of the various rocks under-foot. The trail itself held its own dangers and kept them alert every step of the way because if anyone was lax at any time it promised to send the unsuspecting traveler over the edge and down the preci-pice. As the trail continued to lead them on its downhill journey, the ever-changing switchbacks and narrow and unstable ground surface led them to believe this was mainly a game trail and not for those with unsure mounts. The farther down the steep grade they headed, the farther and farther back in the saddle they leaned in order to give their mounts the balance they needed to ensure each step taken was solid and sure. Down and down they headed till Dillon was beginning to think they were riding towards hell itself. Finally, after that last turn in the trail, he felt Cody level out and was jolted into an upright position, which only meant one thing: they had finally reached the valley floor.

The moment the trail opened into a sparse meadow, both dis-mounted to readjust their equipment and to check animals. It's one thing to climb uphill with a horse fully rigged, with back cinch and breast collar to help keep the saddle in place. It's another thing alto-gether to be descending such a steep grade as they had and not hav-ing a rear britchen attached to keep the saddle from sliding forward, as it was in their case, because after dismounting, they found the saddles had ridden halfway up, or down depending on your point of view, the animal's necks.

As Dillon turned to view from the downward angle of the trail they just left, he knew then and there, another way out of this valley had to be found, because after observing the trail upward, he was not, under any circumstances, scaling that death-defying precipice again, for any reason.

From there the tracks led in a northeasterly direction, right up the valley floor and onward. And as luck would have it, it ran towards the river that ran through it. With equipment properly adjusted, they remounted, heading in the general direction of the river viewed just before they began their descent down the trail. It was a very pretty valley, and if they weren't in such a hurry to find Brina, it would have made a very enjoyable ride. Upon reaching an area where the edge of the clearing met up with the edge of the tree line, they dismounted and set up camp for the night. Traveling at night was a consideration, but under the circumstances the trail would be hard to follow, and they needed all the rest and sunlight possible. The next day was going to be a long hard ride.

After a quick breakfast of jerky and a sip or two of water, they started out in search of the tracks. Dillon asked Cordell once again to take up the lead as he was much better at spotting signs left on the trail. They were about two hours out when Cordell, without warning, slowed from a gallop to a walk, while mumbling something Dillon couldn't hear clearly or understand.

"Dillon." Something suddenly occurred to Cordell that he just had to mention to his friend.

"Yeah?"

"You don't suppose that Brina sacrificed herself, do you?"

Dillon considered his words for just a moment. "Nope. Not with this mission she keeps talking about. Why?"

"Because I can't find a single sign of a struggle. And then what about all that talk about honor, duty and courage. Do you suppose she's using this as a way to prove herself?"

"Naw. You saw how fast...no. No, you didn't see how fast she'd drawn that gun on the snake. Faster than anything I'd ever seen. No. I think she's already proved herself, if not to us, to someone else already."

"What can we do?"

"Stay on the trail. We'll catch up with them eventually."

"But what about *her*?"

Dillon didn't want to think about the possibilities.

XII

a cold day spent in hell

When Brina came out of it, she played the same game; she kept her eyes closed. All of her senses had been put on hold and had been replaced with the world's worst headache lodged unceremoniously between her eyes and at the base of her skull. During each throbbing sensation normally accompanying such ailments came a subtle feeling of not being in familiar territory. For one thing, the surface upon which she lay was not that of dirt but of a hard, unyielding material. The odor that permeated the air around her was that of old and rotting wood. Those two details were self-explanatory. No longer was she in the company of her friends but among strangers, and as she feared, probably those from the night before.

As she lay there thinking of what to do, she remembered one of the very first lessons instilled in her by Dr. Jarlath back at the Academy: If you're presumed unconscious, act that way. Stay calm, keep your breathing slow, eyelids shut, and above all, do not change positions. Unless, of course, their actions towards you dictate it. Therefore, she didn't move. Instead, she tried to evaluate her situation by using the ears and senses the All Mother gave her, rather than giving away her condition to her possible adversary who could, at this very moment, be sitting silently, nearby, waiting for any sign of her waking.

While assuming this unconscious state, Brina allowed herself one simple question. What had happened out there on the trail, and how long had she been here? In reality, those were two distinct questions—oh well, that really didn't matter now. What mattered other than immediate escape was the location of Wolf. For

131

without him, she was doomed in more ways than one. Surely, they would've brought him along and tied him up somewhere. A horse of his caliber was worth a king's ransom. Because whoever had planned this little escapade was more than likely after bounty in one form or another.

The second most important consideration tugged at her conscious mind. What the hell had happened?? How had they managed to get to her without either of them knowing it was coming? Of course, dwelling on that issue could take up more time than she had available. Tucking that away for later consideration, she stopped and wondered whether or not someone *was* watching her. After acutely listening for any sound that'd suggest otherwise, she finally concluded alone she was. Then she tried moving her limbs. She was not surprised to find both hands and feet securely bound. To her advantage, some moron had tied her hands in front of her, instead of behind her back. Her break had come in the form of an idiot.

There's a fool born every minute was one of her mother's favorite phrases she always managed to remember at choice moments. Those and Dr. Jarlath's Colts always gave her the feeling of never being totally alone. And considering the circumstances, she felt the phrase fit the bill.

Once she took inventory, finding herself still in one piece, she opened her eyes to survey her surroundings, get her bearings, and to untie her feet. Not necessarily in that order. With her feet untied *(thanks to that moron)*, Brina was now able to stand, stretch her legs, and as much as the ropes allowed, loosen and stretch her upper body, in preparation for the workout she was sure would come.

Standing in the center of the room surveying each and every corner, Brina found her prison to be approximately 12' x 16' with a fireplace for warmth; a window to open when it got too warm inside because of the fireplace; a table to set dishes, elbows, and books on, which she assumed were never thought of; and a chair to place one's backside upon, while eating the meal placed in the dishes that set upon the table, which was strategically placed in direct line with the door she assumed they brought her through. Because being tossed into a small room by way of a door was most definitely better than being tossed down the chimney, like the gifts in all those ancient Santa Claus tales told late at night during the silly season to small children.

It couldn't be all that bad. At least she hadn't lost her sense of humor. Advantage number one.

With her hands still tied, yet the rest of her loosened up and sorta ready, the next order of business was to try the door. Finding it locked came as little surprise and suggested there was definitely more than one captor on her hit parade, other than the one fool already presumed. With her ear pressed firmly against the door, Brina listened intently for any sounds giving her an idea of what was what so that she could devise a plan for their escape.

Somewhere, on the other side of the door, were heard sounds consisting of the clanking of pots and an unmistakable voice or two. At first, it just sounded as though it could've been one or maybe two, but the longer she strained against the wood, the more she believed it was three. The three *gentlemen* from the other night.

Could it have been just a ploy to achieve a look-see of their camp? Brina believed there was more going on here than met the eye. Why would they kidnap her of all people? She stopped suddenly, realizing what they just might have in store for her. But wait just a darn minute, from the gist of her earlier encounter with them, she assumed they were looking for Cordell, or at least someone of his description.

"Why did they take me?" she asked herself.

"Why not?" she answered herself.

Never before had she considered it, but maybe *she* was the prize. So, not wanting to go there, she refocused back to the problem at hand—meaning, the sooner she found Wolf and made their departure, the safer she'd feel.

With her mind whirling in all directions, she failed to hear the distinguishing sounds of one if not two pairs of boots step up to, then stop on the threshold of her prison.

Lucifer Carstead was somewhere in his late twenties and because of his heritage, of which he was never quite sure of or cared about, had long, stringy, black hair that hung past his shoulders, as well as a beard that almost entirely covered his face. Even though he was abnormally tall, he'd been at one time a likable child and well thought of by his brothers, sisters, and friends. Only after befriending a bad bunch of kids new in the neighborhood did he ever do anything wrong. He couldn't understand at the age of sixteen why Mr. Bloomgarden, who just happened to own the general store and whose daughter, Betsy, was the only girl in town who would speak to him, kept accusing Lucifer of thievery in the worst way. They kept saying something about him stealing Betsy's virginity, but unfortunately, he had no idea what they'd meant. It was only after the bitch slapped him, did he decide to teach her a lesson. Calling to his friends so they all could watch, Lucifer pulled out his knife from its leather sheath attached to his belt, the one his father had made him for doing so well in school and proceeded to slit her from stem to stern.

As Betsy lay there in the grass, feeling weaker and weaker as her life's blood drained from her body to permeate the ground around her, she cursed Lucifer for his acts of betrayal, thievery, and above all, her demise. Then with a venomous promise of retaliation against him and those he rode with, even if she had to accomplish it from beyond the grave, she died.

Lucifer watched Betsy's face as her life slipped closer to its end. And just before her eyes glassed over, he burned her curse and her memory to his own. With the help of his best friend, Rene-with-a-hyphen, they packed the few things they owned and left town, leaving poor, unfortunate Betsy dead in a pool of her own blood.

Rene-with-a-hyphen Quinlan had always, as a small child and a young adult, been kidded profusely about his four-foot-eleven-inch height and the strangeness of his name. His mother had originally wanted to call him Rene-with-an-accent, but his father had the last word in their unorthodox home, and Rene-with-a-hyphen it remained. Because of all the continual kidding since moving to that one little town, Rene became quite shy, insecure, and frightened around all the other children. That was until he was befriended by

Lucifer Carstead, and over time, learned how to turn his feelings from sadness and despair to anger, to rage, and eventually to murder.

Last, but not least was John Deau. John was different than the others. He didn't take out his frustrations on other people; instead, he shared his vast experience and knowledge with the unsuspecting by pulling them into his web of deceit and mayhem. Several years ago, John had the pleasure of meeting up with a young man just boarding the stage in Saint Louise. There they became traveling companions on the long journey west. When the stage arrived in Denver, the two of them were greeted by Lucifer and Rene. That was when the three of the most wanted men in the Rockies became four.

During a holdup in the town of Brokenshire Fields located somewhere along the Platt River, their fourth man was shot and killed. It was again John's job to find another accomplice. Riding into the one-horse town of Lagerville, in the province of Kansas, John stopped at the livery stable to put his horse up for the night. As he stood at the opening of the barn waiting for someone to take his mount, John spotted a shadowy movement just inside the door of someone shoveling horse manure. He could still remember the look on the kid's face when John promised wealth beyond his wildest dreams if he'd meet John in the morning here at the livery, all cleaned up and ready to ride.

John was sure this time he had found the perfect man for the job. Chevalier was a big fella who, he was sure, could defend himself against all odds and would prove a valuable asset to their gang. If it hadn't been for that damn marshal in the town of Eastern-Western in the heart of the Sector 4, they would have gotten clean away. Six months later, they were arrested for robbery and thrown in prison. Lucifer and Rene were sure it was because of that French bastard. John knew different. However, knowing those two as he had over the years, he knew there was no point in arguing, so if they just happened to run across Chevalier in their travels, he was positive either Lucifer or Rene would take care of things proper.

Lucifer was in the lead followed by Rene, with John Deau bringing up the rear as they stepped up to the one room shack that held the unsuspecting woman. As Lucifer reached the door, he stopped suddenly. Because the others were so close behind and weren't paying too much attention, they slammed into each other like dominos.

"What the...where do you think you two are going!" Lucifer hadn't realized they were right behind him as he headed for the door.

"Well, we thought—" Poor Rene. He hadn't realized he was that close, but neither did he think Lucifer would stop so suddenly as to cause him to unceremoniously be met nose to shoulder with his friend.

"You thought what!" Lucifer loomed over him shouting.

Rene stood his ground; then when the sense the All Mother gave him kicked in, he swallowed his pride, turned back towards John, and shoved him unmercifully out of his way. "Come on, apparently Lucifer doesn't want witnesses." With one glance back towards Lucifer, Rene shrugged his shoulders, making sure John was with him, while heading back to their campsite to wait.

After his friends left, Lucifer paused for several moments on the doorstep before entering. He had been the one who did all the talking the other night at their campsite. And while there noticed for a brief moment while she was fixing them all a cup of coffee that very same look *Betsy* used to give him just before he'd take her. A sweet smile it was. *Damn, how he missed his Betsy.* Her sweet and gentle touch, so sweet it made his mouth water as he imagined how it would feel to have her beneath him once again. Just thinking about it again here and now ignited his imagination. He felt his member begin to enlarge, then to eventually throb as it began straining frantically against the tensed fabric of his jeans. His deviate dreams intensified. His heart started racing, and at first, he unceremoniously clutched at himself; then when the desired sensations were not fully achieved, he unconsciously shoved his hands down into his front pockets and began massaging himself while his hips uncontrollably began to thrust with and against the desired sensations, which finally began to surface.

As his impending release appeared imminent, his mind left him in a state of ecstasy. During which he lost all sense of where he was and mistook the door of the shack for the wall—putting all his weight against it while he lavished in erotic pleasure. Well, the lock broke, the door flew open, and down he crashed in a heap on the floor as a surprised Brina looked up.

First, Brina heard a loud commotion outside her door; then things got quiet again. Curiosity being one of her many qualities, she got up from her chair and walked towards the door. Standing there, she could hear something, but for the life of her couldn't quite make it out. First, it sounded like someone hyperventilating, then progressed to the sound of someone moaning or whimpering. Pressing her ear closer to the door, she felt a subtle pressure, which told her to get out of the way. It happened faster than she expected. In the next few seconds, Brina was able to ascertain the snapping of the lock, followed by the sudden opening of the door, and an accelerated descent of whoever was now on the floor in front of her.

"*Betsy*," was all Lucifer could say as he looked up at the woman in the room.

"You'll have to excuse me, but I am *not* Betsy," retorted Brina.

The abrupt landing on the floor brought Lucifer back to reality. It also interrupted his concentration and satisfaction. "Bitch!" Pulling his hands from his front pants pockets, Lucifer came up off the floor with his right fist already swinging towards the woman in front of him.

Brina now knew what the sounds on the opposite side of the door had meant. In that same instant, she knew if she hadn't thought before of stepping aside, she'd better do it now.

It happened almost as though in slow motion. As this man lifted his body up off the floor, Brina spotted his right arm had extended outward, and as it gained in momentum, it headed her way with a fist firmly attached to its end.

Just as abruptly as Lucifer crashed through the door, landing in a heap on the floor, Rene rushed back up the steps to the shack. At the sight of his friend getting up from the floor with his intentions obviously clear, he slammed himself into Lucifer, catching him off guard, which in turn caused him to miss the woman by three feet.

"Lucifer, NO! What if the Reaper came back? What do you suppose he'd do to us? He wants her untouched!" Rene-with-a-hyphen didn't wait another second. Using the hefty tree branch he'd brought just in case, he struck Lucifer a sideways blow. Once on the floor, he grabbed him by the back of his shirt, dragging him out into the open air. He then turned back to the shack and peeked in through the door at the woman. "Best be careful, my beauty. Lucifer here is not too bright sometimes, but also is not the sort to be upsetting."

"What about you?" asked Brina, as if she didn't know better.

"Me? Well, since the Reaper wants you for himself, I'm pretty much out of luck, but I will warn ya, my thoughts on the matter aren't much kinder than Lucifer's." He stepped back outside, closed the door, then added, "By the way, sweetie, don't you be a thinkin' 'bout escaping through this here door just because the lock's now broke. We'll be keeping a pretty close watch out fer ya, and if you do manage to sneak out, what you'll find at the end of all your dreams is something out of your worst nightmares." He left, dragging poor Lucifer behind him.

Brina hadn't believed how horribly atrocious men could be. Oh, she'd had to contend with assholes before, but never on this level. Most of the close encounters she'd had to contend with in the past had usually been things from the void, but as a team player they'd overcome all odds. And before leaving on this mission, she'd been briefed on the period and its not-so-nice characters, but in no way was she prepared for this kind of mentality. It was decided that in the next opportunity for escape, no matter how slim or dangerous it looked, she'd chance it, and from the sound of things, it had better be soon. Not knowing when they'd be back or how many would come, she quickly retrieved her knife concealed from inside her boot to cut the ropes that bound, then returned it to its hiding place. With the leftover rope, she loosely draped it over her wrists, hoping to dupe her captors into believing she was still securely tied.

Lucifer woke later that afternoon with a knot on the back of his head the size of an egg along with total recall of what'd happened. Extracting his knife from its sheath, he gingerly picked himself up off the ground, turned, then went in search for his so-called friend. With each and every step he took, he received a stabbing pain in his head. This brought him back to that woman in the shack who so reminded him of his beloved *Betsy*. *Betsy*. Just the thought of her drove him insane. The last time he'd seen her, *Betsy* had promised to take care of him till the day he died, as he had taken care of her.

How he had missed her, and if anything was to happen before the Grim Reaper arrived, who would be the wiser? Surely Rene would keep quiet on such events, especially if he didn't mark her up *too badly*. Oh, to have her hunger for his touch again. That would make everything worth his while. Maybe, even after several turns with her, he'd encourage Rene to fulfill his fantasies too, and then they'd take her at the same time. After all, *Betsy* was equipped for such encounters. Then the Reaper could do with her as he wished. Forgetting his first intentions, Lucifer decided instead to find his friend and discuss his new plan.

If something didn't happen soon, Brina was going to lose her mind with worry. Not so much for herself, but what if Dillon and Cordell had figured out what had happened and were trying to find her? That would place them at risk, running into this bad bunch out in the open. But where would they look? She was in no condition last night to leave breadcrumbs for them to follow, so it was all up to her. Hearing a sound similar to that of boots stepping up to the door reminded her that her chance had come at last, and to pull this off successfully she'd have to hit first and hit hard. So, she planted her fanny firmly back in the chair with her feet ready, her wrists crossed—as if still tied—and faced the door, looking the innocent and unsuspecting.

The door opened, and in stepped Lucifer. She intently watched him and his knife. Then she spotted the second one behind him. She didn't like the look on their faces, and whatever they wanted or planned on doing she knew she wouldn't like either. But it didn't matter, because she wasn't planning on sticking around anyway.

Lucifer turned back to his friend for just a moment. "Rene, if you don't mind waiting outside, I'd like to have a moment alone with this young lady, before—"

Rene-with-a-hyphen just stood there with his mouth hanging open in anticipation. He didn't want to leave; he had come to watch.

It wasn't what he said, but how he said it that made her skin crawl. In a sort of misguided defiance, she mistakenly blurted out with a chuckle in between, "I'm sorry, gentlemen, was there something you missed last night that you wanted to ask me in private?" She knew this was dangerous, but for some reason, it came out of her mouth before she even knew what she had said. For that she received a formidable slap across the jaw, knocking her off her chair. All in all, she'd managed to keep her wrists together despite the fall.

"Shut up, slut!" Lucifer shouted. He turned suddenly to Rene, and in that same tone of voice, shouted, "GET OUT!" As the door slammed shut behind him, he turned to her and revoltingly introduced himself. "We were not properly introduced last night. Just for the record, I'm Lucifer Carstead, the devil himself, and I'm here for your ass."

Brina thought she was going to be sick. He was so revolting. She could barely contain herself.

"Do you need me for anything, *Betsy*? You do remember me, don't you, sweetie?" Lucifer was having a difficult time distinguishing who this woman really was. They looked so much alike, this woman and his *Betsy*. Had his beloved returned from the grave, or was this someone masquerading as her, or perchance was this someone who just remarkably looked like her? He couldn't grasp much of anything let alone who this really was. The only thing he was sure of was if he did disfigure her, the Grim Reaper would disembowel him, and that was just for starters. "Betsy, you have no idea how lucky you are that I am here to protect you," he said as drool dripped from his lips.

Betsy? What was this Betsy stuff? Who was this Betsy? Although curious, Brina wasn't about to ask. The look in his eyes and the drool spitting from his lips were both something out of a Stephanie Kingford novel she had the misfortune of reading in one of her earlier classes. Then there was this Reaper fella. *What a refreshing name*, she thought. She was just about to open her mouth and insert her foot when she remembered that not-so-old Chinese proverb, *better to keep mouth shut than to lose all teeth.* She was right, she hadn't lost her humor, but she was getting awful close in losing either her temper, her mind, or other precious commodities—she was sure. So, she just smiled up at the creep, while feigning difficulty in getting up off the floor and back into the chair.

"Let me tell you something, Betsy. You depend on us for everything now. You're lucky you're even alive. My partner, the Grim Reaper, wants you for himself. If it was up to me, I'd get your recipe for coffee then let nature take its course."

Then he smiled at her with a smile worth a thousand trips to the bathroom. Not only was he one of the most hideous-looking men she had ever laid eyes on, but he was also missing most of his teeth, and his breath was poisonous.

"But since he won't get here for a few days, I don't see why I can't take advantage of this here situation." He lunged at her.

She was on her feet in no time. He was just as fast. He may look the creep that he was, but he definitely had his wits about him, especially when he thought there was easy prey at hand, or at least what he thought was easy prey. She, on the other hand, had dropped the rope from her wrists, and as he lunged, grabbed hold of his hair pulling him towards her. In the same instant her knee found its target right between his legs. It was obvious he had not built up a resistance to this sensation before, as he crumpled to the floor. She would have thought that most of the women that he had come to know had at least made their feelings known by this line of communication, but apparently not.

Brina dashed to the door. Grabbing the latch, she flung it wide and was met face-to-face with Rene-with-a-hyphen. And before she had a chance to catch herself, she spoke aloud. "Where am I? At the opposite end of the spectrum at the Mr. Universe Beauty Contest?"

While he stood there with this stupid look on that horrible face trying to figure out what she had said, Brina took advantage of his confusion and also presented him with the same little something to think about. *Two down and one to go.* Unfortunately, she knew they would soon recover and be hot on her tail. Thank heavens, the third one was elsewhere. Brina hoped he was unaware of her escape and was preoccupied with something else. If that were the case, she just might have a chance. And believe it or not, that was the case. In her favor, not twenty feet away tied to a tree, was Wolf.

Racing as fast as possible, Brina ran to his side, untied the reins, swung into the saddle, and in a blur, they were off at a dead run. She couldn't believe her luck. Something was amiss. It couldn't have been this easy. One thing for sure, if she made it out of here alive, after those choice gifts she presented, her next encounter with these guys was going to be a very unpleasant one.

XIII

a sight for sore eyes

No sooner were they out of sight and sound from that gawd-awful bunch did Brina find a spot along the trail she thought was safe enough to slow, stop, and finally dismount.

"Wait here." Brina rushed over to the nearest thicket and vomited anything and everything she'd been trying to keep down since that last encounter with Lucifer. Wiping her mouth with the back of her sleeve, she returned to Wolf's side, grabbed her flask of whiskey from her saddlebags, opened the cap, and took a small yet adequate mouthful, swished it around, then spit it out.

"Have you ever…? Yyyeeeeeeyyyuck!" Those guys gave her the willies. Just thinking about Lucifer brought goose bumps to her flesh.

She wiped her mouth on her sleeve again then took two more good swigs. These, she held in her mouth, then swallowed, slowly relishing the whiskey's aged flavor. "Better." Recapping the flask and tucking it safely away in her saddlebags, Brina looked towards the heavens to find the Big Dipper, which led to the North Star. With her bearings established, she turned Wolf southward in hopes that her friends were somewhere out there looking for her.

"All right, my Gray Wolf," she began, then used the palms of her hands and fingernails to scratch and caress both sides of his neck, "if anybody knows where Cordell and Dillon are, you're the one. Let's go find them."

Off they rode into the wild dark blue yonder.

Riding Wolf at a full gallop had always been thrilling to her. The pounding of his hooves, his mane blowing back into in her face, his ears pinned flat back against his poll, the blurring of the scenery around her as he made his way across the territory as fast as he could was exhilarating. He always put everything he had into whatever he was doing, so long as it was for her. He covered so much ground it was almost as though he virtually *flew*. She knew it was because of what he really was that he was able to do this, and for this she was grateful.

The two of them were destined to be together, for always. Their souls were of one body. That was why she put in the special request asking for his help on this one-way mission. She needed him as much as he needed her. The special bond they shared would see them through the difficult times as well as all the others.

An hour or so later, Wolf sensed Brina's need of a break and stopped.

Dismounting, she stretched her aching legs while allowing him a momentary cool down. Suddenly he raised his head in alarm, bringing her attentions to bear.

"What is it?" she whispered.

With ears perked straight forward, Wolf was able to detect another disturbance in the atmosphere other than theirs. Raising his head as far as his neck would allow, he caught wind of it and understood.

Since Brina's seventh sense wasn't as well-tuned as his, it took her longer to pick up on the atmospheric disturbance. When it did come, she realized it was farther off in the distant than assumed. Focusing on its direction gave her time to analyze it. It came to her as a sound. Not just any old sound, but a pounding sound. A three-beat sound. One after the other, at a very accelerate rate. The more she listened, the more she was sure of what it was. It was the three-beat gait of a galloping horse. Thinking it could be one of her friends, Brina almost cried out, then quickly changed her mind.

What if it was someone else?

There was nothing she could do but play hide-and-seek till the moment was right. Quickly and quietly she and Wolf found a clump of bushes in which to hide behind. It wasn't hard blending in; after all, it was somewhere around three in the morning, and even though it was a full moon and the twinkling lights from heaven above were shining down on their world, as long as they remained motionless, detection would be improbable—especially at the rate he was traveling. So, there they stood, still as trees, and as quiet as mice, waiting.

There, off in the distance was the distinct sound they'd been waiting for. A lone horse on the move. And as the animal ran past, Brina saw the rider too. Although the rider never gave them a second glance, hell-bent for leather he was, Brina, on the other hand, had had enough time to scrutinize his stance as well as the face under the hat's brim as best as she could as he sailed past. He may not have seen them, but she saw and recognized him.

"Hell, and damnation!" But before she said anything else, Brina clamped her hand over her mouth. She'd seen that face before, that horrible face somewhere before, but where? As she tried desperately to recall, she began to pace back and forth in hopes of remembering. When it came, as all things eventually do, she stopped dead in her tracks. As she looked up, she was faced with a tree standing directly in front of her. Had she been so deeply engrossed?

"Oh, excuse me," she nonchalantly said to the tree as she began to giggle nervously. "Oh dear, now I'm talking to trees." She returned to the side of her trusty steed. "Wolf," she whispered. "The face of that rider? Think back. He was the one in the chamber I'd wondered about, remember? The one who looked sickly as though he had some sort of disease or something? He was there in the back, standing alongside the main power grid, the day they shipped us out, remember?" She knew this as sure as she knew her name. What was he doing *here*? "Back then he was dressed as a technician." Brina said her words slowly while she stood there with her eyes closed trying to relive those last moments before shipping out. "I thought he'd looked unfamiliar and a little strange. Remember? We'd arrived early, been introduced to the chamber personnel before being prepared. That one stood all by himself on the other side of the holding chamber in a detached sort of way. Of all the faces, how could I have forgotten those cold, hostile eyes and the bloodless pallor of his skin?

That man looked as though he'd been dead for months. Then, while we were in the process of being made ready…"

Now she remembered! Later, as they stood upon the platform, he slowly came forward while it was energizing. That was when she got a very good look at his face. It was the face of death itself with those yellow eyes and that horrible translucent skin that instantly sent chills down her spine. Then while inside the chamber, as they were just beginning to dissipate, she could see the others outside begin to fade. And there, just for a second, she thought she saw that creepy-looking technician raise his arm and hand towards her as a gesture of good-bye, a mistaken gesture of farewell. During that final gesture from the technician, Brina felt sorry for him and his condition. All she could remember after that was waking up with Cordell and Dillon by her side.

That unknown man in the lab coat must have been raising some sort of weapon at her. Why would he do that? Unless…

Wolf again interrupted her thoughts. "What is it now?" Apparently, someone else was coming. She'd worry about the other later. Now was the time to pay close attention to what was going on. They again hid themselves, assumed tree form, and held fast to the ground.

The awaited sound came. This time it was clearer and more precise. It was the slow, sporadic clip-clop sound of a horse's hooves, intermingled with a slow, shuffling sound of footsteps crossing the open prairie. Amid the footsteps were heard whispered words. Brina could identify two distinct voice pitches. Two distinct voice pitches that sounded vaguely familiar. Hoping that it was her two, she waited silently for a familiar tone or expression that would set them apart before making herself known.

Once the men and horses were in sight, Brina recognized Cordell's form as the one down on his hands and knees searching for various signs in the dust. Still being cautious, since the assailant was still within earshot (and sound traveled very well at night), Brina tried something from her Academy days to get their attention. She tossed a pebble. It couldn't have been timed better, because it hit the ground right in front of his nose, but with no forthcoming response. So, she tried again. Same place, and yet he disappointed her again. It was just beginning to turn into a game for her with the question being just how many times would she have to toss a small rock his way, before he'd stop looking at the ground and begin to look around him? But the third pebble did get his attention. And of course, she had to hit him squarely in the nose to get it, but she definitely got it at last. As she watched, Cordell stopped what he was doing and stood to his full six foot four and suspiciously took a good look around. When he looked her way, yet still unseeing, she caught his glance and held it.

They'd been walking the horses for quite some time, and there for a while the tracks were easily read and headed due north. Unfortunately, when they got into that last gully, it got rockier and rockier, so rocky that their tracks became too difficult to see a-horse-back. That forced them to dismount and to continue tracking on foot.

"You know, Dillon. If one of us had taken the first watch instead of her, this probably wouldn't have happened." The whole incident was very upsetting to Cordell. He and Dillon had been discussing it for an hour at least, and they still hadn't come to any definite conclusions.

"We don't know that. If they had been lying in wait for her, they would have gotten to her sooner or later. It was just a matter of time. My question is, why her? Why not you as previously assumed? I don't understand." It made little difference. She was the one they took. Therefore, she's the one they must find. They really didn't need to discuss this; both knew the outcome of a spur-of-the-moment sorta decision. It was just that they were both so worried.

Out of the blue came the dreaded words. "Dillon, I've lost them. Their tracks. They just got up and rode off."

Dillon could hear the despair in his friend's voice. The two of them had traveled for so many hours hoping they could find her, and then out of the blue their trail just got up and disappeared?

As Dillon gazed out over the horizon in search of hope, Cordell had turned his attentions back to the dirt, and as the sun began to rise in the eastern sky, Dillon stood facing it in hopes that his Brina was alive, well, and able to see the wondrous beauty before them all.

Cordell had returned his attentions to the dirt before him, in hopes of discovering the missed clue. So engrossed was he in searching for some telltale sign, he almost missed being hit in the nose.

"What the—?" He stood. What could have done that? Might there be something out there in the darkness he should be aware of? As he looked around him, peering through the darkness, he glimpsed a slight movement off towards his right. When he gave it his full attention, everything suddenly went black.

Abruptly, Cordell froze in midstream. At first, Dillon had thought he'd heard his friend cry out in exasperation, then watched as he slowly stood, then glance around. Once he set his sights on the east, not only did his stance freeze, but so did his gaze.

"Cordell, what is it? Whatcha see?" He didn't answer. Assuming he just didn't hear, Dillon stepped closer, trying again. "What is it? Do you hear something?" Dillon still couldn't get his attention. He tried shaking him out of it. *"Cordell, Cordell. Hello, Cordell—are you in there?"* He couldn't figure it out. It was almost, he was almost acting like how Dillon must have looked when Brina…

Dillon peered eastward, in hopes of discovering the truth. Was it her? If it was her out there, and if conditions were right, she wouldn't be going to all this trouble to get their attention. Something was wrong, and maybe this was her way of telling them. Believing that was the case, he stood guard over his friend, but had he been wrong, they were in big trouble. Standing there, out in the middle of no-man's land, waiting for who knows what to happen, was not a position anyone really wanted to be in.

After a while, he spotted a slight shift in the scenery. It was as though something had swayed in the breeze—only there was no breeze. Dillon took one step forward, drawn to whatever was there. Just as he took his first step, Cordell grabbed hold of his arm, stopping him. He had been freed. As to his warning, there was nothing said, yet Dillon knew to be quiet and not to continue. It was as though he knew something was waiting for them up ahead.

Before they knew what had happened, she was there. At first, he thought it was a ghost or spirit, then realized it was really her walking towards them with Wolf trailing along behind. Not knowing what he was doing nor realizing they were doing it, Dillon's feet took on a life of their own and headed directly towards her. The first few steps were hesitant, but it only took the undeniable grasp of what he really saw to take him from walk to run. Once he could see she was truly visible before him, he threw his arms around her and hugged her with everything he had. She was alive, in one piece, and in their safe embrace once again. Time seemed to stand still. Dillon held her in his arms, looking down into those beautiful steel-gray eyes of hers and saw, what was assumed, the mirror of his feelings looking back. For a fraction of a second it was there; he was sure. So sure, in fact, that it gave him all the incentive he needed. Slowly he...

She gently pushed him away in attempts at reining him in. "Back off, cowboy," she said.

"What? What do you mean back off?" Dillon questioned in return.

"You heard me. Back off." It was a gentle warning.

"But I thought..." He saw it in her eyes. It was there; he knew it was there.

"You thought wrong. Remember, I'm a soldier, not a whore. My training did not include such avenues, nor do I yearn for them."

"Whore?" He must've missed something.

"I'm sorry, but this association must be maintained on a casual note." She could not afford to become emotionally attached to anyone. Not now, not after Lucifer; after having to deal with them, she'd probably never want to be touched by a man again, probably not ever.

Maybe Dillon hadn't missed anything. Maybe it was she who was missing out. He suddenly felt very sorry for her. Not to have ever experienced something so wonderful as love. He was sorry for himself as well, as he'd probably never get to share it with her. At least not anytime soon, and definitely not after hearing *those words spoken in that manner.* That in itself made him wonder what had happened during her captivity, and if maybe it had something to do with how she was acting now? Besides, how in the hell had she managed to escape them anyway? Kinda made him wonder what may have happened, and if given time, would she eventually get over it.

Cordell was shocked at her blunt statement too, but not discouraged. He knew she'd come around eventually. He was pretty sure of that, especially with him at the wheel. He was a patient man after all.

"Brina," Cordell began, "what did they do? They didn't hurt you, did they?" He was quietly raging inside, afraid of what may have happened.

"No. I'm all right. Thanks." She was silent for only a moment. "Those men, the ones who kidnapped me…" She was hesitant in presenting her side. She didn't know if what had happened frightened or made her angrier: her stupidity in allowing capture, her captors themselves and their plans for her, the fact that she had escaped harm, what consequences she may face should she run into any of those jerks again, or the fact that since entering this time period she'd lapsed in her disciplines.

Even though she appeared all right, Dillon's anger rose in leaps and bounds when he thought about what they'd probably had in store for her. He could see the look on Cordell's face as his thoughts matched his own. Then he glanced her way and watched a tear begin to fall so slowly down her cheek. What did this tear mean? It made Dillon wonder if she had ever been in a situation such as that before. He didn't want to believe of the possibility that the experience frightened her more than she was willing to admit, but who knew?

"They thought about doing me harm, and almost did, but I managed to persuade them otherwise. Once outside, I found Wolf tied to a tree, and we made a run for it."

"How did you know which way to go?" This Cordell asked of her.

"It was easy. Wolf knew which direction to go."

"He knew?" were words Cordell muttered halfway to himself.

"Brina," Dillon began.

She turned to face him. "Yes?"

"Those men were the same ones from the other night? The ones who stopped in for coffee and questions?" Cordell and he were fairly sure they'd been the three from the other night, but they had to be sure.

"Yeah. It was them."

She paused in her story, and all Dillon could think of was that there had been three of them. How did she manage to persuade them not to touch her, or do anything else?

"I can't tell you what you want to know, Dillon."

"Why can't you tell me?"

"I can't tell you, because I can't tell you."

He could see the anxiety and fear on her face, even though she tried not to show it.

"It'll never happen again," she stated matter-of-factly.

"How do you know?" asked Cordell

"I won't let my guard down next time. But there is something I can tell you. And that is while Wolf and I were resting, waiting for you, we heard a horse come in from the southeast. He was traveling fast. He rode right by us. Just when we started to relax, we heard you. I didn't want to take the chance that he was still close enough to hear any noise I might have made trying to get your attention, so I threw those rocks instead. I knew Cordell would eventually take notice. Actually, it ended up as kind of a game with me. It took three tries to get one of those pebbles to hit his nose."

"What about the rider?"

"I was able to get a good look at him. I've seen him before." She paused just long enough for that to sink in. "He was in the chamber of the Zodiac Field."

Hesitantly she stopped while looking at Dillon, and at that moment they both knew that she knew more than what she was telling.

Brina knew, even though her better judgment told her other-wise, she needed to be totally honest with Dillon and Cordell. They were becoming close friends, and it just didn't seem right to keep that kind of thing from them. It had been so long since she'd had any real friends that just the knowledge of having two as considerate as these compelled her to be honest. Especially with some of the things she'd learned while in Lucifer Carstead's company.

Cordell had been listening to everything Brina had to say. He knew what kind of mentality she had to deal with. After all, he had ridden with these men for a period a little less than a year. He knew perfectly well what she'd been up against.

"Cordell?"

"Yeah?"

"Do you remember a man by the name of Lucifer Carstead?" Brina couldn't ask about the others, because she was only introduced to the one by the one.

Cordell remembered Lucifer. He watched him on several occasions rape, pillage, and plunder many a fine girl and boy while in Cordell's company. Lucifer had done atrocious things in his past, and Cordell was sure that Lucifer had continued long after Dillon had thrown Cordell himself in jail all those years ago. Yes, Cordell knew Lucifer well.

He nodded.

"Then you know how it was or could've been," Brina added.

"Brina." Dillon, on the other hand, had no clue whatsoever. Cordell had never discussed those days spent with that bunch.

Brina looked at Dillon and knew right away he *needed* to know. "I'd rather not discuss it. Talk to your friend; he knows. I *can* tell you how important your friendship and support is to me, because honestly, if you haven't figured it out by now, I've only had years and years of training. Not until this assignment, have I ever been sent into the field. *Never* have I come up against men so atrocious as those three. *Never.*

"And from what I found out from Lucifer these lowlifes were hired by a creep by the name of the Grim Reaper. To find *me*. Why? I haven't a clue. I'm guessing they just fell on me in search of you. I do know one thing: as long as we stay together, we're all, in danger." The phrase, *together we stand, divided we fall,* suddenly came to mind. It also left just as quickly.

"Hold it!" exclaimed Cordell. "You're not thinking of leaving us somewhere in the dark, are you? Because if you are, I'm letting you know right here and now, we are going to stay together. That means the three of us, four if you count Wolf. We will stick with one another as Dillon and I have stuck with each other throughout the years. We will not abandon or let you leave us because you believe your being here endangers our lives. Do you understand me? I dare say!" Lecturing was not his forte, but he was not about to let her just leave them, and he was letting her know point blank.

Watching each other's back was another attribute instilled into them all, by their teachers. She smiled to herself then added, "If you feel that strongly on the subject, I'll stay for a while. At least until I really have to go. You have my promise."

"What do you mean till you have to go?" It didn't make sense to go through all this trouble to believe, to trust, and agree to assist her if she was planning on leaving. Dillon had come to love and even respect her. She couldn't leave him now! Of course, he wasn't prepared to tell *her* that.

"Nothing. It's all right. You can count on me to stick it out." Brina knew at some point down the road, the inevitable would happen, and she'd have to leave, but for now it appeared things just might work out for the better.

"Anyway, the only one I got the name of was Lucifer. And let me tell you, if I ever run into him again, it won't be a pretty sight. We'd better watch close."

"What about that rider you saw earlier? The one you said you recognized. What about him?" Dillon was beginning to believe there were more players to this game than cards in a deck.

"Yes. There's him too. I think he tried to assassinate me before I vaporized. You did say I was hurt and unconscious when you found me, right?" Brina was working on her math. "He must have decided to take a chance and follow me through the field. You see, if I am killed before I reach Jesse, well, let's just get to him first and not worry about the rest. Right now, I think it would be best if we headed east."

"Why east?" Dillon asked.

"Because I feel like cannon fodder, and it's as good a direction as any." From the moment of Brina's abduction by Lucifer and his associates, she'd dealt with her precarious situations with all the vitality and strength she could muster. However, now that was over and she was again in the confines and protection of her friends, Brina's energy reserves evaporated, leaving her with little or nothing to go on.

"Very well. I don't see anything wrong with east. East it is."

XIV

the best in the west

Cordell was there for her when she collapsed. He'd been watching her eyes as she'd been telling her tale and could see her gradual decline in keeping up the facade. So, when she listed as though about to swoon, he quickly stepped nearer. When she gave into her exhaustion, Cordell was there ready to catch her up, set her back on her feet, then gently guide, and even assisted her in the mounting of Wolf. He knew good and well that if they stuck around here for any length of time waiting for her to rest up, whoever was out there searching for them just might find themselves very, very lucky indeed.

Dillon had no idea she was that tired, but with all that had happened to her in the last twenty-four hours, he didn't blame her in the least. She really needed rest now, as exhausted as she was. If she was correct, the farther east they could get, the better the chances. He also knew if someone was out there looking for her, they'd eventually locate their tracks and be hot on their tails before they were even aware of it. Cordell knew that too. That's why he got her on her horse. With Dillon in the lead, Wolf following behind with slack reins, as Brina being barely coherent, Cordell was left to bring up the rear to best watch their backs.

They didn't stop till Wolf sensed a town on the other side of the next ridge. Dillon still didn't know what type of beast they traveled with; all he knew was how much Brina trusted and loved the animal. How the two of them communicated or how he managed to sense these types of things was another matter. In fact, when it came right down to it, it made little difference, due to time saved and unnecessary trouble.

155

Sitting upon his own trusty mount as they stood atop the ridge, Dillon looked down below at the next valley. There off in the distance, large as life, was a town. Wolf was right again, and he wondered if this place was accommodating to strangers. Dillon was hoping for a hotel for their charge. And if they had one, that meant real beds. Not that he didn't enjoy the peace and quiet of the out of doors; it was just that sleeping on the ground for so long that maybe sleeping in a real bed, in a real hotel, in a real town would remind them all how lucky they had been to be sleeping out on the trail. Town life is convenient, but Dillon had always found living off the land most enjoyable—even though he hated sleeping on rocks and uneven ground.

As much as he wanted to oversee the valley below, he knew he had to get back to Cordell and Brina. After they'd found a place in a little clearing to set up camp, he'd left her in Cordell's safe keeping. Just as he headed out for a look-see at the area, he glanced back to watch as Brina was helped off Wolf by Cordell. Once her feet hit the ground, she fell instantly into him, sound asleep. As Dillon watched his friend lift her as though she weighed but a feather, carrying her closer to where he was to build a fire, Dillon wished it had been him instead of Cordell. Cordell took care of her as though she was a fragile china cup, passed down from mother to daughter over the generations. Dillon had never seen him handle something as delicately as he did her.

When Dillon returned, Brina was still asleep. That poor kid, she really must have gone through an ordeal with that bunch. Wolf had been unsaddled by Cordell and was grazing in the grassy clearing with Baldy. Cordell was, as he had expected him to be, sitting not too far away from their gray-eyed beauty listening intently to all the sounds around them. Dillon rode up to where the other saddles lay, reined Cody to stop, dismounted, unsaddled, then eventually turned him out with the other mounts. Stepping over to Cordell, he informed him of his discovery.

"That town looks promising from up here. Do you suppose you'd mind staying here with her till she's ready to travel? I think I'm going down to scout out the possibility of a hotel, or something of the such." Dillon was sure Cordell would do it; he'd been staying pretty close to her since her escape from Lucifer Carstead and his gang.

Yes, Cordell would stay with her while Dillon checked out the layout of the town. In truth, he wanted the two of them safe, one protecting the other. Just as soon as Brina caught up on some needed rest, she'd protect Cordell with her life, just as he would her. That in itself lessened the strain of his trip down the hill. If this town had the hotel they so desperately needed, he could arrange rooms for them all.

Dillon found the town smaller than it appeared from atop the ridge. At first it looked pretty good size, in a way it was, but many of the buildings were vacant. Seeing a town in this condition creates a sense of curiosity, as to why store owners would pack up and leave their homes and businesses.

It really was no concern of his why they would have left; all he wanted was a hotel—one that could easily accommodate the three of them. It wasn't just the anticipation of feeling a feather bed beneath him, but they were also in need of supplies, and this was as good a place as any to find them. In fact, if they could perchance find a decent packhorse, they'd be able to carry more supplies and not have to locate general stores quite so often.

As Dillon rode down what he had guessed was Main Street, he spotted the hotel across from the stable with a general store nearby. What luck! The sign above it read "Hawthorne Hotel, John J. Hawthorne proprietor." For a moment he wondered who John J. Hawthorne was and if he was still the proprietor of the establishment.

Before checking into the Hawthorne, Dillon thought he'd get a feel for the town first. He wandered for a spell, looking over the various stores that hadn't been vacated or abandoned. The general store was large enough to carry the various supplies needed for a small army. *That was surprising.* If he could find the store owner, he'd ask why. He browsed the store and the second section. There in the back was the owner. At least he thought it was him. What he found was a small man with white hair that circled his head like a halo. He just happened to be standing behind the counter talking to an elderly lady. A closer look suggested a whore, and an old one to say the least. How did Dillon know this? Well, considering she was still in her underclothes and flirting with him with her long fingernails running down into his shirt kinda gave it away.

He must've been embarrassed at Dillon's arrival. The moment their eyes met he turned the brightest shade of red Dillon ever seen. It started at the base of his neck and ran all the way up past his face to the top of his balding head. Yep. Dillon had guessed that was a whore. The store owner in recognition of a potential customer, instead of being a potential customer himself, came immediately to attention, excusing himself to the lady and stepped around to the front of the counter heading Dillon's way.

"Can I help you?" he asked.

Dillon asked why his shelves were filled with so many supplies.

"You a stranger here in town?" he asked.

When Dillon nodded his head and explained that he *was* a stranger to these parts, he explained further.

"Why, we're the only suppliers of dry goods for a hundred miles. The McCauleys, they about twenty miles out, they got five hundred head of beef cattle out thatta way and always make sure they're fully supplied just in case they can't make it in come winter. Then we have a few other large outfits in other directions who depend on us for all their goods. Why, if'n we didn't keep the supplies up, Mr. Dobbs and his bunch would surely bring in another freight line, and that'd run me clean out of business."

Dillon thanked him for the information, gave him the list of supplies they were in need of, and left in search of other little surprises this town had in store.

From Dillon's vantage point on the planked walkways in search of various storefronts, he noticed how similar in appearance and layout this little town reminded him of home. If it wasn't for the occasional vacant stores and buildings, besides the fact that it was much smaller than his own Eastern-Western, he could very well turn this here corner and find…there it was, by golly, the doctor's office. Just like back home! He couldn't believe it. Of course, when he looked up and saw the doctor's name above the door, he knew it for the mistaken fantasy that it was. This doctor's name was Fitzgibbins. Alva P. Fitzgibbins, MD. Well, there was no point in stopping in since he wasn't ailing, so instead, he continued his journey down the walkway, watching and looking for whatever caught his eye.

Marshal Dillon Frasier had spent so many years out on the trail, he'd forgotten the simpler things town life had to offer. Real doctors, churches, schools, families and children—those were the important things in life. He stood on the corner and just watched the people and the goings-on all around. Without a care, he found himself heading off to the left thoughtlessly meandering down more of the streets, browsing through all their little shops, eventually finding himself back on the same corner again. This time, he just stood there, passing the time, watching people.

His attention was diverted when a fuzzy blur came out of nowhere, ran past his leg, and headed up the street. While he was trying to figure out what it was, another larger fuzzy blur almost knocked him over in attempts at chasing the first. It all happened so quickly. It had been a small brown dog that chased a black cat across his path, down the walkway, into the street, and continued down to and around the corner. He watched the cat's attempt at outmaneuvering the dog. That was when he noticed for the first time that one corner building. It was a saloon, and if it wasn't for that dog, he'd probably have missed it entirely. Still having plenty of time before heading back to the hotel, he headed towards the saloon for a long, relaxing drink.

Not keeping track of the time or how many drinks he'd downed, Dillon finally looked up from his corner of the room. Outside the swinging doors dusk had settled. Looks like he'd spent more time sitting around drinking and enjoying himself than he thought. Pushing his chair back from the table, he stood, picked up his glass of whiskey, and gulped down the last swallow. Setting it back down, he turned and headed out of the Red Dog, but before he got all the way out the door, out of the corner of his eye, he thought he saw a single horse standing next to the bar. He must have had way too many drinks. He left, without looking back. Stumbling his way across town in search of the hotel, he spotted directly across the street their sheriff's office. Now how could he have missed that one too? The only lame excuse he could come up with was that the exciting chase of cat versus dog had diverted his attention to the saloon instead. Well, at least they had some sort of law here; however, since Dillon wanted to avoid any contact with someone who just might know him, he headed back towards the Hawthorne. That is, if he could find it in his present condition.

Feeling the center of the street would give him a better view of the town, a better way to hopefully locate the Hawthorne, and a better way to avoid someone who might accidentally bump him on the walkway causing him to crash head over heels into the street, he did just that. He stepped off the walkway. As he recalled, the hotel was located directly across the way from the livery. This meant that no longer was he in search of just the hotel, but now it was the livery too, and him in this condition.

When the sound of pounding hooves penetrated his fuzzy mind, Dillon looked up. There almost on top of him were two riders barreling down the street. If his reflexes hadn't kicked in automatically, as he dove off and out of the way of that deadly encounter, he'd have been run over for sure. Best to get back off the street and back onto the planked walkway, where there weren't no horses.

Behind Dillon, from inside the saloon, came the sound of gunfire. He whirled around towards the sound and drew his own pistol from its holster. Realizing it wasn't needed, he watched as three more men came a-scrambling out through the swinging doors of the Red Dog Saloon.

They never looked back as they charged down the steps and into the street. Reminiscing of times past, Dillon was caught off guard at the heavy thudding that followed their leaving. When he realized that charging out of the saloon was the horse, he thought he imagined, with a rider sitting on top, guns a-blazing, he immediately reholstered his pistol. He wanted no part of what was about to happen, so instead, he sat back to watch the spectacle. The man on the horse, as it turned out, was the sheriff of the town, and whether or not he was drunk, Dillon had no clue. At least the horse in the saloon wasn't a product resulting from his afternoon of liquid libations. And as it unfolded before him, the sheriff, being already mounted on his own trusty steed when those men swung themselves up into the saddles of newly acquired chargers, had a better head start on them than the norm, as he was only inches behind as they made their escape down the street and out through the other end of town.

Shaking his head at the whole silly spectacle, Dillon turned and just happened to have forgotten where he was standing and ran smack-dab into the corner post of the vacant building where he had sought safety from the thundering hooves of only moments before. Quickly he looked around to see if he'd been seen, and since no one was laughing or pointing fingers his way, it was assumed he hadn't. Pretending as though nothing was out of the ordinary, Dillon headed back towards the other end of the street where he hoped the livery and the hotel were.

After trying his hand at appearing to be in a normal state of mind, Dillon tried walking down the walkway without bringing any more attention to himself. Somehow and from somewhere, he managed to acquire news of the hotel's location by overhearing a tall and powerfully built man discuss the difficulty *he was having* trying to purchase the establishment. Since he was already in a heavy discussion on the subject, excusing Dillon's self and his condition, he interrupted, asking for possible directions to its whereabouts so that he could possibly sleep off his condition. It was a good thing Dillon was slightly inebriated because this gentleman was very upset that Dillon had even been within earshot of his conversation on the subject, and had Dillon not been in this condition, he was sure the burly fella would have knocked him flat. No matter, Dillon was still able to get what he needed.

Not being a drinking man at heart, because in his previous profession it can get one killed, Dillon was surprised at his dumb luck in finding the hotel. Especially, since he hadn't stumbled his way off the walkway landing face-first onto the street. For there it was, large as life across from where he stood. Shaking it off as some ill-gotten fate that had been bestowed upon him, prepared to cross over. After straightening and dusting off the front of himself, he stood erect, with head back, shoulders square, and with a momentary straightening of his hat, began his descent off the corner, appearing as though he knew exactly where he was headed and why.

Once through the threshold of the Hawthorne, the first assault on his nose was not the fragrance of food, but a totally unfamiliar smell. Looking around for its source, Dillon noticed instead that the entire interior of the hotel looked larger on the inside than it appeared from the outside. He took a second to again look at it from the outside. It had a second floor as most hotels do, but still from the inside it looked larger, and he couldn't fathom why. Back inside he took a closer look at the foyer. Maybe his answers were right in front of him; unfortunately, he couldn't see them.

Before he stepped too far in, Dillon glanced all around then down, beginning with the floors. They were spotless as though they'd been recently polished. They even had intricate scrolled carvings chiseled into them. Panning to his left was a large fire hole in the wall with stones embedded all around it, and to its right, set into the corner a piano with a hunter's kill mounted on the wall above. As he continued to look past the piano and around the corner, Dillon spotted a beautiful staircase. It seemed to just sprout its way from the center of the floor as if was an unbridled plant working its way up towards the sky branching out in two opposite directions, leading off to the second story and to the rooms above.

He spotted a slight movement from underneath one of the branches. It was a man, with brush in hand, painting. That explained the smell when he first entered. This was fun. The more he looked, the more he found. Tall ceilings, tapestries. Why, they even had a dining room and full-sized kitchen for the convenience of their guests! This hotel must have really been some place in its time. As Dillon returned to the lobby after finding the dining room, he found the front desk. There on a long intricately carved and polished oak front desk was the hotel's register with a quill pen by its side. He stood there in front of the desk and observed the maroon-and-cream-colored wallpaper on the wall behind it and watched in amazement as a distinguished-looking gentleman stepped out from behind a set of matching maroon curtains that he had failed to notice.

"Excuse me, sir, may I help you?" asked the proprietor, John J. Hawthorne. John J. had a rather distinguished look, with a mustache that curled around at the ends.

"Yes," Dillon said, then continued. "Do you have a…" How was he going to do this? It had been so long since Cordell, and he, spent time in a hotel. Did he want a separate room? Or for that matter, what about Brina? Did she want a room to herself, or did they all want to share a room together? After all, they'd been sharing star-lit nights together with just a mere two or three feet separating their bedrolls.

John J. Hawthorne had watched this man enter his establishment. From the very first moment this man crossed the threshold, John realized he was basically a drifter looking for lodging. It was always enjoyable to watch those unfamiliar with this part of the territory enter his hotel and observe the unusual collection of luxuries he'd added just for their comfort and enjoyment. He had taken great pride in his hotel and because of his extensive trips abroad knew the special niceties that are appreciated by travel-weary pilgrims. When this sandy-haired gentleman appeared to have finished his self-tour and headed for the main desk, John J. Hawthorne stepped out from behind the curtains, the ones that matched the wallpaper he'd brought back with him from Europe, to assist. After asking his initial questions and with the troubled way in which this stranger tried to answer, John J. Hawthorne knew he needed more help than normally required.

"Please, sir. Excuse me for asking, but is there a problem? I'm very versed in how things work, and if you don't mind asking a stranger for help, I'll be more than happy to do so."

He had a look to him that Dillon hadn't seen in a long time, honesty. By the twinkle in his eyes and the way he held himself, John J. hinted of a well-educated man of breeding and knowledge. Could Dillon trust him in ways of women?

"Well, sir. Uh, er, I have this problem you see. One that requires a gentler touch."

"I see," said John J. Hawthorne. "Where is she? And have you discussed this with her?"

"Well, no. But——"

"May I make a suggestion, sir?" began John J. Hawthorne and at the beseeched looked in the stranger's eyes made one. "Ask her how she wants to handle it. If she is as important to you as you are letting on, then it is very important how you handle this. During my travels abroad, I've learned a few things about women. Some need to be led, some are very aggressive by nature, and others are independent thinkers. The independent ones are those who must be handled with care, for if the wrong move is made, you may end up with an empty satchel. Believe me, I know."

As Dillon considered all John J. said and was trying to decide which would be the best direction to begin, he heard noises outside. As he turned towards the entrance of the hotel, he saw both Brina and Cordell, large as life, standing together in the doorway to the Hawthorne.

XV

straight from the horse's mouth

Brina woke refreshed and ready to start anew. A new what, she wasn't sure. The only thing she was sure of was that the night before had been disastrous. That moment when she almost dropped her guard and considered a kiss from Dillon had been an atrocity to everything she'd been taught. The carelessness of throwing all caution to the wind was not permitted in either this mission or within her life, and to somehow correct it and to set things on their proper course was all important. That was why she'd told him to back away.

When she found Dillon nowhere in sight, she was relieved. It was true that she hadn't had any desire for love or sex in her past. The second surgery had taken care of most of that. Once her innards were removed, almost all desires had died. The organization had what they wanted, an almost-perfect fighting machine without complications.

Just before excusing herself for some needed privacy, she asked about Dillon's whereabouts. Accepting the news with a nod of her head, Brina stepped away. When she returned, she had a new outlook on her whole situation and the beginnings of a new idea of how to handle it. Returning to her resting point, she once again began her ritual of clearing up her corner of the campsite and to the packing away of everything essential for travel. Once her bedroll, cooking utensils, and other personal paraphernalia were back in their proper place upon her trusty steed, Brina pulled out her Colts and began her ritual of cleaning, polishing, and the eventual practicing of drawing and reholstering them while Cordell watched.

Cordell was amazed how this woman so very diligently cleaned then polished her weapons. Then he watched in total fascination how expertly she handled them. He didn't say a word to her—afraid he'd break her concentration. He just watched and added that special quality to his list of many things he admired her for, wondering all the while who might be faster with a gun, this gray-eyed beauty or Dillon.

When the weight of the holstered Colts upon her hips provided the comfort she'd grown to love and cherish, Brina took one last spin before dropping them into their resting places.

"Thanks, Cordell, for all you did for me last night, and again this morning."

It took him a moment or two to respond. "No need to thank me, after all, you were the one who originally saved my hide from Lucifer and his *friends*." He paused for a couple of moments wondering if certain questions that had been popping into his mind of late should be broached. "Come to think of it, how did you know to hide me?"

"I'd rather not say."

"Why not?"

"Because that's not what's important now. What is important is that you're safe and alive."

She was right about that.

"By the way, how long do you suppose Dillon wanted us to wait here, before following?" If she managed to turn his thoughts to something else maybe, just maybe, they could avoid the information, *das verboten.* Come to think of it, how did *sidekicks* manage to keep time schedules and pertinent rendezvous? After all, by this part of the century they hadn't quite invented telephones, walkie-talkies, telecommunication devices, cell phones, or universal galileolispheres yet, and she was fairly certain neither of them knew how to send smoke signals. How then by chance were they to know?

He wasn't sure how to answer. "I really don't know, usually I just go with him, but because of you being so tired and all, I was asked to hold up with you. You feel like traveling yet?"

Did she? "No, not really."

"Would you mind if we sat for a spell instead then?" Cordell still wanted to ask her all the questions that'd been racing through his mind since meeting up with her.

Brina could see no real harm in that, just to sit for a spell, but just for a spell. Unfortunately sitting usually meant talking. And what would he want to talk about? She'd always been able to sense his feelings for her and had been apprehensive about them since the beginning. Maybe, now was the time for him to bring them up, as it was for her to quell them.

Since learning who he was through the story he told, she now had a very special place in her heart just for Cordell Chevalier. He had been all his name implied—a rope maker, a French rope maker. He didn't have the specialized skills required of one so gifted, but he definitely had the disposition of calmness and the diligence needed of such a profession. Plus, she liked him very much. No, that wasn't quite right. She loved him. But not in the ways of lovers, more in the ways of family, and that meant so much more to her.

Not wanting to hurt his feelings or give away any reasons why she felt the way she did, Brina made that last-minute decision to be completely honest with him.

"Sure, why not?"

Foremost on her agenda was to find a suitable place to sit. If this chat was going to be a long one as she believed it would be, then by golly, she was going to be comfortable. Once situated, Brina stared towards the horizon, giving herself a moment of peace before beginning. "Okay, Cordell, what do you want to know?"

"How did you know?"

"You've had them all along. I can sometimes see things, remember?"

Now he had to actually speak up instead of being able to dream about this moment. Could he do it? He paused as though not sure how to begin.

She remained silent. If there was something he wanted, let him bring it up. She was not going to ruin his moment.

Cordell couldn't believe his luck. Dillon had left him in charge of the most beautiful woman he'd seen in years. He knew why he'd done it and loved him for it. His only problem now was how to bring himself to actually say something to her. He'd wanted to find a way to get closer to this woman since he first laid eyes on her. She and that horse of hers were the most magnificent specimens of beauty he had ever seen, and he wanted to know all he could. His father had been around the world and witnessed so many wondrous things during his early years, and Cordell had seen so little in comparison. He knew right away these two were different from the beginning. Now the doubts in his mind had vanished as to the truth in her words. She wasn't from around here, and he wanted to know all that he could. How was he to begin? Without allowing himself to think further, he took a deep breath and jumped in with both feet.

"Brina, now that we're all alone, will you tell me about yourself?"

"You mean other than me being from Frisco?" she asked.

"Well, yeah."

"What you want to hear is what I haven't yet discussed. You realize most of it will sound a trifle far-fetched."

"It can't be as bad as I've seen or experienced so far. Could it? Please."

She'd committed worse acts during her time here, on this side of the Barrier, what more harm could she cause? How could she turn him down? He looked like a puppy devoted to its master. Could she trust his devotion? What she found when she looked into his soft dark-brown eyes was the *desire to know*. For them, maybe it would be a common bond. Something only the two of them could share, like what she and Wolf had, only on a much smaller scale.

But before beginning this informative little chat, it had to be understood how it was. Very slowly she explained.

"What I'm about to tell you is for your ears only. It will be our little secret. No one else must ever know, not even Dillon. If he learns of what I am about to tell you, then it will never be ours, yours and mine, ever again. Do you understand? I need your word on it." She knew if he was willing to give her his word, the following information would go with him to the grave. But she had to be sure. Some of the information she had was going to shake him up quite a bit.

Without hesitation Cordell said with conviction, "You have my word."

"Fine. Now, to make a long story much shorter, I was born in Frisco. My parents were very loving, and my younger days with them were very good. I grew up very independent, didn't play with other children my own age, just went off by myself. Since I was very small, I'd been showing unusual abilities for intensive learning and unbeknownst to many was receiving spiritual messages from out and beyond the realm of worldly possibilities. When I was about, let me see, with the time change and your rate of measure, I would have been approximately eight years of age, I was recruited by the Organization and placed in the Academy. That's a special school that trains you in all aspects of survival, defense, discipline, etiquette, and many other fields. From the day I was recruited till the moment Wolf and I stepped through the *field*, I have been under a strict training program.

"During my time at the Academy I learned *many* things. Some good, some not so good. Special students with special qualities desired by the organization were taken under consideration by a special staff. The exceptional ones were tested and retested, ensuring their special and unusual talents were true and undeniable. Those who passed the many tests were transferred into the organization's various production programs. To pass on special abilities and/or talents down through offspring was considered one of the utmost accomplishments. Unfortunately, it was found that I was unable to produce offspring." That was a joke if ever she heard one. "That made me one of the expendable.

"Cordell, you have to understand, both my natural parents were descendants of this period. The ancient West and what you call the nineteenth century. I believe that was one of the reasons they chose me for this mission. My roots are here. Once this is over and if I survive, I am to find a place to fit in. The other reason, since I was being sent here anyway, was to find Dillon. I don't know how they figured that one out, or who it was that made that crazy decision, but they somehow knew he would be the most likely to assist me. *You, my friend, were the added bonus—*"

Before she was able to continue, Cordell interrupted, "Will you answer me one question?"

"Sure, if I can," she replied.

"Before you continue, I want you to know how *I* feel." He had always known when he found the right one, he'd instantly know it. "I don't show it, but I'm a very sensitive man, and I have deep feelings for you. I've had them since the first time I saw you in the clearing. For my father, it was love at first sight. I always believed it would be the same for me as well."

Brina was afraid this was the case. "Cordell, please. You don't know what…" *Damn, damn, damn.* Just what she had hoped to avoid. Had there been an easier way to break the news to him, she'd do it. "Look, I like you and all. Certainly, I love you, but not that way. Cordell…" *How did one do this?*

"What do you mean not in that way? There is only one way for a man and woman to love." He was hurt. He now assumed because of her words that there was no place in her heart for a darkie with white blood running through his veins.

When Brina saw tears welling up, she began, "Cordell, I want to tell you a story."

"Never mind. I understand perfectly," he started up.

"No. I don't think you do. Please. If after you hear this story and still feel the way you do, I will accept your decision." She knew then *the truth she held so close and so dear to her heart* must be made known to him and now. Before he had gotten completely to his feet, she was on him—halting his progress by placing her hand upon his shoulder, hoping the gesture would do the trick; unfortunately, she found the pressure needed to prevent his leaving was more than she'd bargained for.

Cordell was so upset with not only her unspoken opinion of him, but also with his lack of control where his emotions were concerned. Then she touched his shoulder. What was he to do now? Should he leave and never speak to her again or return to their conversation only to be humiliated further? He didn't know what to do.

He wanted so much to love her and had expected her to understand. Then when she placed her hand upon his shoulder in a tender yet determined way, he almost melted. Closing his eyes, he sat back down. With them closed, he failed to see the gentle way in which she reached towards him.

Brina was very touched. She was also very confused. Had his feelings for her run this deep? Not since she lived at home had someone visibly shown this much love for her. Was there a possibility of it being something else entirely? She needed to regain his trust and his attention. The telling of her story would explain a lot of his *whys* away. Even though he tried hiding his face from her, and she was sure it was because he didn't want to look her in the eye, she needed his undivided attention, and she was determined to get it. Her feelings ran very deep for this man. Maybe not quite in the same manner as his did for her, but the impact of the truth she was about to reveal would come as a shock to his delicate nature, and he needed to know this truth.

Slowly and gently, she reached out with her hand for the bottom of his chin. She wanted him willing instead of forced. With her thumb, she caressed the side of his face, back and forth among the tears that until now were running down its side. When he, at last, leaned his face deeper into her hand, she knew he was again hers and waited for him to open his eyes and look into her own.

All he could feel were her fingers on his face. He could tell by her gentle touch and the way she caressed his jaw he had been mistaken in his assumptions. She did feel something for him; he was sure. But what was it, and how deep did it go? All he knew at this moment in his life was that this woman had the power to bring his tears to life. He loved her so much it hurt. Dillon had feelings for her as well, but not anything like the ones he had for her. Their only differences? Dillon made his known. Cordell kept his well-hidden. He knew she wanted his attention, but he wasn't quite ready to give it.

When Brina realized he was still frightened of her and the unknown feelings she had brought to surface, she gently let loose his jaw. Instead, she pulled him in close just as a mother would with a young child. When she pulled him to her, she expected him to take flight; instead, she felt him relax against her in such a way that surprised her. When she felt him ready, she let him loose, allowing him to search her face. It was then she took hold of his mind and tried to send him a glimpse of her feelings for him. Then gently let him go.

When he finally nodded his head as a signal that his emotions were once again under control, she finished for him.

"Cordell, please. You are a very wonderful man, and I am honored that you would even consider me as a partner in your life. Don't let what I am about to tell you interfere with your feelings. You need to know I also care very deeply for you. Maybe not in the same way, but the feelings are there, nevertheless. I am a soldier, but once upon a time I was also a normal, everyday, little girl. I'm not void in feelings; it's just that I haven't experienced any honest and true ones for a very long time. And during this mission, I don't want or need them. Without them I am ready; with them, I could slip and get myself or accidentally get someone else killed.

"But the story I'm about to tell you will explain much. It is a story *my mother* told me while I was still very young and living at home. It was just a little piece of family history to tide me over for the rest of my life. She knew about them coming for me for days, so she took me aside, we sat together in the sun, ate cookies, laughed aloud and finally she told me a story, a special story from long ago. She made me repeat it over and over again until I had it memorized. She wanted me to know about my family and how it got started on the Western Hemisphere. It was something she felt I could keep with me, something from my natural-born family that would be mine alone to carry. Something that I was not to forget nor allow the Organization to erase." This time she was the one with tears in her eyes. Did he see and understand the emotions of anguish and love mixed there? Probably not.

"She sat me down and told me of a love story. A very wonderful and touching moment in time for two distinctly different individuals of totally different backgrounds. This story, she said, had been passed down from generation to generation. Mother to daughter. Father to son. To me, she explained that it was a very old and very true story. She told it to me with so much emotion, she cried. She knew what was about to happen in my life and knew the story's impact on me at the time would be tremendous—as it will be now for you." Brina now had his undivided attention.

"Cordell." She gently took hold of his face with both hands so that he could see the honesty in her eyes as she dumped the astonishing truth in his lap. *"He…he was a captain of a French trade ship, and she…"* Brina began choking on her very words, just now realizing how powerful this story was when hearing Cordell tell it that day when she held her guns on them—*"was a slave girl."* Then she added the missing piece. The undeniable proof to her claim. *"He named her Nicole."*

The truth was finally out. She closed her eyes allowing the tears to flow. When she reopened them, she could see it in his eyes. He understood. He knew who she was.

Cordell knew when he'd been forced to reveal his heritage, his mother's name had been left out. Therefore, the only way she could've known was the obvious. "Then, you're…"

"Yes, Cordell. I am."

The tears began to flow unchecked down both their faces. They reached for each other in a way known only to those who realize that they are one. Knowing all that mattered now was that the two of them were together and were bound eternally.

Long after the tears stopped falling, they continued to hold fast to each other.

Brina was the first to finally break away; all the while remaining silent, she wiped away the tears. What she'd just told him needed time to be absorbed. Each of them in their own way had to come to grips with the spoken truth. She herself had been shocked beyond comprehension that day with Cordell's story. Turnabout was fair play, but this time it had affected her just as it had him.

How? How in the name of all that was possible had she managed to run into, of all people, a historical ancestor from her same bloodlines? Of all the totally crazy things to happen, this one topped them all.

Cordell couldn't believe what he'd just heard. He knew she told the truth, because there was no other way she could have known, especially since he had made a point not to mention his mother's name when they'd been forced to reveal such truths. If there was a time for questions, now was the time to ask.

"Brina, ever since that day you held your guns on us, forcing us to relay bits of our past, did you know who I really was to you?"

"No, Cordell. I did not. At least not until after it was all out. I will let you in on a little secret though; from the moment I met you, I knew there was something about you, something I couldn't put my finger on, but something told me you were special. I know that makes little sense, but remember, I just finished telling you. I'm very receptive to unusual messages. If you think about all the things that have happened since our first chance encounter, our whole partnership appears pretty crazy. That is if you understand what I'm saying." Brina was glad most of it was finally out in the open.

"Now do you understand why this must be kept from Dillon? Not only is this to be kept from him for our own reasons, but if he knew we were related, it would allow him feelings about me, feelings I don't want to deal with. Do you understand?"

"Yeah, I git it. I was a little curious at first why you wanted to keep this a secret from him, but now I know. Other than having something special to share, do you realize what else this means?" He watched the way her eyes sparkled in recognition of his question. "There is someone out there for me! Do you know who she is, or where I'll might be a-finding her?"

"No, I'm sorry. Of that I have no idea. Even though you are a part of my family tree, genealogy was not included in my studies." Thank the All Mother for that one. "Whoever she is and wherever she is, it will be a special moment in your life, and you'll know her when you find her."

"I love you very much, my steel-eyed beauty. You have given me a glimpse of the future. My future. It's a wonderful feeling knowing that someday I will find happiness before my life reaches its end. I will always be eternally grateful to you for that. Ya know, this makes us one. I cherish your friendship and love as much as I cherish the love that Dillon and I share."

There was nothing she could say, would say, to break his train of thought. All that was originally feared was now out in the open. Except one, Wolf. That information had to be requested. It was not going to be revealed voluntarily, and she knew with all the other information revealed this day, that question wasn't too awfully far away.

"Brina, there is one more thing,"

Here it comes, she thought.

He paused as though not sure if he should continue. "Since we are revealing secrets to each other, I'd very much like to know about Wolf. What is he?"

He didn't waste any time at all, did he? "Cordell, consider what you're asking. Do you really want to know? I mean really?? Wolf is *very difficult* to explain. I myself don't even know what or who he really is. However, I do know the essence or spirit he is or carries and the power he wields is enough to shake even the strongest of minds." Searching his face, she again found the desired qualities, the need to know and the trust to keep it secret. Without a doubt, he would make their secret his. Was his trust worth the price he'd have to pay for the knowledge? Glancing towards Wolf for any type of hint as to which decision to make, Brina was surprised to find him staring beyond them, as though he was a thousand miles away.

Turning back towards Cordell, Brina noticed the minute change in the way he was looking at her too. On closer examination, Brina believed he wasn't looking at her, but through her. It was spooky, his change in facial expression. He had the look of someone in a trance or of someone waiting for an unknown catastrophe to strike. As she looked back towards her mount again, she felt it there too. Then came the feeling of *contact* as Cordell inadvertently touched her arm. He must have felt it in the air, because all of a sudden, the ground started to tremble, the wind suddenly came up out of nowhere, and high up in the sky, black, black thunderheads filled the sky till all the blue was gone, and the threat of a great storm was imminent.

175

Brina knew immediately Wolf was the source of the theatrics and what was about to befall them. Cordell had asked, and whether he wanted it or not, he was about to experience an unearthly phenomenon, the Gray Wolf.

The Gray Wolf was a spirit of sorts who thrived on theatrics and who was about to befall them both with his unearthly powers. For Brina Louise Grant was positive Cordell Chevalier, a mortal Frenchman, hadn't the vaguest idea who he was about to meet. Because the moment was now in the hands of Aeolus; God of the Winds, Quetzalcoatl; God of the Aztecs, Thorin; leader of the Dwarves, Moza; Keeper of the Trolls, the Great Wizard of median earth; the Divine Sovereign of the Neptune Kingdom, whose name was too difficult to pronounce; and who knew how many others.

At least that's what was told to her in the very beginning, but who really knew for sure?

Once the stage was set, the adverse conditions suddenly vanished. The clouds gone, the ground still, as was the wind that blew only moments ago. Turning back to Cordell, with a twinkle in her gray eyes, Brina asked, "Do you believe in the supernatural, Cordell?" When he returned his worried gaze upon her, Brina knew she no longer had control over what was to come and somehow Cordell knew it too. For what had begun as a simple question-and-answer period had now turned into an experience to be remembered or forgotten—depending on what you thought of it all. For what was about to happen to this poor unaware mortal was nothing he'd ever imagined. *Brina hoped he had a strong constitution.*

It came as a whisper on the wind.

"Cordell,"

It began as a fog-like substance that floated into the clearing, near to where the two of them stood. It tried to take on some sort of shape, as it appeared to breathe with a life all its own.

"Behold."

Cordell first turned towards Brina hoping for an explanation, but when she shrugged her shoulders and nonchalantly pointed towards the horse, he knew what was to happen in the next few moments was something he suddenly didn't want to be any part of. Unfortunately, his feet refused to move. For here in front of his eyes was something out of the deepest part of the subconscious mind. Something he had witnessed several times but had not experienced himself until this very moment. Indescribable terror. What had he done? Turning back to Brina for support, he found, to his relief, she was there next to him if he needed her, with her hand resting upon his. Then when he looked first at the mist, then towards Wolf, Cordell realized for the first time in his life this indeed was a horse of a different color.

Wolf's whisper came across to them, as though it originated from the heavens, descending upon them by way of the trees. Gliding downwards passed the leaves it came, as though it traveled on the wind.

"I, Aeolus, Sovereign of median earth and beyond,

am older than the tallest of mountains.

I have traveled through the ages and across the Great

Barrier in search of one love for all eternity.

Since before her beginnings, Brina's essence, her

spirit, was of my choosing. We are one."

"You. Child of Nicole, ancestral mother of Brina, are

now one with us. As I watch over her, I do now for you."

Then all was as it had been—silent, except for the chirping of the birds.

Well, she thought, at least he now knew the truth. But could he handle the knowledge? Stepping over to her saddlebags, Brina pulled out the flask of whiskey. If any time was a time to start drinking in one's life, it was now. If the roles were reversed, she'd demand one. Returning to Cordell's side, she noticed he hadn't moved an inch. Removing the stopper from the flask, she passed it back and forth under his nose hoping the vapors would bring him around. They did. Immediately he started coughing and sputtering, then grabbed the flask, and downed half its contents. Slowly he descended to a sitting position.

Brina slowly sat down beside him, laid her hand upon his arm, and wisely kept her mouth shut.

XVI

the best way to find a lost stray
is to go to the place you would
go if you were a lost stray

By the time Brina fixed the two of them some lunch and watched Cordell down a couple cups of coffee, she knew it was about time to head on down the hill to meet Dillon. Cordell, her poor friend, still needed time to think about, absorb, and then hopefully accept what he'd experienced earlier, but as the old saying went, *seeing is believing.* In this case, however, what had happened was totally out of the normal spectrum of the period and would take some time for anyone to swallow.

To be able to accept at least the concept of what Wolf was would take some time, and during that transition period, perhaps a ride through the peaceful countryside was just what the doctor ordered. With the continual *clip-clop, clip-clop* of their horses' hooves, the beautiful scenery around them, the singing of birds, and the gentle sea-like breeze that swirled around them and the branches of the great oak trees, they rode down towards the sleepy one-horse town of Dowdyville to locate Dillon and join him there.

Upon their arrival, they checked their horses into the livery stable and found, as hoped, Dillon's trusty mount already bedded down in a safe, comfortable, and dry stall for the duration of their stay. Meandering through town, they unknowingly followed almost the same route Dillon had, only they missed the cat and the chase that followed. When they finally did reach the saloon, the thought of sitting back in a comfortable chair amongst the assorted barflies, listening to all the gossip, and needing a pleasant drink, Brina took the bull by the horns, by nudging Cordell's arm. Catching on quickly, he nodded his head in reply, cocked his hat, took her arm, and together they pushed open the swinging doors and entered the smoke-filled room.

With two feet between them and the outside world, just on the other side of the swinging doors, Brina was caught unawares with a ghastly, horrible, and slightly familiar smell.

"What in the world?" she mumbled to herself.

Once her eyes grew accustomed to the darkened room, all she could see were several grody-looking individuals sitting around, playing cards, smoking, chewing, drinking, and spitting their wads into spittoons, which were haphazardly located on and around several of the tables with many on the floor. Some had been hit, and some were missed, but there was nothing she could see that could've explained that one ghastly smell. Unless, of course, you threw them altogether into a stew pot and whipped them up, smelly bodies included. But smell or no smell, what she was affronted with was just part of the West and an unavoidable inconvenience when entering such establishments.

"I gotta get outta here," Brina said. She could feel the bile rise in her throat.

"No, wait. Just stand here a minute or two. It'll pass, really," Cordell reassured her.

It took more than just two, but he was right. After five minutes or so, her nose and stomach grew slightly more accustomed to the ghastly aroma. Besides, she still needed to refill her flask, and this being the only saloon in town forced her to reconsider. So, there she stood, straddling the doorway blocking thirsty customers, hesitating, reluctant to give up any hope of fresh air, not wanting to enter on her own accord.

Cordell sensed her hesitation. Gently taking her arm in his brought a smile to her lips. And with a nod of acceptance from both, they stepped further into the dimly lit room. Once inside, their eyes adjusted to the dark. Side by side they stepped up to the bar, but before she had time to open her mouth, Cordell spoke, "Allow me, please."

"This time only," Brina responded. He wanted this, so be it, but next time, she'd handle her own whiskey buying.

While they waited for the bartender to see to their drinks, Brina sensed something other than the floor under her boot, and when she glanced down, she saw the source of the smell. Unknowingly she'd placed her boot in a freshly deposited pile of horse manure.

"What the...hell?" She lifted her boot off the floor in an attempt to dislodge the substance from its bottom and at the same time accidentally brushed Cordell's leg.

"What the...?" Cordell hadn't yet looked down towards the floor, which would've explained everything.

"Look. Horse manure, in a saloon." She couldn't believe it. A business establishment with horse shit on the floor? Well, she figured the bartender looked as though he'd been here most of the day; he ought to know something about what she just stepped in and why it was there.

"Excuse me," she addressed the bartender directly.

"Yeah? Whatcha want?" He just glared at her.

That was when Cordell stepped in. "Wait, Brina, let me handle this, you'll just get us thrown out." Without giving her a second chance, he turned towards the bartender, and very politely asked, "Would you mind explaining what this shit is on your floor, in front of the bar? The lady here has stepped in it."

"Oh that. Weeel, the sheriff was in not too long ago. Maybe his horse left it," he said.

Cordell thought he'd misunderstood. "The sheriff was in here with his horse?"

"Yep," he replied.

Brina couldn't believe where this conversation was going and had forgotten all about trying to dislodge the manure from her boot.

"Does he do this often?" Cordell thought maybe the sheriff was addlepated or something. He also began to wonder if maybe the bartender was too.

"Nope, just when he wants a drink, or when there are suspicious-looking strangers here 'bouts." Squinting his bloodshot eyes, he scrutinized the two of them. "You strangers?" This one in front of him was a big one all right, and she, she looked mighty fine with that proud look 'bout her. He was mostly drawn to her ivory skin, her dark-brown-black hair, and her eyes, whose color he couldn't quite figure. He took in all of her until he saw her gun belt. For an instant he stared at the belt but then had a strange feeling something weren't right. Cautiously and with flavor, he followed the contours of her body not missing a thing, finally settling back onto her eyes. He could see them now, see them more clearly. Their color wasn't what he assumed they'd be; instead, they looked like the barrel end of his very own rifle. He was sure of that now. He was also sure that they were staring back at him with the same kind of look his wife had when he'd been caught at doin' something inappropriate.

"Sorry, miss. Didn't mean to be a-staring. It's just that we don't git many in here like the two a you. And well, a…" He didn't know how to apologize to either her or his wife.

Brina recognized his mannerism as being just a man doing his job. And as a man not so well versed with the outside world. She didn't do anything about his behavior, just asked if the manure would be cleaned up soon.

"Weeel, usually when the sheriff comes in with his horse, he gets awful agitated when we start cleaning up with him still standing next to the bar, so we just wait till the end of the day to do the pickin' up," he answered.

"Well, sir," Brina began. "Might I suggest you find some fella willing to clean it up now so we may sit for a spell? Ya know, if your sheriff doesn't change his ways and leave his horse parked outside, I mean, those of them that ain't drunk will find another saloon. Then if you don't have one, they'll find some other town that's got one. People don't stay in shit like this; they go live somewheres else." She tried to sound the part.

As they continued to stand at the bar, Brina watched as the bartender stood for a moment, then motioned to a young lad sitting in the far corner to approach. After silently speaking with him, the lad quickly and quietly began cleaning the manure up off the floor, then, to Brina's surprise, cleaned off her boot as well.

"I'll tell the sheriff what you said." It was the bartender's turn to face the truth. "You're right, ya know. Weee'll die as a town. I'll pass the word around to others, and we'll talk to him about it, 'cause I don't like the smell either." Setting their drinks on the bar, he looked Cordell in the eye. "These two are on me." Then he turned back to his work.

Brina was soon to discover that the taste of mid-nineteenth-century liquor was not as rewarding as expected. All they had for the period was rotgut, which was similar to what she had brought, only theirs had the taste and quality comparable to rank cratier fuel, compared to the last of the fine brandy in her flask. None of the more-refined drinks had been invented yet or hadn't found their way this far West. She found that very discouraging. A glass of fine red wine, cognac, brandy, or maybe even a distinguished liqueur would have been a welcome delight if the time frame would've accommodated. In any case, more of the same ol' rotgut would just have to do; she cringed at the thought.

Both Brina and Cordell knew if Dillon was somewhere within this little town, one of the first places he'd head was either the saloon for a drink or the general store for supplies, and since he wasn't here at the saloon, that meant their next stop was already predetermined.

Entering the general store, Brina's peripheral vision spotted him crossing the street two or more buildings down. There he was, large as life heading towards the hotel. Her heart unknowingly skipped a beat as she watched him walk. So tall and proud he moved. Ever since she'd come to know those little characteristics so well, it didn't take her long to realize something about the way he now walked told her that something was not right. Without a second thought, she nudged Cordell's shoulder.

"There he is, but wait." Gently grabbing hold of him, she whispered, "Don't say a word, just watch 'im. Is it my imagination, or is he walking funny?"

Cordell closely watched his friend for any hint of something out of the ordinary. On closer examination, he also spotted it.

"He's had a few too many. Damn. It's been a very long time since I've seen him do that. He must have spent quite a time in the saloon before looking the town over."

"Well, at least he hasn't gotten into any visible trouble. Let's give him a few more minutes before heading for the hotel. I want to take a look at what the general store has to offer.

The only thing of value Brina found in the general store was a moment of what she called free entertainment. For there, against the counter, fingering what she assumed was the owner, was an older woman still in her undergarments. Large as life she was, right in the middle of the room and in front of all the other customers, flirting with him she was, as though no one else was around. Well, seeing this, Brina couldn't resist a bit of fun.

Stepping over to the fine-looking lady in her underwear she began, "Excuse me. Miss?" When that didn't work, she tried another tactic. This time, as Cordell tried not to look so amused, Brina loudly cleared her throat. "I say." She slammed her fist down on the counter hard enough to be heard by all the patrons nearby.

This time, she addressed the gentleman, "Excuse me, sir. You look a trifle familiar. Do I know you?"

The older woman turned around to glare at Brina with a nasty look on her old yet lovely face. "What? Go away! Can't you see I'm busy here?" Then she turned back to the man behind the counter, who at the time looked very uncomfortable.

The more Brina watched, the more obvious it was to her that this man had been trying to get away from this woman as well as get her out of his establishment for quite some time. After all, from what Brina could tell, the other customers of the store didn't really appreciate the appearance of a whore in their midst; besides, it was bad for business.

"Horace? Is that you?" Now she had both of their attentions. At that moment Brina turned her eyes on her newly created acquaintance, taking hold of his mind. There she learned, the situation as it had been presented to her, was, in fact, more than accurate.

After the older gentleman quickly shook his head, as to clear it from some fog, Brina caught his eye, then winked, hoping he'd understand her intentions. When he winked back, she knew he was ready to play.

"Horace! It is you!" Brina rushed up to the counter, around the whore, and within a blink of an eye hurtled herself over the counter embracing Horace as though a long-lost friend. "My gawd, man, I thought I'd never see you again!" After releasing him, she turned back towards the whore. "Excuse me, dearie, but do you know who you're messing with here?" From the look on the whore's face, Brina knew she'd interrupted at a most inopportune time. At least it was from the whore's point of view.

"Butt out, bitch!" spit the whore.

"Oh, my." Brina feigned fragility. "Horace, catch me. I think I'm going to faint."

Horace's reaction was instantaneous; he reached for the dark-haired woman just as she swooned and caught her before she'd dropped an inch.

"Thank you so much, Horace."

"Get out. Strangers ain't welcome," spit the whore.

Brina righted herself with Horace's help and added, "Forgive me, I'm not prone to fainting."

"Who cares? Just get out. Can't you see I'm busy?"

"I'm extremely sorry if I interrupted something here, but this is…" Brina wanted to be gentle about this.

"…None of your damned business!" yelled the whore.

Brina thought this woman was pushing it. "Now, I wouldn't continue with that line of language if I were you; besides, this here gentleman is an old friend of the family's. You must understand, I'm very protective of family members. Especially when found in the company of folks like you. Now, before you get hurt, I suggest you leave him be."

"Who do you think you are, telling me what to do? Why, you're nothing but a sniveling toad." All the whore had seen was a busy-body lookin' to interrupt.

Brina drew her Colt out of its holster, nonchalantly set it atop the counter for all to see and understand. "Leaving town would be preferable," she said with a sardonic smile.

Well, they didn't have to wait long. The whore stared at the weapon, scooped up what was left of her underdrawers, and ran out of the general store with a shriek.

Expecting Cordell to be as shocked as ever at her shenanigans, Brina instead found him in the front corner of the store laughing hysterically. Taking back her Colt from atop the counter then slipping back into its holster, she hurtled herself back over the counter to join him there.

"Wait, miss!" It was the gentleman behind the counter. "I'm mighty thankful for your help there. Ya know, I've been trying to get rid of that damn whore for ought on three weeks now. Ya see, I'm not married, and all the single womens left in this here town wants my money. Whores included. There's not one of them within one hundred miles that's worth a dime. Here, let me introduce myself to you. Horacio L. Bartholomew at your service. Is there anything I can do for you to show my gratitude?"

Brina first looked at Cordell then back to Mr. Horacio L. Bartholomew. "Horacio? Is that really your name? I just threw out Horace because it was the first name I could come up with on such short notice. Sheeit! I'm sorry, I just couldn't see. What she was doing was horribly obvious, I mean a...er." Brina was flabbergasted. This was one "open mouth insert foot" episode without a logical conclusion.

"That's okay, miss, Miss...?" For some reason, he dearly wanted her name.

"Oh, I'm sorry. It's Grant." At his puzzled look, she made the correction. "Brina Grant."

"Well, Miss Brina Grant, is there anything, anything I can do for you? You've saved me from a fate worse than death," pleaded Horace.

"Not right now, maybe later. I can't think of a thing at the moment, but we'll be here in town a day or so. Maybe something will come up by then. Sound fair?" Friends and acquaintances were hard to come by, and if this man was willing to help her out, then by gawd, she'd keep that avenue open. "We best be going, but I'll stop in periodically to see how things are, and to maybe chat a while. Gotta run." With that she turned back to Cordell, who was in the process of wiping the tears from his eyes. Since his condition was rather unsteady at the time, she had to take hold of *his* arm and almost drag him back out the way they'd come in.

Halfway down the street, Brina heard the bloodcurdling scream of a psychotic woman. Turning instantly towards the sound, she spotted, analyzed, and took immediate action against it. Pushing the still-recovering Cordell out of harm's way, Brina faced the furious whore she had just dislodged from Horacio. This time the whore held a knife the size of a bowie. Not wanting to kill a woman under these circumstances, Brina stood rock-solid still and waited for her. At the precise moment before all appeared lost, Brina grabbed the woman's arm, and using her own momentum against her, flung the surprised knife-bearing woman past herself, then let go—leaving her to crash land headfirst into the dusty street.

It happened so fast that Cordell didn't see it coming. One minute he was laughing hysterically at the antics of his gray-eyed beauty; in the next minute he was on the ground. What was he doing there, and what was going on just a few feet away? As he shook the dirt from his hair and rubbed it from his eyes, he got a glimpse of the spectacle before him. He couldn't believe what he saw. Here was his beloved Brina attacking that crazy woman from the general store with the agility of a highly skilled warrior.

It suddenly dawned on him this must've been how she'd managed to escape Lucifer and his boys. He watched in admiration, the attack, and its end. When the dust settled, he was by her side in an instant. To him, all that mattered was her safety. He didn't see the other townsfolk or Horacio emerge from various buildings around them to watch; all he saw was her.

Moments afterward, Brina felt the appearance of someone directly behind her. When she turned around, there was Cordell looking down at her from his six-foot-four-inch frame, searching her face for...for what?

"What is it?"

He said nothing, just kept his eyes glued to hers. In his stare she saw it. Saw that he understood, at least part of it.

"You've decided to embrace me just as I am, haven't you?" asked Brina.

Cordell acknowledged with a slight nod of his head.

Brina was touched. And as much as it was against her grain, she gave him a bear hug and into his ear whispered, "I luv you too, Cordell." Then let go. Once she finished dusting off and had her hat back on her head, she added, "And as to the other?"

"Mostly." Although, he still wasn't too sure.

With a smile on her face, she turned around to find that the townsfolk had surrounded the three of them: Brina, Cordell, and the whore. Finding him, Brina singled out Horacio.

"You still want to do something for us?" At his knowing nod, she continued. "Get this *lady's* possessions together, purchase her a ticket on the next stage out of the territory, and make sure the driver understands."

"Sounds like an excellent idea, my dear," Horacio said as he took a firm grip of the whore's arm, steering her towards the jail. To the sheriff, he explained the entire episode from start to finish. The sheriff placed her securely in a cell to wait for the next stage outta town.

"Cordell. Let's head for the Hawthorne. I need both a bath and a good-night's sleep." It had been a long day for all.

They both knew they'd find Dillon at the Hawthorne and upon entering found him in the lobby talking to the proprietor.

Brina cleared her throat.

Dillon turned in mock surprise. "Well, if that don't beat all—Cordell, Brina. We were just talking about you."

"Dillon." Cordell stepped up to him taking his hand firmly in his right, as he grasped his upper arm in a reassuring grip of old friendships. "Why in heaven's name aren't you at the saloon? Of all places, that's where we expected to find you."

"I was there for a while, but left after a couple drinks," he said.

"We saw you stagger across the street," Cordell said, smiling.

"Why didn't you call out?"

"Brina wanted a look at the general store."

"Brina, how are you, my luv?" he inquired.

"Just fine, Dillon. Just fine." *Let it go, Brina*, she said to herself. This was not the time or the place.

Mr. John Hawthorne stood behind the counter, patiently waiting for their salutations to end and their decision on sleeping arrangements to be made. When it didn't come right away, he politely interrupted. "Excuse me, miss?" The woman was definitely worth the confusion on the one gentleman's part.

Brina instantly recognized an educated voice from the other side of the counter and addressed him with respect. "Yes, sir?"

Polite too, that was a change. "The room arrangements. Your gentleman friend here was a bit perplexed as to how to handle things. May I be of any assistance?" John Hawthorne felt the situation required a more delicate and refined touch than what the tall one was able to provide.

"Well…Mr. Hawthorne, is it? Mr. John J. Hawthorne, the proprietor of this marvelous establishment?" Brina could tell by the twinkle in his eye this man was, in fact, he. "Very well then. Do you have a kitchen?" At his nod, she continued. "Well then. I would like a private room with a bath and supper brought to me, if that's not too much trouble." She'd read about places like this in her studies and of the accommodations thereof. And now this would probably be her only chance. She knew what she wanted, and she knew she didn't want to be disturbed while enjoying it.

John Hawthorne, proprietor of the one and only Hawthorne Hotel located in the only one-horse town of Dowdyville, nodded his head and added, "We also have a maid to tend to your every whim." Turning towards the room under the staircase, he clapped his hands together twice. Hurriedly from under the doorway stepped a young petite woman carrying a dust rag, wearing a long muslin dress with an apron, and a cute, little, white bonnet on top of her head.

"Oui, Monsieur?" responded the young woman.

"Bernadette, s'il vous plais; veuillez preparer un bain pour cette jeune Dame, et apporter toute les courtoisies necessaires," bid John Hawthorne.

"Oui, Monsieur Hawthorne."

"Go with her, miss. She will tend to your needs. However, there's no point trying to communicate with her. She speaks only French. I saved her from an unknown fate in the streets of Paris so many years ago when I was abroad, and she's been with me ever since. Now, if you would be kind enough to sign the hotel register, she'll be happy to take you to your room. She will also tend to the rest."

After the women left, John J. Hawthorne turned back to the cowboys to hear of their decision.

Dillon couldn't believe his ears. He thought that she'd accepted his slight of tongue as fact and had consequently come around to his way of thinking.

When the proprietor turned his attention back to them, the tall one didn't respond.

"Is there a problem, sir?" addressed John Hawthorne.

"Dillon?" Cordell inquired.

"I thought..."

Cordell didn't dare mention anything pertaining to the true meaning of her requests, afraid he'd spill a bean or two along the way.

John J. Hawthorne knew otherwise, as he'd construed her stately demands as unrequited love. So, to abide this gentleman over until the truth was obvious and accepted, he took a few minutes to explain about independent women.

"Patience, my boy, one must be patient," began John Hawthorne. "Independent women are a commodity only found on this continent. That is something you must learn to understand and accept. If there is enough of a spark between the two of you, she will come when she is ready if she ever is. If you push her into something she's not ready for or doesn't want, it will only end tragically, and you'll have nothing to show for it. Then again, if friendship is what she needs or wants, you'll have to consider that as well. You have thought of that, haven't you? Friendship?"

"Yeah. She'd made that perfectly clear not so long ago."

"Then that might just be your best bet. Friendship."

"Friendship," Dillon echoed.

"Friendship," he finalized.

During breakfast the next morning, Dillon just happened to overhear one of the other patrons mentioning something strange. Excusing his interruption, he asked what they had seen. Their explanation fit the bizarre patterns in which they were searching. It sparked his curiosity enough to believe that they finally had a direction. Once everything was packed, down the trail they rode. Their destination? Northeast. Towards a small community by the name of Mullet Town.

Friendship.

XVII

now enter the bad guys

"**F**ools! You stupid fools! How could you be so brainless, so asinine, so witless as to allow her to escape!" Looming over Lucifer, John, and Rene-with-a-hyphen from his perch atop the step of the shack that once held the woman, the Grim Reaper took kin to a vulture with the explosive tendencies similar to that of a loaded stick of dynamite in the hands of a madman, of which he was very close to being, and knew it.

The Grim Reaper they'd called him since he was a small child. They'd said that his mother had been exposed to Fornax radiation during a military operation. He, in turn, had been at the reciprocating end of her sickness and had suffered for it. With the yellowish, bloodless pallor of his skin and the lack of pigment in the irises of his eyes to boot, his temperament over the years had turned quickly from a demented and tortured child into a severely hateful and deadly being. A monstrous tool used accordingly by Zone 237, a branch organization of the Network, as their own specialist in handling novelty assignments. Yes, sir, if ever there was anyone qualified enough in the artistry of assassinating the gray-eyed one and that damned horse of hers, he was it.

Now it appeared, as Lucifer explained, the gray-eyed woman had escaped. If the Reaper didn't need these three idiotic excuses for associates, he'd extinguished them here and now. It'd only take a split second to reach out to the closest, with the force of a power ram behind his bare hand, to break through the thin layer of skin, shatter the rib cage, and remove the heart. Within the next instant, the second could be staring up from the ground with the Reaper's switchblade protruding from the body cavity with his entrails still neatly wrapped around it. The third, the Reaper hoped that'd be Lucifer. He wasn't ready to kill Lucifer just yet. He still needed him. As hard as it was to imagine, Lucifer appeared to be the only one with any sort of intelligence of the three. He didn't trust him, but at least he had a fairly good idea how his mind worked or didn't. Now, if he did keep Lucifer around, he'd use the twisted fear of himself, which he had deeply placed, to achieve his main goal: to eliminate Brina Louise Grant, the only threat to the zone, and especially at this time, Jesse. Otherwise, the Reaper would kill Lucifer along with the others if he had a mind to and not give a shit about any of them.

"Now let me get this straight. You used that funny-looking green gun and the tranquilizer dart like I showed you. You hit your mark, you got her here, had her all tied up, and now she's escaped, is that right?" The Reaper snarled. He was furious. From the information supplied by Lucifer, it appeared this gray-eyed one had been her. The one he had been sent to destroy. She had been within his grasp and had slipped through his fingers only hours before his arrival to their camp. If only he hadn't taken the time to disembowel that whore in Chapman, he would have been here to take care of things proper. "You had her here in this shack. Then as you entered, she surprised you and made good her escape. That's what you're telling me?"

Lucifer just stood, staring at the ground counting bugs.

"Lucifer. It was the right, gray-eyed woman this time, wasn't it? The one with the dark hair and skin the color of cream? The one I seek rides a massive gray horse. You did get the right one this time, didn't you? Was it her? Was she here?" The Grim Reaper was getting very impatient with Lucifer, but knew at the same time, he had to be cautious. He *was* smarter than the others, but he was also mad as a hatter.

"She *was* here," Lucifer replied.

As he stared at Lucifer from atop the step, he kept his hands off the man's throat, dissatisfying a sudden need to kill.

Lucifer finally chimed in. "How were we to know she would fight back after she woke up? None of the others did. And if John hadn't been occupied at the time, maybe she'd still be here now."

The Reaper sneered. "John? Where is our little Johnny?"

Lucifer and Rene-with-a-hyphen looked at each other and for the first time were extremely happy their names weren't John Deau.

Rene added, "He's gone to town for supplies. We expect him around nightfall."

"Very well," the Reaper replied. "Maybe that's best. Maybe by then I will have found something else to kill. Which of you spent the most time with her? I need to know all the details on the kidnap and what followed. I'll know then whether or not this one was truly the one I seek."

The threesome never really did find out from where this creepy man came, only that it was from very far away. Once Lucifer Carstead and his partner in crime, Rene-with-a-hyphen Quinlan, fell in with this guy, they realized that this was a man not to cross—ever. His personality flaws consisted of everything contradictory to all that was decent in themselves. He did have one unusual attribute of charm; he acted very similar to a rattlesnake right before the fatal strike. If evil could be created on this world in the form of a mortal, this man was it.

Lucifer, of course, had already seen the Reaper, as he knew him as, totally disembowel two other women just out of spite. Those two women had matched the description of the last steel-eyed beauty they'd kidnapped. This last one unfortunately had been the only one who was apparently capable enough to deliver such extremely painful gifts, then make good her escape.

"Well…" Lucifer began. "We happened on them just by chance out in the open. It was in the evening when we came upon their campsite. One thing I've got to say for her, she sure makes the best coffee I've ever drank." One look from the Reaper and Lucifer realized he had better get back to the mainstream of things quickly. "Like I was saying, we came upon their camp, and they offered their hospitality. We hung around long enough for a cup of coffee and a quick look around. John stayed in the shadows as much as he could, as not to be recognized. It was there he spotted the gray horse, and a fine-looking animal he was. Never had he seen one quite like him in all our days of rustling, rape, pillage, and plundering.

"Anyway, after we left, Rene suggested we quietly hide and keep an eye out for any unforeseen opportunities. Once out of camp, we took up different locations and silently waited. It was just a fluke, they were preoccupied for a second, and that was all we needed. We caught them off guard as they took the first watch. From there it was easy.

"By sunrise, she had come around quite nicely. I was greeted by not only a confident and very capable young woman, but also a beautiful one at that. Unfortunately, by the time I made my move on her, she was on her feet and using them quite nicely. Before I realized what was happening, she was out the door, and I was in no position to follow," explained Lucifer.

"Who tied her up?" asked the Reaper.

"John. Her feet and hands were firmly tied." Lucifer stood silently thinking while rubbing his chin. "Now that I think of it, her hands were tied in front of her. But we never expected her to be so resourceful; none of the others were. By the time I arrived, her feet had already been untied. That's why she was so mobile."

The Reaper said nothing. "The Network said she was very resourceful." He had spoken his thoughts out loud instead of to himself. "Have you found her trail?"

"South," answered Rene, knowing what the Reaper wanted.

The Reaper couldn't believe it. She had been so close, and he didn't even know it. "South? I must have gone right by her on my way here. Damn! Gather up your gear. Pack any supplies you'll need for an extended journey. We must find her and that horse."

Interrupting the Reaper again was Lucifer. "There's only one problem—she now rides with two other men."

"Two men? What two men?" the Reaper demanded. "She should be traveling alone. She left alone. Describe them."

As Lucifer described Dillon and Cordell to the Reaper, he could see the wheels turning behind those horrible eyes.

"They shouldn't be too much trouble. We'll just have to watch a little closer and be a bit more discreet in our plans. We'll wait for John to get back with the supplies before we head out. He shouldn't be too much longer."

When John arrived with the additional supplies, they broke camp and headed south.

Three hours later, it was still going pretty much the same. Lucifer was still afoot, reading the trail as best he could for any sign of her.

John knew the Reaper wasn't much on conversation, but something had been bothering him, and he just had to ask. "Why are you so adamant about this woman with the gray horse?" He could understand his desires for the line of work *he* followed, but to search out one woman in particular with such a vengeance was enough to make any man curious. It didn't make sense. Sure, he had pursued women who had wronged him, but not like the Reaper. He had the persistence of a man possessed.

"Shut up. You're in no position to question my plans. 'Cause if you screw up one more time, you will find out the hard way," the Reaper hissed. "Remember, don't cross me. Normally I don't give seconds, so consider yourself extremely fortunate and don't push it." Perched upon his horse, he came up to where Lucifer was searching the ground. "Lucifer, report." The Reaper was getting impatient. First, it was just one; now it was three. Three sets of tracks couldn't be all that difficult to find out here. He knew the risks involved in following her through the *field*, but the alternative was devastating to the Network.

The Network was a special world organization set up by terrorists, assassins, and mercenaries. He reflected on the true reasons why he volunteered for this mission. Jesse had assassinated the international emissary of Cyclops and was fleeing for his life. The Network had been trying to find a way to collapse the intricate world connections of Cyclops for centuries. They knew once that was accomplished, it would cause chaos and the final collapse of the World Protection Organization. Then the Network could move in and take over. Once Jesse assassinated his targeted diplomat, the Reaper knew

Cyclops, a branch of the World Protection Organization, wouldn't stop till Jesse was captured and executed. He also knew the intricate details of Jesse's criminal record. He remembered hearing through various channels Jesse's masquerade as a junior assistant to the leading authority in the Department of Time Travel Research. That was shortly before his escape into the past by way of the Franciscan Lifter. They were hoping once that was accomplished, Cyclops would not continue with their investigations. Unfortunately, that was not the case. They learned of certain elements when information on something called the Neptune Sphere came up missing. Once they put two and two together, they sent her. It was just by chance that he was in the chamber when she departed. He had tried to assassinate her just as she was vaporizing. Unfortunately, he missed his chance to be sure and needed to extend follow-up procedures. By the time the other assistants in the chamber realized what he was up to, he had taken care of them too. No one would be the wiser once he was gone. What Jesse planned to do with that information that he stole was beyond him. All he knew was that he was to kill her. That was his mission in this lifetime. After that? Well, that was anyone's guess.

He was brought back to the present when Rene-with-a-hyphen called to him. "They're here! The tracks, Lucifer's found them!"

XVIII

walking papers

*S*urveying her surroundings, Brina found herself sitting upon a golden palomino horse, high atop a snow-topped ridge. Below rested a vast creviced valley, or gorge, with its shades of brown, mauve, and green interlacing the rocky ledges housing the various feathered friends that had managed to survive the last holocaust. It must've been five miles wide and at least twenty miles long. Its sides in some places were very rocky and steep, with grays and purples intermingling the deep crevices.

She watched from her perch as swallows flew in, out, and around the cliffs and crevices of the steep sides of the gorge-like valley. As her eyes followed the walls down into the great expanse of the valley floor, the great river that wound its way to an unknown destination caught her eye. If she listened closely, the roar of the rushing water could just barely be heard over the silence abounding. Everything else around her was quiet. The sky was the bluest she'd ever seen with white puffy clouds scattered here and there, adding their own special contrasts to the sight before her. It was truly one of the many magnificent wonders of the world. At least what was left of the world.

Suddenly, there was an explosion off towards the horizon just past the beautiful scene before her. As she watched, a gaseous cloud rose high above her vision spreading its deadly form throughout the countryside. She knew right away there was nothing she could do. Wait. That was all she could think of because there was nowhere to run, nowhere to hide. While she watched the smoke billow her way, it took on a new form. It hugged the ground like a blanket, and by the time it reached her valley, the force of its destruction hit her as well. The smell of death hung in the air. She could almost taste it. Everything she had loved in life was about to be snuffed out like a match dunked in a glass of water. Brina watched the blanket unfold its way down the sides of the rocky crevices till it *reached the valley floor. Once it hit bottom and met up with the river, there was another explosion.*

All she could remember was screaming when it hit. Its impact shook her till she was sure all her teeth had fallen out. Then all was quiet.

With her eyes closed, she could almost see a man kneeling before her. She was sure it was Azrael, The Angel of Death. She knew he reached for her. Reached out to take her away from this horrible place so that he could take her away to his horrible place.

Dillon had been watching Brina since the early-morning hours. She seemed to be having a horrible nightmare. He wanted to awaken her, but one look from Wolf, and he changed his mind. It was a look he was growing more and more than familiar with. But when she started thrashing, concern overran caution, and he was by her side in an instant.

"Brina, my luv, wake up."

The sound of her name brought her out of it. Surely Azrael, the Angel of Death, wouldn't have used such a calming tone. "MJ, MJ, is that you?"

"Mgee, no. No, Brina, it's me. Dillon."

"Oh, Dillon. I'm sorry." Her head was clear now.

"Who's Mgee?" Who in the hell *was* Mgee?

She had to think for a minute. "Mgee? No, no. MJ, Master Jarlath. He was my most favorite instructor at the Academy. We had lots of fun."

Those initials rang a bell somewhere, but he couldn't recall it. "Brina. Are you all right now? You've had one dilly of a dream."

"Yeah, I know."

"You do? What was it about?"

Brina knew exactly what the dream had been all about. It was a look at a possible future. It came as a shocking reminder of the importance of her being here. If she failed in executing Jesse, then the Network would take control, making her nightmare a reality, and that could not be allowed to happen.

"Sorta."

"Do you want to talk about it?" Dillon asked.

"No. I don't." Brina rolled out of her bedroll, packed away her things as she did every morning, and excused herself from their company.

"What the hell was that all about?" Dillon asked Cordell.

"Damned if I know. Maybe she doesn't feel well."

"But why be so rude? I was just showing concern."

"Why *are you* showing so much concern? She *is* a full-grown woman. She can take care of herself. Haven't you figured that out *by now*?" Cordell stated a little too strongly.

"I don't get it. In the beginning, all you could think about was her, her, her, and now you don't?"

"Sorry. Maybe I don't feel well either." Cordell didn't. His mood was sour. He'd learned the hard way to look at her differently than before, and that bothered him. He'd been bewitched by this vixen, hoping to make her his, but she shattered his dreams by the mentioning of one name, his mother's. He still loved her dearly yet couldn't have her the way he wanted. And until he could truly accept that…

Brina was frustrated. The pressure of this assignment was getting to her. There for a while she had embraced life spent with Dillon and Cordell. She'd never truly had a life before, other than time spent at the Academy, and she was enjoying this one to its fullest. At least, until now. That damned nightmare had interrupted it. It was reminder to get back to business. That meant that she needed to collect and sort out those involved. She did this while drawing and reholstering her guns. It was a method she used to refocus her attention.

On one side of the coin was Jesse Loame. He was foremost on her mind. He was the main reason for her being here. She must not ever forget that.

Maximillian Rider. Now there was an escapee she knew little about. Jesse's criminal file did list Rider as an associate, and as luck would have it, there was a photo of him in the file. That made him also someone to watch out for, if not to outright shoot.

The unknown lab assistant. The one she recognized out on the trail last week. Who was he? Obviously, he was after her, but why?

The more she thought about it and worked her addition, the only answer that made any sense at all scared the heebie-jeebies out of her. *She had been targeted for execution by the Network.* That was the only logical explanation for all that had happened since they set foot on the platform.

Lucifer Carstead and friends. They were also on her hit parade. What did Lucifer call the ringleader of his gang? The Reaper? Yuck! On name alone, her skin crawled.

How many others had the Network sent?

Surly not Rocky and Bullwinkle too.

On the other side of the coin was Dillon and Cordell. What better friends could a girl have? Friends. Was this assignment too dangerous to be dragging two innocent men with her? Did she have the right to lead them into a situation that could possibly get them both killed? She understood that they too had been sent to catch Jesse, but of the three, it was she who'd read his file. She knew what he was capable of. She knew what they were up against. "Stop it," she said aloud. "Without them, you could've died."

Everything seemed to come at her from all directions and at the same time. She needed to get away and think. Think about everything that's happened and everything that may still come to pass.

There was a noise in the bushes. She froze in her tracks.

Mind and body are one, grasshopper.

Master Jarlath's old adage came back to her in a flash. It reminded her of why they'd sent her. She was a soldier. A soldier of Cyclops. And in her case, one of one. "Mind and body are one." She now knew what she must do. She had to leave these men. Let them search for Jesse; she had more important things to do.

As she stood her ground ready for action, the bushes parted.

There was no one there.

With guns drawn, Brina stood her ground. Then when the bush closed in upon itself with no one emerging, she became suspicious. Unsure, yet not ready to shoot, Brina waited for the assumed inevitable, yet when it came, she was not prepared.

It was a shift in the atmosphere. It moved towards her. She didn't know what to do. Fight or flight? Indecision on her part meant trouble, and she knew it. For just a second, she showed the fear she felt. That moment was all it needed. It moved in and took her.

At first, she tried to fight it but stopped the moment she sensed its origin. Loosening the tension and pressures felt earlier, she began to relax. She released the grip on her guns, allowing them to fall to the ground. There they lay, protected against all, until retrieved.

It engulfed her like a warm and form-fitting coat. It was a gentle caressing gust of wind that only she recognized. This waft transformed itself into a shrouded mist and devoured her in one fell swoop. All that mattered was the warm feeling she got from it. It caressed her like a lover. It was heaven and earth. Life, rejuvenation, trust, hope, conviction, companionship, support, and most of all love. Undivided, unconditional, unyielding love. Love, true and undeniable. Wolf had, once again, come to her at a time when she needed him most.

Once Wolf's formfitting coat retracted, Brina tried stretching away the aches the ground always manages to leave behind. Of all the things she was taught at the Academy, conforming with the ground was not one of them.

How long had she been there with Wolf? Dillon and Cordell were surely worried by now. No matter, Wolf would take care of the situation as it presented itself; he always had. He had also reclaimed what was rightfully his, her. They had reclaimed each other and knew what must be done. Knew it as sure as the sun would come up the following morning. Now she could resolve her conflict within herself reasonably.

She must take control of her situation. It was either go after Jesse aggressively and watch their behinds or abandon Dillon and Cordell. In abandoning them, their kismet would then be theirs alone, just as though she had never arrived—*yeah right*. Sure. They'd know she was out there, on her own, and would worry about her, but that was not her problem.

They were one, she and Wolf, and once again they would go where no man, woman, child, or plant had gone before. They will split up and search together, yet separate from Dillon and Cordell, in hopes of increasing their chances of success.

It was Cordell who noticed the difference in Wolf and brought it to Dillon's attention.

"What is it, what's wrong?" The look on his face told Dillon that something definitely was not right somewhere. He was pointing towards Wolf.

"Watch him," he whispered. Cordell didn't miss much.

Dillon could see what he was talking about. Wolf was most assuredly acting different. Thinking of Wolf brought to mind Brina. Where was she? She had more than enough time to wash up and return.

"Cordell, quickly. We must find her."

Cordell was on his feet in an instant.

They grabbed their guns and took off in the direction Brina had gone. About five minutes out of camp, Dillon started feeling slightly dizzy, sick to his stomach, and apprehensive. Glancing Cordell's way, he noticed a slight waiver in his step as well. He looked like Dillon felt. Suddenly the feeling was gone, and all was quiet. Dillon tried shaking it off as frantic concern, but it was more than that, it was…

Cordell heard and recognized the voice behind the warning as the Gray Wolf.

"You must not follow."

That's when something hit Dillon, hard. Hard enough to knock the wind out of his lungs, knocking him flat to the ground. Sitting on his rear in such an embarrassing position forced him to think twice about the unknown entity within their midst, Wolf. Had he done this? Was he that capable?

"Dillon. I tried for your arm, when I heard Wolf's warning, but missed.

"That was Wolf?" He had to be kidding.

"Yeah."

"How did you know?"

How did he know indeed? "I've heard him before."

203

Puzzled, Dillon pressed him. "When?"

"On the ridge, when you went to town ahead of us."

"Damn."

Everything came back. Cordell, Brina, Wolf, and the reason he was in this position. Then came the sound of approaching horses. There he was, Wolf. He had appeared out of nowhere. Following him was their packhorse. The two animals walked directly past them into the fog-filled clearing, past its invisible wall and disappeared into its misty depths.

Dillon's better judgment told him to let it go, but he tried following instead. Before he got too far, he was struck down a second time by the unknown force. Confused and frustrated, he turned towards Cordell and asked, "What else did you learn while I was away?"

"I can't tell you."

"You can't tell me or won't tell me?" He didn't know what to expect next. Perhaps Cordell could enlighten him a bit.

"I can't tell you. I gave my word."

"Okay then. What *can* you tell me?"

"Some of the things that happened on that ridge the afternoon you rode into Dowdyville, I'm still not sure I want to remember. I swore an oath to both Brina and Wolf that I would never divulge their secrets. I can say that he's more than what he seems."

"That's obvious. What else can you tell me?"

"He…" Before Cordell could finish, the fog vanished, and all was quiet.

"What the…" Running ahead, they ran into the lone packhorse. Brina and Wolf were long gone.

"Damn. Cordell, check the packhorse. I'll search the surrounding area."

"Some of the supplies are gone, Dillon. I found this on the britchen."

He handed his friend a sheet of paper. As Dillon reached for it, he knew what it was before he began reading it aloud.

Dearest Dillon and Cordell,

This letter is one of the hardest things I have done in a long, long time, and that is to leave you.

I've had a vision, and I must follow that vision to an unknown destiny. Had I but known so many things, I would have found a way to stay. Unfortunately, your safety depends on my leaving. I say this because there is another man out there who has targeted me for execution. I cannot risk your lives for that reason. Therefore, Wolf and I will draw the other's fire and leave you free to pursue Jesse.

Your help and friendship has brought me back into the world of the living and back into the position I can hardly ignore.

I have taken the supplies we shall need from the packhorse. Now, Wolf and I travel alone as one in search of the Neptune Sphere.

Till we meet again.
Brina

P.S. Don't bother searching for us, we won't be there.

"Damn her!"

"Dillon," Cordell began. "I know how you feel, but you have to think about the possible outcome of their choice. She is right about one thing: splitting up does give us a better chance at finding Jesse. Not only that, but Brina also knows more than she's telling. That third man out there she speaks of is someone only she recognizes. If he is after her, both she and Wolf will be cautious.

"This is something she feels must be accomplished by her alone. After all, I believe she was sent to us because she needed somewhere to begin. We were tracking Jesse anyway; she just happened to fall out of the sky and into our lives for a time.

"We've learned a lot from her, and she deserves all the considerations due her. Somewhere down the road, I'm sure, we'll meet up with her again. Remember she's not alone. Wolf will protect her with all the power he wields."

Dillon listened attentively to everything he had to say. He didn't want to admit it, but yes, he was right. They were gone, and they had a job to do. Best get on with it.

"Cordell, I hope you're right. I've really become quite fond of that gray-eyed soldier."

All Cordell could think of was the special connection he now shared with Brina and Wolf. "Yes, Dillon, I've grown quite fond of her myself. Let's break camp."

BOOK 2

XIX

don't look a gift horse in the mouth

Brina had a nagging feeling in the back of her head that if Dillon had a mind to, he'd have Cordell track her. But believing her decision to split up was to hopefully increase their chances of catching up with Jesse and that sphere, she rode like the devil himself was hot on her little tail. And because she also believed her dream and/or nightmare revealed the location of the key piece in this puzzle, and a possible end should she not, all the more reason to not dally.

She knew from her dream that particular valley in which the devastation occurred played an important role. From what she tried to remember of her earlier schooling, the rock formation and the distinct plateau region in her dream suggested a northwesterly direction, so Brina headed towards what she hoped were the Montana Territories.

The only thing that bothered her was Jesse's trail. Since leaving Dowdyville, he had been leading them all in a northeasterly direction, when the dream had suggested otherwise. This suggested something else was out there she was unaware of, so covering ground quickly was all important.

She had to remember Jesse supposedly had in his possession a document that told of the location of the sphere and its properties. Finding him and it first was all imperative, because not only did he now have the location, but the guidelines for operating it as well. If Jesse reached the sphere before she, there was going to be hell to pay. That was why she decided to push herself so hard on this leg of the journey.

With so many hours spent in the saddle, Brina for the first time began to realize what it must have been like all those centuries ago when those fearless horsemen rode at breakneck speeds carrying the mail for the Pony Express. Then it dawned on her, *those fearless horsemen of yesteryear were actually making history* directly under her nose along some route south of her, or close to it.

Assuming they'd covered enough country by late afternoon, and since she really did need a break, Wolf slowed to a walk, and while cooling himself out, she enjoyed the scenery around her. It didn't happen too very often, the opportunity to take a moment to enjoy something anymore. There was always something else pending—Jesse and the sphere; Jesse and the sphere; Jesse and the sphere; good ol' Jesse, *didn't it ever end?* But with clear sailing ahead, a direction sorta fixed in her mind, Brina took advantage of the situation Wolf presented her and allowed him his head.

What she saw before and around her was breathtaking. Even though it was summer, the grasses held their own beauty. The browns, golds, and assorted plum-like colors that mixed in with the various shades of green sagebrush plants that sprouted up in illogical places all around the high prairie were awesome. Even the hills had distinct shapes and colors to them. Some took on the appearances of pyramids, loners in this vast land. Their assorted shades beginning at the base of cream to brown with their topping of green from the sparse trees that grew at the top of their own little world definitely made it a sight to behold and cherish.

Without warning Wolf stopped, ears up and alert.

"What is it?" The animal picked up the pace until Brina was finally able to see and identify a structure up ahead. At one mile away, she couldn't be sure of what it was, but knew it was large. Pressing Wolf to his limits they quickly closed the gap.

It was an old, abandoned barn, with a dome-shaped roof that seemed to reach for the sky. Around and on the other side, unseen at their arrival, but later of which she found was the skeletal remains of what could've been the original ranch house—a house with the *Spirit of the West,* she believed, concealed within its walls. And from the way it looked, it had been that way for years, if not centuries.

Out of the silence came a voice. "Is someone there?" It was a man or a big woman with a deep voice.

Before Brina could answer, it came again.

"I repeat, is someone there? I need some assistance if you please." A polite voice even.

It originated from inside the barn. Wolf gave no indication that the situation held silent dangers, but she'd run across stranger things in her day. "Yes, someone is here. Are you armed?" Not that she expected him to answer truthfully, but you never could tell.

"Yes. I have one shot left in my derringer. Am I mistaken, or are you a woman?"

Couldn't get anything passed this guy. There was her sarcastic side surfacing. "Are you alone?" Brina was taking no unnecessary chances this time.

"Well, sorta…" came the answer.

"What do you mean by 'well, sorta'?" asked Brina.

"It's kinda hard to explain," he answered.

"You better talk quick, cowboy, or I'll leave ya where you lay." Brina didn't have time for this crap.

"Okay, okay. There are two of us in here, but I'm the only one breathing."

"Are you hurt?"

"Yes," he replied.

"Do you have any money?" If he was going to be this stupid, why not give 'im a little scare? Even though his voice had a sincere quality to it, for safety's sake she remained leery and cautious. Besides, why be stupid and walk into a barn with an injured man carrying a loaded derringer? It would be just as intelligent as crawling into the den of a starving mountain lion wearing a raw beef steak around her neck.

"Do you need money? I'll pay you for helping me. Please help me. I was thrown when my horse spooked, and I think I've a broken leg."

"What about the other gentleman?"

211

"The other gentleman…hmmmmmm. The other gentleman tried to rob me, and I shot him. Please help me, my supplies ran out day before yesterday."

Brina told herself to not to bother; this man was none of her concern. Unfortunately, she had a soft spot in her heart for injured animals, no matter what the species; besides, the word *please* wasn't normally used by someone who planned on shooting you.

Common sense lost out; she would enter. Slowly she dismounted. Cautiously she stepped up to, then opened the one swinging door, carefully entering the barn. It was light and dark inside, due to the rays of sunshine spilling between each of the old, rotted sideboards, giving the interior a striped pattern on its floor, walls, and on the injured man who lay in the center of the first paddock. *Ya know, kinda like a gigantic zebra rug.* As she evaluated him from above, as he was lying on the ground, with her right hand on the butt of her Colt, Brina noticed he was younger than his voice revealed. Extremely handsome, she thought, with short, wavy, light-brown hair, with eyes the color of a deep, rich and tantalizing chocolate bar.

Her eyes shifted to his leg. It was obvious even for her that the ankle had been injured in some way. The boot appeared smooth and without creases, as it was forced to be the bandage that bound. Yep, there definitely was a problem here, which meant he definitely did need her help. And knowing better than to help an armed man, in a split second she drew her Colt from its holster, had it cocked, and leveled his way. And in a voice, just as polite and calm as in ordering a meal in a top-notch eatery, she instructed him, "Please hand over your derringer and all other weapons you may have hidden, *now*."

With her gun still in its holster, he believed getting the drop on her would be a piece of cake. However, the second before he was able to release and draw his derringer from its concealed location along his right forearm, this woman had already drawn, cocked, and had her pistol pointed at him. Her demeanor forced his hand into submission, compelling him to relinquish his derringer and the knife in his boot. After passing them over, he raised both hands as a signal to her to please not shoot, then sat there disbelieving that a woman had beaten him to the draw. A mere woman, *and a rather beautiful one at that.* He was very surprised and a little awed. Never had he seen a woman that striking handle weapons with such skill. Crestfallen as to the outcome of his assumed win, he swallowed his pride, took a deep breath, then began the telling of his *story*.

"When my horse spooked at something, I found myself in the dirt. I looked up and spied more than dust headed cross country. Gone was my horse, saddle, supplies, and the rifle that was still safely tucked away in its scabbard. This left me with my knife and derringer as protection against any and all attackers."

"You must be very good to have used only one of the two shots allotted in a derringer." Now that he was unarmed, Brina knelt next to him for a look-see at his leg. Gently taking inventory, it appeared to be his ankle and not the leg as he previously assumed. Not knowing too much about broken bones, she did not try and remove the boot to set it; instead, she let the boot do that job.

"I hope it's just a sprain." She wanted to dive into the depths of those chocolate-brown eyes but knew better and didn't. "What's your name, cowboy?" she asked instead.

"Justin. Justin Case III. At your service, my lady." With that he attempted a makeshift bow from his sitting position on the ground.

"Where is your gentleman friend, Justin Case III?" asked Brina.

"In the back. I'm sure by now he's not in the best of conditions. Ya know, you really don't want to see him, especially if you have a weak constitution. He's probably pretty ripe by now." Justin said.

"Let me assure you, I've seen plenty, done plenty, and can pretty much take care of myself." It had been a requirement at the Academy to spend at least 180 days in the morgue viewing and assisting with the assorted cadavers. There she'd had her fill of murdered victims in all ways, shapes, and pieces. Yes, she could handle this viewing just fine.

He held her back a bit longer by asking, "By the way, how are you called?"

Brina had to think about that for a moment. She still had to be careful to whom she gave out her name. Not many things had fallen into place lately; why would she think this would?

"I'm known as Bree." That was pretty close to the truth. It wouldn't be too hard to get used to that one; at least it was closer than her original idea. This guy seemed nice, polite, trustworthy, but who knew? He could be a conman lying through his teeth for all she knew.

"Bree what?"

"Just Bree."

"Okay, just Bree, do you suppose I might impose upon you for maybe having something edible in your saddlebags that I might maybe could eat? Since we're now on first-name basis."

First-name basis, *swell*. She didn't like the way that sounded. A trifle too familiar for a first meeting under such circumstances for her taste and judgment; however, there was something in his eyes that was trying to tell her something. What? She didn't know. Oh well, she'd probably find that one out in time. As to feeding him? Well, he sure looked as though he could use it.

"Sure." What harm could it do? "Wait here." Leaving him, Brina headed for Wolf and her supplies. As she fumbled through her saddlebags for some jerky, she realized that abandoning this man to an unknown fate with that ankle of his just wasn't her style. Upon returning, she again stood in front of him, evaluating him and the situation before her.

"Here, Justin, try some of this while I take a look at your gentleman friend." After handing over some dried meat and her canteen of water, she headed towards the back of the barn where the body was supposed to be. On finding him, she did manage to conclude that he was indeed very dead. Then when she looked closer, she found to her amazement the dead man below her was none other than Maximillian Rider! What the hell was he doing way out here? She knew it was him. She remembered seeing his photo in Jesse's criminal file, along with all those other creeps. She recognized Max's chiseled nose, the square chin, the magenta hair. *In her time there were always oddballs*, and then the one feature that stood out in her mind more than all the others put together, believe it or not, were his eyes. Of course, she had to bend down and open each lid in their turn to be sure, but they were definitely his, for the right was blue and the left was brown.

Not wanting to look a gift horse in the mouth, Brina smiled while thinking, *One down. Thank you so very much, Justin Case III!*

As the last shovelful of dirt settled on its final resting place upon the mound, she began to cry. Silly Brina, she always cried at funerals, no matter whose they were. Cherishing life above all else was another personality trait undesired by the organization. They wanted stolid soldiers fighting their causes; *oh well, can't have everything.*

Brina then turned to find Justin just emerging from the barn for the first time since her arrival. He was in an upright position, barely able to stand, and certainly not able to put much weight on that ankle; using part of a cross piece from one of the paddocks for support, he at least was upright.

One last look at the gravesite again reminded Brina of why she was here. Turning away from it, Brina approached Justin. "Well now, what are we going to do about you?"

"You're not thinking of burying me too, are you?" He was really only kidding.

"No, of course not. Although we do have to make some decisions here. You need that ankle looked at, and I have no idea in which direction the nearest town is. Ya know, it would be much easier if you were dead, like him." She nodded her head in the direction of the grave. "But since you're not, we'll have to think of something else. Let's see. First things first. I know your ankle hurts like hell, but I'm thinking of leaving the boot on. That way it will help support the ankle and give you added protection."

Justin disagreed. "No. It needs to come off. My whole foot, and ankle, feels strangled. The pain is so great that I feel dizzy sometimes. You must help me get it off."

"I'm sorry, Justin, if I help remove your boot, we will not be able to get it back on. It'll swell like crazy. I think you'll be worse off than you are now. Believe me, I know from personal experience. I could wrap the ankle in some rags I have in my saddlebags, but let me assure you, later on, you'll realize your error too late. That is, if I give in to your request, which I won't. You'll just have to believe me."

Now the question was how to get him out of there? Stepping back for a better look, she evaluated his size to be not much larger than her own.

"Yep, it might just work. Since your horse is long gone, and if you're willing to ride my horse, I can walk alongside. We've little choice here." She didn't trust him enough to allow him to ride behind her, and due to the condition of his ankle, he was in no shape to be walking on his own. "I'll get Wolf while you wait here then we'll give 'er a try."

"Wait."

Stopping, she turned to hear him out.

"You have a wolf?"

"No, silly. Wolf's his name," Brina replied. "Ya know, the horse I ride." She knew detaching herself from this man was imperative. Time was running out. If Jesse managed to find the sphere before she did, *damn*. Unfortunately, Justin was turning into the unwanted baggage she couldn't afford. Yet there was something about him that tore at her subconscious mind. Not able to pin it down, she again passed it off as her imagination.

Walking Wolf closer to where Justin waited for easier mounting, Brina then gave the unnecessary command of "Whoa."

Justin was more than surprised at the sight of the woman's horse. "Wow! Where did you *get him*?" Justin was in awe. He had never in all his years seen an animal of that caliber. He was gorgeous. "Ya know, I could use a good horse. Suppose he's not for sale though, eh?"

"You're right, cowboy, he ain't for sale. This horse and I've been together too long. It's not an option. You ought to feel privileged though, Justin Case III, ya know, I've never let anyone else ride him. Then again, he's never allowed strangers to get this close either. You should feel perdy lucky." Trying to ease his apprehension in the presence of a beast such as hers, she added, "Think of it as exploring an uncharted continent. Come on. Hobble on over here. I'll give you a leg up."

"I'm sorry. You'll hurt yourself. There must be another way, a log perhaps?"

"Nonsense. Git on over here, or I'll change my mind and leave you without. Really, I'm stronger than I look—don't fret it."

He was amazed at the strength of this woman. Why, she was no bigger than himself. He thought women were supposed to be weaker than men. She was an unusual find that was for sure, that horse too. Wolf, she had called him, had the grace of a European mount, yet when Justin gazed into his eyes, he was struck with a vision of looking upon a beast of overwhelming power. On size alone he was awesome. Sitting atop his back gave Justin the feeling of a king mounted on his mighty charger surveying his kingdom.

That fantasy shattered the moment she touched his leg seeking his attention. There she was, standing below him. And for the first time since their meeting, he noticed her eyes and their color—that being steel gray. The same steel gray color of this magnificent beast under him. How weird. And as he stared into those depths, he felt... he felt his heart skip a beat.

"Which way now, Justin?" Brina's worries for the moment were gone in the blink of an eye.

"North. I was heading north when that outlaw ambushed me. I would like to keep going that way if you don't mind."

"North it is then. Come, Wolf, we've got territory to cover." Leading her trusty steed down the trail was Brina, all the while rehashing previous concerns pertaining to this delay, and also realizing that decent company was indeed very hard to find.

Once on the trail it didn't take long for her own questions to take form. It was a mysterious situation finding Max Rider dead, after not as much as even a clue to his whereabouts. Then, here he turns up of all places and in the company of some stranger—not even with any of his cohorts, but here he was dead, shot in the head by a wandering cowboy? She was guessing it had to have been an attempted robbery. A robbery? Could Rider really have been that stupid or possibly desperate enough to attempt thievery out in the open? It had to have been just a coincidence, Brina was sure. Either way, she had to take it as a blessing in disguise: the man was dead, out of the way, in the ground, never to be seen or heard from again. And unbeknownst to her friends, who were on the other side of the valley in which she was now walking, this gave them one less escapee to watch out for.

The only other question now was what was she to do with her newly found charge? Justin, she discovered, was a very considerate fellow who unfortunately had befallen an injury in which he needed the attention of someone else. Most importantly it was for her to find him and his ankle a needed doctor. By the time they rode into Daytonville in search of such medical attention, Brina had come to enjoy Justin's company enough to consider continuing traveling together.

Riding double for a spell, Brina now slipped off the back of Wolf as they rode up to the hitching rail in front of the office of Dr. Archibald Paine, resident physician in a small office on the north side of town.

"Justin. If you would be so patient, I'll get the doctor; then the two of us can get you inside. I really don't want to injure that ankle any more than we have to."

Beginning her ascent towards the door of the doctor's office, she momentarily halted when Justin quietly said her name.

"Bree. I know this is a very bad time to ask this, but before you drop me off here in town, would you consider waiting till the diagnosis is definite? If I'm given an almost-clean bill of health, I would be deeply grateful if you would accompany me further on my journey. I find your company stimulating and very enjoyable."

How could she say no to *please?* After all, she was in actuality hoping for the same thing. It was a pleasant change. There were no demands, no romantic gestures, just good ol' companionship. Even Wolf seemed to approve as well.

"Justin, I'll think about it. In the meantime, may I suggest we listen to what the doctor says. Then you'll have to find your own mount. If we are to travel together, we must put miles under our horses. That is if I decide to accompany you. So, if you will excuse me, I'll fetch the doctor." With that she gave him one of those smiles he had learned to enjoy so dearly these last few days. It was almost certain even before entering into the doctor's office what she would decide.

Dr. Archibald Paine was a gentleman from the old-school. Why he had set up practice in such a desolate part of the country was beyond imagining. A doctor, of psychology originally, frustrated in the end by the crackpots in his field, chose to take up residency in a desolate location, which kept his associates to a minimum, if any at all. He found that healing the body was much easier and less complicated than trying to fix those off-balanced minds. Shorter than Brina's five foot nine and much older than expected, Dr. Paine had the charming attitude of a professional who really cared. When he examined Justin's ankle diagnosing a sprain, he commented on the decision of leaving the boot in place, especially out on the trail. Then found it had indeed kept the swelling to a minimum, increasing the support needed and actually aided in the healing. That made Brina feel much better because the decision she had made was a wise one after all—*for a change*. It was final, Dr. Paine prescribed one day, preferably two, of needed rest. He also said that the ankle was to be elevated at all times.

"Bree, please don't abandon me now. Wait the two days or so till I can ride," Justin pleaded.

Why was this man was so determined to remain in her company? Yes, she agreed that waiting was an idea, but for two whole days or more? There was so much at risk!

Once Justin was checked into the hotel for his needed bedrest, Brina came to see him. Three knocks on the door informed him of company. Once permission was granted, she placed her hand on the knob, but before she could turn it, she was interrupted by a lewd remark coming from down the hall.

"Heeey, sweetie."

There, at the far end of the hall was a drunken guest with half of him hanging outside his own doorway, staring at her from under bloodshot eyes, with a bottle in his hand, half full of some such alcoholic liquid. "If you're lookin' fur compnee I'm rite here, sweetie. I've bin waaitin' fur sum nice tart to cum by, but no one's cum, and I'm gitten dawn on drink. Come here an' hep me ot."

Brina couldn't believe her eyes. What a jerk. Probably someone of importance on a business trip who'd just had a few too many.

"No, thank you, sir. I've other things to do." With that said, she quickly entered Justin's room.

Justin was found in a sitting position on the bed with his ankle elevated like a good boy, just as Dr. Paine suggested. "You're following orders. That's a good sign. Listening to what the good doctor says." She still didn't understand why this man wanted her company so desperately. It was imperative she continue on her journey as soon as it was possible and to put as many miles under Wolf as she could. And if that was the case, why in the name of Sam Hill was *she* standing at the foot of this bed instead of being miles away?

"Bree, have you made any decisions yet on what you're gonna do?" Justin was desperate; he was almost pleading.

"Damn it, Justin, I've got to get back on the trail and soon. I need to know why you are so adamant on traveling with me. I will admit we have become fairly good traveling companions on this leg of our journey, but not enough for you to be so damned determined. Justin, I care. Don't misunderstand me, but there is something I must get to before it is too late, and two days may delay me enough to regret our meeting, and I don't want that." *Damn.* Brina was beside herself.

Last time a man had tried to take over her feelings, she wouldn't let him; this time one had without even trying, and she didn't want to admit to it, but she liked it. Maybe she never should have accepted this mission. Too many variables were controlling her decision-making process, and at the same time she realized that Wolf was keeping a safe distance from all determining factors, and that puzzled her too.

"Bree. I…please. I can't explain it, because I really don't know why. I just do."

While Justin paused in his speech, Brina watched his movements. Watched how he looked at his hands, as though the answers to all his worries would magically appear out of nowhere.

"Please, Bree, I can't explain entirely, but I can tell you that it has been a very long time since I've been in the company of someone I feel totally at ease with. I have led a very complicated and lonely life till I met you in the barn, and I'm having a hard time facing the fact that I may lose your companionship and friendship. You see, I've finally reached a stage in my personal journey where I need companionship.

"Ya know, you could have left me there in the barn alone forcing me to fend for myself, but you didn't. You chose to help, and I'm again asking for your help. Bree, please stay. Stay with me till I am well enough to travel, then travel with me. Together we can make it. Alone can only result in unforeseen risks."

Risks. What did he know about risks? She just mentally shook her head. There he sat. This lost puppy she found out on the road. Hurt and alone, asking for help. No, pleading for help. What was she to do? On the verge of sounding like a programmed being, she kept defaulting to her original plan, to continue on in search of Jesse and the hidden sphere. It was going to be a most difficult decision. One that might finalize all of their futures. She chose her words very carefully.

"Justin, you make my decision extremely difficult, but I'll tell you what: I'll spend the rest of today thinking. Then I'll sleep on it. In the morning, I'll see how you're doing. I'll give you my decision then. Will that suffice?"

"Yes, and thank you," he answered.

Outside, the sun was just setting. With Wolf's reins in her hand, she proceeded down the street in search of a saloon. A drink. She needed a drink. A drink just might be the ticket she needed to help her think about the decision before her. At the same time, she believed that drinking and riding were not quite what the beloved doctor would approve of, but hey, she was over 7,665 days; it was allowed.

Wolf was keeping totally out of this one, which surprised her. Moments like this and any other important decisions regarding their mission were objects of conversation that Wolf rarely avoided. Something was amiss here, but she was too sidetracked at the time to confront him with it.

At the saloon, she tied her steel gray to the hitching rail then climbed the steps in search of a glass of whiskey. Not only did she feel in need of a drink, thanks to Justin and his cause, but she also needed to refill her two whiskey flasks for whatever the future held in store.

Stepping right up to the bar, she slapped her dollar down and asked the bartender for a glass. He looked at her as if she was nuts. "Excuse me, Miss, but the owner's not accepting any new girls for hire. You'll have to leave."

"What's this 'excuse me, Miss' stuff? I would like a drink, please." Brina could see right away convincing him was going to be difficult. "I've already given you my dollar. Please do the honors of returning my dollar or giving me a glass of whiskey. I'm in no mood to argue."

"Hey, guys! This here lady, and I use the term loosely, wants a drink! Is there anyone here who would be kind enough to get one for her?"

Two gentlemen from the other end of the bar looked her up and down. The taller of the two stepped away from the bar, heading her way.

Not expecting trouble, she had mistakenly left her gun belt in her saddlebags. That left her again with her knife and her training. Although from the looks of the situation before her and the unlikelihood of finding any one of authority who would take her side, defending herself with a deadly weapon was not a choice she could afford. "Gentlemen, please, if you're going to act inappropriately, I'll just take my leave."

"Not so fast, little lady." It was the one from the end of the bar. "Why, you're pretty enough to eat." He tried to put his arm around her shoulders in a friendly snuggle.

Gently pushing him out of her way and heading for the swinging doors leading into the street, Brina was grabbed from the rear by another gentleman who apparently didn't want her to leave either.

"Wait a minute, little lady, we still have some unfinished business to attend to." He immediately pulled her into his embrace trying at the same time to find his way through her clothing.

Brina knew exactly what might happen if she didn't take some sort of action. Neither being fondled or raped was one of her favorite pastimes—not from any male. Lucifer, these guys, no one. Back during her years at the Academy, she was sexually molested by one of the substitute instructors; unfortunately for him in the process of rape, she managed to break free and crush his sternum with a lucky kick. Here was not the place to attempt such an act; plus, the man she was fighting with probably didn't need that severe a reprimand. She also knew a public pub was not the place to show off her unusual talents and abilities. Therefore, since there was no one in town that Brina could rely on, she took the matters in her own hands and pried herself from his embrace then slapped him as hard as she possibly dared across the side of his face. "How dare you! I'm fully capable of taking care of myself, and I'm entitled to be here!"

Another barfly tried to make a stronger pass at her, not believing her threat, and this time both Brina's fists slammed into each side of his head meeting their mark at the point of each temple, then watched him crumple to the floor. She surveyed the other gawking men in the saloon and asked the curious question, "Who's next?" It was comical. The other patrons standing at the bar turned their attentions back to their previous conversations as though she never entered. The bartender served her a bottle on the house and left her to her own vices. Brina stepped off towards the far corner table to enjoy, contemplate, to savor her bottle, and her position for the evening.

By morning she still hadn't come to any conclusions. The whiskey hadn't helped except to give her a splitting headache. Of course, choosing to remain there for the remainder of the night to watch the assorted town characters wander in and out in such entertaining fashions didn't help matters either. So instead of checking on Justin right away and having to make the decision that chose to elude her, she elected to do a bit of shopping instead, hoping that her expectant purchase would be her deciding factor.

First stop, livery stable. She figured if the perfect mount for Justin could be found by the end of the day, her decision would be to stay with him for the time being. If the perfect mount was nowhere to be found, then she would have done all that was feasible, leaving Justin to fend for himself. She did hope that the perfect mount for him could be found because she'd hate to leave him in an unfamiliar town without any means of transportation.

By the time Brina left the blacksmith, she had the location of the nearest horse ranch that might just have what she was searching for. Her decision, for the most part, had been finalized. Reaching the hotel room where Justin waited for her return, she knocked on his door.

"Come in," was the reply.

Brina opened the door gingerly, not knowing how Justin was dressed and not wanting to interrupt him, but there he was—all cleaned up as though he'd just returned from a trip down the hall. He was freshly shaved, and the aroma of lavender filled the room.

"Good morning, did you have a good night?" Glancing down at his bed was a reminder of her missed sleep.

"Bree, it's good to see you too! Have you made your decision yet?" And again, he was hoping.

"Well, yes and no."

He looked at her cockeyed.

Biting her lower lip in indecision, Brina wondered how to continue. "Before I get into that, I want to ask you something." She put on one of her ornery grins just for him.

"Anything."

"What do I smell?" She knew but wanted to hear him say it.

"Well, that's fairly easy to explain. Ya see, I spend most of my time on the trail, and usually it's not that noticeable because the smell of horse and sweat usually covers it up. Here in the hotel, there are no horses, and I've just gotten out of the tub." With that he smiled.

"You didn't answer my question."

"You didn't answer mine either."

Brina stood silently waiting at the end of Justin's bed for his answer. "I'm waiting."

"Is it that important?"

"No. Not really, but I am waiting."

"Lavender. Do you like it?"

She just looked at him.

"And…?" He waited.

"Yes. I've decided to stay. I don't know why, but I will." It was evident, his feelings on the matter; his eyes sparkled with excitement.

"Now, so you don't get all panicky, I want you to know that I'll be leaving town this afternoon in search of a horse ranch the blacksmith told me about. You'll need a horse for our journey. If I find one that suits me, I'll bring it back. Do you have some extra cash on you?"

"Bree, that's wonderful! Over there in my saddlebags are some bills." He pointed across the room. But before handing over his hard-earned cash, he had to know something.

"But why go across country in search of a horse when they have adequate mounts at the livery stable?"

"Well, let me tell you. I want to make sure you have a suitable mount for the duration of our journey. One that may not be the beauty you hope, but one that is special in his own way and will carry you beyond our friendship. Once again, Justin, I ask you to trust my judgment. In the long run, you will not be disappointed."

Again, he was met with one of her dazzling smiles. How could he refuse her; after all, she had decided to continue on their trip together. "Find me a good one." This was going to work out great, he thought.

"I'll see what I can do. My plan is to hopefully be back in time for supper. If I've not returned, I'll see you in a couple of days. I'm hoping this doesn't take too long, but if this particular ranch is farther out than expected, it may be more."

"What if you run into trouble out there?"

"Don't worry about me. I can take care of myself."

225

"Are you sure?"

"You just wait here. You'll see."

He still looked unconvinced.

"I'll tell you what. When I return let's celebrate with a special supper or an after-dinner drink." At his hesitant nod, she continued. "Fine, and remember, don't worry about me. Instead, think about what you're going to wear when I return."

Just as she reached for the handle of the door, she stopped suddenly. Turning back towards the man on the bed, she slowly approached. With her hand resting on the head of the bed frame, she lowered her head, while diving into his fathomless chocolate-brown eyes. Before he had a chance to blink, before she had a chance to think, she placed a tiny kiss upon his cheek in endearing friendship. And before he had a chance to utter a single word, she had turned back to the door, grasped its knob, opened it, and was gone.

XX

a horse of a different color

It was amazing how quickly the landscape changed around these here parts. Once Brina was out of town, she was surprised to discover that the scenery had taken such a dramatic turn. So much so that she decided to take a moment to enjoy it, for these moments came too few and far between not to.

With the sun almost directly overhead, she gazed off towards the south. There, within the far reaches of the high prairie, she could just see the outline of the town. Gazing off towards the west were rolling hills that looked like waves along a coastline as they gently made their way towards shore. Beyond those were the beginnings of the mountain range whose snowy peaks pitched here and there, finally melding themselves with the sky and her puffy white clouds dotting its panoramic view. What was beyond those, Brina believed, was anybody's guess.

Once she'd discussed with the blacksmith, Matt, what kind of mount she was in search of, he eagerly gave her directions to the Harcort Ranch. This particular ranch was owned and operated by Jason Harcort, a great-nephew of its founder. Furthering their discussion, she learned of its general direction, that being north and that the ranch was nestled in a valley beyond the great rocky cliffs. This was supposed to make it easier for her to find, said Matt, but from where Brina and Wolf now stood, she could see neither the great valley nor the cliffs of which she searched.

Curious, she urged her great beast forward—up towards the top of the hill before them—to survey the surrounding countryside.

As they climbed, the more uneven and rocky the ground became. It was almost as though the rocks underneath the surface had a life of their own and were trying to break free of the different-colored grasses which held firm.

As the Gray Wolf continued his upward climb, Brina kept a watchful eye on the ground and its rocks. Step by step the great beast ascended with Brina leaning as far forward as possible. Slowly and finally the terrain began to change. First, it was the rocks and the grasses; then it was the lack of the same. As they reached closer to what she assumed was the top of the ridge, the ground changed even more.

Atop their climb was a grassy knoll waiting for them. Once the great beast completely cleared the top line of the ridge, she unnecessarily reined him in. There in front of them was a view to behold. The browns, yellows, and grays seen during their climb had transformed miraculously to a powder-blue color of the midmorning sky. Lowering her line of sight towards the horizon, Brina was surprised to see another mountain range. This one melded perfectly with blue of the sky and the white specks of snow that scattered hither and yon atop their craggy peaks.

Brina was beyond words. She had never expected to see anything as beautiful as what was before her.

"Now it is as it once was."

Wolf's words were heard, but because of the magnificent view before her, their meaning was lost on the wind. Dismounting, she held his reins in her hand as the beast behind her snatched a couple mouthfuls of grass while Brina stepped as close as she dared to the knoll's edge. It was by chance, she was sure, that they'd stopped when they did because within yards the knoll on which they now stood dropped off abruptly into nothingness. In awe she looked out across its great divide and downward towards its bottom. There she saw the length and width of a gigantic valley surrounded on three sides by a great expanse of smaller mountains all melded together by various shades of greens, mauves, and browns. The valley itself appeared to be at least three miles wide with lakes and trees of all shapes and sizes along its vast length.

Suddenly she saw it and out of excitement shouted, "There's the ranch!" She pointed farther down the valley. Nestled in a clearing surrounded by trees and not too far down the valley floor was Harcort Ranch, just as Matt described it. But how to get down there?

She mounted her great gray friend, and they traversed the dangerous ledge until they discovered a narrow deer trail that appeared to head down towards what she'd hoped was the valley floor. During her trek down she noted the widest sections of the trail were about a foot. These choice locations were where, she assumed, other animals congregated for who knew what reasons. There were other places as well where they'd lose the trail altogether yet managed to find it moments later by sheer accident. The ride downhill often times turned into a very slippery and dangerous ride for both of them. Not only was the trail itself treacherous because of its narrow and uneven terrain, but the switchbacks and the fist-sized or bigger rocks that were scattered here and there were all balanced in such a way that any careless mishap or step would not only be cause for a small avalanche but could very well end such a scenic and purposeful trip for the two of them.

So absorbed in the trail itself and its impending hazards, the two of them missed the arrival of its end, the coming of the valley floor and the end of their treacherous ride. Relieved, they continued on. Eventually the trail wound its way through and around several large boulders, where subsequently it met and joined up with the main road. And as she later learned, it was the one and only road that connected those of the valley to the outside world, a road she could've taken had she only known where it began.

When finally reaching the outskirts of the ranch, she was met by an older gentleman who introduced himself as the foreman. And after the telling of her tale, she was welcomed and guided the remaining distance to the main ranch house where she was to meet the owners, Mr. and Mrs. Harcort.

Upon arriving at the house, Brina saw a tall, slender gentleman standing alone on the main porch that surrounded the main ranch house who she assumed was Jason Harcort.

Once the introductions were made, Brina told him of her story and what type of mount she had in mind. "I'm in need of a well-broke horse that is able to survive off the land, travel many miles without tiring, can do with little water, has hard, durable feet, and isn't as massive as the horse I ride. Do you have anything like that for sale?"

She could remember from so many years ago, the teachings of the mustang and its survival ratings straight into the Martian year of her birth, 2525. During the period of the late 1800s, the mustang was just another wild horse that shared its existence with the antelope and other assorted wildlife. They were considered tough survivalists—precisely the qualities desired for Justin's mount. When she explained all that to Matt, he knew right where to send her. Even though Jason Harcort was considered a little unorthodox with his ideas of the capturing and training of the wild horses of the plains by many of the townsfolk, Matt seemed to know better. He owned one of Harcort's mustangs himself.

Jason Harcort escorted Brina to the main ranch house, introduced her to his wife, sat her down on a wooden chair in the kitchen, and filled her head with stories of his exploits with the wild horses of the plains. He then told her of a couple exceptional mounts he just happened to have in the barn that he'd been riding these past two years. The more she listened, the more she was willing to follow him out for a look-see. And after spending several hours putting the animals through their paces, she made her decision to buy the red dun gelding. The gelding that she had picked had a short strong back and wideset eyes that fit "The Symbol of the West" description that she remembered from her childhood. Yes, she would choose this one for Justin.

Once the money exchanged hands, Brina began to prepare the young gelding for travel. And after that death-defying descent to the valley floor, Brina thought what better way to truly find out how much heart the breed really had than by giving him an opportunity to prove it by going back up it.

Stopping her in midstream, Jason Harcort asked if she would like to stay till morning.

"The trail you intend to take is a safer one by day. Especially by someone like you, who is unfamiliar with the terrain and the unstable rock formations. Forgive me. I'm concerned only for your safety and that of your horses. Please stay, besides, the wife and I would thoroughly enjoy some unbiased company."

Knowing the information she'd given Justin upon her leaving was fairly accurate, and the fact that the one trail had been a dilly coming down, Brina had no qualms in accepting their invitation to stay the night. Therefore, she gathered her things, unsaddled the gelding, found an uninhabited corral for her two mounts to spend the night and get acquainted in, saw to their needs, eventually following Jason Harcort back to the main ranch house.

The evening was spent in a relaxed atmosphere where they told stories (Jason did most the talking), while enjoying steamy cups of hot chocolate, followed finally by an extremely restful night's sleep. She enjoyed her stay and their company so much that she decided to take them up on their extended invitation and stayed two more days. After all, she'd mentioned to Justin of a possible delay in her returning, so she didn't feel too guilty about the whole thing. Besides, the needed rest that had eluded her the other night would be a welcome change during her stay with the Harcorts.

During the wee hours of the morning just as the sun was peeking out from behind the trees, Jason Harcort found Brina already up and in the corral preparing Justin's new mount for travel. After mounting the newly christened Wyatt, she leaned down and firmly shook Jason's hand while expressing her appreciation for their hospitality, her thanks, and finally her good-byes. Taking the lead rope of Wolf's halter for appearances sake, she reined Wyatt around and headed off down the road in search of that horrible trail and her return trip to town and Justin.

Once back in town, she checked into the livery stable the two horses now in her possession. Again, she thanked Matt for his assistance, then headed over to the hotel to check on Justin. As she walked across the street heading towards the hotel, her thoughts were interrupted when her name was called from above.

"Bree! You've returned! I'll meet you in the lobby!"

It was Justin hollering at her from a second-story window of the hotel where she had left him earlier in the week.

Up the steps and through the door of the hotel she sashayed. Once inside she stood, waiting for her companion to descend the flight of stairs, hoping he would be as pleased as she with her find. Wyatt, the dun-colored gelding, had proved himself unquestionably. He may not have been the prettiest horse on the block, but he'd sure beat 'em by a mile as far as his capabilities went. She had done well. All that mattered now was to convince Justin.

Speaking of Justin, her attention was momentarily averted to the stairway as a distinguished-looking gentleman began his descent to the main floor of the hotel. On closer inspection, Brina recognized the familiar face amid the fancy clothes and new hat. It was Justin. Justin the man she'd left only days before with an injured foot and nowhere to run—let alone walk—was now steadily making his way down the stairs without too much difficulty towards her. Before realizing what she was doing, Brina smartly stepped to the bottom of the stairway where she was able to watch him glide down the steps towards her in his finery.

Justin wore a fancy black dress jacket with a medium-gray vest over a sparkling-white shirt, bolo tie, matching gray arm garters, black boots, and hat. The effect he had on her was mesmerizing. When he reached the last step, without thought, Brina gracefully and with genuine flair curtsied in her gauchos, far and below the customary dip for the period, just as though she was dressed in a floor-length ballgown and was about to be carried out on to the dance floor to the music of Strauss.

To her delight and to a squeal of surprise from her own lips, Justin waited for her to finish her curtsy, took hold of his hat, removed it, spiriting it off into the air to land on the counter of the check-in desk. Turning back to her, he tipped his head to the side, then gracefully offered to her his hand. Captivated with the gentleman before her in his attire, she decided to play along, allowing the moment to carry her off and away by gently and so very eloquently accepting it. Justin confidently took control of the moment by guiding Brina gently yet firmly out to the middle of the lobby's floor where he began to quietly hum "The Blue Danube" only moments before sweeping her around the room to a waltz step.

After several laps he slowed, then stopped, facing Brina with the most honest and delightful smile on his face that she ever did see. He turned loose her hand, then to her continued surprise, bowed with the grace of one born of breeding and status. This man was becoming a continual joy to be around. It was obvious, her decision to stay in the company of Justin Case III had been a good one.

"Well, Bree, you certainly have surprised me. I was a bit curious to see if you knew how to dance. Oh, and by the way, you did waltz wonderfully." Again, he stood there with that delightful smile on his face.

"I surprised you? You surprised me!" Standing there in front of Justin trying to catch her breath, Brina couldn't stop giggling. When she managed to get control of herself, she continued, "Good heavens, Justin, where did you find duds like that? You look delicious... and by the way, did you happen to notice the astonished looks on the other guests' faces? We'll have to do that again some time." Brina was ecstatic. "I also saw how you descended the staircase unassisted, but of course waltzing around the lobby floor was an accomplishment as well. Your ankle must be doing pretty well if you can do all that."

"I wanted to surprise you. The doctor said it was a slight sprain, and I've been, real careful with it all the while you've been gone. It's a little sore now, but that's understandable. Plus, I've been watching from the window for a glimpse of your return. The moment I saw Wolf enter the livery, I quickly changed into this. Then of course, dancing was not something the doctor ordered, but I couldn't help it. Especially after you curtsied." Justin continued to be amazed by

Bree's occasional whimsical behavior and loved every moment spent in her company.

"I just hate to interrupt you right now, but you're now the proud owner of a most magnificent animal."

Justin's eyes grew wide at the thought of the new and wonderful horse Bree had brought him, and before thinking further, he turned and hurriedly gimped past her, heading out the door and down the street in the direction of the livery, in search of his *magnificent* new mount.

Brina watched the sudden shift in realization on Justin's face as the true meaning of her being here with him took form. Then before she could say anything, he quickly headed out the door. There was nothing she could do or say until after he saw the horse. She figured he'd protest the outer cover and not consider what the animal carried inside. That thought always brought back an old adage from her youth, *you can't ride the head*. So, she allowed Justin enough time to lead the way as she moseyed along behind at her own pace.

Once she entered the livery stable, Justin was found standing in front of the mustang with his hand on his chin and a look of consternation on his face. Brina waited for his response. He had been full of so many surprises lately, she decided to stand back and watch to see what this man was all about.

"Bree…I will say this, he's not much to look at compared to Wolf, but then again, no horse is. Yet since you say he's a magnificent mount, there must be something about this animal that isn't visible to the naked eye. What have you named him?"

"Wyatt. It's an Old French name. It means 'little warrior.'" The more time spent with this man, the more she found herself really liking him.

"You've done well, my gray-eyed beau—ty." But before he could catch himself, it was out of his mouth and on the ground before them. "Sorry, Bree, I didn't mean that the way it sounded, really."

"Apology accepted. No harm done. I'm a big girl. I can take it. How about we have that supper or late-night drink we promised each other upon my return?" She ignored the slip.

"Sure, but first, I want to change. These were fun for the moment but are very uncomfortable in spots. That is, if you don't mind waiting?" Justin stood there in his finery waiting for her answer.

"No problem. I know exactly how you feel. May I make a suggestion?"

"Go ahead."

"You might do better if we head on back to the hotel. I really don't think here in the livery you'll find the clothes you're gonna need."

Apparently, Justin had been so wrapped up in his excitement of the horse and her return, he'd forgotten where they were. Being reminded of it, he simply smiled, bowed to his lady, then held out his arm as a gesture of support.

As Brina watched Justin in his finery, bow, then extend his arm, she followed through just as a lady born of high esteem would by slipping her own through his, joining with him on the short gimpy sorta excursion back to the hotel. Once they passed through the portal, Brina paused, halting Justin.

Turning towards each other, Brina said, "I'll be right here."

At Justin's nod, Brina turned, and in finding the nearest chair, sat down to wait for her horse of a different color.

XXI

playing with loaded dice

It had been about two weeks since leaving Daytonville, and Justin's new mount, Wyatt, had proved himself beyond imagination with his inner strength and endurance. Brina knew, once back on the trail, putting miles between them and what lay behind was crucial, especially now that Justin was able to ride once again, and thanks to Wyatt, the ride went easier than expected.

Wyatt, what a find. Even Wolf liked her choice. He was smaller in size to the gray, yet because of his stature, strength, endurance, and easygoing nature, their last two weeks on the trail seemed a breeze. Leaving Daytonville, now that Justin was riding again, eased Brina's mind also. She knew putting a goodly distance between them and what lay behind was all important, and with Wyatt being what he was that helped make that difference.

As the daylight hours slowly faded to dusk, Brina took a moment to behold the scenery afore her—*again*. It was frustrating, she'd been so occupied with Dillon, Cordell, this mission, and now Justin, the passing of the seasons and the changing of the color guards had almost escaped her notice. It seemed like only yesterday, when the scenery of this magnificent land began its spiritual blossoming as the metamorphosis of nature took the old and seemingly dead to magically transform it back into life everlasting. Now everywhere Brina turned, the countryside was changing to its beautiful fall colors. She knew before they'd stop for the night that once again, just like everything else, this beautiful view before her would be gone, and another one, just as breathtaking, would take its place.

Since the beginning of her travels in this unfamiliar land, Brina's appreciation for everything blossomed. Life was no longer just training, drilling, and taking orders. Life, happiness, and the need to be truly independent someday was something that silently took root somewhere deep within the subconscious core of our heroine. Unaware was she of this, which for this time was for the better, as she still had a mission to complete.

Only on this particular night, something strange happened that would change many things. After a long day spent in the saddle, the two of them were so tired they just had enough energy to set up camp, tend to horses, munch on some beef jerky, sip some water, and to sit for just a spell before collapsing for the night. But then, sometime later, during the wee hours of the night, something woke Brina. Not sure of what it was, she remained alert and ready, while waiting for any hint of possible threat.

A moment later it made itself known. Cautiously she peeked a look-see towards Justin's bedroll. There, she saw the blanket flat, indicating no occupancy, and then saw that he was sitting up against the belly of his saddle with legs bent, knees tucked under his chin, arms crossed, with his head resting atop them.

"Justin," in hushed tones, she inquired, "what is it?"

"Nothing."

"Nothing?"

"Nothing."

"Nothing woke you up?"

"Yeah."

"Then why are you up?"

He just looked at her. "You'll laugh."

"No, I won't." The hushed tones turned normal.

"It was a dream."

"A dream?" It was all she could do to keep the sarcasm from her voice.

"Yeah, a dream, or rather a nightmare. It won't let me sleep."

"Reoccurring?" Déjà vu kicked in.

"Yep."

"Want to talk about it?"

"Nope."

Brina noticed him shivering slightly. "I'll get ya another blanket."

"Don't need it." He just stared blankly into the night sky.

"Well then, if you're not cold, this dream must've scared ya fairly good, 'cause you're shaking. Tell me about it."

"Why? You won't understand it any more than I do."

"True, but wouldn't be nice to share it with someone?"

"Not tonight. Not yet."

Not yet, she thought. "Okay." He was an adult; he would decide when, where, and if he wanted to talk about it. So, she said her good-nights and went back to sleep.

The second night it was pretty much the same thing; when she awoke, she found him in the same position as the night before.

"The dream again?"

"Sorry, Bree. Didn't mean to wake ya."

"Want to talk about it now?"

He was hesitant with his answer. "Yes and no."

"Yes and no." At least that was a start. "What's that supposed to mean?"

"Yes, I want to tell you about it, but no, I don't. You'll think I'm nuts."

"When have I thought you nuts?"

With a small smile upon his lips, he mentioned, "How 'bout that night at the hotel, when I wore those fancy duds, and we danced the waltz?"

"That's true, but that was another time, another place, another circumstance. This is different." Her smile held a serious note.

"Yeah, I know. It's just that it's so strange, its meaning eludes me."

"Meaning? What makes you think it has meaning?"

"'Because it won't let me be. It keeps coming back."

"It scared ya pretty good, didn't it?"

He was trembling again. His head lowered, ashamed that he'd been scared shitless by a stupid dream and had been caught at it.

"Want a swig?"

"Whiskey? Yeah, sure." Anything to calm his shakes.

She turned over from her bed and reached for her saddlebags. With one of the two flasks in hand, she passed it on, then watched in amazement as he took three pretty good-sized swigs before wiping his mouth on his sleeve, then handed it back.

He smiled his thanks, and saying not a word, crawled back under his blanket, hoping he could get some shuteye.

Brina returned the flask to her saddlebags, laid back down into her bedroll, and also dropped off to sleep.

As the days passed, so did the landscape around them. Along the trail though, Justin was having a hard time of it. Some days they put miles under their horses. Others, just a few. On those slow days, Brina, either on horseback or afoot, would walk behind or alongside Wyatt, as he precariously carried a dozing Justin in the saddle. Next to him, she made sure she was within arm's reach away; should he decide to slip, she'd be there to grab or push him back into place. Those days made for a snail's pace trip and in her own bizarre way imagined that it was a good thing they weren't racing the tortoise, for on those days he'd surely win.

Each evening during supper as Justin halfheartedly ate, moments before he fell into his bedroll, Brina noticed how he avoided any and all mention of his dream. But then, far be it for her to decide when and where they were to discuss *his* dreams. And since he wanted to play it that way, she went to bed without further ado. For without rest, she'd slip, and that might give any uninvited deviate who came by to party seriously a chance at besting them—especially with Justin being so vulnerable. And even though her time spent in strange and bizarre places dealing with strange and bizarre thugs prepared her for whatever may happen in this time, she always knew it was far better to be safe than sorry.

Two o'clock in the morning, three days later, the shit hit the fan. "BREE!"

In a fraction of a second, the bedroll blankets were six feet in the air. Brina was on her feet, with knife in hand, ready to kill, before

239

she realized when and where she was, and in whose company she was in.

Justin hadn't a clue. All he knew was that his dream was horrible and that it scared him so badly that he frantically called out to her. But now with a clearer mind and fully awake, all he saw was this woman, whom he'd been traveling with for the past several weeks, standing before him with a knife in her hand and a wild look in her eyes. And for a very short second he wasn't sure which he feared more, her or his dream.

"Bree?"

"Justin. Oh dear…I'm dreadfully sorry." Quickly and with no thought at all, she put the knife back in its sheath—inside her boot—rearranged herself and her blankets, then sat down upon them. "What is it?" It was a question filled with true concern.

Gingerly she reached for his hand. Hesitantly he gave it. The solidity of her grip again surprised him, but this time she offered it as a well of strength to draw from. "Justin. I'm here if you need me."

He found the conviction in her voice and her touch reassuring. He took a deep breath, letting it out slowly. Then with a touch of humor in his eyes, Justin said, "I'm sure glad you're on my side." Still, he wasn't too sure about what he'd just witnessed. He'd never seen such a defense mechanism as she had just demonstrated. While in his dream, he'd known enough to cry out to her for help but didn't realize that his calling would initiate such a response.

"Do you feel up to talking about it?" She dismissed her action and instead focused on the reason for it.

"Talking?" His mind was slightly off track.

"About your dream, Justin."

"Uh, yeah…I guess. Can I ask ya something first?"

"Sure."

"What was that thing with the knife?"

For a moment she'd forgotten that he wasn't one of the team. "Ah yeah. Well, I'll tell ya what, I'll tell you all about it someday—maybe, but not now. Now we need to focus on your dream. See if we can do something about it so you can sleep."

"Bree."

"Yeah?"

"You're always coming to my rescue, aren't you?"

"Seems that way."

"Why?"

"I don't know. I think that maybe I like you, Justin." It wasn't often she truly liked someone. "And because of who I am, I want to help. Now tell me about this dream of yours." She was serious now.

Satisfied, he began. "I can't really remember what it's been about these past couple of weeks, but I can vividly remember tonight's."

"Go on."

"Well, I remember I was sitting on a gray stallion high upon a snow-topped ridge. Below me was a vast creviced valley. It was gorgeous. It must've been fifteen miles wide and at least four miles deep. At the bottom was a great river. It was so real. I could even hear the roar of the water rushing through the rapids. The sky was so blue. The white puffy clouds looked like balls of cotton floating in the air. Suddenly the ground began to shake. There was nowhere to run. I called out to you, but you weren't there. Quick as lightning, I saw a strangely dressed old man. I couldn't take my eyes off him. He walked with a staff that was longer than he was tall. He spoke to me."

"What did he say?"

"I can't remember."

"What happened then?"

"I can't remember, but somehow I knew that only you could save me. So, I cried out to you, and here you are."

"You got my attention all right." The dream was so similar to hers it was scary. She wondered if the strange old man in his dream, was Azrael, the Angel of Death, as she was sure it was in hers. That would've explained why he cried out to her with such a ferocity that her instincts to protect him kicked in. "Yet you can't remember what the old man said?"

"No."

"Well, at least this is a start."

"A start to what?"

"Well, Justin. Maybe it'll help if I confess to something."

"You're married." He was really kidding, yet...

"No, that's not it."

"You're not married then."

"Justin. That part of my life is not up for discussion. We're talking about your dreams, remember?"

"Sure, whatever. Are you then going to tell me you're a murderer or maybe a prostitute, have children, don't like me—no, that's not it, you just said that you did. Can't think of anything else right now. What kind of confession?" Of late, while in her presence, and only when he least of all expected it, her closeness seemed to affect him. And even though he rambled on with questions that were untimely, yet honest, he knew they're just a defense mechanism and just to deal with the outcome as it came.

"You're a pill, ya know that don't you?" Smiling, Brina shook her head.

"Yeah. One of my many faults, sorry."

Brina chuckled. A man with a sense of humor. How refreshing. "Actually, I wanted to tell you that your dream is very much like *mine*."

"Your dream?"

"Yeah. My dream."

"When did you have this dream?"

"Before I met you." Finally, something in common. She didn't like it, but maybe it was a common denominator for something.

"Before you met me?"

She just looked at him.

"Did this dream keep coming back?"

"No. My dream was more intensified and much more vivid in detail and came only once."

"Do you know what yours meant?"

"I have an idea, but now that you've admitted to somewhat the same dream, I'm not so sure."

"What was your initial idea?"

"It's hard to say. You see, I think it has something to do with why I'm on this journey."

"You're on a journey?"

"Yeah. I'm in search of buried treasure." It was all she could think of on such short notice.

"Buried treasure, huh?" He had to think about that one.

"Justin."

He was deep in thought. "Yeah?"

"Let's get back to your dream. We can discuss the other later."

With the "treasure idea" locked firmly in the back of his mind, he nodded in agreement.

"I said there was an old man in my dream. Was he in yours too?" Justin asked.

"He was."

"Do you know who he was?"

"I believe so. But I can't be sure."

"Can't be sure?"

"No. I've never met him, nor have I seen him before. And if he is who I *think* he is, I hope to *never* meet him." No one should ever have to meet the Angel of Death.

"That bad, huh?"

"That bad." Thinking a moment, she added, "You said that he said something to you. Are you sure that you can't remember what it was or what he hinted at?" Why she needed to know was beyond her.

"It seems to me that he had several things to say, but none of them made any sense to me. Should we wait another night and see if he comes back?"

"You mean to haunt you?"

"Yeah, to haunt me."

"Justin, why are you now so calm about this dream?"

"'Because I now know you'll protect me."

"I can't protect you in your dreams."

"No, but knowing I've shared this with you should help in defeating any evil that comes about—don't ya think?"

"I get it. Now that I know, subconsciously I'll be with you—and we'll be able to face it together."

"Yeah, something like that."

"That's nice you feel that way."

"Well, after seeing you come flying off the bedroll with knife in hand, in a strange way gives me a feeling of being protected, wouldn't you say?"

"Yeah, I guess it kinda would," Brina responded.

"By the way, where did you learn to do that kind of thing?"

"Years of training and practice."

"Where?"

Where, indeed. The better question was *when*. "A special school."

"In the east?"

If her history served her right, the best schools were always in the east. "Yeah."

"What else did they teach you?"

"How to take care of myself under any and all circumstances."

"What kind of school does all that?"

"I don't know what kind you'd call it, but I started there when I was very young."

"And you still remember it all?"

"I was there for a long time. I was taught by the very best. I was a very good student. And I studied very hard." On a second note, she asked, "What about you?"

"What about me?" answered Justin.

She was curious. "What about your life?"

"There's nothing to tell, really. I just grew up in a normal setting, living a normal life."

Brina, with her past history and mild curiosity, would love for someone to take a moment and explain to her the formalities of a *normal life*. But she wasn't about to ask.

As to Justin, he remained very elusive about his past histories. They were of no one's concern but his own. Everything else was as normal as hers. "I don't like talking about myself, really. Is there anything else *you* want to talk about?"

Brina knew more about skeletons in one's closet than anyone around. Secrecy had become her middle name these days. "Not really. Ya know, instead of talking, how about hitting the trail?"

"Sure. Let's ride." *Buried treasure.*

They rode the rest of the day and well into the night before Justin was willing to stop and set up camp. Try as he might, the dream didn't return that night, nor did it for a full week. In fact, he'd gotten enough sound sleep that they got miles under their horses, miles that they hadn't gotten for days.

"Justin?"

"Yeah?"

"What do you call this place?"

"They call it the Badlands."

"The Badlands."

A week later they began their crossing of this broad expanse of the Great Plains region, now known to Brina as the Badlands. She thought it a magnificent picture with its pastel-painted furrows of fragile soil formed by the wind and the rain, stabilized only by pale patches of prairie grasses, patches of small pines, prickly pear cacti, sage, and yucca plants. It was very different and more interesting than any area she'd traveled before. She found it soothing.

"Nothing of real value grows here, and there's little water if any at all," Justin added.

"What about animals?"

"Prairie dogs, snakes, lizards, and some birds, I think."

"Where do they get their water?"

"They find it, I know, 'cause if not, there wouldn't be critters," he said with a smile.

With a week of no dream and all the sleep he could get, Justin felt born again. And with this renewed feeling he found the strength and the nerve to ask his companion an unorthodox question he'd been pondering since their first meeting.

"Bree?"

"Yes, Justin?" Sometimes Brina would say *yes* as she was taught, sometimes it came out *yeah,* and sometimes, thanks to this time period, it came out as *yep*—she was trying to fit in after all.

He was hesitant with his question.

"Is there a problem?" asked Brina.

The only way he could ask it was to just spit it out. "Have you ever considered settling down?" There. It was out—finally.

Floored, but curious, Brina asked, "What do you mean by set-tling down?"

"Getting married. Having children. Stuff like that?" Might as well get it all out.

"Justin, what are you asking?"

"Have you ever imagined yourself settling down with a hus-band and raising a family?"

Brina pulled Wolf up short. Justin reined in Wyatt. He turned to her as she turned to him. Intently they both stared into each oth-er's eyes. Though Brina did not take hold, she did see in them the sincerity of his question.

Not in her wildest dreams had she ever considered such. She was not capable in any way shape or form to undertake such a quest. Nor was she prepared. Nor did she want to be. She loved her life as it was. To be a loner in *this* vast land, to use her honed skills to do what was necessary at the time it was needed, in whatever place or circumstance she was a part of, was what *she considered* settling down. She took a moment to reflect the life that she led and loved—defi-ance, mischievous, inventive, and mysterious. Full of life and spirit. Ornery, kindly, independent, and dedicated to the cause. The life-blood of the Academy, a capable killing machine. Weapons, strength, agility, and endurance training, hand-to-hand combat, sharp shoot-ing, undercover work, and reconnaissance, mathematics, communi-cation skills, military strategies, etiquette, poise, weapons, and intelli-gence. All intended to ensure a sixth sense of self-preservation into each and every trainee and team. Not to mention the Gray Wolf and the power of her mind. Not quite the qualifications of a typical housewife. Not likely. Nope. Definitely not.

"Honestly and truthfully?" she asked.

"Please."

"Not at this time." *Nor at any time for that matter,* she thought.

"So, what you're saying is that you don't have a beau waiting for you anywhere?"

"No beau."

"Would you consider me, at all, now or at any time in the future?"

"I'm sorry, Justin, the answer to that would be no."

"Can you tell me why?"

Could she? Not on her life. "There's way too much you don't know about me."

"How can I know if you won't tell me? I shared my dream with you."

"That's different. My life, as I choose to live it, is of no one's concern but my own. Don't get me wrong. It's not that I'm not willing to share part of it, but not to the extent that you're suggesting."

"I see." Slightly disappointed was he, but not deflated.

Brina could see the light of hope in his eyes dim slightly, so she added, "We are sharing the trail now, aren't we?"

"Yeah."

"And the way I see it, we probably will be for quite some time. So, in a way I am sharing my life, but as for anything else, I'm sorry I can't do that."

"Well, you can't say that I didn't try."

"Actually, I think it took a lot of nerve to ask. That shows me character. And I've always believed that somewhere beneath that sour exterior was a real character trying to emerge."

"What do you mean sour exterior?"

"Just trying to get a rise out of ya, Justin." Smiling from ear to ear and giggling all through it, she reached his way, administered a playful poke in his ribs, and at the very same time she shouted, "*Race ya!*"

It took only a fraction of a second for Justin to digest what had just happened before he too was off like a shot. Even though they both knew Wolf was the better horse and the fact that they hadn't raced for weeks, he knew what she'd really done. And no matter how much she spurned his hopes and dreams, he truly believed that he would stick to her through thick and thin, till death or worse did them part.

Three weeks later, the dream returned.

XXII

from the bottom of the barrel

"**Y**OU MISERABLE SON OF A WHORE! WHERE IS SHE, AND WHERE ARE HER TRACKS!"

If Lucifer only knew how dangerously close he was to exposing his innards to the Grim Reaper's skill of the knife if he didn't find those tracks and soon, he would just as soon jump off the moon along with that stupid cow.

The Grim Reaper as he was known was not a man to cross, not in any time. He was not only an assassin, a thug, a rapist *when it suited his fancy*, a murderer, hired killer, bomber, a child molester, but was also psychotic. His mind could snap like a twig without a moment's notice. He could kill in an instant and with precision without giving it a second thought. His speed in martial arts was unmatched. His skill with a knife, any knife—long or short—was beyond reproach, as the tie that held back his long black hair denoted; *it was human skin that'd been sliced away from the ribcage region of an opponent's years ago.* The Reaper had learned the ropes of life the hard way. His strength, agility, and skills were remarkable for a man of only five foot two.

The hideous contrast between his yellowish-colored skin, the sneer that never faltered below the mustache he wore, and the translucent pigmented pupils of his eyes made the strongest of men cringe. Those eyes never blinked, never shed a tear, never showed feelings towards any living thing. His demeanor was that of a snake that lay in wait in a dark unseen place, only to strike or to reach out when his fangs were at their sharpest and loaded with venom.

There was also a quiet side to him. A side that was just as deadly, just as unpredictable, just as instantaneous, yet just as controlled as the other. This side was rarely seen. One could say it was the preamble to the snapping of the twig. He had control over this side more so than the other, due to the seriousness of the situations at hand—whatever they may be. He had that now. Now, more than ever, he had to keep his cool. He needed these idiots to find her trail and guide him along in this strange land during these strange times.

The gray-eyed beauty had eluded him for the last time. With dumb luck, she had managed to dodge his bullet in the chamber, recoup from the tranquilizer dart and run, but now that he was hot on her trail—with the so-called help of a few saddle tramps—he would finally find and destroy her. Of course, not before he sliced and diced her up a bit first.

John Deau was the first to learn of the Reaper's skill of the knife. The other two were standing almost too close for their comfort. Since John had been the first to foul up his orders when it came to the gray-eyed one, he was the one who got it. He had tied her insufficiently, so escape for her was child's play. And at first the Reaper tried reasoning with the man, explaining the ways of knot tying, which was something not normally done, but when that failed, he drove his point home. Pouncing, with rope in hand, he trussed John up like a seasoned turkey awaiting the spit. With hands and feet securely tied together behind him and the rope finally fastened around the man's neck so when he struggled breathing was cut off, he stepped back. "How's that feel?" he hissed between missing teeth.

John, at first, tried breaking free of his bindings, but when the noose slowly tightened around his neck subsequently shutting down his air flow, all movement stopped. With eyelids closed tightly, he lay there struggling for each and every breath taken.

When the Reaper's point was obvious to them all, he carefully loosened then removed the ropes that bound.

When the ropes were removed and he could finally take a breath, John gathered all his resolve and exploded. He didn't like the Reaper, never did. And now that the Reaper had made a spectacle of himself, he decided that he'd had had enough. Pulling his knife from his boot, he waved it in a threatening manner towards his intended opponent.

"Put it up," hissed The Reaper.

"FUCKING BASTARD!" John with knife held high lunged at the Reaper.

It was a lucky jab. The knife's tip caught the side of the Reaper's face, cutting him from the corner of his left eye halfway to his jaw.

When all became quiet, John discovered that for some unknown reason, he was extremely tired and lacked the strength needed to remain upright. Not knowing why, he glanced around only to find his friends staring at him with eyes the size of the circumference of one's hat. "Whaaat?" He mouthed the word that had no sound. When his strength began to dwindle dramatically, he looked down only to find the hilt of his very own knife protruding from just below the ribcage of his very own chest. He knew then he'd not share in any future rapes, pillages, or plunderings with his friends and that the Reaper was truly not of this world. With a speed totally unheard of, the Reaper had killed him and his dreams, in less than just a blink of the eye.

Cowering in the presence of the Reaper, watching their lifelong friend die before their eyes, Lucifer risked his own, by asking if he could stay and bury him.

"Leave him," the Reaper hissed.

"What if someone comes?"

"The only some ones will be the wolves. Leave him or stay as well."

Not catching the meaning, Lucifer said, "I'll stay."

"Your choice," the Reaper hissed as he grabbed the lapel of Lucifer's collar, pulling him close enough to smell his fowl breath.

"NO! NO! NO!" he shrieked.

The Reaper expected this. "I thought you wanted to stay."

"Not that way! I just want to bury him."

Knowing he needed all the help he could muster in these strange lands the Reaper released the man's lapel. "Don't be more than a day," he hissed. "Consider what may happen should you not."

Lucifer knew good and well what the implication was here. "Ya can count on me."

"Let's move," spewed the Reaper to Rene-with-a-hyphen, "we've got ground to cover and tracks to find."

It took Lucifer three days to bury his friend. One full day just to dig the bloody hole. The ground was so rocky and almost void of the clay soil indigenous to the region that digging was a major chore. When the hole was what he believed to be deep enough, he struck water. Not in great quantities as one might imagine, but since water in that part of the country was scarce, who the hell cared? Yet since he was not there to farm but to dig a grave, it became a major problem. Damn it all to hell that it'd been his rotten luck to hit the damned stuff. At least this gave him something to put in his canteen besides dirt. It all meant that either he plant his friend in the watered-down hole, or that he start another.

The end of the day brought him nearly to exhaustion. The rocks had been very heavy for even him to move, and amid those rocks was the unseen soil. This he knew without a doubt. The spring water had managed to make mud of the invisible dirt. And if there hadn't been any, as he previously assumed, why in the name of Sam Hill was he now covered with the slimy stuff? Bloody hell.

It took him twice as long to place each and every rock dug out, then some, back in the hole and atop his friend. Since the soil had mixed with the water so completely and the fact that he had no shovel, using as many rocks as could be found was his best bet. He had to make sure the wolves couldn't get to his friend. So, by the time he was finished burying him and before he marked the grave, he had to rest.

By the morning of the third day, he'd finished his task and his marker.

Whilst standing over the freshly filled in gravesite, he gazed out over the horizon in deep thought. Realizing for the first time that as much time as the three of them, he, John, and Rene spent in the saddle together, they weren't as close to him as his *Betsy*. *Betsy*, oh damn, he missed her. He needed her like the trees needed the sun and knew that they'd cross paths again one day and that he'd eventually make her his.

Back to his task, he took the stone grave marker that he'd found in all the surrounding rubble and scraped his message with a second smaller rock with a pointed end. Then he positioned the marker at the grave's head. Even though John was kind of a jerk, Lucifer believed that no one deserved an unmarked grave. "Ya never know, John boy," he began, "I might be back here again someday, and I'll want to find you, 'cause by then I'll have *Betsy* with me. And if you're a good boy, I just might introduce you to her."

After mounting his horse, yet before turning him northward, Lucifer took one last look at his handiwork before heading out. "Not bad for a lefty." Then he read what he'd scraped.

Here Iyz Jon Doe
Gon but not forgot

"Hope I got it right." Then he rode off into the sunset in search of the rest of his gang.

Once back in the company of his associates, after several hours of being lost due to the fact that he'd headed into the sunset instead of north, Lucifer was directed to take the first watch. Even though he was exhausted from the digging, burying, and that horrible ride down the canyon, he knew better than to question the orders given. He didn't want to end up in a second hole or left for dead as John almost had, so he did as told. Especially since it appeared that the Reaper had given him a second chance. A chance he hadn't expected.

The afternoon of the following day found our villains at the crossroads of decision.

"THEY DID WHAT??!"

Cowering in the presence of death in the flesh, Rene-with-a-hyphen hesitantly whispered, "They split up."

"Are you sure?" At first, he thought the tracker was mistaken, but when he himself took a gander at the ground, he saw that he was not. Damn. First, there was one, then three. Now two of the three had gone on alone. He wanted to believe the strangers traveling with her belonged to the tracks that led northeast. The single that broke off and headed northwest had to be her. She was the only one who had a valid reason to do so. She was on the mission. She could travel and survive on her own, not saying that they couldn't, but she had a purpose and probably discovered the strangers got in her way of doing things. She was an independent and determined woman, he'd been told.

But the question kept nagging at him, why did they split? Traveling in such a strange land in such a strange century, one sometimes needs guides to direct. Had she told the strangers of her mission? He thought not. She knew better than to trust those not of her unit. There was no valid reason why anyone should know of her plan. Besides, no one would believe such a cockamamy story as the one similar to his. To himself he thought, "Hi, my name is Pudintain, and I'm from the twenty-fifth century. I'm looking for someone. Can you help me?" Yeah, right on, dude.

But women, who could figure 'em? His past experience with women taught him that most tend to reason differently, act differently, and generally speaking, not think at all compared to the male of the species. Although once in his company, he never considered reasoning with them. His usual appetite was not appeased until well after climax passed, the jugular was slashed, and the blood drained bone dry. But before that, when things would just start to get interesting, they'd start babbling on about something, anything, hoping he'd turn them loose, which he never did.

One of the other considerations was that maybe she'd suspected a tracker or a bounty hunter or even considered the thought that perchance the Network had sent additional assassins to stop her. He hoped not. The thought that maybe she did tell her companions of her plight, or a believable facsimile thereof, came to mind. What other reason could there have been? Men don't leave attractive single women to fend for themselves, no matter how capable they seem to be. Why would this time period prove to be any different than his?

With all things considered, why the split? It mattered not, all that mattered was to decide which trail to follow. What to do, what to do? He knew the importance of stopping the woman; however, if she had told them, how much information had she supplied? What was he to do? He was to do what he always did under circumstances such as this. Follow his nose.

"Lucifer, you and Rene head off in search of those two sets of tracks. Shoot to kill. Don't worry if you happen across the wrong pair. Just kill 'em."

"Where are you going?" asked Lucifer.

"I'm going after the lone rider. It's her. I'm sure of it. And without the added protection of the other two, things might work out just fine." He was hoping to have his way with her before slitting her throat. The thought itself did exciting things to his anatomy. He couldn't wait to catch her.

Just as they mounted their horses, Rene said, "Don't worry, we know who we're looking fer. We've spoken to them before, remember? At the camp? Besides, I'm thinkin' that one of them is the one who gave our descriptions to the authorities after that holdup all those years ago. We intend to even that score."

As the Reaper watched Lucifer and Rene-with-a-hyphen head in their northeasterly direction, he reined his mount towards the northwest and in doing so hoped his intended victim would be there waiting for him.

XXIII

just a little game of hide-and-seek

It was the middle of the night, yet Brina could see perfectly. The moon was at its fullest and directly overhead. Its presence illuminated the sky with lavenders, the craggy snow-topped peaks just beyond with ample pinks and mauves. The smaller but still-magnificent rock formations in their foreground held smoky burnt hues.

As far as she could figure, Brina's seventh sense woke her sometime during the wee hours of the morning. It had alerted her to the fact that there either was to be, or that there actually was, an unknown entity nearby. She rose silently. Without dawning her boots, hat or jacket, she, like an Indian with knife in hand, used the moon's light as a heavenly beacon to, with stealth, comb the area for intruders, yet found not a thing. She did not know what to look for, what to expect. For if they were there, they were as she, cautious, silent, prepared, and alert.

Her seventh sense had never led her astray before. Something or someone, somewhere was hiding from view. Was it a wild animal? Was it a human animal? Were the two one? A sinister being, looking for trouble at this time of the night? She thought not, but until the hairs on the back of her neck laid back down, she would remain awake and alert with knife nearby, as she stood her ground next to the fire and over her friend.

Her friend, Justin.

Silently she chuckled while thinking back to the day of their big race. She reflected on the discoveries made, during and after that race as well. It had been her original intention to get his mind off that blasted subject of her settling down. So, she'd pushed Wolf to the max while Justin was left with nothing to follow except the fading sound of laughter, hoof falls, and wisps of floating dust. By the time she expected him to reach the end of the box canyon, she and her horse would be gone—hidden within the rocks which by then would almost completely surround him. But of course, that was part of her plan.

Instead of, *catch me if you can*, it was now *hide-and-seek*. After all, he who held the rule book controlled the games. She learned that early in life. And since racing had always made her feel giddy and mischievous, so long as she was with Wolf, she'd decided to unexpectedly change the rules.

Now she again was the hunter, but in a rather-playful way. Leaving Wolf in a secure area near to where Justin was sure to stop, she climbed through the rocks searching for the ideal spot from where to watch her prey. The niche she found was perfect. It gave her concealment yet allowed for maneuverability and full viewing. Her plan was to jump out at the last minute and surprise him. After all, it was just a game.

Silently and patiently, she waited, but when he didn't come, she became concerned. What could've happened? Did he not follow her tracks? He saw the direction she'd gone; had mishap befallen him? She needed to know, but her training and self-preservation wouldn't allow exposure. When finally, she did hear the sound of a horse approaching, she crouched down, so as not to be readily spotted—just in case it was not whom she expected. But when Wyatt emerged, he was alone. The saddle seat vacant, the stirrups swinging freely. Suddenly concerned that Justin lay in a heap, injured from a fall, or worse, Brina slowly stood. Once erect, she focused intently on the atmospheric conditions ensuring no immediate threats.

Still cautious, she waited before making her way back to the gray. Once there, her seventh sense again warned of a secondary presence. On reflexes alone she whirled around, knife in hand, ready for the unknown entity. There was no one there. No one to combat her. Confused, she stood her ground and waited. Slowly the feeling dissipated. Nothing was left except the obvious. Justin's mount, hers, and herself.

With the air finally clear, she could inspect Wyatt. Slipping her knife back into its sheath, she took the reins and led the Gray Wolf to Justin's mount. Closely inspecting Wyatt, Brina found no indications of foul play. She did find that the reins were knotted and fastened around the saddle horn. Something wasn't right, she thought. So, after untying Wyatt's reins, she mounted her own mighty steed and turned back from whence she earlier rode.

A hundred yards down the trail, another one of those damn feelings hit. She knew now she was being watched but didn't know from whence it came. With Wolf at a full stop, she stood in the stirrups hoping the elevated position would give her an edge. Suddenly it all came clear. It was Justin. And it was not a watching, but a waiting. She knew now. Justin had discovered a second copy of the game book. His may have listed the rules but failed to include the intelligence levels of the possible opponents that may play.

Reaching out with her mind's eye, she located and targeted his position. He'd found a small rock outcropping out in the middle of the sun-bleached sand and was hiding within its boulders. He had water, she knew this, but had he the determination to stay hidden in the heat of the day, or would he give up his position beforehand? Hide-and-seek was a funny game and could be vital for one's survival. How far would he take this little game of hers? She was trained for these kinds of games; he wasn't. On second thought, was she perverse enough to lock him in? This was supposed to be just a game, but to what extent would *she* take it? It started out plain and simple, but she had underestimated her opponent, as did he. Suddenly it was no longer just a game to her. It had become a minuscule training exercise for the two of them. She would not give in by giving up, but she might break cover in order to force him into surrendering. She was determined and devious when push came to shove. Quietly and to herself she muttered, "If we break him now, he'll be of no use to us later—"

In the twinkle of an eye...

257

Brina considered the unspoken words, then responded in turn. "You're right, of course." Then wondered where the white flag was, and on whose side would it wave?

By evening's early light, neither had budged. Apparently, stubbornness was a trait both carried well. Justin had remembered to take his canteen but had left both rifle and handgun on his horse. His beliefs were that she'd give up the ship early in the battle, thus the thought of him possibly needing weapons didn't register.

Unfortunately, Brina had had all the training, endurance, stick-to-itiveness, supplies, all remaining weapons, and of course, all the food in her possession. Not only that, but to pry her friend from his cover, she stayed hidden until well into the early hours of the morning—long after Justin had given in to sleep. Shortly afterward, she set up camp making sure that both bedrolls were prepared and ready for occupancy. The fire she had going pretty good and had a makeshift table arranged for two standing by.

With knife in hand, she departed on a short hunting expedition. In this she made sure she stayed between Justin and camp, then continued until she came upon and killed two rabbits. The dumb things had been lying in wait under some sagebrush plant assuming invisibility when she stepped on the one. When the survivor broke for the open plains, she threw her knife, and he fell. Her intentions were for Justin to wake to the delicious aroma of rabbit on the spit.

By the time she returned, he was sitting next to the fire. She smiled knowing how hard it must've been for him to surrender. At least she knew he was safe from harm, warm, and hopefully not too out of sorts for company. She remembered asking him if his previous day had been eventful and if his night had been comfortable. He, in turn, sarcastically replied that they had. It was obvious he was frustrated and a bit miffed with her for outlasting the game, but after confessing her judgmental error of him, he, like the Cheshire cat, smiled and forgave her. Apologies accepted, they shared rabbit on the spit for breakfast, along with coffee, and finished it off with a savored cup of whiskey.

Three weeks later she was again plagued with the familiar feeling of something or someone somewhere hiding just out of sight. What was it, or who could it be? It mattered little; she would stay awake, alert, and ready, until long after Justin rose.

The knife she carried had such a sharp edge that had she one hundred times the strength of Hercules, she could equally compete with Paul Bunyan as they chopped down a forest together—he with his ax, she with her knife. All she needed was the upper-body strength to do it. So, when Justin woke, he found her sitting contentedly by the fire with knife in hand, whittling against a piece of wood the size of her arm.

"What are you doing?" asked a refreshed Justin.

"Whittling."

"Where'd ya learn to do that?"

"School."

"They taught ya a lot there, didn't they?"

"Sure did." That feeling still nagged.

"I had my dream again last night."

"Oh really? It must've been quite mild. You didn't stir."

"How would you know?"

"I was up all night." Brina began to explain.

"All night, why?"

"Something was troubling me." *An intruder lurked among them.*

"Want to talk about it?"

"No. I'd rather hear about your dream."

"He was there."

"Who?"

"Your Angel of Death."

If Brina wore eyeglasses, she'd be looking over their tops. "And?"

"He was very old."

"What else?" she inquired.

"He was very tall."

"What was he wearing?"

He thought about it a moment, then answered, "A nightshirt."

"A nightshirt? Are you sure this was the same dream?"

"Yep."

"What else?" she inquired.

"He had a walking stick, and…" He hesitated.

"And what? Justin?"

"You'll never believe this."

She just glared at him.

"His eyes were the same color as yours."

"Mine?" What was going on here? "Justin, did he do anything, say anything, or did he just stand there and stare at you?"

"He spoke."

She was almost afraid to ask, but instead willed him to go on.

"Nothing came out."

"What do you mean nothing came out?" Puzzled she was.

"I saw his lips move though."

She admired him for even talking about it, but found that getting the information out was frustrating. It was like pulling words out of someone's mouth who talked slower than molasses in January. "Justin, we do have all day, but, come on—"

"The truth be damned!"

Shocked, she exclaimed, "Excuse me?"

"That was the message!" He had remembered.

"The truth be damned? Are you sure?"

"Sure as the sun comes up in the morning."

"What that's supposed to mean?" she asked.

"How am I supposed to know? You're the one analyzing this. But now that I think about it, *how about the truth?*"

"What truth?"

"The truth about you."

"The truth about me?" She didn't need this. And why so suddenly was he asking about her?

"That's what I said."

"You want the truth." It was a statement, not a question.

"Yeah. What is your name, really?"

Resigned, figuring they'd been together long enough, she told him what she willed. "Very well then, Brina Louise Grant."

"Grant, huh?" He pondered this for a moment. "Do you mind if I ask more questions?"

"If you don't mind my answers." Whatever they may be.

"Fair enough. Where you from?"

"Frisco." That part was true anyway.

"Where's that?"

Waving her hand indiscriminately in no definite direction, she said, "Out yonder ways."

"That's a great answer." Frustration.

"I cannot tell you everything, Justin."

"Why not?"

"Because I haven't a clue who you really are either."

That stopped him in his tracks. Did he really want her to know who he really was? "Okay, but if we're traveling together, shouldn't we know each other a tad?" *More intimately*, he silently thought and hoped.

"Okay. Who are you, Justin?"

His smile faded.

"You see what I mean? How much are you willing to tell? Unless I'm marrying you, which I most definitely am not, my life is mine, not yours, not anyone else's," she stated.

He now got the gist of it all. "Okay. I get it. Let's change the subject," suggested Justin.

"Fine."

"Can you instead tell me about this treasure you seek?"

"Yeah, I suppose I could, but will I?" At his deflated look, she continued. "Look, I can't really tell you what it is, 'cause I'm not real sure, but I can say that it's also being sought after by a man who shot my father in the back." That was the only way she could fit Jesse into the picture. That way, if they just happened to run across him, then maybe Justin would understand why she shot *her father's killer* on sight.

"Your father was killed over this treasure?"

The emissary had to have been someone's father. Could've been hers. "Yes."

"You want to talk about it?"

"Not really. But I'll tell you what, if by chance we just happen to run across this guy, two could do a much cleaner job than one."

"What do you mean a 'much cleaner job'? Aren't you turning him in?" asked Justin.

"No. When I find him, Justin, I will kill him." It was a statement of fact.

"What makes you think you can do that?"

"I'm quite capable. I'll do what needs to be done when the time comes." *If he's there or not.*

Shocked, but not put off, Justin continued. "Brina Louise Grant." It was also a statement. "Can it still be Bree, or do you prefer Brina?"

"Call me what you want. I'm still the same person."

"Are you?"

She nodded her response.

"And who is that?"

With a faraway look in her eyes, replied, "A visitor in a strange land." On a much lighter side said, "How 'bout you?"

He thought she was kidding. "I'm an ex-Territorial Rider—in search of buried treasure."

"Yeah right." Sarcastically speaking of course.

"Actually, I am an ex-Territorial Rider—in search of buried treasure," Justin stated matter-of-factly.

Interesting. If this was true, why hadn't she picked up on this before? She glanced Wolf's way expecting a telepathic explanation, but when nothing came, she returned her attention to Justin. "What rank?"

"Captain."

"Captain, huh?"

"Yeah. Surprised?"

"A little." *Shocked* was a better word. "You want to tell me about it?"

"Sure, why not. You know, as a captain in the Territorial Riders, I was privy to many things others weren't. About three years ago, I began hearing rumblings about a treasure hidden somewhere up north, and during a chance encounter I just happened to learn a bit more than I had already guessed."

"Go on," she encouraged.

"That's when I broke off from the regiment to search on my own. Come to think of it, if we've both experienced the same dream, there might be a slim chance that we are also in search of the same treasure. Do you think that's possible?"

"What makes you think your dream has anything to do with the treasure?"

"Well, we've both had the same dream, and we're both in search of buried treasure. And I'll bet they're connected."

"I wouldn't think so." Glancing Wolf's way, she added, "But you never know, Justin, the world is a very strange place, and believe it or not, miracles do happen every day."

XXIV

it comes with the territory

Many places in which our companions found lodging welcomed strangers. Her warm, friendly, and honest face, combined with his good looks and similar personality traits, gave them the needed advantage in finding lodging at various ranches and farms throughout the territory.

Brina pushed for such private accommodations as opposed to staying in town, for a couple of reasons. She knew she was being sought after and staying in towns would make discovery easier; second, Justin was not truly aware of her circumstances, being innocent of them, which put him in more danger than her. So, she took it upon herself to convince him that sleeping even in barns would be better than the cold, impersonal, try as they might, unfriendly atmosphere of rickety old hotel rooms and gossipy guests. Then, of course, there was the added plus of home-cooked meals, meeting interesting people, and the exchange of pleasant conversation as opposed to the stuffiness of the contrary.

Brina found it refreshing that even though they themselves were strangers, those who made their living under the guidance and directions of Mother Nature were more trusting of travelers than gossipy townsfolk. Even though countryfolk appear friendlier and more trusting, that didn't mean they were ignorant of scoundrels. Living on and off the land taught those rugged pioneers of yesteryear an insight into the workings of Mother Nature and life itself not normally appreciated by outsiders. When approached with a friendly smile, a warm and sincere glimmer in the eyes, and most of all proper manners, most of those who make their living off the land, whether it be ranching, farming, big spreads or small, welcome into their homes and into their hearts travel-weary pilgrims.

If there were people in the area, or along the trail, Brina found winter no different—if people could be found. 'Cause before she knew it, summer was gone, fall had fallen, and according to the squirrels' frantic gathering of nuts, winter was not far away. And not wanting the squirrels to have all the fun and not wanting to find herself without, Brina looked, found, and collected as many white oak acorns that she could store in their packs, just as the squirrels had. "Better to have and not need than to need and not have" was her motto.

And as it turned out, their travel plans were hindered due to the hard-hitting beginnings of winter. She'd assumed right, thanks to the squirrels. The All Mother's early-warning signals were right on the mark. Winter was definitely here and was hitting worse than ever expected. Thank goodness the horses had been provided with such thick, thick coats this year as a violent snowstorm ushered in at the end of November with thirty-mile winds. To get anywhere the horses were forced to plunge, lunge, and plow through snowdrifts that were sometimes as deep as six feet. There were times when both Brina and Justin were forced to do the same, through such conditions, just to keep from freezing.

Just as she began to waken from a warm, comfortable and restful night's sleep, her mind began to wander back to the last two days and the night before. It had been a ghastly ride; a second storm had hit them unawares. The wind, sleet, and bloody cold had almost taken her. The last warm place they'd stayed was a week past, and she hadn't expected the weather to be so downright freezing since then. Even time spent in the void hadn't prepared her for such weather. Of course, they didn't have weather like this back home, not even in the void. The void had many strange and bizarre attributes and was void of many things, which was why they called it so, but it had nothing like these freezing chill factors, winds, and amounts of snow. And of all the things safely packed away in her saddlebags, her thermals had not made it. They'd been carelessly forgotten by some flunky at the

Centre. And those winds—they blew the snow so hard that last week they finally had to hold up behind a stand of trees until nightfall. Of course, traveling in that type of weather especially at night was a fool's journey, but they had little choice. Their supplies had dwindled to almost nothing, and the horses needed feed, or they'd give out in not too long a time.

So, it was just dumb luck when one afternoon (what she thought was afternoon) when Justin caught a glimpse of what he thought was a flicker of light off in the distance. With hope in their hearts, they rode directly for the beacon, as though it was a lighthouse situated on a rocky coastline, and they the distressed cutter.

By the time they felt it had been their imagination, Brina picked up a faint sound of a dog barking. And if a dog was barking somewhere, that usually meant people, and people in this kind of weather usually meant a warm fire, hopefully a warm welcome, and if they were lucky enough, a place to sleep. It had been so blasted cold, windy, snowy, miserable, and they were both very tired, they would've missed the fence and house, if it hadn't been for the Gray Wolf.

Wolf could see. Wolf saw everything. And with this unexplainable ability, he saw through the blinding snow a warmly dressed man standing just behind a gate cradling a shotgun.

When her trusty steed stopped, Brina knew there had to be a reason. Peering into the swirling snow, she almost missed the gate. Peering closer still, she spotted behind it an armed man dressed in layers and layers of clothing. And not too far behind him, wrapped warmly in several quilts braving the weather, stood a woman, a woman standing on the front porch holding high a lantern to better light the way. And as the husband stepped up scolding the strangers' foolish attempts at traveling in such weather, the woman in the quilts immediately stepped down to approach with her lantern held higher. Pulling farther down the wrap from around her face and eyes, she scrutinized the frozen face above her. Realizing what it was which had encroached upon their secluded domain, she turned to the dog and shouted over the freezing wind, "Quiet, Blue!" Then she turned to her husband yelling at the same volume, "Samuel." As she stepped up to the larger of the two horses, continued. "Help this one down. I'll put her in your chair next to the fire—give 'er a chance to thaw."

"What ya mean her?" hollered Samuel to his wife.

The woman hadn't been married to this man for forty-odd years not to know when to pay him little mind. "Never mind. Just help them down. Hurry up. We got to git 'em inside before they freeze to death."

Even though it's ingrained into all men that they must be the stronger of the two sexes, Justin was just as frozen and weak from the elements as was his horse. As to Brina, she was in reality the stronger of the two with her training and the likes, so as it was, it was Justin who needed to be pried off his horse like a plank off the side of the barn.

"Can ya stand, man?" hollered Samuel through the wind.

All Justin could do was nod as he shook from the cold.

"Lean against the horse till we get 'er down," again hollered Samuel.

Justin did as was told.

Not to say that Brina didn't need to be pulled off as well, but she didn't come down as a plank, more like a limp kitten. On the ground, with frozen feet and legs, she almost fell into the woman.

"Dearie, you're as frozen as that stupid rabbit last year. Here, let's get you inside." With only steps to go, the woman opened her quilts welcoming the stranger into her folds for warmth, then helped her across the yard and into the house.

The house was warm and inviting. Its walls thick, massive and of medium brown. It kept the weather, its ghastly winds, and freezing cold at bay. Brina walked with difficulty, but with determination, with the woman to a high-back cushioned chair that sat inches away from the wood-burning stove. She couldn't utter a word she was so cold, but she didn't have to; the woman knew what was needed. The woman slid herself out from under the quilts leaving them in place before setting Brina into the chair. Sitting so close allowed the fire to warm and dry Brina's boots before the woman managed to remove both them and the socks from her feet. Once off, her feet were wrapped in a small blanket already warmed by the fire. It was like wearing woolen slippers, not at all like the riding boots Brina had been living in of late. Riding boots were great for protecting feet from the saddle rigging, insects, cacti, rocks, and mild weather, but they were not the best for keeping feet warm, and electric socks were null and void in this century.

With the young woman's feet now thawing, the older one raised her head and eyes to meet stranger's face.

Reflecting in the eyes below hers, Brina saw herself in thirty-odd years. Intermixed with the brown irises was an intelligence earned only by years of living a difficult life in such a harsh land. They foretold of happy days, of sad days, and of days yet to come. None of which could be explained. They held a warmth, a strength, a goodness not often found in Brina's life. She was impressed with what she saw there. She also felt an instant drawing to this woman, similar to the one she had with Justin, only this one was instantaneous. The woman's hair was almost white, and her skin was browned and leathery from the sun, wind, and elements. Her smile was cheerful and loving. A warming comfort in this cold, cold land. Not that she normally needed it, but under the circumstances it was a welcome sight.

"You stay right here, dearie. I'll fetch ya something warm to eat."

Outside, Justin was so cold, and the wind was blowing so hard, he could barely hear what was being said. All he knew and felt were the freezing temperatures, the snow pelting his body, the vague movements of others, and the light that could barely be seen through the windows.

"Can ya walk?" hollered Samuel at the stranger as he watched his wife half-carry the woman inside.

Justin himself, half-frozen and covered with zillions of snowflakes from head to toe in the blinding wind, nodded a second time, but when he took his first step, fell into the snow-filled yard.

"Damn city folk," mumbled Samuel. Using strength earned by years and years of chopping and carrying wood, hitching drafts, plowing fields, blacksmithing, living off the land, and building barns, sheds, homes, Samuel knelt down, rolled the man onto his back, eased his arm under the man's shoulders, lifting him to a sitting position. "Come on, man, you don't want the womenfolk seeing you like this." But apparently it made little difference to the man in the snow. Samuel realized that now. Gathering his reserve strength, he grasped the man's shoulders, eased his other arm under his legs, and with a strength not often seen, lifted the two-hundred-pound Justin Case III out of the snow and carried him into the house with little effort, shutting the door and the storm behind them.

"Over there." She directed her husband with his load.

The young woman was in his favorite chair next to the promised heat, dozing. After depositing his load in the second chair, Samuel went back outside.

Not knowing if he could hear her, but for reassurance's sake, the woman spoke to Justin as he warmed to the stove. "Your lady friend was too exhausted to exchange anything more than a warm smile, so I fed her a morsel or two instead along with some hot milk. And by the time I got back to 'er, her lids were already on their way down."

"T-t-t-hhhannks," was the only word Justin could utter.

"Let me git ya some coffee. Warm them innards." Busying herself in the kitchen, the woman returned with a steaming cup. At first, she just held it for the man to take but noticed that his arms and hands were still tightly clasped to his chest. "Here." Prying them apart, she carefully placed the warm cup between his hands, then closed them back upon it, as she closed hers over his. Looking into those deep chocolate-brown eyes, she was surprised to see a tear begin to form. "It's all right," she whispered, "you're safe now." The woman, with love overflowing for all living things, smiled at the man before her.

Justin felt the warmth from both the cheerful face in front of him, and the cup he held in his frozen hands. He felt the heat from the cup itself move slowly up his arms. Shakily and with the woman's help, he managed to raise the cup to his lips, took a sip, swallowed, and felt a delicious warming sensation well up from his core.

In a matter of minutes, his hands had almost stopped shaking. The woman, in turn, let them go.

The older woman gave the man a few more minutes before introducing herself. Still whispering, as to not wake the other, she began, "My name's Fanny. Fanny Albright.

"My husband, Samuel, will tend to your animals. He'll find a warm stall for each, feed, grain, and water them." She wanted to ask what they were doing out there in that storm but decided that it could wait. "We're all damned lucky Blue heard you. Who knows what would've happened had he not."

When Brina awoke, there was just enough time to remember tidbits of the night before—the discovery of the gate, the man, their apparent rescue, the warmth of the stove, the food in her gut, and the roof over their heads—before determining her immediate location. Sitting up, she found herself in a room. Looking around this room, she found it to be about fifteen feet, seven inches by twelve feet, six inches in size, with a wood-burning stove hot from freshly stoked wood not six feet away. Its ornate castings decorating its front were just enough to cause wonder of its origin when she noticed the wall behind it. What a strange-looking wall it was. It was like someone had painted on its off-white surface tiny green figures. A closer look told her that all four walls were the same. The drapes that partially covered the walls next to the windows were heavy, massive, and hung to the floor. Heavy and massive enough to keep the freezing cold from seeping in through the assumed glass behind them. They were a dark green with tassels at their tops that matched the same green of the small figures painted on the twelve-foot-high walls.

She was surprised she could see the room this clearly, but then some kind person had brought in a large fancy lantern setting it upon a small table that when lit did an excellent job of lighting the room, yet left it dim enough to be easy on the eyes. To her right was a tall chest that housed several drawers for who knew what and an armoire for other things. The footboard of the bed in which she lay was also ornately carved as was the stove across the room. The headboard directly behind her, she assumed, was the same.

The person who slept soundly next to her, of course, was Justin. How he'd gotten there was anybody's guess. But then again, where else was he to sleep, and what difference did it make anyway? They'd spent who knew how many weeks on the trail together; then they'd slept almost side by side. Besides, she was sure there weren't more than a couple of rooms in this house, let alone more than a couple of beds. Where else would he sleep, on the floor? That was an option, yes, but why sleep on the floor when one had a feather bed the size of Connecticut to sleep in? She did notice that he lay on top of her covers yet was still under several of his own. Probably his idea, assuming that it'd upset her otherwise, especially after their discussion of weeks past. And how would the Albrights know to put them in different rooms; they had not a clue as to their traveling arrangements. But sound asleep he most definitely was.

Mentally taking inventory on her own sleeping garments, Brina quietly rose as to not wake him. Using one of the quilts left at the foot of her bed as a wrap, she stepped to the window pulling the heavy drapes aside and peered through the foggy glass. From where she stood, she could see that the weather had not changed much since the night before. Those ghastly winds had stopped, but it was still snowing heavily. So heavily, in fact, that the storm doors and shutters below were almost completely covered with the white stuff, as was almost everything else within her view—the fences, bushes, trees, a lot of the smaller outbuildings, and the massive one not far from the house.

Directly next to the window was a chair. The chair was made totally of a dark plain wood with a high back on which lay clothes. Picking them up she found them to be clean, still warm, and not theirs. Theirs had needed attention, thus the replacements. Dawning the borrowed clothing, finding their fit almost perfect, she left the room, leaving Justin sleeping soundly in the cozy feather bed behind her.

The downstairs was just as warm and inviting as she remembered it to be from the night before.

"Good morning," Brina said as she entered the kitchen only to find Fanny finishing up the morning pots and pans.

"Good morning to you too. And how did you and your husband sleep? Well, I hope," came the cheerful reply.

"Wonderfully. Thank you, but he's not my husband."

"He's not?"

"No. He's just a friend. A traveling companion," Brina tried to explain.

"Everyone needs friends." Consternation furrowed her brow, but only for a second. "But you must be starving. Let me get you something."

"That's okay, I don't want to put you to any trouble." Again, noting the dishes in the sink.

"Don't be silly. After all, two days is two days. You must be starved by now," Fanny said as she continued fussing around the kitchen, this time for a plate, then turned towards the fire for the meal that waited to be served.

"Two days?" Brina thought for a moment. "You are joking, aren't you?"

"No, dearie, I'm not. You and your friend's been sleeping for two days. 'Twas night before last when Blue brought you to our attention."

Brina couldn't believe it.

Fanny broke her concentration. "In the shape that you were in, it would've been only a few more hours fer the cold to take ya. It's a thankful blessing you're even here." Then the older woman returned to her fussing.

Brina didn't want to even think about the possible consequences had they missed the light and gate. The outcome would've been disastrous for too many. Accepting her situation as it was, she stared blindly across the room. When her vision cleared and came into focus, she found herself staring at a stove of some kind. It looked strange. Nothing she'd ever seen or heard of could compare to the six-foot-tall contraption that sat within a recessed area of the kitchen wall. It was four feet wide and two feet deep. It stood on four legs with two doors on the front panel, a larger, located almost in the center, with a smaller one to the left. She assumed these were part of the oven. About halfway up was the griddle that had a side platform off to the right for extra pots and pans? She didn't know and was too in awe to ask.

"Is there a place I can wash up?" Brina asked.

"Yes, dear. We have a room under the back stairs with a pump, basin, and whatever else you may need. It's way too cold to go outside."

"Indoor plumbing?"

"Yes, you can call it that if you'd like. It's not what I'd like, but like I said, it's better than freezing your backside on the wooden seat outside."

Brina chuckled on her way to the pump room. She was surprised to find one here at all. Sometimes they had them in fancy hotels but rarely had she seen one in a private home. But after all, necessity was the mother of invention, and she figured that those who lived this far out had to do something.

By the time she was finished and had returned to the kitchen, Justin was sitting in one of the four chairs that surrounded the table.

"Good morning, Bree."

"Morning, Justin." Just as she was about to pull out a chair, he was there, had done it for her, and was waiting for her to sit.

Caught off guard, but not showing it, she thanked him. She wasn't accustomed to such gallantry.

"Anytime."

Griddle cakes, fried eggs, hot coffee, and chops were served shortly before the sound of a door slamming shut.

Moments later Samuel walked into the kitchen. "Damn, it's freezing outside. Mother, I haven't seen this hard a winter since '56." Seeing the two visitors at the table sitting as though waiting for him to join them surprised him. "You go ahead. I already et."

"You did, er, you have?" Justin asked.

"Bin up quite a while. Not everyone sleeps all day round here," Samuel said with a smile in his voice.

"What time is it?" Justin again asked.

Brina thought, *you mean what day is it?* But she didn't voice it. Instead, she watched Samuel in fascination as he pulled an inch-and-a-half-sized watch from his pocket.

Popping its cover to see its face, Samuel said, "Eight o'clock."

"In the morning?" Justin was shocked.

"Justin," Brina began, "be polite."

"Sorry. When did you get up, Mr. Albright?"

Caught off guard with a title he hadn't heard in years, he corrected the visitor. "If we're going to get along, son, it's Sam, or Samuel. Not Mr. Albright. We're just plain folks out here. Don't need no fancy city stuff."

To show him how he felt about the whole thing, Justin pushed back his chair, stood, and offered his host his hand. "I stand corrected, Samuel." The man's grip was amazingly strong. His hands rough and large, so large in fact that they almost swallowed Justin's.

"We'll git along then." Turning to his wife, Samuel asked, "What's for breakfast?"

"Again, still and always," Fanny mumbled.

Justin had sat himself back down by the time Samuel had removed his overcoat and gloves, placing himself at the head of the table.

With food hot on the table, Fanny served Samuel his *again*, then served herself. "How're their horses?"

"Content." The question of the new horses brought forth one of his own. "Say, that's some fancy gray you got out there. Where'd ya find 'im?" he asked Justin.

"He's not mine. He's Bree's."

"Yours, huh?" Taking a mouthful of eggs, he turned towards Brina.

"Yes, sir."

"Would you be interested in selling him?"

"Not on your life."

"I don't blame ya. If he was mine, I wouldn't sell 'im either."

Brina was amazed how well the two of them got on with both Samuel and Fanny Albright. So well, in fact, the Albrights gave them an engraved invitation to stay till the spring thaw.

"It will be a wonderful time, you'll see. I'll tell you stories about what it's like living here in our part of the country, my life, our children and anything else you want to know. It's been so lonely here, these past ten years. You may not know it, my dears, but seeing you out there among the snow and freezing temperatures gave me hope as to be blessed with the sights and sounds of family once again. Not that you're kin, but you could be, and for that, things should work out just fine." Fanny Albright seemed to light up like the night sky as she relayed her plans to her winter guests. "I'll also see to preparing another room so the two of you won't have to share. After all, there are four bedrooms in this house, I ought to be able to find another unoccupied room for one of you to use."

The first morning after both newly found guests felt rested enough to take part in the normal goings-on, Samuel Albright took Justin under his wing to teach him all the ins and outs of living on their ranch in the dead of winter. He explained that of course it being winter the housed livestock need tending, with miscellaneous chores mixed in, but most of it was staying close to the fire just keeping warm, waiting for the spring thaw. So, the following morning long before the sun was due to rise, Samuel woke Justin from a warm and sound sleep so they may both have the morning chores finished before the start of breakfast. With Justin on his heels, Samuel paused at the door to begin his morning routine of preparing himself against the winter temperatures by slowly putting layer upon layer upon layer of clothes on with Justin following suit.

Once ready to disembark for his new job as an apprentice ranch hand for the Cross-Bar Ranch, Justin turned back to Brina, caught her eye, winked, then began, "Bye, Bree, see ya after a bit, after—" Turning towards Samuel, he asked, "Samuel?"

"Yeah?"

"After what? What is it we're getting all bundled up for?"

"It's not a what, it's a who."

"All right, who are we getting all bundled up for?"

"Sarah. She needs milking."

"Who's Sarah? The cow?" Justin had never milked anything in his life.

"Well, we used to have a cow when the children were home, but Sarah replaced Elsie after the kids left. There was too much milk for us and the critters to drink, and since I don't like wastin' nothing, we replaced Elsie with a goat. A goat, Fanny named Sarah."

"Is that all we're going out there for? To milk a goat? Then what?"

"Just follow me, you'll see." Samuel turned to Brina. "Brina. It is Brina, am I right?"

"Yes, Samuel. It's Brina. Justin calls me Bree, but my name is Brina."

"Very well." He addressed both the women of his house, "Ladies, we'll be back in three shakes of a lamb's tail." Chuckling, Samuel opened the door, then gently nudged a most confused-looking Justin out into the freezing elements as he shut the door behind them.

The barn was very large and fully enclosed. It kept out all the elements protecting its occupants completely. It was a warmer, drier, and more comfortable place than outside, where everything appeared to be as though in another world. It was a place where the animals, who spent their winter months within its confines, welcomed all who entered their domain, with their own versions of *good morning, good afternoon,* or just plain *hello.* Even though he was used to the nickering of his horse, Wyatt, over there in the far corner stabled next to Wolf, the various voices of the other horses, the goats, chickens, rabbits and the two orphaned calves was almost like having a family of your own, living outside the house, ready to greet you at any time of the day.

Samuel had explained just last night about the two calves and how two of his first-year heifers had died calving, then had gone on to explain about that in detail, which was interesting, but not necessarily something Justin wanted to dwell on. Then as he stood in the middle of the doorway watching everything with interest, Samuel interrupted Justin's momentary daydreaming by stepping over to another shorter door and opening it. As Justin watched in wonder, in trotted three goats all with totally different colors and patterns to their coats. One he assumed was the aforementioned Sarah, and the other two? That was soon to be explained.

"Quickly, Justin..."

"What?"

"Grab that pail on that there rail and pour the contents in the three stalls there. Yea, that's the one."

Justin had barely enough time to get the contents of the pail into the three separate stall feeders before all three goats had gone to their respective assigned places to eat. "Do they all have names?"

"Yes, they do. That one closest to you is Mongrel; he's the buck. The one next to him is Michelle; she's still too young to breed—maybe this spring. And this is Sarah."

"Do they all come in such different colors and spots?" Justin had never spent any time around a farm or even thought about such things.

"Well, son, back east we used to have many different kinds of goats. Back then we used them for other things, but now they're supplying us with meat, milk, companionship for the horses and for ourselves. They're very enjoyable to be around. These are called Nubians, I think. There are others, but Fanny wanted these for their floppy ears. Silly, huh?"

As Justin sat listening to the tranquilizing droning sound of the goats eating away, Samuel tended to the rest of the animals. The horses got their hay, the goats got hay placed in separate paddocks, (one for the buck, one for the does), the chickens and rabbits got some of the corn put up from last year.

When Justin caught sight of what Samuel was doing and watched as he assumed was an error as the calves hadn't received the same treatment as the rest of the stock in the barn, he asked. "Samuel, what about the baby calves? Don't they get fed too?"

"They'll get some of Sarah's milk, then some of the hay." Samuel picked up the milking bucket from its place on the hook, stepped over towards Sarah, and waited for the inevitable question.

"So, what are you going to do now?"

"Not just me, Justin, you and me. Ya see, we're just beginning."

Back at the house, Brina was in the kitchen with Fanny waiting for her lessons in the wifely duties of pioneer women.

"Brina?"

"Yes, Fanny?"

"Will you be so kind as to take this here bucket over to the fireplace and shovel a few coals into it so I can get the stove going for breakfast?" As Brina did what was asked of her without hesitation, Fanny began gathering the ingredients needed for breakfast from the cellar. A cellar, in which Brina was soon to discover, contained pounds upon pounds of flour, slabs of smoked meat, roots, dried berries, grains, butter kegs, onions, potatoes, and five substantially large barrels of water.

As Brina returned to the woodstove with her bucketful of coals, she heard her teacher making noises somewhere below. "Fanny, is there someplace you want me to put these as you collect whatever it is, you're looking for?"

"Yes, dear, drop them in the firebox. You'll find kindling and other wood already inside, so just place one here and there. It'll take care of itself. Oh, then please close the door. I'll be up in a minute." Fanny was looking for something in particular for breakfast but hadn't found it yet, and thanks to Brina being there, it saved her on wasted time.

Upon Fanny's return, Brina was found standing next to the woodstove waiting for more instructions.

"Oh dear, you want something else to do. Hummmm, let me see, while I prepare the potatoes, you can…"

Fanny's timing was perfect. Even though she had difficulty keeping the temperature in the oven constant, all her years of cooking and taking care of her family made all her efforts look like child's play. Just enough time was left before the cornbread was ready, when the men returned from the barn with fresh eggs. It was almost like watching a magician at work. She had everything down to a science, at least for her time period.

As Justin began to strip off his several layers of clothing, Samuel stopped him with "Now hold on there, son, don't you be a strippin' down too far. We still have work to do today, but first, we get to dig into this here meal."

By the time, the day had pretty much come to a close, both Brina and Justin were pretty much worn out. Justin had spent most of his brisk yet clear afternoon trying to stay warm while he helped Samuel tend livestock, worked in the barn doing various chores, and later in the day found himself chopping wood for what ailed him.

Brina, on the other hand, spent the day learning how to make soap.

That night, after a long, hard day, Fanny decided to entertain her guests with a few stories she knew of while they sat in front of the fireplace getting warm before heading off to bed.

But before she could get started, Brina wanted to ask a couple questions. "Fanny?"

"Yes, dear."

"You said this house had four bedrooms and that your children had left. Would you tell us about them? How many there were, and where are they now? That is, if you don't mind me asking."

"No, child, you can ask. It's been long enough, I think, these past ten years." She then set her sights on some faraway land.

"It's hard for her sometimes, Brina, to remember the children," began Samuel. "You have to understand, we were blessed with a total of seven. Only five lived."

"You mean, they didn't all survive?" Brina was shocked. There was so much she did not know.

"No, dear. They didn't. You see, Fanny and I have been married a very long time. Her grandparents came from up north, and mine, well, they were killed by French trappers. We met at a very young age, got married, and since I was fairly good with animals, we tried our hand at farming in Philly. 'Tis only the All Mother who knows how we ever found our way from there all the way here. You see, our first two boys died at birth, but that didn't stop us. Back then Fanny was a strong young woman, kinda like you, my dear, and she wasn't about to let the loss of children stop her. Over the next ten years we were blessed with five more children who all managed to survive at least till they were old enough to be useful. Jared, the oldest, got gorged by a rank bull during a cattle drive up north for a neighbor friend. Sarah…"

Justin remembered the goat in the barn and wondered if the two names were connected in some way. Then glanced over towards Fanny and found her still staring off into some faraway place.

"Sarah," quietly began Fanny, finally shifting her attention towards her guests and her husband, "was to be my only girl. *My baby*. Even though she was second to Jared and before Michael, Lance, and Luis, being the only girl, she was my favorite. She took a fancy to the horses and loved to ride in the mountains in the summertime. Samuel here rode with her till we both felt her old enough to handle things on her own."

"How old was that?" asked Brina, thinking back on the day the organization stepped in and took her from her family, thinking she was old enough to handle things on her own.

"Oh, about six, seven, in there somewheres. She'd always do just fine. Samuel could send her out after cows, and we never had to worry. She always came back." It had been so long since they spoke this tale aloud, Fanny was beginning to realize it was way overdue. "Then one winter, just like this one, a nasty snowstorm hit us all by surprise. Sarah had gone for a short ride up the canyon and was still up there when the storm hit. It was an unusual winter that year, and we had more snow than we'd ever seen. We waited all day and way into that night for her to return, and when Snowflake, her horse, the one Uncle Danny bought for her that year she started riding came home without her on the third day of the storm, we knew. We just knew."

Samuel knowingly glanced Justin's way. "If you haven't figured it out by now, son, that goat in the barn is named after our Sarah."

"So were nine of them before her," added Fanny. "You see, every spring one of the doe kids that are born in the barn gets christened Sarah. Sound silly? Well, we do that because that way, she's always here somewhere: warm, protected, and loved. Of the other three boys—Michael, Lance, and Luis—Michael is attending school in St. Louise to become a doctor. Lance is partner in a large cattle spread in Texas. He married the only daughter of a wealthy cattle baron and left. And Luis went in search of gold in Kaliphornya about fifteen years gone by, and we ain't received a letter from him in two years."

"Then who runs the place?" asked Brina.

"We get lots of help from the neighbors. Besides, we don't run cows here anymore; we let the Hawkes run their cows. They graze it. Mike and Rachelle Hawke, well, they keep us in whatever we need, for payment of using the land," Samuel explained.

"How much land do you have here?"

"Oh, about"—Samuel had to think a moment to recall—"a thousand acres more or less, I figure."

Brina was amazed. The history books had mentioned "spreads," but the thought of someone actually owning that much land was staggering—especially for her time. "That's quite a lot."

"Oh, not that much. Mike and Rachelle's neighbors on the north, why, they've got millions. Or so I'm told."

"What'd you do with your cows?" asked Justin.

"We sorta let them run with Mike's. But that's been years back. Over the years he's compensated us for them. That's how we've managed to survive here all these years. The land is ourn."

Brina thought for a moment. "Why didn't the children stay? Aren't they needed here?"

"Yes, they are, but when Sarah didn't return that night, it just kinda made it hard for 'em. They lost their appetite for ranching—ya know, the memories? It was just too hard on them. They didn't want to see her at every turn." Fanny was directing her explanation to an unknown and unseen entity across the room.

Startled, Brina too glanced that way, but saw and sensed nothing.

After the first week passed, both Brina and Justin had found their winter chores to be more exhausting than imagined. Yet as exhausted as they both were, Brina, more than Justin, found kitchen chores interesting but asked to be outside. Not that she didn't enjoy immensely the company of Fanny, but she needed the great outdoors to stimulate, stretch, and satisfy her body and soul.

With this unusual request, Samuel at first believed that Brina was just a very active woman. Kinda like their little Sarah, yet as the days rolled on and she complained naught, he became curious. After all, he found her to be stronger than originally believed—she could hitch up and handle the team without help, spent many an hour walking through the deep snow with little effort, and had ample strength and stamina needed for chopping wood. Not only that, but she also had a knack with the animals. Watching her in action kept him suspicious of what she had originally done before she and her friend happened to fall into their lives. Justin, on the other hand, seemed a normal, well-educated country boy. However, until something serious came of their choice meeting and stay, he'd keep his questions to himself and relish the extra help and friendship the two of them provided.

It was around the beginning of December, which meant Christmas wasn't too far off. Christmas. All Brina could think of was the continual kindness and love the Albrights had shown them by bringing them into their hearts as though they were kin, as Fanny called it. Was there something special she could do for them at this time of year? She didn't know. So much time had elapsed since she enjoyed this time of year and the true spirit of giving it brought. Brina on occasion found herself suffering from momentary flashbacks of her early childhood before life with the organization. Some of those moments brought with them vague memories of brightly colored red and green boxes floating haphazardly through the air among laughter and gaiety. It was the only time for her, all those days gone by, when she cherished the true meaning of love and giving for and of her fellow man. Of course, then, she was totally ignorant of what her fellow man was and what he was capable of doing.

Things were different now, she was different now, and she wanted to do something, to make something special, for this wonderful, loving, and courageous couple. She knew Justin was probably thinking similar thoughts as she, and that was all well and good, but she wanted to do something for them, from her alone.

Two weeks before Christmas it finally hit her. *A Christmas tree.* Neither Fanny nor Samuel had mentioned anything about going out and getting a tree for the holiday season. Brina assumed it was because their children were no longer home, but as it turned out, Samuel felt that all the extra effort was just that, extra effort. Furthermore, he didn't intend on tackling the elements for the time it'd take to find a tree, let alone haul it all the way back home. Then again neither one of them had Brina's determination and want of giving for not only them, but for Justin as well. And if there ever was an opportunity to feel belonged and loved, this year was it. It was slightly out of character for her, and she knew it, but she chalked it up to the new time change and the company she kept of late.

The only question now was, how will she do it?

First, she began her plan by meticulously packing her saddlebags with the additional supplies needed for an extended trip to the winter woods. Not that she wanted to spend any more time than need be out there in the freezing cold, but you could never be sure what was to happen. Already in her pack, she kept two flasks of whiskey, Dr. Jarlath's Colts and ammunition, a small hatchet, a skinning knife, her own secret box of wooden "strike absolutely anywhere—even underwater" matches, strips of an old sheet, a micro shovel, a swatch of oilskin, a 250-foot roll of micro-twine, a heat sensory sheet, a few other odds and ends, and to that she added some beef jerky and coffee found in the cellar. It was a good thing no one had ever taken a real good look inside those saddlebags of hers; if they had, they would've been in for a big surprise.

Second, she had to sweet-talk Justin, Fanny, and Samuel into helping her grind the acorns into flour, the very same flour she planned on stashing in her saddlebags.

It just so happened, two mornings later, as Brina was helping Fanny prepare breakfast for them all, the door suddenly flew open, and in rushed Justin and Samuel amid blowing snow and freezing cold air. When Justin finally slammed the door shut behind them, both men rushed over to the woodstove to thaw. "Damn, it's cold out there!" exclaimed Justin.

"Colder than year before last, I'll wager," began Samuel. "That year it was so cold. By the beginning of October, the winter settled in and didn't leave till May. Hundreds of cattle, horses, and sheep throughout the territory were marooned in the October and November snowstorms without grass, hay, grain, or shelter. As a result, many died. And those poor families who ran those spreads moved south towards milder ranges. It's a good thing we had a bumper crop last year, ain't it, Fan?" As Samuel turned, he found his wife standing next to the stove with the eggs in the cast-iron pan ready for scrambling with a twinkle in her eye and a smile upon her lips.

"That's a true story," began Fanny. "I can remember riding out with Samuel that following spring after the winter finally did turn. We found carcasses everywhere, half-eaten by scavengers. It was horrible, just horrible."

"Well, all we have to worry 'bout today is to stay warm till tonight. Then we git to do it all over again, eeh, Justin?" Samuel smiled broadly towards Justin.

"Sounds fine to me, but what are we to do in the meantime?"

Brina's door opened. "I have a suggestion."

Lucky for her, everyone wanted to take part. Not only because it gave them all something to do, but it was also something new and could be substituted or added to flour if need be. And since Brina was the only one who knew how to create this new and exciting concoction, they all were eager to learn.

First, they went through the painstakingly tedious job of peeling away the outer shell of each and every stupid little acorn. Then the acorn's meaty little centers were roasted till they were thoroughly dry, but not burned. They were then pounded into a fine powder that could be considered a flour to be used as needed in various mixtures. Unbeknownst to them, much of this was to be Brina's flour.

Brina was not used to informing anyone of her plans, especially when there was no team commander to report to. So, telling Justin wasn't going to be easy, but she knew necessary. If she left without a word, they'd more than likely try to search for her and freeze to death in the meantime. She couldn't have that. She liked them too much.

She didn't, however, like the way she was beginning to think of late. This was definitely not the way she was trained. To care about others other than teammates was not what the organization intended. Outsiders were expendable and not to be considered. Back at the Academy it was always the mission, the mission, the mission that was above all reproach. But that was before. Now, here, things were different. She didn't have a team or team commander to report to. Now she had, friends? Yes—friends. Friends, acquaintances, and *outsiders* who cared for her, for her welfare as well as their own. Yes, things were changing, but were they for the better? She didn't know, wasn't sure.

She *was* still the soldier, could and would defend herself and anyone else who just happened along. Could it be possible that these outsiders were her team? Could they be considered part of her team and she their commander? Was that possible, or just an excuse to make it easier to accept her attitude changes? It mattered not. Her plan was set in her mind, and approval or no approval of her plan, she was going anyway—her mind was already made up.

Finally, with everything packed and ready to go, including extra grain for Wolf and a few extra layers of clothing, Brina set sail in search of Justin to tell him of her plan.

"NO, YOU'RE NOT!" Justin shouted at her. "You're not going out on a moonlight ride by yourself in weather like this! You'll freeze your ass off or get caught out there and die! Bree, you can't do that, I won't let you!"

"I'm sorry, Justin, but I want to find a special tree for Christmas, and I want to do this by myself. Wolf will be with me."

285

"His going changes nothing. Bree, I'm sorry, but you're not going. And that's that."

She tried cajoling. "Justin, please. I have everything I need in my saddlebags. I'll be fine. Don't do this to me, not now. Not when we're getting along so well." She didn't see herself reach for his hand.

Getting along so well? He glanced down and saw that his hand was now in hers. Searching beseechingly into her eyes, the determination he was afraid he'd find was there. "Damn it, Bree. I don't want to lose you like they did Sarah." Their sad faraway story was now hitting too close to home.

It was so sad. The flood of emotions his eyes held unsettled her. She hadn't realized his feelings for her ran so deep. And she had done nothing nor encouraged such feelings between them. But feelings or no feelings, she was going. If not for this tree, she needed peace of mind, time with Wolf, and time to consider many different things.

Resigned, Justin pleaded, "You'll come back?" He didn't want her to go, but knew she'd do as she pleased.

As much as she hated emotional games, sometimes they worked. Looking directly into those chocolate-candy-brown eyes of his, she answered, "Promise." Picking up on his worried vibes, she added, "It won't be more than a few days, Justin. I promise. I'll be back by Christmas."

"Bree, let me come with you. If anything happened to you, I don't know how I'd go on."

"No, Justin. I need you here to keep the home fires burning; besides, if the two of us leave instead of just me, they'll think we're abandoning them. I need you here. Although I will keep your concerns utmost on my mind. Say you'll let me go. Please, Justin. I really don't want to leave without your blessings, but I will—"

"I know, I know. As long as you know, I don't like it one bit. But if you're all that determined, I ought to feel lucky you've said anything at all. When are you leaving?"

"Shortly. I've already had my breakfast, and I got up earlier making sure Wolf had an early one as well. We're both ready. Tell them not to worry. I'll be fine."

"So soon?"

"Justin—"

"I'll be quiet." What if she didn't return? How would he face the Albrights? Let alone his own conscience?

With nothing further to discuss, as she had already made up her mind to go without him anyway, Justin waved good-bye to his gray-eyed beauty as she set off on that magnificent steed of hers in search of a special Christmas tree just for them.

Brina already had a good idea in which way to head. Her plan was to head back towards the same direction they had originally come from before meeting up with the Albrights. Wolf charged along effortlessly, carrying her through the snow now that he too was renewed, in search of the perfect tree.

Brina had spent a few moments at the supper table the night before mentally guessing at the approximate measurement of the room so the tree she picked would fit perfectly, or at least as was humanly possible without the use of an Elzegraph. It mattered not; they'd be thrilled to see her return with or without the perfect Christmas tree. And even though she was once again alone in this vast winter wonderland, she was ecstatic. The view around her without the added buildings was gorgeous. The air was crisp, the sky was blue, and the air had a clean, dry feeling to it as it caressed her unprotected skin.

By the time she reached the tree line, the vicinity in which she chose to search, Brina was surprised to find that the sun had reached a position in the sky that told her to find a protected place for them to spend the night or to hurry up and build one. Upon reaching a clump of trees that looked as though it'd suit their needs, Brina dismounted Wolf.

The place she found had a grouping of several well-matched trees in size and configuration, giving her a natural wind break on the north side. If this worked right, and she had no doubts that it wouldn't, when this was finished, Wolf would also have a semi-sheltered place to spend a winter's night.

Back to her days at the Academy, Brina could remember during survival training when the instructors would take seasoned trainees up in ancient Hueys, dropping them haphazardly into the middle of hostile territories with little or no gear. Over, and over they did it, until eventually the trainees, those who lived, emerged triumphantly against all odds after many different enemy location drops. Brina thought she'd never get through it. And here she was again. Only this time and place lacked hostile enemies other than the unpredictable wrath of Mother Nature, plus, it was only to be for a couple of days instead of a couple of weeks, and most importantly, she hadn't been thrown out of a copter; she'd rode here willingly.

The one tree in particular that caught her eye was a stout one with a natural crotch at the trunk in which she could lay a main support pole for a debris hut. Here she lashed the eight-to ten-foot branch she had cut from another type of tree to the crotch of her tree. Then she began lying and strapping strong branches upon her pole, beginning at the top and working her way down. Once the frame and the roof were prepared, the next plan of attack was filling the holes. These she filled with wet leaves, smaller branches, moss off the sides of semi-protected trees, and mud, which she found wasn't too awfully hard to find, dig, or thaw, once she got through the snow and slush. Standing back to admire her work, Brina was delighted to see that it indeed was as she planned. The opening was sheltered partially by one small tree, which left room enough for the two of them to enter, one at a time. Not only that, but as she stepped up to give it a strong kick, found it to be as sturdy as hoped, realizing it would stand for both nights, with possibly, just a touch up here and there. All she had to do now was situate herself and Wolf, get a fire going, pull out their evening meal from her saddlebags, and remove her gear from Wolf.

When night fell and it was time to settle in for a good-night's sleep, she asked her great steed to lie down so she could take advantage of his warm and woolly coat. Even though she was tuned to perfection in many ways, that extra layer of fat, which most people take for granted, was a luxury she'd never had. This taught her to take full advantage of whatever was at hand. On this trip? It was her mighty steed.

With Brina now gone, Justin was faced with the difficult task of explaining everything to the Albrights. As he finished his chores in the barn and collected the morning eggs, Justin trudged back towards the house for breakfast and what he was sure to be a most enlightening conversation.

Justin stepped through the door closing it firmly behind him. Once he handed the eggs over to Fanny, he turned to the coat rack to hang his excess clothing.

"Will Brina be in shortly?" asked Fanny as she began breakfast.

"Uh, no. Not for quite a while." Justin was already beginning to dread Brina's absence.

"You might want to call her in. Breakfast will be ready shortly."

"She won't be in for breakfast, Fanny. When I spoke to her earlier, she said she'd gotten up very early and had something to eat then."

"Why in heaven's name would she do that?"

As the conversation began to broaden, the now-alert Samuel sat back to observe. After all, he had been behind the goat gate cleaning up as Brina saddled Wolf and remained there as she came in to speak with Justin, just before lighting out on her own. He hadn't heard the conversation exactly, just enough to know something was going on.

"Well, Fanny." Justin decided to tell them the truth. After all, it was always the easiest to remember. "Samuel, this includes you too."

"What is it?" Samuel calmly asked.

"Brina's gone. She—"

"Gone? Gone where?" Fanny almost dropped the eggs on the floor instead of in the frying pan.

"To the forest. Don't worry, she'll be back," finished Justin.

"How do you know this, son? Just the other day I was telling the two the story about the unpredictability of the weather up here. She could get caught in a storm, be injured, or even attacked by a wild animal. What makes you think everything will be fine?" Samuel was silently losing his composure.

"She's more resourceful than you know." This was, as Justin believed, more truthful than any of them realized.

"Why? What makes her different than any one of us? She'll be alone out there with no man to care for her. Justin, how could you let her do this?" Fanny was beside herself with worry.

"How could I let her do this." It was more a statement than a question. Suddenly he realized that it would be his fault if any harm did come to her. The more he thought about it, the more it tugged at his heartstrings that if anything did happen to his gray-eyed beauty…"You ask how I could've let her do this. I'll tell you." Then in a calm, unwavering voice full of all the conviction he could muster, he finished, "I believe in her." There, it was out. Even though that wasn't exactly what he planned on saying, the moment it was out of his mouth he knew it to be true. He believed in his gray-eyed beauty because anything she had ever said, done, or set out to do had happened. "She will be back. By Christmas Day at the very latest. That's what she said." All he had to do now was keep the rest a secret.

"Why?" Samuel asked Justin."

Shakily Fanny set food on the table silently mumbling, *"Sarah…"*

"She asked me not to tell you. It had something to do with the holiday season. That's all I can say. The rest? Well, we'll just have to wait and see." With that said, Justin took his place at the breakfast table and began to fill his plate.

By 15:3465.2365p the following day, Brina had found, cut, and returned to camp; as far as she was concerned, the perfect Christmas tree to be enjoyed back at the Cross-Bar Ranch. There it had been, as she rounded that last bend, standing all by itself, a young sapling of an evergreen indigenous to its region on the top of a little outcropping at approximately 11:1563.1a, four miles east of camp. Once the comparisons were made between the sapling and the Albrights' room, Brina made sure the tree's growth would continue, long after her presence was forgotten, by making her cuts well above the seventh branch level, where below were found several new growth buds waiting for their turn to procreate.

Once that was completed, she found two rather long and sturdy branches, similar to the one being used in her shelter. Constructing a travois, Brina then fastened it on each side to her saddle, dragged the tree so it rested upon it, fastened it down with some of her micro twine, remounted Wolf, and trudged back to camp. Even though Brina was eager to return home with her prize in tow, the fading light told her that the following day might be a wiser choice for travel plans. So, with the tree still on the travois, Brina unlashed the support poles from her saddle, eased them to the ground, unsaddled Wolf, fed them both and settled down for the evening.

Later that night, Brina and Wolf were both tucked away all nice and warm, thanks to her heat sensory sheet she'd been forced to retrieve from the very bottom of her saddlebags, as the temperature dropped drastically. It was a good thing she'd brought it; it was also a good thing it had various adjustable features, including the latest Bio Block feature, which amazingly kept the two of them insulated comfortably against the freezing temperatures throughout the night. Why she hadn't thought of this while she and Justin were in such a state was beyond her.

By morning, the atmospheric conditions still hadn't changed, yet from what Brina could guess, it was sure to be a sunny, calm, and beautiful day with moderate temperatures, perfect for traveling. After feeding Wolf more of the grain she'd packed for breakfast, Brina started a small fire using one of her "strike absolutely any-where—even underwater" matches.

While that was going, she melted some snow to use in a con- coction her father used to make. Taking some of her acorn flour, she mixed it with minute amounts of water till it reached the approximate consistency of a stiff dough. Taking it in her hands, Brina rolled it until it was long and thin, then wrapped it, creating its own seal, all around an adequately shaped stick. Once that was accomplished, she held it over the fire, baking the dough to a perfect golden brown. Removing the stick from the fire, then the dough from the stick, Brina now had a wonderfully tasting morning roll to hopefully hold her over till she returned home.

Once her shelter was disassembled and the branches scattered, leaving little trace of her ever being there, Brina packed her gear, lifted then fastened the travois to her saddle fastening it in place. Mounting her trusty steed, she proceeded down the trail back into the general direction of the Cross-Bar Ranch and Justin.

It was Christmas Eve day, and Brina still hadn't returned from the back country. Justin didn't want to show it and was doing a fine job of fooling everyone, but the rising anxiety he felt for his friend and the distinct possibility that she may not return at all was getting him down. It had been three days since he watched her ride out into the wilderness, with her ideas of finding a tree for Christmas. And his doubts in her ability to endure such severe winter temperatures on her own were increasing. Sure, she had gone off by herself shortly after they'd known each other a short time, but then she'd gone at a time when the temperatures were mild, and the territory wasn't so deceivably treacherous. By this time, he was no longer concerned about a tree for Christmas; he just wanted her here by his side so he could watch as she chopped wood, enjoyed the animals, laughed with him, and was his all-around companion. He needed his gray-eyed beauty back safe and sound, hoping all along she was well on her way home.

Supper was unusually quiet for all of them, as each silently prayed for the return of their missing member. After Fanny picked up the dishes, Samuel and Justin headed over towards the stove to sit and enjoy the warmth, all the while hearing the wind outside blow its mournful howl, as though the spirit of some lost soul was searching for a place to rest. Justin knew if something wasn't said to break their concentration on the blowing wind, they'd all lose their minds for sure.

"Fanny," Justin addressed Fanny as she'd remained in the house all day, churning butter. "How'd you do today with the butter?"

"Hmmm? What was that, Justin?" She was just as preoccupied with the mournful howling of the wind as he was.

"The butter. How much did you get out of that batch?"

She was still in the kitchen cleaning up, trying to focus on Justin, when she froze in midstream.

And since Justin was questioning her on the day's activities, he was the first to notice the change. "Fanny…what is it?"

"Oh, my heavens! It's Blue!" She was standing still as a church mouse listening to something above and beyond the howling wind.

Justin was instantly silent, straining his ears in hopes of hearing anything that might give a hint as to a barking dog.

Once Fanny was sure of what she'd heard, she didn't waste a second. Reaching for her heavy wool shawl, she grabbed the knob of the door, yanked it open, and was out into the night faster than either Samuel or Justin could get themselves out of their chairs to follow, shouting, *"She's home, our Brina, she's come home!"*

Both Justin and Samuel flew out the door at the same time, only to find themselves on the porch alongside of Fanny desperately searching the expanse of the yard and what lay beyond for any sight, sound, or sign of either Brina or Wolf. As they all, in their turn, stepped down from the porch onto the snow-covered ground, Justin was the first to hear, off in the distance, the familiar sound of Blue barking happily while greeting an unknown entity. Standing in the center of the yard, Justin continued to search the darkness beyond the direction in which Blue had run off, in hopes of spotting a familiar movement of something or someone cherished.

Suddenly Fanny rushed back into the house in search of something she knew would bring the attention of whoever was out there to the homecoming they longed for. When she found the desired item, Fanny rushed back outside, down the steps, and into the yard. There standing as sure as she had been that very first night, when both Brina and Justin came into their lives, was Fanny, holding the lantern up as high as she could to be used as a beacon to bring their lost soul home to rest.

By sheer will and determination alone, Brina reached the outermost boundary of the Cross-Bar Ranch. She knew the weight of the travois behind her had slowed her pace down to almost a crawl but had no doubts in her mind that she could do the task she'd set her mind to. Besides, she'd spent many a day training for just such an expedition, why shouldn't she have taken advantage of her skills on a first-name basis? It was something she had to prove to herself, a test for herself, to see if all that she'd learned still came to her as a second nature, if she so chose to use it. Unfortunately, she had forgotten about the travois. It was a needed reminder to her that all things don't always turned out as planned, and now giggled as she realized her approximate destination time for reaching the ranch had already come and gone several hours past. By her more recent calculations, she estimated her arrival time to be well into the night.

As she trudged on, not sure of how close she was getting, Brina began to hear the very faint sound of a dog barking. Because she'd been traveling all day, fighting fatigue along with the elements, Brina at first believed herself to be hearing things. But as the sound became louder and more distinct, she realized it was not her imagination. Then when the animal found her and realized who, in fact, it really was, Blue's bark changed from that of a warning to his owners into one of joy. It was at that moment Brina realized it was the blue healer, the very same blue healer that was owned by Samuel and Fanny Albright. She was closer than assumed. She had made it. She was *home*. And as Blue reached Wolf's side to happily bark and trot alongside, Brina, with confidence, glanced down at him, saying, "Good evening, Blue, it's a fine night for a stroll, isn't it?"

Between the time Brina leaned down to speak to Blue then righting herself in the saddle, Fanny had gotten the lantern lit and was holding it as high as she could in hopes that Brina would spot it and know where the house was.

By the time Brina returned to her upright position, while chattering nonsensically with the dog, her attention was focused straight ahead. Wolf had his attention already on the light, when suddenly she spotted it too. An earthly star within her line of vision. An earthly northern star sent to her by a celestial angel so that she may navigate her way back home. It could've been no one other than Fanny, who, just like that first night so many weeks ago, was sending her a glimmer of hope to set sail by to bring herself and her charge home.

With Blue running interception ahead of him, Wolf trudged forward until he brought his two charges, Brina and her tree, to a halt in front of the house and the welcoming committee.

"Merry Christmas, everyone!" Brina cheerfully exclaimed as she began to dismount Wolf. "Did you all miss me while I was away?"

Fanny had laid the lantern on the rail and had joined with Samuel as he waited for Brina to dismount. Not hesitating once she was on the ground, they were on her in a flash, welcoming and cursing her absence at the same time.

"Brina, you should never have left. I don't know what possessed you to do so in this weather! Don't you realize you could've been lost, or injured? Didn't you ever stop to think how worried we might have been?" Fanny was so happy to see her yet so upset that she'd left she couldn't stop talking.

Brina didn't understand what the problem was. She was perfectly capable of taking care of herself under almost all circumstances. Then it occurred to her, those who were angry didn't know all the details nor were they going to get them. Breaking away from the onslaught of questions, Brina quietly but firmly stated, "All right. All right already. I get the picture."

Brina turned to Justin.

"Bree. It's so good to see you." He had to be careful. Even though he wanted nothing better than to rush into her arms, his common sense said that if she had changed her mind at all, she would have said so. "I told them you'd return and that I believed in you."

"Thanks. I appreciate that." More than he could ever begin to imagine. Unfortunately, as with Dillon, she was wanted in a way that wasn't possible, at least not now. True trust and friendship always came first; the rest would follow in its own time, if it was to follow at all.

"Looks like you brought us something. What is it?" He'd known all along what she was up to, and because Wolf had a travois lashed to his saddle, he knew she'd succeeded. He also knew, by the way things were going, if he didn't shift the Albrights' attention to Bree's tree, they'd never get back to the warmth of the house.

By the time Brina unlashed the tree and returned the pieces of her micro-twine to her saddlebags, Samuel and Justin had unfastened then lowered the support poles from Wolf's saddle. Fanny continued to hold the lantern as the two men carried and set up the tree in the house. This allowed Brina to take Wolf to the barn and tend to his needs. "Well, I hope they enjoy the tree as much as I enjoyed our trip to the mountains. Whatcha think? Was it worth the effort?"

"Very much so, my beloved. Very much so."

It came to her as a tickling whisper on the surface of her ear, and as she gently rubbed the sensation away, she heard a misplaced sound in the barn. Turning suddenly in the middle of brushing down Wolf, Brina was met face to face with Samuel Albright.

"You did well, my dear."

"Thanks, Samuel, oh, and by the way, Merry Christmas." Brina was a bit taken aback by the way Samuel was standing there looking at her.

"You surprise me, my dear," he continued. "How do you manage the various challenges you've tackled? I mean, most normal young ladies aren't as strong or as educated in the fields you seem so at home in. You puzzle me. It would be very enlightening, I'm sure, if I could understand how you know or how you acquired your knowledge of the various subjects you've mastered. And I'm sure there are more here than just meets the eye."

Brina had to think and think fast. "Whatever do you mean?" Acting the innocent young maiden, in this case, was a good idea but not a very plausible one.

"You know what I mean. As much as I'd like to know about the true you, I'll never get it. I'll tell you this much. I don't think your friend has the slightest inkling as to who…or what you really are. That much I can pretty much guess at."

Brina didn't know what to say, so she stood there till an idea began to form. "You're wrong, Samuel. Dead wrong. When I was a small girl, I was kidnapped and then abandoned." Which was fairly accurate, to a point. "I had to learn to survive on my own. Who I learned with and where I got my education is none of your business, but whatever it is you're assuming, it's just that, an assumption. It's not based on fact, and without fact, you have nothing. If I were you, I'd take full advantage of my talents and my friendship. 'Cause if what you're assuming, whatever that may be, is at all plausible, consider the possible ramifications resulting from it." Then she turned back to her task at hand, tending her mount.

Samuel was rooted to where he stood. He couldn't bring himself to leave the barn or even from the general area in which Brina tended her horse. He just stood there mesmerized as he watched the perplexing and a little bit creepy young woman tending to the most magnificent beast he'd ever laid eyes on.

"Shall we go in now, Samuel?"

It was she. Had he been so spellbound with watching the two of them that he failed to notice her business with the animal had finished? He hadn't even acknowledged her touch when she took his arm, until she spoke, and at the sound of her voice, he looked into those eyes. She held, within those eyes, the look of angels. She appeared joyous, open, and most of all innocent of all things.

"Samuel? Samuel. Are you feeling well?" Brina was definitely concerned. He didn't look too well.

"Brina...uh, wha...what was that you said?" Samuel felt confused and a little dizzy.

"Are you all right? Here, maybe you ought to sit for a spell before heading back to the house. That was an unfortunate fall you took. Here, sit. I'll wait with you, just in case you need me to be near."

When the confused and dizzy Samuel allowed the gray-eyed woman to assist him to the nearest stool, he dropped his head into his hands and held it there.

Brina took advantage of those allotted moments to glance Wolf's way.

There he was. For a moment as she glanced into the face of the Gray Wolf, she could almost imagine herself looking directly into the various faces of Aeolus, Quetzalcoatl, Thorin, Moza, and the Divine Sovereign of the Great Neptune Kingdom. Unbeknownst to her, they and countless others were there, all staring back at her through the gray eyes of a most magnificent animal.

Wondering as to what had just happened, Brina telepathically sent a message his way. *Did I just miss something?*

"All is as it was, my beloved, do not concern yourself."

Back at the house, Samuel seemed to be feeling much better, although neither one of them could clearly remember his fall. All Brina could remember was brushing Wolf then moments later, found herself standing next to Samuel, picking out pieces of hay from his hair. The rest was gone. What had happened out there, and why was Wolf being so secretive? It shouldn't have surprised her; he had a tendency to be very vague about things when it suited him. It mattered little; all that truly mattered was that she was back in the warm confines of the Albrights' home with Justin just now, kneeling by her side with two small glasses of whiskey, one of which he was offering to her.

"Bree, I toast you. We all toast you." Justin then turned towards Samuel and Fanny, who were in the process of raising their own glasses to this unforgettable woman. He then quietly, to her alone, added, "You're also a most remarkable woman. Never have you ever let me down. Anything you've ever said or hinted of has been the truth, and I'll always admire you for that."

"Thank you, Justin, Fanny, Samuel. If it wasn't for your love and respect, I wouldn't have wanted to share a special Christmas memory with you. That is the reason for the tree and why I went searching for one. For you, for all the kindness you've shown us. There's no other way I can show how I feel than to physically bring something special into your lives.

"Before we finish off our glasses, there's a comical saying I learned from the guys at school. Perhaps you'll enjoy it too. Shall we?"

They all raised their glasses.

Brina held her glass about eye level. Then began her ancient recitation. "Over the lips and past the gums, look out tummy, here it comes!" Lifting her glass for a second as a toast to herself, Brina downed its remaining contents in one gulp, as the rest of her friends watched in horror as she did so. "My, that was tasty." She then scooted closer to the fire for its warmth and its fathomless depths where she loved to stare.

Justin realized that both Brina's mind and attention were deep into the light of the fire, after two subtle attempts at talking to her were ignored. Deciding that he still wanted to share time with her, since it was truly Christmas Eve, he joined her in whatever quest she'd chosen to take. So, he sat back with the remaining whiskey still in his glass to stare into the fire with his gray-eyed beauty. Justin found the movement of the flames and the warmth they created had a soothing quality not readily expected. So, when Brina began quietly whispering in a voice so faintly audible, he believed it originated from the fiery depths.

"'Twas the night before Christmas, and all through the house, not a creature was stirring, not even a mouse. The stockings were hung from the chimney with care, in hopes that Saint Nicholas soon would be there. The children were nestled all snug in their beds…"

As Justin sat next to her while enjoying the warm sensations thereof, he was oblivious to everything else in the room, including both Fanny and Samuel. All he could see was the view before him. The delicately shaped pug nose, the length of those incredibly long eyelashes, which enhanced the unusual gray pigment of her eyes, and how beautifully contrasting was the color of her brown-black hair against that incredibly flawless ivory skin. He allowed the smooth contours of her skin to direct his eyes over and down her high cheekbones, down and around her delicate jaw, up her exquisite chin, to finally come to rest upon her coral lips. Staring at those delicately curved, perfectly shaped, desirable, so very inviting lips brought questions to bear. How would they feel against his? Would she put up a fight, or would she come to him willingly? Was he willing to risk the possibility of losing her as a friend and traveling companion if he made love to her?

Justin was so enthralled with thinking about her as a woman, he almost missed the subtle movement and whispering sounds emanating from those very same lips he was admiring. Turning towards her so as not to miss a single word, he silently listened as she continued.

"*...and he whistled and shouted and called them by name: "Now, Dasher! Now, Dancer! Now, Prancer and Vixen! On, Comet! On, Cupid! On Donner and Blitzen! To the top of the porch, to the top of the wall! Now dash away, dash away, dash away all!"* With newly found confidence and joy, as her mind reclaimed the old and ancient poem, Brina's voice gradually increased in volume.

When Justin stopped conversing with him, Samuel assumed he was just tired and wanted to sit back and enjoy the fire. That was until Fanny gently patted his knee for his attention pointing towards the two in front of the fire. When all attentions were finally focused on the fireplace and the young woman sitting there, all became quiet. It was then the words could finally be heard, and as they listened, she continued uninterrupted.

"*He was chubby and plump, a right jolly old elf. And I laughed when I saw him, in spite of myself...*"

XXV

the watcher

*Up from the worlds below was their place of emergence into this world.
Down from the sky world above.
They were brought down on the backs of turtles, up on the wings of eagles.
They climbed a ladder built of spiderwebs.
He, those like him, and the mortals on both sides of the Barrier came
into these worlds as creatures and unbridled spirits placed by a wise
and creative force unknown to all who inhabited the All Mother.
That definition of creation along with many others had
been for those who dwell within their mortal shells,
a convenient way to explain away the meaning of life and eternal beginnings.
However, it had been too many millenniums past, since his
creation, for him to remember the hows and the whys of his
birth, existence, powers, life, and unfulfilled love.
At least until the gray-eyed one's spirit was known to him.
His gray-eyed beauty.
Without her, he was lost.
They were one. One body, one soul.
And he would serve, love, cherish, and protect her shell and all it contained,
until it was time.
Her celestial spirit would then be free to join with him, for the rest of eternity.
Until then, he was—*

*As the watcher observed the joy and gaiety within
the walls of the house, he knew,
now would be a good time to leave for a spell.*

To *leave her in the protective hands of the man of volcanic eyes, at this time,*
would be as if he placed her soul into the hands of the All Mother herself.
For he knew of this man they'd stumbled upon, knew
of the part he played in this little game.
He also knew, as he did of all things, that this man of volcanic eyes,
knew more than he was letting on.
Yet he knew the man would be the same unobserved
sentinel for her, as the Gray Wolf had been and would
continue to be, once he beheld the other for a time.
Once out of the body his spirit soared like the eagle.
Across the mountains of the moon, over the valley
of the shadow, he took to wing.
As he circled the small town of Cascade, where Nicole's child was to be
found, the Gray Wolf glided on the air currents, until a suitable participant
volunteered itself as the receptacle for his vital essence, his spirit.
Once secure, he would observe the comings and goings of all in this place,
without detection.
For Nicole's child must also survive these dark
times, as must the watcher's only love—
if be it by the wielding of the Neptune Spear, be it true—for in the end,
the evildoers will burn in hell, deep within the All Mother's breast.

"So it is written, my beloved, so shall it come to pass."

XXVI

on deadly ground

Three weeks later the Reaper was still on that same trail. Whoever they were, and he assumed it was the gray-eyed one, were better at eluding a pursuer than he ever thought possible. He hadn't even gotten close enough to catch a glimpse of her, but on he rode, determined as ever.

Rounding the bend of a pyramid-shaped hill, he stumbled upon an open plain that held in its center an old barn. He approached, then investigated it enough to determine that it was structurally sound enough to shelter him for the night. After unsaddling his mount, he set up additional bracing for the decrepit corral fence out back, ensuring that the horse would be there come sunup. The Reaper then took a short walk around the barn and corrals checking for any sign of her possible whereabouts or plotted direction.

It was his fate to be here. He knew Jesse. Knew him personally. They'd grown up in the same part of town; both joined the same gangs. When it was heard the Network was enlisting mercenaries and other assorted lowlifes, both of them, along with many others, jumped at the chance. The only mistake Jesse made after that last assignment was to travel to the wrong century. He should've gone forward instead of backwards. Oh well, there was no point in worrying about spilled milk now. But if GR could get to that woman before she got to Jesse, the Network's position would grow stronger.

While considering the possibilities and not watching where he was walking, the Grim Reaper tripped, almost falling headfirst over an unseen object on the ground. Looking down, he found a not-so-very-old gravesite. Since the gray-eyed one's trail led to this old barn, he wondered if by chance she had run into foul play. Perhaps she'd suddenly found herself six feet underground. The only way he could be sure of the idea was to simply dig whoever it was up.

Surprisingly, there was a man's body at the bottom of the hole. Who it was, was anyone's guess. It definitely wasn't who he'd hoped, nor was it anyone he knew. This meant that either she was still out there or that he'd lost her completely and was following someone else's trail entirely. No matter. Come morning he'd pick up their trail again and follow it to its logical conclusion.

The trail he found led him on a merry trek across country to a sleepy little town called Daytonville. There he found answers to several of his questions—*finally*. And as it turned out, he was trailing a woman. A woman who just happened to match the description of the one he sought. Only now, she was in the company of another man. Bloody hell.

After asking around, he was finally directed to a Dr. Paine. There was an oxymoron if he ever heard one. At least the guy was smart enough to help. Of course, convincing the good doctor that she was his long-lost sister was brilliant. Once the good doctor swallowed that one, he couldn't help himself and told all. Unfortunately, the Reaper was still too far away to do any great harm yet knew if he could find a second horse to alternate between the distance would close and close rapidly.

After several hours of searching and bribing, he found one. Its owner boasted that it was the fastest horse in the county. But in order to procure it, he had to pay a very persuasive price.

As luck would have it and before his predicted three-week period had passed, the All Mother deemed it winter. Now, just at a time when he thought there was a chance to catch up with the woman, he had to fight the snow, the slush, the windstorms, and the downright freezing temperatures.

Oh, how he hated this time of year. The only way to handle it, he decided, was to make sure when he traveled during the day there was always a ranch or a town with a hotel or even a livery stable to spend the night. The thought of a livery stable provided him with the option of not having to contend with gabby guests and curious help; it also offered warm-bodied animals and sweet-smelling straw to warm oneself for the night ahead. No, winter was definitely not his favorite time of year. The one thing in is favor, though, was the knowledge that since the weather had slowed him down, so had it slowed them down.

With each day came the question whether to continue or to wait it out till the spring thaw or continue through the winter. The temperature had dropped drastically in the past two weeks and he was sure traveling would only get worse, if not stop altogether. The snow drifts were getting deeper, softer, more treacherous, making it almost impossible for the horses to get through them safely. The other frustration was the certain knowledge of knowing, when the snow thawed, what little trail he'd been following would vanish completely—if it hadn't already.

With each passing day the miles under his saddle became less and less due to the severity of the conditions. Each day he also believed he was getting closer. They weren't as determined as he. She was the weaker of the species and would need a place to rejuvenate. At least, that's what he hoped. So, he rode and rode and rode until one day, the one horse he picked up at in Daytonville finally collapsed under him from total exhaustion and freezing cold temperatures. Apparently, the horse was not as tough as promised.

He left the animal where it lay. Why should he care about the damned thing anyway? He didn't care about anything other than himself. That was why he pushed the horses as he had. They were only tools to be used. To discard when broken. They were there for man's use and had been for centuries. They had no feelings or souls of their own. Why worry about it? His only problem now was that he had only one horse to carry him and his gear on this obsessed quest. No longer did he have the convenience of a backup unit. That in itself made him more cautious.

A month later the weather broke (so much for his predictions), yet it was still cold enough to freeze a certain liquid excrement in midair. But at least the sky was blue, and the winds were calm. The Reaper had packed as many supplies as possible into his saddlebags, added a couple of extra blankets to his bedroll, and last but not least did remember to pack some grain for his horse. This, he'd hoped, would last till he arrived at his next destination, which should be Donegal. He learned of that in the last town.

Donegal, as he was told, was an Irish community, which according to his calculations lay on the other side of the ridge he was just beginning to climb. And at any other time of the year, he wouldn't have considered making another such stop so soon, but he had been warned by the inhabitants of that last town to watch out for Mother Nature and her unpredictable changes of mind and weather patterns. They had also said the temperature could plummet at a drop of a hat along with the sudden appearance of storm clouds followed by severe snow and sleet. Under such warnings as those, Donegal was the targeted stop for the night if he got there before the shit hit the fan.

Unfortunately, the warning he received turned itself into reality around midday. The Reaper had been caught unawares. He had arrived atop the ridge and hoped as promised the community of Donegal would be below, but what he saw below him was snow, snow, and more snow as far as his eyes could see.

As he began his descent down the other side of the ridge, his horse suddenly jumped sideways. When he turned to correct the direction of the wayward animal, he saw movement behind him. It was hard to see at first due to the density of the snow-covered trees, but there, hidden within them, was a form. A closer look suggested a large white bear moving through the forest.

It must have been a bear. He was sure of it. He could vaguely remember looking through picture books as a child. Books of all different kinds of animals that man had so long ago slaughtered or saved due to arrogance. Of all the animals in the books, it had been the bear that he remembered most. Their size, temperament, and their lumbering movements impressed him. Yes, he was sure this was a bear. He couldn't take his eyes off it. The longer he stared, the closer it seemed. It was so close it looked like a dream unfolding before him in slow motion. The beast finally moved, turned, and faced him.

Son of a bitch, it wasn't a bear at all, just a man. A proud man, a tall man. One who stood erect, appeared alert. The skin of his face, leathery, dark, and crinkled. His eyes were cunning, dark, and showed a level of intelligence. His facial structure was chiseled as though from stone. Fearless he was the way he stood his ground.

The Reaper realized that here in front of his very own eyes was a prime specimen of the true and pure Territorial Indian, but from which tribe he did not know or cared. Regardless, he was impressed. He'd read of them but had never seen one of such pure blood as the one before him. There'd been rumors of them in the Academy, strong and silent adversaries, because of their pride, beliefs, and the All Mother's blessings, but it took a trip to the past for him to see one in the flesh.

This one wore a very warm-looking outer garment that just may have been a white buffalo hide, or some such animal. And as the Reaper watched, the Indian slowly raised what the Reaper assumed was his weapon towards him. Having so many layers of clothing on him, the Reaper was unable to draw upon his own weapons for defense, so he just stood his ground and watched.

The item in question wasn't a spear as assumed, but a walking stick. A stick that was pointed towards the Reaper's horse, then out into the forest. When the Indian got no response, he tried using his native tongue. When the Reaper didn't understand the guttural sounds, he decided there was no threat and therefore ignored him.

The moment he turned to head back down the ridge, it happened. He heard it before he saw it. It came as a *whsssssshh* and ended as a *dooiink*. Turning abruptly around towards the tree to his left and slightly behind, he spotted an arrow protruding from its bark with its feathered end still quivering. The son of a bitch had launched an arrow at him and fortunately had missed. Not knowing what the message was, nor caring, he turned to face this new opponent.

Now instead of just the one, there were three standing there. Where had the others come from? Surely, they hadn't been there all along hiding under the cover of the snow-covered trees? Seeing that the one with the staff now stood in the center and that the others had their weapons drawn and ready to fire shocked him. What had he done, or better yet, what did they want? Did they want his horse? Or did they want his life? He finally decided that they wanted his horse. To him, it was the only logical reason for their actions. Then he saw the fourth. It looked like a woman who hid behind the three—of course, being the weaker of the species, she was expected to hide behind the men. Not sure what to do or how to handle it, the Grim Reaper mistakenly decided the woman was a burden to the others' crossing of the freezing harsh land. Therefore, he took the moment to assume they wanted to trade her for the horse. With his appetite for women, any woman, and the fact that they wanted to trade, started his hormones a-racing.

Standing there in the freezing cold, the Reaper grew tired of the standoff. Deciding to get the ball rolling, so hopefully in the confusion he'd kill the men, keep the horse and the woman, he made the first move. He looked to the old one but held out his hand to the female, trying to coax her to him. When no one moved, he offered in exchange the rein of his horse. The message was that the Reaper was willing to trade his horse for the female, or so it appeared. But unbeknownst to him, lust, need, and desire had just countermanded his survival instincts, allowing stupidity to kick in.

When the eldest realized what was being suggested, he turned to the others using a series of hand signals and in an unfamiliar tongue told of the Reaper's intent.

Watching the way the elder communicated with the others made the Reaper nervous. Suddenly he realized that they'd surmised his plan. Not only had their expressions turned from leather to stone, but they'd also taken up the stance of archers. Bodies erect, bows in hand, arrows drawn, and aim taken. All they need do now was send their message.

It must've been the constant freezing temperatures that dulled his senses. Without the hard control that he'd always managed to maintain, the twig snapped. Slowly the reins dropped from his fingers. Seeing it all, but too far out of control, he tried reining in his psychotic anger, but failed. Instead, he took a step backward, then lunged at them.

Three bow strings let go simultaneously. Their arrows found their mark in the center of stranger's chest.

As the Reaper slowly slipped to the ground, he no longer felt the cold of the snow, the frozen air around him, or could he clearly see the trees that towered above him. He did feel disappointment, however. He knew that he was going to die before completing his mission: to assassinate the gray-eyed one. Knowing that, he decided instead to take another. So, when one of the three came to him in the snow to confirm their kill, he was ready. He had pooled his remaining strength, so when the Indian got close enough, he thrust out his hand catching the man unprepared. With his last breath, the Grim Reaper grabbed the Indian by the head and neck and with both hands snapped the spinal column in two.

As his own lights faded like those of John Deau's, the Reaper remembered something Jesse Loame once told him: *When in a fight, hit first and hit hard, and remember, it's virtually impossible to hit any harder than death.* With that last and final thought, the sound of several snarling, starving, blood-hungry wolves reached his ears. At that moment he knew that peace, for the first time in his life, would be his, in only a matter of minutes.

The smell of the Grim Reaper's fear, blood, and impending death, was an announcement to all the carnivores within the territory, that here in this quiet, secluded place was sustenance to hold them over till the next warrior fell.

XXVII

not so dead in the water

Spring sprung like a well-used mattress, and our two travelers were now back in the saddle, having left the company of the Albrights.

"Justin, did I do right?"

Brina had found that leaving the Albrights and their home was more difficult than expected. Their snowy arrival, their treatment afterward, their chores, the tree, the unforgettable Christmas, and Samuel's final acceptance of her talents and abilities had turned the whole experience into an unforgettable memory. A memory she cherished beyond many things.

The whole wintry episode had also turned many of her teachings topsy-turvy. To feel loved and to feel a fondness of her fellow man—those were totally new feelings and experiences for her. She, of course, felt and experienced some of that in the company of Dillon and Cordell, but the fondness she felt here was different. Here were people who accepted her skills and abilities, turning them towards hard work and character building, at least that's how Fanny put it. Her unusual strength was thankfully honed and channeled into anything and everything that could be of use on the farm. Brina took great pleasure in harnessing, hitching, driving, feeding, and cleaning the Belgians Samuel had. She found great love in not only the work, but also the animals themselves. The barn she kept clean as a whistle, finding places outside and away from the buildings to place the dirty straw and manure for the summer garden. She didn't really care for the goats, they were cute and interesting, but their bleating sound over time became very irritating. The Albrights, as well as Justin, found her ability to tell when parturition (birth) was to

310

take place, saving on stress, was uncanny but accepted it as a blessing instead of a curse.

There were other things she loved doing too. She loved chopping the wood, stacking it, bringing it in to set near to Fanny's stove. She loved working with the anvil in the shop, making winter shoes for the horses. She loved the sound of steel meeting steel. Loved working around the intense heat of its furnace, loved the billows. She loved pounding the steel, working it into a shape that fits each hoof in turn, then when the fit was just right, she would drop it in the water barrel to cool.

There, they treated her as one of the family, and as time passed, she began feeling the same way about them. It was a strange and ill-fitting feeling, but eventually it won her over.

As to Justin, over the months Brina began to see him in a different light. Treating him always as before, she now began to watch him closely. The little things he did she took notice of, instead of just ignoring them. Little things like how he watched her when she wasn't supposed to be looking, how considerate he was of her say, how he offered to help when things for her got a bit too frustrating. How he curiously watched as she cleaned her pistols. How his eyes would sparkle when she spoke his name. Little things. Little things she tucked away in her mind to be used at a later date should it come to that.

It was during the Albright-Windslow spring roundup when Brina decided to repay the kindness shown her. But now, while riding down the trail with Justin, she was beginning to second think herself.

"Huh?" His mind was elsewhere.

She saw his absentmindedness and repeated her question. "Did I do right?"

"Oh, I'm sorry. Where?"

"Back at the Cross-Bar."

"You mean worrying us for three days in the dead of winter?" Justin was still slightly ticked about that.

"No. I mean the one about Wolf."

"How many times do I have to say it? You did fine."

On the fourth day of the roundup, Jeremy and Karl Windslow came up to Justin after the cows had mothered up to ask about the gray. So impressed were they with his unusual coloration, temperament, conformation, and most of all his handiness with the cows, they wanted to know if he was for sale. Justin had told them that Wolf was Brina's. In response, they asked if it was at all possible to borrow him for a week or so, so they could turn him out with their mares.

"Remember. It was Jeremy who asked if I'd speak to you about standing or selling him. I told him it was none of my concern. The horse was not mine to bargain with. And look, you managed just fine without me buttin' in. Yeah. It was a good idea. He's not going to live forever 'cept through his foals. It was a wonderful farewell gift."

Brina was still a bit concerned. What would allowing Wolf to breed—to promote himself, his talents, and who knew what else might be contributed—do to the unsuspecting equine industry? Maybe nothing. Maybe everything. Only time would tell.

Being back on the trail brought Brina back to the present. Jesse, the Neptune sphere, Dillon, Cordell, and the ever-present danger of that creepy guy she crossed paths with last fall.

Dillon and Cordell had gone in search of Jesse, not without added stress on her part, but that couldn't be helped. If she could only find that blasted Neptune sphere contraption, maybe she could rectify things, but about that, she didn't know much either. Reading what little she could find on the Neptune's properties gave her an idea of what it could do, but it said nothing about how to harness and use its powers, or what it exactly looked like. She was probably going to have to rely on Wolf for that. Would he help? She didn't know. He was a strange one sometimes, whatever or whoever he truly was.

Wolf. Shit. She needed to tell Justin the truth about herself and her equine companion. Would he believe her? Did he trust her? Did he love her enough to believe the crazy things she'd say? She could use her power, knowledge, and a few magic tricks to convince him, but was the possibility of losing him through it all worth it? She'd grown very fond of him.

Unfortunately, since that creep and who knew just how many others were still out there tracking her, Justin needed a better handle of what was as stake and the danger traveling with her had put him in. It was a long-time overdue, but she finally realized it was a necessity she had to reveal. But when would be the best time to do it?

Justin could tell there was something on his Bree's mind, since she hadn't spoken to him in days, and if she had, it was minimal. "What is it, Bree? You've been awful quiet."

They had been back on the trail just a few hours since leaving Pine Ridge for a night's rest and to purchase needed supplies.

"Oh, nothing." Still struggling with what to say and how to say it, Brina made a suggestion. "Justin. Let's find a cool, peaceful, and shady location. I need..." She was trying to tell him what she needed to do, but it just wouldn't come.

"Bree, there is something wrong. What is it?" He was suddenly very concerned.

"Justin, I, you, we, I need to sit down. Please, let's find a quiet place."

Suddenly her ears picked up on a familiar sound. "Wait. Listen. Do you hear it?"

"Hear what?" He didn't hear anything.

"The water!"

Brina nudged her horse forward while Justin watched her from the rear with the most confused look on his face. How in the name of Jesse James could someone hear water? He couldn't hear anything, anything at all. And if water was really out there, wouldn't it have to be making a hell of a noise for anyone to hear it?

With the water's location pinpointed, Brina broke Wolf into a gallop heading directly towards the sound apparently only she could hear. When she spotted the lake, she pulled back on Wolf's reins, bringing him immediately to a sliding stop. Before Justin realized what had happened, Brina jumped off her mount, hastily unsaddled him, set the saddle down and away from the water's edge, undid the bindings of her hair, then quickly swung back up. Turning away from the water's edge and back towards the way she'd come, Brina again reined Wolf around. Only this time it was back directly towards the body of water.

Just as her peripheral vision caught sight of Justin through the trees, Brina Louise Grant urged her mighty charger into a full gallop directly towards the water's edge. At the last second before Wolf jumped into the lake with Brina on his back, there was heard behind them a shout from Justin.

"BREE—NO!"

Then came the splash, followed by the sounds of joyous laughter.

She was in heaven. Swimming with Wolf was just as exciting as riding him at a full gallop. Swimming, with or without equine companionship, had its own special qualities. Most of which she knew. She also knew that very few people of this period knew how to swim, let alone did it for the sheer pleasure it brought. And for swimming with their horse? That was totally unheard of.

Once they found the deep water, Brina gave Wolf his head and allowed her buoyancy to bring her atop the water so she could float along while Wolf swam. As long as she held onto his mane and allowed her body to remain separate from his, she knew the deep water would not hinder his abilities. When horses swim, their entire bodies except their heads are underwater. Their legs and hooves move them along in the same manner of a dog's. It always amazed her how those little hooves managed to move enough water to propel an animal of such size through the water without sinking. In truth, she didn't really care how they did it, just as long as it worked.

For the first time since pairing up with Justin, Brina finally found a moment only she and Wolf could enjoy. Occasionally she would turn her head towards the direction of shore and see Justin sitting on top of Wyatt in a totally confused state. After an hour or so of peaceful bliss atop the water, Brina decided maybe it was time to return to shore and face the lecture that was sure to come. If she was at all lucky, her plan for the afternoon, before Justin's enlightenment, would become an experience to cherish.

Soaked to the skin, Brina positioned herself back atop Wolf and reined him back towards shore and the awaiting Justin. By the time she emerged from the water, she saw that Justin had dismounted Wyatt and found a grassy place in which to watch.

"DAMNED FOOL! What were you doing out there anyway!" Justin had an unreadable look on his face.

"What's your problem?"

"You've no idea, do you?" If he thought he could get away with it, he'd put her over his knee and spank her for scaring him like she did. He was so mad that he failed to see how delicious she looked in soaking-wet clothing.

Still not truly seeing it, Brina tried to explain his apparent hurt away. "I didn't mean any harm by it. I just couldn't resist. I'm sorry, Justin." Apparently, she had hurt him, and not thinking about her actions bothered her. To kill was one thing, but to inadvertently hurt someone out of ignorance, that was something else altogether.

Justin could read the mixed emotions all over her lovely face. It was like reading pages of a book; she was that readable. "You don't get it, do you? You really don't? Did you ever think that maybe I'd thought you were trying to kill yourself, or maybe that you'd lost your mind? Bree, think. Think about what you were trying to tell me just before you lit off? You sounded so depressed. Then suddenly you head your horse for a large body of water? There's not a soul in this sector that knows how to swim. Drowning is a common form of suicide, accidental or otherwise, here 'bouts, and since you were heading for it, I thought that I had something to do with it. I didn't know what you were doing. Of course, I'm mad." He turned away from her, shaking his head back and forth, punching his fist into his other hand, heading back over to his horse.

She was at his side in a flash. "Justin. I would never intentionally hurt you in such a way. It was an act of impulse, only. When I heard the lake, I felt a wave of release. It never occurred to me how you'd take it. I keep forgetting that most people of this time period can't swim—" *Oh, that was great, Brina Louise Grant. Damn you to hell!* She

315

had done it again. Quickly scanning his mind, she discovered that he, too, had caught the slip.

"Okay. I know what you're thinking. But before I say anything at all and especially before you say anything at all, I need you to come with me." She gently took his hand, turning towards the water. When at first, he refused to budge, she tugged slightly till he began to follow. Brina knew in order for him to believe what she now had to explain, she needed his total trust.

Following blindly out of love alone, Justin let Brina lead him to the water's edge.

When they reached the edge, she let go his hand. "Justin, please. Remove your boots."

He searched the depths of those lovely eyes trying to read what it was she had in store for him. She removed her own drenched boots, then stood there waiting for him to comply—which he finally did. When his footwear was removed, Brina then began removing her outer clothing, keeping the bare necessities in place, then again waited for Justin to follow her lead. "The reason I do this is because when we get in over our heads, swimming comes easier when most of the outer garments are removed." In reality, swimming came easiest in the nude, but she wasn't going to put herself in that position.

Swimming?

After considering her statement, he again followed her lead. He wanted so desperately to trust her. To trust her completely. He needed that.

When nothing but the underwear was left, Brina again took hold of Justin's hand in a firm yet gentle grip, then began her descent into the water. When the water reached just above his knees, he suddenly stopped.

"That's it. That's far enough. I'm not going any deeper. I'll drown." He began to pull back and return to shore.

"No, you won't, Justin Case III. You'll not drown. I'll not allow it. If you trust me, you trust me. You do trust me, don't you?" At his hesitant nod, she resumed her descent into the water with him following reluctantly behind. Brina again felt the wondrous sensation of water rushing into places that normally were void of such pleasures.

When they finally reached a flat spot on the bottom with the water reaching to the middle of their chests, Brina stopped. "Okay, Justin, listen to me." When she had his undivided attention, she resumed. "I'm going to let go of your hand now."

"No, you're not!" Justin began to panic.

"Take it easy. It'll be fine, you'll see." He was so scared he was almost hyperventilating.

It was all he could do to listen to her words and concentrate on his breathing. His eyes were shut tight. He was terrified of standing water in large areas. Didn't like pools of water, didn't like puddles, didn't like streams—unless he was a-horseback—didn't like lakes, didn't even like watering troughs. Now he was in the midst of his worst fears, literally. The only thing that saved him was the sound of her voice. It soothed away the anxiety he felt. Even though the water was swishing around his chest, finding places it didn't belong, its mild temperatures combined with her voice were a cool comfort at his time of need.

Brina sensed his mortal fear. Not wanting it to further itself, nor wanting any of the trust to fade, she led him back towards shore. At just above knee deep, she stopped. "Justin, sit down in the water."

"What for?"

"Since you're having trouble, we'll start very slow."

Relieved, Justin did as he was told. Now the water, instead of being just above his knees, was just below his chin. "Bree?" he said shakily.

"It's all right. Your weight will hold firm to the bottom."

"That's what I'm afraid of. I'll slide down to the bottom of the lake and drown."

"No, you won't. Like I said, your weight will hold you firmly where you are. I want you to get used to the feeling of water at the level of your chin and all around you, but with the security of knowing you're in only two and a half feet of the stuff." Brina sat directly next to him like a security blanket.

Justin listened to what she was saying. And the fact that she was sitting next to him under the same circumstances as he was helped considerably. After he got accustomed to the shallow water, she made him stand up and follow her out further.

"Just relax." He was still frightened of the whole scenario; she could see as well as sense it. "Everything is going to be just fine. Here the ground is flat for about ten feet in all directions, and I'll be next to you at all times."

"How do you know it's flat?"

"I've already been in here, remember?"

"Oh yeah, right."

After several minutes passed, he finally began to relax.

"See?" Brina began. "It's not too difficult, now is it?"

Justin was much calmer now. So much so that he was even doing a bit of bouncing where he stood.

"No. This is easy." He was beginning to really enjoy himself.

She could see that he was having a good time, and since that was the case, she felt it time to move on. "Now, I want you to slowly bend your knees until your arms are floating on the water's surface. Like this." Brina lowered herself, showing Justin just what she wanted.

Justin again did as requested. After all, he was still standing in the same spot as minutes before.

"Good. Now do this with your arms." What Brina was attempting to show him was how to tread water at a depth that was still shallow enough for him to feel safe. Once she walked him through the entire process and treaded water with him for several minutes with his feet off the bottom, she explained and then showed him how to float on his back for long periods of time. After several tries at finding the bottom between ten to fifteen minutes of floating time, it looked as though maybe she could take her craft out to sea.

"Justin, do you feel as if you could keep this up for a while?"

"Bree," he said between breaths, "this is wonderful. I'm sure I could, but I still want you close, okay?"

"I'll be right here." After about ten minutes, Brina decided to recheck Justin's confidence in himself. "How're we doing?"

"Great. This is nice, but the only thing that bothers me is the off-and-on feeling of water running in and out of my ears. Other than that, I'm doing just fine."

Brina had to be careful. She knew he trusted her, but he was still slightly afraid of being in the water and might startle if she didn't prepare him for what exactly she had in mind.

"That's good, Justin. Very good. Now, what I want to do while you're still floating on your back is to pull you with me, out into deeper water."

He was on his feet in an instant, which was just as she feared. That was the reason why she'd mentioned it in such shallow water, just in case he panicked on her.

"What do you mean deeper water? If you take me out farther, I'll drown. You promised I wouldn't drown!" Justin sputtered.

Silly man, he was still frightened. "Justin, don't you get it? That floating position will keep you afloat no matter how deep the water? Think about what I just said, *no matter how deep the water*, you will stay afloat if you relax and do what you've learned."

He considered her words for several minutes. "Okay, I'll try."

"You must go relaxed. If you go out there with me all tensed up, this won't work. Something will make you panic, and the consequences will be disastrous. Float here for a while longer and allow your mind to relax. I'll just pull you around this flat area for a time, and when I feel you're ready, we'll try it." She knew if she stuck to her word, it would all work out, the trust thing, but if she warned him of her descent into deeper water, he'd again panic and they'd be here for weeks on end.

When she felt he was ready, she tried something. "Now. While you're floating, I'm going to swim with you so you can feel what it'll be like when we go out into deeper water. I'll stay fairly close to shore, so if you panic you can touch bottom, but I don't want you to. Understand?"

In a dreamy, relaxed way he responded by mumbling, "Whatever."

He sounded almost asleep; he was so ready. So, under the circumstances, she pulled him into deep water without his knowledge. For two hours she guided him through the water, then gradually eased him back to the shallow area. "Justin, it's time for a break. I need to rest before we continue with your swimming lessons."

"So soon?" He was still on his back in the water.

She couldn't do it with him floating; she had to have eye contact. "Stand up, please, and look at me."

He did so, without question.

There he stood dripping wet, and for the first time in her life, Brina saw him for what he was. A man. A man whose wavy light-brown hair, whether it be dry or dripping, glistened in the sunlight. A man whose mannerisms mirrored someone kind and considerate. A man who towered above her five-foot-nine-inch height. A man physically fit in his two-hundred-pound frame. A man whose deep chocolate-brown eyes held her mesmerized at this very moment. A man who watched her at every turn. A man who months earlier danced the waltz with her in the hotel lobby in all those fancy duds. A man whom she didn't abandon in his time of need, on several occasions. A man who cherished her as much as she cherished to be with him. A man who trusted her.

Her thoughts were betraying her. She, for the first time in her life, had feelings foreign to her and everything she had been taught. Even the pit of her stomach was betraying her—creating in her feelings she was unaccustomed to. What was going on here? This was Justin, after all. He's the same; she's the same. They're the same as they've always been. It was the same man whom she'd been traveling with for months on end. What had suddenly and instantly transformed him into something different, something that she'd look at in a totally foreign way? She had to get her mind off this sudden betrayal of emotions and again act the soldier.

"Bree, stop. I know what you're thinking, and you're right. If you had warned me about heading into deeper water, I probably would've panicked. But since you took it upon yourself to swim alongside while guiding me along out there in the lake, I kept my mind calm, cool, and relaxed. When I finally opened my eyes and saw the trees above me move farther and farther away, I knew what you were doing."

She was relieved. He'd not known what she was thinking, and if he had? What would happen then?

He kept on with his thoughts and ideas totally oblivious to her momentary lapse. "I did what you said and relaxed. It was a piece of cake." When he stopped, he realized the smile on his face must have gone from ear to ear.

"That's wonderful. Ya know, I guided you around the lake for more than two hours?"

He began chuckling. "That's why you need the rest."

"Not just that, but since we're on the other side of the lake, I need to rest before I tug you back to where we left the horses."

By the end of the day, Brina had Justin swimming atop and below the water's surface, not nearly as well as she could, but he definitely had most the basics mastered. And since he was doing so well, and the fact that they were having a great time doing it, they both agreed to spend a couple of days at the water's edge so he could continue to practice. It was also agreed if he did well enough, Brina would show him how to swim with his horse, if Wyatt was willing.

XXVIII

to have and to hold, almost

Instead of a couple of days, their stay turned into a couple of weeks. Brina had Justin so intent in learning about water, swimming, holding his breath while swimming underwater, trust, and friendship it appeared to her that he had forgotten about that slight slip of the tongue she had made earlier.

Brina hadn't forgotten. She sometimes wanted to but hadn't forgotten several items of importance. First and foremost was who she was and where she was. Her plan to tell Justin of her secrets was still in the making. There were things he had to know and believe before they could continue together. She hoped he would understand and accept her story. His growing trust in her would most assuredly help him swallow the unbelievable facts. And because of her concern for his continued safety, as well as hers, she had to say something and soon or leave his company altogether. The other could wait.

The fifteenth day began like all the others. She'd wake before he did and while up would take care of business, clean up, then clean and polish her Colts. After a few moment's practice she'd put them back in their holsters, then grabbed the rifle. With that cleaned and polished, she took it in search of breakfast. By the time she returned with either a rabbit or a squirrel in hand, Justin would be up, dressed, and have both horses caught up, groomed, and had the fire going quite well. After skinning and cleaning her kill, she'd place it on the spit while Justin went in search for more firewood. As the smell of cooking rabbit wafted in the air, Brina went to the water's edge to refill their canteens with fresh water.

When Justin returned, his arms were full of wood. "Bree."

"Yes?"

"Close your eyes. I've a surprise for you."

She closed her eyes as asked, stood, and waited. "What is it, Justin? What did you find?"

He dropped his load on the ground next to the fire, then brushed the debris off his shirt. Reaching into his pocket, he brought out a small round object and held it under her nose. "What do you smell?"

Brina thought and thought. Its smell was slightly familiar, but its name wasn't. "I'm not sure. Can I look?"

"No. Not yet. But don't go away, I'll be right back."

"Justin, you can't leave me in suspense."

"Oh yes, I can. Now you just stand there." Knowing that should he bite into the object while standing so close to her, its sound would give away his surprise. So, taking several steps away and turning his back, he took a bite out of the forbidden fruit, but didn't swallow. Instead, he removed it from his mouth, stepped to the edge of the lake, and rinsed it. Returning to her side, he looked the Cheshire cat. "Want another sniff?"

She stood waiting.

"Try again." He held the fruit, with piece missing, under her nose. "Anything familiar come to mind?"

She knew what it was but couldn't put a name to it. "I give up. Can I look now?"

"No, open your mouth."

She did as he requested.

In it, he placed the piece of bitten-off fruit, then stood back to watch.

Tentatively she closed her mouth and began to chew. "It's an apple!" Her eyes opened in total surprise. "Where in the world did you find an apple tree? This is not their region."

"Let me show you." He took her hand.

"What about breakfast?"

"It's not far. Come. We can fill our pockets and return before the rabbit is done."

Brina was ecstatic. Making sure the rabbit wouldn't burn while gone, Justin took her to the tree.

There standing below it, looking up in its massive branches, Brina suddenly felt strange. Something was wrong. She knew that apple trees didn't grow in this fashion, nor were they indigenous to this region. And there was something else about the tree that bothered her, but not being able to put her finger on it engaged her seventh sense. Perhaps there was something out there she needed to be aware of, but when she didn't pick up any unusual or mystical atmospheric disturbances, she dismissed it as her imagination.

With worries aside for a moment, she stared at the tree's massive branches. They hung low from a height of fifty feet or better. She imagined that one of the branches, the biggest of the lot, had a rope that hung from high above with a tire at its loose end, swinging amid several happy children as they all took turns in its center. She was one of the children playing with the others, without a care in the world.

Then the vision faded, the tree was not as big as she originally thought. The branches not as massive, nor did they hang down in such a manner to make her wonder. It had all been the excitement of the moment that had taken her to her past, at the mention of an apple tree.

Justin watched as his gray-eyed beauty stopped suddenly in front of the tree. He saw the many emotions, wonder, curiosity, happiness, and sadness cross her brow in a manner of seconds.

"Bree? Is everything all right?"

"I'm fine. Really," she answered. Her moment had passed. It was a joy to relive a moment like that from one's past, but her life now was…when? In the future or in the past? It mattered not when her future was, but where it was and with whom. For now, it was in front of this apple tree with a man whose company she enjoyed more than anything she'd ever experienced. "Really and truly, Justin. I'm having a wonderful time. Let's pick some apples. Breakfast oughta be ready."

With breakfast behind them, they both enjoyed a cool dip in their own private swimming hole. On shore, as the sun dried them, Justin asked a question.

"Bree?"

"Yes?"

"Awhile back I asked of your schooling,"

"Yeah, I remember. It was after the episode with the knife."

"Yeah, right. I was wondering, what other things did you learn there?"

She thought of what she could tell him without getting into too much trouble. "I learned how to defend myself. How to find food where there seemed to be none. How to handle a gun, a rifle. Stuff like that."

"Show me."

"Show you what?"

"I've never seen you actually handle your guns, just carry them around and clean them. Show me how well you can use them."

"I don't know, Justin. I'm not used to showing my talents off."

"When then do you use them?"

"When they're needed, for one reason or another." She thought about Dillon and the rattler.

"Since you're always coming to my rescue, Bree, how will I know that I can depend on your protection when push comes to shove?"

"Believe me, Justin. When that time comes, there will be no doubt in your feeble mind."

"My what?"

"Nothing. It was nothing." She wasn't used to having her abilities questioned. Not by Dillon, not by Justin, not by anybody.

"Show me something. Anything. Please. We've got all day."

"Justin. I'd really rather not."

"Bree, if you don't show me something, I'm gonna get you."

"Excuse me? You're going to do what?" Startled, she looked him in the eyes.

He was in a playful mood; she could tell by the twinkle in his eyes. Knowing this helped, 'cause if he managed to tackle her in fun, she knew to be careful with him. Because if circumstances were different, he could die from the injuries she inflicted upon him. And she sure as shit didn't want that.

They enjoyed the afternoon playing a game of cat and mouse. She played the mouse; he, the cat. Round and round they went. No matter how he tried, he still couldn't catch her. Couldn't even get close. Even the water couldn't slow her speed when she dove into its murky depths. There were times when he did gain in ground, but her determination and thrill of the chase kept her adrenaline pumping enough to keep her well charged.

Justin's endurance was just as remarkable. He managed to chase her for hours, laughing almost the whole time. Sometimes he would laugh so hard he'd almost fall. Over hill, over dale he chased her, dodging rocks, around trees, in and out of the water, but he still couldn't catch his gray-eyed beauty. Resigning to the fact that he was indeed no match for her, he faltered in step and finally fell.

Lying on the ground catching only his breath, he waited for her like a cat in the grass. He knew curiosity would get the better of her, and she'd come looking for him once she discovered he was no longer behind her. And when she came, he'd spring his trap.

Brina made it to the apple tree long before Justin was due on the trail. She jumped to its lowest branches then made her way to almost the top. There hidden by the leaves of the tree and its fruit, she not only had a bird's-eye view of the up-and-coming trail but had nourishment aplenty. Long after two apples were eaten, their cores dropped to the ground giving a pursuer a hint to his prey's whereabouts, she grew concerned that he hadn't yet arrived. Had he given up the chase? Had he fallen? Was he lying in wait somewheres, waiting for her to walk by so he could play the cat and pounce?

She was so concerned for his safety she almost missed the feeling that crept over her. At first, it felt like the apples she'd eaten were bad but dismissed that when her seventh sense kicked in. It came as a feeling not unlike the one felt weeks before, when she thought an intruder lurked nearby. Something was out there, watching her. This time she was sure of it, but what it was she had no clue.

Then, just as mysteriously as the strange feeling of being watched crept onto her, it dissipated. Her thoughts then turned to Justin. Again, she wondered if something happened to him, and again she reached out with her mind. She had to find him and find him fast.

Her mind reached through the branches, past the fruit that hung there. It traveled across the dale, dodged the rocks, charged around the trees. Finally, she found him in a patch of tall grasses, breathing deeply as he dozed in the afternoon sun. Well, at least she knew he was safe and sound and apparently asleep. Slowly letting herself down from the apple tree, she made her way back to where he lay.

Silent as a stalking cougar, she approached her victim. Silent as the tree that grows over time, she stood over him, watching, thinking. It was the glistening of his sandy-brown hair that turned her thoughts to the man himself. There lying directly below her was Justin Case III. The man who danced. The man who swam. The man who stayed with her through thick and thin. The man who had trusted her with his life. The man who'd managed to stir her blood, to do what they thought was impossible.

As a woman in this time, she was feeling things foreign to her and everything she had been taught. Even the pit of her stomach was again betraying her like it had been earlier. Creating in her indescribable feelings she was totally unaccustomed to yet craved.

Justin. She hated to admit it, but below her in the grass was the man she'd grown to love. Truly love. He was beautiful lying there in the grass with his eyes closed, their lashes long and thick. His shirt, and what it contained, drying in the sun.

His breathing was steady. She most assuredly believed he was asleep. She yearned for him. Needed him. Desire to kneel down and kiss his eyelids while he slept was tempting. She wanted to do this while he slept so he wouldn't know it was her and therefore couldn't laugh at her boldness. Believing she could get away with it, she ever so slowly lowered herself to a kneeling position. This way, should she decide not to follow through, she could at least be near him when he woke.

Justin heard of her approach from a distance; the birds alone told him of this. He didn't, however, hear her stealth approach to his side, nor did he hear when she knelt down beside him. It was her scent that he'd grown accustomed to that told him she was close. And for him to smell it, *she had to be damn close.*

Brina decided at the last minute to back out. It was too bad; she'd almost made it. She was close enough to his face that she could almost hear the air enter his lungs, then be dispelled by them. He was beautiful, and she the soldier. She was so afraid that should she follow through, she'd falter, he'd laugh, and she didn't know how to handle the feelings that would follow. So, to avoid it all, she started to back off.

Sensing what was happening, since he could feel her breath on his cheek, Justin opened his eyes. Barely inches away from his nose was his gray-eyed beauty with eyes closed, who was just now backing off and away from him. Not wanting this moment to vanish, he quietly pleaded, "Don't go."

Brina, with eyes closed, heard the whispered words. Stopping in midstream, she slowly opened her eyes. Justin's were there to meet hers. They brimmed with tenderness and passion.

With whispered words, Justin pleaded again, "Please, Bree. Don't go, don't pull away from me now, now that you're so close."

Brina was frightened that she'd been caught in the act. "I can't do this." Her whispered words could barely be heard over the silence between them.

"You can."

Brina believed him, wanted him, needed him, and most of all trusted him.

Justin's large hand with its long, slender fingers reached up to and caressed the side of her face. The touch of his fingers sparked emotions never before felt. She stared with longing for him as she searched the length and depth of his soul through the chocolate of his eyes for the truth of his feelings. What she found mirrored hers.

Back at the Academy, this type of thing was verboten to all trainees. Well, she was no longer there under the scrutiny of the staff. She was here with Justin, the trees, the wind, the All Mother. Time was frozen, and her body was responding to the physical and visual stimulant offered by the man directly below her. Ever so slowly she lowered herself back down towards him, halting just short of 2.469843 inches above his lips.

He couldn't believe his luck, if he read her face and actions correctly. He took a chance and gently took hold of her face gazing into her lovely eyes. She was beautiful. Her message, clear.

Brina could see the smoldering passion there. Her lips parted for him, eager and inviting.

Slowly and gently, he pulled her down to him, raising his mouth to hers. Her lips were just as he had dreamed, soft and yielding. There for a moment he felt her stiffen, as though this was her first time; then he continued, slow and gentle. In moments she changed into a woman with emotions and desires obviously untouched by experience. She may not have realized it, but he could feel the urgency in her kisses as those same feelings he had for her reached out to him as well.

Her kiss was urgent and exploratory.

His sent the pit of her stomach into a wild swirl.

She lowered herself onto him. Snuggling closer still, she rested against the warm lines of his body. She felt the hardness of his thigh against hers, as her skin prickled with the heat of his touch. Her whole being flooded with desire for the magnificent man under her. Brina was in ecstasy; the dormant sexuality of her body had at last broken free.

Her desire for him overrode everything else—*except for the double-click sound of a round being chambered.*

Instantly averting her mind's eye from Justin's light and teasing touch to the source of the interference, Brina was able to locate, identify, and assess the intruder's intentions.

As Justin's trembling fingers eagerly sought Bree's buttons, he felt her stiffen. Stiffen like a stout tree. Felt her every muscle tense up as though ready to spring at a moment's notice. Something was wrong, horribly wrong. Her passion for him had vanished. The heat of their lovemaking, squelched. He hadn't even gotten started, before suddenly he found her attention elsewhere, eyes on the horizon, no longer with him. In her place was an immobilized doe. He tried bringing her back by blowing softly in her ear, but when that didn't work knew that she was far, far away. "Bree? What is it?"

The sound of her name brought her back, but only long enough for him to see her face. What he saw there put a scare in him. He was about to ask but was silenced by her dark, angry expression. Her mouth was tight and grim; in her eyes was a faraway look, a lethal calmness tinged with indefinable emotions. It was not in her to be this way, but because of their learned trust and shared experiences, Justin knew to pay heed to all that she said and did—no matter what the circumstance, whatever the conditions be.

Brina returned to the present but came back with feelings foreign to her. Feelings of anger, rage, hate, loss, emptiness, a protectiveness for Justin, a burning desire to annihilate the intruder into a million pieces, and surprisingly enough, fear. A fear not just for herself, but for Justin and what may now befall him. Not liking these feelings, not now, not ever, she suppressed all but the self-preservation instilled in her for the team players by the Academy.

No longer the lover, she was but again the preserver, the warrior, the soldier, the protector—just like her name denoted. And having a certain task to perform, she mentally ran through her options. Since ensuring Justin's safety was first and foremost, it was imperative that he understand the validity of the situation, so while pushing him back into the tall fescue, she drove her point home.

"Don't you fucking move, soldier." Her words were cold, exact, and edged with steel. Her eyes smoldered with fire.

Heeding such a cold-blooded warning, Justin had no choice but to crouch back down in the tall grass, thus hiding his entire form from view.

As the intruder rode into the clearing, Brina's battleplan was already in play.

XXIX

the fastest gun in the west

They called him the Executioner, and they did it for a very good reason. He was trained by the best, grew up in an upper-class family, attended the best in scholarly and military institutions, had been in the fighting force for years, and had all the proper connections. He was substantially more funded and better equipped than most to handle himself under any circumstance and could and would do any job asked of him, killing quite efficiently.

The Network, his employer, paid well, had promise, and their plans were boundless. Their primary consideration was for themselves instead of others the world over. This appealed to him greatly, especially since he grew up with a weakling father who directed those under him with standard practices and procedures dating back to the seventh conflict instead of just getting in there and kicking ass like he thought ass should be kicked.

Now, thanks to opportunity, he was on the trail of an enemy of the Network. And on this particular assignment, he'd been given free rein to pull in his objective: Brina Louise Grant. With regard to her, he had an advantage. He knew this woman, knew her well. They attended classes at the Academy together. He was there for different reasons than she was, but they were both there, nonetheless.

He'd learned many things about her back at the Academy. During sessions of survival training, military strategy, and hand-to-hand combat, he had ample opportunity to observe her. He saw how her mind worked, how she physically fought, how she survived under horrific conditions, yet continued to wonder how she managed to bring her team back safely and as a whole without so much as a broken nail.

But now, he was the Master, and he'd beat her at this game. He'd hunt her down, dismember her, and return home with a personal memento providing proof of completion.

Since traveling in this simple time zone, the Executioner learned how to plow through all sorts of obstacles, whether they be rain or shine, snow or sleet, feast or famine, uphill or downhill, dirtbags or churchgoers, plow boys or cowhands, broke horses or broncs, open country or dense forests, as well as the blasted heat of the day. He did, on occasion, slow down to compare common folk of the past to its cleverer and more deviate scoundrels of the same time period. He also found time to chat with unwary countryfolk.

There was one couple who gave him valuable information vital to this particular search. They were an elderly ranching couple who were more than eager to tell him, or anyone, of their winter escapades while in the company of a young man and woman. A young woman who, after listening to their stories of her great strength, and endurance not to mention that blasted gray beast she still shared company with, could've been no one else but Grant.

The fact of the matter that she was now traveling with a second wouldn't hinder his objective either. Instead, the whole experience would bring him more enjoyment because of it. To kill two birds with one stone was his idea of a win-win situation.

And now he was closing in for his kill.

With Wolf gone, Brina was totally on her own. And being on her own, knew that the only way she could survive the upcoming encounter with this *particular* opponent was to use her wits and the pistols at her side. So, as he rode into the clearing, she stood at ease with gun belt fastened, Colts a-gleaming, cylinders loaded, attitude adjusted, the sun at her back.

Peeking through the tall grass, Justin could see his Bree strap on her Colts and get serious with their feel. Not being able to hear but understanding the severity of the situation since she had never spoken to him in such a way before, he knew to keep as silent and still as a church mouse.

The man who approached rode a chestnut gelding that stood 16.1 or better. He sat tall in the saddle. He was of formidable size and obvious strength. His attire was all black—*as was his attitude, no doubt.* The brim of his hat was wide, wider than most. Wide enough to hide from view those deadly, calm, green eyes. But since Brina saw him approach from afar, she knew who hid under that wide brim. She knew better than most how he thought, how he handled himself, what his personality was like, his reputation, and how his techniques in fighting usually gave him an edge, but what she didn't understand was why he was here to kill her? Who sent him, and what were the reasons behind his betrayal of Cyclops and his father?

But her not knowing wasn't going to change anything. Caring only for her life and Justin's, Brina Louise Grant's weapons were ready to bear when David Michael Seneschal VIII, the chief director's son, rode into their clearing.

She watched him approach. When he got within 49.45627 feet, she stepped towards him and the gelding. Feigning surprise at his sudden arrival, she spoke.

"David? Is that really you?"

"Yep. Sure is." The Executioner rode to within forty-five feet and dismounted.

"Why are you here? Did they think I needed help?" Brina acted nonchalantly while focusing her seventh sense on any atmospheric disturbances from him, whether they be audio or visual.

"In fact, just the opposite." As he took a step closer, he reached out with his hand as though to offer it in friendship.

Brina heard the click of the mechanism as it sent the derringer towards her opponent's waiting hand. And at that final moment before he could put his finger on the trigger pulling it back, she drew and fired both Colts, simultaneously hitting their mark directly in the midsection of her former classmate.

The shock of the impact knocked the man's hat off and splayed him backward upon the ground. With guns still drawn and barrels smoking, Brina approached the fallen assailant, bent over, and removed the loaded derringer from his hand.

Barely able to see due to the sun, and barely able to utter a word between spitting up blood and his weakening condition, the Executioner tried speaking. "How did you know?"

Brina looked down at him with disgust, hatred, and pity. "The derringer?"

The Executioner nodded.

"I heard the mechanism." She saw no reason not to explain it. He'd be dead shortly.

"Heard it?" His words could barely be heard.

"Yes, David. I heard it. I also heard you coming."

"Heard me, how?" His lights were fading fast.

"It doesn't matter. It's over. Your reign of terror is kaput. You'll not kill again," Brina spoke matter-of-factly, without a trace of remorse.

The Executioner missed most of what she said. He was stone-cold dead. Drowned in his own blood, he died in the very way he'd planned for her to die—miserably, horribly, and in ghastly pain. He wanted her and that gray thing that followed her to the ends of time to die. To disappear, to vanish, to exist no more.

But unfortunately, he had again underestimated her ability to bring home her team without so much as a broken nail.

XXX

somewhere between here and there

If someone had asked him yesterday, Justin would've said the pearl-handled Colts strapped to his Bree's hips hung there just for show. Even though he'd witnessed her daily routine of cleaning, polishing, loading, unloading, drawing, and reholstering, he never truly believed she could actually shoot the damned things, let alone kill something with them. But only moments ago, she'd proven beyond a doubt that she could handle her guns and their bullets in a most lethal way.

Moments ago, his Bree managed to beat to the draw a stranger without so much as a blink of the eye. His Bree. He was totally floored and a trifle in awe with the lightning-fast speed in which she drew and fired both weapons simultaneously at the man who was now stone-cold dead on the ground. And for him, seeing was believing. Jumping up from his vantage point in the waist-tall grass, he ran to her side. "You did it, you did it!"

"I told you I could protect you if push came to shove." Brina didn't like killing but could be just as effective as the man at her feet.

"I should've never doubted you." Justin was suddenly very serious.

Brina stood as silent and as calm as a hundred-year oak, while staring at the dead man on the ground.

Justin gave him just a glance, then turned to her. "You know him?"

"Did I know him? Yeah. Yeah, I knew him." She wondered what could turn a man so.

"Where'd ya know him?"

"School."

"You were friends?"

"No. I had no friends at school."

Surprised, he inquired, "No friends?"

"It wasn't that kind of school, Justin." The sound of her voice ended that line of questioning.

"An enemy, perhaps?"

"There are always enemies, but no, not him. At least not then."

"Why would he want to kill you?"

Now was the perfect time. Could she tell him? "Because I'm a hunted woman."

"Because of the treasure?"

"No. Because of who I am. Because of whom I'm hunting and why, and because of what I can do that others can't." That just about summed it all up as far as she was concerned.

"What do you mean?" Justin didn't understand.

She was so tired of this charade but didn't know if she could tell him outright. "Justin, have you ever wondered about me?" Heaven knows others had.

"Of course, I have." He took a step towards her.

Since the killing of the Executioner, our heroine had been transformed from the mild-mannered, *aroused,* gray-eyed beauty Justin knew back to the soldier, the warrior, the protector as her training dictated. And as protector, she had no time for his foreplay. She wanted to get this crap out of the way. "No, Justin. Not now." Her tone was most definite.

The look on her face stopped him dead in his tracks. He was confused, hurt, and miffed. Being all the above, he stood there glaring at her, staring into her deep, gunmetal gray eyes, thinking, wondering.

Brina, on the other hand, didn't have to concentrate too hard to get the gist of his thoughts. "Justin, have you ever wondered how I can be so warm one minute, then turn cold as ice the next?"

"You mean like now?" It was a cruel stab at her lack of feeling towards him and his feelings towards her. Yet since the emotional jab didn't seem to bother her, that drove the knife deeper.

Unbeknownst to Justin, Brina was in the midst of her own inner conflict. Part of her wanted to take him here and now and forget everything else. The other part of her knew the consequences should she follow her heart and forget the whys and wherefores. That part of her was stronger. That part had more control. That part of herself she hated but loved at the same time. For without it, there would be no Justin for her to love, and for that reason alone she stood her ground and took his cruel stabs in stride.

"Justin." Ignoring the shaky ground on which she tread, blurted out several facts about herself. Some normal, others not so. "Did you know that I can kill a man with my bare hands if I have to? I can get breakfast, dinner, and supper without going to a diner. I can hold your attention so firmly you'll miss the obvious. I have a seventh sense that allows me the unimaginable. I travel with a beast from a distant place. And have you noticed that my boots are blue?"

Caught off guard, Justin missed most of what she said, except the last. Looking down at her boots, he saw their color and remarked on it. "No, they're not. They're brown, just like mine." It was laced with sarcasm.

Brina broke the tension in the air, by chuckling at his observation. "Only because they're filthy. Let me show you." With a determined step, Brina went to her saddlebags and pulled out two pieces of cloth. One was a piece of an old sheet from the Albrights; the second, a swatch of oilskin. Over to the water's edge she headed with a miffed Justin still standing where she left him. Once the dirt and grime were rinsed off, she dried them as best as she could with the old sheet, then used the oilcloth to bring out their true color and what little shine they had left. Looking down at her feet, she saw that the boots weren't quite as blue as they were when she stepped through the field, but they were certainly more blue than brown. Before showing them to Justin, she rinsed out her piece of cloth and put back the oilskin. "Now, smart guy, now what color are they?"

He had to get down on his hands and knees and inspect them closely. The color she suggested was there and that bothered him more than he was willing to admit. "So, what if they are?"

"That's not what you're thinking." It was a statement of fact.

337

"How do you know what I'm thinking?"

"I have a seventh sense that tells me." Another statement of fact.

"Seventh sense, seventh sense. What the hell is that?" His irritation was growing.

"Why are you so angry? Just moments ago, my seventh sense saved our butts."

"Your Colts killed him, not your…sense thing."

"You're right about that, the Colts did the killing, but I heard him come beforehand. If my seventh sense hadn't alerted me, we'd both be cannon fodder."

"How do you know?"

"David was the best. He was the most efficient killer, assassin, murderer, hit man of his time. If I hadn't heard him, we wouldn't be arguing; we'd be decomposing." A true and undeniable statement of fact.

"You keep saying you heard him."

"That's right. I heard him."

"What exactly did you hear?" Justin was curious.

Not wanting to go back from whence they came, together, in the grass, her with her tongue in his ear, him eagerly unbuttoning her shirt, she stated just what she had heard. "I heard the double-click sound of a round being chambered." Her answer to his question gave her pause.

Justin also gave it some thought. "A double-click sound."

"Yeah. A *double-click sound.*" Her wheels were spinning faster than sound. Then suddenly it hit her. "It was the double click sound of a round being chambered into a rifle. *David had no rifle!*"

"*DROP YOUR GUNS AND REACH FOR THE SKY!!!*"

The unseen man with the rifle rode out from behind a tree, leading a second horse, with his Winchester leveled their way.

With wonder, curiosity, and complete shock, Brina watched as the rider approached. It wasn't until he cleared the trees and rode into the full sun that she saw the face below the hat. There, hiding just below the brim were a pair of eyes she'd never forget. They were hideous black dots that stared out towards the world with an intensity and hatred that instilled foreboding. "Lucifer" was Brina's only whispered word.

"I SAID DROP 'EM! OR I'LL SHOOT!!!" Lucifer Carstead took aim on his two unsuspecting victims while urging both horses forward.

The only thing Brina could think of at the moment was to protect Justin, and to do so was to step directly in front of him.

"What are you doing?" Justin asked of his gray-eyed beauty.

"Stay behind me."

"I'm not letting you protect me. Not this time. You're not the only one that can handle a gun, you know."

"I know that, but yours are way over there." Brina indicated their direction with a gesture of her head.

Believing he had time, Justin made a dash for his guns, only to be stopped dead in his tracks by a small explosion of dirt directly at his feet.

"STOP WHERE YOU ARE!!!"

Caught totally by surprise, Justin did as Lucifer ordered. He didn't like it, but he did value his hide beyond all else.

"Get back where you were!" Lucifer hollered. He knew of their potential threat, he saw the outcome of the gunfight, but because the sun was in his face, he couldn't see clearly enough to recognize who he was riding up on, only that there were two, and both were his.

Brina watched as Justin first reached for his guns then subsequently for the sky. It wasn't until after she heard Lucifer's next words, did she transfer her attention back to the problem at hand.

"Drop the fucking guns, bitch!" Lucifer still hadn't recognized the woman's face but could tell that one of the two was female. The curvature of the one body gave most of it away, so did the long dark hair that tumbled down a foot or so from under the dark hat. And it was the female who had won the draw. It was she who was the threat. The unarmed second could be handled in a pinch.

By the time Lucifer rode within a hundred yards, Justin had returned to Brina's side. And now that he was there, Brina again stepped directly in front of him as though she could shield him from any and all lead projectiles that just happened to be sent their way. "This time don't move," she whispered with an authoritative voice.

"I'll not—"

Brina had had it. "You will." Frustrated with the whole scenario and with Justin's total disregard for common sense and his own safety, she whirled to face him and drove her point home—*telepathically*.

All Justin could see was something that looked like the end of a double-barrel shotgun. A shotgun that was only inches from his nose. The rest of the clearing and what was going on was naught. But the muzzle's color matched the dark gunmetal gray color of Bree's eyes. A deep gunmetal gray that bore into the darkest recesses of his brain with an intensity that terrified him. A gray so dark, so intent, so threatening he wanted to pull away, but couldn't.

What he saw, what he couldn't tear away from were her eyes. Her very own eyes. Their gunmetal gray color hit him like a dark force that penetrated the very center of his brain. They were both paralyzing and mesmerizing. So mesmerizing, in fact, that he didn't see her lips move as she spoke, but the words were heard and understood, nonetheless.

"This time you will stay behind me!"

Brina knew Justin got her message by the fact that his eyes were the size of saucers as she spoke. "Do you understand me now?" She verbally asked in a sarcastic way, just before turning her attention back to Lucifer.

Justin didn't know what to think. And he was so shocked at what he had just heard, yet didn't, and how he'd heard it that he couldn't bring himself to move out from behind his protective shield.

Lucifer approached with rifle leveled. When he reached his two victims, he reined in his horse and dismounted, with rifle still cocked and ready.

"I said, drop the fucking guns!" Lucifer approached Brina with eyes wild and blazing.

Brina, having a pretty good idea of what Lucifer may have in store for each of them, in their own good time, should she not act soon, began backing towards the water's edge.

"What are you doing?" whispered Justin as he was gently pushed backward.

"We're getting you in the water."

"Me? What for?"

"Don't ask stupid questions. Just do as I say." Brina had little, if any, time at all to get Justin out of Lucifer's unpredictable reach.

"What about you? Are you coming with me?"

"No. I've got to stay."

"Stay and do what? Get yourself killed?"

"Nah. I'll be fine." Spoken like a true optimist.

"Then why can't I stay and help?" Brina was pushing Justin closer to the water's edge.

"He'll kill you. Now stop arguing with me, or I'll have to kill you myself." Brina was just kidding really, but then again.

"I won't repeat it again! Drop the Fucking guns!" Lucifer was taking aim.

Brina hadn't dropped either gun, neither had she made a move towards her gun belt. She wasn't planning on disarming herself until Justin was well out of harm's way. Then and only then would she temporarily offer herself in his stead. She could handle Lucifer in a pinch, as Justin could not begin to do.

"Remember the swimming lessons?" Brina asked Justin while facing Lucifer.

"Yeah, so what?"

"Remember them and make for the opposite side. Keep down and don't worry about me. I can take care of myself and have been for a long time. NOW GO!" Brina whirled on Justin, pushing him into the water with all the strength she could muster.

Justin, not knowing what else to do for the moment, did as instructed. Remembering the lessons, he dove into the shallow waters then headed for the deeper water. Once there, he remained underwater, surfacing only when absolutely necessary for air and swam for all he was worth. He didn't look back until he reached the other side and then only from deep within the bull rushes, reeds, and sedges that lined the opposite bank. There he waited and watched in horror as the confrontation unfolded across the waters.

Closing the gap as fast as he could, since he was too far out of range, Lucifer fired several shots at the man in the water, missing every time. By the time he reached the gray-eyed beauty, the man had disappeared, and he was almost out of control with anger. "Come outta that water, bitch, but first, drop those hoglegs!!"

Brina did as told. She had to. Reluctantly she unfastened her gun belt letting it and both her prized Colts fall in the three-foot-deep water. If she'd joined them, along with Justin like she wanted to, Lucifer would still be out there, gaining on her, especially since he now had her in his sights. Not only that, but she still had the Grim Reaper to deal with along with who knew how many others, and she desperately wanted to lessen that list if at all possible. So, she stepped towards shore to face him.

Finally reaching the woman, Lucifer peered into her face and recognized her for who she was.

"Betsy," was spat at Brina with all the venom of a pit viper. "Bitch! Didn't you hear me the first, second, and third times? I said drop the fucking guns!"

The moment she was out of the water and within reach, Lucifer stepped up to his gray-eyed beauty and punched her directly in the jaw with his fist. He wanted to use the rifle butt but needed her alive and not too damaged.

Reeling with pain and seeing stars, Brina lay where she fell. When the stars finally fell from the sky, she continued to lie as though unconscious. It had worked before; perhaps it'd work again.

In the meantime, Lucifer walked around as though searching for something.

"Where's your gray steed, my dear?" When he couldn't find him, he gave up. Assuming the remainder of the situation was under his complete control, he whistled a happy tune after what he found, and then started going through her saddlebags, blankets, and clothes. He stopped short when he found the whiskey flasks. "What have we here?" Forgetting the saddlebags, Lucifer opened the one flask and downed its entire contents. "That's mighty too good for the likes of you to be carrying." Tossing it aside, he grabbed the second and followed suit.

Brina watched him closely. Believing that no one could consume so much of that stuff she'd been carrying in such a short time without falling on their face, she began inching her way towards her rifle, which was not four feet from where she and Justin lay earlier. With Lucifer not quite himself, she was able to reach it without too much trouble. Unfortunately, as she picked it up, but before she could get her fingers in the trigger guards, he spotted her.

"Don't do it!" he hissed as he brought up his rifle leveling it her way.

"You do better drunk, don't you?" asked Brina to Lucifer.

"Never drunk. Just slow sometimes," he responded lucidly. Drink did strange things to strange people, and to him, Brina found its effects interesting.

With a stick of dynamite without its fuse lit looking down on her, Brina got up and stood her ground. "Now what, asshole?"

"DON'T YOU EVER CALL ME THAT, BITCH!" Lucifer exploded, slapping the woman with the back of his hand with such force that it sent her reeling backward several feet.

Lucifer could remember the last time he dealt with this woman. He also remembered when last he saw Betsy. The problem he was having was separating the two. He couldn't remember if this woman was the one the Grim Reaper sought, or if she was the woman he sought. It mattered little really, for she was here, and he was going to do with her as he saw fit. The Reaper could go find his own woman and go to hell at the same time.

Brina's cheek and jawbone were on fire. She dearly hoped the bastard hadn't broken her face. That would definitely hinder any future investigating. Then she remembered something her mother used to say, *Remember, hindsight is twenty-twenty. Think of that before you speak.* Perhaps, she thought, she ought to consider its meaning and be nicer to strangers with psychotic tendencies—especially if they're taller, built like Brobdingnagian tanks, and carry a cocked rifle, ready to fire upon the unsuspecting. Yes, maybe she'll be nicer.

Screw it. She'd be nicer when Lucifer and those like him were buried in hell.

"You're lucky I don't shoot you. But I will if you push me!" Lucifer shook with rage.

Glancing over towards the opposite shore, Brina, with her mind's eye, found Justin safe, sound, and well hidden within the reeds.

It happened quicker and harder than she ever imagined. Just for looking back across the lake towards the man she helped escape, Brina was knocked to the ground by another vicious slap, this one, thank the All Mother, was not quite as bad as the last.

"ME ME ME!!!! YOUR ATTENTION IS SUPPOSED TO BE ON ME!!!" Lucifer was still shaking from rage, and her looking towards the opposite shore and hopefully her friend sent him over the edge. **"Don't go thinkin' 'bout escaping today, 'cause it ain't gonna happen!"**

Brina's opposite jaw stung immensely, and neither the rubbing of her hand nor the reality of her entire situation could still the anger she felt rise from the depths of her soul. Keeping her mouth most assuredly and securely shut, as any outburst on her part would result in more pain, and even, heaven forbid, death, she glanced momentarily at Lucifer, then looked directly towards Justin. When their eyes met, without a second thought as to what she was about to do, she again took hold of his mind and spoke to him directly and calmly.

With a voice full of warmth and love did she cross the threshold of time and space to arrive at the basis of the trust they had established over the past year.

"Justin"

At first Justin though he heard insects buzzing around his head, but when he looked around and saw none, looked Brina's way. When he caught her staring directly at him, he couldn't believe that it was happening again. Out of total disbelief, yet a yearning for it to be truly real, he beseeched her face for any chance of hope. When she nodded an acknowledgment, he found himself giving way to a much larger fear. A fear that suggested that she was, in fact, very different from all the other girls he'd known in his lifetime.

Inasmuch as he was afraid of this discovery, the words and the sound of her voice inside his mind struck a chord within him. With the trust and love he felt for this woman and the danger she was now in, he decided that it made no difference how, why, or what he was hearing. What mattered most of all was that it was her voice, her words, her message to him.

"Justin, just like the swimming lessons, you must,
again, place your total trust in me.
Do not move, do not be frightened, do not utter a sound. He will kill you.
Nod your head if you hear me."

Out of bewilderment, Justin Case III slowly nodded his head. Shocked as he was, with this newfound discovery, he accepted it as just another of her extraordinary talents and abilities.

Then he thought of the woman herself. Brina was a woman who did what she said she was going to do. A woman who survived a snowstorm by herself. A woman who found food and water when there was none. A woman who danced with him in the hotel lobby. A woman who found an amazing horse for him when she hardly knew him at all. A woman who carried him from harm to a doctor's office. A woman who stuck with him through thick and thin. A woman who taught him how to swim and how to save himself. A woman who wore blue boots that were covered with so much mud and dirt you couldn't tell their true color. A woman he trusted with his life. A woman he loved beyond anything else. A woman he was about to lose.

As Brina Louise Grant received a momentary glimpse of a thought being sent to her from over the airways and across the lagoon, she realized no matter what the outcome with Lucifer Carstead, the feelings that she and Justin Case III held dear would remain with each of them as each traveled towards their own destinies.

When Brina focused her attention back to Lucifer, he slapped her again for old time's sake. With her head spinning, Lucifer pushed her face down onto the dirt and held her there with his boot, then whistled for his mount. When the animal came and stood next to his side, Lucifer reached into his saddlebags, pulled out a piece of rope, and tied her hands securely behind her back. He was not going to make the same mistake John Deau had made last year. Once that was accomplished, he did the same for her feet. With her securely trussed up like a spring buck, he left her where she lay, while he went in search of his packhorse. When he found the animal, he was surprised at the additional animal that stood nearby—Wyatt.

There were at least two problems that hinged on catching the extra horse. One, try as he might, he couldn't catch the damned animal. Two, he wanted to shoot the fucking thing for running from him. The worst was realizing his gun was nowhere to be found, when shooting him seemed the best option. So, he gave up and settled on what he brought.

With both his horses standing tied to the ground, Lucifer lifted the trussed-up woman lying facedown over his packhorse, then tied her securely in place. He wanted no surprises this time.

Try as she might, Brina couldn't escape and knew without Wolf's help, she could be in big trouble. So, one last time, Brina Louise Grant telepathically spoke to Justin.

"Justin, when we are gone, retrieve the Colts from the water. Let them dry while you catch both horses. Clean and polish them extensively. Look at them closely and read everything that is engraved upon them. What you will learn from their cylinders will tell you much about me. I want you to set up camp here and wait for an old man. He will tell you what needs to be done."

Before she could say more, Lucifer mounted his own horse, then turned him back from whence he came, pulling along his packhorse with a bound Brina in his possession.

XXXI

definitely on the right track

It had been rather quiet and lonely riding without Brina, but Cordell and Dillon had managed. Both missed her continual wildlife observations, her gunmetal gray eyes, ivory skin, and dark hair, but they had other things to think about.

Their continued search for Jesse eventually led them to the musty little hole-in-the-wall community of Mullet Town. There, they were handed a tangible lead in which to follow.

They left the horses at the livery stable, not knowing how long they would be in town, then sauntered down to the town's one and only saloon for a drink to tide them over until the sun went down. After being there several minutes, there came a horrible commotion outside, followed by the sounds of several shots being fired. By the time Cordell and Dillon got to their feet, the entire assemblage of the saloon was standing in the doorway, and they couldn't see a thing. Suddenly from behind and above came a woman's bloodcurdling scream. Both men turned in unison, and there above them hanging from the railing of the second floor, where the whores conduct their business, was a man with a knife protruding from his back and two whores standing back, aghast. Both had hair to their waists. One was blonde and was crying; the other one's hair was red.

To Dillon's and Cordell's horror and surprise, the redhead heaved the remainder of the *gentleman* off and over the railing onto the floor below them, which dumped him directly on their table, spilling their whiskey everywhere and shattering its bottle as well. After the unfortunate victim rolled off the now-tipped table, finding his way to the floor with a sudden crash, Red spit over the railing onto him, while hissing something about his sexual preferences and tastes thereof. When all was quiet, she gently guided the blonde away from the ghastly scene and towards the staircase. But at the last minute before reaching the first step, there was another interruption.

Another whore, or at least Dillon assumed that's what she was, stepped through a second opening atop of the stairs. She'd also been interrupted by the commotion going on outside her door. Not appreciating it, made mention of it by stepping up behind Red, grabbing hold of her hair, yanking her back and away from the steps. To their added surprise, there began a moderate-sized skirmish, right up there at the top of the stairs—*whiney women without song.*

"You bitch. You filthy bitch! He was my best customer! He took care of me proper! You'll pay for that one, you'll—"

As it turned out, the redhead was a survivor from the old-school and had been around the block a few times. It took her only one minute to disable her attacker by elbowing her in the midsection, by which her hair was suddenly released. Then, as Red whirled around to face her new opponent, she made a grab for and caught the uppermost portion of the other's corset, which caught her opponent off balance, making slamming her into the wall a much easier task.

"He may have been your best customer, but he almost killed Mabelle here. And if that kind of fun is what you look for in customers, especially with your preferences, then you ain't worth spit neither! Bitch!"

Then with all the strength she could muster, Red curled her right hand into a fist, pulled her arm back like a spring, and let it fly like a kicking mule, hitting the other whore on the side of the head right above the ear, which in Dillon's book should've killed her instantly.

Dillon never really knew the other whore's condition until it was all over. She had been so close to the staircase, the force of the blow to her head had propelled her sideways, and down the stairs she tumbled. Head over heels she fell until she reached the bottom landing and remained there, as the previous two stepped over her, stepped over to the bar, and had a celebration drink.

Dillon had watched them descend the stairway, and when they both stepped over the still form, his attention shifted towards the entrance of the saloon and the noise outside. Not wanting any part of that either, he returned his gaze around the room, and to his surprise, found only Cordell, the bartender, himself, and of course, those two remaining whores were the only ones left in the saloon. Everyone else had left to join in the shooting, fighting, shouting, stabbing, and naturally the cussing at each and everyone else outside. Believe it or not, that made Cordell and Dillon extremely happy to find themselves in a saloon with two whores, a bartender, a stabbed *gentleman,* and a very dead whore.

"Pardon me," Dillon addressed the bartender.

"Yep, what can I do for ya?"

"Shouldn't we…" Dillon pointed to the still form at the bottom of the stairs.

"Shouldn't we what?" he responded.

"Shouldn't we get 'er off the floor and put her somewhere?" Even though she was a whore, her presence on the bottom of the staircase was distracting to the saloon's decor.

"Nope. They'll take care of him later, after all the hullabaloo," he stated.

"Him?" Dillon asked perplexed.

"Yeah, him."

Dillon could tell by the expression on his face he meant what he said. They had to get outta town fast. "Do you have a back door?"

"The only way out, sugar plum, is past us!"

Dillon whirled around, and there standing in front of him was the redheaded whore again, holding her blood-dripping knife. Apparently while their attention had been diverted elsewhere, she'd stepped over to the fallen *gentleman* and retrieved it.

Dillon was beginning to wonder what that couple they had run into days before, had been doing in a place like this, and what in the world had stuck out in their minds as being strange. The whole bloody town had the freakish nature of an unsettled mind.

"Why, stranger, don't you be a lookin' at us like we was crazy! This here town's what's lost it! Why, Mabelle and I just stopped in three days ago, when we was forced off the stage two miles out. Why, we ain't been in no trouble till that crazy loon met up with us. Why, the way he talked, one woulda thought he wasn't from round these here parts. With all his braggin' 'bout killin' all them riders and searchin' fer buried treasure an' the likes, why, there ain't no treasure round these parts. All there be is rape, pillage, and plundering. That's all them creeps want to do out there in that there street. Can't ya hear 'em? Sheeit, bartender! Give me and Mabelle here a glass of yer best, or I'll introduce you to ma Portia here." With that, she held up her knife in a threatening gesture towards the bartender.

Now the bartender was no fool. He didn't hesitate a second in handing over two glasses and a bottle of his finest. They all watched as the redhead took 'em, then led her friend over to a table, sat down, and began their drinking and celebrating. When he could see that they were preoccupied with their drinking, he motioned for Dillon and Cordell to follow him back behind the bar and through a door, which eventually led to the outside. The bartender then explained to the two a way to get to the livery stable without being seen, then headed off in another direction entirely.

"Dillon, those two ladies sure were an interesting pair, don't ya think?" Cordell had actually enjoyed the little scare they'd just experienced.

"Did you hear what that red-haired whore said? About that man they had met up with, the one that bragged about killing all them riders? The one who's searching for buried treasure? Cordell, she said *all them riders*. That would've made it Kane's regiment. Don't ya see?" They were at last faced with something tangible, no matter what the source. Even if it was told to them by a whore who'd just killed a…a…*damn*. Dillon didn't want to think about what it was or what he'd learned in there.

"Dillon, you head on over to the livery stable, get the horses, and meet me back here as soon as you can." Cordell had a plan.

"What are you gonna do?"

"Don't ya know? With the information that *little lady* has in her possession about that stranger, I thought I go back in and buy her a drink or three. Don't worry, I'll be careful of Portia." Cordell smiled.

Dillon left him there and headed over to the livery stable by way of the directions the bartender was considerate enough to provide. When he arrived at the livery, found to his surprise Cody and Baldy had already been saddled and ready to go. When he found the proprietor of the livery sitting in a back room with a bottle, he couldn't resist. "How did you know to rig our horses for travel? And I see you've provided us with more supplies than we came with. You want to tell me about it?"

"Well, sir, I knew when you rode in here the two of you were strangers to these parts. No one in their right mind would travel through Mullet Town on their own accord. We do have some clean and law-abiding citizens, but they live on the outskirts of town or way out. Them folks only come in on Sundays to pick up supplies and go to church to pray for the souls of the damned. Ya know, those damned that continue to thrive in this here town?" Then he started chuckling. "Then on the other hand, I heard the fighting and shooting begin, and I knew that if you two had a lick of sense in those heads of yourn, you be here in no time. That's why I got them horses ready. I may work in this town, mister, but that don't mean I'm stupid like the rest of 'em. That'll be fifty cents please." He held out his hand, waiting for the change he knew would come.

Returning to the back door of the saloon, Dillon was pleased to find Cordell there waiting for him.

"How'd it go?" He waited in anticipation. This was the first solid clue they'd had in quite a while. Dillon wanted to get started.

"Nora—that's the name of the redhead—well, by the time I returned to the saloon, she wouldn't have known what she'd been drinking. After I left my five bucks on the bar, I took a bottle of something from behind it and set the bottle down with a thud, in front of her nose. Since she was heading in the direction of total inebriation, if I hadn't set it down so loudly, she'd never known I was there.

"But to get on with her story, a few days ago, as she told it, the two of them had been on the stage. And believe this or not, even the stage driver skirts this town, depositing his passengers five miles out at an old stage stop due east of here. It's crazy—even the stage line avoids this place. There, they ran into this character who apparently was drunker than they are now. Being the kindhearted whores they are, as they have shown us to be, they tried to get a little friendly with this guy, but apparently, he was no fool and saw what they was up to. Told them he didn't need them 'cause he had better things to do now that he had killed all them riders. Then told of a treasure map he'd removed from the leader's saddlebags and that all he had to do was to search for the buried treasure. From there, he headed northeast. At least that's what Nora said. They tried to get friendly and to steal his wallet but decided anybody who thought there was a buried treasure around these parts was clean out of their cotton-pickin' mind. That, my friend, was their story."

Cordell, Dillon could tell, had done a bit of celebrating along with them in order to get the information desired. He also found out, and told Dillon later that night, that Nora and Mabelle hadn't always been whores. But as luck would have it, finding a decent living in the West for a man was difficult enough. A woman, or even two lone women trying to find decent work, was as easy as finding buried treasure. And according to the story Mabelle told, the two of them at one time, about five years ago, had been schoolteachers.

This to Dillon made everything more confusing. One minute, Nora was speaking as though educated; the next, she slipped into more ignorant-like expressions. It made no sense.

Cordell continued his story. "On their way west in search of their fortune, their stage was held up by a gang of outlaws. In the process of the holdup, the stage overturned when the driver attempted a sharp getaway turn at breakneck speeds trying to elude the bandits. After the stage overturned, the horses ran off, leaving the driver and the guard dead. When the holdup men found both of them, Mabelle wouldn't continue with her story, but we can pretty much guess what happened. The only other thing she could remember from their attackers was that the ringleader was a sandy-haired man with green eyes.

XXXII

always accept an outstretched hand

The farther on down the trail they rode, the more they heard of, well, Dillon wouldn't exactly call it Jesse's escapades, but it was mighty close to that. Whoever he was, he seemed to be in the habit of leaving a very similar trail as Jesse had, which is why they thought they might be the same. Only now, they were finding thievery followed by the now-familiar, execution-style killings.

There was a difference that was becoming obvious. Whatever kind of projectile he originally used had apparently been exhausted because within the vicinity of each body was now found standard casings. Oh, this character was defiantly particular in which brand of ammunition he chose, because they still all had the same stamping on their bottoms, only now they appeared to be of standard issue instead of those odd-colored casings. Yes, Dillon was sure this man's trail was their Jesse's.

What was exciting to Dillon was knowing that the gap that kept him from his brother's killer looked to be closing. It wasn't just because of his brother that he was consumed about this case, but because of all the other innocent young boys who died as well. Oh yes, Dillon forgot to say, one of the other choice pieces of information Major Northrup told him was that most of Kane's regiment had consisted of new recruits out on their very first assignment. How very sad it was to have lost all those young men whose lives were just beginning. Yes. Dillon was hoping the gap was closing quickly.

Now that they were getting closer to the end of this bloody trail, Dillon had to make a few decisions. If he turned Jesse over to the authorities, alive as they had instructed, they'd give him back his badge, his old job, and add a retirement package to boot—or so they said. However, from what he'd managed to learn of Jesse and the execution-style murders he's committed, not to mention whatever else he's done, why would they want him back alive? That, in itself, was idiotic.

As a bounty hunter, most wanted men are turned in dead as opposed to alive, just to make things easier for all concerned. But in this case, because of what he learned from his gray-eyed beauty, he was beginning to question the orders given to him by his superiors.

His next question, did the government want true justice for the people, or did they want Jesse and what he supposedly had done for their own selfish reasons? He knew getting him off the streets and into safe custody would be the ideal plan—only what about the victims and their families? Didn't they deserve to know the murderer had gotten his just rewards?

Then there was Brina. Dillon often wondered where she was, what she was doing, and if she was safe. Brina's mission in this life-time was to find Jesse and to witness or be the cause of his demise. The more Dillon thought about all the things he and Cordell had learned in her company, the more he realized her plans for Jesse mir-rored his own. The only difference, Dillon wanted revenge, disguised as justice. She wanted justice, plain and simple.

Once his decision was finally made, he was able to focus on the problem at hand.

As the weather changed to cooler temperatures, the two men decided to push their mounts and supplies to the limits of the weather. They both knew once the rain, snow, and utterly lousy con-ditions eventually hit this part of the country, they'd lose Jesse for sure. So, at the last little town stopped at called Thornhill, known for its beautiful flowers, they packed up enough supplies to hopefully get them through till the first frost.

That was when the unimaginable happened.

Just shortly after Cordell and he packed all the extra supplies purchased for their continued search, they stopped in the local saloon for a short drink before heading out. Both had been in there a short couple of minutes when Dillon just happened to look towards the swinging doors and saw his old friend Territorial Marshal, Glen Harper, enter.

"Glen!" Dillon stood, pushing back his chair. "What in the name of my great-great-grandmother, Rebecca M. Rivers, are you doing in this neck of the woods?" he hollered his way.

When Glen heard the words, saw the man, he approached the table. As he approached, his hand was extended, expecting Dillon to take it, but just before contact was made, he broke the gesture and instead pulled him into his arms. He hugged him like a bear, right in front of all the other patrons. He didn't care. He was in no position any longer to care about much of anything.

"Dillon, my friend. How the hell are you these days? Ya know, a long time ago I told old man Stewart you were the best. He thought I was joking. Hey. Let's you and me find a quiet and secluded place to talk—"

That's when he noticed Cordell sitting at the table watching everything with a very curious eye. "Pardon me. Dinna mean ta interrupt," Glen said in hushed tones.

"Don't be stupid," Dillon said as he waved his hand in the air as though the thought was totally absurd. "I want you to meet a man who is as close to me as Kane. Cordell, may I present to you another Territorial Marshal, Glen Harper. Glen, Cordell Chevalier."

"You can forget the marshal part. Now it's just ol' Glen," he said.

"Wha'?"

"That's part of what I want to tell you, Dillon. We need to find somewhere that I can share some confidential information. What I've learned you'll want to hear, information that's sure to change your mind—on lots of things."

Glen was serious. Dead serious. There had been too many strange things Dillon needed to know of since the last time they met. "And since Cordell here is that close to you, you might as well bring him along."

They made one last stop for a few additional supplies, paid the livery attendant, then left town. Once they found a creek with a panoramic view, they stopped. Looking at Glen, waiting for his story, Dillon saw for the first time his eyes having a haunted look to them. What in the name of the All Mother had he learned? He was just about to get off Cody when Glen's words stopped him.

"Stay mounted, gents. We'll have a better vantage point if we remain a horseback. I'll tell you why. Because should the right person ride by and see me talking to you, we could all very well find ourselves in front of a firing squad, accused of treason." He gave that a moment to sink in, hoping one of them would ask why. Glen had been trying to figure out a way to tell Dillon the forbidden information, and since he couldn't bring himself to tell him outright, he knew Dillon could pry it out of him.

"What do you mean treason? What firing squad? What has happened?" What did this man know that the retributions would be that severe? "What do you know? Come on, spill it, man—and be quick about it." Dillon pressed.

"Dillon, what I'm about to tell you, I believe to be true. I learned it from several different sources."

He waited for Glen to finish.

"According to several people in the Ivory Tower, *these are rumors* I might add, but rumors with substantial evidence behind them."

"What, Glen, what is it?"

"The third person I heard this same thing from was a Marshal Charles Maidenfern—CJ's supposed right-hand man. He told me that it was Carl J. Stewart who, with a gang of his own, ambushed and slaughtered the regiment of riders and your brother—searching for some treasure." It was finally out. Whether it was true or not, Glen wasn't sure, but continued, nonetheless.

"And according to someone else high in rank, Carl didn't find it, so after hearing of this outlaw named Jesse Loame, who by the way *is wanted for countless atrocities*, accused him of the dastardly deed. And knowing he wouldn't be able to track him himself, he convinced you—I wasn't included in the lie and hadn't a clue as to the truth or the rumors being spread. But since you've taken so long in finding, catching, and incarcerating Jesse, Carl is now out there trying to find the treasure himself. He and a bunch of thugs.

"And from what I understand, this treasure is a hell of a find. Worth a king's ransom."

Dillon's head was spinning. "Are you sure of all this?" He couldn't believe his ears. Had Carl J. Steward played him a fool, or had someone else played Glen the fool by convincing him of this ridiculous charade, and in turn, have him pass it on to Dillon? This didn't sound right.

"Like I said, I'm fairly sure of my information. The people I've talked to are good friends and associates; they wouldn't tell such elaborate tales if they weren't true."

"What about the assassinations of Jesse's gang members? What about those strange cartridge cases lying about?"

"I can't tell you what I don't know."

Dillon had to think about this for a moment. He closed his eyes bringing back those words said on that dreaded day. Stewart spoke of his brother's killers and asked how determined Dillon was to track them, but never did he mention anything about Kane's body. The guy had Dillon so fired up about the assignment, he totally forgot the importance of family responsibilities. Stupid. Damn, damn, damn, damn!

"What about *Kane?*" Dillon had to know.

"What *about* Kane?"

"Was there proof of his death? Was there a body to be retrieved for burial?"

"Are you kidding? It took them weeks to clean up the bodies of men and horses alike. I don't have the final count, nor do I have the final list of those identified. Only Carl has that. And that list was supposed to be in his office desk, but according to those in the know, it's gone. He must have it with him. They couldn't find any evidence of it being there, even after tearing everything apart—his home too. I'm guessing it's because he doesn't want anyone to know who was found at the site and who wasn't. I'm also figuring, if there were missing bodies, he's on the look-out for those walking, talking witnesses. He wants no one alive to tell of his dastardly deed, and the treasure? He wants that for himself. That's what I'm guessing at."

Smile when you say that, stranger.

"But what about all that other gobbledygook he told in the beginning? That of John J. Nobody, the ransom, and all that stuff?"

"I honestly don't know and therefore can't tell you, my dear friend. All I can say, I've turned in my badge to Marshal Charles Maidenfern—for if what I've heard was the truth in any way, shape or form, I couldn't live with knowing you were tracking a lie. So, I decided to track you down as best I could to tell you of this unsettling discovery. After all, you were there for me when my Maggie died. I owe you, man."

"I don't know what to say." Dillon couldn't believe all the things he was saying. "Does this Jesse feller know anything about the treasure?"

"I haven't a clue, he might."

"What do you suggest then?"

"Well, if what I've learned is true, my best guess is to follow your nose. During your search for that Jesse feller, did you happen to learn anything about this treasure?"

"No."

"Then my second, third, and fourth guesses would be to follow Jesse's trail anyway. If anything, he'll lead you towards places you've not covered. He's not likely to retrace his footsteps if he's trying to outrun the law. And maybe in the meantime, we'll come across Carl's trail or hear news of the treasure."

"What if we come across Carl? Whatcha got in mind?"

"Well, if he did slaughter the Territorial Riders' regiment with Kane in the lead, he's as good as dead as far as the Ivory Tower is concerned, if and when they find him. We could bring him in for bounty. Make it simple for all concerned. Maybe even find the treasure too!

"We?"

"I might as well come with ya. I haven't got anywhere else to go. After all, I'm sure it won't be long before Carl's associates hear of my breach in security and be hot on my little tail. And if we find Carl, he should have the list with the names and dates on him. Clues to your brother's whereabouts—be he dead or alive—and others whose families are waiting to hear news. That, my friend, is our proof of insurance. If we can catch him with that list, we'll have it all. All the evidence needed for his incarceration and proof of our innocence."

"Our innocence?"

"Well, mine, really, but yours too."

"Come again?"

"If you decide to follow this second direction, this truth of sorts, it will eventually be learned by those with bigger guns than us. They'll believe we're in cahoots together—which we are—and with my learning of it, perceive it as a threat. They'll do whatever they can to ensure we end up like those boys in blue. But if we can get that list and Carl, we could end this charade. Whatcha think?"

"What do I think?" What did he think? Dillon hated to think it, but what Glen said made some sorta bizarre sense—*although*...after all, no one of any substance had seen or heard of anyone matching Jesse's description, at least any credible person they'd run across. Most had been whores or drunks, and who can believe half of what they have to say? Were they looking for another man and just not know it?

It was obvious the Ivory Tower wanted the Neptune sphere so very badly and probably planned on finding out how it worked and what it really was. On the other hand, there was the possibility that they knew nothing of the sphere, and it was only Carl and his fellow thugs who knew of it and were desperate enough to kill for it.

Brina was the only one who truly knew what it was, and Dillon was sure she knew how to use it too. Did she know of this lie that had surfaced? Did Wolf? He couldn't be sure of what he was hearing and didn't know what to do.

"Cordell," Dillon began, "what do you make of all this?"

Cordell had been listening in earnest to all that this Glen fella had said. He, too, was a bit skeptical. But in a strange way, it made some sorta sense to him too. After all, they'd not seen hide nor hair of this Jesse. And according to his lifelong friend, the only person who brought this Jesse fella up other than Brina was this Carl guy. He, too, wondered, if Brina knew and just hadn't told them, or if she, too, had been led astray.

"What about the treasure? What are you planning on doing with it if it's found?" Cordell wondered.

"Hadn't given it much thought. My main concern at that time was finding supporting evidence as to the rumors told, which has been confirmed as far as I'm concerned, by those of higher authority—not much higher, but those worth their salt. As to the treasure? I don't even know what it is. I'm assuming it's some sorta of solid gold or silver ball. After all, that's what a sphere is, isn't it? Round? As to the size? Could be anything—could be pocket sized, could be as big as a bread box. But no, other than that, I really hadn't given it much thought as to what I'd do with it, if and when found."

Standing around with fidgety horses got them nowhere. "Either way, we've got a trail to follow, boys. Shall we see where it takes us?"

They were now three. And as three, they headed off again in a northeasterly direction heading deeper into the winter winds and hopefully towards Jesse, Carl, the Neptune sphere, or whatever it was they sought. Maybe they'd even be lucky enough to find the list that held that special clue as to the whereabouts of Kane.

XXXIII

the stage is set

Three weeks later the snow came, and with it, a drastic drop in temperature. Our newly found threesome just happened to be walking out of the hotel lobby in Cascade when they were hit with a blast of Arctic air. Well, Dillon's mother raised no fools. He knew enough after that; Cascade was where they were to hold up for the winter. And since there was nothing they could really do about things as they were, made the best of their predicament by, unfortunately, hiring on as the town's peace officers.

It was a simple job since the size of Cascade wasn't any larger than a cow camp. Not to say that stranded cowboys, miners, and local shepherds when met face-to-face during times of card playing, whoring, drinking, or just meeting each other along the walkway didn't incite fights. If those occasional challenges weren't met, the three of them would've been bored out of their minds.

It brought back memories of days spent back home in Eastern-Western. Only on a much smaller scale. And as Dillon's mind faded back into the past, it seemed like only yesterday when he watched history in the making as the first cattle drives arrived from Texas.

The town was in an uproar. Ol' Mike Johnson had gone out for a look-see hoping to spot any sign of the approaching herd. He wanted to be the first to see the masses of cattle head towards town so that he could race back hollering that he'd seen them, and they were on their way.

Everyone would wait till the last minute, finding safe havens from which to watch the thundering hooves make their way through town to the stockyards beyond. There, the herd would stay until the new owners arrived with their own hands to take them to their new home ranges. Some of the drives brought cattle as breeding stock for new spreads; sometimes they'd bring them in to help feed the Territorial Riders and settlers. Nevertheless, they'd come.

The coming of the cattle from Texas and beyond brought with them cattlemen, cowboys, and vaqueros as they made their drives northward from Texas. They were a tough bunch. Men of simple pleasures and honest values whose only goal in life was to tend their charges, cattle, and horses on their long journey north across rugged and dangerous terrain. A country where water was scarce, Indians were plentiful, days were very long, nights were very, very short, and Mother Nature's sense of humor was unpredictable. From blistering heat to severe winter conditions, no matter what the weather, the cowboys and their cattle continued.

Sometimes it was exciting, sometimes it was boring, and sometimes it was deadly. There are countless stories of rattlesnake and roping accidents, unpredictable cattle, as well as mounts, unexpected incidents involving cowboys, stray cattle, hungry mountain lions, and even an occasional bear.

Much the same can be said for sheep, shepherds, and their dogs. Although, since Dillon knew little about sheep, as per his choice, he assumed the shepherds' and their flocks' travels across the prairie were similar, if not worse, than the great cattle herds, due to the size and vulnerability of sheep.

Both cattlemen and shepherds are survivalists in a harsh land, and their livelihoods depend on Mother Nature. With plenty of rain, the grass grows abundantly. Without it, many of the animals starve, leaving the weak and young as prey for the predators. The same can be said during the winter months. If the animals manage to live through the harsh winter climate, the calf and lamb crops are sure to be profitable for those who make their living thereof, being predator or man.

It isn't always so trying, for they do have their advantages: the beautiful country in which they live and work, the joy of companionship between themselves and their partners (being the horse or sheep dog), and the simple life that they lead, tending to those under their safekeeping. Only those who have dedicated their lives to those two totally different, yet similar, ways of life know their own advantages and disadvantages.

Once the drive reached town and the stockyards, the cowboys and assorted help usually found their way to the Tumbleweed Inn and Saloon—a fine establishment located in the heart of town. The fights that would break out—resulting from the confrontations between the various cowboys, cattlemen, and shepherds—were endless. Dillon knew this because they kept him hopping every night.

What needs to be understood about the differences between the two types of livestock is that cattle eat the tops of the tall grasses as they grow across the prairie. Sheep, on the other hand, eat the entire plant right down to the ground. So, to preserve the grass lands, cattleman wanted the shepherds and their sheep out of the territory, if not, outright dead. Not only did their eating habits make the sheep unwanted by cattlemen, but they also have an undesirable aroma to them different from cattle and horses, one in which cattlemen find offensive. This gave them an additional reason why the animals and their keepers weren't wanted. Therefore, and again, since sheep have just as much right to the grass as cattle, the fights, arguments, and shootings were endless.

Yep. Dillon admired the cowboy on the trail; it's just the cowboy who is celebrating and looking for a fight, that's where he has a bit of trouble.

Here in Cascade, on the other hand, it wasn't quite that bad. They only had a single drive that had reached town, and that was long before our threesome arrived. Unfortunately, the cowboys, once they came around after blowing their wads on drink and whoring didn't have sense enough to leave town before the early-winter winds set in. Being cowboys, they always enjoyed life to the fullest, so through the winter they played.

Shortly after Cordell, Glen, and Dillon accepted the jobs of peace officers and broke up the first of several fist fights resulting from bored cowhands, they were to learn of mysterious rumblings hidden under the surface of their newly adopted home. Rumblings of an old and mysterious woman who lay dying in some basement of an old withering house on the outskirts of town were whispered of. At first, Dillon was the one who wanted to check in on her, wondering if anyone at all was tending to her needs and if she possibly needed anything, but somehow, he never got around to it.

Rumor had it that she'd been abandoned by a traveling medicine man during his journeys through this here neck of the woods, but that was just about all they knew. No one seemed to know how old she was or seemed willing to find out. However, being one of the newly appointed peace officers, Dillon felt it was his job to know his town and the people in it. So, on occasion, he would watch the old house for signs of activity. He wanted to see for himself whether the gossip was true or not. Was there really an old woman dying in that house?

Dillon's stick-to-it-ive nature brought him the results needed to further his investigation. After watching for about a week or so, the only person he saw enter or leave this house was a young wisp of a woman. Seeing her sparked his curiosity further. By chance, one evening he decided to shadow her comings and goings and find out for himself. Standing on the corner of the crossroads of town, while snow gently fluttered down from the sky, he watched this mysterious woman amble her way down the street about nine in the morning or thereabout from the old house. Curiously, the more he watched her, the more he realized she reminded him of his Brina. Only this one wore a long muslin dress that more than showed off her slender form, instead of pants, vest, and gun belt.

The closer she got to town proper, the more Dillon figured she was heading for the general store. So, across the snowy street he meandered, entering the store before her. Along the counter near to the door, he dallied until he heard the sound of light footfalls outside. He had hoped his guess was correct and was happy to see that it was, as this young and pretty woman opened the door and entered. He was so enthralled with watching her, he failed to see where he was standing and suddenly found the door unceremoniously whacking the tips of his boots upon opening.

The young woman realized only too late she had opened the door and accidentally struck someone standing almost directly behind it. Believing they had both grabbed for the door at the same time and it was she who had been a second faster in entering than he in retreating, apologized.

"Oh. Forgive me. I'm extremely sorry. I didn't see you back there. If I had only been a second slower, this may not have happened." It was then she saw his face. It was a very beautiful face in its own rugged way, with hazel eyes at its center, a well-defined nose resting slightly above a tender yet strong jawline and mouth, and under the typically cowboyish hat for the period lay a mop of brown hair. Then she noticed the badge.

Dillon didn't know what to say or do. The sudden slap of the door broke his concentration for the moment. Here he'd found himself standing in front of yet close enough to so that he could see every detail in her face, the mysterious woman in question. She was beautiful. Her eyes were green, a true green with skin the color of true cream. Her hair was a shimmering mass of light red that framed her lovely face with soft curls, which continued to cascade down her back. It took all of Dillon's control not to do or say something overly stupid. She was a tiny thing, no bigger than a minute, yet the intense strength behind those eyes caused him to take a step back.

"I'm sorry too. I don't know what happened. Is there something I can do to repay you for your kindness?" Words were coming out of his mouth that made little sense.

She was confused. Wasn't it she who'd accidentally hit him with the door? "I think you've got that bassackwards, sir. It was I who hit you." Then to help break the sudden tension between the two of them, she offered him her hand. "Let me introduce myself. Mary Beth Robinson of Bangor, Kaliphornya."

Dillon was a bit taken aback. This gesture was something his gray-eyed-beauty would've done. Maybe the stories he'd heard were true after all; she was as crazy as a loon. Wait a minute, that was supposed to be the old woman who lay dying in the basement of that withering old house, not the one standing before him. What was he to do? Well, to start things off, he took her hand. Just like he'd taken Brina's. "Very nice to meet you, Mary."

"That's Mary Beth, if you please," she responded.

"Very nice to meet you, Mary Beth. I'm Dillon Frasier."

It only took her a minute to recognize the nationality of the name and the badge on his vest. "That's a nice Irish name, Dillon Frasier. May I ask, Dillon, are you the new sheriff here 'bouts? 'Cause if you are, your help is way overdue."

How could she have known of his heritage? "Yes. I am one of three newly appointed peace officers for the winter. My friends and me will be headin' out come spring."

"I'm sorry to hear that. I mean about heading out come spring, that is. This town sure could use a full-time, capable gun on our side of the law to protect us law-abiding citizens. But if you'll excuse me, Dillon Frasier, I've got to pick up some supplies and head on back to the house. It's been nice chatting with you. Perhaps I'll see you another time."

"Before you go, I'd like to ask ya something."

"Yes?" Suddenly she was suspicious.

"Well, I really don't want to pry, but I hear there's an old woman dying in that withering house you came from. Is that true?"

"You've heard the rumors too, huh? Nothing is sacred in this town. Remember that, Mr. Frasier, nothing is sacred."

"Please. Call me Dillon." Sauce for the goose.

"All right, Dillon. Now if you'll excuse me." Then she turned to the assemblage within the confines of the store and announced, "What do you think you're all doing? Do you realize you're gossiping about me again to total strangers? You have no clue whatsoever, do you?" Shaking her head in total disbelief, Mary Beth Robinson turned away from the newly met Dillon Frasier, back towards the center of the store and continued with her business.

Since Dillon really didn't want to be in the store to begin with, he gingerly opened the door trying not to let anymore cold air in than necessary, then left. Walking back towards the center of town gave him time to think about the rumors he'd heard. Were the stories true? It really didn't matter for the moment; all that mattered was that he had gotten what he wanted. A good look at Cascade's mystery woman. The only thing that bothered him now was his curiosity about her.

About three days later, Dillon did, late one evening, spot a fairly young-looking man sneak over towards that end of town as if he didn't want to be seen. From what Dillon could see, he wore a hat similar to those of the local cowhands. He would've followed him on over, curious that he was, however, at that moment he was rather busy. His hands were full trying to detain a drunken cowboy by the name of Marlboro Smyth of the KCD Ranch. He was one of several boys stranded in town 'bout the same time as themselves. Dillon had hold of his ear in an attempt at hauling him off to a quiet place to sleep it off, after he smashed an empty whiskey bottle over the head of a shepherd who'd just stopped by the saloon to wet his whistle. By the time Marlboro was safe and sound within the confines of a cell, the marshal moseyed on back towards the saloon. There, Cordell, Glen, and he were to meet for a relaxing drink before the evening came to its exhausting close.

Since the sheriff's office was conveniently located near the Moonlight Saloon and close to Harry Jordan's Bar and Grill, the slippery walk through the slush was a short one. As Dillon pushed open the swinging doors, he spotted Glen seated comfortably at a table near the front window.

"Evening, Glen," he said as he waved and stepped himself up to the table. "I see by the look on your face and the size of the bottle here it's been a very eventful day."

"You don't know the half of it, Dillon. Sit." Glen then waved the bartender over, asking for a couple more glasses.

No sooner did Dillon sit, there was the sound of shots being fired somewhere out in the street. Instantly both their chairs were pushed back and out of the way as they jumped to their feet. With guns drawn they were ready for action. Upon reaching the swinging doors, both men dove for cover, not knowing who was firing or from where it came. And as Glen peeked around the corner in a crouched position while Dillon covered him, Cordell appeared out of nowhere.

"Who's shooting?" Cordell asked.

"Damned if I know. One minute it's the cowboys; the next it's the whores. One thing's for certain, we ain't bored." Then gave a quick chuckle.

"Can either of you see anything?" Dillon asked.

"Nope. Not a darn thing," Cordell answered.

Then off in the distance Dillon heard something. Only this time it wasn't the sound of shots being fired; it was the sound of a woman's voice.

"Now stop it. Both of you. This isn't worth killing each other for. Damn it, listen to me, the two of you. If'n you don't stop all this foolishness and put your guns away this instant, you'll never hear the end of any of them. And that's a promise. Clear out before someone gets nosy. Go on, git."

Dillon could tell the voice came from somewheres near the general store, but from whom and exactly who was involved in this incident, he couldn't rightly tell. Neither could he make any sense of what was heard, and apparently neither could anyone else. After a few minutes had passed with nothing following, the three of them straightened up and headed towards the middle of the street finding it empty. Whomever had taken part in the little commotion was now long gone, and only silence remained. "Damned if that don't beat all." What had it been all about and where had they all gone? At least all was quiet again and no one had gotten hurt.

The three of them just stood there in the middle of the street for no one could remember how long before they all, in turn, reholstered their guns and reentered the saloon. A second before allowing the doors to swing all the way closed so they could close the storm door, Dillon spotted movement out of the corner of his eye. "Go on in without me. I'll be in shortly."

"Whatever you say." Cordell was relieved nothing had happened out there in the pitch-dark. After all, he had been in the center of that earlier fight with Marlboro Smyth and those other cowboys. Why, he'd figured he'd had his fill of excitement for the day if not the week. "Come on, Glen, buy ya a drink." Then turned to his old friend. "Dillon, you keep your wits about you out there in the dark."

"Sure 'nough." Slapping him on the back in fond friendship, Dillon headed down the street in search of what he thought he may have spied earlier. Then again, if there was nothing out there other than his imagination, well, that'd meant he'd just taken a pleasant stroll for nothing.

Glancing momentarily out the window due to the pain in his head and behind the eyes, Marshal Dillon Frasier noticed the sun was just beginning to show itself for the first time in four days. And there he was, still within the warm confines of his bed when he shoulda been out on the street making his early-morning rounds.

"Damn," he said aloud. It had been another late night spent in the saloon playing poker with Marlboro Smyth and Joe Hastings from the KCD range, Glen, and some drifter who wandered in all cold and tired from being caught up in a storm not far from town. Then when he spotted their game, sat down and joined right in. Feller won ten-dollar off'n Dillon. Lucky bastard.

Oh, how his head hurt. He must have drunk two bottles of the most foul-tasting whiskey he'd ever wasted time drinking. Once out of bed and finally dressed, Dillon staggered down the stairs anticipating a hot breakfast. Entering the dining room, he was met with just that. Then later, after his stomach was pleasantly filled to capacity, Dillon stepped outside the door, and again, ran directly into Mary Beth Robinson.

"Mornin', Dillon Frasier."

"Mornin', Mary Beth." Tipping his hat.

"I see for the first time in a few days the sun has decided to come for a visit. Maybe if we're lucky, it'll stay a while and raise the temps a bit." Mary Beth loved this time of year.

"That would make it pleasant enough." What to say, what to say. Every time he found himself close to her, his voice failed. And since he couldn't think of anything clever to say, he again tipped his hat saying, "Good day to you, Mary Beth." Then turned and headed for the jail. Damn. Why couldn't he say anything intelligent to her?

It just didn't make any sense at all. Dillon had no trouble talking to Brina. Then again, Brina held guns on them, giving him all the incentive needed to talk straight and sure.

Maybe that was it. It was Brina's strength that drew him to her; this woman acted differently. She was polite yet strong of will. Stop it. Stop it. Stop it. They were there to enforce the law and keep the fighting to a minimum. Not to look at pretty girls during the winter months with…beautiful green eyes, long soft hair, delicate features—damn it! It was almost as though she had cast a spell upon him. Dillon believed he'd best be finding a fight to break up.

Mary Beth Robinson was a little confused at first with the Irishman's reaction to her. That was until she thought about it a bit. He was tongue-tied around her. That's all it was, which must have meant he had had little practice conversing with intelligent women. She understood that completely. There had been many a day and gent call on her back home who suffered from the same malady. She recognized it. Thought about it. Then tossed it out the door with the rest of her worries. If he was interested at all, they'd both know it in time. If not, *c'est la vie.*

By the end of November, the winter had hit with a vengeance. The snow wasn't too awfully deep, but the air was so cold, the horses' coats were as thick as bear fur. If it hadn't been so blasted freezing outside, it would have been a perfectly beautiful day. It had snowed for five days solid. The first morning after the snow had stopped, it brought the promise of sunshine. A bright and shiny day it was, which made the snow that covered everything around Dillon look all sparkly and pretty.

It was about ten in the morning when Dillon spotted Mary Beth Robinson trudge down the street, step up to and enter the Stage, Telegraph and Freight Office. He couldn't believe his eyes. What was she doing here in town in weather like this, with only a light shawl for warmth? But since it was really none of his concern, he turned his mind to other business. Not just that, but because he was always tongue-tied in her presence, to stop and try to talk, even about the weather, was a ludicrous idea.

Mary Beth was so excited. She'd watched from the window of her old decrepit house as the stage made its way through town. She had thought because of the storm, the stage line would've closed down till the weather broke, but since it hadn't, she made a point to rush into the office shortly after its departure. Maybe there was a notification for her on the special shipment she'd been expecting for three months. It had been so long since she had something new for the cowboys who frequented her home, keeping their attention and enthusiasm fresh was becoming increasingly difficult. Upon entering the office, she stepped right up to the counter with a sparkle in her eye and a delightful smile upon her lips. "Mr. Hoganberry. Please, is there anything for me in that satchel?"

"Why, Mary Beth. I didn't hear you come in." Mr. Hoganberry was an older gentleman who had worked back east when the stage line first started. After his wife died at an early age, he decided to move away from all the places his memory of her rekindled. When he asked the stage line if there was someplace way out west they may want a clerk, he'd be the first to volunteer. Therefore, when they'd decided on Cascade as one of the many stops for the Stage, Freight, and Telegraph Office, he jumped at the chance.

"In fact, there is a little something here addressed to you," he said with a gleeful voice. "Let's see." Reaching for the mail sack, he opened, then began to sort through it, searching for the desired envelope. "I node it's here someplace. Hmmmm…" He knew he was giving her a bad time. She knew it as well.

Mary Beth Robinson was a patient little thing, with an appetite for life who had mysteriously appeared out of nowhere. The town had grown since her arrival, yet many of the folks who stayed on still found her strange. Mr. Hoganberry, on the other hand, found her delightful, friendly, full of life, and very intelligent. *He also knew she had secrets abounding.* He didn't care because she treated him fairly and always made him smile. As for the shipments she'd been receiving the past two to three years, he never questioned what was in them.

Although once in a while of their contents he did wonder because every now and then her shipments would come in either single or several moderately sized boxes. These boxes were oftentimes heavier than she could manage; therefore, a man's strength was required to help lift them into and out of the buggy she sometimes brought. On the other hand, if the buggy was not available, sometimes a local got volunteered.

"Mr. Hoganberry," began Mary Beth.

That was something else he liked about her. She always called him *Mr. Hoganberry.* Not like some of the other folks in this town who just hollered at him, using whatever they felt like calling him that day. She always had respect for him. It kinda reminded him of what he would've liked to see in his own child if Kate had lived. "I know, I know. I'm searching as fast as I can," he said with a smile on his lips. "Here! Here it is. I knew it were here somewheres." Straightening up from his bent position, Mr. Hoganberry handed to the young woman with the sparkle in her eyes and the radiant smile upon her face the patiently awaited envelope.

"Thank you. Thank you. Mr. Hoganberry." Mary Beth was so excited she didn't wait a second before ripping open the envelope right there in the office. Reading the notification as fast as her mind would allow, she squealed with a sound of delight as the desired information was finally revealed. "Oh, how wonderful."

"What is it, Mary Beth? What's in those envelopes that makes you so happy?" He really didn't have any right asking her this, but they'd been doing business with each other for so long, he almost felt himself a friend. A friend to share secrets with, maybe? Heaven only knew, he'd never, never repeat a single word to anyone in town what was in those shipments of hers.

"Something special, Mr. Hoganberry. Some things that are very, very special."

"Would you tell me? I won't tell anyone. Really." He truly thought she would tell him.

"Hmmmm. Not yet. Although I will tell you someday. Then, on the other hand, you'll find out on your own through the gossipy townsfolk. They think they know everything, but I'll tell you what—they don't know how good they've got it living the way they do. I've seen things. Things that'd make your skin crawl. Cruel things that only the devil can devise. The people here are wonderful. The countryside is wonderful. Even though they gossip about me all the time, I really don't care. Even when they spread rumors around town that eventually end up in the minds of strangers who think I'll explain their curiosity away, I don't care. I think they do that because they don't understand me. I think maybe they're a bit afraid of me too, because they don't understand, but I'll tell you something, Mr. Hoganberry, I'm going to help them understand and soon. Yes, I am. Then they won't be afraid of me any longer. I promise. Good day to you, sir, and thank you for finding my letter for me." Mary Beth smiled at him, slipped her envelope into the bosom of her dress, readjusted her shawl, turned, and left poor Mr. Hoganberry standing there behind the counter in a state of bewilderment.

Dillon was sitting on the porch of the jailhouse when he spied the young woman leave the freight line office. Even though she was down a-ways from where he sat, that slender form wrapped in a light shawl, with that shimmering red hair, could only belong to Mary Beth Robinson. Why was he so enthralled with this woman? Was it the mystery that surrounded her? Perchance, could it have been his dumbfounding attempts at carrying on sensible yet simple chats with her that kept his mind a-whirling? Whatever the case, he stayed where he was and continued to watch her as she headed back towards the old house.

Just when Mary Beth reached the other side of the general store, Dillon caught sight of a small girl running in her direction, splashing and crunching through the snow-covered street. He thought Mary Beth had been too far out of earshot but apparently not, for she stopped then turned in the center of the street and waited for the young girl's approach. There she knelt in the snow and spoke to her for several minutes as though chatting a summer day away. The young girl then turned away from her, and before getting too far down the street, turned and waved to her in a way recognized only by innocent children.

That's when Dillon turned towards our mystery woman. She had gotten to her feet, and as she clutched the shawl tightly around her with one hand, Mary Beth Robinson was waving back to the small girl with the other.

The child. That adorable little girl, Becky Lindsey. She had actually stopped Mary Beth in the center of the snow-covered street to chat with her. If her parents had only known. Mary Beth hoped the parents would find out when the time was right and only at a time when she was ready for them. Becky, like the few others who came to her, had given her word not to reveal the secrets that lay hidden within the many walls of Mary Beth Robinson's weird old house.

Two weeks later, the general store received its freight shipment of dry goods, hardware, hard candies, and miscellaneous items. Within the confines of the wagon, hidden beneath a stack of woolen blankets, was a package addressed to a Mary Beth Robinson, Cascade, Southern Section of the Dakota Territories. Dillon knew this because Mr. Hoganberry brought it to his attention, asking if he would be kind enough to deliver the parcel out to Mary Beth's house. She had been in just that morning looking for it, shortly after the stage had arrived, believing her parcel to be there. When it didn't appear to be, she headed back on home. So out our hero trudged with the package in hand. Through the snow and sleet, he walked with his many layers of clothing to guard against the windy, rainy, and miserable weather just to deliver a stupid package.

When Dillon reached the house, it was as they had said: "Shabby and run-down with plants growing haphazardly all around the yard." At one time it could've been a very lovely place. But as the years passed by and its care nil, it looked like a broken-down, old homestead, forgotten by the rest of the town and seldom seen by travelers passing by.

He opened the small front gate of the old decrepit fence that surrounded the house, closing it behind him. Turning, he glanced at the house for a second before walking up to its door. There were two windows to the right of the door with green curtains, but for the most part, this afternoon they were closed. Stepping up to the porch, he noticed the floor as he stepped across it. It was solid and sound, not in need of repair as expected. That was funny, he thought. From a distance the house looked as if it was older than the All Mother herself, but now that he stood on its threshold, found just the opposite. How curious.

Up to the door he stepped, paused, then knocked three times upon its face. Nothing. He waited a couple of minutes more, then tried again, only this time he knocked four times.

The door creaked opened.

There was no one there to invite or to turn him away. Regardless, since the wind had turned for the worse, he stepped through the opening as though it was a giant monster waiting for an unsuspecting victim to step into its hungry mouth. The moment he was inside, the door slammed shut with a solid thud, then bolted itself. He froze in his tracks, not knowing what to expect. When nothing did happen, he peered through the darkness. Eyes adjusting to the dark interior, he realized the room wasn't as dark as previously imagined. There, built into the wall to his left was an open fire pit, with a fire crackling, hissing, barely lighting the room.

"Welcome, Dillon Frasier, to my humble abode," came her voice from behind him.

Startled, he almost dropped the package. Whirling around, he was met face-to-face with the ghostly visage of Mary Beth Robinson.

"Would you like to sit and chat awhile?" she asked.

"Jehoshaphat, Mary Beth! You just about scared me to death!" If he ever had anything to say to this woman, now was not the time.

"I'm sorry, Dillon Frasier. I didn't mean to scare you."

"Then why all the mystery?" His wits were just beginning to find their way home.

"Well, you did come here expecting the unexpected, didn't you?" she asked.

"Ah well, yeah. I guess so."

"Well, I just figured that since you were brave enough to give us a try, I didn't want to disappoint you. Especially since Andy Simms followed you out here." At his bewildered look, she continued. "Yeah, he followed you from town. As I expect, when you get back to town, they'll be new rumors floating about." She really didn't want any uninvited company, but since he was here anyway, she might as well make the best of it. Besides, as cold as it was outside and as wet as he had gotten walking all the way from the center of town, he should be allowed to get warm and maybe a tad drier before heading back to all those gossipy townspeople so he could tell his stories. She had hoped this wasn't the case with this man with the hazel eyes, but you never could tell 'bout folks.

"I'm sorry, Mary Beth, for all the stories they spread. I, myself care little for what they say since me and my friends plan on leaving come spring anyway. But you know how folks is." After all, Dillon had spent several months in the company of Brina Louise Grant. The strangest woman anyone had ever spent any time with. This secretive woman and his gray-eyed-beauty had nothing in comparison, but after spending months with Brina and that damned animal of hers, he could handle anything Mary Beth planned on throwing his way.

"Well, if that's the case, would you like to sit a spell? I was just in the middle of something, but I can set it aside. That is, if you'd like to stay and warm up a bit before heading back. Really, I don't mind." She knew he wanted to but that he was also slightly afraid of her. Moreover, she knew it was a different kind of fear than what the townsfolk felt. She would see if being in her house and seeing her for the kind person she was, would help him relax enough to allow his charming self to come out, the side she was sure was there hiding just below the surface.

Dillon felt a little uneasy about being in this woman's house, especially without enough light to guide him than from just the pit. Then as though she heard him, an oil lamp was lit followed by several candles, one by one until the room was aglow. And as his eyes again refocused on the room before him, noticed again the fire pit, and since now there was ample light in the room, he could see that it was just a standing woodstove with its front door opened wide. On the wall directly to his left was a desk of some sort, a chair, and a candle already lit on its corner. Around the room his eyes roamed, not missing a thing. Over in the corner, against the facing wall, were two doors. Both were open. He spied a small room with a place to eat, a place to prepare meals, and a...

"By my aunt Abigail Heathrow, Mary Beth. Is that a water pump here in the house?"

"Yes, it is, Dillon Frasier." He was very observant, this man of Irish ancestry.

There was a couch to his right, but when Dillon spotted the circle of six chairs directly in front of him, he suddenly stopped. Within that moment of stillness when all was silent, he heard the sound of a cowbell ringing. The suddenness of it almost caused the marshal to drop the package. "Here, Mary Beth, you'd better take this before I drop it."

"Oh, thank you. Dillon Frasier. Thank you very much for bringing it out. Would you set it on the desk for now? I'll get to it later." She wasn't ready to be explaining her packages to anyone. "Excuse me for a moment, Dillon Frasier, but I must attend to something in the basement." Mary Beth gestured for him to sit down and wait while she headed towards the other side of the room. Upon reaching the door that led to the descending stairway, Mary Beth took hold of its knob, turned it, and when she had the door open, there came another woman's voice from its mysterious depths.

"Mary Beth. Is someone here?"

"Yes, Toby. Someone is here." Turning back towards Dillon she saw that he was suspended halfway into and out of the chair using his hands and arms to support him as they firmly grasped its arms.

"Dillon. Can you wait just a minute?"

"Yes, of course," he answered.

Turing back towards the opening, Mary Beth asked the voice from the basement, "What is it, Toby?"

"The final shipment has arrived. Do you want the vase broken?"

"Are you sure it's the last?" At least Toby understood that there was someone with Mary Beth; otherwise, she wouldn't be so careful as to what she said and how she was saying it.

"Yes. I'm sure. With it came a completion notice," she said.

"Yes, Toby. Smash it into a million pieces for me, will you, please?" Mary Beth Robinson replied.

What was she smashing? He was lost. None of the conversation between them two women made any sense. Suddenly there came a *KABOOM!* The loud blast was followed immediately by the rattling of the windowpanes and glass, along with a rumbling feeling within the room and under his chair. Smoke filtered through the doorway. When everything stopped, he looked to Mary Beth for an explanation. What he got instead was the look of a beautiful cream-colored face staring off into an unknown place far and beyond the window, the curtains, and what lay beyond them.

After several moments thinking of what she'd done and her reasoning behind her decision, which didn't make a hill of beans' sense, Mary Beth Robinson returned her attention back to the man in front of her. Dillon Frasier, the man of Irish descent. What was he thinking of her now?

When her eyes came back into focus and rested on his own, he blurted out the question of his fears. "What in the name of the All Mother was that?"

Now it was her turn. What was she going to tell him? She really hadn't expected that much of a racket. "Dillon Frasier, can you keep a secret?" This wasn't the smartest thing she'd ever done.

With all that he'd been through in the last several months? "Yeah."

"Better yet, how are you at giving your word, and how good are you at keeping it?" It was now time for the moment of truth.

"My word is my life, Mary Beth."

"The reason I ask is that you obviously need an explanation of sorts—especially since you are the law."

Dillon found himself now more curious than fearful with an explanation coming, no matter what the outcome.

She waited a moment before continuing. "You see, for the most part, the mystery that surrounds this old house and my life here lies at the bottom of this stairway in the basement below us. Are you willing to trust me by handing over your word of honor that what you are about to see will not be revealed to anyone outside?" She was taking an awful chance with this man, but unfortunately, between herself and Toby, there was little choice.

What was he to do? He couldn't ignore the voice, the explosion, and what followed. Was this part of the rumors that were whispered behind her back where no one was willing to tread? He had to know. His curiosity was eating him up alive. As he has said, his word was his life. Was he willing to give it to this mysterious woman and the voice below? What had he to lose? They would be gone by spring anyway. Who was he gonna tell other than maybe Cordell? "No one?"

"No one," she responded.

If that was what she wanted, that's the way he had to accept it. "Very well. I give you my word of honor. I will keep silent." There. He'd said it. Let the rumors spread. Marshal Dillon Frasier was going to learn something this day.

"Good. Very good. I believe you, Dillon Frasier. Now, if you would, follow me and be careful of the stairs. There are no lights other than my candle, at least until we reach the bottom floor." Reaching for the brass candleholder, the one that sat near the door, Mary Beth stepped over to the fire and lit her candle.

With not so much as a word, the mysterious woman cautiously made her way down the flight of stairs with the light of the candle distorting the walls of its interior, followed by a wary and very curious Dillon Frasier behind her.

XXXIV

for all intents and purposes

All Dillon could see as they descended deeper and deeper into this cavern of hers was a flickering of light from something far below. Halfway down the narrow, long, and winding staircase, Mary Beth retrieved the source of this light—another candle, one that rested on a nearby ledge. With the second candle in hand, they managed to reach the bottom, without mishap, where they were met with a door.

With Mary Beth Robinson in the lead, Dillon followed behind as she opened, then passed through the doorway into a long and narrow corridor, a corridor with sides constructed of rock and green-gray moss, which he found interesting, but not as interesting as the very large and spacious room at its end. The room in which they stood was very large, larger than the house above, and was lit with many lanterns that hung suspended from various locations on the craggy ceiling above. Looking around, he also discovered three more separate doors on the opposite wall from where he stood. This suggested a more spacious area beyond. It was as though she had found a cavern deep within the All Mother, far and below the world above them all.

When Mary Beth reached the bottom of the stairs, she listened carefully. First, she listened for Dillon Frasier, making sure he was still behind her, then for any indication or sound as to how Toby was tending to the broken item. When she picked up the sound of sweeping, Mary Beth continued down the corridor until she reached the library with Dillon a few feet behind her.

Toby was just finishing with her sweeping when Mary Beth and a tall gentleman stepped into the room. Ignoring the gentleman,

Toby directed her attention to her companion. "Mary Beth, may I speak to you privately for a moment, please?" Now may not be the time, but communication regarding the noise and what had made it had to be known.

The concerned look on Toby's face forced an interruption. "Will you excuse me for a moment, Marshal?" Without waiting for a reply, Mary Beth turned away from the man of Irish descent to give her full attention to Toby.

Mary Beth spoke to Toby in hushed tones. "That's all right, Toby. No one knew it would make that much racket. I sure as hell didn't. It's over now. Well, we'll just have to fix it later." When she heard a throat clearing, she immediately corrected her rudeness. "I'm sorry. Dillon Frasier...may I present Toby Bicker." Then reversed it. "Toby, this is Dillon Frasier, of Irish descent."

"Nice to meet you, ma'am," he said.

"Dillon Frasier of Irish descent. Nice name, Dillon," Toby responded.

Toby Bicker was an older woman, who was half Dillon's height. She had white hair, deep-brown eyes, dark-brown skin, and a very mischievous look about her. He couldn't describe more of her, as she turned serious while tending to whatever pieces she had picked up from the floor—which was where his attention was momentarily fixed. Curious as to what had happened and what had broken, Dillon watched her pick up, carry, and pass through one of the other three doors the many pieces just recently retrieved from the floor. And just as she quietly closed this door behind her, his eyes were averted to something hanging, or shelved, on the far wall next to that one door. Still being curious as to all the mystery, he slowly walked across the room towards that wall to investigate further.

Mary Beth knew Toby's intentions were to draw Dillon Frasier's attention away from the incident and focus it elsewhere. And as Mary Beth echoed in this man's footsteps as he stepped across the room towards the wall next to where Toby just exited, she pondered the man before her. Might he be the one she had searched so long for? Was he even worth considering? The next few minutes would tell her many things about this man of Irish descent.

The wall Dillon headed for was dark and gloomy, but within just a few feet, every nook and cranny came into focus. He couldn't believe what was there. There he was, at the threshold of something he'd only heard about.

"Would someone's Aunt Martha look at this," he whispered to himself, for the entire wall in front of him was packed with books, books, and more books. Turning, he saw that all the walls of the room were the same. He was so surprised he'd forgotten all about the woman behind him.

It was Mary Beth's turn. "Do you like my collection, Dillon Frasier? They're mine, you know."

He whirled at the sound of her voice. "I would think so, since they're in your basement," he replied.

"No. You don't understand. Pull one out." Mary Beth added.

He did as she said. The first book he pulled out had a leathery cover with fancy lettering on its front. Its front read *Short Stories of Heroic Adventures, Volume XXVII by Mary Beth Robinson.* "Is this you? Did you do this?"

"As a matter of fact, yes, yes, I did. Pull out another," she said.

He didn't put back the one in his hand, instead reached for a second and found another one very similar yet still different. The second read, *Ghost Stories from Our Past Lives, Volume V by Mary Beth Robinson.* Dillon just looked at her, *really* looked at her. "How many of these have your name on them?" He was beginning to feel a bit dizzy.

"They're all mine, Dillon Frasier. All of them." She watched as the wheels turned behind those hazel eyes. "I've been busy. Don't you think?" The smile she held deep within her core began to surface as the reality of this man and his ability to remain composed was brought to light. She had been correct in her assumptions the day they met in the general store. But was he the one?

Dillon didn't know what to think. It would take someone ten lifetimes to collect if not write all these books. She was a young woman. How could she have done all these? Unless she was lying. "Impossible."

Mary Beth Robinson half-expected this. If he hadn't said it and had accepted her explanation flat out, then he would have branded himself a fool in her eyes and not worth her time. "I'll tell you what. Give me those two and I'll return them to their proper place in the bookcase. What I'm going to do is ask that you randomly pick and choose any or as many as want, look at them, skim through them, *investigate* all you want, Marshal, 'cause believe you me, Dillon Frasier of Irish descent, I've got all the time in the world."

He did as she suggested. For the rest of the afternoon and well into the night, he did just that. Each book had a different title, her name, and was about an inch to two inches thick. Dillon didn't pull all of them down, but almost. He eventually found himself sitting in one of the chairs in the room reading as best as his schooling allowed. After a time, he began to feel the urges of sleep pull him away from his appointed task.

Mary Beth Robinson watched from the other side of the room as Dillon Frasier thumbed through quite a few of her books. Then when he sat and began one, she knew in not too long a time he'd tire and finally fade off to sleep. After all, he was using her favorite chair, the one Toby had found for her those sixty or so years ago when they first met. The one she countless times fell asleep in herself, while reading, editing, and putting together the finishing touches before sending her various transcripts on their merry way to her publishers.

Oh, how she loved thinking of the help and understanding she received from the Establishment in which she used to live and thrive. How that special lottery had found for her a new life to enjoy instead of the turmoil of those times. The years before 2386 had been acceptable, yet they lacked the true meaning of life. She had always believed, ever since she was a small child, that she had been born in the wrong time, the wrong century, the wrong everything. Yes, she had her dreams of writing, but there was nothing of interest to write about there at home, unless you were a historian, and that period was chaos. So, when the Establishment had a lottery, offering "An Escape of a Lifetime" to the winner, she jumped to the opportunity, paid her dues, and to her surprise, won.

For her, since she did have a remarkable talent for writing, they added a special exception clause to the winnings. With the aid of a transference device, she was asked to travel to all ends of the All Mother, the Barrier, and sometimes even to that one solar system that housed those ten heavenly bodies, to collect and write about various stories and/or happenings. Stories of folklore, fantasy, nonfiction, fiction, and those special stories the historians always managed to find boring, unimaginative, even unbelievable, and therefore, ignored. Then off she'd send them through the transference device to the Establishment's leading publisher. Once they had the first copy in their historical museum, they'd send her the second copy right off the press and her payment in gold bullion to boot, hence, the many books on her shelves and her extremely large bank account in St. Louise.

The device also had given her a special treat that she hadn't expected, immortality for its users. As long as the device was in working condition, she could live forever. However, after those many centuries of visiting all those different places, times, planes, and realms, Mary Beth discovered that to live on the move always without a partner to share it with other than Toby was just not worth the effort. She had been everywhere and had written countless stories of unusual happenings and not-so-unusual occurrences. Now, she believed she was ready to settle down for keeps.

Once the termination slip, and her last payment arrived, she knew the Establishment was content with the collection she had provided, and since she wanted to remain in this part of the time continuum, she had asked Toby to smash the device, but instead, the still had blown. It was on its last leg anyway.

Originally Mary Beth had planned on smashing the device, tired that she was of traveling through the ages. But since coming to this century, this world, and this little town with its plain, simple, strange, and sometimes very interesting folk, found new meaning to her dulldrum life and her writing. Those who were born here, grew old here, and eventually died here had stories unmatched by those in other places, other times. That and those not afraid of her would sit for hours and listen intently to stories she'd written millenniums past.

They and Mr. Hoganberry were the reasons she was glad that the still had blown before Toby broke the device. Now all she had to do was notify the Establishment that her book writing was to start anew, and she'd be off again on some other foolish adventure.

The only thing that was missing was a man to share in her life. She had done quite a bit of searching for a compatible man during the times and places she had visited, but most of the men were too complicated for her tastes. Hopefully, she'd find one here in the next few years, and if not? Well, maybe she'd move on to another town, another world, another time, and start her search anew.

Returning her attentions back to the man in front of her, she realized that the afternoon had passed by without hardly a word spoken between the two of them, especially since this man of Irish descent's attention was elsewhere. Mary Beth, then, took just a moment to consider the possible outcome resulting from her momentary loss of common sense in allowing Dillon Frasier access to her basement. If she hadn't fallen so hard and fast for this damnable man of Irish descent who, unknowingly to him, had stolen her heart the moment she'd first laid eyes on him, she might have had more time to feel him out. Instead, she had played the fool and allowed him past the threshold of time and space. The more she thought about the whole situation, the more she realized that some sort of correction need be taken. So, as the afternoon progressed, a plan took form.

When she realized this Dillon Frasier of Irish descent was falling asleep as she figured he would eventually, she snuck out of the room and commandeered Toby's help.

"Dillon. Dillon Frasier."

A soft whispered voice came to Dillon from what seemed so far away, and as he stirred, it came again.

"Dillon."

"Hmmmmm?" He wanted to, but couldn't focus.

"Come. You can't sleep here." Try as she might, her words were not getting through. She could've dumped a bucket of water on the man's head, but not only was that no way to begin a friendship, it would've ruined her favorite chair. So, with Toby's help, the two of them pried a half-asleep Dillon Frasier from his chair. "By the All Mother, he's heavy," Mary Beth added as they continued to painstakingly begin to half-lead, half-carry him up the stairs and away from the secret rooms below.

The moment they stepped through the threshold of the rooms upstairs with Dillon still half-asleep and leaning almost all his two hundred pounds on Mary Beth, Toby turned back towards the opening to the basement.

"Toby, wait. Help me get him to the couch first," Mary Beth said.

At the couch they laid down, then covered, the unconscious Irishman with a blanket. When still he didn't stir, they knew he was out for the count. As Toby took the first vigil, Mary Beth headed back for the basement and returned with several selectively chosen books from downstairs. Some she stacked along the baseboard. A single, she gently placed upon the Irishman's stomach. This one she left open, as though partially read. Toby then hurried over to the basement door and pulled the lever, which closed the secret panel, making the door invisible to unknowing guests.

With everything in place, she and Mary Beth headed towards the kitchen for their nightly ritual of toasting to themselves, to their other enterprising and profitable hobbies, then finally to the man of Irish descent on the couch, and to the fortune he may bring to them all.

XXXV

early one bright morning...

It had been two days since Dillon's mysterious encounter at Mary Beth's house. Thinking back to that day, what he could remember didn't fit with what he thought happened. He remembered entering her home with a package. A package Mr. Hoganberry asked him to deliver, which he did. From there, Dillon remembered a dark stairwell and corridor followed by a room where the walls were lined with a thousand books. He could remember words describing gray-skinned creatures from somewhere, entities with wings, star-lit skies, cows and moons, and dancing owls, but from there on in, his memory failed him.

He remembered waking up on Mary Beth's couch covered with a blanket and an open book resting, binding up, on his stomach. A book he vaguely remembered looking at the night before. But the room. The room with all those other books that lined the walls, the one in which he could distinctly remember, was now nowhere to be found. Not only that, but the house was silent, as though dead. After waking, he searched the house and grounds for either Mary Beth or that other woman, as well as the entrance to the basement and that room, but couldn't find crap. He did find evidence to Mary Beth's existence, but from what he could tell, she just wasn't home.

Had it all been a dream? Dillon was beginning to think so, until he ran into Mr. Hoganberry on the afternoon of Dillon leaving Mary Beth's house. When Mr. Hoganberry stopped him, he inquired as to Dillon's success with the package. That in itself said that his visiting her was real enough. All he had to do now was find her and clear up the rest. It wasn't until Dillon began picking up on the latest gossip that he began to really wonder if finding her was going to be possible at all.

It was just his luck that Cordell had all the latest gossip recently learned at the general store.

"Dillon," began Cordell.

"What is it, my friend?"

"From what I've heard, you'll not be seeing Mary Beth anytime soon. She and Toby Bicker left town. At least, that's what I hear."

Cordell had been concerned for his friend during the time he was away, until he spoke to Mr. Hoganberry at the freight office. There he learned many things, most of all that the fears he held for his friend and his safety were totally unnecessary. Mary Beth was good, a wholesome and honest girl who arrived in this part of the country many years before there even was a town. Inasmuch as the townsfolk believed she arrived after they established Cascade, she was actually here long beforehand. Also, Mary Beth had many shipments delivered to her over the years. No one knew what exactly was in those boxes, or from whence they came, only that they were extremely heavy and that they were packed and freighted with strict instructions as to their care. Cordell had also been told that Mary Beth and Toby usually left town this time of year for a few weeks or so, returning just before the first break of spring. Then they'd go again in midsummer. This, he explained, was a yearly occurrence as far back as Mr. Hoganberry could remember. This got Cordell a-thinking. That was when he asked Mr. Hoganberry about who took care of her place while they were gone. His answer surprised Cordell.

"This year, I believe, she hired Andy Simms," answered Mr. Hoganberry to Cordell.

All this, Cordell passed on to Dillon.

"Left town? In this weather! Is she coming back?"

"From what Mr. Hoganberry said, they've been doing this twice a year for many a year now," Cordell added.

"What do you mean many a year? That woman is a mere child, Cordell."

"That's what he told me," Cordell said.

"Where does she go? When will she be back?"

"He said they usually return before the first spring thaw; as to where they go and why, no one knows."

"Damn her hide!"

"Dillon?"

"Yeah?"

"You're sounding a tad attached. What are your feelings towards her?"

"I don't know. I really don't." As Dillon ran his fingers through his hair, he thought about Cordell's question. Dillon really didn't know the answer. Sure, he was attracted to her. Any man in their right mind would be. However, he had too much to do and too many things he'd learned in the past before he could or would let himself consider a woman, any woman. Let alone one of questionable normalcy.

"You must feel something for her; otherwise, you'd know. Dillon?" Cordell began.

Dillon didn't know how to answer Cordell's question or what to think at this point. There were too many veiled paths and not enough distinct thoroughfares.

Cordell could see the befuddlement on his friend's face. Taking the reins in both hands, he tossed him an alternate thought.

"Ya know, we could…after this thing with Jesse, Carl, and the treasure is over with, if you want, we could come back here, to Cascade. Maybe by then you will know which road to take. We might even have jobs waiting for us." Cordell had been thinking again.

Dillon thought about this. Thought about it a lot. "Ya know. You might be right. And if'n we catch Carl, Jesse, or find that blasted sphere, I'll wager we'll be needing jobs." That made him think for another moment. "Speaking offhandedly of Glen, where is he anyway? I haven't seen or heard of him since that last blast in the street."

"Dillon, all you've seen is Mary Beth Robinson. Even when you're with me, your mind is on her. Glen found himself a whore and has been keeping rather busy between meals. Correct me if I'm wrong, but this is a small town located far from anywhere, and this is the middle of winter. If I wasn't so damned sure that I was going to find myself a wife someday, I'd find myself a whore to keep me warm too."

"What makes you think one of them whores isn't what you're looking for?" Dillon asked.

Cordell thought a moment. "Ya know, I never thought a that. Maybe I'll have to check them out."

As to the other, Dillon guessed he just hadn't seen the whole picture until Cordell had brought it up. "Really been hung up on her, haven't I?" He reached over and fondly squeezed Cordell's shoulder with his hand.

"Coffee?" Cordell asked.

"Sure." At that they pulled up a couple of chairs, poured piping-hot coffee from the pot resting on the woodstove into two cups, then sat, and talked of times, and friends, past, present, and future as the cold winter days slipped by.

Three days later came a knock on the jailhouse door. When Dillon opened it, there stood a very cold and wet Mr. Hoganberry with a letter addressed to him.

"Come in out of that weather and stand by the stove, man; you're freezing!" The moment he stepped into the jail, Cordell took his coat and hat and quickly placed a piping-hot cup of coffee, with a shot of whiskey in it from the saloon, then placed him directly next to the stove.

"Brrrrrrrr. I'vvvvve ggggot a lllettter here fer ya, Mmmmmister Fraaaasier. Itttt's ffrrrrom Maarrrry Bethhh, I thinkkk," was all Mr. Hoganberry could get out.

Dillon gingerly took it from him. He didn't want to let on how anxious he was to read what she had written. Forgotten was Brina's devastating letter to the two of them since his feelings for her had been thwarted and assumed over. As he held the packet, his hands shook.

Cordell watched as his friend with anticipation and stepped in. "Dillon."

All Dillon could do was raise his head, looking into his friend's eyes. Cordell knew what Dillon was momentarily thinking, when he slowly extended his hand sending the packet Cordell's way, understood the gesture, and gently took it.

Cordell pulled the letter out and slowly unfolded it, but before he could read it aloud, Mr. Hoganberry momentarily interrupted.

"I just tthhought, I oughtta llet you know, there were three other lletters from her, adddresssed to others in ttown." As Mr. Hoganberry was warming up, his speech was improving.

Dillon had to know. "Do you remember who got the others?"

"One was adddressssed to the town council, one was addressed to mmme, and the other one, well, I'm sorry. I'm not allowed to say. I'm also not at liberty to say what mmmine was about, but I've ggot a prettty good idea what yours and the tttown counciiill's say."

At least Dillon now knew that he wasn't alone in this. And as he watched Cordell unfold the letter, he began to read it aloud:

To Mr. Dillon Frasier of Irish descent,

Forgive me for my sudden departure from town and your side.

We were called away, as it is normal for this time of year. I do not know if we shall see you before you leave Cascade. But I would like to think that should we see each other again, we would become good friends. Should you decide to return to Cascade and those who live here after your business abroad is finished, I, as well as others, would welcome you and your friend, Cordell Chevalier, back. We all need your friendship, courage, and protection against those who would do us otherwise.

Consider us, please.
Mary Beth Robinson

As Cordell wound up Mary Beth's letter, he turned his eyes towards his friend. "Well, Dillon, that's not quite what you expected, was it?"

"No. It wasn't." That's when Dillon turned to Mr. Hoganberry.

"Don't look at me, look towards the town council. They, more than me, can answer your questions—that is, if you choose to ask them," said Mr. Hoganberry. "And I want to thank you for the warmth of the fire and the coffee, but I should be getting back. If you'll be kind enough to retrieve my coat, as soaked as it is, I'll be leaving."

Dillon did as bid, then thought about her words as he watched Mr. Hoganberry step back out into the storm.

"Dillon."

Dillon closed the door to allow the storm to continue its wrath outside as he pondered the letter in his hand.

"What do you think?" asked Cordell.

"About what?"

"The letter, man, what do you think I mean? Don't ya think it says more than you read?"

"What difference does it make anyway? We're not going to be here. And who knows, Jesse or Carl just might kill us all in the process of apprehending either. There are too many things that can happen before I can think of"—he paused for a moment as his line of thinking changed in midstream—"her. Although it would be nice to have someplace to call home when this is all over, wouldn't it? If this all goes as planned, Eastern-Western will no longer be home. You and me, we'll need a place, and we'll need money. Perhaps, Mary Beth Robinson has given us the answer to our prayers. That is, if the same thoughts have been passed along as Mr. Hoganberry suggested. By the way, does he have a first name, this Mr. Hoganberry?"

"As a matter of fact, it's Walter. But I wouldn't be a-calling him that until everything is settled. He's just as secretive about his first name as Mary Beth is about some of the things she does."

That sparked Dillon's curiosity. "What things?"

"What things what?" Turnabout was fair play to Cordell.

Sometimes he could be so exasperating. "What kinds of things is she secretive about?" Dillon hadn't told Cordell of his experiences or that dream he assumed he'd had at Mary Beth's house.

"She just is. No one in town, other than Mr. Hoganberry, knows anything about her. And he's very limited in his knowledge. Maybe it's just that she seems that way because she keeps to herself. She doesn't visit or spend any time with anyone else in town other than the children and a few of the cowboys. Have you noticed that?" Cordell felt that some of his learned information needed to be heard now that Mary Beth was out of the picture for a spell.

"The children." Then abruptly, it came to Dillon. "The child!" He told Cordell about that day he spied Mary Beth in the middle of the snowy street with nothing but a shawl on and the little girl. "And now that you mention it, I have noticed how polite and considerate some of the cowboys are to her and how they heed what she says. I've even overheard a couple of them talk about her, and it's not in the same way as the townsfolk talk of her. Cordell, what…who is this Mary Beth Robinson?"

"Dillon. Let's head over to the saloon for a drink. I think we deserve one. We can further discuss this there."

The atmosphere in the saloon had a more hospitable feel to it than they had experienced since their first arrival in this little town. Once the storm doors were closed against the freezing temperatures outside, both boys stepped up to the bar and asked the bartender for their usual whiskeys.

But when their drinks came, it was Cordell who first noticed the different smell of his. Questioning its contents, he stopped Dillon from drinking his too. "Don't drink that."

The statement was ludicrous, but the sudden distress in his voice did the trick. Without pause, they both called to the bartender.

"Yes, gentlemen? Finished already? Would you like another?"

"This isn't whiskey. It doesn't smell like whiskey. What is this stuff?" Dillon demanded.

"I'm sorry, sir. Do you not wish a taste of our very best brandy? It is made especially for this saloon and this saloon only. It is our very finest. Please follow my example, and I will be happy enough to show you how to enjoy it to its fullest."

They watched in fascination as the bartender filled another glass with his elixir of their "finest" quality.

"I love this stuff," began the bartender. "Now, gentlemen…"

They followed his example as he held the glass to his nose smelling its fragrance, which they did find to be exquisite. Then, as he took a small sip of the liquid, they watched until they were sure it wasn't going to kill him, then followed suit. He was right. It was heavenly. "Where did you get this stuff, and what is it called?"

"It is called blackberry brandy, and from where do I get it? That, gentlemen, is something I'll never tell. Even in death."

Well, that summed it up. They were never to learn who his supplier was, but at least they could and would enjoy the blackberry brandy until and after the day of their departure.

As it turned out, Cordell purchased two extra canteens of that exquisite elixir. One was for the two of them after they left Cascade, and the other, Dillon was to learn, would to be his gift to Brina Louise Grant. It was to replace the brandy she had brought with her from the future, and since Cordell was so sure that they'd all meet again, he filled and kept the other just for her.

The coming of spring was just around the corner, and still there was no sign of Mary Beth Robinson or Toby Bicker. Without her in town, but still in Dillon's thoughts, gave him the time needed to question certain cowboys and children, especially Becky Lindsey, about her.

The cowboys told him "'Twas none of his business." The children, on the other hand, were a bit more cooperative.

"She reads us stories," was what Becky Lindsey told Dillon. "Stories of faraway places," she had added before walking off.

What she said kinda took Dillon back to some of those books he was sure of in Mary Beth's home. Maybe his dream was real after all. Some of those stories were of faraway places. Other than that, no one would say.

Although, about a week later, both Dillon and Cordell were approached by the town council. They wanted to know if, after their previous engagement was completed, they would be interested in returning to Cascade. It was almost as though Mary Beth's thoughts and words to them had been placed into the hearts and minds of the local townsfolk.

Perhaps they had been. Mr. Hoganberry had mentioned something about it a month or so back. Perhaps Cordell was right, and there was something else on her mind.

Spring finally hit, and with it came another letter from Mary Beth. Only this time, Dillon was the only recipient of her words. It read,

> *To Mister Dillon Frasier of Irish descent:*
>
> *I take pen in hand to write you a short note to apologize for my absence during this time. Springtime is my favorite time of year, and there in Cascade it is most beautiful. I am extremely sorry that I am not only missing the coming of spring, but I'm also missing your leaving.*
>
> *Not only have Toby and I been called away to meet with a supplier, but other things are pending as well. As I have mentioned to you in the past, I have traveled much in my life and have met many people. However, there have been few people who have touched a special place in my heart as you did that first time I almost hit you in the nose with the door in the general store.*
>
> *You, Dillon Frasier of Irish descent, have been on my mind of late, and that is why I must get this to you before you leave Cascade. As I have written to you before, in regard to your possible return to us, I have also mentioned my thoughts to the town council. This you may*

already be aware of. It is your decision and yours alone, whether or not to return.

I therefore send via this letter all the hopes and dreams you have set aside for yourselves and may all your future rainbows be colorful.

Yours very truly,
Mary Beth Robinson

Dillon took Mary Beth's letter and carefully folded it placing it in the same packet he had placed Brina's last letter to them. Then he took time to write a letter to her of his own, leaving it in the possession of Sir Walter Hoganberry, as Dillon found him to be of royal blood from a place so very far away and across the great waters to the east, as he knew he'd give it to Mary Beth upon her return.

To Mary Beth Dillon wrote,

Mary Beth,

Words have always escaped me. Not so with prisoners.

My life is in the hands of the All Mother and only She knows what the future holds.

Until the day arrives when Cordell and I ride back into your town, you must not forsake others. Promise me.

Dillon Frasier
(of Irish descent)

XXXVI

you can't get there from here

Three weeks following their departure of Cascade, they rode into Marcus. At first glance, the town didn't look too bad, but as they rode in further, saw neglect everywhere. The buildings' storefront windows and doors were all broken, bashed in, or boarded up. The wooden sidewalks were in shambles, the boards were out of alignment, and some were even missing. In some places, old and rusty nails were sticking straight up—not a safe place to walk at all. There were pieces of blown-off roofs scattered in watering troughs, walkways, middle of the streets, everywhere. The sides of the buildings themselves told the rest of the town's story. Again, here there were boards missing, and many were even losing their paint—blue, gray, brown, and white paint. Everywhere they looked, the stuff was peeling and hanging off Marcus's buildings in strips. It was a sorrowful and very sad sight.

The whole town reeked of abandonment.

About halfway down the main street's mess and debris, they found what was at one time the sheriff's office. Being the law themselves, decided to investigate. Ya never know what kinds of decorating ideas you can pick up while checking out someone else's home or place of business. Besides, who was going to stop them?

So, Dillon tied his trusty steed up to the rickety, old hitching rail out front, then stepped up to the door. What he found left him open-mouthed. The glass of the window, the wooden door and its hinges, the paint that covered, the wooden walkway upon which he stood, and even the curtains hanging inside the window were all extremely intact, fairly clean, the wood floor appeared well oiled, freshly painted, safe to walk upon, and clean as a whistle.

Dillon turned back to Cordell and Glen. "Just hang tight, I'm gonna try the door." Dillon stepped over to the door, gently grabbed its knob, turned, and pushed it in. It swung with a horrible *skrrreeeeec-cch*. That, he found, was quite interesting, especially since the hinges looked to have been recently oiled as well—a seemingly unimportant and forgotten-for-the-moment notation.

But the rest was not soon forgotten. What Dillon found inside was a sheriff's office in usable condition, neat, tidy, and with no cobwebs. The floor had been recently swept, the stove in the middle of the floor not only was clean but was also stoked and had a coffeepot resting on its ledge. The office had even been recently painted!! So strange compared to the rest of the town.

Dillon didn't walk in further as planned. Instead, turned back towards Cordell and Glen and told them of his find. It was at that moment when Dillon noticed, down a block or two on the other side of the street, a lone horse stood tied to a hitching rail. This led him to believe there was, in fact, a living, breathing soul hiding, drinking, or existing somewhere in this musty place. But instead of mounting with the others, he took hold of Cody's reins and proceeded to lead him, followed by the others, down to that one building where that one horse stood.

Once there, Dillon inspected the animal. The solid-black mare stood about fifteen hands was of good flesh and quiet. She was bridled with a modest headstall and reins, one of which was tied to the hitching rail, suggesting her rider to be inside. The saddle was a Territorial Rider's-issue McClellan, which is a very light and compact sorta rigging—making several things easier for the horse and rider.

The building the horse stood in front of was also freshly painted and sound. The sign above its opening suggested a saloon. Glancing around he found Cordell and Glen right behind him as he began his short climb up the steps, which were also quite sound as were the windows of the establishment. Apparently, their curiosity had gotten the better of them as well for Cordell and Glen dismounted, then tied their horses next to Cody.

Following Dillon's lead, they entered the Tumbleweed Inn and Saloon. It was funny. There they stood, the three of them at the threshold of this establishment feeling like *the three musketeers*. Dillon was in the center and flanking him, standing ready and able to take on the world, were his faithful companions. As they all glanced one another's way, each smiling from ear to ear, together, they stepped up and proceeded in unison into the saloon.

Once inside, their eyes adjusted to the dim lighting. There standing behind the bar was a bartender with several customers milling about. The customers paid their little group no mind, nor did the man behind the bar. The barkeep appeared to be very diligent in his task as he cleaned and polished each and every drinking glass with the filthiest rag Dillon had seen in years. He was dressed in a clean white shirt with fancy garters three quarters up his sleeves—quite a sight. The man wore an exquisite black vest that came together in front with two gold chains. On one side, both chains hooked on separate buttons then draped across to the other side with the lower chain mysteriously ending up somewhere within his pocket. The other held fast to a button on the opposite lapel. His blonde hair looked wet, but Dillon guessed it was waxed up against his head in a way that had created the curl right above each eyebrow. His mustache was also waxed and stuck out from under his nose three inches or so in each direction, with a curl on each end. His height was around six feet, Dillon wasn't real sure, not knowing if there was a floor-shelf behind the bar or not.

They watched him finish with one glass, then pick up another starting on it without giving them the slightest notice. Dillon even went so far as to step up to the bar as though wanting a drink (which would have tasted very good even in a dirty glass) and still got no reaction. He acted as though they weren't even there.

Dillon was about to say something when a noise was heard behind them. They slowly turned around, and there, leaning against the opening of one of the swinging doors, was a woman. She looked to be about five foot, five inches with mousy-brown hair. She wore not a dress, as most would expect, but pants similar to their own, a long-sleeved shirt, vest, hat, and had slung across her arm a dou-ble-barreled shotgun. On her vest, she wore a star—*a sheriff's star.*

"Excuse me, gentlemen. Would you mind telling me what you're a-doin' in town?"

She leveled her barrels their way. "We just stopped in for a drink and a rest, Sheriff. Then we'd be on our way." Plain and simple.

"Fine. Since you're here in the bar, I'm assuming you want a drink? Has Preston acknowledged you yet?"

"Who?" Glen was confused.

"Preston. The barkeep. Preston!" She loudly addressed the bar-tender. "These here gentlemen need attending. If you wouldn't mind finding a few *clean* glasses, I'm sure they'd appreciate a drink before their ride outta town." She then slung her shotgun back over her arm and walked out.

While she was addressing him, their attention was also focused on Preston. But when Dillon turned around to thank her for her time, she was gone. He stepped outside expecting to see her walking down the street but found nothing but tumbleweeds rolling along with the never-ending, ever-shifting dust. The horse was still there, but she was long gone.

When he turned back around to Cordell and Glen, he found them standing at the bar with Preston tending to whatever they asked of him, so Dillon sat down and joined them.

"Preston. Preston!" He seemed to be ignoring them again. That was at least until Glen slammed his fist down on the bar as hard as he dared.

The barkeep looked at them like it was the first time that day. "I'm sorry, what can I get for you, fellas?"

Was this man addlepated or what? "We already have our drinks; you've already brought them."

"I'm sorry, sir, would you like another?" Preston was standing behind the bar with his arms stretched out and his palms resting on the bar leaning their way, waiting for a reply.

Something wasn't right here, yet Dillon answered him all the same. "No, thank you. I think we've had enough for right now." Dillon wanted to finish his drink and get the hell out of the saloon as fast as his legs would carry him—something about this place gave him the heebie-jeebies.

"Shall we head on over to the sheriff's office for some answers?" he addressed his friends.

Instead, it was Preston who responded to Dillon's query. "Would you like me to come too, sir?"

"No. No, thank you, Preston, I think you'll do better staying here," Cordell told the barkeep.

"Whatever you say, sir."

Glen just looked at Preston while addressing his friends. "I thought you'd never ask." He was visibly relieved to be leaving and swallowed the last of his drink in one gulp, set his glass down on the bar along with his dollar, and joined Cordell and Dillon on their way out into the street.

"Dillon, what was with that nutty bartender? He sure was acting strange," Glen asked once outside.

"Speaking of spooky, how about that sheriff? And what about the people of this town? Where are they? Aren't there any? Surely there must be more than that bartender and that female sheriff—if that's what you want to call her." Cordell didn't like Marcus at all.

"I can't answer any of your questions. But I'll tell ya what, if we want answers, we'll probably get them at the sheriff's office," Dillon said.

"What if the sheriff is that woman?" asked Cordell.

"If she is, she is," said Glen.

"Let's see what we can find out." They untied the horses from in front of the Tumbleweed Inn and Saloon then turned back in the direction of the sheriff's office. Once there, they left their mounts in front and entered the office. There was not a soul to be seen. As they poked around the interior, Dillon spotted paperwork on the desk, with an ink well and pen. Being the so-called marshal that he was supposed to be, sat down in the sheriff's chair and began thumbing through the wanted posters, letters, and assorted garbage lying there. About halfway through the stack, he found a wanted poster, or a drawing, of a man who stirred memories. The man in the drawing held a strong likeness to Kane.

"Cordell. Come. Look at this." As he joined Dillon alongside the desk with Glen behind him, Dillon showed him what had just been found. "That's Kane, I'm sure of it." The only thing that set it apart from any other wanted poster was that there was no name and no reward being offered. It was just a drawing.

"Let's get out of here, see if we can find some answers." They left just as quickly as they arrived. They didn't even wait around long enough to check out the rest of the jail.

There was only one other building in town that appeared to have been preserved through time. There was a small boarding house on the same side of the street as the sheriff's office down the walk-way a tad. Still needing a place for the night our three cowboys took a chance, along with their horses and headed in that general direction.

Above this structure's door there was its carved sign: *Balistine Boarding House*. Inside they found a rather-clean establishment, but no one was there to check them in.

"Are you surprised?" asked Cordell.

"Not really," Dillon responded to his devious smile and question.

"Maybe we'll just wait a few minutes, and someone will come. After all, we are the only newcomers in town. There's bound to be news of our arrival," said Glen.

"Yeah, sure. Who's going to tell them? Preston?" Dillon was still perplexed as to what had happened in the saloon.

Regardless, it seemed a good idea at the time, so they wandered a bit. The Balistine boarding house was just that: someone's home. It was a small two-story building that, upon entering, one was greeted with a desk for registering, and behind the desk was a rather-long dining table. Behind that, Dillon assumed, was the kitchen, and to its left, the staircase that led to the rooms above. Here, again, the cobwebs were nil, the floor recently swept, yet all the furniture was dusty. The room though was freshly painted in yellow and white, which Dillon thought were horrible colors, but who was he to tell them what colors to paint when all they wanted was a good-night's sleep.

And since no one arrived right away to check them in, Dillon occupied himself for a time by reading the interesting signatures of those who'd been here before.

Molly Bolt	January 15, 0001821-ctmk2
MONTY MAYHEM	MARCH 3, 0001841-JKTO7.4
Patty Kake	June 27, 0001836-4etvk8
Emily Post	April 1, 0001840-jmip
Theodore Baire	June 15, 0001855-emytg3
Bea Cause	July 18, 0001862-mk
Otto M. Beale	August 98, 0001863-
Misty Waters	September 22, 0001871-
Sally Forth	January 30, 0001873-. cqyt3
Kane W. Frasier	April 1, 0001872.-cgqt4

Page 54

Chester Orland	June 1, 0001872
Sandy Hill	June 17th, 0001872.5 ~dsdqtdd
Jim Dandy	July, 000 1872 ~ pfm
Gertrude Lipshits	'tis none of your business when I was here!
Willy Makitt	September 13, 0001872~maybe
Scott Free	October 21, 001872~dggwexcc
Rusty Wyre	February 28, 001873~dwsddf
I. M. Warrington	June 26, 0001873ttgww6
Pierce Arrow Esq.	July 4, 0001873~note this date in history!
Slim Chance	August 33rd

Page 55

Hank O'Cheefe	no date
Dotty Matrix	U/wouldn't believe me anyway <grin>

There were more pages and more pages and more pages of folks whose signatures Dillon couldn't make out. Then as he turned to page 53, there it was, his first solid clue.

"Cordell! Glen! Come quickly!" As both rushed to his side, Dillon pointed at that one entry in the Balistine Boarding house register. There it was larger than life:

Kane W. Frasier, April 1, 0001872.—cgqt4

Dillon's brother was here in this town! Maybe even standing on this very spot! That meant he was indeed alive. And if this be true, what the hell had happened out there, why was he here, was it him who actually signed, and what the hell was he doing in this neck of the sector? Too many questions. Not enough, if any, answers.

They could stay there for the night. After all, it was a quiet little town away from the main road, even though it had its strange sides to it. What could go wrong other than everything? Dillon had to think of their stay as another delirious adventure.

Brina would've loved this place and this leg of the journey. Brina. Dillon often found himself thinking of her and Wolf—whatever or whoever he really was.

Later that evening in Dillon's room, he thought back to the shocked expressions not only on his own face but also on the faces of Cordell and Glen as they found clean silk sheets on all the beds in their rooms. After a short investigation, they found all the other beds in the boarding house were made up in the same manner. They may have been around for some time, but they were all real silk and all quite clean. This strange little town and its occasional surprises baffled them all.

While Dillon was taking comfort in his room and its surroundings while just finishing off a quiet drink before retiring, he heard footsteps outside and below his window. It couldn't be Glen or Cordell; they had already retired for the evening. Curious, he pulled on his boots, headed out of his room, and descended the stairway that led to the hall and the front door. There he stopped to listen more closely.

There it came again, the distinct sound of boots on the wooden walkway. It sounded as though it was coming from the opposite end of town, from an area not yet explored. The footsteps came sure and strong. Though dark, the moon shed enough light that if someone were to walk by the window, Dillon just might be able to identify them. The sound grew closer. He kept trying to see around the window's glass and down the walk hoping…hoping to get a glimpse of the owner of those boots; unfortunately, anatomy doesn't work that way.

Dillon was just about to reach for the knob when the sheriff walked past the window. Not being able to help himself, he turned the doorknob and stepped out into the night, as though walking out of a building that time of the night was a normal occurrence. It turned into a bigger surprise than expected when he was met with a pair of shotgun barrels pointing at him from about chest high.

"Wait, don't shoot!" It was her all right. Braced and ready to fire.

When she realized who it was and remembered she had run into this stranger down at the saloon earlier that day, she relaxed her stance a bit before addressing him. "What in the name of tarnation are you doin' up at an hour like this? I figured you for a more intelligent person."

"I'm sorry, Sheriff, I was just dozing off when I heard footsteps, and since there are very few inhabitants here 'bouts, I thought I'd take a look-see." They didn't even know her name. "What do they call ya?"

"They used to call me Sheriff Camille Donnelly. But no one calls me anything now days 'cept Preston. Regardless, I am still the sheriff of this town, and it's my responsibility to keep an eye on folks who visit and to patrol the sidewalks. And when that fateful day comes when I find him, he'll be here instead a me. If you'll excuse me, mister, I've got ma rounds to tend to."

Sheriff Camille Donnelly turned back towards the direction she was heading and continued her rounds, as she put it.

What did she say? *When that fateful day comes when I find him, he'll be here instead a me.* What was that supposed to mean? Dillon's instincts strongly suggested waking Cordell and Glen then leaving this town on the double. But since they had already retired, and the "sheriff" was making her rounds, well-armed and able, he felt relatively safe enough to return to his room. Regardless, come morning, they'd pack up and leave town, pronto.

Neither Cordell nor Glen had heard anything last night. Dillon wasn't really surprised. He was beginning to believe it was all in his head anyway. Taking heed of this mental warning on their way out, he decided to make one final stop at the sheriff's office for one last look at that so-called wanted poster of Kane.

After tying the horses up to the hitching rail, they all dismounted. Up the steps they tread; Dillon, being in the lead, reached the door first. Just when he was about to grab the knob, the door flew open. There standing in front of them was a very old gentleman with a broom in his hand and a sheriff's badge pinned on his shirt.

"Excuse me," Dillon began. "I was expecting to see Sheriff Donnelly. Are you her deputy?" The older gentleman looked about as old as the mountains with hair the color of new fallen snow. He wore brown pants, a blue shirt, a pair of spurs on his boots, and an old, ancient, and decrepit hat.

"Sheriff Donnelly? You mean Sheriff Camille Donnelly?" He looked at them with a smile across his old, wrinkled face. He hadn't seen her in years.

"Why yes. Isn't she the sheriff of Marcus?" Dillon was curious at his reaction.

"Actually, no…have ya seen her lately?" It had been a long time since this had happened. They didn't get visitors in Marcus 'cept once in a blue moon and sometimes not even then.

This conversation was just as strange as everything else Dillon and company had come across so far. "Actually, we ran into her at the saloon yesterday. You see, we were having a bit of trouble getting the attention of the bartender, and she was kind enough to bring us to his attention. Then I talked to her last night when I heard footsteps on the walkway. She was making her rounds at that time and didn't want to chat. Why?"

"Maybe the three of you ought to come in and have a seat. You'll need to be sitting down when I tell you *why* I ask." It always used to amaze him how she would continue to haunt this town after all these years.

"Well, yeah. We would appreciate some answers to some things. Especially the wanted poster sitting on top of her desk, or is that your desk?" This was going to be interesting.

"Well, it's actually my desk now. I'm Sheriff Robert Preston, and I've been sheriff of this collection of tumbleweeds, dirt, and strange occurrences for nigh on fifty years. Come on in, gentlemen, have a seat." He led them into his office and pulled the few remaining chairs left in town back away from his desk for them to be seated.

Glen was the first to ask. "If you're the sheriff, who's Camille Donnelly?

Sheriff Preston believed with the occasional retelling of Camille's story, she never would leave him, nor would she ever truly die.

"That, gentlemen, is an interesting tale. Once upon a time, back in the years of my great-grandmother, there was in this town a sheriff named Myron Blacksmith. He was a gentle and kind man who in reality had no business being sheriff. He was in love with a whore named Camille Donnelly. Unfortunately, Camille was in love with Preston Cole. Preston was the barkeep of the Tumbleweed Inn and Saloon.

"Although Myron knew of Camille's love for another man, his love for her ran deep. Wanting to save her soul from hell, since she was a whore and all, he established her in a position of high esteem. You see, his love for her was not physical, but because of who she really was and how the town felt about her, he was worried about her safety. So, he went against everyone in town and made her his deputy, thus believing he was saving her soul at the same time. As his deputy, she served him well and continued to see the bartender.

"Camille and Preston would have made a wonderful couple had she lived long enough to see her wedding day. Shortly before they were to be wed, there came the dreaded day when a drunken gunslinger was making trouble in the saloon. After Myron was called in to break up the fight, he headed back down the street towards his office. Out of the saloon the gunman staggered, saw Myron walking down the street, and shot him in the back.

"In three shakes of a lamb's tail, Camille heard of the dreaded deed and confronted the gunslinger. You see, even though she was in love with Preston, she still loved Myron deeply and was devastated upon hearing the news. Well, she went after the gunslinger with a vengeance, but her chance for justice was short-lived because it was over before she had much of a chance. She was no match for the gunslinger, even though he was drunker than a skunk.

"Preston later killed himself because he had lost his only true love. However, before he died, he declared his love by promising never to leave her side, even in death. It is his ghost who served you fellas your drinks there in the saloon. If he spoke to you at all and I'm sure he did, you now know why he didn't make much sense. The same goes with Camille. You must remember, gentlemen, they are not of this world, yet reside here in Marcus forever.

"They will never leave this place, and neither will I. You see, my great-grandmother was Camille's sister, and I'm the last of that line. I will stay here till it's my time to join them." Then he was quiet.

"That's quite a story, Sheriff. Do you also keep up the appearances of the saloon and boarding house?" Dillon was sure it was him; who else would it be?

"Yes. I do all that, too. Not many folks see that trail that takes off the main road and heads over this a-way. However, there are those out there with a daring spirit who would take any trail that hints of adventure. That, gentlemen, is why I stay here and keep certain establishments clean and neat. There are people out there like you who enjoy a good scare. Then, of course, I'm always here to still their fears and put them to rest with a good bottle or glass of whiskey followed by silken sheets till the morning lights. Sometimes the sheriff from out Park City way comes and stays for a day or two too. She feels sorry for me and keeps me well supplied for the year, knowing if there be any troublesome characters on the trail, I'd send her a telegraph and warn her. Yeah, I do that too—one of the jail cells, you probably didn't venture in too far, has a telegraph in it so I can keep in touch with the outside world."

"There is one more question." While he had been telling of his tale, Dillon had glanced over the top of the desk for that wanted poster they saw yesterday, noticing it was no longer here.

"Anything I can do for ya, just ask," Sheriff Preston stated.

"Yesterday, we found a wanted poster or a drawing here on top of your desk. It had a likeness to that of my brother. While we've been listening to your story, I see that it's gone."

"I never saw nothing on top of this here desk this morning or last night for that matter. Ya see, I was asleep over there in one of the cells, and I never heard nothin'. Did it have a name on it?" he asked Dillon.

"Isn't that a tad strange? Us seeing it and now it's gone?" Dillon inquired.

"It might've been Camille. She gets kinda silly sometimes. Plays tricks on folks. Once, a long time ago I was sitting at my desk here and heard that door squeak. When I looked up, I watched it slowly open about two or so feet, then slam shut. I nearly jumped out of my skin. I was sure it was Camille, 'cause when I got up to look outside, there was no one there—and the winds were not.

"Besides, 'twas their office. Now's it's ours, hers and mine. We share it, and occasionally she feels she has to remind me that it was hers at one time. Sorry, gents, I've no such drawing." Sheriff Preston had also on occasion found certain things in his office misplaced and scattered. Camille even went as far one day as to shuffle his deck of cards, dealing five hands of poker, knocked over the coffeepot on his stove, knocked over his broom, and piled tumbleweeds in the center of his floor. This is one reason why he no longer makes coffee in his office unless he plans to stay until the last drop is drunk. Nope. Nothing she did surprised him anymore.

"Hmmmmm. Okay. But back at the boarding house there's an entry in the register dated April 1, 0001872.cgqt4. Do you remember, by chance, the man who signed in?" Dillon wondered.

"Well, let me see. Like I said, we don't get many visitors around here, at least those willing to sign in. What was his name? Maybe that'll help." If he was only younger, maybe he could remember things easier.

"It's signed, Kane W. Frasier. Ring a bell?" Dillon was hoping.

Sheriff Robert Preston took a deep breath and exhaled it slowly, as though his memory might reveal something along with it. "Sorry, son, my mind just don't work the way it use-ta, and I don't remember names too well anyway other than the ones in Camille's story. On the other hand, I do seem to recall a couple of visitors back about that time. Ya never know, he just might have been one of them. Can't rightly say. But if you're saying your brother's name was in the boarding house register and that drawing you thought you saw yesterday was also of him, maybe he was here after all."

"We all saw the drawing," Dillon added.

"Well, fella, the only thing I can think of, and I'm sure you're gonna think I'm the one that's crazy, but maybe Camille took a fancy to him while he was here; she also liked to draw things. Who knows?" As he pulled his pocket watch out, opened it up, and glanced at the time, said, "Sorry, son, but I got to run. If'n you'd be kind enough to excuse me, it's about time for my nap—take one every day about this time. I sometimes need the extra energy come evening. Never know what Camille's got planned." With that he got up from his chair, headed back towards the cells, opened one squeaky door, then lay down on one of the cots, and closed his eyes.

They took the more than obvious hint, then turned to leave. Dillon called back over his shoulder, "Sure enough, Sheriff. And thanks for the story. We'll be on our way, and uh, take care of yourself and give my regards to Camille." Dillon couldn't keep from smiling, because Marcus had most definitely turned into more than any of them thought it would be.

BOOK 3

XXXVII

the die is cast

Once upon a time, in a land terribly far away, lived a man named Jesse Loame. Jesse was a man who was about six-four, with blonde hair, green eyes, and weighed in at anywhere between 200–240 pounds.

Jesse was a fighter. He was a planner. He was a survivalist. He lived well. He resided in a rather large estate, in a well to do neighborhood, with a pool, his own private yacht, a bird sanctuary, and lots of trees to hide behind. No one in the neighborhood knew him. No one in the neighborhood saw him. There were always rumors spread of what lay behind all those trees, but those who braved the fifteen-foot rock walls that surrounded the place, that were in front of those trees, never returned to tell of their find.

This was a very strange man. A very determined man. A very lonely man. This was a man without family. He had no wife. No children. No friends. He had had no brothers to beat-up, no sisters to molest. He was born in Foggy Bottom, TNesi, fourteen hundred miles east of Sector 5. His mother died at childbirth. His bastard father he killed on a camping trip when he was very young.

In the beginning, life was not easy for this man without friends, without family, without connections. And because of that, Jesse became a loner. He learned the only one he could trust was himself. He tried everything and anything just to get by. He found himself very diversified in his talents, in his abilities. He cleaned floors. He cleaned sanitary stations. He played doctor. He planted geraniums. He was a pilot, once. He pulled teeth. He played a medium at a séance—*ghosts and all*. He taught kids to play the guitar. He worked in the slave markets. He mined ore. He repaired small mechanical contraptions. He worked in financial institutions. He made a lot of connections over the years. He did a lot of favors for lots of folks. He learned to safely handle all kinds of weaponry. He did a bit of teaching in marksmanship. He worked on both sides of the law. He even masqueraded as a police officer once. He did such a good job at it, they promoted him four levels.

Having such vast talents and abilities eventually brought him to a group of mercenaries who hired out from time to time to anyone who'd pay their price. With them, he learned to do just about anything, whether it be marksmanship classes, teaching hand-to-hand combat, improving weaponry skills to those in need, pulling teeth, stitching wounds, or removing tonsils. In time, he escalated to highway robbery, high-tech thievery, from hit man to assassin, and sometimes a master of torture—disemboweling enemies of those paying him. Anything for cash. He needed a paycheck, needed the dough. Moneys received were usually laundered, then used to pay off his tree-lined estate and other fineries, finally making them all his.

Life was to be wonderful—for the man named Jesse Loame.

Then his big day came, or so it seemed at the time. From far away he was contacted and asked to come to Sector 4, where he was contracted by an organization he didn't know too much about. They had heard of his expertise in various fields and said they wanted him for a special job. The communiqué indicated a simple job, and a simple job it was supposed to be.

Well. If this simple job had gone as planned, he'd be sipping tequila under palm-lined, silky-blue skies right about now. But unfortunately, it hadn't, he wasn't, and wasn't about to be. Instead, the proverbial shit had hit the fan. He wouldn't have believed it possible, back then, but sure as shit, he knew it now.

He knew it now, because not too long ago he was forced to pull in some old favors for additional information on this particular hit. His informants said it was the Network who was behind the mess-up. They had done this to him. Jesse's other connections confirmed it, were sure of it. Sure as the sun would rise and set at the beginning and end of each and every day.

The information his connections had offered revealed that only the Network had the ability to carry out such a task. No other organization had those kinds of connections, that kind of pull. Jesse had some but apparently not to the extent of theirs. The Network had bottomless reserves, immense power, a zillion informants. They held mega money. They had the extensive agenda. They knew what they were doing. And above all, they had complete and absolute control over Sector 4's northern area.

Unfortunately, Jesse had not known any of this, and because of his ignorance, they had played him a royal fool. Played him as brilliantly as any flunky on a game board. Played him like a joker, a dice, a chess piece. And as with any game piece, these people strategically maneuvered him into position, manipulated his talents and expertise, then discarded him in one fail swoop once *their* winning play had been made.

He should've known. Should've seen it coming but hadn't. More than likely, the ploy had been in the works for months. He should've known all along they'd double-cross him. Absolute power corrupts absolutely. So those in power should never be trusted blindly.

The Regulators with whom he dealt set him up from the very beginning. Of this he was now sure. *They were the Network's best.* After all, he didn't fall off the turnip truck yesterday, he had friends, and his friends told him as much. The Regulators' jobs were to enlist, to fool, to deceive, to maneuver. Their job was to dangle a carrot afore his nose expecting him to snatch it, which he did—hook, line, and bloody damn sinker; in this they did very well. They took advantage of his good nature, his greed, his desperation, his need of a well-paying job.

He should've been more cautious. Should've read between the lines. Should've dissected the small print but hadn't. He'd been so oblivious to everything, except the proposal, the target, and especially the promised compensations that he'd missed the obvious—*it was all too good to be true.*

The ancient phrase "Hindsight is twenty-twenty" was often used to explain away many stupid maneuvers made by its participants after the fact—as was the norm. The problem was, no one made good of its premise back then, and unfortunately neither had he. Had he known what was to happen, he would've bade those involved farewell and left the sector, never to be seen or heard from again. But he hadn't. Instead, he allowed his greed and his desperate need of a good job to lead him to a most valuable lesson: *trust no one.* And because of who taught him, how they handled it, and especially because he hadn't followed his own rules regarding *trust,* Jesse decided right then and there *there'd be no more chances for anyone, anywhere, anytime, ever—none, nada, forget it, no way, José.*

To the original arrangement:

The original arrangement included an assassination, a place to hide, and a new life once the kill was made and recorded. Included also were terms regarding his return trip, his payment, and all accommodations thereafter. It was touched upon that such accommodations and arrangements were usually engineered specifically for each individual situation as was warranted. Yet they failed to state where exactly the safe house was, just that it was where no one could find him, where he would be safe, and out of harm's way. Such specifications of any and all negotiated agreements were always documented in writing, with blood oaths taken and imprinted upon all copies of the written contracts. *(Such a contract was worth its weight in gold; thus, Jesse kept his copy, in a secret pocket hidden deep within his very own knapsack, assuming it would be his insurance policy should the shit hit the fan at a later date.)*

After the assassination:

Jesse was told to infiltrate Cyclops's Time Room, where both the Zodiac Field and the Franciscan Lifter were stationed and operated. He was to secure the area, then set the dials on the lifter to 00001872.xxt--55893866-5. Then he was to stand on its platform and wait for transport.

He knew exactly what to expect. The Network's representatives didn't elaborate on where exactly he was going or what he was to find there, *other than the assumed safe house.* Jesse, being in no position to argue—*being on the government's ten most-wanted list*—believed them, but not so much that he ignored old habits. Instincts told him to take his best rifle and as many cartridges that his knapsack could carry. In it he took additional provisions, such as water, crackers, peanut butter, jerky, a hat, and a few extra clothes. He didn't expect trouble, but you never could tell.

When he arrived at his "retirement site," he was floored. There was no safe house anywhere. Nothing as far as the eye could see. Just a vast land covered with gray-brown grass and stupid rocks. The absurdity of it all, what he was seeing, what he was finding, was getting the better of him! He felt his initial irritation manifest itself into rage. At what? Rocks? He became obsessed with the objects and with the vegetation he was forced to traverse. Thousands upon thousands of stupid, ugly, and colorless rocks. Some of these horrible rocks were round, most were jagged—all were gray, green, brown, ugly, and stupid! The massive round ones he had to climb over and around, the smaller jagged ones he had to walk and stumble across— eventually they worked their *magic* through the soles of his boots, through his socks and eventually blistering his feet. Damn, damn, damn, damn!

Over time and many miles, the landscape did finally change, but not to his satisfaction. All he wanted was to find what he'd been promised—*the safe house.* Unfortunately, where he looked, there was nada. No vibrant colors, no refinement, no cities, no nothing. Nothing he expected, but a foreign and desolate land covered in nothing but those bloody, damn, shitty, crappy, stupid rocks, and ugly red and green weeds.

The more he thought about the whole situation and what he'd found, or better yet what he wasn't finding, the more pissed he got. This crappy land he had found himself in was brimming with antiquity. There were no powered vehicles, no personal means of transportation, no transport devices. There was no oasis, no sand, no palm trees to sit by, no umbrella drinks, no mild temperatures. There were no women to his liking; there was no one to meet or greet him as planned—no one. No one at all.

Something was up. The feeling was all wrong. *Not completely wrong, after all, the sun did rise and set when it was supposed to.* But *this place* was totally out-of-place with what he'd expected, what he'd envisioned, what he'd been told. It was a horrible place. A place he wanted to get out of, to leave, to depart from, to vacate, to bid farewell to, to split from, and for it to happen now!

Unfortunately, nothing could be done without help from the other side. And when he left the chamber, all were made dead.

As per his instructions…

He wasn't in the future as promised; he'd been exiled to the distant past.

The Network had placed him in a faraway place all right, and at the same time, put away the playing pieces and packed away the game board.

Once the initial shock wore off, he realized he had no other choice but to go forward. To go forward meant survival. To survive, he learned to blend in. Whether it be in the mountains, on the prairies, over hill, over dale, through the heat of the deserts, the freezing temperatures of the winters, he made a go of it. He watched the people around him, learned from them. He learned to imitate *their* habits. He accepted and wore *their* garments, mastered *their* phrases, became familiar with *their* cultures, ate *their* foods, ingested *their* beverages, discovered and expanded upon *their* monetary exchange values—hating every minute of the above—and indubitably broke *their* laws.

His first experience with the locals proved invaluable, as was his first town. There, he found a rather small, minuscule sorta village in size, with little refinement and/or wealth. Curious, he investigated. He checked out every building: store, bank, school, resident, house of ill repute, nook, cranny—everywhere. North to south, east to west, attic to basement, aft to bow, starboard to port—he searched the town. First and foremost, he needed some friendly release. The rest—travel supplies, money, food, and a means of transportation—

would be procured shortly thereafter. Some gave willingly, others not so.

When he finally did decide to leave, he did so in a hurry, and atop an animal not of his choosing. The beast wasn't as difficult to deal with or to maneuver as were the bank tellers and mercantile clerks, and it did save wear and tear on his feet, but the sucker had a mind of its own, and he had to fight with that constantly, proving beyond a measurable doubt that this place was not to his liking. Not to his liking at all.

He didn't like the clothes, didn't like the footwear, didn't like the hats. He didn't like the vegetation, didn't like the weather, didn't like the modes of transportation, didn't like the insects biting him all the time, didn't like the lay of the land. He didn't like the way the people talked, didn't like *their* hairstyles, didn't like them themselves either. He didn't like *their* food stuffs, didn't like the dirt and dust, didn't like the antiquity of the weaponry, and especially didn't like the posses, or *their* intent.

For months Jesse shot up many an outrider, trying as they might to ambush, track, corral, or capture him while he hightailed it into and through the wide-open spaces, between small well-placed jobs here and there. Those who placed bounty on him for all his thievery, shootings, butchering, murders, and rapes even went as far as sending messages, across ancient telegraph wires, assuming *their* urgent messages would reach the next town before him, in hopes that someone could and would try *their* hand at his capture, but it never happened. He was too smart for them.

His skill with his own rifle and the efficiency of its ammunition foiled all attempts at bringing him in. At least until the titanium blues ran out. Once those were gone, he had to rely on *their* ammunition, and *their*s wasn't as accurate as his. His was the same caliber, but *their*s didn't compare. *Theirs* loaded and performed well enough but didn't carry the same push, the same accuracy, nor did they have the same velocity as the blues. It was unfortunate really, the titanium blue hollow points with their gray casings had given him the additional edge he thrived on, needed, in this hostile, foreign, and desolate land. But now, they were exhausted. And so were his carefree days. He now had to rely more on *their* antique ammunition, the blasted animal he rode, his instincts, his learned skills, than to rely totally on the Blues.

Jesse knew, and logic dictated, that it was only a manner of time before he'd get careless in his flight, or that the authorities would get smarter and cleverer than he in their pursuit of him. He knew they'd eventually catch or kill him, but until that fateful day arrived, he would continue his merry search for wine, women, and song, followed by murder, mayhem, thievery, fun, profit, and adventure.

As per his instructions…

XXXVIII

hold yer horses

Cordell, Glen, and Dillon had been in the saddle way too long. Dillon's butt hurt, his ankles ached, his throat was parched, his back was killing him, he was hungry, and the sun's constant heat was frying his brain like a burnt steak. And of course, thinking in those terms didn't help his appetite none. And if he felt that bad, imagine how the rest of his party felt. They needed water, the horses needed watering, all of them needed a place outta the sun, a place to lay back, some decent food, rest, and someplace to put their feet up for a spell. They needed a break, and badly. Unfortunately, there had been no watering holes, no trees for shade, and no relief from the blistering heat since high noon two days ago.

The hot sun. Hours spent in the saddle. Combined, they can alter a man's mind, just like a good woman. They can make you see things that ain't there. You can search the horizon for a glimpse of anything other than nothingness and find a lone barge floating without water somewhere between the pale earth and the lifeless, gray sky.

They trudged onward, each in their own private and silent hell. What went on in his friends' minds was beyond knowledge, but Dillon's wandered back to times spent with Brina, then on to Mary Beth. Both women held a special place in his heart, for each had brought forth emotions thought long ago buried. Then there was Kane and their childhood together. Was Dillon ever to see any of them again? He didn't know. Those questions and many more bounced in and out of his thoughts for several days.

Upon reaching the top of a grassy knoll, they all stopped their mounts to survey what lay ahead, hoping it was different than the last hundred miles. It was, but not in the manner expected. Behind them was a country they thought was an endless prairie. Below and beyond lay a land as white as salt. Dillon would've said snow, but it was the wrong time of year—too hot. *Waaayyy toooo hot.*

What was there was a sea of sand, and it was the whitest stuff he'd ever laid eyes on. Miles and miles of white. It stretched ahead like the future. On and on, as far as the eye could see. Never-ending, even after death. Even the sky took on the color of the ground. A ground that only moments ago was flat, brown, gray, green, and rocky now had the gentle curvature and color of a good woman's breast—only without comfort, without contentment, without solace. And at this time, and in this gawd-forsaken place, Dillon could've used a good woman's breast to give solace, contentment, and comfort. Anything to keep him from losing his mind.

But that's not what he had. That's not where he was. He was in the middle of nowhere with two friends, three horses, scant supplies, two flasks of brandy, and sections upon sections of white, white sand. White. White. Endless white sand. This was something he didn't expect—something he did not want to see, something he did not want to cross, but had to. For Jesse's trail had led them here, and sand or no sand, this great expanse of white was where they were to cross. So, ride on they did, reluctantly.

By late afternoon, on this one of many long, long days spent in the saddle, they'd traveled countless miles without seeing a single blade of grass. If Dillon had been a horse, he would've bucked off his riders at the last watering hole and stayed there—or run for the last livery stall visited. This attitude and knowledge made them all very tired, irritable, and concerned for what lay ahead. They had scant supplies in their saddlebags other than the brandy acquired for Brina, and that Dillon wanted to save. Neither had any of them seen or heard a single bird, rock, plant of any kind, any body of water, or animal during the day or night. It was as though their entire world had been swallowed up by this massive sea of powdery matter that billowed and filled the air with each gliding step the animals below them took. Cordell, who was riding point, wasn't affected by this too much, but the rest of them coughed, hacked, and blew their way west. They were lucky at first. There was little wind to speak of—just that powdery matter from the sand, and a very slight breeze letting them know they weren't so awfully alone.

On the fifth day, the winds picked up. In the very beginning they weren't so bad, but only moments later they became horrible, blowing hats, hair, manes and tails. It made their trip miserable. It blew the sand everywhere. It was in their hair, eyes, ears, clothes, noses. It was hard to breathe even with handkerchiefs over their faces. The horses were covered and not happy at all. They couldn't see shit. They had to stop. Dillon didn't want to, but they had no choice. They couldn't ride blind. It just weren't smart. If they didn't stop, they could end up in Timbuktu on the far side of the eastern slope of the sector if not careful, so stop they did.

Dillon wanted to stop at the base of a small gully, but Cordell would not allow it. He said that should the winds increase in strength they could find themselves buried under ten feet of the dirty silt come the morrow. So, against Dillon's better judgment, they found a flat spot on a downhill side of a dune facing south and planted themselves there. Knowing horses as he felt he did, he believed they'd be most comfortable with their butts facing the wind, so that was how they were placed. Dillon considered leaving them saddled, but thought should they spook, all their meager supplies would disappear into nothingness, along with their only means of transportation. He also believed they might use the saddle blankets for partial cover and protection. So, with the reins gripped tightly in their hands, they dug into the saddlebags for halters and lead ropes, placing them accordingly. Now they had three leads to cling to, instead of two for each horse. Leather would break if pushed hard enough; the rope leads were more reliable. The horses were then situated between the north wind and our boys, on the downhill side of the dune where they sat down tightly together to ride out the storm. The decision to unsaddle the horses and sit together in their paths might not have been the smartest, but in this case, it worked quite well.

As Dillon sat huddled with his friends trying in vain to heed the blowing sand, he thought of where he was, who he was with, and why they were all here. It made sense two years ago, but under the circumstances made little now. Through all their past experiences—the letters, their discoveries, the towns, finding Brina, meeting the Gray Wolf, stumbling upon Mary Beth and the other inhabitants of Cascade, all the invisible leads regarding Jesse and Kane— Dillon still found it very hard to believe they had nothing to show for their troubles, but the miserable sand in their hair.

By the following morning, the wind had ceased its bombardment. It was still. Although alive, all of them found sand in places no one wanted to admit, but at least the horses were still there. One could barely see them for all the sand and dirt, but they were standing like faithful dogs, right where they'd held them. After brushing them, shaking out clothes, dusting off the riding gear as best as they could, our boys saddled up, and off they rode.

Dillon's brain was still working overtime. Were they to get across this great expanse with their minds and bodies intact? Fate had brought all of them here to this place. Fate put them together. And fate put Dillon in charge. Fate, Kane, Jesse, and most of all, Brina. They all brought Dillon here as sure as the sun would rise on the morrow, if only to bake their brains like an overly done apple pie—crusty on the outside, dry and sticky on the in.

"Dillon! Look!" shouted Cordell.

Snapping back to the present, Dillon saw him pointing off towards the horizon.

"Trees!" exclaimed Glen. "If there are trees, there's sure to be some kind of water."

Inasmuch as they all wanted to race to the trees, Dillon couldn't bring himself to do it. What if it was another hallucination like that barge? Cody was not the only thirsty and exhausted member of their entourage, and Dillon couldn't take the chance of finding nothing there but misery and disappointment. It would be an added drain on their hopes as well as their strength and especially reserves if they raced the distance. Yet as they forced the animals to walk on, the trees became larger and greener, and their hopes and expectations continued to climb.

Suddenly, Cody's ears shot forward as his head and neck stretched higher and higher as though there was something he didn't recognize up ahead. He began to snort and blow air in and out of his nostrils. Instead of walking forward, he started dancing and fidgeting sideways and backwards. If that wasn't bad enough, his fear was transmitted to Glen's horse instantly. As they all began to act spooky and the likes, Dillon wondered what the hell lurked up ahead within the many trees.

Suddenly a shot rang out, and seconds later, the sand exploded at their feet. Cody leapt sideways. To keep from falling, Dillon's knee had wrapped itself around the saddle horn holding him three feet from four dangerously frantic hooves. "Cody, whoa! Whoa, son. Damn it, horse—whoa!"

Glen's mount wasn't doing much better, but at least he had some sort of control and was still in the saddle.

Baldy, on the other hand, was totally at ease and unafraid, with a very surprised Cordell sitting atop his back. So, without further ado, Cordell eased Baldy over towards Dillon and his mount, grasping the bit, bringing Cody to his side, thus allowing the calming factor of his own mount to calm his friend's so that he could again regain his seat and some control.

"What the hell?" Dillon demanded.

"Don't know." Cordell didn't understand either. But of course, nothing in this crazy sea of sand made any sense to him. Not finding another living creature for miles, let alone a single blade of grass, then unexpectedly finding a stand of trees in the middle of nowhere? All he could do was shake his head.

Glen's horse, on the other hand, had bolted with him gripping the reins.

"Glen, are ya still with us?" Cordell yelled after him.

Finally gaining some control, Glen answered with a "Yeah. I'm still here. What the hell is the matter with these damned beasts?"

"Damned if I know. But I suggest we take a firm hold of these frightened puppies as we ride closer to them trees. Whatever spooked them could still be there, and if it is, we could be in for a hell of a ride." Planting his backside as deep into the seat as possible, Dillon took a firm grip on the reins, as did the others. Then onward they inched, closer towards the trees ahead.

"Hold yonder seats, gents," came a loud, booming voice deep from within the trees.

Suddenly, without warning, another shot rang out, again followed by another explosion of sand directly in front of our boys. This time, they were ready, and even though the horses lunged sideways, all except for Baldy, they managed to remain seated.

"Hold your fire!" Dillon yelled back.

"Go way," yelled the voice.

"We can't. We need water!"

"Go way," the voice yelled again.

"We can't, there isn't—" Dillon wasn't given a chance to finish, when another shot rang out.

"Dillon." Cordell looked at his friend for a moment. "Let me."

"You're kidding. You can't just—"

"I can." Cordell let go of Cody's reins as he turned his own mount towards the trees and away from his companions. Baldy stepped sure and steady as Cordell coaxed him towards the trees and the unknown voice. He didn't really have the nerve to continue, not knowing what lay ahead for them, but continue he did. Knowing full well and good that if someone didn't, they'd eventually all die of thirst before the week was out—especially if this was the only source of water in this sand trap. That and Baldy's unusual undying courage of this particular unknown gave him a false feeling of being invincible.

"Stop! I'm warning ya fer the last time, stranger! D-d-don't come any closer!" hollered the voice. A little less booming.

Cordell stopped Baldy momentarily. "All we need is some water," he said in a calm and friendly voice. "We've traveled many days across this great land, our supplies are low, and all we want is some water for the animals. Haven't you got a heart for dumb, thirsty critters?"

The voice was silent.

Cordell, realizing that the voice hadn't answered, cautiously urged his mount forward one step at a time. When he got within twenty or so feet of the trees, he not only saw movement of some large gray form from somewhere behind the trees, but also got a whiff of a ghastly and totally unfamiliar smell that forced a halt to all forward motion. "What the hell is that?" he muttered aloud.

"Oh. Thems my Tirza," answered the voice. "She no hurtz ya. She just—" Just then came a horrible sound from the other side of the trees, followed by a louder crashing sound.

Baldy was still steady and sure. To the complete confusion of Cordell, of course, his trusty mount continued to remain as solid as an old oak tree.

In amazement Dillon watched the episode unfold from several yards away and still couldn't believe his eyes. Here was an animal that appeared fearless against an unknown force, which hid itself within the stand of trees ahead. Something wasn't right, but for the life of him, he couldn't imagine what it could've been.

"Scairt," the voice said.

Cordell, not wanting to back down, dismounted Baldy, then led the horse towards the trees.

Nothing further was done to frighten off either of them.

With Baldy's reins gripped firmly in one hand, Cordell cautiously led his mount up to then around the stand of trees. What he found on the other side blew him away.

"Howdy, pard! Now that yer here, how 'bout a drink?" it said.

The voice emanated from an old and faded cavalry officer's uniform with an ancient-looking individual inside it, resting against a large boulder. The man's trousers had red stripes down the sides of the legs, and his boots were cracked and caked with mud as was the rest of him. The hat he wore was of military issue but was green and purple in coloration. Cordell assumed that was either from the dust off the trees, its antiquity, or something else altogether. The old man's face was leathery and crusty, but his green eyes showed an intelligence that pierced through the stubble on such a leathered face.

"Who are you?" Cordell asked.

"Sarg Sam Osburn. At yer service, sir," the crusty old officer answered as he saluted the stranger, then held up towards him a canteen.

Cordell looked at the canteen. "Water?"

"Water," answered the officer.

"May I?" asked Cordell as he gingerly reached towards it.

"Let me ask ma Tirza," he responded.

Cordell was about to question the statement but stopped short when the boulder the officer was leaning up against began to move. "What the...?" Cordell, not knowing what was about to happen or what the boulder was, quickly backed his horse several feet.

Baldy, of all animals, was the first to respond to it, with a nicker. Cordell watched in total amazement as his own horse, the one he'd been riding for the last several years, nickered to the boulder with ears up and alert.

The large boulder began to rock to and fro, as its eight-foot-long neck emerged from its hiding place from the other side—away from Cordell's initial view. It had a head that could've been about a foot long, which was shaped not too much unlike a horse. To Cordell, it looked as though it tried to stand, as the hindquarters ascended first, like a cow's, with the front following. Once on its feet, it proved to be an awful sight. "What is a Tirza?" he questioned hesitantly.

"Tirza?" The officer glanced at the beast. "A Tirza is a *grkdkuu*."

"A what?" Cordell again asked.

"A grkdkuu," the officer answered proudly.

Cordell assumed the man was addlepated, and therefore, ignored the explanation. "What's it used for?"

"She used for," responded the officer.

Cordell didn't understand at first but caught on quickly. "She, okay...what's she used for?"

"Don't ya know? We had a whole troop of 'em at one time. But when they decided to disband, we left. Ya see, Tirza and me? Well, weze in luv."

Oh great, Cordell thought to himself. A military uniform and a walking rock—in love. It was then Cordell looked closer at the grkdkuu. The thing stood six feet taller than his own mount at the shoulders, had a rounded back with a long, stringy tail at its end. Its feet had a broad and cushioned look to them. Its hair was very long, brittle looking, and its coloring matched that of the sand. He wondered what a sight it would be to see an entire troop of these animals. Any enemy in their right mind, upon seeing such an assemblage, would instantly flee. If one could stand the smell and their looks, it could just work.

"What does she eat?" Cordell was curious.

"Whatever she wants," answered Sam Osburn.

"Whenever she wants to too, I'll wager," Cordell inadvertently commented with a grin on his face. Then he added, "Sam, is there any major water here 'bouts?"

"Yep."

"May I?"

"Huh?"

"My horse, their horses too, need water. May I?" That wasn't all they needed, but since the sarge responded kindly to dumb critters, Cordell used Baldy as an excuse.

"Tirza said it was okay, didn't ya hear her?"

Now he knew for sure the officer was addlepated, crazy, or had been in the sun way too long. "Thanks, you're mighty kind." Cordell then looked around assuming it would be close by, and finding nothing but the trees, the officer, and the grkdkuu, asked, "Where is the water?"

"The, what?" asked the old cavalry uniform.

"The water, for the horses. Where is it?" Cordell was beginning to feel as though this officer was related to Preston.

"Oh. The water for your horse." The old officer held his chin for a moment or two as though trying to remember. "Near the empty lake."

Cordell was a patient man, but this walking, talking, leathery military uniform was exasperating. "The, what?"

429

"The empty lake. The one over that rise." The officer pointed in a westerly direction from where they stood. "That's where I sent that other feller."

Cordell was instantly interested. "What other feller?"

"The one Tirza bit."

"When did this happen?"

"What time is it?" asked the officer.

Cordell glanced up into the sky, ascertaining the approximate time of day from the location of the sun. "Late afternoon."

"Day before yesterday. Tried to steal my Tirza he did. That's when she bit 'im. Ran 'im off we did." The tired old military officer nodded his head as he retold Tirza's story.

"Do you remember what he looked like?" Cordell didn't think this Sam Osburn could remember anything important, but you never could tell.

"Let me ask Tirza. She'll remember. She remembers ever' thin'."

Cordell didn't say a word as Sam Osburn consulted with his grkdkuu. While he waited for an answer, he heard horses trudging through sand. Turning, Cordell found Dillon and Glen on their snorty mounts with horrified looks on their own faces as they all stared at Osburn and his grkdkuu.

Cordell whispered Dillon's way, "Don't ask. I'll explain everything later."

"Don't worry, I won't." Then to himself, wondered, *What in the hell was that horrible-looking thing, who was that man, and why did they look like they were talking?* Dillon looked it over carefully from his vantage point of a thankful ten yards or so.

"She says his hair was the color of grkdkuu foo with eyes like mine. And that he was tall, lean, and mean. That's why she bit him," he said with an expected look of excitement on his leathery face.

Cordell was afraid to ask. "What is grkdkuu foo?"

Just then Tirza began to urinate.

Sam Osburn pointed at the yellowish-colored urine on the sandy ground before them. "That's grkdkuu foo." As if on cue.

Cordell believed the old man was describing a man of green eyes and blond hair and knew that Jesse matched the old man's description, but so did a lot of other men, as they had learned last year in Mullet Town. "Is there anything else she can tell us?" Cordell asked skeptically.

The more Dillon listened to this conversation, the more fascinated he became. Imagine finding someone like this crusty old antique with a very stinky and strange critter way out here in the middle of all this white stuff. Not just that, but the old fool talked to it. And from what could be gathered, the two of them were discussing someone that could very well have match the description of the elusive Jesse—their someone.

Cordell was satisfied with the information he'd received, no matter how it came. "Now, are you sure there's water over thataway?"

"He dropped this," inadvertently added the sarge.

Cordell reached out with his hand to retrieve the item in question. His eyes lit up when he realized what he now held in his hand. "Do you have any more of these?"

"Nope. Just the one. He dropped it when he was cleaning his guns. At least that's what Tirza says."

Tirza.

Cordell, even though he believed this Sam Osburn to be addlepated, he kinda liked the old fella and his…grkdkuu. "Do you have any food? Food for you and Tirza?"

"Food? Oh yeah. I'z got plenty hidden away. Doan you go worryin' 'bout us. Me and Tirza here have been here long time. If you're finished now, you can please go way. Tirza and me like bein' alone."

Cordell couldn't tell whether or not the antique officer was telling the truth or whether he'd just been in the sun too long. It mattered little, Jesse's trail was fresher to them now than it had ever been, and they needed to be on their way as soon as possible.

Our boys followed the old codger's directions that supposedly led to the water supply. It was funny, really. Dillon had halfway expected not to find anything, but as they all rode over the next rise, lo and behold, there it was just as described. And it did look something like an empty lake, or a very large hole in the ground. Next to it was the spring and a small pond of clear blue water, just like the old fart said. Surrounding it, though, were the strangest-looking trees Dillon ever did see. They looked like large branches that someone had placed haphazardly into the ground, then placed hats on their ends to shade them from the hot dry sun.

After dismounting next to the pond, they allowed the horses their fill, drank deeply themselves, then filled all water canteens to capacity.

Then it was a short dip in the cool water, a break to dry off, collect and eat strange fruits off the trees, and let the horses nibble on the assorted grasses nearby. Once our boys were all rested for a spell, they returned to the horses, remounted, and were back on Jesse's trail.

Only this time, they headed west, because the casing Sam Osburn had found matched all those others in Cordell's saddlebags.

XXXIX

just a little trip into no-man's land

If their Brina was right, and Jesse was from the future as was she, he was as brainless as a block of wood. Dillon believed this due to what he was finding at each of Jesse's campsites—scattered among the debris were more of the very same casings from previous findings. Dillon found this to be very stupid. Had it been him, he'd surely collect any and all unusual evidence believed necessary and dumped it in the nearest trash receptacle on his way through various towns.

Now. Who was Brina Louise Grant anyway? Where did she originally come from, and why the hell had she come? The answers to those questions had become considered a hush-hush issue. Mostly due to if the truth be known, her life wouldn't be worth a plug nickel. That was why she left the boys, and that was why none of them talked about her or of the animal or whatever he was with anyone.

As to Glen, he was an old friend of Dillon's from years past, but Dillon hadn't seen him for a long time. Dillon didn't know from where he'd been, who he'd been with, slept with, ate with, drank with, or anything else recent about him. Due to these unknowns, Dillon didn't dare trust him enough to confide in him such stories as Brina's—yet he was beginning to believe some of Glen's so-called rumors about Carl.

During the several weeks spent in the saddle during their ongoing, never-ending, frustrating, exhausting, exasperating, bug-infested, freezing, sweltering search for Jesse, the weather, the countryside around them, and the horses on which they rode changed dramatically. Gone were the damp mornings, boggy pastures, and bug-in-

433

fested meadows with their cool days and chilly nights. In their place came the drier grasses, cool mornings, welcoming meadows, and the warmer days of summer. The horses' long thick coats had also shed, leaving them with cooler, shorter, shinier summer coats.

Just short of reaching the Missouri River and Banyard's Ferry, as the trail led our boys farther west, they came across a freight wagon. Its driver and team of blondes were resting peacefully under a shade tree near the river's edge. As the teamster was not with the others just recently passed, Dillon assumed he was either enjoying the shade and cool breeze while resting his team, was waiting for someone, or he was in no hurry whatsoever and was just enjoying the view. Hoping he might welcome some company, since his was the only shade available, Dillon and his friends decided to approach and to share in his find.

Later that afternoon they were again on their way west. As they rode, they discussed the new information recently learned from Dillon's chat with the incessant wagon master.

Moses Fishburn had supposedly been a man with a mysterious past, hearing him tell it. At least until the day he discovered gold. He said that day changed his life forever. He had been digging post holes in the yard for a fence he'd promised the missus, when shockingly, there it was. The biggest damned nugget he'd ever seen in his whole darn life was staring up at him from the bottom of the hole. From that moment on, he knew he was destined for wondrous things. So, the following day he'd packed up all his belongings, left his wife of twelve years and their eight kids, bought a train ticket to Frisco, was robbed of his money and ticket before boarding, got drunk, spent that night in jail alongside some smelly derelict, then landed himself a job as a mule skinner for a freight-hauling company the very next day. Followed eventually by an honest-to-goodness job as a teamster the following week. He told them of his travels, of his newly acquired family, and of a small community of teamsters nestled someplace near Indian Valley where he now called home. Then went on to tell Dillon of his experiences while driving freight for a Capt. Kincaid

Lansky, who, according to Moses, could hit a fly on a mule's rump with the crack of his bullwhip without even disturbin' the mule.

He rambled on and on until Dillon began to nod off, when finally, out of the blue, Cordell coughed, making Dillon aware of Fishburn again and what he was saying. He was in the middle of talking about some feller who'd moseyed on into his camp for a cup of coffee three days back. Dillon, of course, perked up right away and listened intently as Fishburn described this guy as tall and wearing a fancy two-gun rig. As to their urging, he went on to describe to a tee whom they believed was their elusive Jesse. Then after some urging on Dillon's part, Moses was kind enough to point them into the direction in which he rode.

"Yep. That young feller come on me all sudden-like, like he weren't nowheres before." In the middle of explaining to these three cowboys, Moses shivered as though someone just crossed his grave. "He seemed nice 'nough, and weell, I was lonely and weren't gonna chase him off none. So, I shared ma coffee with 'im and a scrap er two a jerky. Now I ain't stupid ir nothin', but he had a look about 'im. Them eyes is what got me. But he never done me no harm. Just chatted, rested a might, then left."

"Which way'd he go?" Dillon tried to keep his voice calm.

"Mmmmm, let me thin'. I thin' he mentioned sumthin' about... somethin'. Lemme thin'. Somethin' about that there...place," Moses mumbled.

"Which that thar place where?"

"Thems what they calls the valley of the...sumthin' er anuthr. I can't rightly remember." Then scratched his head with his fingers.

Dillon waited for his reply in a state of controlled excitement. Here, at last, was proof that they were on the right trail and closing in.

"I 'member now. 'Twas due west towards that there Valley of the Fire Moon," Moses proudly stated now that he'd remembered.

Dillon had heard of the place, but not from folks who'd ever been there. According to legend, the Valley of the Fire Moon is supposed to be the fabled sanctuary of the All Mother herself. A valley inaccessible to all but the most powerful, whose tallest mountain peak, Ashur's Pinnacle, rises high above the fog to take vigil upon all who accidentally find their way through the mystical tunnel of Arapath.

The many stories, which have been passed down from generation to generation, from crazies and tricksters to storytellers and old Gypsies tell of a vast valley whose lands mirror the crimson color of its night sky and moon. A realm filled with hidden dangers, strange occurrences, and ghosts. It is also rumored that the sun never shines and that only the light of the fiery moon supposedly illuminates the land within the realm of its guardian: Ashur's Pinnacle.

Such stories were mainly told to children, of course.

For three weeks since parting from the teamster, they rode. And as each day came to a close, Dillon dreamed they were actually getting closer, maybe even downright around the bend from Jesse and even maybe to the end of this story.

Then one day, as our boys approached the prelude to the gray green mountain peaks of the ridge before them, their luck miraculously changed. You see, the tracks they'd been following began to fade as the trail wound its way around the foothills that guarded those green-gray mountainous peaks. As they rode, the climb got rockier and steeper with every switchback taken. And if that hadn't made their trip harrowing enough, Glen had taken the lead and was getting farther and farther ahead.

"Glen, hold up a bit, will ya?" Cordell hollered.

"Ain't waitin'. Can't take the chance of slowing down now. Not if Jesse's this close. And if'n you two don't get with the program, I'll find 'im without ya," came Glen's sharp reply.

He was pissing Dillon off. "Damn it! Can't you hold on for just a moment or two? He's not just around the bend waiting fer us. We'll catch 'im." Why all of a sudden when they were closing the gap was Glen becoming such a pain in the ass?

Thank heavens he slowed and waited for them to catch up. When they did finally catch up with him, they knew why he'd stopped. The trail had up and vanished.

"Which way now?" Dillon asked of Cordell, since he was the one who could read such squiggles in the dirt.

"Hell, I doan know." Dismounting, Cordell carefully surveyed the rocky ground. He knew no matter how rocky the terrain, there should be some sort of message left behind by their quarry. And as his friends stood off together and chatted or argued—he couldn't tell which nor did he care—Cordell relentlessly searched the ground for a sign. When nothing was found, he looked along the sides of the trail—up and down the steep sides—just in case their quarry had suspected trackers and had tried to conceal his tracks by making a go of it cross country.

"Cross-country indeed," he muttered, wondering why anyone would consider such a stupid idea. The terrain, in all directions, was solid rock. Either it ran steeply uphill or promised to be a most fatal fall downhill. Either way, Cordell believed, would prove to be disastrous if tried. So, for the next hour he kept looking at the rocky ground 'til his eyes crossed. Eventually he did spot a scoring on one of the rocks nearest his left boot; glancing upward, scrutinizing each and every rock, he found more of the same. All of them seemed to lead straight up the craggy rock face. There could've been no other explanation; they had to have been the scoring of a shod horse. Jesse's or some other darn fool's.

"Dillon...here."

At the sound of Cordell's calling, they shut up and listened.

"I've found it. The trail. At least, I thin' this is it." At the approach of his two friends, he continued. "If'n I'm reading all the signs right it leads off that-a-way." Cordell pointed towards the top of the rock face.

"You've got to be kidding." It was more a statement than a question. For where he was suggesting was insanity.

He looked at it again. Yep. That was it. He was sure of it. "It can't be that hard. He did it, and if'n he can do it, we can do it." At the look of total disbelief from his brother, Cordell continued. "Aw, come on. If we take 'er slow and easy…"

"Oh, that's just fine. What do you think we are, mountain goats? I ain't a-gonna climb that bloody rock!"

"Either that or you give 'im up. You want to do that now after all we've been through?" Cordell had it in the back of his mind that although the climb may be difficult, even a bit dangerous, they could do it if they were extremely careful. Their horses were in excellent condition, and he had all the faith in the world in his mount's ability to take him safely to hell and back if need be. Even if it meant this skyward journey—*especially of late.*

Dillon closed his eyes momentarily and silently prayed for guidance from the All Mother herself. "Let's set up camp, get a fresh start come morning. At first light we'll give 'er another look." The sun was setting. Climbing such a rugged mountain peak such as this, under any conditions let alone towards nightfall, could prove deadly—*if not just plain stupid, suicidal, ridiculous, idiotic, insane. The list is endless.*

Shortly after sunup, after Dillon's third cup of coffee, he felt he was ready for anything—even the rockface. After all, they hadn't gotten this close to Jesse without taking chances before, and as much as he didn't like the idea or the direction, the taking of the rock was still the only way to go.

"Well, Cordell. This was your idea; you go first."

The three of them had gathered around the same spot as the day before, where Cordell had discovered the scoring on the rocks. And as much as he wanted to take the lead, Cordell was still very apprehensive about the whole damn thing. Especially after sleeping on it. But not wanting to say anything to the contrary, nor to give them a glimpse of his newly discovered yellow streak, Cordell slowly reined Baldy towards the rock, gave him his head, then asked him to move out.

At first, as Dillon watched from behind, the ol' bald-faced horse refused to move. Then as though under some spell, the animal gingerly yet with the surefootedness of a mountain goat, stepped up onto the rocky surface and proceeded slowly upwards across it instead of directly straight up it. "I'll be damned," Dillon muttered under his breath.

"I heard that," responded Glen. Then added, "Shall we watch for a spell, see if he makes it?" He had no nerve for such climbs.

"I don't know about you, but I'm gonna take advantage of that horse's willingness to lead." Without a second thought, because if Dillon had thought about it at all, he would've turned tail and left the territory; instead, he reined Cody in directly, yet at a safe distance, behind the bald-faced gelding. And sure enough, if he weren't right. With a confident animal in the lead, the horse Dillon rode cautiously followed, placing each hoof in succession just as solidly as the one before it, never faltering in his ascent.

"Easy, son. You can do it. Come on, one step at a time…" Dillon, in order to calm his own nerves, spoke to himself as much as to the horse. And with each step taken, he held fast to his mane with a grip not soon to be forgotten, all the while leaning forward to help balance the animal.

As much as Dillon knew Cordell was up ahead, he was afraid to look. He was also reluctant to look back, checking to see if Glen was behind. All he cared about was getting to the top of the rock so he could git off and kiss the ground. Mesmerized with the rock formation before him with its outcroppings, stones, and pebbles, as well as holding on for dear life, Dillon failed to notice the moment they reached the final plateau.

"Yippee, Kie Yay!" Cordell hollered. "We made it!!"

They *had* made it. And by the time Dillon finally was able to break free the death grip he had on Cody's mane, reins, and horn, he saw Glen and his horse just step over the rise.

"Sheeeeiiiittttt!!!" exclaimed Glen as he almost fell off his horse, grabbing onto the horn for support. His whole body was shaking from the sheer fear and excitement of the climb.

Glen had sat on his horse at the bottom of that bloody rock as both horses ahead of him began the dangerous climb upward. His had fidgeted in place as he held fast to the reins trying to keep it still. He knew all along that if he allowed the horse his head, he'd follow the others up the harrowing rock face. And Glen was terrified of heights, slipping off the rock, stumbling, possibly even falling to his doom. Finally, he had given the horse his head. With slack reins, the horse followed his friends and brought Glen to safety just like the others.

"How 'bout a drink? I could certainly use one." Without waiting for an answer, Dillon stepped down, reached into his saddlebags, and pulled out one of the several flasks of brandy he'd purchased in Cascade. "To the rock and our success. Gents, a toast." Dillon passed the flask to Glen, who took quite a large swig, who then passed it to Cordell, who followed suit; then it was returned. After wiping his mouth on his sleeve, shortly following a hefty swig himself, Dillon returned the cork, then put it away. "Well, shall we continue?"

Round the next bend, Cordell spotted a strange-looking dirt trail. It was just wide enough for man or horse, and its sides were lined with red-gray rocks the size of saddles, as though showing them the way.

As it turned out, the painted rocks showed them how the trail skirted along the mountain's outer perimeter, and they, the tourists, enjoyed the view. It was as though our boys were on top of the world.

Cordell was confused. Why a trail this high in the mountains? And why be laid out in such a fashion? His mind was jumbled with so many questions, he almost missed their one solid piece of evidence as to someone else's passing. When he heard the clank of metal hitting metal, he reined in his steed. With reins still in hand, he stepped down off the horse and onto the trail. There below was spotted the evidence in question: a recently thrown shoe.

"Dillon! Glen! Look what's here!"

With the evidence now in hand and the horses rested, Dillon took the lead following the trail with an excitement found only at the bottom of post holes. But at the next turn, the trail and the rocks that led all just got up and vanished.

"What the...?" Dillon began. "Now what? Where do we go now?"

Cordell eased alongside until he was once again in the lead. Dismounting, with his nose to the ground, he followed the seemingly invisible traces of Jesse's trail. After several minutes, he turned to back to Dillon. "This way." Then without uttering another word, rode on until he reached an old, single, and craggy tree that covered a shadowy section of the rocky hillside. "In here, Dillon. The trail leads this way."

"What do you mean, in here Dillon, this way? In here where?"

With a smirk on his chocolate-brown face, Cordell Chevalier turned towards the only friend he had in the whole world. "Dillon—"

"What."

"You're never gonna believe this…"

"Never believe what? Whatcha got?" Dillon could tell from the smile on his chiseled face he had found something special.

"It's a cave. The tracks lead inside," he stated.

"A cave?" Dillon asked, with a surprised look on his bewildered face.

"Yeah." Not giving his friend much time to think, Cordell stepped back into his stirrup, remounting his trusty steed, pushed aside the brushy tree using the leverage gained from the weight and size of his mount, and gestured with his hand for his friends to enter. Then as if on cue, he released the tree seconds after following them into the cave's dark interior.

Once inside, their eyes readjusted to the faint light. That's when they realized they were in a large and long tunnel, not a cave. A tunnel that at its end was a reddish light, which puzzled Dillon no end. A tunnel that reminded him very much of that dark staircase that led down into Mary Beth's basement, only this one had no steps—*and this one was real.* This one's walls and roof were smooth, rounded, and were taller than expected, as the three of them were able to sit upright, as they rode cross the threshold, of what could only have been the Valley of the Fire Moon.

Such stories were for children…

When they reached the other end of the tunnel, they found themselves beneath a star-lit night sky. The view was magnificent. "Will my great-aunt Wendy Windmill look at this. Ya know, I've heard stories and rumors of this place, but this is the first time I'd ever believed it was real…" There wasn't a word that could or would describe what they saw. It was like…like envisioning all those uncharted places that silently hid themselves within the many pages of the thousands of books on all those shelves in Mary Beth's basement. Because what lay before them could only be construed as a place like no other found on the All Mother.

Everything they saw was a dark-reddish pink. The trees way over yonder, were a dark red-black as were the mountaintops that loomed above them. The sky was crimson, with light-pink thin clouds that hovered and moved. And the water of the lake, well, its dark red-black color gave Dillon the creeps.

Stories for children…

With this eerie view came a feeling that they were not alone. Dillon felt eyes everywhere. He was sure they were being watched—watched by a living and breathing thing that whispered unto them its message of death and despair with bone-chilling assurance. When the hairs on the back of his neck literally stood on end, Dillon decided to leave this place and fast. They all must've been on the same wavelength as they all turned in unison to make good an escape. It was then they discovered the entrance to the tunnel had mysteriously vanished into thin air!

"What the…?" began Glen.

"Shit! Where'd the bloody tunnel go?" Dillon was now more than spooked.

"Dillon. I don't like this," stated Cordell.

Each one, in their turn, stood rock-solid still in total amazement while staring at the brush-covered hillside. Nowhere was the tunnel they'd just exited, which meant there was nowhere else to go, except forward, into the heart of the Valley of the Fire Moon.

children...

In fear, curiosity, and total bewilderment, Cordell and Dillon rode forward into this unknown land as Glen followed close behind. They rode until they reached the bottom of the slope, meeting the tree line. At the tree line, they discovered an additional trail that banked off the great expanse of water Dillon had spotted from the tunnel's opening. *Ya know, that tunnel that was no longer there?*

In front of our boys was a huge body of water, surrounded by trees. Any place else, this would've been a beautiful valley; however, the color of this lake on whose bank they stood mirrored the yellow, gold, and red colors of the sky and moon above. High up and beyond the trees, trapped within a wall of fog, were the tops of two craggy mountain peaks. The fog that encompassed all was also of the same crimson hue as everything else, and it shifted and moved as though alive!

As the three men glanced around the lay of the land before them, they noticed a trail that led out and away from where they stood. A trail that had been placed along the water's edge that looked as though it led directly up to and into that mysterious fog that rested at the base of the mountain peaks beyond.

"Dillon," began Cordell.

"Yeah?"

"There are those tracks. The ones we've been followin'. And one's missin' a shoe. Thataway..." Cordell pointed farther on down the trail.

"Let's go. But not too fast. In a place like this, I'd hate to accidentally run into something sudden-like. Ya know what I mean?"

"Yeah, gotcha," answered Cordell.

With the horses at a moderate pace, the three of them trotted down the lakeside trail in search of their quarry, and hopefully, a way out of there.

Their ride took hours. Hours spent in a land whose scenery around them never wavered. Every turn looked like the last as they continued along the lakeshore. Not only did the landscape around them cease to vary, but the colors of crimson red were everywhere.

The trees carried the darkest, deepest shade of it, while the clouds above were mottled with variances of the same gold, orange, and red that were mirrored in the sky and the water as well.

the water...

Of all the creepy things they came across while riding along its bank, the water itself was the most unsettling. At first glance it looked like any other body of water, other than its coloration of course, but as they rode along its edge stranger things began to happen.

It did things. Made sounds. The first caught Glen's horse unawares...the ol' horse jumped sideways, bolted, and almost ran amok at the sound.

"Whoa! Whoa, horse. Whoa." It was all Glen could do to keep his mount from running away with him. When he was finally under control, Glen turned towards Dillon as he caressed his horse's neck with calming reassurances. "What the hell was that, and where did it come from?"

Dillon couldn't answer his question. No one could. Dillon's eyes were riveted to the water's surface.

Tag, you're it.

"Dillon, what *are* you looking at?"

It was the water. This time it was doing things, and all Dillon could do was point at a spot twenty feet or so from shore.

Cordell didn't see anything at first, so he readjusted the brim of his hat, then looked again. "I don't see..."

Unexpectedly, the water somehow began to shift, forming small whirlpools right before their eyes. Something told Dillon to move on. Trying to ignore a sinking feeling in the pit of his stomach, they turned and rode nonchalantly down the trail, away from the water as though nothing was wrong. But curious as they were, Dillon took a chance to look back and found that as they moved down the trail, so did the whirlpools.

The water also held strange-looking rock formations that seemed to grow directly from its surface. They were about fifty yards out. Their bases were wide and oddly shaped. They looked like single piles of manure that some horse had dumped on for years, without some stall hand cleaning them up. They could've been a grayish-red in color, but out here where everything was blood-red, who could tell? Some were tall, and some were short. Some looked like stalagmites found in vast caverns; others looked like kitchen funnels. All looked like they had warts. And surrounding each and every one of them were winged creatures that Dillon had never seen or heard of—even in Mary Beth's books.

Cordell saw it all too, then pointed them out to Glen.

And without another word, the three of them regained control of their thoughts, glanced at each other, turned back to the trail, and frantically urged their horses into a full gallop as panic seized the moment.

...while a woman's gentle laughter floated on the air...

They were still at a dead run, when the trail veered off towards the dark, dark, mysterious interior of the forest. It wasn't until they were within the trees far and away from that mysterious lake and its water, did they stop and take a breather. As shaken as our boys were, they looked first towards where they'd just come, then at one another. This episode of nervous exhaustion manifested itself into hysterical laughing as the realization of what their overactive imaginations had concocted passed.

"Can you believe us?" Dillon asked.

"Give me a minute to catch my breath." Cordell wheezed.

"Never mind that, now where?" Glen asked.

"Hell if I know. I just know, I ain't goin' back towards that lake. That place gave me the willies," Cordell exclaimed.

"Well, I doan know about the two of you, but I've had it!" Glen's panic was still grossly evident and because of it turned tail and sunk spur.

"Damned him, anyway," Cordell began. "Do we go after him?"

"I'm gittin' tired of his shit. We'd better. No telling what trouble he'll find," Dillon replied. "Ya never know, he might even crash into Jesse."

But before they'd gotten too far, a single shot rang out, followed by several more.

"What the...?" Assuming he knew where they originated, Cordell urged Baldy ahead, deeper into the trees.

Dillon made the mistake of assuming he knew where he was off to and followed without thinking.

Anxious to find Glen, afraid he may be hurt or in a shoot-out with Jesse, Dillon tried keeping up with Cordell, but the deeper into the trees he got, the denser and thicker they got. Traveling was way slow, and because of the long, slight tree branches and tall bushes, Dillon had to pull his handkerchief up onto his face to avoid cuts and scrapes made to his good looks.

At every turn in the trail, Dillon and Cody had to duck under low-hanging branches, jump downed trees, while winding their way through and around boggy areas filled with creatures and flowers never seen before—creatures with long scaly necks and clawed feet, others with feathered ears, small ones with paddles for tails, and rainbow striped birds. On the other hand, the flowers Dillon didn't really see too much of—as he was watching the foot-long dragonflies as they flittered from the one scaly creature to the other one with feathered ears.

Stories for children, indeed...

When he caught up with Cordell, they rode in unison. In the middle of the next meadow, they found Glen standing, pointing his rifle at something off in the distance.

"Glen. Are you all right? What the hell are you shooting at?" Dillon hollered his way.

Glen never heard a word, so infuriated was he with his inability to hit the damned bull moose in front of him. He was sure he'd hit the critter three times, as he'd reloaded his rifle several times. However, not only didn't the animal fall, but none of his bullets had appeared to have pierced his hide—and he was only fifty yards away.

At the sound of hoof-falls, Glen whirled, with his weapon still in the ready position.

"Hold it, Glen! It's us," Dillon quickly said. "What in the name of the All Mother are you doing?"

"Are you crazed or somethin'?" It was Cordell.

"It was that damned bull moose over there. Tried to attack me, he did." But when they all turned to look, there was no moose to be found.

"Attack you? They don't attack unless they're with young. What happened? Did you come on her too fast?" Cordell asked.

"It weren't no cow, 'twas a bull, and the biggest sucker I'd seen in years. Had a spread on 'im of more than twenty feet! Damn thing charged just as I was roundin' the bend," explained Glen.

"Twenty-foot spread? I don't thin' so," Cordell stated.

"'Twas twenty feet, I tell you! Like I said, he was the biggest sucker I'd ever seen!!"

"Glen—" Cordell began.

"Cordell," was all Dillon had to say. If Glen was sure the animal had a twenty-foot spread on him, let him think that. Who was he to argue, especially after seeing rainbow-striped birds and creatures with feathered ears?

"Okay, okay. I get it. You think I'm nuts.".

"We didn't say that."

"But you were thinking it."

"What do you expect? You run off, you shoot your gun, we have a hell of a time getting here—"

"What do you mean a hell of a time getting here? The trail's clear," Glen stated matter-of-factly.

"No, no, no. We had to make our way through underbrush, downed trees, and rocks just to get here."

"Not me."

"How'd you get here then? Which trail did ya take?" Dillon asked.

"I came the same way you guys just come!" *And these guys are leading the way? Idiots*, he thought to himself. Who the hell cared how they'd got here, certainly not him. All he cared about was that damned bull moose he'd missed. "Damned thing must've moved off.

Shot him 'bout twenty times, and still he didn't fall," he absentmindedly stated.

It was obvious to both boys, Glen was so concerned and excited
about the moose, he'd forgotten how he'd come and why he'd left
their side.

Cordell looked Dillon's way, knowing they were thinking the
same thing. "You must've missed him."

"Missed him? The hell I did! He was just over there." Glen
pointed just a short distance away.

"Let's go take a look-see," Cordell suggested. After all, Glen
was adamant in his assumptions, and after all, he did shoot at something. "If he did wander off, they'll be tracks. We'll find him."

And find him they didn't. Not only didn't they find any tracks,
but there was no evidence of him ever being there. No droppings,
no eaten grass, no nothing.

"It must've been your imagination. There's nothing here,"
stated Cordell.

"I know what I saw. He was here. Biggest bull I'd ever seen."

"Well, he's gone now." Dillon figured it was an overexcited
imagination. "Let's go."

Reluctantly he agreed.

Now that they had Glen back in their sights, Dillon wanted
to keep him close. He was at a loss as to these new obsessions he
was noticing in Glen. The almost frantic way he was now with the
Jesse issue, and now that damn bull moose, and his bullheadedness
in believing it was truly there when they found no sign. Maybe Glen
was just tired of the continual tracking. Maybe he wanted the whole
episode over with so he could go home, *which wasn't such a far-fetched
idea*. They'd catch Jesse, Dillon was sure of it. The gap was closing,
and he figured they'd spot sight of him within the next couple weeks.
Maybe even sooner, then they could all go home. Dillon was more
than ready to go home.

So, move on they did. Back through the dense trees, the way
Cordell and he'd come—hoping they'd rediscover the tracks that led
into this strange and bizarre place.

It took them forever to get anywhere, and then again nowhere. Not only did they have to fight the damned underbrush again, but when they assumed it was time to be where they started from before entering, they weren't. They covered ground Dillon never imagined. They didn't find the water's edge, which was fine by Dillon with all its strangeness, yet they never seemed to get themselves out of the deep, dark, dense woods either.

Realizing they were getting nowhere, went ahead and set up camp in a quiet area filled with more of the same unusual plant life Cordell and Dillon had found within the trees, and retired for the night. As Dillon lay there, beneath the stars above, he let his mind wander to the afternoon's discoveries.

First, there'd been the tunnel and its sudden disappearance. Then there were the kitchen funnels that grew out from the glassy water. Next, there was the mysterious whirlpooling in the water alongside the trail. Thinking of that, Dillon remembered something else. Something he hadn't thought of before. There had been…a sound, just as they broke towards the trees, yet, however hard he tried to remember it, the foggier and more elusive it became. Something had happened, or some sound had voiced itself, just as their panic took hold. And no matter how hard he tried to remember it just wouldn't come.

By morning, such thoughts were just a memory to be replaced by a most beautiful scene. Gone were the crimson colors of the day before. In their place were the most vibrant colors imaginable. The greener-than-green grasses, the blue-green leaves of the trees, and many of the previously unseen purple, red, yellow, crimson, white, pink and black flowers. The sky was its bluest, with stark-white clouds floating haphazardly everywhere. He couldn't believe his eyes. Everything was simply gorgeous.

Glancing over, Dillon noticed Cordell was still asleep. Checking Glen to see if he, too, was enjoying the scenery, was shocked to find him and his horse gone. "Damn," he issued under his breath.

A half-asleep Cordell heard the muttered word. "Hmmmm? What…what is it?" he mumbled in a sleepy state of mind.

"Glen's gone again."

Cordell was immediately awake. "The fool. What does he think he's doing? What does—" Cordell's sentence halted in midstream when he noticed the brightness of the day and the colors abounding.

"Dillon."

"Yeah, I know. Magnificent, isn't it?" Dillon still couldn't get over how vibrant the colors were and how they had miraculously changed from those gloomy blood-red colors of the day before. "I guess those stories are just that, stories."

...from somewhere came the sound of a woman softly laughing...

"What was that?" There it was again, that sound.

"What was what?" replied Cordell.

"Didn't you hear it?"

"Hear what?"

"The laughing."

"Nope. Didn't hear a thin."

For a moment Dillon thought maybe it was Glen he was a-hearing, so he called out to him, with no return reply. For the most part, it was soon forgotten. Had to remember the main objective here was finding Glen Harper. That little choice maneuver of his overruled anything and everything else.

Two days later, they found his trail, or at least someone's trail.

"Yep. Them's two sets of tracks all right. But I don't know. Something's not right here," began Cordell.

"Explain."

As Cordell examined the trail and the tracks found, he too was having trouble. "Well, what we have here is a set of horse's hooves, which I'm assuming is Glen's, but there are other tracks here too." Then he paused for a moment. "The others look as though they were left by someone either barefoot or wearing...*moccasins?*" he questioned.

"Moccasins? Are you sure?"

"Yep. Small ones. A woman's or a small man's," Cordell continued.

"We haven't seen any indication of *her children*, here 'bouts. I wonder whose they are."

On the far side of the next rise, they found another mystery. There, standing all by itself in an inlet of flowers was what Dillon had learned in school as a "heel" stone. A stone that rose high above the ground twenty feet or so and was as wide as the length of his horse. The two rode closer. It looked as though it had been there since the dawning of man. Its edges were worn from the elements, and its face had something carved nearest its top. And as Cordell steadied Cody for Dillon, he stood in the saddle while leaning against the side of it and read aloud its worn and ancient message carved in stone.

We, the People of Dorrit-Boreas,
came into being from the sky world above.
We came upon this world as creatures,
placed here by the All Mother herself.
It is She who reigns forever over all who inhabit this land,
this,
our Valley of the Fire Moon.

"Do you suppose the stories we were told as children really are true?" Dillon asked his friend upon finishing the scripture.

"Hell, I doan know. But if they are, the way I've always looked at life everlasting has suddenly reached an abrupt halt. Good grief, Sandy Claws, it's just a big rock in the ground. The words could've been someone's bizarre idea of a joke and not for the reader to take as truth," Cordell absently said aloud.

"If that's true—"

"Let's leave this rock and its ancient nonsense. If we keep following the tracks, they may still lead us to Glen and whoever is following him. Besides, this stone gives me the creeps," Cordell said.

"Fine and dandy. Lead on, Macbeth, I'm right behind ya." With Cordell back in the lead, Dillon was left to silently consider the words carved onto the big rock in the ground.

Shortly after lunch the following day, they again heard a single rifle shot. Urging their horses into a full gallop, as they had just broken into a wide clearing, Cordell took the lead as they rushed to what was hoped to be Glen and another of his invisible targets. Only before they could get too awfully far, Cody spooked, unseated, then dumped Dillon unceremoniously onto the ground with a thud.

Spitting grass and dirt from his mouth, shaking his head as to clear his mind, Dillon glanced around only to find that neither Cordell nor his own trusty steed were anywhere nearby. Cordell must've been too far ahead to see or hear of Dillon's sudden departure and was long gone. Brushing off his pants with his hat, Dillon stood, placing it back upon his head. Not having anything better to do, Dillon walked down the trail towards the direction they'd headed to hopefully meet up with his faithful horse.

Needless to say, 'bout ten minutes passed, and there was still no sign of either of them. Onward Dillon trudged until he heard the snapping of a branch to his right. Stopping instantly, he glanced thatta way and to his amazement found a young girl. She was a slight and pretty thing, wearing a deerskin dress with all different colors of beads decorating its front. Her hair was as black as the night sky and was worn in braids that hung past her waist. Around her forehead was strapped a headband with the same colors and pattern of the beads on her dress. As mesmerized as Dillon was with her beauty, and her sudden appearance, he took in all of her, including the moccasins she wore. Perhaps they were the same moccasins Cordell had mentioned earlier?

"Who are you?" Dillon asked, hopefully in a manner that would not frighten.

the young Indian maiden smiled at the man with the hazel eyes—

When she didn't answer, he tried again. "Are you alone? Where are your people?"

the young maiden's eyes bore into his, with joyous curiosity—

"I'm not here to hurt you. I want to help. Let me help you." Dillon didn't know what to say to her. He didn't know if she even understood his intentions. He didn't want to hurt her, but if she was here alone, he didn't think being alone in this strange valley was a safe place for anyone, let alone someone of her age and beauty.

Seconds after he took his first steps towards her, Dillon heard Cordell calling his name.

"Dillon! Dillon! Can you hear me, are you hurt?" came the words from down the trail.

Dillon took his eyes off her for only a second. "Here! Here I am. Not hurt, just shaken up a bit. Cody spooked at…" Dillon was still hollering at him, forgotten for a second was his latest find.

"…the wearer of the mocca…" At the word *moccasins*, Dillon had turned back towards her, only to find that she, too, had vanished. *Just like the tunnel.*

"Did you say moccasins?" Cordell had found Cody and was leading him back across the trail hoping his friend wasn't too badly hurt from the fall. What he found instead was his friend whirling around, searching frantically through the grasses and the trees of the clearing for something. "Whatcha looking fer?" Cordell asked.

"She was here! The Indian girl. She was standing here smiling at me. I saw her. The one who wears the moccasins we've been tracking." Dillon knew he sounded like a babbling idiot, but damn it anyhow, she was real, and she was here. He wasn't crazy.

"I know. You can stop searching."

Dillon stopped suddenly. "What?"

"I saw her too."

"You saw her? Where? When?" Dillon was flabbergasted.

"Only moments ago. Down the trail. Just seconds before I found Cody. That is, if it's the same one." Cordell had stumbled onto her like a cricket in the night. He had only seen her for a second before she vanished into thin air, right before his eyes.

"Do you suppose Glen was shooting at her? Not knowing who she was or what she wanted?" This valley and its legendary stories were beginning to get to Dillon.

453

"Don't think so." He left it at that. "Dillon. She's the least of our worries. We must find Glen. Is it normal for him to act this way?"

"Ya know, I haven't seen or heard from Glen Harper in years. So, I really can't answer you. I do know he can take care of himself."

Cordell thought about it for a moment. "It might be something else, ya know. Maybe somethin's got him bugged with this Jesse and Carl thing." Cordell didn't know Glen from Adam and didn't trust anyone other than his friends Dillon, Brina, and that damned horse of hers. Besides, this just wasn't the way a posse was supposed to work. It worked together or not at all. At least that was the way it was when he and Dillon rode and worked together all those years back.

"Glen's just high-strung, that's all. Besides, you just can't discount all he's done fer us, can ya?"

"It's just…I don't know. I just don't." After a moment of reflection on everything that'd happened, Cordell reached for his brother. "Forgive me. It's just that I don't know him. That's all. If you trust him, then I'll try to trust him too."

But did Dillon trust him?

"Well," began Cordell. "git back on that horse a-yourns and let's see if'n we can find 'im."

As hard as Dillon tried, he couldn't get his mind off that Indian girl, her youth, beauty, those beautiful leathers she wore, and the fact that she was out there all alone. It troubled him some, knowing that he knew nothing about the All Mother's *children* other than the varying stories of his youth. But there she had stood. An innocent-looking girl who appeared as though she couldn't possibly have hurt a fly.

By noon the next day, neither Dillon or Cordell had come across any traces of Glen or his horse. Cordell suggested that there could have been a possibility of him being thrown in the same manner Dillon had; unfortunately, there were no tracks, no nothing that hinted of any such happenings. It was as though he and his horse had vanished into thin air, just like so many other things they'd come across in this here valley.

Regardless of where Glen was, our boys decided to take a relaxing break from the day's journey by unsaddling and unbridling the horses, allowing them freedom to roam and graze at their leisure. They set up camp at the northern end of another of the many meadows encountered since their trip through the mystical tunnel of Arapath. There, the two of them relaxed by reclining onto the underskirts of their saddles, then chanced a short nap on such a peaceful afternoon.

By the time Dillon woke, Cordell was saddling and bridling his horse. "What time you suppose it is?" Dillon asked.

"It's high time you're up and about. There's smoke over the next rise." Cordell continued packing away all his leavings then waited for his friend to follow suit.

"Smoke?" Dillon was on his feet in a flash with saddle in hand, heading towards Cody.

"Yep. I figure it's Glen," he added.

"Glen, huh?"

With everything ready to go, they swung into the saddles and down the trail they rode. "Where'd ya see it?" Dillon asked, after a few minutes of hard riding.

"In those trees yonder!" he yelled back.

Up ahead was another wall of trees. And from somewhere beyond them, Dillon was able to spot the waft of smoke as it rose halfway to the sky.

From the moment our two boys fell into this valley and its mysteriousness, Dillon began to believe it was a place where only the All Mother herself watched their every move. It was either that, or someone else was. Because from the moment they entered the wall of trees, Dillon had another distinct impression that they were definitely under the scrutiny of something or someone hidden deep within their confines.

The horses were snortin' and blowin' at every little thing as they were urged forward. They side-stepped through the low-hanging branches, leapt over the densely matted undergrowth, and charged around the numerous brushes that tried to hinder their progress towards their unseen destination.

Then it all ended as mysteriously as it appeared. It was like a door just opened to another world, closing behind them. Not only were Dillon, Cordell, and their horses surprised, but so were the several spotted horses at the abrupt appearance of newcomers into their secluded hideaway. There all the horses stood, with heads erect and ears pointed towards each other. Counting them, Dillon found there to be fifteen. Brown, gray, cream, and bay-colored ponies.

They had been surprised so abruptly with the animals' sudden appearance, it took a moment or two for our boys' peripheral vision to pick up another flash of movement. This one was farther on, just past the ponies.

"Look...there's our smoke..." Cordell mentioned.

"Will the All Mother look at this," Dillon whispered. For what was before them on the opposite end of the small herd of ponies was a village. "The All Mother's *children*," Dillon again whispered. Tepees and all. Why, there must've been a dozen or so of 'em. All backed up against the continuing line of trees that surrounded this fourth secluded meadow.

By the time the spotted horses had accepted our boys' presence and returned to their grazing, Dillon and Cordell had urged their own animals forward towards the village. The closer they got, the more that could be seen. And what was there was amazing.

There were more of the tepees than first imagined. And they were scattered haphazardly throughout the clearing. All of them made up of the same brown material, some animal hide—Dillon guessed. Each one was the same yet different in its own way. Each had its own adornments whether it be feathers, animal paintings on its side, or that of colorful stripes, shapes, and patterns. Some were even being set up by women as they approached. Others had children playing around their openings while older women were sketching basic figures on them while others were coloring them in. The women seemed hard at work. There were also young men or braves meandering about on their horses, with no apparent destination in mind.

There were others there too. Young Indian braves, their women, and younger children milling about, gathering sticks for firewood, and a multitude of other chores, as their never-ending work seemed to keep them forever occupied. So occupied, in fact, they never gave our boys a second glance.

Not even when they rode past one of the young braves mounted on a pony, were they stopped, questioned, threatened, or even looked at. It made no sense. Neither did it after they rode directly into the heart of the village. They still weren't noticed, stopped, or questioned.

In the center of camp, Cordell dismounted, handed his cohort Baldy's reins, then began to explore the surrounding area on foot.

Dillon remained seated upon his trusty steed and watched the people. The children played contentedly as some of their mothers were seen carrying firewood and water, while others were tanning and stitching hides. *Those hides*, Dillon assumed, *would be made up as replacement covers for several of the tepees around the village, if not clothes.*

He watched the children playing. Over in a corner, he caught sight of an elderly woman as she sat silently in front of a lodge of some sort. A lodge that was different from all the other structures. This one's construction was that of twigs and brush, which made it look rather like a thatched house. Looking around, Dillon found it to be the only one of its kind. The individual herself was a sight to behold. She sat cross-legged with pots scattered about her frail frame, weaving a grass basket to carry the unknown treasures of her homeland. Her eyes never left the horizon, as disciplined fingers diligently maneuvered each individual grass or reed into its proper place. Dillon was so fascinated with her handiwork and her diligent fingers, he unknowingly urged Cody, with Baldy alongside, forward until they were standing directly in front of her. Expecting her to look up, as he was now blocking her view of the horizon, Dillon was mildly surprised when she looked through him and still didn't pay him any mind.

"Good afternoon," Dillon said, dismounting.

"Good afternoon to you too," said a voice behind him.

Dillon whirled around at the suddenness of the words, only to find a smiling Cordell directly behind. "What the…?"

"Easy, son," he began as he tried to still the mirth behind the words. "I couldn't help myself." Then gestured towards the woman, and with a more serious tone, he said, "Dillon, they're all just like her, all the Indians in this village. No one looked at me, threatened me, or even acknowledged me. It's as though they're not really here, or that we're not really here. Ya know, like a hallucination or something?"

"That's crazy. I see them…you see them…how can we both be having the same hallucination?" Were they seeing things?

…from nowhere and everywhere came the sound of a woman's soft laughter…

"Wait. Did ya hear that?" Dillon asked.

"Yeah, I heard it. It's been with us ever since we entered this valley. Who do you suppose it is?" asked Cordell.

"Someone with a very sick sense of humor, I suppose."

"Dillon, I think it's a good idea to leave." Cordell suddenly had the feeling he was being intently watched.

"We will. Just as soon as we can find the trail and Glen. There's gotta be someone here 'bouts who can help us—someone who can see us."

"I do."

Both whirled around at the sound of a woman's voice.

The flap on the tepee directly behind the two had been tossed back onto itself, and there, stepping through its opening was the same Indian maiden from the other day. Her beauty went beyond anything imaginable—more so than what Dillon had envisioned. "Did you just say something?"

"I did."

Dillon didn't know what else to say, but Cordell did.

"I'll be damned." It was her. The one from the trail. "Who are you, and why can't anyone see us?" he asked.

"What makes you think they don't?"

458

"They don't act the least bit curious, nor do they look at us. They just seem to look either directly past us, or through us. As though we're not here." Dillon stated, then began again. "Come to think of it, how can you see us, and they can't? And why did you run off the other day? It was you, wasn't it?" He was full of questions, but was he to get any answers?

"Run?"

"Yes. Back at the clearing. Just after I was thrown. I saw you there, and then you were gone." Dillon watched her eyes sparkle with amusement, as she considered his words.

"I did not run. There is no need."

She stood there in all her innocence, just like a whisper on the wind. Her face was lit with a wholesome goodness, with an air about her that was intoxicating, with eyes that glistened like the morning dew. "I wasn't going to hurt you, ya know."

"I know."

Dillon was so mesmerized by her beauty, the fathomless depths of her deep dark brown eyes, and by the way she smiled that all the answers to his many questions seemed so very unimportant.

Cordell watched his friend, amazed at the power this young Indian maiden held over him. Not knowing what else to do, since they did need answers as well as someone's help, he broke her concentration by speaking up. "Excuse me...miss?"

"The one you seek is no longer in our valley."

At the sound of Cordell's voice, the magical moment was lost forever. "How do you know this?"

"Does it matter?"

Intrigued, Dillon and Cordell looked at each other then back at her. "Describe him to us," Dillon asked, assuming she was just guessing.

"Are you asking or telling?

From some place in the corner of his mind, this question reminded him of something Brina Louise Grant would've said. "I'm sorry. Asking."

"Better. The one in which you seek hath hair the color of the daisies at your feet, with eyes to match their stems."

What? What kind of a description was that? Glancing down, he found it. The answer to his question. Where both of our boys stood, was in a patch of yellow daisies. Yellow, blonde. Eyes to match their stems. The stems of the daisies were green. Blonde hair, green eyes. The same facial characteristics of the elusive Jesse. "Was this man wearing a two-gun rig?"

"Yes, he is clothed with such things created by her children for the destruction of her children, and because of what you must, your presence here disturbs her—she wishes for you to leave. Come."

The two men just stood there in mock confusion. Someone was again saying things that made little sense. It seemed that over several months they had found many of those same kinds of folks.

Then again, Dillon thought of her words, *our presence here disturbs her? Her who?* And why would their presence disturb whoever it was? They hadn't done anything that would warrant a leaving, yet as much as her statement confused him, it also relieved him. There was really nothing Dillon wanted to do more than leave this valley and the strange feelings it gave them both. "But what about Glen? What about our friend? Have you seen him?"

"He is also gone from our valley."

"How do you know this?" How did she know of Jesse and of Glen? Had she and her people hurt them, killed them, done them harm? Dillon wanted to know, needed to know and understand.

Without another spoken word, the young Indian maiden momentarily stepped behind the tepee, only to emerge a moment later mounted atop a gray, spotted pony. Beckoning them to follow, she reined the animal towards the outer most boundary of the village, urging him forward towards the mountain and its all-encompassing fog.

children...

XL

enter a realm of enchanted danger

"So it is written, my beloved, so shall it come to pass."

*I*t *was now time for the watcher to return home to the body of the gray charger.*
The same gray charger who hath carried his spirit, his soul, his essence,
for nearly a century.

As he leaves the body of the bald-faced steed,
satisfied with all they have shared,
he again takes flight.
This time it is an invisible winged dragon that brings him
across the tall mountains, over the deep-creviced canyons.
He spreads his majestic wings wide soaring the skies effortlessly.
Flattening his wings against his body
he abruptly dives like a plummeting meteor into the fathomless depths of
the deepest waters.
Submerged, his powerful wings move like pulsating fins
forcing his immense form ever forward.

Erupting the water's quiet and glassy veneer,
he rockets skyward high up into the atmosphere—
shrieking victoriously.
'Tis a resonating sound that emanates from the bowels of hell itself,
creating such a commotion, such a disturbance,
that all within sight, sound, and sensation
flee.

THE ASSIGNMENT

In flight,
he stretches his neck straight and tall,
holding his head most regally,
as his magnificent wings spread wide
lifting him up towards the celestial sphere far beyond.
As he reaches the outermost boundary of the stratosphere,
he does slowly descend to a more comfortable level,
where he allows its atmospheric currents
to not only dry his leathery hide,
but to also carry his great form home to the gray.

XLI

fancy two-gun rig

As frantic and horribly upset as Justin was by the abduction, he had to focus elsewhere, and yet it wasn't until after he retrieved Brina's Colts from the lagoon did he truly think about her words in their entirety. Because not only had they come to him in a most bizarre way, but when he considered all that he'd learned and experienced in his life, he also decided that her words and how they had come were to become just another reminder of what brought him here. He chucked for a moment thinking what an odd way to be looking at his latest adventure.

So, as the Colts were left to dry in the sun, Justin went in search of the Gray Wolf and his own horse, Wyatt.

Justin trampled through the various grasses and wildflowers on his way towards the meadow, taking time to reflect on the wonders the *All Mother* provides to those who could see, like his Bree. She was one who could truly see…

During quiet times when daydreaming, talking to herself, or enjoying her surroundings, she would absentmindedly describe to no one in particular little details most miss as they pass through the All Mother's window. Like the different blues, grays, and green colors of the various sagebrush grasses, the rock formations that keeps one guessing as to their origin and the many flora and fauna that lived and thrived within the regions they traveled across. Those and so many other little details they passed by and/or saw, only she seemed to *see*. Not because others couldn't, it was just because they refused to look. *Really look*, like his Bree had.

His Bree had the ability to see things that others couldn't, and that had always amazed him. She always took special pleasures in everything around her. It seemed strange to him that she could be so deadly, yet so kind, gentle, and understanding of the innocent or helpless, her being the soldier and all.

For example, she had taken him under her wing after finding him injured in that old and deserted barn, and in the end had helped him get back on his feet when he needed it the most. She found him a horse to ride. She consented to be his partner on this leg of his journey. And as their trust and friendship continued to grow, he began to see many special qualities in her.

It was only earlier that very morning after she'd snuck up on him in the grass—without his knowledge, when she was suddenly inches from his face, her eyes blazing with hidden yet wild desires— did the true meaning of their continued compatibility and/or friendship begin to take form.

Then when her life was threatened by the nut case with the gun and taken from him, he finally saw and truly accepted the fact that he was in love with his best friend.

Now, she was most definitely gone. That horrible, creepy, and ugly nut case had taken her from him. Why? Justin didn't know. Neither did he know anything about the man or the reason behind the venomous act. Obviously, his Bree knew, and because of such knowledge, and her fear for Justin's own life, she sent him away— almost throwing him into the water—sacrificing herself. In the midst of all the terror, him now on one side of the lake, Brina on the other stalling the nut case, in a most bizarre way she told him what to do next. The most unsettling part was how the words came to him. They came to him mentally, in his head, with her eyes locked onto his eyes. He would have given that idea a bit more thought if the words she sent hadn't come with such conviction, such sincerity, such fortitude—all of which hinged on the trust they'd established in times past. Therefore, with all considered, his conscious and subconscious self had no choice but to keep to his unspoken word by nodding his head in understanding, with the promise that he'd follow through with her orders.

The beauty of the countryside with its haphazard flower arrangements and the majestic landscape surrounding the meadow where he found the horses grazing was invisible to his senses. All he could think about was the sound of her missed laughter as she had splashed into the lagoon on that first day they had arrived at this beautiful campsite. Her laughter, her smiles, and the sound of her voice had always been taken for granted. That was until now. Now she was in mortal danger with a man he didn't even know; furthermore, her orders for him were to hold up till help arrived in the form of an old man? He couldn't for the life of him understand the meaning of those words. However, if she did have the ability to see things he couldn't, perhaps…

Once both horses were caught and securely tied, Justin pulled out from Bree's saddlebags *the kit*, as she called it, for the cleaning and the polishing of her weapons. And as his hands searched her bags for said kit, Justin Case III found a treasure he hadn't expected to find.

"Good grief, Molly Bolt, will you look at this!" He couldn't believe his eyes as he gently pulled out everything from within her saddlebags. As he found them, Justin gently set them on the oilskin he'd pulled out first, thinking it was the cleaning rag. Upon it he placed a skinning knife, which was found to be razor sharp as he extracted it from its sheath examining it carefully; several strips from an old sheet; a small hatchet; some beef jerky; two empty whiskey flasks; some matches; her gun cleaning kit, which he set next to the Colts; extra ammunition for them and for her rifle; and finally three additional items he had no names for nor did he know how to describe them.

After cataloging the items to memory, Justin placed each item back into her saddlebags, all except for the cleaning kit, which he was to use. The other items unfamiliar to him, perhaps she would explain upon her return.

Positive thinking was the only way to fly.

Once Justin finished the internal cleaning of each barrel and cylinder of each of Bree's Colts, he cleaned, then polished their exteriors as well. He hadn't been paying much attention to the inscriptions or the ornate engravings that engulfed each piece, nor did he look at the engravings on the guns themselves until the last oils were added. While holding one of the pistols in his hands as it received its last rubdown with the gun oil and rag, Justin noticed an image of a rearing white horse on its cylinder.

On closer examination of the weapon, its detailing and the white horse, Justin stared in wonder. It was a weapon he'd never seen before. Of course, he'd seen Colts before, but nothing like this one. To make sure his mind wasn't playing tricks on him, Justin picked up the other weapon, finished its last buff; he examined the two of them together. It was just like finding those other unfamiliar items in her saddlebags. With his mind's eye set, he re-examined each weapon finding them to be identical. It looked as though his mind had not been playing tricks on him after all. Both guns were ornately engraved with fancy scrolling. Each of their cylinders held a white horse rearing within a circle with the words *Colt 150* next to the animal. Not just that, but just short of the cylinder, on both weapons, was a man's picture. A man, whom he did not recognize.

Justin then found three distinct areas on the Colts that truly gripped his attention. Directly below the circle with the white horse in its center were engraved numbers, and those read *1836-1986*. On the barrel there were more engravings, such as *150th Anniversary Model.*

If that wasn't enough to throw him off a tad, an additional engraving on one of the pearl-handled grips did. It appeared to be a message. A message that had been engraved in a different hand from that of the original engraver. He read it aloud, "Brina, if you need me, I'm here for you. MJ"

"Who is this MJ fella, really?" Justin asked aloud.

The very moment Justin Case III was asking of no one in particular about the mysterious engravings on the butt of Bree's Colts, the Gray Wolf in the form of the great winged dragon Remsiy Hywalfin broke through water and air, discharging such a ruckus that its reverberation reached the sensitive ears of Justin and all the other animals within the surrounding area…

Without knowing the source of the commotion, or that of his reasoning, Justin instantly whirled towards both horses. There, still grazing among the knee-deep grass was the Gray Wolf. As to Wyatt, he was long gone. Nothing but a cloud of dust and the fading sound of thundering hooves were left of the animal in question. As to the Gray Wolf? There he stood all the same.

"What the hell?"

Suddenly all was quiet. Not a sound stirred from any direction. Justin could feel it. It gave him chills. It was almost as though time had frozen. Everything around him had come to a complete halt. Nothing stirred, not even the leaves on the trees. The water stopped sloshing against the shore. Even the birds had stopped all of their sound, and with Justin standing as still as a single blade of grass, he quietly began to panic at the unknown of it all.

He couldn't even begin to guess.

As Justin contemplated the reason for the freeze in time, a sure-fire creepy feeling of uneasiness moved in and settled into the entire area. When the hair on the back of his neck literally stood completely on end, he was sure that something within the meadow had changed. The panic that firmly held him earlier had finally loosened a bit, eventually remolding itself into a morbid curiosity. Now with his mind still a bit shaky, yet alert and ready to react, he waited for the inevitable. When nothing happened after a few minutes, he relaxed.

Unexpectedly, he felt a presence behind him. Whirling around again he was met face-to-face with Bree's gray charger. The animal stood not ten feet away, curiously calm, and with his gaze intent upon him.

The air around the horse seemed to move and churn.

Justin couldn't see anything, but cocked Bree's pistols all the same.

Something else in the air shifted.

"Who's there?" Goose bumps began their run up and down his arms. Something was amiss, and he tried to shed an instant feeling of anxiety.

The air shifted again.

This time Justin was sure he was no longer alone. "Whoooose there?" he shakily asked.

The answer came, but not as expected.

"Do not fear me, for I shall not harm thee."

It came from everywhere, yet nowhere. It came from his left. It came from his right. It came from above and below him. It came to him more as a feeling or as a whispered echo from someone on the outside looking in, or from the inside looking out. It seemed to come to him from within his mind, but wait. He knew better.

"You think so?"

Justin's eyes grew to the size of saucers.

"What the...?" Justin jumped at the spoken words. He frantically looked in all directions expecting to find someone nearby yet found nothing. Nothing, except the gray horse still where he'd last seen him, the lagoon forever in its place, the all-encompassing trees, and his campsite. Nothing was out of the ordinary.

Hoping that it was nothing, he questioned his thoughts. "Is someone there?" When no answer came, he again relaxed, lowered Bree's Colts, releasing their hammers, then slowly lowered himself to the ground. There he sat, cross-legged with his hands in his lap and Bree's Colts still in their grasp. Taking a deep breath, he exhaled slowly, then looked again at the ornate carvings on each gun.

"Bree, your kidnapping must be weighing heavy on my heart for my mind to play such bizarre games on me." Justin's conscience worked against him as he stared, while reading all the numbers and all the words before him.

Again, he voiced his thoughts. "Oh, Bree..." At the sound of her name, his eyes began their fill with tears of woe. "If only I knew how to save you..." Without even being aware of it, a tear trickled down his right cheek. Subconsciously he wiped it away and continued to ramble on, "...as you saved me on that fateful day."

With the Colts still firmly grasped in his hands, Justin, without knowing why, whirled around and began to crawl frantically towards the gray, sitting directly under his belly.

The animal never moved.

Shortly thereafter, with confusion clouding his thoughts as to the reaction of both him and the animal, Justin crawled back out from under him, stepping slightly away. Once upright, he stopped, turned, and considered the animal before him.

"What is it about you, or better yet, what is it about me that makes you stare so? Do I have horns growing out of my head? Have I sprouted a tail? Do I look like the jackass I feel?? Ya know, horses don't normally do what you're doing. Horses normally don't let crazy people frantically crawl up to then grab onto their legs for support. Horses don't usually act quite the way you do. What is it with you, Wolf? What makes you so different from the rest? Why am I asking you?"

The horse continued to stare at him.

In his desperate search of the truth, Justin had unwittingly become a participant in a mystical experiment—*equine style*.

Justin continued talking to the gray steed. "Is it you? Are you the cause of my anxiety? My feelings of being watched? Not only have I lost my Bree, but because of you I'm losing my mind as well."

With no answer forthcoming, he returned his attention to the weapons in his lap. The Colts. He knew that the truth behind the weapons she carried played an all-important role in this whole escapade. She as much had said so.

"It is time."

XLII

have gun will travel

Justin whirled around, guns ready, hammers cocked.

"All right. I've had it. Step on out here where I can see you."

His attention was on the horse, but because that was really kinda stupid, he swiftly turned around. When no one was behind him, he again turned back towards the horse. To the animal he demanded, "You're in this too. Right? Right up to the top of your pointed little ears."

Poor Justin, he never got a shot off.

Before the animal had a chance to kick, bite, charge, or lower his head to nibble on choice grass blades, a figure stepped out from the *middle* of the horse.

"Who in the hell are you, and where'd you come from?" Justin stood his ground ready to fire.

He was so focused on the man himself never did he think from whence the gentleman came. This guy was like no other Justin had encountered in his lifetime. This fella stood in the center of a shimmering light that pulsated around his every breath. A pulsating light that began to fade, then finally to dissipate. That's when Justin got a better look. He was a dapper sort of fellow whose face was long but whose features were overshadowed by the unmistakable and vibrant gray-blue color of his eyes with long curly eyebrows resting upon them. He stood well over six feet tall with a lean yet robust frame. He stood like someone of high station: regal, majestic, or proud, Justin wasn't sure. But sure as shit, Justin knew that this guy wasn't from around here. Couldn't be, not with that outfit.

471

The old man wore a black-and-silver banded hat that rested atop a mop of thick, grayish-colored hair that draped in soft curls around his shoulders and fell halfway down his back. His shirt was of the same gray-blue color of his eyes, which Justin wanted to see more of, but couldn't because of the exquisite, yet simple, black vest that covered most of it. Lowering his gaze, he spotted a ring on the old gentleman's right index finger. Moving to the rest of the outfit, noticed also that the man's pants were of a material that Justin hadn't seen before, and with a tinge of surprise noticed that their color also matched that of the vest and ring. The pants were held in place by a fancy-looking belt and from what he could see a fancy type of buckle. When he reached ground zero, Justin noticed the color of the boots. They again matched the shirt and were of the same gray-blue hue as the gentleman's eyes.

Justin broke his gaze from the gentleman only to place it upon the beast the gentleman stood near to. This was when he noticed the gray-blue color of this man's eyes, shirt, and boots, matched perfectly with that of the Gray Wolf's coat.

With that, he returned a very bewildered and curious gaze back towards and upon the face of the stranger before him.

"Now that you've looked me up and down, do you approve of my attire?" the older gentleman nonchalantly asked.

"What?" Justin was caught off guard.

"My attire. Is it appropriate? Do you approve of the selection?"

"I don't understand." Justin didn't.

"Humph."

"Who are you?" Justin repeated his original question.

"Don't you know?"

"Am I supposed to?" If Justin wasn't confused before, he was now.

"I am from your dream," the old gentleman said matter-of-factly.

"The man from my dream," Justin said with a hint of sarcasm. "I beg to differ. If you were the old man from my dream, you wouldn't be dressed like you are."

"I didn't think that outfit would be appropriate for riding," the older gentleman replied just as sarcastically as the young man before him.

Justin didn't reply, instead returned his gaze to the Colts and the engraved message on the one butt.

"She wanted to tell you, you know—"

"Who?"

"Your Bree."

"She was going to tell me what?" Justin responded a bit more harshly than expected.

"Many things."

"Was she going to tell me about you?" A hint of jealousy crept into his voice.

"She didn't have to, your first impression of me was accurate enough."

"My what? No. I'm sorry, we've not met."

"But we have."

"I don't remember meeting you. And believe you me, I would've remembered that meeting."

"It was not a normal introduction as you're assuming. Let me reawaken your first impressions of your Bree and myself…

"As I recall, you found her to be an unusual find, which she most definitely is. Actually, she's much more than that. Of the horse, you found him to be of unusual standards. You believed he had the grace of a European mount, yet when you gazed into his eyes, you were struck with a vision of looking upon a beast of overwhelming power." He paused just a moment before continuing. *"Your first assumptions were very accurate, for I am the gray."*

"Yeah, sure." No hint of sarcasm this time. This time the statement was laced with the stuff.

"You don't believe me?"

"What do you take me for? A fool? Only fools and small children believe such nonsense."

"Are you sure? Come closer. Remember, I will not hurt you. I want you to look deep into my eyes and tell me what you see." Talk about old clichés.

The old man allowed Justin to approach. Cautiously, and out of curiosity, Justin did just that, he looked him in the eyes. At first, he didn't see anything but the deep gray-blue color of the old man's eyes. But then something down inside the irises moved. Something was down there. Something caught Justin's attention. Caught it in a way never experienced, never heard of before. In a flash, the old man had a firm hold on Justin's mind. Held it in a way that wouldn't spook, wouldn't cause flight. But take it he did.

Realizing the sudden shift in control, Justin tried pulling away. But no matter how he tried, he couldn't tear his eyes from the grays that bound. Giving in to his predicament, especially since trying had got him nowhere, eased the pressure. With the battle now won, the depth in which Justin was being pulled intensified. But Justin didn't want to go there. He didn't want to play this game.

Justin was spooked more by the strength of the hold than what he was being forced to see, to experience, to live anew. Slowly and out of curiosity he took a step closer. He wanted to taste the feeling, live the feeling. Maybe a small taste then, he thought. The one wasn't too bad. A second perhaps, a third taken. After a moment he found himself swallowing everything on the offered plate. His eyes widened out of wonderment, amazement, fascination. They became the size of saucers. He could see it, feel the sensations, smell them. He was one with it. A fathomless depth of an age-old wisdom whose origins Justin could not begin to explain or even guess at. Deeper and deeper the old man pulled Justin down until he remembered. Knew where he was. It was vaguely familiar this place. It held a panoramic view of that very first day when Bree and the Gray Wolf stumbled upon him in the barn.

Justin could smell the sagebrush, the scene before him seemed so real. Suddenly it all changed. Changed to another time and place he'd never been, yet he lived it just like she had.

Jason Harcort escorted Brina to the main ranch house, introduced her to his mail-order bride, sat her down, then filled her head with stories of his exploits with the wild horses that roamed his spread.

The scenery changed again.

During the day they managed to put several miles under their horses, yet each night Justin continually woke from that same bad dream. Dreams he wouldn't discuss. Brina was getting more and more worried, because for each night he was denied needed rest, the following day he'd continue to wane in energy and enthusiasm.

And again.

As Justin sat next to her while enjoying the warm sensations thereof, he was oblivious to everything else in the room including both Fanny and Samuel.

But the very last one told him much more about his Bree's concerns for him and that dream. This one hinted of her and of the gentleman before him.

Wolf. She needed to tell Justin the truth about herself and her equine companion. Would he believe her? Did he trust her enough to believe the crazy things she'd say. She could use her power, knowledge, and a few magic tricks to convince him, but was the possibility of losing him through it all worth it? Unfortunately, since that creep, and who knew just how many others were out there tracking her, Justin needed a better understanding of what was at stake and the danger traveling with her had put him in. It was a long time overdue, but she finally realized it was a necessity she had to reveal. But when would be the best time?

Suddenly all the visions stopped, and all he could see was a gray-blue color of someone's eyes.

Justin swayed. "I've got to sit down." All he could think about was what he'd seen, not the power that bound and the intensity of it. What he'd been through was just like he'd ridden every mile, taken each step himself, and felt, or witnessed, in the flesh, each experience the old gentleman had shown him. The old man then led Justin back to his fallen log where he patiently stood while Justin slowly sat.

Looking up at the old gentleman, Justin made some profound statements. "You definitely aren't from around here, are you? How you've shown me what you've just shown me is proof of that."

"Have you learned anything from your travels?"

"Yeah, but first I need to know something."

"Anything."

"What's your name so that *we* can stop referring to you as the older gentleman, feller, guy, gent, old fart, stranger, figure, old man, squire, chap, dude, fellow?"

"Are you sure you named them all? If given enough time, I'm sure we can think up some more."

"And I thought I was being sarcastic."

"Two can play that game."

"Sorry. I'll try not to be such a fool in the future."

475

"Be that as it may, my names are very unusual. Perhaps you would like to use one of your own. It matters little what I am called."

"What does Bree call you?" asked Justin.

"Brina calls me Wolf," the old gentleman added.

"Wolf. Is that short for something, or is that a nickname of some sort?"

"I am known as the Gray Wolf."

"Wait. That's the same name as Bree's…horse…"

"Justin. We are one. Brina's gray horse and I are one in the same."

After everything he'd just been through, experienced, saw, felt, tasted, through the eyes of a single man, Justin thought he'd believe almost anything. "That's the second time you've referred to her as Brina."

"Brina Louise Grant."

"Then she wasn't lying, that is her real name. Then what about the engraved message on the Colts, that's…?"

"It is."

"Who's MJ then?"

"His relationship to her is both teacher and friend."

That explained some of the weapon's mystery. The rest came without Justin having to ask.

"The weapons that have sparked your curiosity are easier to explain. How they came to be here is one of many questions I will answer for you."

"Tell me, please," asked Justin.

"These are exquisite weapons, are they not? Look at them closely and listen. I am not going to give you a history lesson on their centuries of turmoil. I am giving you a basis from which to draw your own conclusions.

"Once upon a time in the not-so-distant future, on a world light-years away, exists a species whose development closely resembles your own. During one of their early evolutionary periods, weapons such as the ones you now hold were devised with an insinuating fact that they would create equality within their species' ranks. After quite a colorful passing of time and history, this particular gun, and at this time I am speaking of the one without the message, was created in the year 000001986rtmp, as a 150th year anniversary exhibition gun, cel-ebrating its creator's name and achievement. The rearing white horse is Colonel

Colt's official mark, and the picture is he. Officially this weapon is called The Colt New Model Army Revolver, Peacemaker.

"Over time and space this weapon fell into the hands of a forefather of Brina's teacher, Master M. Jarlath of the Academy. And consequently, the weapon was passed down from generation to generation until MJ gave it to Brina in hopes that should she need protection, he, in his own way, would be there for her."

To Justin there were still pieces missing. "You said there was just the one gun. If that is true, what about this other one?" Justin gestured with the second.

"They are still not sure, but when the one was confiscated, the second mysteriously materialized and was therefore seized as well, adding it to the collection."

"Why have you deemed it necessary to tell me the entire story? I thought you said that you wouldn't."

"I like telling stories when it suits me. Besides, it is an interesting story, is it not?"

"Sure." This story did just that; it sparked Justin's curiosity. Justin, now very curious about the whole episode, wondered about Brina, Wolf, why she was here, who that creep was who took her...

"Wolf? If that is to be your name and what I am to call you?"

"It is. And yes, you will."

"I will what?"

"See her again."

"You knew what I was gonna say?"

"Always."

"You can read my mind then."

"When I choose."

Justin thought about this. "Can you place words there too?"

"When I choose."

"Then it was you earlier."

The Gray Wolf only smiled.

"You said I would see her again. Does that mean you and I will go together and find her?"

"No, young Justin. I will not be searching. I know where she is. It will be your adventure, your findings of the truth that will bring you both home to rest."

"What? I thought..."

"You thought what? That I would allow you to miss your own undiscovered destiny and go get her myself? I will not help you. This adventure is yours."

This royally pissed off Justin. He picked up both pistols he'd dropped earlier, held them cocked and fast. "You will help me rescue Bree!"

"You think so? Where are you going to look?"

"You showed me the past. You can see things! You can probably do things too!"

"Yes, young Justin. I can see things. I am able. I know things. I know she will escape harm. I could step in, but her fate is already written. Your fate is already written. We will not rescue her. She must endure this journey herself. Without my assistance she must prevail. Otherwise, there'll be no future for us."

"What do you mean for *us*? Surely you're not suggesting—"

"Of course not. Brina is mine only after her death."

"Explain."

"She has her own life. She will live it as it is written. As she sees fit. As she chooses. Once her corporeal existence is over and her corporeal form is laid to rest, her soul comes to me. Together in eternity we will love."

"Eternal love. How beautiful." Justin was momentarily touched.

"Yes, it is, is it not?"

Justin's *moment* lasted only a moment.

"But what about now? What about her life now!" He was back to being angry again.

"You need not concern yourself. She is in no better hands."

"Where…where is she? Does he still have her? Where is she now? *I demand to know!*"

"Children—"

"What? Are you calling me names now?"

The Gray Wolf sighed. *"No, young Justin. You are far from being a child. You are just upset about a beloved friend and want to do all that you can. It is for me to say that you do not need to worry. Remember, I see things. I know things. And I tell you that Brina is in very capable hands. She will heal and will meet with you again, in this life. I promise. Trust me."*

"Has he ruined her?" This was something he had to know.

"Not in the manner you are suggesting. No. I will not lie to you, Justin. He has done her considerable harm, but nothing she cannot fully recover from."

With the wind knocked out of Justin's sails, he lowered himself to the ground and cried. There was nothing else he could do. He could not save his Bree. He could not go to her in her time of need. This mysterious Gray Wolf would not help him do anything. There was nothing for him, except to get the frustration, aggravation, fear, hate, anger, and despair out of his system. And from learned experience, crying seemed to help considerably. At least it seemed to last time. It would this time as well.

By evening, after Justin had recovered and had spent some time thinking, the Gray Wolf had the fire going and had something cooking on the spit.

"Feel better?"

"Yes and no. Thanks."

"You can eat anytime. The meal is prepared."

"You cook?" Justin asked.

"Sure can. Had many a millennium to practice."

Justin sat across from the Gray Wolf. "You gonna eat?"

"I do not eat."

"Why is that?"

"Justin, I am not a corporeal being. I am spirit. What you see before you is what I want you to see. Nothing more."

"Are you solid?"

"I am what I want you to see. If it be solid, I am solid. If I need to be liquid such as water, I will run freely downhill and puddle at the bottom. If I need to be gaseous, I can do that too. But I do not eat or drink. I am spirit."

"Were you always like this? Spirit?"

"No."

"Tell me about that time."

"Sorry, no."

"Why not?"

"There are more important things to discuss here."

"Like what? You said Brina was in good hands, and therefore I needn't worry about her. What else is there for us to do?"

"What about the treasure?"

"The treasure. Shit, I forgot all about that."

"I figured as much."

"You know about the treasure?"

"Do I know about the treasure? Think about who you're asking."

"Of course, you know about the treasure," Justin said with a grin on his face to match all grins.

"There is no treasure. It does not exist for you."

"What do you mean there is no treasure? It does not exist for me?"

"It was a ploy. A scam. A spelling error." The Gray Wolf started to chuckle thinking back on it all.

Justin didn't understand.

The Gray Wolf kept laughing, chuckling, chortling, cackling.

So much so that Justin was getting very pissed off.

"What are you laughing at? What do you mean there's no treasure? What scam? What ploy? What do you mean a spelling error? What are you talking about?"

After the Gray Wolf finally calmed down and wiped the tears from his face, he tried to make clear the muddy water.

"There is no point in explaining the situation. The important fact of this matter is, is that there is a treasure, but it is not what you've been told. Life is the most important treasure there is. And with my abilities, I was able to give a wondrous and special life to my Brina by manipulating those from whence she came. The 'treasure' of which you speak is not round like the sun, as you've been told. It is long, heavy, sharp, and has special attributes associated with it. It is also in a mystical place far, far from here. The one who holds and on occasion wields it, I know personally, but as far as others finding it, they never will, you never will."

Justin wanted to believe there really was a treasure. A treasure to match all treasures. What made this "spirit" think that there was no treasure when all those soldiers had been killed because of it? What about all those other people who were out there looking for it? Could they all be wrong too? Or were all of them right, and this guy had it hidden somewhere just to collect it at a later date? But if this guy was truly a spirit as he claimed, why would he need something like that of such value? Dead people don't spend money. Dead people don't need money. Was this a wild-goose chase? Had he been chasing this stupid goose all these years for nothing?

"I would not be calling my Brina nothing."

"You heard all that I was thinking?" Justin was shocked.

"Remember who I am, young Justin."

Resignation.

As much as he really didn't want to believe, Justin knew what this spirit said was the truth. Why would he lie? There was no treasure. There was not to be a pot of gold at the end of this rainbow this time. "You've seen it? The treasure I mean?"

"I know of its existence, yes."

"But…"

"There are no buts to be considered here, other than your own. And speaking of your butt, young Justin, where is our next stop?"

"What do you mean, 'our next stop'? You said yourself, you travel with Brina. Get back in your horse, if that's where you came from, and go to her."

"I cannot."

"Why can you not?"

"I could get there, but not as the steed, not without special assistance. And where I go, he goes. It is as simple as that."

"What are you saying?"

"We will travel together. You and us. We will travel until we find Brina. Then I will leave you for her."

"Will you be riding as me, or will you travel incognito?"

"It all depends. What would you like, young Justin?"

"I would like for you to stop calling me young Justin. Justin is good enough."

"Very well, young Justin."

Justin sighed, resigned to the fact that the Gray Wolf would do as he wished, call him as he wished, no matter what he himself wished.

XLIII

where the sun doesn't shine

Yesterday morning when he looked his Betsy over, Lucifer decided perhaps she'd ride more comfortably if her hands had been tied in front of her. She looked awfully uncomfortable, bleeding, and so unresponsive that other way. This way instead of having to truss her up like a freshly killed buck, using all his rope, he could just tie her bound hands to the off side stirrup, thus draping her over the saddle, securing its tied legs to the nearside stirrup and saddle strings. That way he only had to tie and untie a couple of knots instead of a whole bunch.

So, on the following morning, when Lucifer got Betsy down off the packhorse, all he had to do was untie her feet and legs. With that done, he moved to the animal's off side to loosen from the rigging the straps that remained. With the mare standing rock-solid still, like the good girl she was, Lucifer gently pushed, then watched as his unconscious Betsy slid ass-side down to finally land with an unceremonious thud on the valley floor.

The woman did not move. She did not grunt, groan, or bat an eye. Curious, he moved to the near side of the mare to look at and inspect his most recent catch of the week. There on the ground it lay. Believing it was playing opossum, he kicked it. It still didn't move or make a single sound, so he kicked it again. Nothing. Nothing did it utter. After several attempts at rousing the fallen figure with his booted foot, he finally gave up. It lay as though dead, and therefore, he believed it to be true. Perhaps the last forty-eight hours tied to the packhorse had done it in. It was too bad really; there was so much more he had planned. The only thing left to do now was to bury it and get on with more important tasks.

He wasn't sure when he'd started thinking of her as an it. Probably once it stopped trying to reason with him, state its complaints, requests, needs did he begin to think of it otherwise. He did feed and water it, but only when he felt like it, in small amounts and when it was convenient, but as to its other requests, they were all denied.

Leaving her still form, Lucifer went in search of a place to dig the hole that would hold his dear and beloved Betsy safe, sound, and secure for all eternity.

Brina felt no pain, only a numbness. There was no hunger. That sensation was long past gone. Yet vital fluids were somehow being quenched by trace amounts of internal and external moisture. Internal injuries were miraculously regenerating, reforming, healing. All internal bleeding had stopped. Sleep, induced. The conscious mind withdrawn, leaving only the seventh sense alert, aware, and ready.

The body was in a state of healing, a regeneration of being, of light, of strength, and of wakefulness. If death was the victor here, so was life. And in this lifeless condition, Brina Louise Grant lay stolid against this foe of foes— her special talents and abilities aided by a mystical force, regenerating in her a strength, during this momentary period in this life, to do battle with the foe before her, and win.

Lucifer picked up, carried, and then laid his beloved Betsy on the ground next to a spot freshly dug where he'd decided to bury her should it still refuse to awaken. Once the hole was ready for occupancy, he stared at her lying there next to it, while quaking with rage.

"You fucking bitch!" Out of anger and frustration he kicked the body again and again.

With anger spent, he straightened out the body laying it flat on its back. This way, he could look at it when he chose, and then again when it was time to get it in the hole. All he had to do then was give it a slight shove with his booted foot, and it would roll right in.

Even though the body lay flat and was still, its look bothered him. There was something about the way it lay that troubled him. Not knowing what it was exactly, Lucifer looked it over closely. The legs were extended and slightly apart, *ready and waiting*. Its hands were tied and extended above the head. Its dirty and smudged face lay slack and unfeeling against the ground. Its hair uncombed and snarly.

He gave it a second look. No. There was nothing out of the ordinary. But something was definitely wrong with the whole picture. The whole scenario. He wasn't sure what it was. Could it have been the filthy clothes it wore, or could it have been the lack of a fight for life struggle on its part? *That* could've been it. For most of his girlfriends in the past dressed like real ladies but didn't act like that when he tried to take them—they fought tooth and nail. But here, there would be no fight. This one was different. This one was Betsy. His Betsy. And his Betsy loved him beyond anything else.

He straddled the body with knife held ready. Looking down at her face, her body, he fantasized what it was going to be like to enter her. Without life, there'd be no battles for him to fight, no sharp nails to avoid, no screams to silence, no begging and pleading to ignore. Just the endless climatic pleasures that followed the joining. Just the thought of it excited him greatly. So much so that he began to swell and enlarge. His trousers grew too tight for comfort. They were becoming too restrictive for his tastes.

He had to get busy. Had to remove her trousers before it was too late. He lowered the knife towards Betsy's middle. Pausing for only a moment while his own grew increasingly uncomfortable, he sliced the belt that held hers in place. Needing to unbutton and rip her trousers down and off, since his member had taken on a life of its own, he began to frantically search for the top button, its hole, and the corresponding ones that followed.

He couldn't find the fucking buttons! He double-checked the area in question. When they were not found, he wildly checked the sides. Those were simple seams. He was almost delirious with need. He tried searching the back, but they were not there either. He was rabid with need, running out of time. So again, he frantically searched the front of her trousers. This time, he did finally find something there, but they were not the fucking buttons! They were something else entirely! But before he could investigate further, his member's desperate need for release forced him to drop and bury his head and mouth against her clothed pelvis. His member strained against the fabric of its cell wall, demanding immediate attention. Primal instincts drove his pelvis hard against the ground in hopes of finding a willing partner to stroke, rub, and handle the top, sides, and bottom of his swollen member. His whole being rocked to the pulsating beat of the reddish-black gore that raged deep within his veins.

Momentarily spent, furious, frustrated, angry, and more determined than ever, he continued his frantic search for the fucking buttons that had to be there.

Finally, he found something. Only it wasn't what he thought. It was a single smaller metal tab, followed by a metal contraption six inches in length.

"What the fuck is this?"

Brina's seventh sense had been working overtime with the mystical force. The vibes they'd picked up kicked in her last reserves. Her eyes flew instantly open.

"That's my zipper, you fucking asshole!" she screamed at him.

Brina's hands clenched into rocklike fists. With all the strength the force allowed, she slammed them down with a crunching blow at the base of Lucifer's neck, stunning him momentarily. Her second came as a wrecking ball as it swung sideways, striking Lucifer's temple—knocking him off her. This gave her time to roll, then jump to her feet, and spot the knife still clutched in her opponent's right hand. With speeds unheard of, especially of one so injured, she kicked out with her booted foot, making contact with the center of his knee—shattering several bones. This, most assuredly, forced him to let go of the knife and cradle his leg and knee, while moaning, groaning, and rolling around in agony.

Grabbing for the knife, Brina spun away only long enough to quickly sit, hold the knife point up with her booted feet, and cut the bonds that bound. With her hands now free and knife in hand, Brina stood to face her opponent with eyes a-blazing.

"You son of a bitch! You wanted to be fucked? Well, you're fucked now!"

"My knee! My knee! You fucking broke my knee!" The injuries Lucifer sustained did nothing but infuriate him more.

The shattered bones and their pain should've stopped him, but he just kept coming like the devil possessed. "You bitch!" Lucifer charged at his attacker with no weapon 'cept the strength, hatred, and blindness of a madman gone over the edge.

Brina's strength was dwindling. She knew she couldn't last much longer. The source from whence she drew her sudden strength and agility was fading, draining away, leaving her with little or nothing to work with. She had to do something, and fast. So, as Lucifer Carstead charged directly her way—fingers like claws, hands reaching to kill, arms extended towards her, with the strength of an efellent and the mind of a rabid timber wolf, Brina backed up several feet, then hurled Lucifer's knife back towards its owner. Unfortunately, due to her fading strength and weakened condition, the throw was bad, and the knife missed its mark.

Lucifer continued to charge.

Brina's remaining strength failed her. She slipped, then caught herself moments before she expected Lucifer's fingers to make contact with her throat...

Lucifer threw himself in a last-ditch effort to kill the bitch who'd broken his knee, his life, his deviate plans, and his heart.

With the last of her resolve, Brina dropped to the ground and rolled while grabbing for her own knife, hidden well inside her boot. In those last remaining seconds, she steeled her exhausted self for what was to come.

When Lucifer hit, he hit as dead weight.

"What the hell?" Brina could barely utter the words, for her strength was almost gone, as was her conscious self. There was Lucifer, dead at her feet. She didn't understand why, how. She'd been ready and was waiting for him to attack so she could plunge her knife into his awaiting chest, but something went awry. Her kill was already still. What the hell had happened?

There was a sound in the brush. A twig broke. Brina glanced towards the sound but saw nothing. She was too tired, too exhausted to care, to comprehend. She was unable to bring forth any remaining energy, strength, endurance, or fight for life. All had vanished. Her resources from which to draw were deteriorating. Her strength, her ability to reason, to think, to visualize, to see Justin again, to enjoy Cordell's laughter—all those, and much more, were draining away much too quickly for her to grasp, to hold, to cling to. She took one last look at the fallen Lucifer. It was then at that very last moment before darkness overtook her, she saw the rocklike spear handle that penetrated clear through the ribcage of the man at her feet.

Lucifer Carstead was killed by an ornately carved, petrified, ceremonial spear, complete with razor sharp titanium barbs at its metal end. The ancient spear was hurled from the darkness into the light, to pierce the core of Lucifer's demonic heart. The decision for such a kill occurred only moments before he launched himself at the gray-eyed one.

His body and soul were pronounced dead at four feet nine inches from ground level—three feet from the woman. His life's blood drained from the body to pool at the base of her feet, to pay homage to the one so great.

But before Lucifer's body was rolled into the very hole and covered with the very soil it had intended for the gray-eyed one, the ancestral spear mysteriously dematerialized.

In the deepest darkest recesses of the All Mother's breast, Lucifer Carstead's wrecked body, along with his evil, deranged, treacherous and tormented soul, was encased in its own grave below forty meters of bedrock, topped with seven layers of rock clay, then sealed for all eternity under twenty-four feet of topsoil.

Where had Brina's savior come from? Who was he? Who sent him? Why had he intervened at this particular moment in time? And why save her? And where had the bloody weapon gone?

XLIV

only the shadow knows

*T*he gray-eyed one felt no pain, only a numbness. Broken bones were mending. Bodily functions, stabilizing. Internal injuries, healing. Bleeding halted; the excess absorbed. The conscious mind, a comatose-like state. The seventh sense, asleep. The body, in a state of regeneration of being, of light, and of strength. If death had been the victor here, life, in its greatest form, could not be offered. Yet be it given life.

And so, in this healing and lifeless condition, the gray-eyed one lay silent and unseeing, blind to the shadowy form who tended her every need.

He was as silent as a church mouse. His every step quiet, calm, without noise. His every movement kind, gentle, caring. It was he who kept her warm. It was he who nourished her. He touched her heart with the healing hands. He bathed, washed, and dried her. Her clothes were made anew. Her blankets free of pests. Her head, he cradled. Her hand, he held reassuringly. It was ordained this life be restored. Brought home. Healed.

He was the shadowy form the gray-eyed one could not see—must not see. He was the one who did not speak. He was the one who followed them, hid in the bush. He was the one who hurdled the ceremonial spear. He was the only one. The sum of them all. And it was they who would bring her home.

The All Mother sent them. She knew the great one. She knew of the connection. She gave him the healing hands—a gift as precious, as mysterious, and as wondrous as She. There was no reward here. No recognition. No favors. Only devotion, admiration, loyalty, love, traces of humor, and of playfulness. To return the gray-eyed one unharmed, healed, alive, and now would be a noble, honored, and sacred gift to a friend so great.

To save their best, it was imperative She send an accumulation of her best. *With them, She bestowed the great honor of carrying and using the sacred ceremonial spear to thwart the attacker, the destroyer. If death were to occur, let it be the destroyer.*

It was dawn. The tall, slender, agile, and shadowy figure knelt beside the woman. His strong arm and hand gently eased up her shoulders and head. He tilted the head back. With caring fingers, he worked her lips apart. He dribbled the sparkling-clean water held in the small earthen cup into her mouth. She swallowed. He held her close. He cradled her. He brushed the hair back from her face, away from her swollen lips. Her skin, hot. The sickness, still present. The healing would take time.

They had the time. All the time in the world. She had ordained it. She entrusted the gray-eyed one's life to them. They were her saviors, her warriors, her escorts. They would bring her home. And it would be there, she would rejoin the living.

Seven suns passed.

It was almost time. The horses accepted him. The travois ready. The mare accepted the travois. The gelding, his hands. The sickness lightened, yet hovered. She would travel this day. Their homeland was a moon away. The journey hard. The shadowy form caught the horses. He fed and watered them. He saddled the gelding. The mare, he prepared. He secured the travois. He packed their belongings.

It was time. He tied one hide to the travois. He tended the gray-eyed one. He stepped to where she lay. He looked down upon her. She was still frail, small, weak. She was dependent. He fed her the elixir. Fed her small amounts from last night's meal. She took water. She gave water. He cleaned her. He dried her.

She was light. Her frail form warm. He wrapped her in the blanket and the second hide. He laid her upon the first. He secured her. He eliminated proof of their presence. He mounted the gelding. He led the mare.

Each day, the sun grows stronger. Each day, the gray-eyed one grows stronger. Her skin cools. Her mind now foggy. His concoction quenches the hunger. He holds her reassuringly. Her sleep, now peaceful. His form keeps her warm.

He bathes her. Makes her clothes clean. Not much longer. Finally, they cross the south boundary. The encampment still four days away.

She is in control. Her powers are great. She hath clouded the minds of others. She holds the land and its people in her hand. In her heart. It is She who hath allowed them safe passage across the outside frontier. It is She who wills them here. The gray-eyed one cometh. Her lifelessness restored. The great one will be pleased.

Glen was sick and tired of traveling with both Dillon and Cordell. Neither of which he really enjoyed riding with. He only traveled with them because they were his only link to finding the fabulous and mysterious item in question. In the beginning, before anyone knew of Carl J. Stewart's involvement or the rumors, Carl had offered the assignment to Glen but backed out at the last minute. Carl had stated, back then, that he, Glen, was too unreliable and too shady a character to be given such an important task.

So, Glen did what any shifty person would do; he instinctively cheated. He may not have had all the facts, but what he had and heard led him to Dillon. CJ had said they'd find someone else to carry out the task, and after much waiting and watching, his hunch finally paid off. Then when Glen heard rumors of Dillon joining together with some old friend, Glen knew they'd travel together in search of the mysterious sphere he'd heard so much about. It would be stupid not to.

So, what if Carl was the instigator in the massacre, instead of this Jesse fella? The treasure still existed he was sure. So, to ensure its procurement, Glen came up with a plan. In order to accomplish what he wanted, he had to concoct some sorta silly, half-assed, halfway believable, bullshit story to again gain Dillon's trust. Once the trust was earned, or the story believed, he knew Dillon would allow him to join in on this most exciting quest. Unfortunately, Glen's travel plans were cut short, thanks to several unnerving experiences spent in that horrible Valley of the Fire Moon. That's when Glen broke away to search on his own.

Yet Glen still had a strong tie to Dillon. Years ago, when Glen's Maggie died, he was distraught. There was no one to turn to except Dillon. None of his family was in this part of the sector, nor did they ever write each other. That, of all things, was the main reason why lying was so difficult. That's why he left to search on his own. He also couldn't bring himself to kill Dillon once the sphere was in hand, as Carl J. Stewart had wanted, so to avoid it all, he left. He had to escape. And escape he did.

If it hadn't been for the sphere itself, his feelings of making amends to Dillon and the fact that bringing in Jesse Loame and whomever else was out there would be bringing in a king's ransom, he wouldn't have put up with so much crap. That horrible winter in Cascade with that idiot woman and those drunken cowboys. That horrible ghost town, Marcus. Then there was that ancient and crazy guy in a military uniform and his whatever the hell it was he talked to. That hair-raising climb up that damned rock face. The tunnel that led in, but not out. The swirling water that followed their every move. The bull moose that no one saw but him. The creepiness of that whole valley, those he rode with, and Dillon's endless search for that stupid brother of his. Glen had had it. He had to get out. Had to get away. Had to find Jesse and the sphere on his own. Make his own gold. Find his own destiny.

Carl J. Stewart had planted the original idea in Glen, which brought Glen to Dillon. Dillon got Glen to this valley. And this valley would eventually lead Glen to the Neptune sphere. He knew the sphere was here. It was fabled to be here. Carl J. Stewart said it was here. And Glen Harper believed that. Once he had it in his grimy little paws, he'd get to Jesse. And once Jesse was caught and was handed over to the proper authorities, Glen would be rich beyond imagining. Dillon could find his own bloody gold.

Once out and away from his party, though, things got really creepy. Not only did the forest grow totally silent—no birds chirping, no underbrush rustling from small animals, no moose to see, bull or otherwise—but his horse began to spook at every turn. He was finally forced to dismount and lead the stupid beast hither and yon. He could've just turned the damned thing loose or shot him for being such an ass, but once he got outta this place he'd have no transportation whatsoever, and he needed reliable transportation to pursue Jesse.

Three days and fifteen miles later, after the forest regained some of its noise and normalcy, Glen was found riding along paying little attention to anything when he spotted smoke as it curled and rose above the tree line for the clouds high above.

"Let's take a look-see at that, horse."

Not believing Dillon and Cordell had come this way, nor this far, decided to investigate himself. Tying his horse to a nearby tree, he drew his hogleg from his gun belt, cocked it, and was ready. Not taking any chances, he slowly crept closer and closer to its source and the assumed occupants surrounding the fire. Hoping it was Jesse.

The shadowy form had just lain Brina's cooled body down for the night. Her scant morsels of rabbit ingested; the sparkling-clean water sipped. Her cleansing complete. The sickness, almost completely gone. Her improvement, remarkable. So remarkable that his own aura told him that hers was fully awake, functional, and ready to act, if need be. Yet she was not yet strong enough to tend her own self, nor was she totally alert. Her eyes could not yet recognize objects. She could see, but everything was out of focus, without color, with no definite shape. Her mind could not see either. Could not function. Objects were totally without form.

As it should be.

Brina's seventh sense was more than just awake; it was alive. It was so alive that it was incessant in showing her the *hows, whys, when, where,* and sorta with *whom* she now traveled.

The *how* reminded Brina of her blessed time spent with Justin. The love they felt for each other. The appearance of the Executioner. She watched herself best him. Watched the tender and angry moments with Justin that followed. She again heard Lucifer's voice. She relived those moments when she sacrificed her safety for Justin's. She suffered the pain at their parting. She heard herself tell him of the old man from his dream. She felt the stinging blows Lucifer inflicted upon her body, her soul. She was aware of the humiliation, injustice, pain, and betrayal while in his company. She relived those horrible two days spent on the back of the horse without so much as a moment to quietly relieve herself, stretch, and/or scratch.

Finally, Brina watched in horror the attack on Lucifer by an unknown force.

Her seventh sense explained of her condition thereafter and how lucky she was to be alive. It told her that without her savior, she would surely be dead. It told her that some unknown force had deemed it imperative that she live, be allowed to fight another battle, another day. *This told her why.*

The *when,* indicated how long she'd been in this condition. It told her how long it had been since Lucifer's attack. She knew how long they'd been on the trail. She even knew about how long it would be before she'd be back on her feet again.

Her seventh sense felt it necessary she relive this part of her journey. The sights, sounds, smells, and experiences. It told her of the terrain they traversed across. It showed her everything. It showed that everywhere she looked was solid rock. In places, it ran steeply uphill. Other places, it plummeted drastically downhill. The ground was rocky, with boulders the size of buildings and rocks the size of hand grenades. The trail, ancient—wide enough only for man or horse. Its sides were even lined with rocks as though it was designated so.

She remembered the tunnel lit with a reddish glow—its walls and roof, smooth, rounded, and tall. She could see the ancient petroglyphs carved into its surfaces. Surprisingly enough, at its end she was hit with a feeling of being watched, looked after, guarded. Her senses had also picked up a presence that lived, breathed, cared, and on occasion could, would, and if need be, kill efficiently.

Brina's seventh sense allowed her to hear, feel, and vaguely see a great expanse of water surrounded by trees. The water and the colors it held were as vivid in her mind as if she saw them herself. Their yellow, gold, and red hues were mirrored from the sky and moon high above. From below and atop the water's surface grew wide, thin, and oddly shaped rock-like forms. They looked funny, like they had warts or something, and were grayish-red in color. Some were tall;

some were short. All had beautiful birds flying around them. The trail ahead led out and away towards the mysterious fog that rested at the base of the mountain peaks beyond. A trail in which he led her mare behind his gelding.

Yet who was this masked man? She didn't understand, couldn't see. All she could see of him was darkness. His form was entirely black. There were no definite lines to follow. No hues to distinguish between. She couldn't see the changes of colors or textures between clothes, hat, boots, and skin—for there weren't any. His hands were just extensions of the upper-torso limbs, his boots were feet upon which he walked on or hovered over the ground. She couldn't tell which—his form was too fuzzy, too hard to track. She never saw his face either. Every time she'd try to get a glimpse of his eyes or the color of his skin, her mind would shut down—confusing her.

His touch, though, was gentle, reassuring. There were no malignant forces in this mysterious and shadowy form that tended to her every need. No harsh words were spewed from its lips. No nice ones either. He never verbally spoke, yet his touch told her much. It told her of his healing abilities. It told her of his gentleness, his kindness, his concern for her well-being. It told her many things—except who he was, who sent him, and why was he dedicating all his time and effort on little ol' her.

Who in the hell had her in his possession?

The last leg of their journey was expected to pass quietly now that they were across the barrier. Once across the barrier they were granted refuge. Their land was protected.

Their land was under the guidance, protection, and watch of the mysterious entity who never slept. A mystical being who never showed itself yet was known to reside within all, and everything. Every rock, tree, drop of water, molecule of air. Every living, dying, and dead thing. Every creature, every flower, every insect—everything. Everything was scrutinized by the mysterious entity who inhabited the place they called home.

So why was it when the shadowy form was off gathering herbs, berries, and water for the making of his magical elixir was the stranger allowed to enter their camp?

XLV

as long as the grass grows and the rivers run free

*I*t was fabled to be the most beautiful valley in the land. Few had been there; many more had not. Few remembered its beauty, its location, and their experiences while there. Others tried but failed. Those who could told stories of what they saw, what they thought they saw, and what they hoped was there. Some embellished on their accounts, some exaggerated upon them, some played them down, and some were afraid to divulge their tales. Many of these folks were considered jokesters, pranksters, storytellers, fabricators, and liars.

Others believed the valley was a figment of someone's bizarre imagination and did not exist at all.

Yet the fabled stories continue, nonetheless.

Many of these fabled stories have something tangible in common. Some tell of rocky peaks, tinged with shades of gray, blue, green, and soft whites that tower high above the serene valley below. All tell of a gorgeous sky that is supposed to be the bluest, and seems so close one could reach out and touch it, with wispy clouds floating endlessly on its gentle breezes. Many believe the air that churns high and low within its lower atmosphere is both crisp and warm, both at the same time. All tell of a fire-red moon that seems to appear and disappear, on consecutive nights, at consecutive times.

All of these stories are true. Yet it is only the chosen who know the truth. And the truth is it all depends upon which pebble you stand, and with whom.

The valley's fabled water supply runs endlessly. Many a river begins from deep within the rocks lying just below the crust of the All Mother's breast. Many end there as well. The lakes and the many ponds that dot the landscape hold water that is always sparkling clean, crystal clear, and as fresh and as icy as the *driven snow. Their colors are mirrored only by the bluest skies, the greenest of the trees, the pond grasses and reeds, the wispy clouds high above, and distorted shadows that flicker, glow, and swim below the water's surface.*

Such shadows often play havoc with weaker minds.

The valley floor is wide and green. Its grasses, weeds, flowers, reeds, trees, and bushes all grow as though there is no tomorrow. Their configurations flourish in all shapes, sizes, and depths. Their varying shades of green, brown, blue, orange, yellow, pink, and reds all burst forth with a wild and clean scent, soft and everlasting.

The creatures that inhabit this valley prosper in every detail—even those not of normalcy. Many of the animals that dwell in this region are from far away. Many exist nowhere else. Some are known. Some are unknown. Some are common. Some are evident. Some are secret. Some lay hidden. All thrive.

Yes. This valley, its lands, and its inhabitants are beautiful and bountiful. There is no doubt about that. And those who thrive, survive, and reside intend to keep it that way.

The one with hair the color of daisies with eyes to match their stems passed through untouched. The twosome—the new moon and the full moon—still wander undisturbed. The single entity is closely watched. The evil one, destroyed. The gray-eyed-one, her actions and reactions, observed and ignored. More to arrive. Others, long gone.

She knew all. The land, its greenery, its creatures, and its people—hers. Nothing happened she did not know about—did not partake in. She created it, the land. Watched it evolve.

She knew her world. Knew it like none other. Knew its flora. Knew its beauty. Partook in its pleasures. Knew what could happen—if, when. She knew the fauna. She bestowed upon them all a natural instinct for survival. Fight, flight, procreate, eat, or be eaten. She flew the skies with them. Hunted and killed with them. Walked in the sunshine, the moonshine, in the rain showers, against the winds with them. Drank the sparkling-clean, clear water with them. Browsed the tall grasses, the trees, and the brush with them. Their beauty. Their innocence. She knew the soil. Its minerals. Its rocks. Its properties. She knew what it could sustain. What it could produce. What it could endure. She swam in the ponds, lakes and rivers—played with its glowing and multicolored creatures.

She knew of the people. All within their valley. Some outside their land—across the great Barrier. Knew a great many of them, personally. She saw it all. She saw the goodness. Witnessed the evil. Some had intelligence. Some had little. Some had none. Many were arrogant—all consuming. Others were kind, gentle, giving. Some were strong. Others, weak. She knew what they were capable of—or not. She knew what may happen to her land, its flora, and fauna—depending...

She designed their world. Their land. This valley, other frontiers. She watched, listened, and laughed. She decided many things. She intervened when necessary, or when not. She questioned. She tested. She judged.

Here she was the protector. The sentinel. The designer. And as sentinel, it was her business to know or to learn of her lands' visitors. Learn of their intentions. Their goals. Their loves. Many came; many went. Many were harmless. Many were not. Some were tested—proving their worth. Others ignored—not worth her time. Few were destroyed. She watched many. Watched few. Watched certain individuals long and hard. Knew of their wants and desires. Knew of their treachery. Knew of their plans. She knew of their deception, their lies, their betrayal. They were always seeking the easy way out. Always searching for riches. Always looking for something. Something that usually belonged to someone else.

This time, they searched for a fabled treasure. This time, She smiled and silently chuckled at what they sought. She knew of its existence, or lack of, depending. She knew where it was. What it was. How it was used. How it worked. How well it worked.

This time would be interesting.

So, it is written, so must it come to pass—

XLVI

let sleeping dogs lie

Whomever it was who held Brina in his possession tended her every need—this shadowy form. It bathed her, fed her morsels of cooked game, herbs, berries, flower petals, and traces of dirt. It quenched her thirst, cleaned her, washed her bedding, and cared for her.

He came and he went. He was there one minute; in the next he wasn't. She could feel him come, feel him go. Even though his motions were without noise, she was still able to sense his movements. She could smell his aroma. It was clean, almost floral, or that of a forest, woodsy. That distinct scent, aroma, that smell that was his alone, helped her to track his every move.

Unfortunately, she could not yet see him. Not clearly, at least. Her general vision was improving. She could see the flora and fauna that shared their campsite, but his shape or configuration she could not pinpoint. He was without substance, without definite lines to follow. He was just as described, a shadowy form that seemed to float as it moved about. She did not understand but accepted him at face value, as she did others of mystical origins from her past. The Gray Wolf was just one of those examples.

The Gray Wolf was a mystical being. A mystical being with legendary powers galore. Powers that hath allowed him to take on unbelievable tasks, journey to fantastic places, to see and control the obscure. One who is able to take many different forms—able to change from a solid to a liquid, from a liquid to gas, from a gaseous state back to that of solids. His shape changes from round to square, from three dimensional to two, to zero—if he so desires. He could change from animal form to plant form, or to expand to greater than the universe, or to dwindle down to microscopic proportions.

These powers he wields are great, they are stupendous, they are unmatched. They are unheard of, unimaginable, and beyond logic. He can do the impossible. He can command the elements. He can halt the rain, flood the land, burn the crops and forests, direct the winds. He clouds up the skies. On a whim he can bring in the storms, send down the lightning with great force and destruction, and blow ocean-side cottages to Kansas. He fogs the mountains, fogs the valleys, and sometimes fogs the minds of mortal man. He places barriers, walls, confines, around or in front of what he chooses. With a wave of his mighty hand, he is able to heal the sick, kill the disease, destroy the evil, or might be the cause of it. He moves wherever, however, and whenever he chooses. Such an iron grip, such might, such energies to wield, are vast. Such extensive and colossal powers are used only when he chooses.

He knows many of the mythological forms and entities that inhabit the universe. He knows many of the mortals as well. He travels through time, space, across planes, whenever he chooses and with whom. He has been around for many a millennium. He hath loved many a woman yet hath chosen only one.

He came into Brina Louise Grant's life at a very early age, and never left. He is with her, everywhere. He stays with her, protects her, takes her places she's never imagined—good and bad. He teaches her, learns with her, and asks nothing of her, except to be allowed to stay at her side.

He has taught her much. He has taught her how to keep secret any and all special talents and abilities, and if the need arises, how and when to use them. He has taught her to be strong, independent, confident, caring. He gives her love, understanding, comfort, when in need. They talk of many things. They communicate telepathically; they are forever on the same wavelength yet sometimes speak verbally. They are forever friends, lovers, buddies, confidants. They need each other as the flora and fauna need water and air to breathe. They are forever joined.

Yet he allows her many things as well. He allows her mortal friendships, lovers, companions. He allows for nature to take its natural courses with her. He allows injury—mental and physical, heartache, and great loss—to her, in hopes that she grows stronger, more independent, more seeing. He allows for her life to continue as she chooses.

He does all this because of what he is, what he hath been, where and what he hath seen. After all, he is

Aeolus, God of the Winds,

Quetzalcoatl, God of the Aztecs,

Thorin, Leader of the Dwarves,

Moza, Keeper of the Trolls,

The Great Wizard of Median Earth,

The Great Winged Dragon Remsiy Hywalfin,

The Divine Sovereign of the Neptune Kingdom,

the watcher,

and many other unknown, unbelievable, and mysterious entities.

And ya can't get any more mystical than that.

As to the other mystical being in her life, this shadowy form, Brina tried communicating in all ways, shapes and forms with this shadowy form but got nowhere. He was as void in words and conversation as she was in strength. She tried sitting up, but he insisted that she not, by easing her back down. She even tried feeding her own self, but he would not allow that either.

"Let me," she would endlessly plead, but never would he allow it.

Finally, she just gave up. It was obviously clear that no matter what she did, tried to do, or say, this shadowy form would not let her tend herself. He was adamant about that.

Damn him anyway.

Brina wasn't used to being treated this way. Wasn't used to being the invalid. She'd always taken care of herself. Always had. Before the Academy she could, thanks to Wolf. Under his wing, she had learned much, had done much. At the Academy, there were ruffians, upper clansmen, and thugs to contend with. Previous teachings and experiences had prepared her for such opponents. She knew how to handle them. She knew how to defend herself, how to win, how to cheat. These learned skills turned possible failures into attainable victories. Especially during combat training, on the battlefield, and in the void. Such learned skills and abilities gave her a feeling of having the power she needed to attain her goals. And she liked that. To have the strength and ability to sustain survival. The strength to endure. The power to control your own destiny.

Unfortunately, that ability to care for one's self had been temporarily put on hold, once with Lucifer and now while in the company of this shadowy form. And that sucked.

Days passed by. Weeks. At least, it seemed like weeks. They would travel for miles. Cross hill, cross dale. He on the gelding, she still on the travois fastened to the mare. Then he'd rest them all for several days. This monotonous escapade droned on and on and on, until she totally and finally lost track of time, space.

Glen approached the campsite, wary. He'd been watching something, someone, move in and out of his line of vision up ahead for quite some time now. He couldn't make out its form but clearly watched as it would leave for a time, then return. It would then move from one side of the camp to the other, stopping on occasion at different locations within its center. Curious, he decided to investigate further. He had to get closer. Had to see what was going on.

Leaving his horse tied to a nearby tree, he approached the camp cautiously and silently. Didn't want to spook whatever it was into fleeing or shooting him. He wanted a good look. Wanted to make sure it wasn't his imagination, like that stupid bull moose apparently was.

Step by step, inch by inch, he crept closer. Finally, he reached the edge of the clearing. Cautiously, he parted the branches for a better look-see. There in the center of the camp lay a body. A body clad in blankets and hides. He peered around the camp, hoping to spot the other being, but he or it was nowhere in sight.

He stepped through the brush into the clearing. He managed to do this without making too much noise. With stealth he approached the body. Standing above it, he saw that it was a woman. A woman clad in nothing but the hide she wore. Her eyes were closed. Was she alive, or was she not? He assessed her condition. Her hair was a dark brown, almost black, with flawless ivory skin. She was quite attractive, in her still condition. Eager to learn more, he lowered himself close enough to press his hand and fingers onto her neck, discovering it warm. She was alive. But what about the shadowy form? What did it have to do with her being here and in this condition?

"Go away," mumbled Brina without opening an eye. She could sense someone near to her.

"You can speak," whispered Glen.

Brina was instantly alerted to the unfamiliar speaking voice. "Of course, I can. Who the hell are you?" Brina spoke as loud as her weak voice would allow.

"My name is not important."

"The hell it isn't."

"I've got to get you outta here. Can you walk?"

"Go away."

"I can't leave you here with that thing." Glen was concerned for the woman's safety.

"Go away. What's going on here is none of your business." Brina was getting irritated. Her eyes flew open.

She could see!

The man before her had brown eyes and long brown hair. His height was hard to tell, being bent over like he was, but she figured it to be about six foot and his weight to be about two-forty. "Who the hell are you?" She tried tuning in her seventh sense about him, but it was nowhere to be found.

503

"Doesn't matter. I've got to get you out of here."

"I said go away," Brina said with a hint of anger in her voice.

"I'm not leaving you here." He couldn't leave her. Not with that thing.

"I'm in no danger. Buzz off."

"Not in any danger—like hell you say. Don't you know what holds you here?"

Who cared? Surely not her. He'd been taking care of her for weeks now. It was her savior, her well-giver. He would not harm her, nor she him. "Leave. Go on git. Go about your business."

"No way. I'll not leave you with that thing. Are you crazy or what?"

Crazy. That was a good question. She didn't have time to explain her situation to him, nor did she have the desire to. "I'm perfectly fine. Now, get lost, cowboy." She hoped her refusing to go with him would deflate his ego and send him on his way, but it hadn't.

"I'll not leave you." Glen was insistent.

"Arrogance. Master of his race. Shit," Brina said in exasperation.

Without warning, the woodsy scent returned.

Glen caught a glimpse of something approaching out of the corner of his eye. He immediately stood to face it.

Unthinking, Brina's muscles and tendons tightened like a bow-string, ready to snap.

The shadowy form entered the clearing. Its indistinct form floated towards the intruder.

Glen drew his gun. He was going to protect her, along with himself, one way or another.

The shadowy form froze.

Glen pulled back the hammer, cocking the weapon.

"No. Don't," was the strained warning issued from the woman on the ground.

The shadowy form took a step towards the intruder.

Glen took aim. "Don't come any closer!" He didn't want to shoot the creature but would if he had to.

Not waiting a second longer, Brina threw back the covers, preparing to lunge at the stranger.

The sudden movement to his left caught Glen's eye. He instinctively turned her way. With the gun still in his hand and cocked, it accidentally went off, missing Brina by inches.

Brina's years of training at the Academy, honed instincts, and time with Wolf had given her something this man knew nothing about, *her*. Her protective instincts kicked into overdrive. Not only for her, but for the shadowy form as well.

According to Brina, this man had had his chance when he was more than encouraged to leave but had lost that when he refused to do so. Now he was hers. And she was going to kick his ass.

Once both blanket and hide were thrown clear, Brina quickly rolled her nude body to the far side of her bedroll. Hearing the bullet *pssssst* past her ear, she jumped to her feet, whirled clockwise, lashing out with her bare foot making contact with her opponent's abdomen. Clear of her attacker, Brina stood poised, ready for any attack. She was a tad shaky, but at least she was vertical.

The air was knocked out of Glen, but not quite enough to slow or knock him down. Brina's weakened condition had caused her blow to hit much softer than anticipated.

"Whatcha do that for?" a perplexed Glen hissed between gulps of breath.

Brina ignored his words, as he had ignored her urging to leave.

Now he was getting angry. "Damn it all to hell! Bitch, can't you see—"

The words were lost on Brina. All she could see was an armed man taking his anger and frustration out on a mysterious entity whose only purpose in this lifetime was to help a poor, defenseless female. Shit. If she was going to do anything in this life, she was going to teach this guy a little respect.

At first, all Glen saw, was a woman with gunmetal gray eyes standing toe to toe with him. A color not lost on him. Behind them was an angry fire ready to take him on. He couldn't believe it. A woman, a mere woman wanted a piece of him, and not necessarily in a form he was accustomed to. And if he read those gray eyes right, she would take him apart piece by piece if necessary. Not knowing this female, Glen understood that he couldn't underestimate any skills and/or abilities she might have. Second, he had a healthy respect for her boldness, if not her arrogance or her bravery. He didn't care why, he was there only to protect, to serve, to assist those who needed it. And by the looks of things, he might have been mistaken. It might be himself who needed such assistance.

After evaluating his situation, his second look at her told him much. His second look told him that not only did he have a beautiful woman to contend with, but also a well-built, sinewy, slender-of-stature, gray-eyed, dark-brown-haired woman clad with nothing on but her birthday suit. Damn, she was beautiful! When was the last time he was with a woman? Any woman? In any situation?

Brina's senses kicked in telling her of the change in him. It infuriated her—why in the hell hadn't the dumb thing shown up at an earlier time? Why did it lay in wait until now? What difference did it really make now; after all, it was here now, when she needed it most. And if she hadn't been so horribly mistreated, beaten, and sexually attacked by Lucifer, perhaps she'd feel differently about this man before her. Not too differently, but not so damned dirty, not so horribly degraded. She hadn't felt that way at all, until now. Until he looked at her that way—*that way*. It just drove home how Lucifer had looked at her, how he had treated her, how he had touched her. And that made her more than angry, more than dirty, more than wanting to kill; it made her want to literally rip this guy to shreds.

Up it came. All the rage, the disgust, hatred, betrayal, of being handled like a fucking piece of meat. Damned that Lucifer! Damned him all to hell! And now this. Naked or not, she would take this guy out. How dare he think of taking advantage of a naked woman who'd been sick and injured, protected and nurtured by an unknown entity. How dare he, indeed!

"I'm warning you, back off, jackass, or your ass is gonna be grass," Brina hissed.

"Are you threatening me? You?" Glen was amused.

"Leave, while you've got the chance." Brina began to circle the man before her, like a cat on the prowl.

"Or you'll do what?" Glen was sneering now.

Without warning, the ground began to tremble, shake, and lurch. Glen was knocked off balance and fell to the ground. Brina managed to stay afoot. The ground shook, rattled, and rolled for a full minute. Then without further ado, it stopped. Dead silence surrounded the campsite.

The momentary tension breaker gave Brina a moment to reconsider her condition. Her nakedness. She was mentally vulnerable in such a state. Quickly she turned back towards her bedroll, glanced around, spotted, then snatched up a light cotton shirt that was not there moments ago. Dawning it, she turned to face her opponent, feet spread wide, balanced, and ready. "You still want a piece of me, asshole?" Being partially covered lessened her feeling of exposure. It brought on more of the strength and determination not there moments ago.

Glen was stunned. What had done that? A quake? Was the sky about to fall? He wondered, since the tremor occurred at a most timely manner, had she something to do with it? He'd heard many a bizarre tale of this valley; were any of them true? Was it possible? Was she a witch? He'd read stories about them.

He needed his gun. Where was it? He needed it in his hand. Needed to feel its heaviness, needed to feel its steel. Needed the weight in his hand, on his hip. He needed it so he could get out and away from this insanely half-naked woman, her world-shaking powers, and her floating whatever it was. Frantically he searched the spot he thought it had fallen.

"Looking for something, buddy?" Brina asked of Glen. She stood facing him in her cotton shirt with his very own pistol nonchalantly held in her right hand.

"Hand it over!" Glen demanded, believing his words could make the woman cower.

"Not on your life." Brina chuckled. "What do you take me for, a fool?"

Glen took a step towards her.

"I wouldn't if I were you. I know how to use this." For his benefit, Brina checked its cylinder for loads, snapped it back in, and took aim.

"Wait, wait. Don't shoot. I've got kids!"

"Do you now?" Brina wondered but cocked the weapon anyway.

"You wouldn't dare."

"Are you willing to bet your life on that one?"

Was he? Screw it. He lunged at her, trying to grab the gun away. She fired.

XLVII

off the beaten path

T he wooded glen of Dagon was hidden deep within of the Valley of the Fire Moon. Its green forest held many beautiful and wondrous things. It was the hub of all that flew, climbed, crawled, stepped, and swam. It was where the sum of them all, their horses, and the gray-eyed-one journeyed.

When Brina awoke, she heard bird song. Yawning, she stretched the night's kinks away, then opened her eyes to greet the morning. She sat bolt upright from whence she lay. She was no longer under the moon and the star-lit sky of only a few nights ago; she was here, in an unfamiliar closed-in place, in unfamiliar bedding.

"Where the hell am I?" she demanded to know of no one in particular.

Looking around, Brina saw that she was in a rounded enclosure of some kind. Its sides, smooth and tall, tapering as they rose upward, eventually closing onto each other at the very top. There were bowls on the earthen floor containing pasty colors of goo, all matching those of rainbows. The interior of the enclosure was kept warm by a small hearth of small red-hot coals that burned, smoldered, and glowed effortlessly at its center. Her bed was a soft hide the color of burnt wood, with smaller pelts nearby, many white, some black, and a single red.

Her condition, as she guessed, was clothed. Clothed only in the long light cotton shirt of the other day. She felt fine yet was still a tad tired. She checked herself over. There were no broken bones, no bleeding, no bruises, no hint of concussion, no vision problems, no scrapes, no scratches, no injuries of any kind. What was going on here? And where the hell, was she? Who had her? What was she doing here? Where was here? And how was she to escape? First, she must find out, and then do so—pronto. The other answers could wait.

Cautiously she checked the earthen floor for holes, cracks, and crevices. There were none. She checked the smooth sides of the enclosure, checked them against the earthen floor. Finally, she found what she was looking for. An opening. A door. A way out.

She listened for any sound of a guard nearby. When she detected none, she peeled back a corner of the material to peek outside.

She gave the area a general once-over. What she found was surprising. There were more of the same enclosures everywhere. They were scattered haphazardly all around. All were made up of the same material—softened leathers, just like hers. Each was the same yet different. Each had its own adornments, whether they be feathers, animal paintings on their sides, or that of colorful stripes, small and large circles, and other strangely jagged patterns. Some were even being set up by women as Brina watched. Others had children playing around their openings while older women were sketching more basic figures on their sides, and still more were coloring them in. The women seemed hard at work. The children hard at play.

Brina watched as many of the women diligently drew the different animal forms on each of the structures. At first, she couldn't put her finger on what had grabbed her attention about the drawings, but eventually it dawned on her. The majority of their drawings consisted of wolves, deer, bear, horses, and other figures, yet some were different still or appeared quite deformed. More of them than not were familiar. Some she'd studied, some she'd seen, many she'd tracked. A lot she hadn't. Amid the unfamiliars, these women were drawing winged beasts. Beasts with massive wings, long necks, four to six legs, hoofed and/or clawed feet. Some had long pointy teeth, some not. They were really strange. Those appeared very, very tall, with rounded backs and long stringy tails. It was fascinating just thinking if these things had really existed at one time. Yet as bizarre and dangerous as these creatures could be, if they did truly exist, it mattered little, for these were just drawings on leather and not real.

Shifting her attention away from the women, their strange drawings, and their triangular structures, Brina surveyed the rest of the encampment. Milling about were boys on spotted ponies, clothed in leathers of various lengths, designs, and colors, with no apparent destinations in mind. Additional young men, women, and younger children were also drifting about, gathering sticks. Even more were doing a multitude of chores, as their never-ending work seemed to keep them forever occupied. So occupied, in fact, they never gave her a second glance.

Out of curiosity, Brina left the enclosure, keeping low to the ground. She didn't want to be too conspicuous. But instead of escaping as she had first planned, Brina stopped, sat directly in front of the opening of which she just passed through, crossed her legs, sat back for an hour, and watched.

It was a wonderful setting. Children played contentedly as some of their mothers carried firewood and water. Still more women were tanning and stitching what Brina believed to be animal hides. These, she assumed, were being made up as replacement covers for several of the enclosures around the village, if not for clothing themselves.

Over in a corner, Brina spotted an elderly woman as she sat silently in front of a lodge of some sort. A lodge that was different from all the other structures. Its construction was that of twigs and brush, which made it look rather like a thatched house. Looking around, she found it to be the only one of its kind. The woman sat cross-legged, just like Brina, with pots scattered about her frail frame as she wove a grass basket. Her eyes never left the horizon, as her disciplined fingers diligently maneuvered each individual grass into its proper place. Brina was so fascinated with her handiwork and her diligent fingers she stood, walked over, and stood directly in front of her. Brina expected her to look up at her, but she never did. She just kept diligently working.

"How are you feeling?" said a woman's soft voice behind her.

Brina whirled around at the suddenness of the words, only to find a young maiden atop a spotted pony. An Indian maiden who had rode up to where Brina stood, from far beyond, and was just now dismounting.

Brina looked her up and down. She was a very young and pretty thing who wore a long-sleeved deerskin dress with all different colors of beads decorating its front. Her hair was as black as the night sky and was worn in braids fastened at the bottom with leather thongs, which hung past her waist. Around her forehead was a headband with the same colors and pattern as the beads on the dress. The skin of her face, neck, and hands was smooth, flawless, and very tanned. Her eyes glistened like the morning dew. She stood before Brina like a whisper on the wind.

"Better. Thank you very much."

"That is very good. We were all very concerned."

"Concerned?"

"Yes, very."

"Why?"

"You do not recall?"

Brina didn't, or at least couldn't, and therefore shook her head indicating thus.

"We are not surprised. You were so very sick, for so very long."

"Sick? I don't remember being sick."

The Indian maiden recalled for her, her abduction by Lucifer Carstead, his deviate intentions and actions upon her person, their arrival and actions thereof, and touched lightly on her healing process.

Brina interrupted. The last several weeks were coming back a little too quickly. "Wait. Stop. I've had enough." The bile rose in her throat at the thought of Lucifer and what he'd done.

"We will give you a moment to gather yourself."

Brina swallowed it back down. It stayed there—thank the *All Mother.*

"He is gone now."

"Yes. I know. His body was at my feet, bleeding profusely. I remember."

"That is good. You remember. You must remember. Remember everything."

"Why should I remember *everything?*"

"The remembering will make you stronger."

Brina considered her words. "What about the spear? It disappeared shortly thereafter. What about that?" Brina asked, for she remembered that vividly.

"Of course. It is as She planned."

"Excuse me?"

"The ornately carved, petrified ceremonial spear that was hurled through the air into your attacker belongs to her. She who ordained it."

"Her, she, who she?"

"Why, the Mother, of course."

"The Mother."

"Yes. The Mother of this land. It is She who rules and protects all."

Brina paused in her questioning. Was it possible? Was this young maiden speaking of the one, the only? "Surely, you're not suggesting...?"

"She is here, with us now."

Brina spun around expecting to see another, but there was no one there. "You're kidding, of course."

"If it is proof you need—"

"That would be nice."

"It will not be forthcoming. She does not need to prove her presence. She is here, with us. All who reside here within this valley know of her presence."

"How?"

"They see her everywhere."

"What do you mean *everywhere*?" Brina was anxious to know all she could.

"Look around you."

Brina did. Closer than before. At first, she didn't see anything. But then it came to her in bits and pieces. She saw it on their faces, in their eyes. The people around her were truly at peace with the land, with the animals, with themselves. There was a merging of togetherness. A feeling of serenity that bound the people, the animals, the mountains, the trees, and its valley together. It was something she had not seen before or experienced anywhere else. It was almost musical, harmonious, instrumental. She could see it. She could feel it. But she didn't understand it. And that kinda frightened her.

"Do not be alarmed. We will not harm you. On the contrary."

"It was you then." Brina had been giving the last month considerable thought. "You. You brought me here."

"We brought you here."

"There was only one entity."

"Are you sure?"

"Of course, I'm sure."

"You could not see. How would you know?"

"How do you know I couldn't see? You weren't there."

"We were there. She was there. She is everywhere. All of the time."

This was getting confusing. "We, we, she, her, we. I don't get it. I only saw only the one."

"The one what?"

"The shadowy form. He was the only one who tended me."

"Let me explain."

"That would be nice."

"Come back to the tepee. We will talk there."

Brina followed her and her spotted pony back to the tepee, where she learned of many things. Some unbelievable, some enlightening, some revealing, some amusing, some things that didn't surprise her. Nope, didn't surprise her at all.

"They were here? In this very camp?" Brina had just learned that she had missed both Dillon and Cordell by mere days. "I can't believe it!" She couldn't. They had been so close, but now they were so far away. As it turned out, she was recuperating from her last encounter with that fella who'd entered their camp only days before. All three of them had been meters apart and didn't even know it.

All those days spent in their company flooded back to her in a torrent. Her mission, the real reason she was sent here, her head injury, her new and exciting friendships, her blood tie to Cordell, the apparent love Dillon had shown for her, how hard it was to convince the one but not the other, the Hawthorne Hotel, its proprietor, and that helpful maiden, whose words were not understood, yet whose actions were. Time spent in Dowdyville with that crazy sheriff who drank with his horse in the saloon, her escapades with Horace and that bitchy whore. Her horrible revealing dream, her departure from her friends, followed by her discovery of Justin, and their escapades since that time. What a time it had been. What a time, indeed.

And she'd just missed them by days.

"Your very own destiny awaits you. Theirs follows a different trail, one that will eventually lead them full circle."

"How will I get there?"

"You have two horses."

"My horse is not here. You know he isn't. You even know who he is, what he is."

"Yes. We know. You are very fortunate to have one so great be so close. Very fortunate indeed."

Brina thought it comical. "Thanks. He means more to me than you can imagine."

"We can imagine quite a lot," the Indian maiden said as she broadly smiled at the gray-eyed one. *"Quite a lot indeed."*

Brina smiled. "Somehow I don't doubt *that* for a second."

"Come. We must prepare you for the remainder of your journey."

"What will I find there?"

"You have most of your answers. We have given you those. The rest, you will find on your own."

"You didn't tell me about the man who entered our camp."

"You misread his intentions. We had to intervene."

"What do you mean misread his intentions?"

"He feared for your life. His wanting to save you was sincere."

"Who was he? Did I kill him?"

"You missed him."

"I couldn't have. It was point-blank range."

"We know. We were there, remember?"

"You said you intervened. You made me miss?"

"We did."

"Who was he anyway?"

"He was an associate of your two friends."

"Where is he now? What did you do with him?"

"We relocated him to another sector. It will take him many days to return. Many days. That is, if he wants to."

"Where did you send him?"

"We will not say."

"Surely you didn't kill him."

"Silly one, no. His life is worth more than death. He is where he wants to be. He has his gold."

"His gold?"

"His gold."

She smiled serenely at the one with the gunmetal gray eyes.

XLVIII

morning star of paladin

Brina left the Valley of the Fire Moon in the early spring. She had to. She had a life elsewhere. Leaving wasn't going to be so bad. She'd made so many friends, learned so many things, and had seen so many strange and wondrous things. None of which she would ever forget.

She was prepared to leave. She was mentally ready to leave. She'd made peace with herself and with Lucifer's memory. What she needed now was to get on with her life, her mission. She was again strong, vital, ready for that mission—*what was left of it*. She'd worked hard getting there. Many hours were spent getting back into shape, building up her endurance, her strength. A dozen or so of *her children* helped in these tasks. They played games with her. Games of chase and games of chance. These helped Brina immensely. *Her children* could run for hours without tiring, and over several weeks' time, Brina finally managed to do the same. She took on many of the chores of both the men and the women. She chopped down saplings, working her way up to the larger ones. She worked wood, scraped hides. She hauled building materials, water, rocks, baskets loaded with goods. She even practiced throwing hatchets, axes and knives—hitting their marks dead-on (*after a whole lot of practice*). She even got a chance to hone her own knifing skills using an ornate hunting knife belonging to one of the young men who, by the way, had a crush on her. It all turned into a contest of sorts. Yet to let a woman beat the men of the village was totally unheard of. But in this case, they allowed it. It was written.

Getting used to Lucifer's guns was another matter. They were in top shape, clean and primed, but not of the period of her Colts or of the rifle still with Wolf. These were really antiquated and not too very accurate. Brina was surprised how anyone could hit anything with these oddities, especially after being so attached to her pearl-handled babies like she was. But in the end, getting used to these handguns was like anything else. One could do it if one dedicates the time and effort. Which she did. Same with Lucifer's rifle. The four of them would make an efficient team.

Brina decided to leave Lucifer's horses with the All Mother and *her children* too. She didn't really want to part with the mare, but it was for the best that she did. Not only would his animals constantly remind her of their *dear departed owner* and all that he did, but here, in the valley, they'd have a special, protected, and a sacred place where they could roam free, graze to their hearts' content unbridled and with spirit. And for Brina that was just as important. In the mare's place, the All Mother bequeathed her very own spotted pony and a second be taken. Brina said she would be proud to accept such gifts, and therefore it, too, was written.

Several of *her children* accompanied the gray-eyed one back towards the tunnel of Arapath. Together they passed the swirling waters, passed the funny shaped rocks with their small and beautiful winged dragons flying about, passed the trees and the fog-lined mountaintop. Once back through the tunnel, Brina was told not to follow the trail of her friends but to retrace backwards the original trail leading in. Once at the bottom of the mountain, she was to turn northwest towards Banner Mountain and finally north to the Valley of the Sun. There she would expect to find many of the answers she sought.

By midsummer Brina had passed through Banner Mountain and was almost on the eastern horizon of the Valley of the Sun. What a trip that had been.

When she first came upon Banner Mountain, she saw a craggy mountain range with rolling hills at its base, whose slopes were dotted haphazardly with the many different shapes and sizes of trees that were indigenous to the region (like most mountain ranges she'd come across). Little had she known at the time, but Banner Mountain was at the southernmost boundary of the valley she was to cross, and supposedly in it, find her answers.

Months ago, she thought entering the Valley of the Fire Moon was interesting. Had she known that this place was to be more treacherous, the trail more unsure, the experience more unnerving, she might have ridden south after the winter.

The trail, as it turned out, was a fissure of sorts that ran right through the base of the bloody mountain itself. It was the only way to get where she was to go. She knew this because she'd tried other avenues. Matter of fact, she looked for hours for another way, but there were no other ways to cross or get around the mountain. Every turn, every trail she took ended up as a solid-rock wall. A wall whose face was flat and seemed to extend straight to the moon—with no way around it—unless one had wings. So, she gave up on that idea and headed back to the fissure.

The trip in started out simple enough, but once inside the darkening interior of the mountainous caverns, Brina was instantly seized by a force of unknown origin. It was as though something from the deepest reaches of the All Mother was singing to her inner soul a mysterious song that drew her deeper into the cavern's depths.

The horses did fine. There were no complaints there. Even though the trail led in a downwards direction, as though heading for the devil's domain, the horses moved on like it was the thing to do. Brina wanted to believe the All Mother had had a hand in that one and silently thanked her for such stable animals.

The lighted path began to darken as the trail swooped and turned farther and farther away from the outer world. Finally, the entrance was gone, and so was the light. Darkness. The horses trudged on nevertheless, with level attitudes, with steps sure and unwavering as if the tunnel was brightly lit. They walked on like they knew exactly where they headed as they took Brina deeper and deeper into the cavern's blackest depths.

On one turn, Brina spotted a tiny spark of shimmering light that rhythmically beat against the up- and-coming rock wall along that she rode. Anxiety turned to hope, as dreams of sunlit skies, green grassy knolls, and vast horizons took form. Unfortunately, she was not to get her wish, as the song in her head was growing stronger now, more demanding as though calling her in. But calling her in to what?

Without fail, the next turn of the trail brought her directly to the source of the light. One moment she was riding the trail; in the next she had entered a large, round, cavernous room with ceilings reaching way beyond one hundred feet high. There in the center of this huge room was the source of the singing and of the light. It was a circular object resembling a sphere, which put forth a blinding light, yet when Brina entered, it dimmed slightly so. It hung suspended from nothing, supported by nothing. It floated five feet three inches from the earthen floor. Surrounding the object was a rock wall, not three feet high, short of a foot wide, which rested solidly and silently upon the terra firma upon which she and her entourage also stood. This, Brina assumed, was a barrier of some sorts, protecting small animals and those unaware from either falling in or from the hovering object itself, or vice versa.

Ten feet from the light she reined in the mare. Dismounting, she dropped one rein, assuming the animal would stand, then slowly stepped closer to the lighted sphere behind the rock wall.

The closer she got, the more intense the vibration in the room, in herself. The high-pitched song she'd been sensing since entering the mountain screamed at her. When Brina got within inches from the rock wall, all sensations ceased. The song was gone, the pull had released, all the vibration—in the room and within herself—stilled. This was when she got to take a look at what was on the other side of the wall. Looking over the edge, she found no floor. Nothing 'cept a bottomless expanse that dropped beyond her view. It was like looking into a dark, dark and very deep well.

"Who comes to me?"

After all Brina had been through, all her training, all the places she'd been, and of course traveling with Wolf, she was used to having entities speak up at the strangest moments. So, she wasn't too surprised at the deep, rich baritone voice nor the question that came forth from the well. "'Tis I. Brina Louise Grant."

"Why have you come?"

"I'm on a journey, a quest. I seek your wisdom and guidance."

"Who sends you my way?"

Brina though she was the one to get answers, not the other way around. "The All Mother sends me this way. It is through her and you that I am to find answers to my questions."

"Is it She who sends you to me?"

"Yes. It is *She* who sends me to you." This was getting old, fast.

"Take the left fork.
It is through there you will find the way out."

"Am I not to receive answers from you? I was told that I would."

"You are mistaken, I direct, I do not provide."

Answer my questions indeed, Brina thought to herself. If this was where she was to receive answers to her many questions and this entity was not to provide them, then where in the hell was she supposed to get them?

"Search your heart, for your answers are there.
So, it is written. So, shall it come to pass."

Another one who spoke in riddles. That's all she needed, splendid.

Brina was about to ask another question, but just then the vibration and high-pitched song returned with a vengeance. So much so, she tried covering her ears to block it out, but the sounds were from inside her head, not outside. Apparently, whatever resided in this cavern was now wanting her gone. "Well, at least he gave me a way out," she mumbled to herself.

Not knowing what else to do, since the reverberation was almost too much to bear, Brina turned back to her mount, threw herself on its back, grabbed for the lead of the second, and rode around the walled-in hole towards the tunnels behind. There she found three openings. The far left she took, wondering all the while what exactly was the entity behind the light, why was he there, and was he directing her towards something worse or something better. Why had she been directed here in the first place? There was only one way to find out.

Daylight hit her full force two days later. She wanted to believe in the entity and the directions he gave, but after the first several hours of her second leg of her trip through the mountain had passed, she became increasingly anxious. Several times she'd tried turning back, but at each turn in the tunnel, she'd again find the same thing she'd found outside: a solid-rock wall that reached to the top of the ceiling. It made no sense. Finally, she resigned herself to her own thoughts and prayers. And thanks to the All Mother, not only had she two fine solid, bomb-proof horses under and alongside to carry her on this incredible journey, but she'd also been riding under tons upon tons of rock and soil, seemingly in circles with no way out 'cept the directions from a very well-lit hanging basketball with a deep voice who liked scraping metal objects down chalkboards at full volume. Good thing she didn't have a baseball bat with her; otherwise, she'd have batted that sucker to hell and gone. But surprisingly enough, the entity had come through for her in the end. The tunnel in which she rode did, in fact, emerge into full sunlight and the prettiest valley she'd seen in ages—much more so than the Valley of the Fire Moon.

And so here she was. "Now what?"

The All Mother had told her to head north once leaving the mountain. And since there had been no answers to her questions in Banner Mountain, she'd just continue riding that way until something else came along directing her elsewhere.

BOOK 4

XLIX

my gun hath bullets, see?

*T*he unseen man with his magnificently shaped hands lifted and tilted her head so their eyes would meet. There he searched the depths of her soul through his own eyes for an explanation.

In the beginning, he could not believe his luck, if her face had read correctly. Believing it mirrored his own feelings, he took the chance as it was presented; he was sure there would be no next time. Taking gently her face into his hands so the lovely eyes could be gazed upon, he stopped to hold onto it for just a moment—taking it all in.

The face looked up at him and was beautiful. Her message, clear. Her lips parted as though to speak, but he knew better. Her lips, eagerly inviting him to join unto this special moment. Slowly his head lowered, and his mouth gently brushed her cheek. From her cheek he followed down the contours of her face to her lips. There he took them gently in his. They were as one had dreamed—soft, yielding, floating. There for a moment he felt her stiffen. He slowed his racing heart, slowed his eagerness, backed off a tad, and gave her a chance to relax, and she did.

She may not have realized it, but the urgency in that small kiss offered and the soft moan that followed reached out and touched the unknown man before her.

Yet, who was this man before her? She could not make out his features. She could not see his face. She could not tell his height, weight, or coloration. His scent was void. Who was this masked man who was falling for her, falling from her, falling away from her, falling into her? Who was this guy? It really mattered not, for whomever he was, she and he were together finally. And whatever was about to happen, she was going to let happen, because it was written.

The man now knew this was his dream come true. And from the sheer pleasure in knowing, chose to tread cautiously and to explore his find slowly, com-

pletely. Just for a moment he broke from his next attempted kiss so he could pick her up off the ground in his strong arms. He wanted to take her to a secluded location and take his time with her, explore every nook and cranny, every hump and bump, hither and yon, over and under, port to starboard, side to side; over and over and over again he wanted to search and make love to her.

But at the last second before any of it could begin, Brina Louise Grant woke up forgetting most of what she dreamed.

Brina took her time heading northeast. She knew most of what she came to learn with the exception of Jesse's whereabouts, of course, was from the help of the young Indian maiden. According to her, as far as the Neptune sphere was concerned, there was no such thing. According to what she'd been told, this all-powerful item was not the object she was originally told about by the chancellor. *Sure, why not? After all this way, she was chasing what? Ghosts and their magical tools?* This sphere thing wasn't even something she could hold, touch, or for that matter, retrieve. According to the waif, it was the weapon that had mysteriously vanished after it was used by the shadowy form to kill Lucifer Carstead. It was the ornately carved, petrified, ceremonial *spear* complete with razor-sharp titanium barbs at its metal end, which Brina found to be quite an interesting description to say the least. *It had been a spear, not a sphere*—could it have been a simple spelling error? Did they know of this back home? Had they just wanted to rid themselves of her, or were they just as naive and accepting of those in high places as she once was? There were so many unanswered questions—if any of what she'd been told had any truth to it—many unanswered questions, indeed.

"And do we always believe absolutely everything we're told?"

The waif had also said that the mission she supposedly had been on all this time was a farce too—all these months turning into years for nothing except the adventure. None of it except for the part about Jesse. His part as far as being an assassin was apparently real, and from what the waif said, Jesse had made quite a terrible name for himself while in this time and did, indeed, need to be stopped, and permanently.

"If you have so much control over everything, why not stop him yourself?" asked Brina of the waif.

"*Some things, some peoples, and their fates, along with many events must follow their own paths, their own courses, to their own conclusions. That is also written. She cannot do everything, nor does she want to.*"

Or so Brina had been told. So much for that bowl of cherries. Oh, well.

This new trek of hers, since leaving the village, had taken her deep into a tall mountain holding in its center a strangely lit basketball shaped hanging basket thing with a deep, deep voice that she wanted so dearly to swat with a stick or a baseball bat. If she had one, she would have sent it clear into the next century for sending her on such a rotten three-day ride through its mountain with its sky-high walls that blocked her every turn. Eventually, she did manage to find her way out, but no thanks to that damned basketball thing. She had found her way out strictly because her seventh sense, and her need of such had led her to the sun. *So there.* At least that's the way she wanted to see it. Anyway you looked at it, she was now heading northeast as per its instructions.

At first, she thought it was her imagination, that strange looking sapling tree thing way up ahead, but as they grew nearer, she could see that this was no ordinary piece of wood. This small tree walked, often times tripped, while it tried carrying what looked to be a saddle across its shoulders as it crossed the open prairie. A horseless rider she assumed it was, as opposed to a horseless carriage—*not another man, please*—

Apparently, whoever it was, spotted her as she came from afar. She watched as *another man to meet and to deal with* laid his saddle down upon the ground and sat down along with it to wait for her. The closer she got, the more he came into focus. From what she could tell, he had exceptionally long black hair. It must've hung down to his waist. She'd seen hair like that on men before, not for a long time and certainly not in this time period. Nevertheless, one was here before her.

"Howdy!" the long-haired fella hollered and waved as Brina rode closer.

"Howdy back atcha!" Brina responded. "Lose your horse?" She was still far enough away for safety's sake—just in case.

"Yep. Several miles back. Found ourselves in the midst of a hailstorm, and the animal spooked with me on 'im, tripped, and broke his damned leg. I had to shoot 'im."

"Bad luck that," Brina began. "Where ya headed?"

"Was headed back to Eastern-Western, but without a horse, might take a bit longer than I expect."

"Where 'bouts is that?"

"Up yonder ways. 'Bout a hundred miles or so."

"What brings you out here? On your way back from somewhere in particular?" This conversation gave Brina a good chance to give this guy the once-over. She needed this chance. There was something about this guy that rang a bell with her, but she just couldn't put her finger on it. His eyes were black. Coal black. He had facial hair so thick, and there was so much of it that she couldn't distinguish his features. There was something else about him too that bothered her, but again, she couldn't put her finger on it.

"Where're you headed?" the stranger asked of our heroine.

"Northeast."

"That'd be about Eastern-Western way, if I'd know my way around these here parts."

"Been around long then, have you? Visiting relatives and the likes?" Brina wanted to sound as nonchalant as she could.

"Nope. Just been wandering, looking, seeing what's out there."

Not wanting to assist someone she knew nothing about, especially after that encounter with Lucifer, and more especially, not having Wolf around for insight, she was reluctant to offer any help—her being a woman and all *(hahaha—like that made a difference)*. But then again, she could let him walk the ground while she took the saddle and placed it on her second horse—out of politeness, per se.

"Need a hand?"

"Sure, if you've the room."

"Well, since I am a semi-defenseless woman on this here high prairie of yourn and that I do have some extra room on my second horse, I could take the saddle, making your travels easier, if you don't mind walking?" Brina had Lucifer's pair of guns strapped around her hips for insurance's sake across this barren land.

He came along the side of her to stand for a moment. "Mind if I tighten the cinch enough to hold my weight and allow me to climb aboard?" asked the tall, very dark, and hairy stranger.

"Actually, I do mind."

"Why be that?"

"Frankly, it would be too much weight for her to carry, and too precarious a load. Not to mention the fact that I don't know anything about you. You could be a bandit in disguise, wanting to steal my horses, kill me." Brina laced it with sarcasm, while never breaking eye contact. Besides, she liked him better afoot.

"Never." The man was slightly put off but was still wary due to her wearing a double rigging of pistols.

"We'll see how things fly, play it by ear—see how it goes," Brina stated matter-of-factly.

He decided to let it drop for now, at least until maybe later when he could get the drop on her.

"Nice looking guns."

"Thanks." Only reason Lucifer's guns were nice was because she had always made sure her rigs were always cleaned and ready, and she had worked hard on these two—because they weren't as nice, modern, and their actions weren't as smooth as her Colts were.

"Might ya want to sell 'em?" He could always use another set of guns.

"Don't think so. Might need them against wandering folk." *Smile when you say that, stranger,* she thought.

"Know how to use them?" he slyly asked.

"In a pinch." The seriousness of her words came out like a viper's tongue.

"Just checking, just checking, no offense. Just wanted to make sure, if'n we ran into some of them desperados, if'n you could protect me—since I am afoot." He was starting to feel a tad nasty at this broad with the two horses who made him walk while his saddle was cinched on her second horse all the while she rode bareback. It wasn't setting right with him, not at all. "Where ya from?" the stranger asked of Brina.

That was a good question, she thought. She often wondered that one herself. "Of late, or originally?"

"Either, neither, however you want to answer. I'm just conversing to pass the time away while *I walk, and you ride.*"

The way he said it and what was said was not lost on Brina. She stopped the animals.

"Would you rather…"

He was waiting for her to ask the obvious question and approached the second animal.

"Would you rather that I dumped your saddle here and now, then hightailed it down the trail leaving you to steam like a train all by your little ol' lonesome? Or would you be kind enough to keep a civil tongue in your head and walk a few steps off, keeping your nasty comments to yourself?" Brina had had enough of this kind of man. Justin was a different matter, Dillon was a different matter, Cordell was a surprise and a most definitely different matter. This guy was being a real jerk and was probably a mental case to boot. She was not going to put up with any more jerks, wise-asses, or deviates. Not on this trip anyway.

Still steaming, but reining in his anger, the man stepped away from the stirrup and off to the side. "Better?"

"Better." She still hadn't lowered her guard and watched him out of the corner of her eye.

Fifteen minutes of silence later, she attempted to converse. "What's your name, stranger?" Funny. It sounded just like those old ancient B-Westerns she watched with MJ.

"Ma friends and acquaintances call me CJ, and you?"

Of course, what did she think he was going to ask in return? Great. Now what? What was she going to call herself now? Brina Louise Grant was beginning to be a name too well known in these parts. Bree, on the other hand, was a name she'd given to Justin only and really didn't want that to be used by any other Tom, Dick, Harry, or CJ for that matter. What was she to call herself? Then it came to her.

"Pixie. Pixie Woods."

"Strange name for a gal."

How she hated being called "gal," but it fit the times (*argh*). "I had strange parents." Which, in a strange way, was absolutely correct.

Now that he had her name, he gave her a closer once-over trying to fit the two together. Pixie. The name didn't fit her. "Pixie" sounded like something attached to a two foot tall, red-headed, freckle-faced child with a look of innocence, long pointed ears, and ivy growing out of her head. Not someone tall like this beauty, with dark-gray eyes, ivory skin, and dark hair. Pixie? Naw. Bet it wasn't her real name—and unless she had a sector identification card, one with her photo that she'd let him see, he'd never know, or for that matter care, for innocent or not, bitches in this time had no ID cards.

But, innocent? Over twenty-one? Never. He wondered if he shaved some, if she'd find him attractive enough to mount, just like her pony? "Well, Pixie, shall we mosey on down the trail?"

"Sounds like a plan, CJ."

The two continued in silence for miles on end.

Come evening, Brina handled the stock as usual. Not wanting to show her masculine side, that being the hunting, skinning, "bringing back the bacon" sorta girl, asked if he would be kind enough to find dinner.

"Are you kidding? I don't provide meals. I go to restaurants, bars, and cafés for that. Here, I've got some jerky from last week in my saddlebags if ya want to chew on it."

Brina settled on the jerky. *This time.*

Come morning, each took their turn at the spring Brina found a half mile or so back. CJ was kind enough to allow her the time she needed first, her being the woman and all. Thinking this was a more gentlemanly thing for him to do and perhaps she'd note that for later should he decide to get a tad more "friendly." But the one thing he hadn't expected, happened.

By the time CJ had returned to camp after taking his turn, Brina (or Pixie if you'd rather) had camp all cleaned up, horses rigged for travel, and their campsite void of any traces of their passing.

"What the hell is this?" He had spent extra time at the watering hole to do just as he was thinking the night before. His hair was still awfully long, yet for her he'd tied it in the back, but the facial hair was gone and in its place was a chiseled face with pockmarks here and there from some explosion he'd caused in his earlier years spent with the Network.

Brina took one look at him and knew instantly who he was! Within a fraction of a second, Brina had drawn, cocked, and held ready both guns on the man before her.

"WHAT THE HELL ARE YOU DOING?"

"CJ, my ass! You're Dillard Pickle a.k.a. Carl Jaster Stewart, a.k.a. Sonny Beech, a.k.a. Jack Ash, a.k.a. Lane Duck, a.k.a. Teddy Baire, a.k.a. Otto Control. Did I miss any? Change your name to something altogether different when you crossed over, did you? Correct me if I'm wrong." The moment Brina saw that chiseled face without all that hair, she recognized this man instantly as Dillard Pickle, one of Jesse Loame's associates. A photo of him, along with all the other lowlifes she was to watch out for if not outright kill on the spot, was in Jesse's file the day the chancellor briefed her.

The man was in shock. How the hell had she known? With beady eyes he stared her down, or at least tried to. "I don't know you!"

"I will answer all of your questions in just one or two words. Cyclops. The Academy. Do these words ring any sorta bell to you?"

"That's three words, and you're not—"

"I was sent here to take care of you and your friends. How's that for spoiled milk?" She winked, sneered, and raised her eyebrows up and down a few times at the man calling himself Carl J. Stewart.

"Don't shoot! I know where there's a treasure!"

"Treasure, huh? Be it known as the *Neptune sphere*?"

"Yeah, how did you know?" he questioned with a surprised look on his chiseled face.

"Cyclops, the Academy—weren't you listening, you idiot?" She couldn't believe he was so thick headed. "And besides, you can't get it. Not now, not ever. No matter how many people you bamboozle into searching for this damned thing, it ain't gonna do you no good. You're never gonna see it. I've seen it. I know where it is, I know who's got it, and besides, I've seen it in action. And I ain't gonna tell you shit."

"I know where there are instructions on how to use it, if you could lead me to it!"

"It won't do you any good. Those instructions were a hoax, a ploy." *Boy, did she ever get the lowdown on this story from someone close to the source.* "Those instructions were written by an unknown entity who wanted to play a joke on the establishment. And he knew the only way to get a handful or two of us, outta dodge, including and especially myself—giving us all a more exciting and better—hahaha— life, with cleaner and sweeter-smelling air to breathe, (*essence of horse manure*), clear and sparkling water to drink, (*without all the pollution*), all the pretty horses to ride and pet, open ranges to see, to enjoy, and uncluttered scenery to behold was to lay down and eventually set in motion such wild rumors as you've obviously swallowed and run with."

"You don't know what you're talking about."

"Don't I though? Ya see, I know of several of those poor fools out there searching for this nonexistent thing—several of which are associated with Jesse—ya know, like you? And you're not the only fool out there, ya know."

"I don't know what you're talking about."

"What about that marshal you sent on this stupid quest three years past?"

He had to think hard and fast on that one. "Frasier? You know Dillon Frasier?"

"One and the same. Now if you've got anything to say to the almighty—forgiveness for sins against anyone, any woman, or any poor sheep, any such subject matter—better git with it now, 'cause in a moment you'll be as dead as the jerky we had for breakfast." Brina waited.

"You know he now travels with a black bastard," sneered CJ Stewart.

Brina fired, head shot. Point-blank range. Brain matter spattered from the hole in the back of his head to parts unknown. No questions asked. No time for explanations, no arguing, no accusing, no remorse.

Now all she had to do was bury this name calling, murdering, son of a bitch, stinking bastard, sleazebag deep within the ground, or let the wolves have at him and move on to Eastern-Western, with a nice new saddle to put atop her second pretty pony.

One down and who knew how many more to go.

L

getting there is half the fun

 T hree weeks later Brina rode into Eastern-Western for the first time ever.

   It was a much smaller place than she'd expected, yet its clean and surprisingly wide streets, well-maintained sidewalks wide enough for three to walk comfortably side by side, tall and beautifully trimmed dark-green trees lining both sides of the road leading into town gave her the feeling of entering an old friend's house for tea.

   With all things considered, she'd half-expected a sprawling metropolis with sculptured landscaping everywhere—more so than just on the trip in, but that was not to be the case. Apparently, the only plant life other than the occasional tumbling tumbleweed were just those entrance trees—*pity, she thought*. Folks must've had other more important things to occupy their time than to garden and plant trees.

   And instead, and despite the way Dillon had talked, Brina found more of a quaint, quiet, little town nestled near and about in the northwest corner of the Dakota Territories than she was originally led to believe. This particular settlement was located in the heart of sector four of the United Sovereign Territories, zone #55893866-5. This was all with an assumed population of nine hundred—*she believed the count actually included all town characters, dogs, cats, squirrels, and rats*. All of which were trying to survive along the west bank of the Missouri River, whether it be in the middle of winter when the water levels rose dangerously above normal, or in the summer when the mosquitoes were as big as sanitation trucks—trying a million times

537

a day to snack on folks about. In addition to the mosquitoes and according to the map found on the wall outside the sheriff's office (where she was getting most of her information), to the west of them was the Montana Territories, and somewhere hidden within its boundaries was the famed Miles City, known for its sheep, its cattle, its cowboys, Fort Keogh, and its history (not necessarily in that order).

After making herself known to the livery stable owner, Cornelius Thatcher III, with detailed instructions as to the care of her animals and their rigging, Brina headed for The North Star Saloon and Inn, which, according to the owner, was built just two years ago to accommodate visitors from faraway lands. When Brina inquired which faraway lands—her origin being about as far away as one could get—the owner blindly stared out into space as though searching for an answer. Any answer.

Eastern-Western, a real Western town. She was finally in a real live Western town. Not to say that all the other towns she visited these last couple of years weren't Western: it was just that this time she could actually see it for what it really was instead of having her attention divided between horse, mission, and the gentlemen (whichever one it was at the time), with whom she traveled and set up camp with.

Her dear, sweet, traveling companions. Dillon had been from Eastern-Western; she had crossed many a mile with him. She didn't know from where Cordell had originated, nor did it matter for this story. Justin was in the same boat; Brina didn't know from where he originated either. But then she asked about herself. What about Brina? Brina Louise Grant originated from Frisco, and what a distance she's traveled since then. From a safe and secure home in Frisco, followed by procurement to the Academy, through the Zodiac Field to this time, then on to Dowdyville, Mullet Town, Daytonville, Harcort Ranch, the Badlands, the Albright Ranch, Pine Ridge Lake, Valley of the Fire Moon, Banner Mountain, Valley of the Sun, and finally to Eastern-Western.

But why Eastern-Western? Why in the hell here? Why this town? Brina guessed some of the answers, or at least hoped many of them, would come just like the setting sun—when *She* felt it necessary. Either that, or Brina would be gone come fall. No point in waiting around for Christmas.

On the sidewalk, leaning against a decoratively carved wooden pole in front of the inn, Brina let her mind wander back in time, back to those wilder days of yesteryear as the events and the lives of several townsfolk Dillon spoke about—all those many months passed, played out in her mind's eye.

First, there was the chaos of life surrounding the setting of town. Cowboys riding their horses up and down all the roads, the drunks, the townsfolk meandering everywhere, the buckboards and their drivers, the freight wagons being pulled by their team of hefty horses backing in, unloading goods, dust rising and swirling in the breeze, tumbleweeds tumbling, dogs chasing cats, cats chasing mice, mice scurrying from small screaming and delighted children while frantic mothers watched—the sights and sounds were endless. Then, all of a sudden Brina pictured the original "Marshal Potter," the one Dillon spoke so fondly of—long dead now—stepping off from the sidewalk as though crossing the street. She could see the scene unfold as though it was happening before her, now or then, depending on whether you were now dead or still alive.

There he sauntered. Marshal Potter. Stopping to stand in the middle of the street with his back to the sun, too slow for the whiskey-trading gunslinger who beat him to the draw yet was later hung for the deed. The local schoolmarm, Annabelle Drearylane, a determined woman who knew how to shoot a shotgun and hit what she pointed at; that other teacher (whatever his name was) who was found dead on the classroom floor beside an empty bottle of whiskey—Brina wondered for a sad moment who had found him, hopefully not a child. And that man by the name of Joshua C. Baylock and the cowardice he showed to everyone in town—who was probably later rode out of town on a rail-tar and feathered. *What a funny sight that would've been.* Then there was that Mrs. Fitzwilly and her collection of cats. Brina remembered this one pretty well, as they once had cats at the Academy to dispatch the rats (*not normally walking upright*), which were sometimes found in the showers doing some cleanup work with the other rats (*those who did normally walk upright*).

She remembered Dillon speaking of the whores in town, a few of whom she planned on talking to later on—gathering gossip on who to watch out for, when and where they hung their hats. The names Bertie, Louise, Dierdre, and Cassandra all rang a bell; she hoped she remembered them right—to address them thus and have her be wrong would not be proper for a lady of her or their distinction.

Then there was "Johnny Soars Like an Eagle" rather Johnny S. Hartley—newly appointed deputy by Marshal Dillon Frasier. If Brina was ever in need of anyone before settling down for a spell in this town, the deputy was one she had to contact. She wondered for a moment whether or not he was still dating…what was the name Dillon mentioned…? Oh yeah, Ellie Broomdale, daughter of one of the storekeepers. Dillon never really said Johnny was dating anyone, but Brina, in her infinite wisdom, assumed they were. As to the townsfolk? Brina also believed no one else knew, because it was supposed to be a great big secret.

After Dillon left Eastern-Western in search of his brother, John Hartley was made honorary Sheriff. A job he's held since then. He loved his job. Loved the respect he'd earned from the townsfolk. Loved the work itself. It kept him busy. Kept him in the hearts and minds of the people, of the children, of their parents, the storekeepers, and visitors. Kept what he truly was, a half-breed half-Cherokee bastard, at bay. Not to misunderstand, but to grow up between two worlds, neither of which wanting to lay claim, both hurling threats in all shapes and sizes, Johnny was thrilled to have had Dillon on his side. In him, Dillon saw an inner strength, an inner pride, and honored his friendship, and because of that, Johnny carried himself like a king. After all, when one grows up hard, and is eventually found and admired for himself, whether it be now or later, one can feel like a king. So, when he heard there was a newcomer in town, one who rode in with two spotted ponies, the king was intrigued. He had to find the ponies, see 'em, talk to 'em; see who rode them, who it was, meet him, shake his hand. Sheriff Hartley liked spotted ponies and always checked out strangers. It made for a better understanding between all.

Yet somehow this stranger had been able to avoid contact with anyone of any importance. They were still in town; John knew this because the beautiful spotted horses were still in the livery being taken care of by strict instructions of their owner. He found that part rather amusing. Yet, at the same time, he never gave it a second thought that their owner wasn't a male. He never talked of the owner to Cornelius, as Cornel was always too busy shoveling manure or some such menial task, never wanting to be bothered for mere chitchat.

John checked out every nook and cranny of town for this invisible stranger. Even at the North Star, he discovered the signature was too hard to read, and the bellboy who'd originally tended them had been called home to take care of his sick ma, so he was pretty much a dead end as far as that information went. Assuming the gentleman was in the assigned room according to the register, John climbed the stairs and knocked on the designated door, getting nothing but a hollow and empty sound. Curiosity getting the better of him, he tried the knob—slowly. Pushing the door open and stepping inside discovered nothing but an empty room with a twenty-dollar gold piece resting on the dresser with a note of apology and a request of immediate checkout, again signed by the same hand as the unreadable name in the register.

Where was this "masked man" hiding? Johnny wondered.

Brina had originally checked into the North Star Inn, but while signing the register, she began to have second thoughts. What if the reason she was summoned here was to meet or find an associate of Jesse's? What if someone from the Network was near and just might recognize her or her signature. What if, what if, what if. There were too many "what ifs," and if any of them held water, other than just an over-imaginative mind, she needed to cover some of her tracks.

Thus, in the middle of signing her name, she decided to make it illegible by definition so no one would be the wiser. And to better hide herself and any future tracks, she decided not to stay at this particular inn either, and instead left a puzzling note requesting release from the room along with a $20 gold piece for their troubles on the dresser and headed down the street in search of the house of ill-repute. When Brina asked Cornel if they'd had anyone in town by the names of Louise Shifter, Willow Tree, or Cassandra Banks, he had directed her to "The Pussy Willow Inn and Massage Parlor." Being a stranger and all, Cornel insisted that she talk to the owner, Justin Thyme, who always had a firm "hand" on everything going on, *or in,* his establishment.

This she did. And after reacquainting her friendship with Willow Tree, after meeting Justin Thyme, who happened to be a dropout from the Academy and relocated thus, not only did Brina get the scoop on everyone in town but was also given a nice and totally frilly private room, usually reserved for important dignitaries from far away, where she could hang her "hat" until it need come down.

Which was why Sheriff Hartley couldn't find her.

Brina stayed in her room and was waited on hand and foot for five days in a row by the owner, Willow, and especially the other girls. She did this because she was still so very exhausted from her trip. Riding the trails, seeing beautiful scenery, enjoying the steed you share your campsite with, even spending the winter with wonderful folks is unforgettable. But to sleep in a real room, in a real bed with real sheets, clean sheets, with a locked door to keep away the rats, as opposed to night after night after night sleeping under a mere blanket for warmth on the cold hard and rocky ground—the bed, my friend, was the only way to fly.

Brina got updates on the care of her stock. Even though they were just horses, they were still special and treasured gifts from the All Mother, and she wanted the best for them. Brina's meals came twice a day, which was sometimes more than she needed, but since Willow came with them, along with her witty personality, charm, and conversation, Brina didn't care an iota; it had been years since she and Willow spent quality time together.

During quiet times, usually in the middle of the night, Brina would sometimes sneak outside, find a quiet location away from town, and work out. From there, she'd head to the nearest well or stream and with her seventh sense tuned in for any wandering derelict, would strip down, and wash herself from head to toe—enjoying the frosty air, the freezing water—then in the nude would sneak around town and check out its design, just for fun. Later, she'd return to her bath-site, redress, and head back to her room. There she'd work Lucifer's guns and rifle, making sure they were clean, making sure her lightning-fast draw and their dry firing were still honed to perfection. Ya never knew when such talents and equipment would come in handy. Even though the rifle was kind of a pain to practice with, along with getting it to work right, she did the best she could with it too.

On the sixth day Brina donned her best pair of cotton blue jeans, gray shirt, boots, and hat, and headed down to the livery in search of her horses and their rigging. Her plan for the day was to get the horses some exercise, enjoy the sunshine and outdoors, and maybe even get a bite to eat.

At the livery, Cornel was just opening the back gate that led into a large corral when he spotted Brina.

"Howdy, miss, lovely day, ain't it?"

"Cornel."

"Come to check out? Your beasts have been very good. I'd be sorry to see them go."

"Naw," Brina said. "Just going for a short ride, that's all—see a little country."

"Sheriff's been asking about ya. Trying to git me to gossip, I guess."

"Idle gossip. Seems it's the only way a town communicates. You say anything?"

"Naw. He sure do like your ponies though. Him being half-Indian and all has something to do with it, I reckon."

"You like my ponies, don't ya?"

"Sure do. Them's mighty nice."

"You're not Indian, are you?"

"Nope. Not that I know of, anywhoos."

"Then ya don't got to be Indian to like ma ponies." Brina smiled as she reached for a brush setting it near to where the mare stood.

She was almost done saddling the mare when she picked up the sound of footsteps approaching. Knowing Cornel was out back, Brina continued cinching up the mare but kept her attention glued to the opening of the barn door.

"Knock, knock. Anyone home?"

It was the approaching voice matching the approaching footsteps. Brina could tell they were the same, common sense dictated, yet she didn't respond. Why? Whomever it was was sure to find her when they entered—regardless of what she uttered.

The sun-outlined silhouette of a man stood in the center of the barn entrance—its portrait darkened and unreadable.

"Evening," greeted the illuminate form.

"Morning," Brina said, correcting in return.

"Is it still?" asked the dark form.

"Is there something I can do for you?" asked Brina, wanting to get to the point so she could get on with the day's activities.

"Yes, there is, as a matter of fact." He paused for a moment, then continued. "You're new here, aren't you?"

"Sorta."

"Been working for Cornelius a few days, have you?"

"Don't work here at all."

"Then you're helping him out."

"Nope. Not that neither."

The voice entered the interior of the barn, closer to where Brina was preparing her mounts.

"Then what are you planning to do with these two ponies?"

"I'm preparing them for a ride. Is there something I can do for you?"

"I'm sorry, Miss. I was looking for either Cornelius or the gentleman who owns these here ponies."

"Cornelius is not here right now, and the ponies are mine." Brina stopped what she was doing and turned to face the face that was just now becoming distinct. He was the same height as she was—about five-nine, dark hair, dark complexion, high cheekbones, pronounced nose, proud. Must be the sheriff.

"Pixie Woods, Sheriff." Brina held out her hand in friendship.

He was impressed. "How'd you know I was sheriff?"

With a smirk on her face and sheer pleasure in her voice, Brina replied, "Well, Sheriff, for one, the badge is a dead giveaway."

He chuckled at the realization of it all.

"And I knew a guy who once lived here who knew you as a deputy, and since he's been gone from here more than three years, I figured you'd probably been promoted a tad."

"Who did you know?"

"Not important now. Too many memories passed."

Curiosity put that thought in the back of his mind for later use. "Johnny Hartley. Sheriff Johnny Hartley now."

"Congratulations, Sheriff. Like your job?"

"Love it."

She couldn't resist. "Still dating Ellie?" The shocked look on his face confirmed her previous suspicions.

"Actually, we've been married a year now—baby on the way."

"Cool." Brina beamed for him.

"Cool?" asked the sheriff.

"Just a figure of speech, Capt'n—oops, sorry, that's just another figure of speech. Don't mind if I call you Capt'n, do you? It kinda just fell out. And besides, it sorta fits ya."

Johnny thought about that one for a moment too. Captain. Sounded good. "Nope, don't mind at all."

"Good. Well, Capt'n, my pony is saddled. I'd like to tour the country a tad before lunch."

"Know your way around?"

"Not really, but I'll figure it out."

It was then he noticed the guns she wore. "Expecting trouble?" He gestured towards her hips.

"Never know."

"Know how to use 'em?"

"In a pinch."

"Good, bad, or mediocre?" He was anxious to know.

She had him dead in a fraction of a second—had she intended it thus. "Fast enough for ya, Capt'n?"

"Shit. I didn't even see it coming. That's fast!! Where'd you learn to draw like that?"

She wondered what she should say. "Years of practice."

"Running from the law or fighting for it?"

"Kinda in the middle, I guess. Been mainly on the better side, but I'll tell ya what, Capt'n, when I get back from my ride, I'll look you up, and we'll sit down somewhere you feel comfortable, and we'll discuss what you're thinking—fair?"

Sheriff smiled. "Fair. Enjoy your ride." He would look forward to their little chat.

"I will, thanks." With that, she re-holstered her weapon, grabbed her mount's left rein, hoisted herself up into the saddle, grabbed the halter rope of the second horse, and out the open door they trotted.

LI

smile when you say that, stranger

By lunchtime, everyone in town had heard about the incident at the livery. After all, Cornelius just happened to come around the corner of the livery door and froze when he oversaw Pixie and the sheriff talking and then saw the gun be drawn like lightning. Things like that just didn't happen, at least not in this town. And since it was totally unheard of in these here parts, he couldn't resist gossiping to everyone he knew about what he'd seen.

The countryside was beautiful, yet different, especially after seeing what she now called the strawberry mountains. The rich red mineral deposits that ran throughout their centers made them such a special find compared to all the other mountains and/or hills she'd seen other places. And what about those loose shale pieces she rode across with their small hiding places for rattlers? One in particular, she just happened to startle awake while he was enjoying the sun, which explained the warning created by those rattles at the end of his tail. A sound she unceremoniously received for intruding upon his quiet sanctuary. Curious, and cautious, Brina watched the reptile as big around as her forearm slither its brown-and-dark-brown scaled body further back into his hole as she crept by. Yes, indeed, it was a hugely different and beautiful part of the country still needing to be cherished and remembered.

Yet, for the most part, Brina was troubled. Under normal circumstances, some things wouldn't hold a candle to the beauty of the countryside or the spotted ponies she rode, given to her by someone very special—but there were some issues that were really bothering her. First, she didn't like lying about her name. Using Bree wasn't too much of an offshoot from Brina, but this stupid Pixie Woods crap was hard for her to swallow and accept. After all, that name really didn't fit her. Its sound fitted a small, pointed-ear, winged, elf-like creature, not at all unlike some of those dark-purple and black, twenty feet tall, winged demons found in the void (where she was summoned from when all this took flight), especially those of them that breathed fire and smoke. No. Pixie did fine for out on the trail when running into straying folk, but in this town, and especially if she planned on staying awhile, wasn't something she wanted to be addressed by. So, after just a short bit of time out on the trail thinking, she decided to rectify that one little issue upon her return to town.

Then there was this other issue of this town and the reason(s) why she was directed here. Eastern-Western of all places. Why Eastern-Western? Why the originating place of Dillon's search of his brother? Did it have anything to do with him or them, or was that just part of her overactive imagination? Was she perhaps to meet someone else here, was she to settle down here, was the Gray Wolf coming here? Or was it just a place to hold up and rest until she again was forced to leave and continue her search for Jesse? If it be that, how long was she supposed to stay? Too many questions, not enough answers.

Back at the livery she unsaddled the mare and let loose the pony, then decided to just sit things out and wait for whatever it was that was to come.

Brina had been sitting at one of the smaller tables in one of the local restaurants named the Gunslinger Tavern *(where'd they get the names for these specialty establishments, outta an old book of Western slang or were they just someone's warped sense of humor?)*, and of all places for her to stop at was the *Gunslinger* Tavern. She was just finishing off her potatoes and gravy, after downing her beer and beef, when the Capt'n entered.

"Capt'n, nice afternoon, ain't it?"

"Sure is, Miss Woods, mind if I join ya?"

"Barkeep, another beer please!" Brina addressed the gent behind the bar thus.

"Why, thanks, don't mind if I do." With that, John pulled back a chair across the table from her and sat.

"Capt'n, I've got to get something off my chest—sorta speak."

"Somethin' bothering you?"

"Yeah…" The bartender arrived with the second glass of beer for the sheriff then left to tend someone else. "It's my name."

"Don't like it?"

"Actually, I do like it, which is why I've got to clear this up before things get too dicey."

"Your name on a wanted poster or sumthin'?"

"Oh no. Nothing like that."

"What then?"

"Pixie Woods is not my real name."

"It's not? Gee." Sheriff wasn't too surprised.

"No. My name is Brina Grant."

"And why are you telling me this? Ya know, there's lots of people who change their names."

"'Cause it just don't sit right with me. And besides, if we're going to be honest with each other"—Brina thought about Dillon's opinions of this man. "I got to set things straight with ya."

Sheriff thought about it. "Okay, Brina Grant. Anything else you want to git off your chest?" It wasn't like she'd robbed a bank and killed a guard in Tuncson or something.

Brina thought about it for a moment. If she were to be here in this town for a while, she'd need a job. Staying with Willow in such a nice, quiet, and frilly place as they've offered was just that, a nice, quiet, and frilly place to stay, and for the most part not being bothered is nice, but it sure as shit wasn't a line of work she was interested in—even with the pay offered. So, in order to git herself through whatever time she had to spend in this town, she might as well do something she was good at and liked.

"Need an extra gun?"

"Why, you want to sell yours?"

"No, silly. I'm looking for a job—gotta make ends meet, ya know."

"You plan on staying in town for a spell?"

"Kinda looks thatta way, maybe—ya never know."

"It would look kinda funny to have a woman as a deputy, unless you just want to clean up my office and jail."

"That kinda cleaning up wasn't what I was thinking about. But as to being your deputy, think about it this way: the bad guys would never expect a woman backing you up, or never expect a woman could beat them to the draw."

Those last few words brought back that surprising and terrifying moment at the livery. The one Cornelius was telling everyone in town about. Unfortunately, for him it was rather embarrassing to have a woman beat him to the draw and have everyone in town know it, but the contest hadn't been fair, as he hadn't expected it. *Hadn't expected it.* Now that he thought about it, and as she had put it, would the outlaws expect it either? But what if that episode had been just luck? What if she had been here in town as deputy long enough to give her either a reputation as someone capable, or if the contest rules were nonexistent and someone surprised her, dying as a woman deputy on the spot, proving herself to be a charlatan and him having poor judgment in the matter? It certainly wouldn't look too good for him hiring a woman who was shot and killed the first time she stuck her head outta some door by some crackpot drunk deciding she should've been more "friendly." She'd be an easy target, just like old man Potter. John wasn't liking the way that thought, or the scenario as it was, might play out. Then again, what if she was just what the doctor ordered? Remembering back, John had received an unexpected chance at one time from an unlikely resource, from a Marshal Dillon Frasier.

Brina saw the wheels turning. She knew her offer was tempting, but the indecision on his face and in his eyes clued her in to his possible second thoughts.

"Tell ya what we'll do, Capt'n. We'll have a contest of sorts."

John thought about that one for a long time too. Sitting directly across from her, wondering, thinking of everything that could go wrong with this should he take her up on such an offer, he sat unmoving, concentrating, staring into her eyes—those gun metal gray eyes—trying to decipher whether or not she was pulling his leg or whether she was real, her offer true.

"What kind of contest did you have in mind?"

"Whatever you want, Sheriff. It's up to you. After all, you're the one with the concerns, the doubts. You're the one who's got to contend with the rumors going around town. I'm just willing to help you squelch them in the bud. Understand this though. I am fully capable of handling any situation or surprise you may want to initiate in this 'open-ended, no rules need apply' contest."

"What if you're injured, or heaven forbid, killed?"

"Ain't gonna happen."

"How can you be so sure?"

"The only way you'll know why I'm so sure is to put me to the test...Capt'n." Brina smiled when she said that to this stranger.

"No regrets?"

"None expected."

"You're sure?"

"I'll even sign a release. You have a judge? I'll make it official."

"That's something I hadn't thought of, making it official with the circuit judge. Let's see, he's due in next week. You want to wait until then?"

"It's a date."

Waiting for the circuit judge's arrival gave Brina a week to enjoy what this town had to offer. After all, there always is that rare possibility of a lucky shot, and heaven forbid, some idiot would kill her. But she was thinking not. As the All Mother led her to believe, there were other reasons for her to be here. So, after taking inventory of the town, finding a nice, secure bank-like facility to open an account in for this new job she was soon to be taking, she checked out the other stores, people, and entertainment this town had to offer.

She was really surprised at her finds. They had a small group of singers who often sang harmony at their worship place, but who also gathered on corners to sing real songs—songs like "Oh Suzanna," "Red River Valley," and "Don't Fence Me In." There was also found a couple of fiddlers who sometimes played along with said choir or by themselves, and a gentleman who played guitar as best as possible. She was *really surprised* to find an old European gentleman who played excellent piano and was well versed in the "classics and waltzes" like Strauss, who also accompanied the small choir on occasion—when they were willing to sing at the inn. That was fun.

She enjoyed different sorts of meals consisting of fish, beef, lamb, something called a crayfish (something new and exciting), grouse—prepared in a tomato sauce instead of over a spit. She got to see and thoroughly enjoy a hometown play put on by the local school kids—forgetting the name of it, like it mattered—and finally met and instantly took a liking to John's very pregnant wife, Ellie.

She found the foundry and the blacksmith to be well equipped with anvil, metal wheels for wagons, and found that he also made horseshoes for needy customers (the horses). She found a gunsmith, who might be willing to trade a better set of guns for the ones she carried, just in case she was interested, and she found the general store to have everything imaginable for just about anything you might want to cook, clean, sew, sweep, mop, fix, drain, fill, carry, drink, wear, shovel—just about anything. Anything but a flying carpet—those she could've gotten back home had she the cash.

All during the week, Brina kept in mind the rules of this contest that she so eloquently set in motion *(none, nada, zip, open season),* which meant there were less of, or an equal value of chances that could, would, and might be set in motion before the circuit judge arrived in town. After all, an "open-ended, no rules need apply" contest is just that; she might just as well have painted a circled target on her chest.

Sheriff John Hartley, on the other hand, was of a proud people and because of *who he was,* believed he'd "given his word" on holding off on this little contest of theirs until after the circuit judge, JJ

Hatchet, arrived. And at that time he was going to ask for an affida-
vit to be written up, signed, witnessed, and made legal—just in case
there was an accident. This was, of course, after filling the judge in
on the details of this little arrangement and the consequences upon
which he and Brina had agreed.

There was only one problem. A few days later, to be precise, the
pieces to this chess game were drastically altered.

LII

johnny on the spot

It was six o'clock Friday morning, three days later when two very distinct yet at the same time very questionable-looking men rode into town together, bearing a third riderless horse. After making their way to the livery, told Cornel they'd be in town for a least a month. They also said, which was the really odd part, that the soon-to-be arriving judge would be settling their account with him later. That got Cornel wondering whether or not these two unscrupulous-looking strangers with their long, yellow, scraggly manes of hair and their torn and weathered clothing riding thin ill-kept mounts would be associated with the circuit judge. Such questionable statements encouraged him to wait till they departed for town proper. He then quickly unsaddled and tied their mounts to the rail (of which he'd brush, feed, and pay more attention to later); then, as fast as he could, sought out and told the sheriff.

"They looked like what?" asked the sheriff.

"Like them come out from under a rock or sumthin'."

"Said the judge'd take care of things?"

"Yep."

"JJ wouldn't be associated with such ratty-like characters. Sure, they just didn't need a bath or something?"

"Not with the likes of 'em. Them horses looked like they hadn't been fed in months, their clothes dirty and rotting, saddle blankets on crooked with holes—nope. I thin' they're scoundrels."

"Scoundrels, eh?"

"Yep. Thinkin' you might want to take a gander fer yersef. That's why I headed here right away."

"Where'd they head?"

"Saloon, of course."

"Where's Brina?"

"Brina?"

"Yeah. She'd be good to watch 'em. Like she said once, they'd never suspect a woman."

"Right. I'm thinkin' she's around somewheres. I'll find 'er. Want me to send 'er to you?"

"Yeah. Tell 'er to come see me."

"Will do, Sheriff."

Cornel found Brina just emerging from the Pussy Willow, just fitting her hat for the sun.

"Cornel. Nice day for a hanging."

"What?"

"Just kidding. Just sorta fell outta ma mouth. What's up?"

"Sheriff wants to see ya."

"Because why?"

"Er, a, because he asked me to find ya and send ya to 'im."

"What's going on, Cornel? Somethin' wrong?"

"Strangers in town."

"Strangers, eh? Does he want me to watch 'em, or did he send them to test me?"

"Naw, he's waiting for the judge—make it legal. I seen them come in. Brought their nags to the livery. Poor nasty-lookin' things they is. Says they gonna be here for a long time. Said the judge would take care of their bill. Didn't sound right. Told the sheriff. He wants to see you."

"Okay. Tell the sheriff I'll be over straightaway, but first, let me get my second gun, check my ammo."

"Okay."

"Last Cornelius saw, they headed for the saloon."

"Gee, am I surprised?" Brina replied to the sheriff's statement, sorta wanting a drink herself. "I'll tell ya what, if they do anything out of the ordinary, I'll either shoot first or just wait, watch, and keep you updated."

"Good, on any, either or all. See ya fer lunch?" They had gotten in an almost habit of having lunch together—all four of 'em. Johnny, Cornel, a very pregnant Ellie, and Brina. All turning into pretty decent friends.

Brina sauntered into the saloon, sweeping her eyes around the large room until they settled upon the two in question. Once their tables were located and noted, she stepped up to the bar and asked for a drink, tossing her coin towards the barkeep.

He caught it. "Good day to ya, missy. Regular?"

"Sarsaparilla today, Mike."

"Sarsaparilla it is then."

Brina thanked Mike as usual, taking her glass over to one of the smaller tables in the front left corner of the saloon where she could see the whole room and all its occupants. Brushing back her long hair just before sitting, she got only a single glance from the "gentlemen" at the opposite corner as they quietly chatted with their heads no more than a bridle bit away from each other while drinking their whiskey down.

Mike, on the other hand, swooned. He did this every time she came into his saloon. He thought her *quite special*. He had at one time tried to persuade her to join him for supper, but she wasn't having any part of it. Said she wanted to be friends only—had had enough of men trying to get into her pants. He backed off willingly, saying he understood completely. Instead, he decided to wait. She just might come around to see things his way if he stayed distant, being ever patient, courteous, and sweet.

Leaning back in her chair, legs extended, feet resting on the second of four, leaving an invite open for anyone wanting to join her—*almost*—Brina watched the two for a few, before an approaching sound broke her concentration. The stage was drawing near, heading to town, only a mile or two away—she knew this to be true. Curious if the "judge" was on board, curious as to who he actually was, what he looked like, and curious as to what may unfold once the "three" were reunited (she, the sheriff, and the judge).

Just then, Abby Crabtree—the red-headed, four-foot-tall, ninety-eight-pound, fifty-year-old telegrapher—charged herself and her cane through the swinging doors of the saloon frantically searching for someone, letting both doors hit her on the ass just as she spotted her objective, Brina. Abby ran to her table and just as quickly, whispered in her ear.

"He what?" said Brina.

The two "gentlemen" looked up suddenly, their attention now riveted on the older whispering woman and the younger one with the guns on her hips who'd been watching their every move since she sat down, trying at the same time to look inconspicuous in the process. Wondering all along if the noise was of newly discovered "gossip" concerning either of them, of the soon to be approaching stage with their surprise cargo aboard, or of something else entirely.

Brina shot up from her seat, forcing her chair backwards. Not being totally without manners, she quickly picked it up, placed it back against the table, then left the saloon in a rush. Sending Abby back to the telegraph, Brina quickly headed for the livery and her best spotted pony.

The two gentlemen, curious, stood up and headed for the swinging doors where they could see over their top, watching her direction. Obviously, it wasn't to the sheriff's office, so they felt reasonably safe for the time being. But where did she go, who was she, and why was she watching them? Probably because of their appearance and because they were strangers in town. They probably always watched strangers here 'bouts. After all, you never know what strangers might be up to.

Brina brushed both horses lovingly. She knew the two had watched her heading, watched her movements, curious as to her attention on them. Strangers are nothing more than people outta place, out of their own personal comfort zone. Regardless of the fact, they were still people. Just because they were strangers to this town didn't mean they were stupid—no matter how they were outfitted. The condition of their horses sorta told her to be alert, because those who treated animals that way, were to be wary of, watched carefully, and in her opinion hung from the highest tree. But what the two of them didn't know about was her having a seventh sense, one that would allow her to pick up on the idea that they too were wary and watching anything out of the ordinary—like a woman packing two guns instead of being in a dress heading for a ball or just the general store. This was her ace in the hole and the reason she left the saloon. After all, her seventh sense told her *they posed no immediate threat.*

The stage arrived. Its seven passengers disembarked, circuit judge included. The other passengers were locals and were known by those meeting the stage. Yet, as circuit judge, he was unseen by those who were there, by those who should've been concerned, and most importantly, was missed by those who were looking for Hatchet. Why was this possible? No one expected him, no one knew him, therefore no one of consequence bothered to meet the stage. No one bothered to see where he headed—directly to the saloon. A place—had he been real, honest-to-goodness real, and officially official—he'd not frequent, unless accompanied by someone of similar judicial authority, such as the sheriff of this town, a marshal perhaps, or even a low deputy.

Inside the saloon, he saw his awaiting cohorts, his friends, his partners in crime. They had only glanced his way, when the doors swung wide, when he spotted them thus. Confidently, yet with great caution, ready to spring into action at a moment's notice, he stepped over to their table, sat down with his back to the wall, and cautiously took part in their drinking, conversation, and laughing, all the while him keeping a lookout on the door.

The hat worn could camouflage a standing world globe, its brim so wide, keeping the face indiscernible under such a veil. The normally distinct facial features were blurry, without definite lines. No one could see the blonde hair, the green eyes. No one bothered to guess at the six-foot-four frame, his two-hundred-plus-pound heft, his fairness of skin—good thing too. Had they seen him, had the impossible happened, had someone recognized him, the tide would've turned for the worse.

His clothes, as usual, were fancy. His dark, black slacks were perfectly pressed, creases centered. His shirt snow-white with its long sleeves and their French-like frills—crisp, smooth, and silky. The white shirt was made of a light and extremely expensive material sent directly to him from Spain. His light-gray, black-lined vest with the dark black embroidery on its pockets was striking and sophisticated looking to those of lower standards; it, too, was from Spain. His boots, usually solid black, today were a tad dusty. But who could expect perfection when one is forced to use, or only has available to them, such common and antiquated transportation as they had here? They, on the other hand, were local and used to such atrocities.

Living the lie of a circuit judge was as simple for him as pulling teeth, being a doctor, or flying across the friendly skies with a cargo of drugs. Living the lie of a blacksmith, however, before this present and overly simple impersonation, was a bitch. Folks constantly complained; he could never keep horses sound or wagon wheels secure. The constant heat was miserable not only from the ovens and bellows, but the townsfolk as well, although everything else rode like clockwork.

When Johnny heard rumors of a stranger who was dressed to the hilt, he automatically assumed it was Circuit Judge JJ Hatchet trying to impress him again. Last time he arrived in town, he was dressed in fancy-schmancy matching browns; this time, they were saying black and gray was the combination. Good ol' Hatchet, always trying to put on the show.

Unfortunately, that was not whom he found upon his entrance to the saloon. Expecting Hatchet and no one else, he had let down his guard, entering without a care, with a smile from ear to ear. For this, he was rewarded with a now-vacant saloon, except for the bartender and three very unfamiliar strangers sitting at the back-center table of the saloon.

"Please sit down and join us, Sheriff," said the wide-brimmed hat. One couldn't see the eyes; the hat was pulled down so, but the unsettling smile was definitely there.

"I'm sorry, but you're not Judge Hatchet." John had looked forward to Hatchet's company. He had even planned on introducing him to Ellie, inviting him for lunch, making it a fivesome.

"Nope. He was unable to make the trip. I came instead. Judge Bobby Catt. Rob or Robert, if you don't like the other."

The man offering himself as Judge Catt hadn't extended his hand in greeting, and that bothered John. That, and the fact he sat with two other scroungy-looking characters, and no telegram sent added up to suspicion, although John showed no sign. Not thinking, he *offered his hand* in "friendship."

The hooded gentleman didn't take it in return.

"Sheriff John Hartley, at your service. And I'm sorry, I'd love to sit and chat for a moment with you and your friends, but the little one is due any day, and I like checking on her often."

"Well now. You hear that boys? The sheriff here's got a missus at home with a bun in the oven. Isn't that nice, real nice," the hat said with a sneer.

John just realized he'd slipped more information than he should've. Must've been the last several years of clean livin', no outlaws, and a quiet town that caught him off-guard. Damn. Must find Brina. Find out why she wasn't watchin' these fellas like she was supposed to. Why she didn't inform him of the judge's arrival. *If she was anywheres as good as she boasted.* He excused himself and left the saloon.

The capt'n found Brina at the livery, brushing and tending her spotted steeds.

"Brina?"

"Capt'n. Nice morning, isn't it?"

"Why aren't you watching those two characters like I asked?"

"Why, it is a nice morning. Thanks for bringing it to my attention…Brina," she returned.

"Why ain't you watchin' them two strangers like I wanted?"

"Cause, Capt'n, I didn't see any need. Besides, they were watching me. I believed they knew why too. So just in case, I had Abby cause a commotion loud enough to get their attention, and I hurried out. If they didn't care, they wouldn't have gotten up to see where I went, but Abby watched them for me from across the street and told me they seemed very curious, watching me from them doors. I figured, since I didn't feel any immediate threat, I'd wait here for a spell, then head back. Anything else you want to discuss?"

"Sorry. It's just that I'm sorta scart."

"Scart? What's that? Stomach bothering you? Butterflies in there fluttering around? Something not right?"

"Yeah. For one, that's not Judge Hatchet. Hatchet didn't come. And no telegram to notify me of the change in plans. That's just not like JJ. We've been friends since Dillon was here. He would've sent word."

"No telegram, eh? What's this feller look like?"

"'Twas hard to tell. He was sitting down in the saloon with those two shady strangers. I think they're friends. They was talking, laughing, carrying on like they was. I don' know. His hat has such a wide brim, you can't see his face nor the color of his hair, it must be real short. No ponytail, no facial hair, no nuthin'. But that smile, it was wide, thin, and unsettling. I could just barely see it below the brim. Brina! I even made the mistake of mentioning Ellie and the babe—what am I going to do?" The true meaning of fear, fear for his own life, for that of Ellie and the babe just kicked in. What if he lost them or vice versa?

Sounded like the only thing he didn't tell him was where he lived. Brina didn't like this. Didn't like the various thoughts bombarding her from all directions. Something was rotten in upper Locany again. The capt'n was really shaken, and that was saying a lot for a man of his stature and this situation at hand. "You mean, what *are* *we* going to do."

The look of calm determination from the gunmetal gray-eyed, ivory-skinned beauty standing in front of him with a finishing brush in her hand, for a moment, was comical, if the situation be different. However, knowing her like he'd learned these last couple of weeks strengthened his very soul. She amazed him. His confidence for the outcome of the situation at hand increased as he watched the brush be put down; the gun belts checked, tightened; the holster strings secured; the guns drawn, cocked, released, and reholstered in mere seconds. It was all he needed in this time of hour.

"What's your plan?" he asked her.

"What's your plan, Capt'n? You're the one in charge. I just follow orders." Brina never wavered in her staring at an unknown and unseen entity across the empty barn but did turn to wink and give a small grin at the capt'n, letting him know all would be well in the end.

The sheriff thought a moment. "Well, let's just watch for the time being. If he is an impostor, he probably doesn't know we know. JJ knows lots a folks. Besides, the telegram just might be late. And if this guy's just here to meet these two creepy dudes and move on, there should be no trouble, hopefully. If it's not, and there is trouble afoot, our guard will be up."

"You should probably tell Ellie to stay close to the doctor. Hate to have her give birth alone and without help should the shit hit the fan."

"I'll tell her to be careful and stay close. But she might raise a stink, me being in danger and all."

"Tell her I'll make it my business to watch your back."

"Thanks. That'll help, I hope."

Ellie had her baby girl by lunchtime, making Johnny Hartley not just a very proud papa, but also the first man in town to watch and take part in the blessed event. Brina had strongly insisted. Said Ellie would need him and his strength to draw from, as having a baby was quite an ordeal. *Brina would grab a bite to eat somewhere while keeping an eye out, and if it be a dire emergency, she'd fetch him pronto.*

The doc gently handed the capt'n his new daughter, Dusty Rose, named for the windy day and the color of her hair, wrapped loosely in a small blanket. Johnny never knew such happiness. He would've preferred a son but knew he and Ellie had plenty of years ahead of them—many laughing and dearly loved children expected—if he wasn't killed by week's end.

Brina knew the funny feeling in the pit of her stomach wasn't the beef sandwich and beer she had for lunch at the Inn. It was her seventh sense that had stirred up the butterflies in her stomach, making it seem like a wild and crazy party no one invited her to.

Something was up, something was terribly wrong, and something nasty was coming. What it was, she still wasn't sure. She did know it wasn't Ellie's condition. The baby was healthy, the mother fine. On the other hand, the anxiously awaited telegram still hadn't come, the town seemed on edge, the three strangers were suspiciously nowhere—yet their horses were still at the livery, meaning they weren't too far off—and the capt'n, after leaving his wife for just a moment to check on something, hadn't been seen or heard from since.

"I said *sit down*."

"Listen, I don't take orders from—"

The wide-brimmed hat held a gun on him. Pointed it at his head. Threatened to kill his wife and new baby if he didn't follow his instructions to the letter. All the other patrons who had been shopping in the general store had been herded up, frightened into silence with the threat of death looming at the door, and ushered into the back storeroom, locked in, followed by more whispered threats.

The wide-brimmed hat did all the talking. The second one was one of the two from the saloon. Where the other was, what he was doing, who else he was threatening, John wasn't privy to. All he knew right now was that all their lives were in danger. And without making himself a martyr, he had no way to warn Brina or anyone else in town of the pending situation here at the store.

"What are we going to do with him?" The words came out like a whispered growl from the man he overheard being called Buzz Saw, a small man, an extremely nervous man, with strange black eyes. One of the eyes was constantly in motion, the other remained locked in place. His hands were nervous too. They were constantly moving from pants pockets, to gun, to waist, to shirt pockets—almost as if the guy was frantically seeking something yet never finding it.

"I've got an idea—git over here, Buzz," he with the wide-brimmed hat whispered in Buzz's ear.

John sat as ordered and tried, ever so hard, to pick up anything tangible they were discussing. Had to find a clue. Had to find a break to escape. Had to warn Brina. Brina. He hadn't even been able to test her true abilities in a real contest—instead, the contest was turning into a real life-and-death situation today, now. It was one they all, he, or his family, might not live through. He didn't know which was more frightening, knowing he could be dead by the end of the day leaving no support for Ellie or Dusty, or not being able to get any sort of word or signal off to Brina for any help she could provide. He almost wanted just to take a weak moment and cry it out—make room for the sudden determination he knew was hidden somewhere below the surface.

"Poppy Seed going to be there with the horses?" asked Buzz Saw.

"She'd better be, if she knows what's good fer 'er."

Her? Thought the sheriff to himself. *That was a woman sitting there in the saloon with that other creep? Or was this Poppy hiding somewheres in town all along, without anyone the wiser?*

"What do you want to do to those in the back room? Shoot 'em all—kids too?

"Don't you go thinking 'bout such thins. They'll stay quiet. I told 'em if they didn't, I'd be back with a machine gun and blast away at all of them. Didn't matter if only one was the troublemaker, they'd all die. I figured that ought to have gotten their attention, ya think?" the brimmed hat assured.

"That'd work, if Poppy weren't high on laudanum again. You sure she can do this?"

"Let's have a word with the sheriff."

John had heard his name mentioned. He was trying not to, but he was suffering a mild case of the shakes, and his anxiety level was rising quickly. He was the most scart that he'd ever been. Never had Dillon or anyone else for that matter trained him to handle this type of criminal. One who conned, one who threatened, one who beat that poor little girl blind till her mother shut up. No, Brina was right. All outlaws must be stopped permanently. Especially outlaws with guns at their disposal, and more so, those who molest or harm children.

The one with the brimmed hat stepped next to the chair where the sheriff sat securely tied. Kneeling down in front of him gave

John an opportunity to see this man's face, to permanently fasten it to his mind's eye. If he lived through this, his would be the face he'd never forget, never...until he caught and gleefully watched him dangling dead from the highest tree.

Little did the sheriff know of the plans of the threesome. The wide-brimmed hat left Buzz Saw with the sheriff for just a moment, so the hat could check out the street. He figured the best time to hit the bank was either right before it opened or shortly before it closed. If they walked, the three of them—sheriff, judge, and Buzz—down to the bank in a line, carrying on a conversation between themselves, and with Poppy bringing the horses down, they could pull this off. After all, this bank was supposed to have the largest payroll in the sector. The hat thought it curious that it wasn't guarded by more than just this upgraded lowlife deputy, but also knew his gang knew nothing about this deputy guy. This half-breed might be the best shot in the West, and if that be the case, 'twas he and his cohorts who were in for a big surprise. But this time, they held the guns, and the sheriff had no ace in his hole. They would be fine. The horses Poppy had procured were big horses, with plenty of girth for moving plenty of air. Plenty of air could handle long distances when chased. Yesiree, they should make a fine killing in this town.

"Git up, Sheriff!"

"I ain't getting up for no one, no how."

The chair upon which the sheriff sat was abruptly kicked out from under him. "I said git up, Sheriff, and if you don't, you'll find yourself over there against that wall, upside down!"

"Buzz off."

The brimmed hat quietly watched from five feet off. "Sheriff," when he got his attention he continued, "if'n you don't get up and walk with us across town like there's nothing wrong, I'll send Buzz Saw to the back room and let him take his first pick of the day, the smallest and cutest child and make things not so nice for them. Are you understanding my insinuation?

"Git up!!"

John had no choice but to stand. His mind was running in all directions silently, yet with urgency, calling out to anyone for help, not expecting anything, but what else could he do at the moment? None of the avenues he wanted to use were available, and any break he might take would only endanger either his life or someone else's in the back storeroom further, or heaven forbid, his family. He wanted to cry. He'd been so stupid with these three. He should've immediately telegraphed JJ's headquarters seeing if he really had left or had he just been sent elsewhere. John should've handled this with a little more finesse, yes, with a little more finesse, indeed.

Brina wanted him out in the open where she could get at him. She wanted her back to the sun, her hat securely in place, her guns cleaned, oiled, smooth, and well-practiced, waiting in anticipation. She planned to be in the center of the street, where she could see him coming. It was he who was coming. It was he who was here. She knew now why she was sent here. She understood now who it was under that wide-brimmed hat. It was Jesse Loame. And it was time for her to end this.

"Come along now, Sheriff, time's a-wasting," said Buzz Saw as the threesome stepped out of the general store, off the sidewalk into the street, their destination—the bank. The man with the wide-brim hat was on the far left of the trio, confident this heist would fall into place just like all the others he'd pulled. The sheriff, Johnny Hartley, was held firmly in the center of the three with a very small handgun held to his middle, concealed within an old handkerchief, threatening to end his life should he try anything stupid. It was Buzz Saw who held it. They were making sure their withdrawal slip didn't blow away in the breeze before it was time. They needed to procure some traveling money to make it to the next sector since Jesse was getting too well-known around these parts. Had to move on.

Brina wasn't sure how to handle this. Sure, taking Jesse and his ratty companions out would be easy, but with John being held with a gun against his gut by one, or both? She watched them approach from her position at the opposite end of the bank, sitting in a chair along the wall of the Pussy Willow Inn and Massage Parlor, like a cat ready to pounce on its prey.

She thought of Ellie and the baby, knowing John would protect them till his dying day. The thought of sending him a message crossed her mind, but what would she say, and would it throw him off more than she needed? She believed should Jesse get to the bank, use John to help procure funds, he'd kill everyone inside before making a git-a-way. Only now, the third outlaw could be seen riding out of the livery leading the other two horses, all saddled, packed, and ready for travel—also heading for the bank. *Wait.*

Wait. There was something peculiar about this third rider and the gear they had. For one, that third horse carried Brina's saddle, and the other oddity was the way the rider held themselves as they rode—it was a woman! That's why Brina had missed her earlier. She hadn't expected a fourth one. Where had she been hiding? And where was the other one? The one she saw in the saloon. Dead somewheres, she suspected.

John Hartley was thinking similar thoughts as Brina while they held him at gunpoint on their short journey down the street. He knew their plans. Any idiot could figure them out. After all, just to prove a point to all in the store, they'd slit the throat of the other outlaw, leaving him to bleed to death on the floor, while keeping the hostage situation quiet. It was a silent threat of death should anyone holler or scream or make a warning noise of any kind to anybody. They were good people in this town and loved their families; they promised to keep their mouths shut.

Johnny spotted Brina on the far upper side of the street. After all, it was early still. Not many folks up and about yet. They locked eyes, him trying to convey the situation at hand while still being forced to walk "hand in hand" to the bank.

Brina found her moment in John's stare, and for a moment, he stumbled, almost falling, but his comrades held him quick.

"Stand up, Sheriff, we're almost there."

Brina sent John her message.

"I feel sick."

John was not ready for the thought that suddenly entered his mind. After all, he really wasn't sick; he was just totally and completely scart outta his mind. Too many butterflies, too many concerns, too many worries for loved ones pushed the half-assed thought away.

"I feel really sick."

Brina sent him another stronger message. She had to get him to almost collapse, to throw the other two off just enough.

John did stumble. His stomach was suddenly in a whirl. He'd never felt this crappy before. Was it a character flaw during time of stress? Was he weak and unable to hold his job as sheriff?

"I'm going to throw up now!"

There was no way he could ignore this message Brina sent. No way in hell. John, with both hands on his stomach, bent over and lurched up his early-morning coffee, steak, and eggs. Over and over and over he did this, until the dry heaves hit, and both Buzz and Jesse were forced to let loose their hostage. They tried dragging him off the street, them not yet to the bank, but at the last moment and out of the corner of his eye, Jesse spotted movement up the street and dropped the heaving sheriff.

There was a form walking easy down the middle of the street, sun at their back. The form could not be defined, other than it being a clothed, slender person wearing a hat. A person who he assumed posed no threat, but it was still early. Still curious as to who in the hell would be out and about, making a beeline for their locale, Jesse's concentration on the approaching form was momentarily interrupted when John fell as his stomach lurched again.

By now John was curled in a fetal position in the middle of the street still heaving up bile, stomach muscles cramping, innards in an uproar. It was the only way Brina could think of to get him down and outta harm's way, leaving Jesse and his cohort exposed to the sun's blinding ability and her deadly aim.

"Son of a Bitch, Jesse, what we gonna do now with this damned sheriff? Folks'll start opening shop doors, start meandering about."

"Shit, Buzz, ya think I'd known he was so weak hearted? Maybe we ought to just shoot him here, put him outta his misery, and rush the bank."

"Screw it. Leave him. He ain't going anywheres, he don't have the strength to get up, let alone fight or warn anybody. Let's get this over with. Git them funds like you said, git outta town. Here comes Poppy with the horses."

As Brina approached her side of the bank, the woman and her three horses came in from the side street, still bent on the bank and the threesome in the middle of the street. With one message aimed directly at the horse the woman rode, the gelding reared straight in the air, too high and too off balance. Not injuring the animal, it fell over backward, crushing and mangling its rider.

Jesse saw this. "Quickly! Get that fucker up. We gotta get to the bank, or this is a wash!"

As John still lay on the ground, stomach in knots, feeling like he was dying, another message came through.

"You're fine. Git up!
Quickly find and take the shorter man's gun.
KILL HIM! *If you don't take his life, he'll take Ellie's!"*

With his pain and misery vanishing as though it was never truly there *(except for the evidence in the dirt)*, all Sheriff John Hartley could see were these strange words in his mind. These strange words conjured up a horrible image. An image of this short outlaw taking his wife, slitting her throat like they did that fella in the store. That image lasted just a fraction of a second, yet it was all the encouragement he needed to carry out the deed with precision.

John's sudden recovery and attack on Buzz Saw caught Jesse off guard. That and the commotion at the end of the street with

Poppy Seed and the horse made him stop short. Something was happening, something not of his control. That was when he noticed the stranger with the hat standing in the middle of the street with the sun at their back.

"Drop it, Jesse." Brina's hands were on her hips, riding deadly close to the butts of her pistols.

Well, he didn't drop it, but he did give her his full attention. Moving well into the street, away from the commotion created by that damned and conniving sheriff, he addressed her. "Ya know, I still can shoot the sheriff."

"You can, but do you want to take that second away from me?"

"And who in the name of Sam Hill do you think you are?"

"I'm the one they sent to track, find, and kill you, Jesse Loame."

"You know my real name then. How?"

"Been on your butt for too many years. Caused quite a stir here and at home, haven't you?"

"What do you mean at home?"

"Let's take a moment for a quick history lesson. You were born in Foggy Bottom, Illinoizy, weren't you? As you matured, you learned to masquerade as all sorts of characters so you could build and secure that walled-in estate no one can breach. Let's see, you were a junior assistant to Department of Time Travel Research, rode with Max Rider, assassinated the international emissary of Cyclops, escaped prosecution, escaped into the past via the Franciscan Lifter. And now, here you are. In Eastern-Western. Standing me down in the street, like any other Western outlaw about to be beaten and killed by a mere woman."

"Like hell!"

"Hell hath no fury like a woman scorned, remember that, Jesse Loame. And ya know, I'm damned sick and tired of chasing your ass all over this countryside. Let's end it—*draw!*"

He did.

Brina was surprised. Jesse Loame's aim and speed with a gun was very, very good. After all, he, too, had attended the Academy at one time long, long ago. He, too, studied under MJ. She'd forgotten this one small tidbit. She remembered it now—of course, as she sat on the ground with her limp and bloodied arm resting in her lap. There had been a small note in his file, words she found scribbled on a small blue piece of paper. It seems that Jesse's time spent in school had been noted in a barely decipherable hand by some unknown entity, stapled on the back page of some stupid report card, in a file, lost on the very bottom of many folders.

Jesse Loame must've suspected Cyclops would eventually send someone from the Academy, someday, some year. And knew he had until then to hone his skills. But apparently, he'd forgotten about the man on the ground. Her friend, John Hartley. It put a smile on her face knowing a man like this, one she hadn't known very well, except just of late, but one who saved her in a pinch as she had expected to save him. No. Jesse was not quite as good as both she and John Hartley, simultaneously.

At the last minute, John had rolled into Jesse—throwing off Jesse's aim enough, allowing the bullet to just graze her shirt, wounding her in the arm, while her shots were still able to make their mark, shooting him dead.

Mission accomplished, finally.

Although, after the dust settled and Jesse's things were gone through, there were no copies of the operating instructions for the sphere to be found. But she knew that—the All Mother had told her as much.

LIII

here comes the judge

The body of Judge JJ Hatchet was found in a pile down the hill in a cutbank, back behind the horse corral at the last stage stop. He had worn his best brown pants, vest, boots, hat, and cream-colored shirt—all for John. John, Brina, and the townsfolk all learned of this when they dropped the bomb, telling of his death to his wife and three boys.

Hatchet's throat had been severed from ear to ear, thus one would believe he bled out before falling to the ground. This placed Jesse behind him at the time of the attack—the assumption being to not only discourage any overly noisy gunfire or outright hand-to-hand fighting, but to hold secure, ensuring death before leaving the scene, then changed out of his bloodstained clothes into the fancy duds he brought, and running, like the proverbial cheetah did in folk-lore without effort, for his rendezvous with the stage.

Those who rode the stage that very day Jesse met them on the trail, without a horse or saddle, asking the driver for a ride, weren't paying attention to the particulars. It didn't concern those who sat in the already-cramped, dust-filled compartment that they had to move over, making room for another, as long as they got to where they wanted; they didn't care, so therefore the facts of the matter were forgotten.

Apparently, Jesse and his band of outlaws had planned the mur-der of the judge, the bank robbery, and the get-away months ago. All except for Poppy Seed, who was high on opium most the time, and surprisingly enough had been working undercover for the last few months at the massage parlor right there in town. She had been higher than a kite as usual, *which was why Brina hadn't picked up on it.*

The new circuit judge, William BJ. Power, wasn't the dresser Hatchet was, nor did he have an expensive taste in clothes like Jesse, but he did know the law and his way around the sector. Short, gray-haired fella that he was, spent an entire week in town talking to all the townsfolk about this one particular shooting, killing, and kidnapping incident, getting all the various details in all their shapes, sizes, and colors. Then he cleared Brina Louise Grant of "hunting outlaws without a license to kill." After a long talk with John Hartley, his wife, Ellie, and playing finger games with little Dusty Rose, he officially gave the office of *Deputy Marshal of Eastern-Western and its surrounding territory* to Johnny Soars Like an Eagle Hartley and appointed to Brina Louise Grant a semiofficial position of *Marshal of Eastern-Western within its limited surrounding jurisdiction.* At least until she, too, was gunned down like ol' man Potter (which he didn't figure was too far off, her being a woman and all—thus placing Johnny back in charge).

In the meantime, until fate or kismet dictated otherwise, Brina decided to stay in this little podunk part of the sector, in this more than important position, with her new friends, her painted ponies, and her still-healing arm wound.

Brina thought about moving out of the brothel but decided to stay put. Instead, they had an extension built onto the newly christened marshal's office and jail, increasing its size, just in case room was needed. If time permitted and things worked out, maybe she'd either find a house in town or a small spread just a tad out of town to inhabit for a spell. Because after spending life as she had since the Academy, she'd been a pretty busy little girl. Who knew if she was ready to settle down or not.

One thing she did know, she'd bide her time here in Eastern-Western until the Gray Wolf again found his way north to be by her side.

LIV

cause and effect

"**F**REEZE! Drop them guns!"

You've heard of the phrase "cause and effect"? Well, this demand made by a seemingly unknown was what you could consider the cause, the true cause—the cause that would set in motion events none who survived that day would soon forget. As Dillon looked back on that miserable morning, the card dealt to both boys from that fat poker-faced dealer in the sky was nothing short of a single ace of spades. And as to the hand drawn from that one single card, of which they were about to play, was to be a dilly.

Our boys started out the morning sore and still tired from the previous day's ride. The breakfast that they did get, the one Cordell started their day out with, that of overly burnt coffee, black and way too crispy bacon, cremated potatoes without seasonings, with little else to add in, along with them having to contend with drenched bedrolls, soaked clothing, drippy saddle blankets and cranky horses, was just the beginning of a very frightening, interesting, and unbelievable day.

Yesterday, they'd ridden hard. Dillon had gotten a tip from some poker-playing dude in the last dry place they stayed about a feller who kinda sorta matched the description of that blasted Jesse they'd been trying to apprehend for forever. It sounded good. It was good. At least he kept telling himself it was a good lead. But at each place they stopped, this feller seemed to be just minutes or hours ahead or had vanished into thin air, so instead of pulling in the reins, taking a breather, they sunk spur and tried to catch up.

Needless to say, by late last night, they'd still not caught up with this masked man of yesteryear—Brina's yesteryear, their present target. So, of course after their miserable night's sleep, having everything soaking wet and smelling of old army blankets from the downpour, topped off by the rotten breakfast, their day wasn't starting out too great, especially if you also added in yesterday's empty catch.

By midmorning, they were caught unawares by this jerk and addressed as mentioned above. And as Dillon was later to learn, after everything calmed down, this outlaw who came to be "the cause" was the last of the last that they had to worry about out of the original bad bunch who haunted them or rather who haunted Cordell from years gone by.

"Don't move! Drop them guns and reach for the sky!" Rene-with-a-hyphen couldn't believe his luck. After all these months upon months upon years of tracking that black bastard who betrayed them all—all them years ago—he himself, all alone (except for his horse), had finally tracked down, found, caught up with, and gotten the draw upon these two, surprising that fucking Frenchman and that interfering bastard of a marshal.

"Where's Jesse!" Dillon demanded to know. It may have not been the smartest avenue to take, but at the moment, Jesse was the only name on their exhausted minds, and after that rotten breakfast, of which Dillon ate little of, there was no fuel available for clear and precise thinking.

"What? Who? Who the hell are you fucking talking about? Jesse who?" came the reply from the man of few feet, dark-brown eyes with ugly, stringy, brown hair to match, whom no one, for obvious reasons, liked as a child.

"Jesse. Jesse Loame, you fool!" Dillon shouted in a not-too-brilliant fashion.

"I don't know no damned Jesse Loame!!"

Venomously the small man whirled on Cordell and shot him in the chest, point-blank range. "FINALLY GOT YOU, you little tattle-tale—hahahahaha!" Rene, in all his glory had forgotten all about Dillon,

575

Cordell being his one true love to kill, and was jumping in circles of joy, waving his arms and hands, giggling for all he was worth. He had finally gotten that black French bastard who betrayed them all!

"CORDELL, CORDELL! HELP HIM! HELP ME! SOMEBODY HELP!" Dillon yelled at the top of his lungs at the bleeding man on the ground. He was in total shock. Was Cordell still alive? Was he dead? Dillon couldn't believe this asshole shot him without hesitation, without a fight. Dillon ran to Cordell's side, knelt down to check the wound, listened to his chest for a heartbeat, but was stopped by more than just the sound of that little shit ass's voice.

"Don't you dare! You're next, buddy! Drop your guns slowly, slowly get up, look at me with them angelic hands raised to the moon!"

Time was running out for Cordell. Dillon had to do something and fast. Without further thought, he turned and lunged at the small man, grabbed his arms, wrestling him to the ground.

Had to git them guns before he had a chance to pull the trigger. Unfortunately, he was more agile than Dillon ever imagined and apparently had gotten a better breakfast than he or was stronger than appeared or just damned bloody lucky. While Dillon was grappling with him, Rene managed to get those short little legs up close to his body while Dillon was trying to pry the guns free and managed, with all his might, punched them into his abdomen, forcing all breath into the next county—forcing Dillon to let go as he collapsed down alongside his dying brother.

As Dillon lay on the ground gasping for air, Cordell surprised all by the sheer fact he was still alive. Dillon knew this because Cordell turned his head Dillon's way with a fight for life still in those deep browns of his. His slavery mother had given him strength after all, if only to shed a single tear in good-bye.

Cordell felt the life draining from him. He knew Rene had shot him squarely in the chest with that dreaded .45 he always carried. He knew the reason behind the attack, but sadly it had not been him who'd turned the threesome in to the law back then. Back then it'd been some other sucker who'd overheard them talking about their next conquest—some lucky dipshit who collected the bounty and probably to stay out of harm's way moved east to spend it.

Cordell wasn't ready to die. It wasn't his time. Brina had told him as much back when they'd first met. She said he was a part of her, her destiny. Without him alive, she would surely die—and of all the things in this life, whatever was left of it, if only seconds or minutes, Brina Louise Grant's life and loves were worth everything. He could not die. Not now.

In a flash, right before his very eyes, during those last seconds of consciousness, Cordell relived that last cherished and enlightening conversation he had with Brina Louise Grant, his great-great-great-great-great-great-granddaughter.

"The story I'm about to tell you will explain much. It is a story my mother told me while I was still young and living at home. It was just a little piece of family history to tide me over for the rest of my life. She knew about them coming for me for days, so she took me aside, we sat together in the sun, ate cookies, laughed aloud and finally she told me a story, a special story from long ago. She made me repeat it over and over again until I had it memorized. She wanted me to know about my family's beginning on the Western Hemisphere. She said it was something I could keep with me, something from my natural-born family, that would be mine alone to carry. It was something that I was not to forget, nor allow the Organization to erase.

"She sat me down and told me of a love story. A very wonderful and touching moment in time, for two distinctly different individuals of totally different backgrounds. This story, she said, had been passed down from generation to generation. Mother to daughter. Father to son. To me, she explained that it was a very old and very true story. She told it to me with so much emotion that she cried. She knew what was about to happen in my life and knew the story's impact on me at the time would be tremendous. As it will be now for you." Brina now had his undivided attention.

"Cordell." She stepped close, inches away. Gently taking hold of his face with both her hands, she tilted it so that he could see the honesty in her eyes as she dumped the astonishing truth in his lap.

"One of my very far-removed grandfathers was a captain of a French trade ship, and his true love was," Brina began choking on her very words, as now

realizing how powerful this story was when hearing Cordell tell it that day when she held her guns on them. "…was a slave girl." Then she added the missing piece. The undeniable proof to her claim: "Her name was Nicole."

The truth was finally out. She closed her eyes allowing the tears to flow. When she reopened them, she could see it in his eyes. He understood. He knew who she was.

Cordell had turned his beautiful face to Dillon, as they both lay on the damp ground. Cordell dying from a gunshot wound, Dillon in agony from Rene's kick—with a pain so severe it felt like it was radiating all the way to his spine.

In those seemingly last moments of Cordell's life, he turned his head and looked Dillon's way. Flat on his back he was, with a small spot of blood in the center of his shirt growing larger with each second. Dillon could feel the tears in his eyes start to form, as memories passed before him as though living them again as though yesterday.

"No, Cordell. I'll not let them harm or put ya away. The circuit judge is due come spring, how 'bout I wire him about your situation. Perhaps, instead of sending you to prison, maybe they'll let you work off your time helping me, without pay of course. Don't worry, though, I'll see to it that you'll have a place to sleep, are taken care of, and receive three square meals a day.

It was done. Cordell worked faithfully under Dillon's direction for three years then alongside him for three more. They became as brothers. Dillon's real brother Kane and he hadn't seen each other for ten years. Cordell had now filled that hole.

Sadly, he was now about to leave it.

LV

the sky is falling, the sky is falling

Yes, it appeared that Cordell indeed was about to meet his Maker. And there weren't a damn thing Dillon could do to prevent it. The blood was flowing too fast, and they were way too far from a doctor's care to stop it or even slow it. Dillon had never been faced with anything like this in his life. He didn't know what to do, how to begin.

Not to mention the fact that the little shit in front of him, the one who took Cordell's life without a thought, with his gun—out of revenge, the one who beat Dillon at his own game with his feet in his middle—was also the one who was about to blow Dillon's brains to kingdom come as well.

But just as that last second appeared to be imminent and loved ones were sure to perish, the air cracked around them with such force you could actually feel it, taste it, almost touch it; and its sound so very loud to hit upon them so abruptly and suddenly Dillon actually thought for a moment that the sky was about to break into pieces and fall upon their heads.

Up from the worlds below was their place of emergence into this world.
Down from the sky world above.
They were brought down on the backs of turtles, up on the wings of eagles.
They climbed a ladder built of spiderwebs.
He, those like him, and the mortals on both sides of the Barrier came into
these worlds as creatures and unbridled spirits, placed by a wise and creative
force unknown to all corporeal beings who inhabited the All Mother.

579

That definition of creation along with many others had been for those
who dwell within their mortal shells, a convenient way to explain
away the meaning of life and especially its eternal beginnings.
However, it had been too many millenniums past, since his creation,
for him to remember the hows and the whys of his birth, his life, his
death, his existence, powers of both, and his unfulfilled love.
At least until the gray-eyed one's spirit was known to him.
His gray-eyed beauty.
Without her, he was lost.
They were one. One body, one soul.
And he would serve, love, cherish, and protect her shell and all it contained
until it was naturally wasted.
Her celestial spirit would then be free to join with him, for the rest of eternity.
Until then, he was—

Nicole's child must also survive these dark times,
as must the watcher's only love—
if be it by the wielding of the Neptune Spear, be it true—
for in the end,
the evildoers will burn in hell, deep within the All Mother's breast.

"So, it is written, my beloved, so shall it come to pass."

The Gray Wolf felt the blow upon Nicole's child as if it was upon himself. It was at that moment, after he and Justin had just agreed to join together in this journey of journeys, did he instruct him to immediately and without question catch Wyatt and pack their gear for a journey of great importance, of great speed, of great urgency—*quickly, quickly.*

Without asking why, Justin did as he was told in record time. He knew, just by the demeanor of the creature before him, the need was great, the cause imminent, the effect disastrous—especially in that tone.

With the saddling of Wyatt, with all Brina's possessions in the saddlebags along with anything else he could find, he turned to look for the Gray Wolf, but the old man had vanished like he had so many times these last few days. The only thing he saw was the gray horse patiently standing there alongside his own, saddled, and ready to ride.

Of course, Justin failed to even consider looking directly above him. For above him was the belly of a monstrous creature, held in place by two massive, scaled legs bigger around than any tree in the sector. Trees with strange roots that rested upon the ground, where nothing was only moments ago. Both of which were at that very moment only a few feet from the water's edge, straddling Justin's position. But no, not until the beast spoke did Justin look up and see.

"Are you ready, young Justin?" came the voice from above.

Justin heard the old man's voice but didn't see him anywhere. His glance took him all around the immediate area, but still, the old man could not be found.

"I am above you. Do you not see my legs that straddle you?" asked the old man.

Justin finally looked up, looked up, looked up, and continued to look up. He could not believe his eyes, but he did believe them. After all, within the last couple of days, Justin saw and learned of several things this old man could do, of which he never dreamed of, and of which he now believed, but this gargantuan winged beast above him?

The great winged dragon, Remsiy Hywalfin, stood over Justin waiting for the okay to load his passengers and be on his way. Thinking nothing of it, he failed to realize just what his massive presence could or would make one not of his own kind think. The shadow in which he stood, poised, ready to take flight would lay to waste to any sane person. He stood almost hundred feet tall at the shoulder, visible for all to see—his length almost twice that. His skin was scaly like an alligator's, his tail long with spikes protruding from its topline. His vast wings extended, stretching, waiting in anticipation for immediate departure. His feet huge with talons long, curved, extremely sharp, and deadly to anything they seized. The creature's head was at least ten feet long, five feet wide, his mouth open, teeth long, sharp, and deadly. His scales shimmered with silver and green, the blue-gray smoke billowing from his nostrils stank of death and destruction, as did his breath. His eyes were large, all-seeing, yet were protected in a sense by delicately curled eyelashes, which gave them an almost-feminine look. His tongue was long, thin, and surprisingly bright pink in color. His long neck curved slightly when looking down at and addressing Justin to the call.

When Remsiy spoke, Justin recoiled.

"What is it, young Justin? You know we have no time for silliness."

"Your breath…"

"What's wrong with my breath?"

"It's terrible. It smells like last month's vomit."

"Hmmm, that bad, eh?"

"That bad."

"I'll work on it, okay? Let's go. We gotta go now." Remsiy, if you could call it smiling with that scaly mouth and all, grinned the widest grin he could, showing off those long and pointed teeth, just for Justin; then he batted those long feminine-like lashes up and down his beautiful dark-gray-blue eyes.

The color of those eyes were what Justin recognized, and in the end trusted. They were the same identical color and showed the same intelligence of the horse he came to love and respect, the very same gray steed of his beloved Bree, the very same color of hers as well. The eyes were also of the same color and intelligence, intellect, personality of the old man he was talking to only moments ago. It was unbelievable, but in a manner of speaking all three of whom he loved were of the beast before him.

"As you've said to me on many occasion, are you ready to ride? We must leave now if you are to join me."

Justin could only stare with mouth agape and eyes as wide as saucers.

"I guess that means yes," said the green-scaled dragon.

Justin could not move. He could not conceive for a minute on how this was to take place. How he was to travel? How the horses were to travel? How this was even possible?

The dragon asked once more, "Are you ready, young Justin?"

The words that broke the camel's back broke Justin's hesitation. *"Sure, why not."*

The dragon, the old man Remsiy Hywalfin, Aeolus; God of the Winds, Quetzalcoatl; God of the Aztecs, Thorin; leader of the Dwarves, Moza; Keeper of the Trolls; the Great Wizard of median earth; and the Divine Sovereign of the Neptune Kingdom (whose name was way too difficult to pronounce); and who knew how many more was about to take Justin Case III to places unknown, on an unthinkable and unbelievable form.

The temperature again turned cold, almost freezing. The air around the dragon began to mist, form, and pulsate. The consistency of the air began to thicken, to change, its color turning from a light gray mist to a green-blue fog. Wyatt was visibly nervous, yet the gray steed stood rock-solid still. Justin also stood that way, not because he was used to what was about to befall him, but because of sheer terror he could not move. Suddenly and without rhyme or reason, both horses vanished into thin air. Justin, on the other hand, found himself in a front-row seat, directly on the withers of the great winged beast—a place so far and away from anything he had ever imagined, he could do nothing but watch what was about to unfold, from a place found only in a dream.

The wings began to slowly pulse up and down, back, and forth. Without further ado, the power and strength of this great beast, gently yet with vast powers unknown to anything in this time, lifted his great form off the ground, taking them all into the air. It was an experience Justin would never forget. He was terrified yet at the same time fascinated, thrilled, excited beyond belief. His stomach was churning, but not from sickness, from the sheer raw power of the whole experience! He couldn't believe, wouldn't believe, was unable to truly believe where he was, until he looked down and witnessed for himself the mountains and streams pass under him. The beast flew effortlessly across deep-creviced canyons, spreading his majestic wings wide, pushing air back and them forward. Moments passed. They were in another valley. A valley that had he gone by horse or carriage, it would've taken him weeks if not months, yet the passing was accomplished in only a matter of seconds.

Abruptly and without warning, the massive beast flattened his wings against his massive body and dove like a plummeting meteor towards a lake below. All Justin could do was watch in horror as the water grew bigger and nearer and closer and more frightening, and then the sudden *SPLASH!*

Submerged, secure, and yet unbelievably with air still to breathe, Justin, still upon the withers, rode this beast whose powerful force moved them through the water, with wings like pulsating fins forcing his immense form along with its passenger ever forward. Finally, they erupted the water's quiet and glassy surface and rocketed skyward high up into the atmosphere, both of them shrieking victoriously. Justin was beside himself with glee. The dragon's sound of course was much louder, yet as always was a resonating atmospheric disturbance that emanated from the very bowels of hell itself, creating such a commotion, such a disturbance that all within sight, sound, and sensation bolted and ran for cover.

During flight, the Gray Wolf stretched his neck straight and tall, holding his head most regally as his magnificent wings spread wide, lifting them up towards the celestial sphere far beyond. As he and his passenger broached the outermost reaches of the stratosphere, the Gray Wolf slowly descended to a more comfortable level, where he stayed for only a second while allowing its atmospheric currents to not only dry his leathery hide, but to also carry both of them to Cordell's side.

LVI

and a-wwwaaayyy...we go

"**H**ang on, young Justin, this is where it can get real interesting."
The Gray Wolf's head had turned around to just offhandedly mention, so he would know to prepare.

"HANG ON? HANG ON TO WHAT?"

"The harness, silly. The one right in front of you. Grab on tight! Going down—*ladies foundations, luggage, bedding, home furnishings*—tag, you're it, fella. *Your ass is mine!*"

Justin looked down and saw the tightly secured piece of leather that wrapped around the beast's neck, at the base of where he sat with his legs straddled. *That was funny; it wasn't there a minute ago.* Amazingly enough, the harness *built for a dragon's passenger(?)* apparently came equipped with reinforced handles for hands and stirrups for feet, both just big enough for Justin to slip each through, pulling and grasping with fists tight, and pushing in the stirrups as best as possible, as dragon and passenger began a nosedive with mouths agape, fire and brimstone shooting forth from the dragon, screams of terror mixed with excitement coming from Justin, and an ear-piercing scream also from the dragon to deaden the senses of all living beings to whatever end was intended for them both. It was like riding a roller coaster to hell.

Rene-with-a-hyphen heard and felt the same thing Dillon had. Whatever it was, it hit him so hard he lost his footing and fell with a thump ten feet from the marshal. If he could've, if he had it in him, Dillon could have jumped at the chance, catching him off guard, snatching the gun away, but it was not his time to do so. It was also

585

not of his mind to do anything at that moment, for the sound of the sky falling brought with it an intense heat that was stifling. It did not come from a direction in particular, but instead engulfed the entire clearing in which they all were.

It began as a foglike substance that floated into the clearing, near to where the two of them stood. It tried to take on some sort of shape, as it appeared to breathe with a life all its own.

Wolf's whisper came across to them, as though it originated from the heavens, descending upon them by way of the trees. Gliding downwards passed the leaves it came, as though it traveled on the wind.

"I, Aeolus, Sovereign of median earth and beyond,

am older than the tallest of mountains.

I have traveled through the ages and across the Great

Barrier in search of one love for all eternity.

Since before her beginnings, Brina's essence, her

spirit, was of my choosing. We are one."

"You. Child of Nicole, ancestral mother of Brina,

are now one with us. As I watch

over her, I do now for you."

Then all was, as it had been, silent, except for the chirping of miscellaneous birds. Brina's two horses walked directly past them into the fog-filled clearing, past its invisible wall, and disappeared into its misty depths.

It was too coincidental. Could it be? It couldn't be, could it? Naw, it couldn't possibly be. Dillon's mind was trying to associate common denominators of this moment with those of their past, bringing all into focus, but with such a racket going on all around and them trying to evade dislodged trees, rocks, and flying furbearers made it very hard to think straight.

The crackling sound of thunder was everywhere. The air encircling their little clearing began to churn and pulse. Rocks, boulders, and trees were being uprooted and flung in every direction, during which followed an ear-pounding barrage of turbulent winds, explosions, near misses with flying squirrels, deer, bear, and other blurry shapes all sailing past—upside down—and the horrible dust that made seeing one's own hands next to impossible. The air was almost unbreathable; it was either that or the oxygen itself was being sucked right out of Dillon's lungs.

When the winds finally lessened and the breathable air was again available for the taking and giving, the rocks and the trees fell to the ground rolling, finally stopping in haphazard piles. The miscellaneous furbearers—squirrels, bears, deer—and stringy snakes all hit the ground, tumbling, running for their lives, darting away as fast as their little legs or scales would carry them.

It was as though the sky had fallen, and they were the survivors.

Yet, on the other hand, when the turbulence of everything stopped, Dillon noticed there was still a gentle pulsing of air. The heat that had surrounded them all also grew weaker, but not enough to forget. Now he could feel from which direction it came. And the really strange thing was the direction it came was from above.

The problem was did Dillon want to look?

Actually, Dillon had no choice in the matter. That decision in whatever form it took was taken away from him. In the end, he didn't have to look. The source of the heat shot forth in the form of hellfire, engulfing their attacker, Rene-with-a-hyphen, burning him into a little crispy critter, faster than you could say, "Helen Gone."

It was then Dillon saw the real change. First came the greenblue fog down from the sky, engulfing the whole area just on the far side of where the largest trees fell. Then he heard and felt through his feet and legs a very heavy thud upon the ground. Then he heard voices, not loud, more on the quieter side, yet believed them to be impossible, or at least thought it was impossible. *What in the name of momma Pearlbody was happening this time?*

There came a shift in the atmosphere. It came as an unknown force. It moved towards Brina. She didn't know what to do. Fight or flight? Indecision on her part meant trouble, and she knew it. For just a second she showed the fear she felt. That moment was all it needed. It moved in and took her.

At first, she tried to fight it but stopped the moment she sensed its origin. Loosening the tension and pressures felt earlier, she began to relax. She released the grip on her guns, allowing them to fall to the ground. There they lay, protected against all, until retrieved.

It engulfed her like a warm and form-fitting coat. It was a gentle caressing gust of wind that only she recognized. This waft transformed itself into a shrouded mist and devoured her in one fell swoop. All that mattered was the warm feeling. It caressed her like a lover. It was heaven and earth. Life, rejuvenation, trust, hope, conviction, companionship, support, and most of all, love. Undivided, unconditional, unyielding love. Love, true and undeniable. Wolf had, once again, come to her at a time when she needed him most.

The green-blue fog split, leaving part of itself where it descended; the rest of it condensed, becoming a smaller, more controllable, workable size for the job at hand. In this form, this consistency, this measurement, it could engulf no more than the size of an elephant if it had a mind to, yet the opinion of this gaseous form was not to seek out said elephant; instead, it needed to only envelop the darkly skinned, bleeding man who lay dying on the ground just a few feet away.

The green-blue fog billowed its way past the last-known remains of Rene-with-a-hyphen, that being the still-smoldering pile of ashes. It surged forward past the pile of trees and rocks, past Dillon, towards Nicole's child. It surrounded and converged upon him quickly, silently, and without prejudice. It took him like a deadly plague. It clothed him from hatless head to booted feet, from a foot above his almost-still form to a foot below the soil. It pushed all else aside. It wanted him alone. Nicole's child was in need of his most precious gifts. He held tight to him, gave him all he could.

Dillon, on the other hand, stayed on the ground and watched in horror, in fascination, and mock disbelief what was happening before him. He would've stood, but his innards were still on fire, his breath just now returning to a regular state. Plus, had he managed to get to his feet, he wouldn't have been there long. So, it was either pass out and injure himself further in a fall to the rocky ground or stay right where he lay until it was over.

Dillon could remember so many times before the mysterious powers of the Gray Wolf. Although it never occurred to him at all that he'd have such vast abilities and/or power to do what was now happening in front of his very own eyes, but there was still so much he would never know about many things. This had to be him though. It had to be. There was nothing on this world during this time in history that could perform such miracles as that creature before them all could and was doing, as Dillon watched.

As the process continued at what Dillon thought was a snail's pace, he spotted movement out of the corner of his eye. Emerging from the still-green-blue fog, which rested on the opposite side of the clearing, walked a man leading two saddled and geared-up horses, one of which Dillon recognized instantly as Brina's gray charger—the Gray Wolf; the second was an unknown steed.

Forgotten was the miracle behind him. Besides, if it was the Gray Wolf behind him working miracles, Cordell couldn't be in better hands. What now had his attention was the fact that the gray steed was here, but Brina was not. There comes a time when one's adrenaline or emotions or not giving a damn runs roughshod over such inner pain as what Dillon was experiencing, along with the miracles happening all around him, that a sheer need for answers propelled him up and forward to investigate.

Justin had been filled in on most of the story by the Gray Wolf himself on the situation at hand while in the air; thus he knew of the dire need for the hurry and knew pretty much what was going on, although it was not the whole story, he was sure. However, at this moment in time, Justin was sure there were few if any at all in this land who knew of this great winged beast, this classy dresser, this patient and understanding old man with the beard, who could see all and on occasion would help others to see. So, when he saw the second man get up and hobble his way, ignoring the wondrous act the green-blue fog behind him was performing to the injured man, Justin Case III believed the best way to handle this was that of open honesty and friendship.

With the reins of both horses still in his left hand, Justin Case III extended his right in friendship as the other man approached.

"You must be Dillon Frasier," began Justin.

Dillon paused for just a second to size up the man with wind-blown hair. Of the reins he held, the one tethered behind was the Gray Wolf. And the last time he remembered seeing Brina and her gray steed was that day when she left to do her own bidding, her own search for the Neptune sphere. Leaving our boys alone to find Jesse.

"Yes, I am Dillon Frasier, and you?" Dillon extended the same courtesy offered by the man approaching.

"Justin. Justin Case III. At your service, sir, or is it still marshal?"

Dillon thought it scary. The man before him could pass as Kane, except this man was a few inches taller and had brown eyes whereas Kane's eyes were blue. The next question that occurred to Dillon was how does one approach any subject when one is faced with someone who'd just exited from a green-blue fog and whose company shared is that of a mysterious entity?

"You've been talking to somebody."

"Yep. On our trip over here, the Gray Wolf filled me in on several things, not many, but for the most part, the *whys* part of this leg of our journey." Justin didn't elaborate on the mode of their transportation; he just let that drop.

Dillon took his hand in friendship. It was all he could do. After all, if the Gray Wolf had him as a companion and passenger, had he not all his confidence and trust? What all of them in this story had in common was at some point in time, they had been privy to some aspects of this mysterious being known to them all fondly as the Gray Wolf. And through this commonality, they were all brothers under the skin. For who is anyone to argue the knowledge, power, ability of with whom they have all come to love in one form or another, including she who rode atop him?

"You know of the Wolf?" Dillon asked.

"We've met," responded Justin with a grin.

"How much of him do you know?"

"More than I care to admit." Justin snickered at the thought of the ride of the century.

Dillon was about to ask about Brina, but Justin continued.

"How's your friend over there?" Justin pointed towards Cordell. "The one just now sitting up."

Dillon couldn't believe his eyes. Forgetting Justin, he immediately went to Cordell's side, knelt beside him asking how he felt.

"I honestly don't know. It was so strange. What happened?" Cordell had slipped into unconsciousness, a coma if you will; the blood was seeping from his chest wound, life seeping from himself. What little he could feel—cold, vacant, dark, alone—were just the beginning of what he was sure was the end. When all was assumed lost and seconds believed were all that were left, he again began to sense life. Only this time it began as an indescribable warmth surrounding him. A sensation like none other he has ever experienced before. He wore it like a warm coat against the freezing mid-February temperatures. It brought him back to life. Its tender touch stopped the blood from pooling atop his chest, on the ground. Stopped it completely. He felt the excruciating pain ease in his chest. Felt it eventually dissipate. During the minutes this change occurred, this resurrection happened, enough of his strength returned to allow him restful sleep. A sleep that for him lasted weeks, when in reality it only lasted the time the Gray Wolf required to heal him. His lungs could again take in needed oxygen. He could feel his fingertips, his toes. He could even wiggle them. His breathing became deeper, stronger, more regular. He could focus his thoughts. Through it all, and eventually, Cordell Chevalier—rope maker, trusty sidekick—found the strength to open his eyes and try and sit up.

"Well, to start with, that guy over there shot you. I thought he killed you."

"What guy over where?" asked Cordell.

"Why, that pile of ashes over there. That's what's left of him."
This explanation was going to be interesting.

"Left of him? What happened?"

"Well, maybe I'd better let this here fella tell it." Dillon asked
Justin over.

"Who's he?"

"He is an intimate friend of the Gray Wolf."

"The Gray Wolf?" Cordell remembered who exactly the Gray
Wolf was and who he revealed himself as—to him alone.

"The very same. I think maybe the two of you might have
things in common." Dillon was thrilled beyond reason Cordell was
again alive and well. The reasons anymore mattered not. The fact
that he would live was all Dillon cared about. And should he and this
Justin fella have a common bond, whether he be included in it or
not, also didn't matter. After all, it's life that matters. And when one
is faced with the death of a loved one, the torment, the inner agony,
the tears, the fears of loss, nothing can compare to the miracle of life
given to that friend, relative, life's match. And when Dillon watched
as Justin exited the fog, he knew who had control of the situation.
And knowing thus gave in completely to that confidence. If the Gray
Wolf traveled with Justin, then Justin was okay in his book. And
after he gave him time to talk to Cordell, he was sure Cordell would
be tired and again need rest. At that time, Dillon would tuck him in,
using one of the blankets on Brina's saddle; then Justin and he would
talk.

LVII

to the bitter end

Cordell was sleeping soundly, finally.

Dillon thought maybe now would be a good time to get some answers from this Justin Case fella, but as it turned out, it was someone else's turn.

Unexpectedly, Dillon felt a presence behind him. He whirled to meet it. There behind him stood the gray steed. The animal stood not ten feet away, curiously calm, and with his gaze intent upon him.

The air shifted from warm to chilly.

Then it shifted back.

Justin knew what was going on, what was about to happen to Dillon, as he'd been through this same charade several times before, but he was sure Dillon hadn't and was also sure it would be a big surprise to him.

"Do not fear me, for I shall not harm thee."

It came from everywhere, yet nowhere. It came from the left. It came from the right. It came from above and below. It came as a feeling or as a whispered word from someone on the outside looking in or from the inside looking out. It seemed to come from within his own mind as well.

After giving his head a quick shake to clear his mind, Dillon asked again if someone was there. That's when he spotted him. Another man amid the green-blue fog. The fog that now shimmered and pulsated, finally dissipating.

Dillon could barely see this man at first, but as the fog dissipated, his vision sharpened. This gentleman who now stood before Dillon, looked to be a dapper sort of fellow whose face was long but whose features were overshadowed by the unmistakable and vibrant gray-blue color of his eyes. He stood well over six feet tall. His frame was lean, yet with strength. He stood erect, regal, majestic, or proud. Regardless of how he appeared, sure as shit, Dillon knew it just had to be the Gray Wolf. Had to be. Especially with that outfit. No one here 'bouts dressed that way.

He wore a black-and-silver banded hat that rested atop a mop of thick, grayish-colored hair that draped in soft curls around his shoulders and fell halfway down his back. When he reached ground zero, he saw the boots. Not only did they match the shirt and were of the same gray-blue hue as the gentleman's eyes, but they also matched the color of Brina's horse that first day they found her in the clearing. It had to be him.

"Well, Dillon Frasier, now that you've looked me up and down, do you approve of my attire?" the older gentleman nonchalantly asked.

Dillon just grinned. He was right. It was the Gray Wolf.

"Having fun, are you?" he asked him directly.

The Gray Wolf returned the grins, extended his hand, and when Dillon stepped forth to take it, the Gray Wolf surprised all by embracing the man, who in turn returned the gesture.

"It's been one hell of a trip and you? Did you ever find Jesse Loame in your wanderings?"

"Nope. Never found him. We heard rumors, chased shadows, found evidence, but never saw him. Not once." It was very discouraging indeed.

"Well, you needn't worry any longer. Brina got him last week."

"Brina got him? How do you know—*wait*. You two are in constant contact still, aren't you?"

"Yep. No matter where I am, and no matter where she is, we are one. It's nice you remember."

"How'd it happen? Where'd she find him?" This was exciting.

"Well, ya know, she's back in your old stomping grounds. Eastern-Western."

"You're kidding, is she really?"

"Yep. She and your deputy…Hartley, is it? She and he killed him during a bank holdup."

"I'll be damned. A bank holdup. Of all the things. Wait a minute. If he was in Eastern-Western last week, who the hell have we been chasing these last few years?"

"Who knows. Probably shadows as you just mentioned. Could've been someone else, could've been your imagination, could've been a decoy, who knows?"

Dillon raised his eyebrows in question. "Was that *your* doing?"

"No. My attentions were focused elsewhere." The Gray Wolf glanced towards Justin.

"Speaking of elsewhere, how is Brina? She well?"

"As can be expected. She's been through hell and back several times over, of late. But all in all, I think she'll be okay."

"Did she ever find that Neptune sphere thing she was looking for?"

"She not only found it but saw it used before it mysteriously vanished. And by the way, it's called the Neptune spear, not sphere."

"Really?" That pulled Dillon's string. "Saw it used? How was it used?"

"It was used to kill Lucifer Carstead before he could get to her."

"Lucifer Carstead, huh? The same Lucifer who rode with Rene-with-a-hyphen all those years back?"

"The very same. He was a very bad and demented man. Deserved to perish as he did in the fashion that he did." The Gray Wolf stated matter-of-factly.

"Who wielded it?"

"That's kinda hard to say. You could say a messenger sent from the All Mother. Yep, that's how I'd describe it anyway. Besides, she owed me a favor." He grinned and winked at Dillon.

"Interesting." So many questions, so many eons to learn the answers. So many that didn't matter—*to Dillon anyway.* Brina was saved by the same-type of entity that has now saved Cordell. Who was he to question it?

"You say it mysteriously vanished too?"

"Yes indeedy. Mysteriously vanished. As a matter of fact, right into thin air." The Gray Wolf again grinned and winked at Dillon.

"Does she still think of me, Brina?" The unasked question was asked.

"To be honest, she does once in a while, but not like you're hoping. With all she's been through, her priorities have changed. She's looking elsewhere now for her answers." It was the truth, without telling the whole truth. Why complicate things?

"Well, if she no longer thinks of me, which direction should I travel when Cordell is ready to ride, ya suppose?" Dillon was so tired of traveling after ghosts; for the first time in his life, he needed someone to give him a hint in which direction was the rest of his destiny.

The Gray Wolf smiled. *"Dillon. Take a moment. Think about what you've done, what you've been through, who you've met, who you've traveled with. Think about it. Give it a long hard think. Then follow your heart; your instincts will lead you to where you belong."*

"What about Cordell here?"

"Cordell has his own destiny to follow. In time he will find his true love, but I cannot tell you or he the outcome, for his is another story to be told later."

"What about this fella? This Justin Case. Who is he?"

"Don't you think it's about time to ask him yourself?"

LVIII

loves lost and found

Justin's story to Dillon covered all the bases for a storyteller to tell. It covered sadness, glory, triumph, friendship, fear, great fear. It was thrilling, terrifying, and mesmerizing.

His account of Dillon's brother Kane and his exploits were the most enjoyable. Sadly, he was there when Kane was shot and killed, and of course buried him where he fell. Dillon knew this because there was no other way he would have had in his possession Kane's final letter to Dillon, written in his own shaky hand.

With tears in his eyes, Dillon read Kane's last letter to all within this realm:

Dillon,

> *I take pen in hand and write to you again in loving memory of our beloved parents, who unfortunately were unable to tell us what we so desperately needed to know, if any unforeseeable tragedy should befall them or either of us. First and foremost on my mind, I love you more than life itself, and your safety and security are all important to me.*
>
> *I have accidentally discovered a secret organization of illegals, hidden deep within the confines of our own governing body, far and above the First Citizen. This secret organization is in the process of taking control of our*

lands under the unsuspecting noses of those supposedly in charge. This group, through deception, is manipulating everyone within this entire investigation and beyond. They call themselves the Network.

It is because of your safety I'll not reveal how I know this and more. All I can do is ask for you to be cautious of everyone and use the sense the All Mother gave you to be on the alert for bitter deception and betrayal.

Before I continue, I must introduce to you the bearer of this letter. He is my dearest friend and traveling companion, Justin W. Case III. He and I have been through many an adventure and escapade since you and I parted all those years ago.

He can be trusted explicitly, and if this letter is in your hands by way of him, that means death has befallen me. Should you not discover my remains, there is a reason for this. My identity was made known to a Carl J. Stewart and a Maximillian Rider, two men who are positioned deep within this secret organization. Who it was, who tipped them off, I don't rightly know, but I have my suspicions. That discovery forced me to travel under the alias of I. M. Warrington. Should you find a grave with that name carved upon its headstone, that, my dear brother, should be mine.

Furthermore, what is written here and what cherished moments we shared as children you must always remember and keep to yourself. Dillon, listen to me, brother, to ensure yours and Justin's safety, you must burn this letter. With it will go its secrets.

Your beloved brother
Kane

Forgive me.

The contents of the letter brought more tears and feelings of loss than Dillon had ever expected. Justin had pulled the envelope out of a secret compartment in his shirt, handing it to Dillon. After reading it, Dillon showed it to the Gray Wolf, knowing and hoping he could fill in some of the missing holes. Alas, he would not. He did pull Dillon into his eyes and showed him what Brina saw, what she found after her leaving. The very day she found Justin Case III.

It was an old, abandoned barn, with a dome-shaped roof that seemed to reach for the sky. Around and on the other side, unseen at their arrival, but later of which she found was the skeletal remains of what could've been the original ranch house—a house with the Spirit of the West, she believed, concealed within its walls. And from the way it looked, it had been that way for years, if not centuries.

Out of the silence came a voice. "Is someone there?" It was a man, or a big woman with a deep voice...

It originated from inside the barn. Wolf gave no indication that the situation held silent dangers, but she'd run across stranger things in her day.

"Yes, someone is here. Are you armed?" Not that she expected him to answer truthfully, but you never could tell.

"Yes. I have one shot left in my derringer. Am I mistaken, or are you a woman...?"

"Are you hurt?"

"Yes," he replied...

Even though his voice had a sincere quality to it, for safety's sake she remained leery and cautious. Besides, why be stupid and walk into a barn with an injured man carrying a loaded derringer? It would be just as intelligent as crawling into the den of a starving mountain lion wearing a raw beef steak around her neck...

Common sense lost out; she would enter...

Her eyes shifted to his leg. It was obvious even for her that the ankle had been injured in some way. The boot appeared smooth and without creases, as it was forced to be the bandage that bound...

With her gun still in its holster, he believed getting the drop on her would be a piece of cake. However, the second before he was able to release and draw his derringer from its concealed location along his right forearm, this woman had already drawn, cocked, and had her pistol pointed at him. Her demeanor forced his hand into submission, compelling him to relinquish his derringer and the knife in his boot. After passing them over, he raised both hands as a signal to her to please not shoot, then sat there disbelieving that a woman had beaten him to the draw...

"Interesting," Dillon offhandedly mentioned.

Dillon wasn't too surprised to see that one, especially after witnessing firsthand the episode with the rattler. That was his Brina alright. He sure did miss her. He could take a moment or two to reminisce about her, but now was not the time. Now was the time to ask other questions. Thinking back on how he got started with this whole mess made him wonder about the short little jerk who coerced him onto this case.

"Ok, but what of Carl J. Stewart? After all, it was he who originally sent me on this *assignment*. Is he still alive?"

"Young Justin, please come here. Look into my eyes with Dillon, and you both will see."

Justin did, and in minutes both he and Dillon knew the truth about many things.

At first, she thought it was her imagination, that strange-looking sapling tree thing way up ahead, but as it grew nearer, she could see that this was no ordinary piece of wood. This small tree walked, oftentimes tripped, while trying to carry what appeared to be a saddle across its shoulders as it crossed the open prairie. A horseless rider she assumed it was, as opposed to a horseless carriage— not another man, please.

Apparently, whoever it was spotted her as she came from afar. She watched as another man laid his saddle down upon the ground and sat down along with it to wait for her. The closer she got, the more he came into focus.

"Howdy!" the long-haired fella hollered and waved as Brina rode closer.

"Howdy back at ya!" Brina yelled. "Lose your horse?"

"Yep. Several miles back."

"Where're ya headed?" Brina asked.

"Up yonder ways. 'Bout a hundred miles or so."

"What brings you out here? On your way back from somewhere in particular?" This short chat gave Brina a good chance to give this guy the once-over. She needed this chance. There was something about this guy that rang a bell with her, but she just couldn't put her finger on it...

"What's your name, stranger?" Brina asked.

"Ma friends and acquaintances call me CJ, and you...?"

By the time CJ had returned to camp after taking his turn at the stream cleaning up, shaving, and the likes—hoping she'd take a more intimate liking to him, Brina as usual had camp all cleaned up, horses rigged for travel, and their campsite void of any traces of their passing.

"What the hell is this?"

Brina took one look at him and knew instantly who he was! Within a fraction of a second, Brina had drawn, cocked, and held ready both guns on the man before her.

"WHAT THE HELL ARE YOU DOING?"

"CJ, my ass! You're Dillard Pickle!"

The moment Brina saw that chiseled face without all that hair, she recognized this man instantly as Dillard Pickle, one of Jesse Loame's associates. A photo of him, along with all the other lowlifes she was to watch out for if not outright kill on the spot, was in Jesse's file the day the chancellor briefed her.

"I don't know you!"

"I was sent here from the Academy at the Centre to take care of you and your friends."

"I don't know what you're talking about."

"You don't, huh? What about Jesse Loame, the treasure, and that poor marshal you sent on a wild goose chase to find them a few years back. What about that? Remember now?"

"Frasier? You know Dillon Frasier?"

"One and the same. Now if you've got anything to say to the almighty—forgiveness for sins against anyone, any woman, or any poor sheep, any such

subject matter—better git with it now, 'cause in a moment you'll be as dead as the jerky we had for breakfast." Brina waited.

"You know he now travels with a black bastard," sneered CJ Stewart.

Brina fired, head shot. Point-blank range. Brain matter spattered from the hole in the back of his head to parts unknown...

Justin wasn't too awfully surprised with what had unfolded with his Bree and this gentleman they called CJ, especially after what he had witnessed firsthand with that other feller who showed up before the creep did. Although, shooting someone at point blank range in the head without thought, *that* put his Bree in a special category all to herself.

Dillon, on the other hand was quite shocked. He didn't think she had it in her to just shoot someone in that manner. It wasn't even a fair fight. But learning of Carl's villainy, along with how Brina felt about Cordell, he might have done the same thing himself given the same circumstance and frame of mind.

With all that was said and done, our boys holed up for a week before Cordell and Dillon headed southeast. What they were to find on their trek, they weren't sure, but under the circumstances there was no point heading home. Might as well see if they could find Kane's grave, say a few words, then move on.

Justin, on the other hand, knew exactly where he would go. Both men knew exactly where they would hang their hats—without saying a single word. So, without further ado, as our boys rode east, so did Justin Case III and his newly acquired companion, the Gray Wolf—the old man; the Great Dragon Remsiy Hywalfin; Aeolus; God of the Winds, Quetzalcoatl; God of the Aztecs, Thorin; leader of the Dwarves, Moza; Keeper of the Trolls; the Great Wizard of median earth; the Divine Sovereign of the Neptune Kingdom (whose name was way too difficult to pronounce); and who knew how many more—headed north to Eastern-Western, where both their destinies hung her hat.

LIX

when the heart skips a beat

They said she'd been ill for quite some time. Those who really didn't know. They didn't know the cause; they knew it wasn't the gunshot wound in her arm from the robbery. That was too far from her heart to kill her. One day she just collapsed. Her body temperature climbed sky high within minutes. Try as they might, they couldn't bring it down. Not even after submerging her into ice water would it budge.

To all who came to know her and love her, Brina Louise Grant was dying of an unknown disease, infection, malady, or some such illness. No one saw it coming. No one could treat her. The doctors were baffled. They quickly called in specialists. No one could find a cause, let alone a cure. All they could do was leave her in her own bed with Ellie at her side, comforting her, mopping her brow, and listening to her senseless ravings.

The morning she collapsed had started like any other. Brina woke up refreshed from her wonderful night's sleep. You see, she was in a real bed now, in a real room of her own, with real curtains, with her own dresser, her own bed warmer, one which was now cold. She always started the day out with a good outlook, a spring in her step, a howdy for all who passed her way. You see, Brina was now living in her very own cottage on the outskirts of town. She had found it during one of her sightseeing rides. It was there, just waiting for her to come see.

It was an older house, with pansies growing haphazardly all around and other flowers here and there, ones she had no names for. There was a large tree in the front and another one in the back, both of which would give lots of shade for the hot summer months sure to come. Long ago it had been painted a light blue, whose layers of paint were now peeling off in flakes the size of feathers in a down pillow, much of its color faded, thanks to the wind, the elements, and from the sun. It was a two-story, with several rooms she'd probably not use for quite some time if at all. It mattered not; she fell instantly in love with this place. What made it even better were the corrals in the back with a small barn to store whatever she chose—whether it be exercise equipment or hay for Wolf, *if he ever came back to her in that form*, or for her spotted ponies to stay warm and out of harm's way when those horrible winter winds came.

Yes, Brina was in love.

After finding this treasure, she rode directly to the bank where she talked to Mr. Forni, an Italian gentleman who'd relocated to their sector for untold reasons. The two of them talked of this house, and it was then she learned of the stories that were told in secret about a ghost who supposedly lived in one of the built-in bookcases. She was told that the previous owners had seen him occasionally walk—through walls just to get back to his case, and about other times when his reflective form was spotted walking from room to room while folks were looking out the windows watching their children at play.

And as you can guess, after the ghost made his appearance more often than not, making himself well known, the house was sold, time after time, because no one wanted to live with a ghost. Brina, on the other hand, while living in Wolf's company, had accustomed herself to dealing with such unknowns. Thus, she had no problems, no misgivings when it came to signing the papers transferring ownership of old man Hill's haunted house to her.

But when she took ill all of a sudden, folks began to wonder whether or not it was the ghost's doing. Had she bought into a haunted house whose dead owner didn't want her there? Had she accidentally picked up some bizarre virus that hid in the basement just waiting for the unsuspecting to investigate? Was the house cursed? Had some wicked goblin placed a magical spell upon her? Had it been something she ate at one of her meals? The food issue was dismissed right away, since no one else came down with this mysterious malady, but maybe she picked up a deadly disease at the Pussy Willow? But again, that was dismissed, as no one else had anything that slightly resembled these particular symptoms ether.

What did she have? Would she live, or would she die? No one knew.

On the third day she woke up. Was it Ellie's soft-spoken voice, or was it the babe's laughter that woke our Sleeping Beauty? What had they done different to have brought her back from the dead? No one knew. Some doctors were confused, others baffled, all were relieved. The specialists took notes for future reference. Within the week, Brina was again strong enough to work out in the mornings in her little barn, behind her haunted house, the one she was lucky enough to find still standing, not to say that some of the towns-folk didn't threaten destruction due to superstition. She even had the heart and endurance to run around town three times before tiring. Her guns again were hers to draw, clean, and polish. She was again herself.

The town threw a party in celebration of her wellness. Everyone from miles around was invited. The cattlemen, the shepherds without their flocks—both promised each other during this time there would be no fighting among themselves over such silly issues as fences, grasses, water, sheep smell, etc. Everyone was to have a good time. The marshal was again on her feet.

They were so excited to have her back, they partied all week long. Brina Louise Grant had even agreed to join in the festivities. Although she knew she had nothing to wear, but dear sweet Ellie, would of course help her find something for each night, which given time, she might use again. It was always a good idea to have a dress or two in the closet for times needed. Besides, as Ellie so eloquently put it, if need be, a robber might expect trouble from a woman wearing a two-gun rig, boots, hat, shit like that plus a marshal's badge on her vest, but they sure wouldn't expect anyone wearing a floor-length dress as they walked down the street with their gun concealed in the folds of their skirt. It was a great idea, Ellie thought. Brina, on the other hand, had never had a dress, let alone worn one. But, as this whole life in this time taught her, there's always a first time for everything.

The first dance was hosted by the Millers. Their grandfather had originally homesteaded the place Brina was now in, although at the time, their family's name was Hill, but to avoid controversy about the house and its ghost, they changed that first letter and then some. As to dancing, Brina learned that night not only did she have two left feet while trying to dance with Rathbone LaRue who in turn had six left feet and was tripping her up most of the time, but also, she learned a tad more about the house and its ghostly occupant. Mike Miller, during small talk, also suggested she fill the case with books and take out her weapons and boots. He said his grandfather had built it for books, and from there the story grew vague, but he said his grandfather had believed in order, everything having a place of its own, thus perhaps rearranging things would stop the hauntings. Brina, on the other hand, enjoyed the hauntings and said she planned on leaving things exactly as they were.

Those who provided the music for the dance the Millers hosted called themselves The Musical Two. They were none other than the two fiddlers Brina saw one day while walking around town months past. They were pretty good, their fiddles fast and tunes catchy. She really had a good time. In her bright-blue dress with the lace around the end of her short sleeves and around her modest bodice, Brina found herself to be the object of every single bachelor in town. She must've danced a hundred dances—all with men looking down the front of her dress, watching her rising and falling chest. It was like they'd never seen a girl before. She thought maybe it'd be best to stick to her jeans and shirt on the next go around of dance parties.

When the night was over, instead of being happy, she was saddened. The last time she'd danced was with Justin. Oh my. Had it been that long ago they waltzed across the floor of the Daytonville Hotel together? It was like watching a dream unfold as she replayed it in her mind.

Brina recognized the familiar face amid the fancy clothes and new hat. It was Justin. Justin, the man she'd left only days before with an injured foot and nowhere to run—let alone walk—was now steadily making his way down the stairs without too much difficulty towards her. Before realizing what she was doing, Brina smartly stepped to the bottom of the stairway where she was able watch him glide down the steps towards her in his finery…

To her delight and to a squeal of surprise from her own lips, Justin waited for her to finish her curtsy, took hold of his hat, removed it, spiriting it off into the air to land on the counter of the check-in desk. Turning back to her, he tipped his head to the side, then gracefully offered to her his hand…

Brina was a firm believer in holding dear to one's heart memories of times past. After all, memories were to be cherished and remembered for all times—good and bad ones. Bad ones teach; good ones bring joy. And for her, even the memories of time spent with Dillon and Cordell were cherished and brought her many moments of joy. The times spent with Justin, however, did bring many moments of joy, but it also brought feelings of loss. Of all the men she'd met and grew to know in her lifetime, Justin's smile would be forever branded on her mind—never forgotten. Where was he of late, she wondered. Had Wolf found him, saved him from that ill-fated day when Lucifer caught up with her? She had left him in the water, on the opposite shore, hiding in the reeds. She had sent him a "direct order" to stay there concealed and to wait for an old man. She thought he believed her to be nuts. But she knew Wolf did come to his rescue, yet at the same time wasn't sure of the outcome. Wolf was still in constant contact with her, but that didn't mean he was forthcoming in information. He oftentimes kept things to himself, allowing her to live her life as she saw fit. So, as far as where Justin was, where Dillon was, or where Cordell was, was anyone's guess, and the Gray Wolf wasn't telling.

Looking back at her illness, hearing the stories of no one knowing the cause, having doctor upon doctor upon specialist being called in to diagnose and to hopefully find a cure for her near-death illness, and them not finding a blasted thing meant two things. Either it was a totally unknown illness or that Cordell had been injured in some way and near death. Only with Wolf's expertise, knowledge, and mysterious powers could Cordell have survived; thus, she regained consciousness and strength. In this, she knew Cordell would be fine. And knowing this, believed Dillon wouldn't be too far away. But where had Justin wandered off to? She wondered, yet knew it mattered not. He, like herself, had his own destiny, his own plans. And in order to make one's own self happy, one must follow their own path.

The second dance that week was put on by the group singers. There were twelve of them now, all having a great time of it trying to sing the songs of the times while drinking glass after glass after glass of sour whiskey down. Needless to say, with them drunk as skunks, there'd be no way in hell they'd be able to either sing the right words to the music, or could they get the tunes right, which none of them could. So, with the tipsy and more often than not drunk singers screeching their merry tunes, the other participants decided to partake in drink as well, dancing, staggering, and falling all over the dance floor laughing all the way. They all had a great time, but such a fun time left everyone with horrible headaches and hangovers the next morning.

For the third and final dance, Ellie surprised Brina with the most beautiful skirt and blouse set Brina had ever seen anywhere. "The black grenadine skirt had a beautiful floral design that was lined with pink taffeta. The outside material was a sort of transparent fabric that showed off the pink lining thus producing a very stylish effect." At least that's what Ellie read from the old Sears, Roebuck & Co. catalog. The shirt, or what the catalog called "Ladies Waist," had "tiny light-purple, violet, and lavender flowers." It was supposedly made in the very latest style with what was described as a "two-point yoke, plaited back and front, with the newest puff top sleeves, laundered cuffs, and plain-white linen detachable turn-down collar." Also read directly from the old Sears, Roebuck & Co. catalog.

When Ellie took the pair out of the box to show Brina,. Brina thought they looked horrible. And when Ellie held them up trying to make it look like one piece, showing it off better, Brina thought they looked worse. Although Brina didn't say a thing. After all, it had been a gift to Ellie from Johnny before the pregnancy, but since she still hadn't lost her "baby fat" after the babe was born, she could never fit that waist, and since she didn't want to waste it, decided to give it to Brina as a get-well gift.

The evening of the last party given for her miraculous recovery and welcome back to the world of the living was the best—especially with Brina wearing this new combination dress-skirt set—making her the talk of the town (even though she had nothing on her feet 'cept her riding boots).

It was the old European gentleman who played the excellent piano and was well versed in the "classics and waltzes" like Strauss, who performed at this last dance. Brina, on the other hand, with this new dress set on, was more than a little uncomfortable. Not because of the music, not because the people were staring at her in this new and delightful getup, but because she was a tad worried some drunken cowboy just might spill his drink on her or his dinner or vomit—since they always served alcohol at such functions, and some of the partygoers weren't too sober upon their arrival—or fondle her. So, for most of the night, she turned down the offers for a great time and sat it out to just enjoy the music.

Brina was getting bored. Even though her foot would tap to the music she missed being out on the dance floor. She now wanted someone to ask her to dance, but after turning down every eligible bachelor in the room at least four or five times, she knew they'd pretty much leave her alone—probably figured she was worn out from all the other parties that week. She thought she could always get up and dance by herself, that in itself would be enough to get someone to again ask her, but Ellie had said that kinda thing was not ladylike, and since Brina was dressed as a lady this night, she reluctantly resigned herself to remain seated and to enjoy, or at least she tried to enjoy, what was left of the party.

Justin, Wyatt, and the Gray Wolf finally arrived in Eastern-Western just before midnight. He was tired. About fifteen miles back

Wolf decided he'd had enough of being in corporeal form, changed back into his fog, and again engulfed and then once again became the gray steed.

Justin, alone now, rode into town hoping to see some life somewhere. There were always those who lived the nightlife and those who woke up with the chickens. He was looking for those rare individuals who walked around at night. Perhaps they could tell him where the best place to stay was until he could find out information on his Bree.

Lo and behold, just as he was tying his horses to the hitching rail, one staggered around the corner, down off the walkway, almost tripping and falling into the gray horse.

"Watch it, friend!" Justin warned the passerby.

"Watch it your own self, buddy," responded the tipsy cowboy.

"Sorry, just wanted to save you from running head-on into my horse. He's kinda funny about strangers trying to dance with him."

Funny Justin had chosen those words, for it had brought back to life the party the drunken cowboy just now left.

"You been there? Seen her?"

"Been where, seen who?" Justin asked.

"At the get-well party. The one for the—*hic*—marshal."

"Marshal? Sorry, don't know of anyone in this here town."

"Weeell, if'n you head on over to the party—*hic*—you might get her to dance with ya. I couldn't, but I figure she'd rather—*hic*— keep that pretty dress of hers all clean and sparkly. Hehehe, ya see, I've been carrying this here bottle of—*hic*—whiskey around. She probably didn't want it all over her pretty new dress." With that, he passed out and fell in the freshly dumped pile of manure Wolf so eloquently provided at just the right moment.

Party? There was a party? With dancing? For the Marshal, in a dress? Justin put on his thinking cap, picked up his saddlebags, and sauntered over to a vacant watering trough to clean up before attending.

The cake still had not been served. Brina was yawning now, barely keeping her eyes open, her thinking blurry. This was way too late for her. Nights like this were fine, if you were riding after or away from some lowlife, but to just sit and listen to nice easy tunes could sometimes put you to sleep, which was exactly what was happening to her now.

There was a slamming of a door somewhere off in the distance. She really didn't care; all she wanted to do was leave the building before Ellie saw her. Brina got up, but before she could get turned towards the exit door, Ellie spotted her and came over at a trot. The honored guest of the party could not abandon them at this still-early hour. She rushed to her side, averting Brina's attention away from the slamming door, which was just now welcoming a new party guest who was just now entering the main room.

"Where are you going?" asked Ellie.

"Home. I've had enough party to last me a lifetime."

"You can't go, not yet."

"Why not?" Brina was pooped; she'd had enough.

"The cake's not been served. I slaved all day making it. You can't leave now, please. One bite, please."

"Very well. Just for you I'll stay."

Fifteen minutes later, it was the same story. The cake had not been served. Brina tried to leave; Ellie saw her and came over to talk her out of it again. Ellie, as much as Brina loved her, was a persistent little twit, especially when she couldn't take the hint that all Brina wanted to do was go home, change, fall into bed, and sleep for a week.

Finally, she saw her chance. She stood, looked all around for Ellie. She didn't see her anywhere, so she made her break for it, but her escape plan was momentarily averted to something over in the back corner by the entrance. With eyes half-closed from lack of sleep, she peered that way. It was just another partygoer in her opinion, another gent there to enjoy the party, to take part in the whiskey-drinking contest. Although she didn't recognize him, it mattered little; there were still so many folks who lived in the area she had yet to meet. And this one she really couldn't see either. The brim of his hat was too wide, and he had it pulled down just enough where his facial features could not be viewed. It mattered not; she was about to

611

leave anyway. Although she had to admit, he did stand out from the rest. He was, after all, the best-dressed gent there. Too bad he was just arriving as she was just leaving.

She didn't get too far away from brouhaha before Johnny intercepted and gently guided her back to the dance floor. Johnny saw the look in her eyes and recognized it instantly.

"Having a bad night, Brina? Am I that bad a dancer that you'd want to leave?"

"Oh no, Capt'n. It's just—"

"Humor me. Let me have this dance with you before you retire. You're so pretty in that dress set I gave to Ellie before she got with child. No point in wasting the moment, eh?"

Brina smiled. What could it hurt anyway? Johnny Hartley and she had been through so much, one little dance wasn't going to hurt nothing. Besides, she really did want to dance, just not with every Tom, Dick, and Harry in the room.

With Brina momentarily engaged with one of the best dancers in the room, and this new partygoer without a partner, all the eligible young womenfolk gathered around him, hoping for a dance with the fancy-dressed dude.

Justin found not just beautiful music, beautiful women, a piano, a European pianist, several ranchers' daughters all wanting him as their dance partner (the shepherds' daughters had been quietly threatened to back off), but he also found all the information he needed to devise and finalize his plan for the evening—*and that his Bree was in a real dress*. The outcome was going to be brilliant, especially if his target was indeed here, and he hoped she was still.

He could hardly wait.

The music stopped. Her dance with Johnny was over. Brina excused herself, and John let her. She again tried to leave the dance floor, but at that very last second, the cake was served. Not wanting to disappoint Ellie again, Brina resigned herself to finding another unoccupied chair and placing her fanny in it until the cake was served to everyone so she could enjoy her one promised bite and finally make her escape home.

In the middle of a mouthful of cake, the pianist began to play. This time it was something Brina recognized instantly, "The Blue Danube" by Johann Strauss Jr. It's funny, she thought, how hearing certain pieces of music could and oftentimes would take you back in time to that very place, that very moment when you first heard it, or during a special time in your life. This particular piece brought back to Brina, Justin and their dance.

Daydreaming away, with eyes closed, Brina relived that very day when that lost soul she rescued came down those stairs to dance with her in all his finery. Lost in another world, during another life, Brina failed to see the gentleman standing in front of her with his hand extended, asking for this dance.

The dance floor was vacant. Everyone was in awe at the sight of this gent with the fancy duds. Watching his approach of the marshal, the onlookers stepped back, allowing him the hopes of winning the full length and width of the dance floor. You see, Justin had again worn his fancy black dress jacket with a medium gray vest over a sparkling white shirt, bolo tie, matching gray arm garters, black boots, and hat—just like that day long ago.

With the sudden silence of the room—all except for those eighty-eight keys—Brina took the chance and opened her eyes. There standing in front of her in all his finery was the familiar face of her Justin. She shook her head to clear it, thinking her eyes were not open and she was still dreaming. But, no. Here was Justin Case III, the man she'd left months ago in the water, safe from Lucifer's grasp.

"My lady?" asked Justin with his hand extended asking for the dance.

Brina was aghast at his presence before her. Never in her life had she ever expected to see him again.

"Justin?" It was a whisper.

"The one and only, my love. Would you honor me with this dance? It's our favorite tune, ya know." He bowed to his lady with eyes twinkling with a smile that reached from ear to ear. "Please, would you accompany me to the dance floor?"

When he again asked for her hand, without thought, Brina gracefully and with genuine flair stood, put her cake on her seat, turned to the gent in the fancy clothes, curtsied in her fancy skirt herself, *far and below the customary dip for the period*—just as though she was dressed in a floor-length ball gown, just like that day in the lobby of the Daytonville Hotel.

To her delight and to a squeal of surprise from her own lips, Justin waited for her to finish her curtsy, took hold of his hat, removed it, spiriting it off into the air to land surprisingly enough atop Ellie's head! Ellie, just like everyone else in the room, allowed and watched in pure joy the event that was about to take place with the one they all loved. Turning back to her, Justin "tipped" his head to the side, then gracefully offered to her his dance hand. Captivated with the gentleman before her in his attire, she allowed the moment to carry her off and away by gently and so eloquently accepting it. Justin confidently took control of the moment by guiding Brina gently yet firmly out to the middle of the dance floor where he swept her around the room several times to the familiar waltz step.

After several laps he slowed, then stopped, facing Brina with the most honest and delightful smile on his face that she ever did see. He turned loose of her hand, then to her continued surprise, bowed with the grace of one born of breeding and status.

"Happy to see me?"

In front of everyone in the room, Brina, on tiptoes, reached up and kissed Justin like he'd never been kissed before, all the while pulling him into her as to never let him go again.

"I'm so glad you've come home," she said after parting, after finally catching her breath.

"So am I, my dear. So am I."

"So, it is written.
So, shall it come to pass."

The great winged dragon,
Remsiy Hywalfin

LX

to a screeching halt, we come

When our boys left the site of where the Gray Wolf and that other fella saved their butts, after spending lots of time exchanging information on both adventures, Cordell and Dillon moved on. Everything was done. Jesse had been taken care of, the sphere was nonexistent, at least to them, and Kane's whereabouts in a nutshell were confirmed by Justin; he was very much dead, and a proper burial was given. Therefore, not having any true direction to now follow, our boys headed towards Marcus to see if they could actually, maybe, hopefully find Kane's grave, say a few farewell words of wisdom, and move on with their lives.

They headed for Marcus because Justin had hinted that was where he'd buried Kane, but the dip didn't say exactly, where. He'd been very vague about that. Said there was a headstone of some sort, but who knew if it was still out there, visible for anyone to find. He didn't specify why he was so vague, just that it was out there somewhere between where the Gray Wolf turned Rene-with-a-hyphen into a crispy critter and that little ghost town of Marcus. Dillon wanted to believe it was out of protection for Kane's remains, why Justin was so vague, either that or since it had been such a long time, he just forgot. Maybe there wasn't anything in the area that would stand out and be remembered to be used as a reference point for recognition purposes. Maybe the area looked just like the next hundred miles. Who knew? But when one thinks about it, when someone is buried where they fall, after several seasons of rain and wind and fire, finding such a place might be impossible, but Dillon had to look one last time.

They never did find the gravesite but did find Kane's alias, the one he referred to in his letter, in that hotel register. It was there all the time. Our boys just didn't know what to look for, never had considered him changing his name, never considered the danger he may have been in, the crooks he had to contend with. It never occurred to Dillon that maybe someone else was looking to find him too, to kill him for what he knew.

Dillon, on the other hand, was just scouring the countryside looking for him while searching for an outlaw who, according to Brina, had supposedly murdered and stolen something of great value. The funny thing is, now, other than the known criminal acts of Jesse during Dillon's time, fifty percent of the rest was supposedly a fabrication, a piece of someone's bizarre imagination, someone's warped sense of humor?

So, since they were so close anyway, with Cordell still at Dillon's side, they headed onward to Cascade to at least see if Mary Beth Robinson was still living there writing her many books, which she was, and to inquire as to whether or not the sheriff's job was still open.

It worked out great. Cordell took the sheriff's position, and Dillon married the now Mrs. Mary Beth Robinson-Frasier. Seems she had her own ideas of how things should be. As it turned out, not only was she very much different from all the other women Dillon had known (at least almost all of them), but Mary Beth was also from the future. She had been scouring the centuries searching for anything and everything to write about. She also had in her possession a small portable time machine she and Toby used to travel all those many miles to get all those many stories for all those many books in the basement.

And as luck would have it, through the using of the time machine, Mary Beth was immortal, not just in Dillon's time, but in her time as well. Both she and Toby, the two of them, were best of friends. They originally met in a small community somewhere on the West Coast, in a hot, rocky, foothill region. Even then, she had said, it was secluded and boring—few stories to tell.

Dillon learned a lot from her as they traveled the centuries past. She tried teaching Dillon her wares, how to work the fingers on the keyboard—trying to get the words to flow, to make sense. He tried very hard, but each time she would rip the pages recently typed. Too windy, too many sentences to say a simple thought, she said. It was frustrating, but Dillon tried anyway. Eventually he did manage to write a simple manuscript, but not till after it was turned down time after time by various printing houses—too windy, too many sentences to say a simple thought, they said.

Oh well—*c'est la vie.*

Epilogue

homeward bound the traveler

It was time to leave. Time to go home. Time to come home.

Many of the institutions Mary Beth dragged me to, over the decades and across the barriers, were museums. It was said she found her best inspirations for writing through the resources offered in their many books, file cabinets, microfiche, computer programs, videos, audio equipment, etc. Museums of natural history, museums of the gold rush age, museums of mechanized transportation devices, science museums, planetary observation stations—the list was endless.

Within the walls of these many institutions visited, all types of technology were displayed. Of course, being from the middle of the nineteenth century myself and being as stubborn as a boulder when it comes to learning new things should give you an idea how well I embraced these sciences. I just couldn't fathom the advantages to every button, every key, wave of the hand—whatever their meaning, what it did, and the consequences that usually followed when applied. To put it bluntly, almost everything I saw and had explained to me was useless. It was all way beyond my thought process and my desire to create one. The question Mary Beth kept asking was whether or not I wanted to learn, to use what all these times could teach me. Well, my response was not really. Not unless it included a horse, saddle, and a range to cross. This line of thinking drove Mary Beth nuts. Of course, turnabout was fair play.

You see, I had always loved my life as it was, back in Eastern-Western, back in the Dakota territory, back in Sector 4, and wanted to live it simply—far and away from any inkling of what I had learned in the many years with Mary Beth Robinson, my wife. Traveling with her and Toby Bicker had brought me many things. Many wonderful experiences, places never seen by mere man, triumphs, defeats, personal tragedies as well. Knowledge beyond what normal folks learn in their own lifetime, I had experienced in many of my own lifetimes. I could elaborate on my travels now, but the importance of this story lies in the desire for what I missed most and what followed.

I needed my old life. A much simpler life. A familiar place where I could hang my hat, where I was at ease with my surroundings, where I was welcomed to wear my badge proudly, protecting those in need, enforcing the law. I needed my horse under me—riding the range once more, my old and dear friends by my side. What I didn't want was what the new science, the new technology of the periods visited offered. I didn't care an iota for any type of such advancements, other than the telegraph, my guns, a secure cinch, saddle tree and horn, and most of all the way a real honest cup of coffee should be made—over the campfire or a wood burning stove.

The life I was presently living took a turn for the better at one of the museums we visited. We had been to thousands of the places, and I was getting burned out on all of them. This one in particular proved to be much different. Here, because of what the new science (there's that well-oiled word again) brought in sight, smell, feel, sound, the experience as a whole was unbelievable, unfathomable. I think what got my attention the most that day and what initiated my homesickness and the desire to go home more than wanting to stay at Mary Beth's side was the vision in that room, that experience, that moment.

It was our turn to enter. We had been waiting in line for hours. For her, I don't know what was there, what happened, what she saw—it didn't matter. What mattered was what I experienced, what I felt, what I saw. We walked in side by side. It was the same room, mind you, it was the same time—three thirty, but for each person who enters, a moment from their past, something they either loved or lost, is waiting for them in that room.

The moment I walked in the room and its contents vanished. The floor had changed from polished marble to that of red clay. The walls, ceiling, and chairs were gone. It was as though I was dreaming in color and 3-D of a place long ago where I had maybe kissed my first girl, walked alone heavy in thought, rode across on my dearly missed, trusty steed, Cody. The ground upon which I tread was covered in a zillion small bright-yellow flowers with green stems only one inch tall. It looked like a flowing carpet of yellow that went in all directions. The sun above, shining brightly, enhanced that beauty. The water oak with its trunk diameter of at least three feet stood majestically in the middle of them all—its tall and massive branches reaching out over each flower as though lovingly protecting them from the elements like an opened umbrella. Part of this canopy of green, gray, and brown hung over the one end of the weed-covered pond not seen moments ago, with its cattails, all its aquatic life therein, reminding me too much of home. A feeling too strong to be ignored. I was almost dizzy at the sensations experienced. The fragrance of everything was fresh, of course, none of the individual aromas stood out in their own right, but their own individual beauty together brought what was only moments ago a simple room in a gigantic building to life. To me, my life, and my losses, my needs, my loves. *Home*.

I kept this from Mary Beth. Oh, we talked lightly on what each saw and felt in this room, but the deep feelings I held was not something I wanted to share quite yet. I needed time to digest it all—my feelings, my losses, my gains, and my emotions in regard to my life with this woman. Would she be willing to divorce me, let me go home to Brina, Cordell, Cody, Eastern-Western? Would Brina and Cordell be willing to allow my life to reenter theirs? Mary Beth and Toby were wonderful people. Life with them had been wonderful, exciting, complicated, yet stressful at times.

I took just a moment and changed places with Mary Beth. I tried to see me from their eyes, from their experiences in the vast universe via what that little time machine could do. As much as I loved the man I was with, knowing he wasn't as happy in traveling as we were, would I feel that anchor attached to my foot? Would he be dragging me down, and I not know it because of the hope I had, that he felt as I did, wanting to share in my life for eternity? It was definitely something to ponder.

Later that day, my concerns and my decisions were answered in a simple sentence or two found on a simple page in a history book Mary Beth had found for me. It was apparently written during a troubled time of the Old West. Mary Beth knew of my origin and knew what I might be interested in. Being in a museum, many of the books were bound instead of just electronic. This one room and its walls were just like the many I had found that one night in that basement of hers back in Cascade—books, books, everywhere books. I heard there were other floors just like this one—three of them supposedly consisted of nothing but bound books, and seven floors were dedicated to the electronic versions. But we didn't go from room to room. Mary Beth had centered her research project on the one floor, and while I was looking at old photos of the nine-teenth century, with a touch of homesickness here and there, she came to me with a single bound book in her hand. Taking my arm, she gently led me to another large room, full of occupied, and some unoccupied, chairs with other folks reading. She again wanted me to sit and enjoy. To take some idle time reading, while she and Toby were busy elsewhere.

It was a history book she had handed me. Funny. Me, being as close to history as I am, especially for this time, I could relax in this chair. Really relax. It made me feel like being home. I could forget where I was and just focus on the contents, the story, the facts, the words spelled out. I began skimming through it, looking for dates, names of folks I may have known at one time or another. Once in a while I would find something that reminded me of my past, but rarely. After a while I felt myself beginning to nod off, when some-thing caught my eye on the top of page 4883. There it was, in black and white. One of the reasons I had to get home. It was an obituary, dated two weeks after the three of us had left Cascade for the wide-open spaces via the time machine. Apparently, the only reason it had made it to the history book was because this person was the first woman of that time period to be appointed such a position. It read, "Marshal Brina Louise Grant. Stabbed in the town of Eastern-Western by an unknown assailant after leaving a celebration party. Died shortly thereafter. She was survived by her betrothed, Justin Case III. There were no children. Services were held at the Eastern-Western grange hall."

My heart jumped into my throat. I had to find Mary Beth. Had she known about the entry, the circumstances surrounding it? I had told her about my time with Cordell and Brina and all that we had learned in one another's company, although I conveniently left out the part about the Gray Wolf. Who in their right mind needs to know about something no one need know about? What he was, what he could do, what he had done to Rene, what he had changed into, etc., etc., etc. She didn't need to know any of that, at least not from me. But, as to who Brina was and from what time she originated and her mission, I felt that would be easy for Mary Beth to fathom—being from the future herself and all. So, I had told her everything I dare.

I sprang from my chair, with book still grasped in my right hand. I was so excited and frantic at what I had read and at the same time furious as to who may have done this dastardly deed. I wasn't there for her. I should have known she was still in danger. I had to find Mary Beth somewhere in this maze, but it was no use. I couldn't find her. I looked everywhere. Agitated, I began running from aisle to aisle, forgetting where I was, almost tripping over someone's feet. That slight mishap was followed by the obvious "Slow down, fool, can't you see we're reading?" It brought me back to where I was. Regardless of almost breaking my neck running at a frenzied pace, my goal was still to find Mary Beth and learn the truth of this matter. She had been around the block, she had traveled through time and sometimes space, and she and Toby were writing all those books. In her travels, she must have been at the Academy at one time or another. Being as well informed as she was, maybe—just maybe—

she would know something. I finally found her and Toby in a section filled with those stupid electronic doodads, all of which I just hated with a passion.

I urgently whispered her name, "Mary Beth!"

"Yes, love. What is it?"

"The book." I was trying to catch my breath as well as control my excitement.

"The one you have in your hand. Is that the one I brought you?"

I nodded my head.

"You found the entry." It was a statement of fact.

I again nodded my head.

"And you want to do what? She has been dead for centuries. So, has he."

It's funny what kind of games the mind plays. Here, I had just read it for the first time, yet seeing her name in print brought back all those memories I had of her and my life before leaving Cascade, never realizing it had indeed been centuries since that entry had been made. My mouth dropped to the floor, and subsequently nothing came out. Mary Beth stood there staring at me, allowing my brain to absorb her words. Centuries.

Mary Beth saw the wheels turning. She knew what I was about to say, long before the words began spilling out. "We need to talk, Dillon, my love. But not here. Wait until Toby and I finish our research project for today. Then we will talk this out—you and I."

My bubble was burst. I wanted to talk about Brina *now*. Now, while everything was fresh again in my mind, just like that weird room and the longing for home I felt afterward. "I would like to talk now." It was not a demand, as I had already learned you can't do that with her and still feel alive at the end of the day. It was more of plea. At least that's how I tried to say it.

"Love." Mary Beth reached for me, embraced my shoulders gently, and with great affection kissed my cheek. "I promise. Give us a few hours to finish this. Find the curator—he knows me personally. He will do this for you. Have as many of those pages as you want copied—manually or on their antique Xerox machine—and hang on to them. Fold them up, put them in your pocket or wallet. Once the information I need is obtained, I will be free for the rest of the day. Toby has another errand to run for me later, so you will have me all to yourself. Then, my beloved, we can talk as much as you want about this."

I knew there was no point arguing with her. I found the curator; he graciously carried out the task (with great care of course). It was interesting to see this machine at work, especially since I had not paid the slightest attention before. Of course, again, this type of machine I didn't do. It wasn't a horse, it wasn't a telegraph office, it wasn't a campfire or woodstove heating up that good ol' pot of plain coffee. It just wasn't me.

There was a small café on the edge of town we frequented. I just loved their prime rib with all the fixings—something we didn't have at home, my nineteenth-century home. This place fixed the steak just the way I liked. They, of course, thought I was absolutely out of my mind asking for "rare to raw," but since the meat was certified pure beef without being fed hormones, additives, by-products, and being as expensive as it was, I didn't care and believed it perfect. Some foods you just couldn't get past me—yuck, like those raw oysters Mary Beth and Toby loved. Gag. Just looking at them, thinking of how they went down (then back up again) made my stomach do cartwheels. No, thank you very much. I'll stick to dead cow.

There she sat across from me, waiting for my questions. My Mary Beth Robinson. The woman who almost hit me with the door that first day I met her at the general store. The woman who willingly took me to her basement, then thought better of it—leaving me asleep on her couch with a book in my lap—and when I woke, confusion kicked in. I was confused because the house was then empty and no one in town knowing truly where the two had gone. Then, it was like they had vanished into thin air. Later, of course, just before we were married, she told me she and Toby had used the time machine and did just that—vanished into thin air. They had skipped back to her publisher to inform him of recent events and the possibility of a new inspiration in her life; thus, the writing would continue. He was thrilled. I also had learned from her that day of the supplier of that wonderful elixir, the one the saloon provided its customers. The still in Mary Beth's basement, the one that blew that same day as their disappearance, had been the source. She and her sidekick, Toby Bicker, had been concocting and supplying the town with blackberry brandy, for years.

I must have had a blank look on my face, so deep in thought was I. It was Mary Beth who broke it.

"You wanted to talk about the entry in the book. Do you still have those copies the curator made for you?"

I just looked at her for a moment, wondering if I really wanted to stir this up. Yes, in my own way, I did love Brina. In my own way, I also dearly loved Mary Beth Robinson. Which direction did I want to take this? Did I owe Brina anything? In death, she would go with the Gray Wolf. He had declared that from the beginning. With her dead, there was nothing I could do anyway. And if I did decide to go back home, would Mary Beth let me go? Would she understand? Would she hate me for it? Did I want to stay by her and Toby's side for the duration? No. I didn't. I was tired of traveling. I wanted to go home. I missed Cordell. I missed Cody. I missed the simple life. I missed stability.

It was again Mary Beth who broke his concentration. "Would you like to voice your thoughts?"

It was hard. I looked deeply into her eyes, longing for love lost. There was nothing there. It was as though she knew what I was about to ask and had accepted the outcome whatever it may be. "I don't know what to say."

"Talk to me. Tell me what you are thinking. I promise, I won't get mad."

I spilled my guts. I told her I wanted to go home. I almost cried it. I told her about my feelings rising to the surface when reading that entry but not of the experience in the room.

"I know how you feel about her. Those feelings are written all over your face. They always have been," Mary Beth said.

"But I've never said anything about her during our time together. Yes, I did try and get closer to her at one time, but she pushed me away. I accepted that. I didn't like it, but I accepted it. After all, she could have killed me had she wanted to, had I been too persistent—and with her bare hands, mind you. She was a soldier, trained for hand-to-hand combat. I did tell you about the snake and her guns, didn't I?" At her nod, I continued. "So, after Kane's grave, finding not a trace, I came home to you. I wanted so desperately to belong to someone, and as it appeared from another learned source, she had found her own love. I was no longer in the picture." Stirring up those memories, my voice cracked.

Mary Beth changed the direction of the conversation. "Then why do you want to investigate her death?"

She knew me so well. "Because I am or was a marshal. That was my job, my love. Your job, your love, is traveling and writing books about what you have seen, what you have done. You and Toby travel to places so unbelievable it boggles the mind. Please understand, I do love you so much, but this traveling and these things, these machines, the sciences out there are just not what I want to pursue. It was nice for a while, something different, but I need a purpose in my life. And at this moment, my desire is to find Brina's killer. I owe her that much."

Dillon's words were not the first she'd heard—different reasons, but the true meaning was there. Mary Beth had been in the company of many a gentleman traveler in the past. It always turned out the same. She had the endurance, the drive, the true love for writing and traveling and combining the two, making it work. But that type of life isn't for everyone. Toby was a different matter. She didn't care where they went, as long as they were together and stayed far and away from her homeland. You see, Toby was from Transylvania. Toby was a vampire and a hunted one. But that's another story and not one to be told here.

Mary Beth was curious. "Why do you owe her this? What had she done for you in the past to justify this type of decision."

It was my turn. "Why do you let Toby stay with you? Look at what she is. What she has probably done to others. What has she done for you to justify your decisions where she is concerned?"

"Touché. Sorry. That, my love, is why Toby and I worked so hard today. The research project we both worked on was to find a place for us to start our search into your Brina's death."

I again was speechless.

"Caught you off guard, didn't I? Dillon, my love. You are not the first man who has time traveled with me. You will not be the last. As you know, the time machine has granted me immortality, because it is mine and because I carry it. Toby is already immortal. Her heritage dictates that, unless she runs into a wooden steak as opposed to a beef steak. I knew from the beginning you were not completely mine. Part of you was always elsewhere. I expected it would be a woman's love lost, but I had hoped the excitement of our time together would bring you to me—heart and soul. Unfortunately, no matter how hard I tried, there was always a part of you that was somewhere else. A woman knows these things. Especially one you spend so much time with. Us women, we have a sense about us. It's called woman's intuition. With this built-in tool, we know about such things. It was only a matter of time before you got tired of traveling or something like this notation caught your attention, making you homesick enough to want to leave my side. I understand. Remember, I said I would not get mad, and I am not.

"Actually, it throws everything into a different light. Not only did I see this coming, thus the research today with Toby in full swing, but it gives me another completely different direction in which to travel and write. You and I can start this adventure together. Once we have most of the puzzle pieces, Toby and I will go our own way, and you, my love, can go home and do what needs to be done."

"You knew? You found the book, read the entry yourself, then set your plan in motion by giving me the book to also browse through, and hopefully make that second find?"

"Yes. I did."

"When did you first discover the entry?"

"About one week ago. It has taken Toby and me since then of on-and-off research to track down the one person who can help you."

"I thought you said Brina had been dead for centuries."

"We have the time machine, remember? We can go back in time. We will use it the same way as we have used it in the past. Then when it's your turn to go home, we'll do that. We'll send you home to Eastern-Western to finish the job."

"I love you," I whispered in her ear.

"Yes, I know," she whispered back.

Acknowledgments

With all my heart I want to thank

Randy Slawson
Betty Mayberry
Tammy Samson
&
Rick Kappel

All of those whom have had the honor to read this novel
in its entirety. Their wanting and begging for more pages,
more chapters, and/or the entire raw manuscript kept
me writing for years before I found a publisher.
To all my other friends and relatives who received samples or parts
of this manuscript during this same period whether they are still
with us or have passed into the fabled Valley of the Fire Moon, *the
All Mother's Realm*, I thank you from the bottom of my heart as well.

In addition to the above I give hugs, honey, and a special thank you
to my very wonderful friend

Theresa Morton

for without her I would be lost in this maze of editing
"The Assignment."

"So much fun! Don't want to stop reading to make dinner.

HAHAHA Dr. Horacio Dimwit, HAHAHA. Chapter IX was fun! It was a smooth transition into their friendship. It starts out nicely. Good exchange of data. Good caring about each other. Insights into how each feels, but not so much as to qualify for a sappy chick flick!

You actually have quite a few really funny lines! The characters have a great time being themselves!

I'm astounded how much fun it is. It's beautifully written & such a pleasure to just read. It flows.

I don't feel the need to suggest adding anything.

It was awesome! So magical. So fun. So perfect. I love it! It's excellent. Don't change the story in any way, shape, or form".

About the Author

Jill M. Slawson was born Jill Marie Barthelmess, a California native raised by relocated late depression era Montana ranchers. From an early age she was encouraged to embrace the family history dating back to the early west of the 1800s. Her uncle's family still runs the Range Riders Museum in Miles City, Montana where Fort Keogh's skeletal remains reside. With major stress fueling her inner fire, and her subconscious mind taking over her fingertips, she wrote this novel—off the cuff. She and her husband of 45 plus years continue to live side by side with love and friendship between them.

Contact the author:
The.Gray.Wolf@cncnet.com